I0604403

THE REVOLUTION WILL BE ISEKAI'D

BOOK 2

THE REVOLUTION WILL BE ISEKAI'D

D. D. WEBB

All rights reserved. No part of this publication may be reproduced, stored in a retrieval system, or transmitted in any form or by any means electronic, mechanical, photocopying, recording, or otherwise without prior written permission from Podium Publishing.

This is a work of fiction. Names, characters, places, and incidents are either products of the author's imagination or used fictitiously. Any resemblance to actual events, locales, or persons, living, dead, or undead, is entirely coincidental.

Copyright © 2024 by D. D. Webb

Cover design by Dalia and Sam

ISBN: 978-1-0394-5783-6

Published in 2024 by Podium Publishing
www.podiumaudio.com

THE REVOLUTION WILL BE ISEKAI'D

1

In Which the Dark Lord Gazes Into the Abyss

All right, everyone's tired, so let's make this quick."

This was my first use of North Watch's conference room, and in fact the first time it'd been clean enough to *be* used; previously it had served as storage for decomposing furniture and spiders. Now fully lit by bottled light slimes on akorshil stands in the corners, its atmosphere was improved by the spicy-sweet fragrance of Fflyr tea.

"My main goal up to this point has been to recruit the women of Cat Alley," I continued, "and now they're here. More the worse for wear than I'd hoped, but at least I have time to make it up to them and the ability to protect them from more reprisals from our enemies in the city. We now pivot to the next stage of the plan, and now that it's no longer just me and a handful of bandits out here, I'd like to go over our situation, our needs, and our strategy with all of you."

"And have you planned all the way to the end-of-world conquest?" Miss Minifrit drawled.

"I'm sure it will be a great comfort to you to know that I'm making this up as I go," I said with a pleasant smile. She raised a wry eyebrow, and Sakin laughed. "However, we are still within the realm of matters I *have* a strategy for. The next step is securing control of the entire criminal underworld on the whole island. That means killing Lady Gray and destroying or recruiting whatever's left of her organization in Gwyllthean, and doing the same to the various bandit gangs active in the countryside."

"You'll need a plan to deal with Clan Olumnach if you mean to take over their stranglehold on the local bandits," said Aster.

"I have one. Or more accurately, I have several, depending on how things shape up with regard to them. We'll put off addressing that in detail because I don't want to commit to a specific course if events might still push us in a different direction. That's exactly how Gray kept tripping me up. Likewise, before coming to the end of the current phase I mean to have the next step laid out, but right *now* we're going to focus on the more immediate term."

I paused to take a sip of my tea. By this point I'd learned to actually like the flavor, though it was strong and wildly different from anything I would have called "tea" back home in Japan.

"First things first," I said, setting the cup down. "Now that it's not just eight people in the forest, an actual chain of command is needed. For that, I simply want to formalize the arrangements that have sprung up naturally. Aster, you're my second-in-command."

"General of the Dark Lord's armies," she murmured, lifting her own cup and holding it under her nose without taking a sip. "Oh, if only my dad could see me now."

"Life is strange for us all," Minifrit said with a wry smile, then took a long drag on her ever-present pipe. The smell of it actually wasn't unpleasant, a nice counterpoint to the tea—in fact, it had a similar spicy-sweet aroma. Not that I intended to cease nitpicking at her about the constant smoking. Having personally healed her of what I'm pretty sure was lung cancer, I felt entitled to make all the comments I wanted.

"Miss Minifrit," I continued, "if you are amenable, I would like to continue relying on your administrative abilities. You are now in charge of personnel; you'll be responsible for organizing our people and mediating conflicts in the ranks. Preventing conflicts from arising in the first place, if you can manage it, but I'm not going to ask for miracles."

She inclined her head. "I'm flattered by your confidence, Lord Seiji. I shall do my utmost."

"First thing is to get everyone trained and ready to deploy," I continued. "Right now we're not planning to field a professional army; banditry requires competence rather than mastery. Training will continue, and I'd like to increase everyone's skills as much as possible over time, but at the *moment* I need people ready to start raiding caravans and taking down other bandit gangs within a week."

"One of those sounds rather more dangerous than the other," Minifrit said.

I nodded. "We use ambush tactics and goblin alchemy to minimize any hand-to-hand combat, but that's still assuming everything always goes according to plan, which it *never* does. I'll be leading operations against gangs myself, so anyone along on those can be Healed at need. For the rest, I want to be able to delegate and have units able to function autonomously. So! What we need now is to get people able to hold their own in a fight, the *way* we'll be fighting—with crossbows and alchemy. Some of it they'll have to learn in the field, but weapon and general combat training we can do here at North Watch."

She took a drag of smoke and blew it off to the side. "Can you be specific about your needs, expectations, and timetable?"

"First, I need you to organize a training schedule, identify anyone who's already skilled enough to teach, and put them in that role. The system you'd already set up with the girls from the Alley Cat seemed to work, but now, in addition to more people to train, we've got another handful of Lady Gray's former fighters. Leverage as many as you can, in groups as small as possible, to maximize the education everyone's getting. In one week I mean to make a move, for which I'll need everyone who's *ready* to move by then. I don't expect more than a handful to be talented enough to be ready at that point, but a handful should suffice for my next step. Additionally, over the long term, it'll be your responsibility to organize teams to operate together. That means watching for people with leadership potential and setting up the groups themselves." I hesitated before adding my final thought. "Try, if you can, to mix people up. I don't want factions within my organization, so don't collect too many people from the same brothel into one team."

"A certain amount of that would be necessary, anyway, if we are to organize people by aptitude," she mused, "but I'll keep it in mind, Lord Seiji. Very well, I can begin as soon as everyone is awake."

"Thank you, Minifrit. I realize this indirectly places pressure on you to form the entire rest of the chain of command, so reach out to me for anything you need. And just . . . generally. I want to be kept informed of progress and any decisions you make. For the time being, while everything's in flux, we'll meet daily to go over it."

She nodded again with that same dry little smile she so often wore.

"With that, there's just one other post to arrange at this early stage of planning," I said. "Kasser, I'm placing you in charge of facilities. That means everything related to the maintenance and repair of North Watch itself."

He blinked, straightening up in his seat. "Wh— Me?"

"You," I said solemnly. "You'll answer directly to me, or Aster if I'm not available. Eventually, your job will just be to keep everything clean, oiled, and working well, but right *now* you also have a campaign ahead of you, given the state of this place. Keep me informed of anything you require to continue the project; I will try not to have unreasonable expectations of you, but I would like North Watch fully cleaned and repaired as soon as we can manage it."

"Some of that we straight up don't have the capacity to *do*, Lord Seiji," he protested. "There are multiple places where the masonry itself is broken and we don't have a thistwright on hand to oversee that. If you get me mortar and akorthist blocks, I can stack the one on top of the other same as anybody, but as a craftsman myself, I'm here to tell you that putting a job like that in the hands of someone not trained in it *will* cause you even bigger problems down the road."

"I'm aware," I said, nodding. "Do what you can. I'll see about finding an actual mason for us, but barring that, you have my blessing to make any patch jobs with akorshil so you'll be able to guarantee the quality and also remove them later if we're able to fix the masonry properly in the future. The battlements might look weird with plank walkways and barriers, but I prefer that to the holes they have now."

I returned my attention to Minifrit next.

"So Kasser's job is also going to affect yours, Minifrit. He needs people to work with. I'm not gonna ask him and Harold to rebuild this entire fortress with their own four hands. For now, while this place is still such a mess, I want people to have cleaning shifts as well; that'll be everyone's job in addition to combat training. In the longer term, I want a dedicated staff to look after the facilities. Kasser, form a plan and come to me with an estimate of how many you need. Until we have that, Minifrit, please be on the lookout for people who are unsuited or disinclined to combat. I know we've picked up a few who hate fighting, and I don't want to either waste them or force them to do something that'll make them miserable."

"Ah, if I may?" Kasser lifted one hand. "*Also*, Miss Minifrit, if you could please keep an eye out for people who seem to have an aptitude for construction or crafting, or who particularly want to learn? I'd sort of prefer not to end up working entirely with the rejects and washouts."

"I can do that," she said, smiling with warm amusement.

"Yes, good point," I agreed, "though, let's not call people rejects and washouts, please. Everyone out here has taken an enormous risk throwing in with me, and the first and most important job I have for all of you is to make sure they're all treated with respect and dignity. That's the best thing we can do to differentiate our organization from . . . well, the entire rest of Fflyr society."

Everyone nodded solemnly, and I took a break to have a long sip of tea.

It wasn't blood tea, which was probably for the best, as I think I had minor heart palpitations in the first few hours after downing three cups of that. I didn't know what plants the Fflyr were brewing with, but at least one of them had more caffeine than coffee. After the exhausting daylong hike back to North Watch with a hundred refugees in tow, and the battle in Cat Alley before that, I felt like I was on the brink of collapse. I'd considered putting off this meeting 'til everyone was awake. But I wanted to have a plan in place for *when* everyone was awake, and when I discreetly asked, Aster had admitted she was as wired from our recent adventure as I. Minifrit had been safely back at the castle at the time, Kasser seemed okay, and I didn't really care how Sakin felt. So here we were, finishing this business now.

"With that settled, plans. First of all, our strategic position. Sakin?"

"Defenses need to be a priority," he said, all business for once.

"Indeed," I said. "Kasser, how are the doors coming along?"

"Harold and I have the one to put across the goblin tunnel almost built," he reported. "We'll have to install it inside the tunnel as the masonry around it is too crumbly to give us a proper anchor. Maugro will definitely notice us doing construction work in there. I hope he doesn't take too much offense."

"He can live with it. Maugro of all people understands the importance of security. How about the front gates?"

"I haven't had a chance to go over them in fine detail yet, but I think the gates themselves are still solid. There are no visible cracks or holes; they probably need a fresh varnishing, but I can do that, no problem. The issue is the hinges and bar mounts. Those are made of iron, and rusted as hell; what hasn't disintegrated entirely is frozen in place. That's a problem, Lord Seiji. Aside from how expensive iron is . . . I don't think there's even a blacksmith on Dount, and there's no way to buy gate hinges that size without everybody involved in the transaction knowing you're building a fortress. *That'll* catch Clan Aelthwyn's attention. Possibly the King's, if we're extra unlucky."

I leaned back in my chair, sipping tea again. "Can hinges be made of akornin, if I get Harold big enough pieces?"

Kasser grimaced and made a waffling gesture with his hand. "In theory? I guess. Door fastenings on peasant houses are usually made of akornin. The thing is, Lord Seiji, iron is used for fortress gates because it *lasts*, so long as you keep it properly oiled and maintained. Iron fittings can survive decades, even centuries, of use with the right upkeep. Akornin is more brittle and, uh . . . biodegradable. If we take the best care of it we possibly can, it'll still wear out within five years, ten at the most, not to mention it'll break a lot faster if somebody takes a ram to the gates. Nobody wants to mount a gate that size that often, especially not when your fortress might come under attack."

I sighed and drummed my fingers on the table. "All right. Have Harold write down what he needs to make hinges and fastenings that size, and we'll get to work. That'll buy us five years to lock down a source of iron." Not to mention, I might not still be using this old heap in five years. I hadn't thought that far ahead. "Sakin, what else do you recommend?"

"Regular patrols and watch shifts, obviously," he said. "We need people on the battlements and towers at all times, keeping an eye on the surroundings. Also, for that purpose, we need some repairs done to the walls just so they *can* be walked on; there are impassable stretches. I think your idea of akorshil patch jobs should suffice, Lord Seiji. As for structural repairs, I actually wouldn't prioritize that. The fortress itself is solid, and all damage to the walls is up at the tops. Nothing's in danger of falling in. More to the point, nobody's going to get siege engines out here through a century's worth of wild khora overgrowth; honestly, there's no force on Dount, and possibly not in Fflyr Dlemathlys, which is even *capable* of properly besieging North Watch. What we need to worry about is subtle insertions."

"Hence the patrols," I said.

He nodded. "Also, we need to cut back the khora closest to the walls. There are several places where there's a convenient path right to the battlements or a window for anybody able to climb. We should recoat the upper parts of the exterior walls to deter climbers, too; theuryct paste is pretty cheap, and I bet the goblins have a bunch of it. That'll make it too slippery to clamber up, even for squirrelfolk. It's what the Clans use on their fortresses."

"Felling live khora will require some tools we don't have, but those are obtainable," Kasser added. "Actually, Lord Seiji, that can work in our favor. Most of the khora outcroppings closest to the walls are species whose shells I can work with. If we cut down and stockpile those, that'll cover our material needs for the foreseeable future."

"Good! Get me a list of implements you'll need, and I'll make that a priority next time I see Auldmaer."

"Will do, Lord Seiji."

"What will be our next threats, do you think?"

"I told you what I figured would be Gray's next move against you," he said.

"Right, Blessed with Magic."

"As many as she can round up, yes, with Gray herself waiting to deliver the killing stroke if she can. *But*, the other pressing question is whether she *will* attack you again."

Minifrit emitted a scornful smoke-scented laugh. "Oh, I assure you, she will."

"Without question," Sakin agreed with an easy grin. "But will she do so *now*? Quite aside from the fact that this has gotten deeply personal and she probably wants Lord Seiji's head more than she's wanted anything in years, there's the fact that after he smashed half her organization in one night *and* publicly fought her to a standstill, forcing a humiliating retreat, she's lost a lot of face, which she can only regain by killing him. And for someone working in the areas she does, reputation is everything."

"That's true for anyone working in any areas," Aster opined.

"Right, but here's the thing—Lady Gray has got *other* pressing concerns." Sakin folded his hands on the tabletop and leaned forward. "Now that Lord Seiji has what he wanted from the Gutters and has pulled them all back to here, she's gotta go well out of her way to come after him, and she may not be in a position to *do* that right now. She's lost money, personnel, and respect, all in large amounts—*and* she's still in the middle of a bitter feud with Clan Olumnach, who *will* press the advantage as soon as they smell weakness."

"What do you think she'll do?" I asked quietly.

"Too close to call, since I don't know her intimately," Sakin admitted. "If I were in her position, I could go either way. Taking the fight to you is important and could improve her position for taking on the Olumnach bandits, but that just might not be feasible for her right now. And even if it is, she might still make the call to set you aside until she's dealt with them."

"Then my original strategy still holds," I said. "Both ends against the middle. Now that Gray is weakened, it's time to hit the Olumnach gangs in the back as soon as they try to close in on her. That addresses our other immediate needs, too. All the supplies we've stockpiled would've kept us going for a year or two before, but with a hundred-odd mouths to feed, we'll run out within three weeks. We need income, and Auldmaer's little trading company can't support a group our size anymore. We have no choice but to leverage our numbers. Next move will be to crush the outlying gangs one by one, take over their territory, and start funneling the spoils that were going to Clan Olumnach to us instead."

"So you and Gray are in sort of a mutual position," Aster noted. "You *also* have a need to finish her off . . ."

"And it is both strategic and personal," I agreed. "She's a hazard I can't have active on my island, but also after the various shit she's pulled, the knowledge of her *existence* makes my brain itch. However, I've got pressing material concerns which require my attention to be turned elsewhere for the time being."

"There's another faction you need to consider, Lord Seiji," said Sakin, again falling into an uncharacteristically serious tone. "It is fuckin' weird that we haven't heard anything from the catfolk at all. Rocco's arrangement with them gave them a monthly tribute to let us live here without trouble. You haven't paid them."

"*You* said they'd come asking for it when it didn't show up! I don't even know when or how he delivered those payments."

"Yeah, that's why I said it was strange. I figured they *would*. But here they haven't been paid in two months, and they've neither asked politely for it nor started trying to cause us trouble. I can't figure out their position, much less their next move."

"Any insight on this?" I asked, turning my attention to Biribo. "You're supposed to be my Ephemera tour guide."

"Well, that's a hell of a way to put it," he grumbled. "I don't have any specific insight into the actions of particular beings I don't personally know, but we can get a few hints just from the overall situation of beastfolk. Right off the top of my head, strength is a factor. You're a powerful Blessed at the very least, and so is Aster; any scouts watching us would be able to pick that up. North Watch is a defensible structure even in the sad state it's in. And *now* we've got enough sheer numbers to make any tribe on the island think twice about getting shirty with us."

"So it all comes down to power in the end," I murmured.

Biribo flicked his tongue out. "It's hard to say for sure without hearing from 'em directly, boss, but . . . my advice in the absence of better data—well, first of all, is to *get* better data. There's gotta be somebody on this island who's familiar with the ways of the cat tribe. Aside from the cats themselves, I mean."

"The King's Guild would be the place to ask about that," said Aster.

"Right, good thought. But *pending* that, I recommend leaving them alone and letting 'em make the first move. It's a common convention among beastfolk, orcs, and others who're forced to scrabble on the outskirts that whoever makes the approach is in the subordinate position. Believe me, boss, you only wanna deal with them from a posture of strength. Eventually, one way or another, they *will* come to you."

"And if their method of coming to us consists of arrows out of the forest?" Minifrit asked pointedly.

"Like the lizard said, they're not likely to try that *now*," said Sakin. "For people who live as close to the edge of survival as the beastfolk tribes do, starting shit with a dangerous group that rivals theirs in size is a desperate last resort. Based on what little we know *and* Biribo's insights . . . I reckon what's most likely is they're hanging back and watching us to figure out what's going on before they do anything. Every change we make around here will put off their making an approach, but one way or another they'll eventually come introduce themselves, if only because leaving us as an unknown this close to their village is dangerous."

"So," I said, "the consensus is that we should continue ignoring the cats for now?"

"Well . . . sort of," Sakin hedged. "This *does* raise an issue—our food situation. We can trap crawns, so we're not gonna starve until hibernation season, but the biggest way to supplement our food stores would be to hunt and forage. Doing *that* in territory the catfolk have claimed as their own is an unequivocally hostile move. That's the leading cause of tribes going to war against each other."

"Mm." I frowned, thinking. My brain felt slow. The tea was no longer helping as much as it had been; I needed to wrap this up and collapse into bed. "Well, that's also something we can kick down the road. Taking out bandit gangs and taking over their territory will also open up areas for hunting and gathering."

"That's true," Sakin acknowledged.

"Okay," I said, standing up and pushing back my chair. "Thanks, everybody. I think this gives us a starting point. Everybody know what they need to get to work on first thing tomorrow? Any other urgent issues? Good, I suggest everyone get some rest. We've got the next week or so to catch our breath, but after that it's back to violence and mayhem."

"I love this job," Sakin practically sang, already sauntering toward the door. Kasser heaved a sigh, folded down hands at me, and followed Sakin at a circumspect distance.

"Actually, Lord Seiji, there is something I wanted to ask you," said Minifrit, intercepting me just short of the door.

"What's on your mind, Minifrit?" I asked, suppressing a yawn. "Scuze me. It's not the company, it's the hours."

"Of course," she replied with one of those feline smiles of hers. "I won't keep you long, my lord. But while I have your attention, I'm afraid my wardrobe is somewhat diminished since I was forced to leave the Alley Cat in such a hurry. Do you think my dress is . . . suitable?"

I started to irritably demand why the hell I should care about this, but before I got as far as opening my mouth, she was already tracing one fingertip into the very low neckline of her dress, drawing my eyes inexorably to the mostly exposed expanse of her chest.

Minifrit's chest was . . . worth seeing. She was the most buxom woman I'd met on Ephemera and possibly ever, except for maybe that rude goblin who worked for Miss Sneppit. Zui, that was her name. Unlike Zui, Minifrit dressed to flaunt her assets. Also, while the traditional Fflyr prostitute's uniform tended to resemble a loose dressing gown wrapped around the waist with ribbon, I could tell Minifrit's had some kind of internal support, because those things were way too high up and perfectly shaped for their size and her age.

I realized, belatedly, that I'd been staring for a couple of silent seconds. Dammit, I had better self-control than this; exhaustion is a hell of a drug. But just as I started to shrug off that momentary distraction and look for an answer, Minifrit deliberately shook her shoulders in a way that set her bosom to bouncing in the most bewitching—

The memory of so many screams; they all ran together as one chorus of agony, the smell of rot and sickness—pleading eyes, gaunt faces full of despair, blood running—

I gasped and stumbled back, bracing myself against the wall and clutching my head. This time, it took a lingering moment for my vision to clear. The echoes didn't vanish instantly, fading over the next few seconds. I realized that Aster had darted to my side, reaching out, but then hesitated to actually touch me.

Anger pierced through the fog of remembered trauma, and I welcomed it as a preferable alternative. *Again* she pulled this shit? I was no longer amused.

"Listen, you—"

"*You listen to me.*" Minifrit surged forward, reaching up to take my face in both her hands, gently. When had she put down her pipe? She was always carrying that damn pipe . . . "Lord Seiji, you have never once condemned or judged any of the women of Cat Alley for the injuries and diseases caused by the lives we led there. You just healed them. No one whose opinion matters will judge you for this, you understand? It's an injury of the brain, nothing more or less. One your magic can't fix by itself. It is *no* diminishment or reflection upon you as a man, or a leader. But it *is an injury*, and one which *needs to be dealt with.* Even if you're stubborn enough to dismiss your own suffering as unimportant, this causes a predictable reaction which *can* be recognized and exploited. Look how easily I did it! Lady Gray is definitely savvy enough to spot something like that and take advantage—and let's be real, you're the Dark Lord. *She* is far from the most dangerous person you'll ever have to fight. You *need to address this.*"

I drew in a long breath, hands twitching at my side; I had started to reach for her wrists, but abstained, unsure how well I could moderate my strength in that moment. I didn't want to hurt her, especially by mistake. And her hands on my jaw and neck . . . What was the last time a human being had touched me without homicidal intent?

"And how, pray tell, do you propose to do that?"

Minifrit finally relaxed, lowering her hands from me. I hated myself a little bit for immediately missing the contact. "I am no priestess or healer; I won't claim otherwise. But over the years I have been responsible for more than a few traumatized people. Not every case *can* be healed. Still, there are ways. I will put my full expertise to the task, if you'll let me. I can't make promises as to results, and I might still fail you, but I can swear it won't be for lack of effort. Even if nothing I know can *fix* this, I am still confident that I can at least *help.*"

I forced myself to breathe evenly and control my expression.

Vivid flashbacks, caused by stimuli associated with the initial trauma— in my case, all the misery and pain of the lives of prostitutes in a medieval hellhole, which I'd seen firsthand over the last few months as I regularly treated them in my guise as the Healer. So, the trigger was . . . potentially anything sexual, apparently. Yeah, this was PTSD. It was pretty textbook. I had resisted acknowledging that increasingly obvious fact because . . . Well, where the hell did *I* get off being traumatized? All these women had been *living* with this for years now, and they had found enough gumption to pull together and fight back just the night before. All I'd had to do was *see* it, once a week for two months. And I was the one having flashbacks now? Ridiculous. *Pathetic.*

I'm sure a proper therapist would have opinions about that, but I didn't have a proper therapist—and neither, I suspected, did anyone else on this entire planet. The closest I had was a middle-aged ex-prostitute who I was pretty sure would react with pure anger and contempt if I revealed the detailed cause of this. Who wouldn't?

"All right," I said aloud, stepping back from her, "I'll think about it."

Minifrit narrowed her eyes to angry slits. "Young man—"

"I think you mean *Lord* Young Man."

Aster cleared her throat loudly. "Ah, Minifrit? I'm sure you're aware that when most men say they'll think about something, they mean they want to drop the subject and ignore it. Lord Seiji actually is pretty good about thinking over things in his own time. And if he doesn't," she added sweetly, turning a sunny smile on me, "I will *remind* him. As many times as it takes."

"Great," I said sourly. "Thanks, Aster."

"As always, my lord, I have your back."

Minifrit heaved a sigh that did interesting things to her neckline, which I steadily looked away from so as not to have a repeat of . . . that. "Well. I suppose that for the time being, that will have to do. Thank you, Aster. A good evening to you, Lord Seiji. Rest well."

I nodded, a little stiffly. "Oyasuminasai."

Aster gave me another pointed smile before following Minifrit out of the conference room, leaving me alone with Biribo.

"It's my own fault, you know," I said aloud. "I'm the one who had the bright idea to surround myself with women."

"Yeah . . . Keep sayin' stuff like that, boss. That should help smooth things over."

2

In Which the Dark Lord Makes it Rain

I watched the slime sail away into the sky, arcing down into the khora forest, and frowned.

Holding out my hand, I cast Slimeshot several more times, sending more of them flying into the wild blue yonder. It was easy; casting the spell without a target was nothing.

"Considering we're planning to normalize relations with the catfolk, I hope none of 'em are standing in that direction," Biribo commented.

I ignored him; what were the odds of that? It was a huge forest. I did, however, turn around and put the battlements at my back so I was facing the fortress, with the courtyard spread out below my current perch atop the walls.

Just within my field of view there were five "classes" in session during this afternoon period, groups of people separated by a reasonable buffer of space, with still more around the corner of the fortress and a final group outside the walls, being led by Sakin in the art of moving silently through the khora forest. Below me I could see teams of young women, mostly still dressed as prostitutes because that was all they owned, each unit being drilled either by one of the former Cat Alley bouncers or one of our recruits from Lady Gray's organization. Unarmed fighting, knife fighting, and swordplay, with two groups practicing crossbow archery against targets along the walls. Each group, at my insistence, had a nearby bucket containing the pink glow of a healing slime.

Frowning in concentration, I extended my hand toward the upper walls of the fortress itself, high above the heads of my people practicing down below. Flexing my outstretched fingers, concentrating.

This wasn't working.

Mostly out of frustration, I gave up and just shot North Watch itself with a bullet-velocity slime, taking some small satisfaction in the way goop splattered from the impact.

"Aw, *come on!*"

I winced at the sight of Nilli, one of the women who'd joined up with Khadret and had been walking a group of former prostitutes through some basic sword forms. She now hurled her akorshil practice sword to the ground in rage, using both hands to claw tiny fragmentary slimes out of her hair.

"What the fuck! Who's throwing that—"

Nilli froze and went silent as she beheld me on the battlements.

"Sorry!" I called. "They should come right out if you push 'em off; just don't let them burrow into your hair. Gomen nasai!"

She hesitated, then folded down her hands at me and started combing fingers more aggressively through her hair, a couple of her students stepping up to help. I had to wince; it made a certain amount of sense that my followers were afraid of me, all things considered. I guess I'd just have to make it clear over time that nobody would be in trouble for getting mad when I did shit like dump slime on them.

"What're you trying to do, exactly?" Biribo demanded. "I'm getting a little tired of having to say this exact thing, boss, but *maybe* I could help you if I understood what you needed."

"I doubt it," I murmured. "I'm . . . grappling with the reality of how much my mental state affects my ability to do magic."

"Well, I mean . . . Of course it does. You do magic with your brain. It's just like how the strength of your arms affects your ability with a sword."

I sighed, turning again to scowl out at the khora forest over the battlements. "Spell combination is a lot easier when I'm in a calm frame of mind. Which makes me wonder if there are some more combinations I could have unlocked by now if I wasn't neck-deep in life-threatening bullshit every minute and could *actually relax*. But anyway, this right here is just an extension of that. Lady Gray has that artifact that blocks spell targeting, right? I was thinking . . . Maybe I could aim Slimeshot at, like, the air right in front of her."

"Like I said," Biribo exclaimed, "I coulda told you that wasn't going to work! It's not even the spell itself, just the nature of human cognition. You can fire it at nothing, but if you're wanting to fire it *at* something, no amount of rules lawyering is going to fool the target blocker."

"So I discovered," I admitted, glancing back at North Watch. I'd been unable to shoot the air right in front of the fortress while thinking about shooting the fortress. "This seems like a gateway to broader issues, though, Biribo. I need to figure a way to control . . . Well, I've got bad habits that keep rearing up. My whole life I've tended to shoot my mouth off under stress. That's the last thing you want to do in a place like Japan, but in Japan the worst that happens to you is social disapproval and isolation, unless you're dumb enough to sass a yakuza or even be somewhere you might meet one. I feel like compulsive shit-talking is going to cause me some *real* problems here. And it is compulsive—it's like something takes over, and . . ." I trailed off, then heaved a sigh and reached out to rest my hands on the battlements. "Fuck's sake, I got carried away and actually offered Lady Gray a place in my organization. What the hell would I have done if she'd said yes?"

"Slit her throat the second she dropped her guard, I assume," said the familiar, buzzing forward to hover in his usual spot at my shoulder. Below us, we could see Sakin leading a column through a patch of the thorny, red vines that passed for underbrush in a khora biome. "Look, boss, I think it's a good thing you're considering stuff like this. Beats blundering around without a plan or any self-awareness. But you might be misdirecting your worry, here."

"How so?"

"Well, if you ask me, it's a mistake to think in terms of having strengths and weaknesses. What you've got are character traits, which are more useful in some situations than others. Yeah, letting your mouth run away with you under stress can cause problems, but on the other hand, you being witty and charismatic is responsible for nearly all of your successes here. Also, for example, remember that night during the battle? While you were confronting Lady Gray, she *also* stopped in the middle of fights to make speeches at you. *Twice.* And didja notice how nobody *shot* her either time?"

". . . hm." I frowned, remembering. Now that I recalled, that was exactly what had happened. "That's a point. How'd she get away with that?"

"Reputation, and charisma. Everybody present aside from you had spent years being terrified of her, and Lady Gray also *knows* how to put on a spectacle. No offense, boss, but she's noticeably like you in several ways."

I just nodded, having realized that myself. Lady Gray's commitment to melodrama and the frustration she'd expressed with the venality of human nature were . . . uncomfortably relatable.

"Still," Biribo continued after a moment, "I think you're not wrong to be concerned about your overall mental state. That's gonna affect *everything* you do. You should really take Minifrit up on her offer, boss."

I let out a little huff of scorn. "What's she gonna do exactly? If I had access to a proper psychotherapist, maybe, but . . . Look, I don't doubt Minifrit is good at what she does, but this is an entirely different skill set."

"Boss, you're talking about a woman who's been a prostitute and a business owner managing dozens of employees. In the absence of a proper mind healer or priest, you're not gonna find much better than that for dealing with emotional problems."

My fingers tightened on the battlements, the smooth texture of akorthist under my skin reinforcing just how alien everything here was. How far I had been flung from anywhere I belonged. "I can't tell Minifrit of all people how I'm reduced to gibbering impotence by the faintest shadow of what she's been through. She'd stab me on general principles, and I wouldn't even blame her."

Biribo flicked out his tongue at me. "Boss, I don't think you're giving yourself *or* Minifrit nearly enough credit. Should probably work on that. Speaking of which, here she comes."

Seconds later, the door to the tower several meters to my right opened and Minifrit herself emerged, just as predicted. Pipe in hand, she sauntered toward me with that rolling, feline gait she was so good at, trailing fragrant smoke from her nostrils like a sexy dragon. I didn't *think* she was trying to seduce me; I was starting to think playing the vamp was just part of her self-image, something she couldn't stop any more than I could keep my yap shut when under pressure.

"What's this I hear about you dropping slimes on people?" she asked, coming to stand beside me.

"I apologized," I protested. "It was a simple accident. And it's not like anybody got hurt. Slime's pretty harmless . . . well, at that size and velocity, anyway."

Minifrit slowly inhaled another long streamer of smoke.

"You should really find another vice," I lectured for at least the third time that day. "There have to be ways of having fun that don't involve slow-roasting yourself from the inside out."

This time, she ignored it. "The slime itself is not really an issue, Lord Seiji. People here are understandably nervous about . . . many things. I would hope you would have the basic courtesy not to practice your spells in a direction where your own people even *might* be caught up in it. They have all seen how deadly your magic can be, and don't need anything further to worry about."

"All right, fair enough," I admitted. "I'll be more careful. I was just trying to think of a way around Lady Gray's antitargeting artifact. I needed something big to test a theory against, and hey, there's a fortress right over there."

She slowly blew out a cloud, staring off over the huge branches and plates of khora spreading out before us, many with fluffy-looking fronds swaying in the breeze.

"What a shame there was nothing in *this* direction big enough for you to shoot at."

I enjoyed Minifrit's dry wit, when she wasn't using it at my expense. "Was there something you needed?"

"You did say you wished me to report to you daily," she said, giving me an amused sidelong look. "This seems as good a time and place as any. Plenty of fresh air."

"There *was*, anyway," I said pointedly, waving away a cloud of smoke.

"Morale is high," she reported, gazing distantly out over the forest. "I see no reason it should not stay that way, provided we are careful and thoughtful. The key will be keeping everyone busy, while also providing them with leisure time in which to socialize, relax, and have some fun. Having enough people to get a proper sing-along going during mealtimes has been a boon. We need to avoid giving people time to brood, while also not overworking them. A careful balance, but a feasible one. The one matter that concerns me is the shock which ensued at the revelation that the Healer these women agreed to follow is the Dark Lord. For *most*, I think it will not be a problem—whores are not, as a rule, the most devout of citizens. Still. It's early, but I will be looking out for the deeply religious Sanorites among the ranks. There are always a few."

"And . . . what do you intend to *do* about them?" I asked warily.

"That will depend on the individual and the situation," she said, blowing another drifting cloud of smoke. "I am reasonably confident that most can be brought around. The fact that you have manifestly done more for all of them than Sanora or her church ever have will weigh heavily."

"And the others? I'm not comfortable . . . preemptively 'silencing' people on the grounds that they *might* prove disloyal."

She gave me a scornful look. "I can always tell when you've been talking to Sakin. It's me, Lord Seiji. Minifrit. I assure you, I can handle this. If it comes down to needing to dispense punishment, I will consult you. For now, I will work to avert that situation."

"Good. I prefer that approach."

"I would not have agreed to serve you if I thought otherwise. Oh, and you should know that Gannit has unilaterally taken over the kitchen. As she's a better than decent cook, I haven't seen any reason to challenge her on this, and I would encourage you to endorse the arrangement."

"Gannit, huh." I narrowed my eyes. "Wait a second. I *thought* the food was spicier than usual today."

"Gannit has firm opinions on the health benefits of properly spiced food," Minifrit said solemnly.

"You *fucking* Fflyr and your peppers. It's like you all have your sinus cavities coated in tar! What is *wrong* with you people?"

"A great deal, Lord Seiji, though personally if I were to draw up a list of complaints about my home nation, it wouldn't start with the food."

"Of course not, you're used to it. Hang on, what about Donon? He was more or less in charge of the kitchen."

"Donon seems a good lad," she said with a smile. "No real ambition and not a territorial bone in his body. If anything, he seems to enjoy having someone else in charge. He and Gannit are getting along swimmingly, last I checked."

"Well. I guess that's . . . something."

"If you'd like," Minifrit said, her smile turning mischievous, "you can ask Gannit to specially prepare you a less-spicy plate at meals. Surely being the Dark Lord has its privileges."

I narrowed my eyes in suspicion. "Uh huh. And if I were to do that, exactly how much shit would I then get from Gannit and every other wench in this place?"

"Approximately all of it."

"Yeah, that's about what I figured."

"On the subject of morale! When you get Kasser his tools and start felling those big khora shells, please make sure he gets enough pieces of the right size and shape to carve more bathtubs. The competition for the *one* you have set up is fierce, and there's plenty of space in that old stable for more."

I had to blink twice. "Wait. Competition? People *like* the bath now?"

"Many of the women do, at least," she drawled, giving me a sidelong smile. "I think most of the resistance is due to your decision to translate whatever the original word was as 'bath.' When people think of bathing, they think about getting clean, which is clearly not what's happening in that tub."

"Well, yes. You're supposed to wash off *before* getting in the bath."

"Right, exactly. But once there? It's just a tactile pleasure. Your original bandits may have been averse to trying outlandish foreign customs, but whores are open-minded and very acquainted with the joys of the flesh. I have to say, Lord Seiji, it would not have occurred to me to stew myself like a fresh-caught crawn as a way to relax, but having tried it, I am very much impressed. And rueful," she added with a grimace. "Oh, the money I could have made by installing one of those at my establishment. I wonder what other delights from your homeland you could introduce to us?"

"Well, there's no rice or fish here, so that rules out a lot. Come winter, though, I'm definitely going to try to put together a kotatsu."

"Concerning that," she said with a faint frown, "this may seem like a change of subject, but . . . Kasser and Harold are a couple, right?"

"Yep. Is that going to be a problem?"

"Not for me, or *most* of those you've brought under your aegis. As I said, no one is more open-minded than whores. But . . . you are *openly* allowing their relationship?"

"What's to allow?" I said irritably. "I haven't got time to take an interest in everybody's personal business, and theirs is no more a moral failing than having blue eyes. Attacking whole groups of people like that is just one of the ways incompetent rulers cling to control. Do you *want* to listen to me rant, Minifrit? Because I've got at least five solid rants on this subject alone."

She grinned. "I believe I already grasp the gist, thank you. No, in fact this dovetails with the bath, and that . . . peculiar chant you've been using before meals."

"Itadakimasu?"

"Yes, that sounds familiar. Lord Seiji, I think one of the most important things for us to do out here is establish a *culture*. No doubt we'll be absorbing more Viryan influences as we come into contact with them, but nobody here has any idea what Viryans are actually *like*, and even then, I think converting directly to the ways of the local dark elves would be a hard sell."

"For the dark elves, too, boss," Biribo added. "They'll just try to take advantage if you adopt a subordinate posture like trying to absorb all their customs over your own."

Minifrit nodded and took a pull from her pipe. "So. Culture. This is not something on which I encourage you to rush, my lord, but do think about the *way* you will have your followers live. After-dinner baths and embracing gay couples are a good start to differentiate us from Fflyr society, but more will be necessary. And if you don't have a *plan* for what we are to become, we'll end up turning into some random amalgam which might or might not serve our best interests."

"Hm. You make an interesting point . . . Thank you, Minifrit. I'm not sure any of that would have occurred to me. Any suggestions for how to make a start?"

"Well, off the top of my head, try reciting your meal chant more slowly, and enunciating. I've already seen some of the girls trying to mouth along, but they're probably afraid of getting it wrong and offending you."

"I . . . don't think that trying to turn these people Japanese is . . . a good idea."

"In principle, I agree. But I see no harm in importing a *few* customs from your homeland for them to latch onto. It will give them something, at least, from which to create a new identity."

I had to pause and chew on that one for a minute. Some time ago, I'd specifically decided to start introducing some little Japanese courtesies and customs to my bandits, back when there was just the handful of us Rocco had left behind. And sure, Fflyr society in general urgently needed some civilizing touches. But now that the actual prospect was upon me, I couldn't help wondering if trying to convert a nation of people to my own customary ways wasn't an incredibly bad idea. That specific thing had been behind many of Earth's greatest historical atrocities.

No, Minifrit was right. We did need to establish some kind of cultural identity, and I didn't see the harm in it having some Japanese components, but it would be much better off being something *unique*. And ideally, something to which other people could be converted easily. Something it would be *desirable* for them to convert to.

I would have to give this a lot more thought.

My attention was caught by frantic barking. Turning around, I beheld Junko zooming furiously across the courtyard, disrupting several in-progress classes as she went, and fortunately not getting whacked in passing by an errant practice swing. Still barking her customary greeting, she skittered on the turn at the gates and raced outside onto the old road.

"Ah, my messengers must be coming back," I said. "How does she always know?"

"Dogs have good senses, boss," Biribo reported.

I gave him a flat side-eye. "*You* didn't notice. Isn't that your entire reason for existing?"

"Just cos I didn't say anything doesn't mean I didn't notice," he said defensively. "You were in the middle of a conversation, and last I heard, you weren't expecting any pressing news from 'em."

"Messengers?" Minifrit inquired.

"Lord Seiji!" A very young woman leaned over the battlements of the tower closest to us, waving at me. "Aster and Kastrin are coming up the road!"

"Thanks, Iredi," I called back, and she disappeared, no doubt returning to her position overlooking the gate. I hadn't asked her exactly, but Iredi couldn't have been more than sixteen. Every time I saw her, I was torn between horror that she'd been working in a brothel and guilt that I'd roped her into an insurgency.

"I sent them to the Kingsguard waystation to send a message to the Auldmaer Company," I explained to Minifrit, who was still watching me with raised eyebrows. "An updated list of some stuff we need, and also he needed to be warned about Lady Gray. She seems to have figured out who the Healer is, and from there it wouldn't be hard for her to find out who Lord Seiji has been talking to in town."

"I do hope someone reminded you that this is still Fflyr Dlemathlys, and thus corrupt as the revels of hell," Minifrit said pointedly. "The couriers read everything that's given to them, and will sell the contents to whoever might be in the market."

"Yes, we spent the extra time to come up with a roundabout phrasing, don't worry. I'm going to have to get down there and explain to Auldmaer what's going on in more detail soon, but right now I need to be here overseeing the early training. I don't want a repeat of what happened when I left you and your girls alone right after dragging you out here. Besides . . . the situation with Lady Gray is going to make it difficult for me to get in and out of Gwyllthean in any disguise. It'll be a risk when I do go back, and I need to figure out a way of avoiding her notice."

"Mm, I see," she said noncommittally. "It's probably best that he's aware enough to invest in some extra security, but it's doubtful attacking the Auldmaer Company is among Lady Gray's possible moves."

"Yeah, that's what Sakin and Aster both said. Forgive me, but after my own, admittedly brief, dealings with Gray, I'm skeptical about any reasoning that boils down to 'she wouldn't dare.'"

Minifrit grinned and took another long draw on her pipe. "It's not even about her, but about the Clans. Nothing is more important to them than the status quo which keeps them in power. Lady Gray is allowed to run her business in the Gutters because the Clans don't care what happens to the lowborn down there. By the same token, banditry in the countryside is just the natural consequence of their disinterest in spending the money to properly enforce the peace. But if a Gutters crime lord attacked a middle ring trading company, even a small one? That's no longer about the Auldmaer Company; I doubt anyone in power cares about them. That is an affront to the system itself. It's a lowborn forgetting her *place*. Tantamount to rebellion. Lady Gray had the sense not to directly antagonize Clan Aelthwyn, even at the height of her power; she will definitely not provoke them now that she's wounded and hounded."

"So they told me, more or less," I admitted. "That's why I was willing to take this risk."

"Mm. Because clearly they know you're always more persuaded by an explanation which hinges on how rotten people are."

I gave her an irritated look, not missing her smirk or the way Biribo flicked out his tongue at me.

"Well, since you're reporting in, any suggestions for who'll be ready to roll out by the end of the week?"

"It's only been a day, Lord Seiji. Don't worry; I'm on it. If nothing else, you have your original bandits and now enough recruits from Lady Gray's organization to make a solid strike team. Though . . . I well understand how you might be reluctant to trust a group of entirely those."

"There's that," I agreed, "and also, I have a specific need to include as many Alley Cats as possible. From as wide a selection of brothels as can be managed."

She gave me an inquisitive look, and I leaned on the battlements, staring out at the horizon.

"This isn't going to be just me seizing power, Minifrit. It can't be; every asshole in Fflyr Dlemathlys is trying to do that, and I have to be *better*. That's the entire point, and what I promised these women when I brought them here. I aim to continue what I began in Cat Alley. We're going to advance our strategic position, yes. But more importantly, I am going to serve these women some *vengeance*."

3

In Which the Dark Lord Plays to a Captive Audience

The thing about vengeance is the "best served cold" part; there's a lot of fiddly, detail-oriented, and frankly, boring prep work before you can get to the grand catharsis of seeing your enemies kneeling broken at your feet.

Which is why, at the end of the week, I found myself leading a small team through the dark khora forest at the end of a long day's hike, trying not to trip or give away our position. Thanks to Sakin's coaching, we were doing okay, so far. It helped that Ephemera never got as dark as Earth.

"Almost there," Biribo murmured, hovering right next to my ear. "Should be able to see the lookout up ahead. That one shape there . . . look, she moved."

I nodded in silence, then looked past him to my right. In the darkness, Kastrin also nodded, indicating she'd heard and seen. She raised the tiny one-handed crossbow, taking aim. Most of the team were some meters behind us; for this advance I'd brought Kastrin for her sharp-shooting skills and Aster to back me up if this went sour and we had to just slaughter everybody.

With my spells and artifacts, I was not concerned about the danger this group of bandits posed. Failure here would just mean having to kill them all without extracting the intelligence I needed.

Kastrin was still aiming after a few seconds. I waited; she knew what she was about, and this was a shot we could not afford to miss. That tiny thing—a "stinger," Sakin had called it—couldn't be terribly accurate to begin with. It also had basically nothing in the way of stopping power, being useful only to deliver poisoned darts.

Even the twang of it was quiet when she finally released, probably not even audible to its target several meters away. I could only tell the vague shape was a person because it had moved and emitted a strangled sound—a soft one, thankfully—staggered for a moment, and then slumped downward.

"Biribo," I whispered.

"On it." He buzzed off into the night.

I patted Kastrin on the shoulder, getting a pleased grin in response. She always responded so well to praise; I definitely wasn't going to tell her I was mostly just relieved this harebrained scheme had worked. I had been skeptical, due to the fact that tranquilizer darts (at least for humans) are Hollywood bullshit. Anesthesia is far too complicated, and the margins of error punishingly tiny. Deliver slightly too little juice and the target won't go under and might not even be inhibited that much; a hair too much and they just die. It *probably* wouldn't be a problem if we'd killed the lookout, but the other outcome . . .

Of course, Kastrin's stinger darts were dipped in a concoction provided by my goblin allies, and as far as I could tell, the difference between alchemy and chemistry was that in the case of the former, the underlying scientific principle was "fuck you, magic."

Biribo returned moments later with his report. "Success! Lookout's fully under, nobody else on watch, and the rest of the gang are asleep."

"Perfect." I wetted my finger in my mouth and held it up to the air, testing the direction of the breeze. "We need to get upwind. This way."

Next came more silent picking through the dark khora. A lot more of it, as we had to swing wide around the bandit encampment, with Biribo guiding our hesitant steps through the darkness. This took longer than our initial approach by far; I was placing a lot of trust in Youda's sedative. Supposedly, one dart's worth would keep a human-sized target down for an hour. If the lookout woke up too soon, we were screwed.

No outcry was raised by the time we finally reached a point at the northwestern edge of the camp, practically opposite its entrance, which would put the prevailing breeze behind us. It wasn't *much* of a breeze, but considering what we were about to set off, we couldn't risk having it blow into our faces. Biribo did another quick check to make sure everyone was still out, and then Aster began carefully making her way up the slope alongside us.

This gang had built their camp inside a bowl-shaped shell, which had once been one of those dome-like khora that resembled brain coral. It had been a huge specimen, bigger than any of the ones I'd seen on the khora plantations where they were cultivated; dead, the lower remains of its broken shell provided a nifty little nook in which to hide, with one single crack big enough for a person to walk through, serving as its entrance.

It wasn't particularly defensible, though; the outer walls sloped upward and were easy enough to climb. These guys were taking a lot on faith by only posting one lookout at the entrance. Aster made it easily up the slope, moving slowly so as to be silent, and at the peak pulled a cantaloupe-sized cloth bundle out of her bulging coat pocket. One-handed, she lobbed it into the camp. Kastrin was our best shot, but this task didn't call for nearly as much accuracy, and Aster had stronger arms.

The little missile landed with a soft thump—soft, but audible even to us out here. Immediately following it came a faint rustle, as if someone was moving around, and all of us froze, Aster ducking back down below the broken lip of the shell wall.

Seconds of silence ticked by. Biribo buzzed up to peek over the edge, then swooped back down to me. "We're golden, boss."

While Aster climbed gingerly back down, I passed her going up. It wasn't hard; the rough texture of this particular khora species provided abundant handholds and stepping places.

I wondered why Lady Gray hadn't attacked them yet. I knew she knew where this camp was; after accidentally discovering it myself back when we'd set fire to the Crown Rose caravan at the Kingsguard waystation, I had led a few of her people here to get them ambushed by the local bandits, and then let them live to report back to her. Gray worked hard to avoid being put on the defensive, so why hadn't she cleared out this nest? It wasn't like her to leave enemies alive and intact. There must be more factors involved in this gang war than I was aware of.

Hopefully I could get some answers about that tonight.

Reaching the lip, I peeked over, letting my eyes adjust to the lesser gloom inside. They had a fire going, burning low with a smokeless asauthec blend that put off just enough light for the occupants to walk without tripping. There were about twenty of them, more than I recalled; it was a little cramped with that many plus their various belongings.

It took me just a minute of scanning to spot the bundle Aster had tossed, full of what had become one of our standard weapons. For this one, we hadn't bothered with the shimmer powder that would disguise it as a rock. I finally spotted the little pile of cloth, lying near the center of the open space.

Perfect.

Spark!

Ignited, the sleeping powder bomb went off with a deep *pfoomp* and a huge cloud of dust that enveloped the khora basin. I threw myself back down the slope without waiting to see that, casting a self-Heal to negate the effects of any sleeping powder I might have accidentally inhaled (and the effects of falling onto hard khora outcrops, because ow). There came a few abortive yells from inside the camp, but they ended swiftly.

The ensuing silence told us they were all out. *Thoroughly* out now and would stay that way no matter what we did to them. Perfect.

"All *right*," I said with a grin, not bothering to moderate my voice. "Biribo, go fetch the others."

"You got it, boss!" he chirped, already zooming off into the night.

"C'mon, ladies, let's go see what we've caught."

I had brought eleven women from North Watch, in addition to my side-kicks, Aster, Kastrin, and Adelly, who were here to do the actual heavy lifting. Adelly had stayed behind to organize the rest while we went ahead to knock everyone out. I'd let her carry the Lightning Staff since Aster and I already had artifact weapons we preferred, even though if anything went even slightly according to plan, there would be no need for her to fight. She had the Blessing of Might, and it made her happy to have an actual artifact in her hands, since she'd never gotten one during her adventuring career, so I'd already decided to assign her that one whenever she went on a mission.

Our other find from the battle of Cat Alley, the Featherweight Tunic, had been left behind. I could see the utility of it in very specific situations, and all three of us had been training with it, but that fucking thing was a pain in the ass to use, not to mention incompatible with many other artifacts.

In short order, my troops were binding the sleeping bandits' hands and feet. We'd brought extra long ropes with us and were trussing up our victims by hobbling their ankles together and tying their wrists behind their backs, while also keeping them linked together in groups of five or six to further impede their movements once they were awake. Kastrin had another sleeping dart loaded and was keeping watch with her stinger in case there were any early risers.

"Hey, hey," Adelly said sharply, stepping forward and pointing the staff at a woman who had drawn back a fist at the man she was supposed to be tying up. "Not yet."

"He . . . this is the one who . . ."

"I know," Adelly said more gently, bending to squeeze her shoulder. "He'll get his, Mierit. Lord Seiji's promised. But *wait*. There's a time and place; you need to follow the plan."

Mierit took a couple of deep breaths to compose herself, then nodded jerkily and resumed binding his wrists. Probably way too tight, but neither Adelly nor I said anything. From that performance alone, we already knew he wouldn't be needing the use of his hands again.

I spotted a few other sets of bared teeth as they finished binding our new victims, but there were no further delays, the rest being apparently willing to wait for the proper moment. Soon enough, the work was done and my people stepped back, leaving four groups of snoring bandits tied up in neat little rows. They regrouped to stand in a line covering the entrance to the hollow, and I moved to the center. Biribo took his position over my shoulder, Aster and Adelly striding forward to bracket me from a step behind, and Kastrin lounged against the wall to one side where she had a clear field of fire over the entire group.

Finally, I extinguished the Orb of Light, whose clean white radiance I had been using to let the women go about their work.

There were, all told, twenty-two bandits. I formed the mental weight that was **Heal** in the forefront of my consciousness, and pushed it constantly, letting my gaze flick to each of the shadowed bundles I saw lying in the darkened camp. Chain-casting it was surprisingly easy, once I'd taught myself how in the aftermath of the battle of Cat Alley. A tiny flick of the eyes and the pink radiance burst around a new target, wiping away the sleeping drug and bringing them to wakefulness. It took no more than three seconds to sweep across the entire group; the lot was done by the time the first were blearily opening their eyes.

In the dimness of their fading campfire, there came outcries, cursing, and increasingly frantic struggles as the bound bandits awakened and began to realize their situation.

There it was—all the preparation for an ice-cold dish, finished. And now came my favorite part.

Showtime.

I held up one hand in the darkness and ignited a Firelight above it. The orange glow revealed myself and our followers to the bandits, prompting more yelling and cursing, but also a fair amount of stunned silence.

"Little lost lambs," I intoned, projecting powerfully despite the close quarters. "For so long now you have wandered in darkness, but no more. I have come to Heal your confusion, and to weigh your sins. The price shall be paid this night. And when it is done, we shall see who will join the crusade, and who will join Hell's revels."

Off to the side, one man in particular began to scream in abject horror. I was in my Healer getup, foregoing the mask but with my dramatic longcoat and hooded cloak over that, leaving my face in shadow. Apparently the look and the voice were enough for him to recognize me, though. No surprise; I recognized him, too, and well remembered having left a lasting impression. His name was Rugin, and he'd shot me with a crossbow.

Then I'd Immolated him.

Rugin tried to get away, which, of course, was futile; he could move neither his arms nor legs, and his thrashing did nothing but piss off the other men bound to him. Lucky for him, they were in no position to bludgeon him silent, either.

As usual, I had to do everything myself.

Windburst.

They were already on the ground, so the spell merely flattened them— as well as flinging every loose object in the camp around, including the embers of the fire, which made a merrily burning spray halfway up one wall. Asauthec-soaked fronds such as those weren't going to stop burning until the oil was fully consumed. Luckily it hadn't landed on anybody.

"Silence," I ordered. I was obeyed, for the most part.

"You're that . . . guy," one man said slowly, sitting upright and leaning forward to squint at me. "That crazy preacher. With . . ." He peered around at my followers, the women still mostly dressed as they had been. Clothes tightened up as much as they could be, but apparently there was an entire language to the details of those robe-like garments Fflyr women wore, and a prostitute's dress was immediately identifiable even if you covered up a bit. "With a bunch of whores? Okay, obviously I'm still dreaming. Would've preferred a sexier dream, but hey, I'll take it. Least it's not the lions again."

"Understandable, but no," I corrected. "Kastrin, pinch him."

She swiftly unloaded the potioned dart from her stinger, slotted in an untreated one, and shot him in the leg.

"*Augh!* Motherfucking—you little—I'm gonna—" He swiftly tried several things, including doubling over and pulling the dart out of his leg, none of which worked due to his bindings. Quickly enough, the guy settled for staring up at me with bared teeth, breathing heavily. Without poison, the dart was really just a large akorshil splinter, currently embedded a couple of centimeters in his thigh. Doubtless painful, but it wasn't going to do him any lasting harm. With the initial shock past, he seemed more annoyed than actually suffering. "All right! Point made. Goddess's tits, that seems excessive. So, you got us, Mister Healer. What's the big idea?"

"I told you. I am here to judge your sins."

His grimace turned into a sneer. "Oh please. What gives *you* the right to pass judgment on us?"

I recognized this guy, on closer inspection. He'd been present during my last encounter with this bandit gang. In fact, at the time he was clearly the leader, at least of the small group who'd ambushed Lady Gray's trackers. To judge by the way everyone else fell silent and let him talk, it seemed he was the boss of the whole operation. Good, probably—at the time he'd impressed me as a fairly levelheaded chap, as bandits went.

"The right?" I answered sententiously. "Nobody on this broken wreck of a world has any rights. I get to judge you for the same reason you get to beat people up and take their stuff—because nobody I'm doing it to has the power to stop me."

I let that sink in for a moment. The bandits all stared at me in dread; Rugin was actually whimpering.

"But take heart, my lost little lambs," I said finally, spreading my hands in benediction. "I am a *fair* judge, and when I can be, generous. I understand very well the vicissitudes of life that can leave people like you in a place like this. You live in a country where everything is stacked against you from the outset—where one turn of bad luck or the whim of some inbred blonde can rip away what little you have and stomp upon you until you are either crushed or forced through a crack and out of society entirely. Believe me. I know."

I folded my hands in front of me and bowed my head.

"Each of you has been pushed out of a normal life by the failures of those who would call themselves your betters. You have had to make terrible choices and do terrible things merely to survive, all with no hope of ever making your lives *better*. I understand. So it is for us all. *But*."

Raising my head, I held up one chiding finger.

"*Some* of you have done much more than survive. There are always a few who grab the opportunity to spread their misery around, and try to make life harder than it needs to be for others. Don't you worry, little lambs. I will test the weight of your souls, and consider all factors. For many of you, one day you will look back on this night as the moment when your lives finally took a turn for the better." Pause for effect, beat, beat . . . "But *some* of you fuckers are about to have a *real* bad time."

The silence stretched out for a few more seconds, and then someone started weeping. Somewhat to my surprise, it wasn't Rugin.

I really hoped they didn't *all* fail the tests I'd prepared; this whole operation was based on my gamble that at least some of them would know the positions of other bandit camps. Maugro wasn't going to spill the beans, so if I didn't get *some* intel out of this group tonight . . . My next moves suddenly became very uncertain.

The gang's boss was staring up at me through narrowed eyes, but his expression was intently curious—he seemed neither angry nor frightened, and no longer showed any signs of pain despite the steady trickle of blood making a spreading stain on his leg.

"Who the hell *are* you?" he asked.

I raised one hand in a languid gesture to indicate Biribo, who was still hovering in place. "Do you know what this is?"

The bandit leader's eyes shifted to Biribo; he squinted harder, and then shrugged. "I dunno, some kinda weird-ass pet?"

"Oh, look who's calling who weird," Biribo shot back, making the guy jerk his head upright in surprise.

"Biribo," I explained, "is my familiar. The physical sign of my Blessing of Wisdom."

"Your— Wait." The boss was frowning deeply now. "You're Blessed with Magic. Aren't you? I *saw* you cast spells. We all saw it!"

"Indeed."

I explained no further than that, just standing there. Waiting.

Due to how rare it apparently was, I expected that not everyone here would even know that the Blessing of Wisdom was a thing. No doubt some others would be too dense to put it together, but even so, I began to hear the hisses of indrawn breaths as various bandits proved fully capable of applying the logic. I was not surprised that the leader's eyes were the first to widen in comprehension.

"It's the Hero," a woman's voice said with an audible quaver. "The Hero's come to save us!"

"Does it look like we're bein' saved, Jenit?" a man near her spat, squirming against his ropes.

"I'm ready to be judged!" Jenit called, trying to struggle forward and earning an angry elbow in the side from the guy next to her. "Lord Hero, I swear—"

I held up one hand, and waited. To my immense satisfaction, my *presence* proved powerful enough that my wordless command for silence was obeyed.

Not instantly, but they did all fall quiet and stop trying to wriggle out of their bindings.

"I am not," I enunciated, "the Hero."

Another beat of silence.

"Oh, shit," someone whispered into the silence.

"Whuh?" another voice said more loudly. "I don't get it."

The guy next to him leaned over and whispered into his ear. His eyes widened and his dark face turned an amusing shade of gray.

"Oh, *shit*."

The bandit leader was now staring up at me with the first expression of overt fear I'd gotten from him since he woke up. I took two steps forward until I stood directly in front of him, then crouched on the ground so that we were eye to eye.

I lowered my hood, finally, and smiled. To judge by the twitching of his right eye, he did not find this reassuring.

"So, my little lost lamb. Tell me your tale."

4

In Which the Dark Lord
Passes Judgment

"My . . . tale." The bandit boss's eyebrows drew together in confusion.

"Not many people are born bandits, I imagine," I said in a genial tone. "Even fewer aspire to it. You don't see many children scampering through the farms, villages, and city streets, *dreaming* of one day slowly starving to death in the forest, with no future but the certainty of an early and violent demise, hated and outcast by all of society. Or did I just describe your youth?"

He grimaced and dropped his eyes.

"And yet, here you are. It must have been a long series of escalating misfortunes that brought you to this point. Tell me the short version. To begin with, I assume you have a name?"

"Name's Auron." He shook his head once. "I dunno what to tell you, man, it's not much of a story. I fell into debt, then ended up indentured on a farm. Then ran away. This isn't a great life, no, but it beats that."

"Ah, so you were a slave."

"Indentured servant," he said, not without a note of bitter irony. "There's no slavery in Fflyr Dlemathlys."

I reached out and smacked the side of his head. Lightly. To judge by his expression, he seemed mostly confused by this.

"Don't do the work of the Clans for them, Auron. They don't need any help. They can pass a law that turds are called dumplings, but you still wouldn't want one for lunch."

"Yeah, yeah, I get what you're saying." Auron actually grinned at me, still with that hint of bitterness to the humor. "People get got by crooked judges for debts they don't owe. Yeah, it happens all the time. I worked with some folk like that in the fields, and I've met some here in my, uh . . . third career. But that wasn't me, preacher man." He managed to straighten up enough to raise his chin pridefully. "I *owed* what I owed. I took the loan knowing full well what'd probably happen, and when it did, I went to court and took what I had coming without whining."

"A man of integrity," I mused. "And yet, you ran away."

Auron broke eye contact at that. "Yeah, I ran. It's just like they say—you don't know whether you'll take a devil's bargain 'til one appears before you. Well, I found out the price of my integrity, all right. I ran cos I couldn't survive, working those fields. Nobody can. Nobody *does*. An indenture's lucky to pull in five harvests before their bodies just fuckin' give out. They drop dead right there in the wheat, or stop breathing in their bunks one night. A lot get their hands on a sickle and draw it across their own throat before the overseers can grab 'em. I'm not proud for scarpering on my debt, but fuck it. I'm not ashamed, either. It's not like I'm gonna live much longer out here, right?" He raised his face again, that dark grin returning. "Least I get to go down in a good scrap. I've gotten to punch a few rich merchants on their fat chins, too. Even a highborn, once. Got a little of my own back before I join the revels. Fuck it all, I'll take what I can get."

A stir had gone through the women behind me partway during his recitation; for the most part, the captured bandits still seemed too scared of me to do much, but by the time Auron came to a stop, even a few of them were muttering.

I let them, for a moment, while I gathered my thoughts. Fuck, the situation on these farms was way worse than anyone had told me. My reasoning for recruiting the Alley Cats held—the powers that be would not expect the Healer of trying to turn prostitutes into an army—but I now wished I'd known about this before I launched that plan. Not only would farm laborers be stronger and tougher, it sounded like they were in much more urgent need of rescue. *Five years?*

"That must've been a steep debt," I finally said aloud. "Gambling?"

Auron's face closed down again. "It's not— Ahh, what difference does it make? I dunno why you even wanna listen to this, but fine. My mum was sick. Spores from nahkta khora in her lungs. You know what that means."

"I don't, actually."

He squinted up at me. "Seriously, man?"

"Do I *look* like I'm from around here?"

"Well, fair enough," Auron said with the faintest huff of almost-laughter. "Some khora you have to be real careful harvesting, or various shit in 'em gets into you and messes you up. Nahkta drops spores that can root in your lungs and . . . Well, anyway, it's deadly. Pretty easily cured, though. Just takes the right medicine."

"Ahh, and let me guess. Since the medicine can save one human life, it has the same going rate."

He nodded. "Only guy on Dount who makes it is a Gwyllthean alchemist who's infamous for doing this shit. He'll sell to highborn cos they're good for the money, and to everybody else on credit cos he can then sell the debt to his highborn customers whenever harvest time rolls around and they need a few more warm bodies. I knew what I was getting into, but it was my mum. You know?"

That was a not-so-subtle gesture toward common ground, but I was not interested in diving into my own relationship with my mother, least of all with this guy. "And so you reckon what happened to you was fair."

Auron shrugged. "What the fuck in life is fair? No sense whining about it. It's no worse a deal than most people get. I *told* you it wasn't much of a story, preacher man, and there's nothing special about it, either. Everybody here's got a story a lot like that, some of 'em a lot worse. There's a couple dozen stories like it in every village in Dlemathlys. You try to listen to 'em all and you'll never get anything else done. Rich people being greedy is not a problem that can be solved. It's always been that way, and always will be, everywhere. What's the use complaining?"

My legs were starting to ache in this position, but before standing I reached out and ripped the dart out of his leg.

Auron hissed and jerked. "Ow!"

"If you don't complain," I said, finally straightening up, "how's anybody supposed to know you need help? **Heal**."

I couldn't directly see the effect of the burst of pink light, as the wound was covered by his trouser leg, which was already soaked with blood. Auron glanced down at it and then back up at me.

"I know, I know," I said before he could speak, giving him a wry little smile. "You're not accustomed to anybody bothering to help. And that, my friend, is just one of the ways they keep themselves in power without ever having to go to the trouble of deserving it. A hopeless populace is much easier to keep in line. Tell me, have you ever heard of wage garnishment?"

"The . . . what?"

"Garnishing wages. When someone falls into debt, their creditor obtains a court order, which is then presented to their employer, requiring a portion of their earnings to go to the creditor, leaving them just enough income to live on. It's better for the debtor, obviously, because they retain their freedom. It's better for the creditor because it extends the duration of the debt, thus increasing the interest and their total profit. Certainly better for the economy itself; a slave on a farm isn't buying any goods or services or paying taxes, while a free citizen is doing their part to keep capital in circulation. That helps everyone who has anything to buy or sell."

Auron blinked twice. "Uh . . ."

"And then there's the fact that slavery is the least cost-effective way to run a workforce," I continued, glancing up and down the row of tied bandits. A few looked confused, many intrigued, but I had everyone's full attention. "There's a whole science of human motivation. An effective laborer is a healthy, well-fed, fully rested, properly socialized laborer. In particular, people are by *far* at their most productive when they can gain pride and a sense of belonging from their work—something to truly invest themselves in. When you look at the data, these intangible incentives make a *massive* difference in the bottom line. Nobody's work is more inefficient than a slave's—somebody with nothing to look forward to and no stake in what they're doing. Not to mention that if you keep a slave, you're responsible for their upkeep—a big, unnecessary expense. Ending indenture in favor of garnishment would even save the government money in enforcing it; everything's done by the same bureaucrats who'd be drawing up these contracts of service. No need to employ guards to haul people away in chains."

"Yeah, well . . . I guess that idea hasn't made its way here yet."

I barked a laugh full of derision and void of humor. "Oh please. Any legal system sophisticated enough to have and enforce contracts of indenture can execute wage garnishments with a lot less effort. But then, you see, they wouldn't get the *satisfaction* of putting people in chains."

Auron straightened again, frowning at me. "You actually think—"

"That is the great misconception," I said, "no, the great *lie* at the heart of corrupt power. The idea that the people brutalizing this country—any country—are just *greedy*. Greed is something anyone can relate to; thinking of our self-styled masters this way masks the depth of their monstrosity. Greed is already a vice in and of itself, so the pretext of it dissuades people from looking deeper, keeps us from realizing just *how* vile they truly are. It prevents us from seeing the reality—that these 'greedy' people are willing to *pay extra* to inflict greater suffering. They could be making *so* much more money, enjoying so much more *power*, if they actually ran this country in a way that made any fucking sense. It's not all that hard! Even lowborn have enough business sense not to fuck everything up as badly as the Clans—you can tell, because of how many lowborn actually *run businesses*. If you can manage a successful bandit gang, you could run a Clansguard better than anyone actually doing that."

I could feel it happening again; it was running away from me, the words spilling out and projecting so powerfully through the night that I really hoped nobody else was out here hunting for a bandit camp. Give me an audience and something worth ranting about, and my self-control started to suffer. At least I was having exactly the effect I intended. I could tell from the rapt expressions all around me, some of the bandits seeming almost to forget I was holding them prisoner as they nodded along with my rant.

"If you're honestly greedy, if you reduce the value of life to the coldest calculations, a human being is good for fifty to sixty years of solid labor, at least. Any system that's working them to death in *five* isn't greedy; it's comically wasteful for the purpose of being *sadistic*. The point of those farms isn't the wheat you brought in, it was the pain and deprivation you suffered to do it. This country is the way it is because the mansions and diversions and comforts of the powerful just don't *feeeeel* as *special* if they can't look down on people living in abject misery. Its core governing principle is that they can't get hard if they can't hear someone weeping! They're not even *human* anymore. There is nothing inside them—just a bottomless appetite for more shit they don't even really want, for the pain it causes others to supply it, and the hollow satisfaction of feeling *better* than someone else. Toppling the Clans, slitting every last aristocratic throat, and making *fountains* of noble blood wouldn't even count as murder! What else can you *do* with a bunch of *rabid fucking animals?*"

At that, I actually got yells of approval—from the bandits I had taken prisoner and just threatened to kill. God *damn*, I'm good. I mean, sure, I was capitalizing on countless years' worth of built-up misery and resentment, but still. Doesn't mean I'm not good.

But I had admittedly strayed off my planned curriculum for this event, and now I needed to bring things back on point.

"But of course, this creates a . . . *dilemma* that must be reconciled." I surveyed my captives for a long moment, relishing the way I had commanded abrupt and total silence simply by changing my demeanor. "None are free of sin. All of us, merely to survive, have preyed on those whose only crime was being too weak to stop us. We must bear responsibility, and be mindful of the debts we have incurred, but there is no benefit in recrimination. Keeping us all at each other's throats is how *they* stay in control. Unless we are willing to forgive and embrace those who have been our enemies, we will always be either slaves or outcasts. Only in solidarity can we achieve our revenge on those who have oppressed us."

I held up one hand to silence the displeased stirring that I could hear from my own followers, not looking back at them.

"But."

During my next three-second pause for emphasis, one of the bandits audibly whimpered. Splendid; it was so nice to have an obliging foil to play off.

"Some actions go further than can be suffered," I said, putting on a grim tone and folding my arms. "Some among you have lost yourselves in your misfortune, forgotten what it means to live as a human being, and mimicked your own oppressors by wallowing in pointless cruelty. I have come to bring judgment, and absolution, for those I can. For the rest? I hear the cries of those you believed you had silenced. For those who have let themselves become monsters, there is only *vengeance*."

Finally, I turned halfway around, putting myself in profile to both the bandits and my . . . well, bandits, I guess.

"Who has an accusation to bring against those here?"

It did not surprise me in the least that Mierit was the first to step forward and point at one of the prisoners, her outstretched hand trembling in barely contained fury. I glanced down at the object hanging from her other hand; well, now I knew what she'd been doing with the excess rope while I'd been talking.

"*Him*," Mierit spat. "He's been to Cat Alley half a dozen times. He likes to *choke* girls. No asking if they're up for it, let alone paying for rough stuff. It's gotta be a *surprise*. Every time he leaves bruises, at *best*. This son of a bitch is the reason Lairit can't sing anymore. He *killed* Tamnyn—she was my *friend*. He's killed one other woman that I *know* of! And nothing worse happened to him than being banned from half a dozen brothels. Women are *dead* so this piece of shit could get his rocks off!"

The man at whom she pointed was big and broad-shouldered, with enough of a paunch that I figured banditry must be going pretty well. Or more likely, he'd been taking food from weaker members of the gang, some of whom were painfully scrawny. He was now frowning at Mierit in slack-jawed confusion.

"I see." I raised an eyebrow, turning to sweep a critical look across the captive bandits, coming to rest on Auron. "And does anyone speak in this man's defense?"

Auron just sighed softly, gave a tiny shake of his head, and refused to look in the direction of the accused.

"And you?" I asked him. "Anything to say for yourself?"

The man's eyebrows drew together in a look as if he were physically pained by the effort of following this conversation. "What? I don't . . . They was just whores. I paid! That's what they're there for. What's the big deal?"

The collective indrawing of breath from the women behind me promised imminent violence.

"Raec," Auron whispered in a tone of pure awe, "you *stupid* motherfucker."

I had to agree. This was not going to be any loss to the gene pool.

"Mierit," I said, turning to her. "I don't have to tell you the sentence. Do you claim the privilege of carrying it out?"

She nodded at me once, her expression so furious I imagined she might be having trouble forming words. Mierit stalked toward Raec, raising the hand in which she held the recently tied noose.

"Hey, wait," Raec protested, beginning to struggle against the bandits bound to either side of him—who, in a display of classic bandit solidarity, were both trying to pull as far from him as they could manage.

"This one's a heavy-looking side of beef," I commented. "Mierit could probably use a helping hand or two."

Three more women strode forward immediately, bearing out Mierit's accusations; she clearly wasn't the only one who recognized this guy.

With the four of them working and none of the nearby bandits daring to interfere, she got the noose around his neck with only minimum trouble. Mierit wrapped the rope around both her hands for traction, planted one foot against Raec's back, and *pulled.* He outweighed her by a fair bit; it took two of her comrades to help hold him down and the third to join in tugging the rope, but they did it.

The execution was carried out in grim silence. All four women pushed and pulled according to their respective positions, unrelenting and in the cold silence of well-earned, vindicated hatred. Not one of the other members of the gang raised so much as a peep of protest, whether out of fear of consequences or because none of them felt any sympathy for Raec, I didn't know, though I suspected a bit of both.

I watched the man die, choking and twitching and turning blue, with an impassive face. A couple of months ago, I'd have had to work at keeping my expression steady. By this point, I had seen too much death and dealt a lot of it myself. I just didn't have enough sympathy left to cover the likes of this asshole.

Mierit was gasping when they finally released the rope, leaving the lifeless bulk of Raec to topple against the next man, who kicked him off with a grimace of revulsion.

"Well done," I said. "Who else brings an accusation?"

It was a grim night's work, all told. In the end, I was both proud and a little appalled at how efficiently it all went down. I repressed the latter in favor of the former. I ended up repressing a lot these days . . .

Apparently, bandits didn't get to visit Cat Alley very often, and enough of those who did behaved themselves, more or less. There were only two more executions based on accusations from the women I'd brought. In both cases, there was not a peep of protest from their comrades. That gave me reason to hope the next stage would go well.

It went almost *too* well. I had picked up on hints that there wasn't a lot of solidarity or camaraderie among this group, but if anything, I'd underestimated how eager they were to turn on each other, to judge by how fervently they did it when given the opportunity. We actually had a bit of trouble getting this witch hunt organized once I started it by asking the bandits if any among them deserved vengeance.

I was well aware that what I was doing here was a mockery of justice, but I'd been careful not to promise justice—in fact, I had very specifically told my people not to expect that. I promised them revenge, nothing more or less, and that was what I handed out.

A couple of obvious personal feuds I ignored, in favor of the much greater number of unanimous condemnations. Overall, the members of the gang who made a habit of going too far were well known to their comrades, who, if anything, seemed *eager* to throw them into the fire.

I killed eight more based on the overwhelming testimony of their own fellow gang members. Bullies, sadists, murderers, rapists . . . Fucking hell, why were there *always* rapists? Everywhere I went, more of these stains had to be put down. Was this just what people *did* when there wasn't a legal framework in place to stop them?

Auron, perhaps sensing which side of his bread was buttered, proved quite useful. I took to consulting his input on the cases I judged, taking his word as a tiebreaker in the few cases when there was a disagreement. Apparently, he commanded at least some respect from his followers, if not actual loyalty; not a soul objected to his judgments, except the specific people he condemned. For his part, Auron showed no attachment to the men and the one woman he affirmed to me deserved the rope. I got the distinct impression he was relieved to be rid of most of them.

Not that we used the rope, after that first guy. I had an artifact rapier that could find a lethal spot to stab with a mere thought. And yes, I did my own killing, after the first three whose deaths provided catharsis to the women who needed it. I had instigated all this; I deemed it my responsibility. No one else needed to bloody their hands over my own unjust decisions.

It helped a lot that my Wisdom power kicked in after I impaled the first screaming man through his left eye socket and the brain behind it. Traumatic dissociation turned into a cold, blank efficiency. All unfeeling judgment and no emotion.

My old buddy Rugin was among the condemned. Apparently, he liked to shoot people when there wasn't a need—he was particularly fond of shooting them in the back while they tried to run. In my Blessing-induced fugue, I felt nothing as I silenced his tearful pleading by whipping the tip of my rapier through his throat.

The entire thing was . . . a blur. I was aware, dimly, of the importance of this. Both strategically, and in the sense of more stains on my soul that were never going to come out. But I coasted through it in a detached fog, as if skimming a passage in a particularly dull book. Screams of terror and anger washed over me, blending together into meaningless noise. I opened enough bodies that the dirt under my feet squelched with blood at every step. And I just kept going.

Until I found I had flicked the tip of my sword through Auron's bindings and cast another quick Heal on him, allowing him to stand up before the rest of his surviving gang. There were now eleven, including the leader.

"So . . . what now, preacher man?"

I stared at him in silence. The dispassionate state induced by the Wisdom effect seemed incompatible with my innate tendency toward theatricality, but in this case, it worked. A blank, cold stare had exactly the result I wanted.

"I mean . . ." Auron cleared his throat, grimaced, and ducked his head, making an abortive gesture that looked like it would have been folding down hands had he finished it. "Dark Lord."

"That depends on you," I said at last. Suddenly, I was beginning to feel twinges of emotion returning and suspected I had better get through the rest of this quickly before I ended up embarrassing myself in front of all these people just when I'd gone to such trouble to impress them. "Each of you has a decision to make."

Auron narrowed his eyes.

"So, is this what you're gonna do?" he asked. "Revenge? For everyone?"

"When I can, and when it's earned. I want to be as clear with you as I have been with those who came here with me—I do my very best to protect and care for my people, but we are about a bloody, brutal business. There will be no safety, no justice, no guarantee of freedom. In the end, probably a violent death. All I promise is the chance to *strike back*."

He rubbed his recently unbound wrists, frowning pensively. "That alchemist in town."

"If he's still there when we take Gwyllthean?" I nodded. "Sounds like the bastard has it coming."

Auron shifted his head to look aside at his remaining followers.

"Fuck yeah, boss!" the woman identified as Jenit shouted.

"Sounds like it beats the shit out of our current, uh, backers," added another man.

"Speaking of that," Auron said, looking back at me. "We have an . . . arrangement with Clan Olumnach. A pretty one-sided one."

"Oh, you had better *believe* I have plans for them." Yep, it was wearing off. The icy relish in my voice was unfeigned, and on its heels I felt a welling horror at what had just transpired. I had killed eleven people, most of them personally but all at least at my order, and the whole thing had passed like some kind of bad dream once I got done putting on my little show.

Auron laughed aloud, an outburst of sheer confused emotion. "Well, fuck me running, boys and girls. Looks like we're joining the Dark Crusade. Who woulda thought?"

I nodded at Aster and Adelly, who began untying the surviving bandits I had just press-ganged from the corpses of their companions who hadn't made the cut.

"We have a lot to talk about, while we clean up here and depart," I said to Auron, the former bandit boss and my new subordinate. "Tell me about Clan Olumnach."

5

In Which the Dark Lord Gets the Lay of the Land

Of course it couldn't be that simple.

Time was dragging on, and the hike back to North Watch wasn't insignificant, so after a relatively short exchange of words, in which I figured out that my questions were going to take some time to get answered, I opted to put that aside and move out. This involved cleaning up the camp by removing all the food and money, and what weapons we could carry, as well as a few other sundries that might be useful. The bandits didn't have much, but we took most of it, along with their remaining personnel.

What was left looked like what it was—a bandit camp that had been attacked, destroyed, and looted, with the bodies of the slain left where they'd fallen. We took the precaution of removing the bloodied ropes, and I had left none of my hallmark slimes on the site, so whoever found this shouldn't be able to connect it back to me. The plan was for Clan Olumnach, when they learned of this, to assume it was Lady Gray's handiwork.

Hopefully.

At any rate, once we got on the road I was able to walk at the head of the column along with Auron and ask him some questions.

"Oh, that wasn't when Lady Gray learned about our camp's location," he said. "I figure she's known for a while. Couldn't tell you why she never made a move on it, but I guess she's got her own reasons. Nobody *else* has made a move on it cos Highlord Caldimer keeps the Kingsguard and the King's Guild paid off to leave it be, and with us bein' on Olumnach land, nobody else has the authority to make a move unless they wanna start more shit than they're ready for."

"So your location was kind of an . . . open secret?"

"Maybe not the *exact* location, but c'mon. It's a patch of khora forest not far from the waystation, and people get robbed around there. I assume most folks who matter had it figured out. It's not heart surgery."

"I guess not," I acknowledged. "What kept the other Clans from deploying their Clansguard? I understand Olumnach's hold on the bandits on Dount is another open secret. I gotta figure everybody's tired of his shit by now."

"Fflyr Clans don't fight each other," Auron said, shrugging. "As to why, you'd have to ask 'em—I don't exactly get my ass invited to high tea. I don't understand noble politics, but I do know that whatever's going on between the Clans, they keep it to meddling in each other's business interests and spreading scandals. No open war, and no assassinations. Nobles don't spill noble blood."

"Hm." That was very much contrary to everything I knew about aristocracy as a concept. "Aster, any insight?"

"Do I look like I get *my* ass invited to high tea?" she demanded. "Auldmaer might have some knowledge of that. Or Minifrit, for that matter."

"Good idea, I'll ask around."

"Whatever the reason, it's a big deal," said Auron. "Our only standing orders from Highlord Caldimer came down to that. We were ordered never to attack highborn under any circumstances, and handle 'em *real* careful-like if a few turned up in merchant caravans we raided. Orders are not to kill highborn for any reason, no excuses allowed, and try not to ruffle 'em any more than absolutely necessary if things went bad. And the boys were not to put their hands or anything else of theirs on highborn women. No exceptions. The Highlord made it clear that if those rules were ever broken during a bandit raid on our turf, the next thing that'd happen is the Olumnach Clansguard wiping us out like the filthy nest of rats we were. His exact words," he added with a little smirk.

"If those were the 'standing' orders, I gather there would be specific ones?"

"Yeah, from time to time. He'd send Clansguard to deliver 'em. Not on any regular schedule, just whenever he was cooking something up. Orders to attack or not attack this or that caravan, or to avoid the road during a certain period. Occasionally hunt down a smaller target moving around our turf, or be on watch for something like that. It was always something different and we never understood it. Options for us were to do as we were told or get butchered. Guess which choice we picked."

I nodded, thinking. Yeah, it made sense that Auldmaer and I weren't the first people to try this. You can manipulate the hell out of the markets if you can determine which shipments do or don't get where they're heading. Never mind acquiring the shipments themselves; if you're one of the people moving capital around in significant amounts, the opportunities are limitless.

"Were you ever able to identify a pattern in these orders? Anything that would hint at his overall goals?"

"I, uh . . . Sorry, Lord Seiji. Not beyond the overall objective of 'make money.' I'm sure it would've all made a lot more sense if you've got a scraw's-eye view of Clan politics and the trade networks, but . . ."

"Yes, we've addressed the subject of your ass and high tea. Hm . . . I'm interested in developing a better general understanding of this Highlord . . . Caldimer, was it?"

"Caldimer," he enunciated.

"That's what I said."

"You said . . . Carudimeru? I'm not sure where the extra syllables—"

Aster cleared her throat loudly. "Lord Seiji does *not* have an accent, Auron." I'd have appreciated the show of loyalty more if she wasn't smirking at me. Or if Biribo didn't laugh himself out of the air.

"Ah yes, of course. That's my mistake, my lord, I'm sorry. I don't hear so good anymore. It's rough living that does it."

I wasn't sure whether it was a good or bad thing how quickly he got over being afraid of me, though I was starting to get the impression that Auron, at least, was going to fit in just fine with the crew.

"Yes, well, anyway. I'll ask you for more details about him in a more comfortable setting, when I have the luxury of devoting my full concentration to the subject."

"I never met the man, Lord Seiji, but I'm happy to empty my skull for you," Auron assured me, nodding. "Just from secondhand knowledge, I got a more'n passing impression Caldimer Olumnach's a shitty piece of work, even for a highborn. Be my pleasure to contribute any tidbit that ruins his day."

"That's something to look forward to, then. In the meantime, I need intel on other bandit gangs on Dount. Most importantly their locations, but anything else you can add will help."

"Oh, that I can do. Yeah, it's like how I said with our camp—I couldn't walk you right to their front door, but I know enough from talking with others in the trade where generally a few of the camps are. Close enough to track 'em down, if you've got a decent tracker."

I nodded, glancing at Biribo. Sakin was a decent tracker, but in this case a familiar was even more useful.

"What about around here? I need to expand the territory under our control—we need the income from raiding, and also the food from having space to hunt and forage. But your camp is the only one whose location I knew, and I chose to abandon rather than seize it because it's hell and gone from our home base. Next priority is to annex territory closer to us."

"Yeah, makes sense," he agreed, nodding. "You don't wanna be trooping back and forth through other gangs' turf; that's askin' for an edgewind full of shit. Yeah, Lord Seiji, I can point you to a few camps, like I said. Let's see, we're in the great western forest out here . . . Depending on how far north we are and your base is, there's either one or two gangs between you and the waystation camp. Up north's a crew based in the ravine maze that's probably not too hard to take down. They rely on the terrain around 'em for defense, and don't even raid trade roads, just hit the outlying villages and farms. Way I hear it, they're sneak thieves rather'n proper bandits. Pushovers, once you root 'em out."

"Good to know. But that's up north; what about more directly between here and the waystation territory?"

"That news is less good," he said, grimacing. "Yeah, that's another group. I've got a general idea where they're located, but those fuckers are bad news, Lord Seiji. *Bad*."

"How so?"

"It's . . ." Auron paused, narrowing his eyes in thought. "Well, actually, you laid out the exact problem, back at the camp. That was a good speech, by the way. But yeah, there's basically two kinds of bandits. You got the folks who had shitty luck or just couldn't fit in and got chased out of, uh, normal society. And then you got the fuckers who *love* being out of normal society. The ones that *live* to gut people and generally wreck their shit. Different gangs have a different . . . balance, let's call it. My group was a pretty even blend cos we had high turnover; we were right on Olumnach's actual owned lands, so they'd send us new people directly when they found 'em. There's gangs like the one I mentioned up north that actively try not to cause any more trouble than they gotta to survive. Hell, I've heard of a group way out east that only hits highborn and tries to help out peasants when they can."

I nodded. "I'm familiar with that group. In fact, I've already reached out to them. But I'm getting the impression that you're leading up to a reveal that the nearest gang is the opposite of that."

"Yeah," he said, grimacing. "The reason is, that's Clan Yldyllich land, Lord Seiji. The Yldyllich Clansguard do *not* fuck around. They catch you doing shit on their turf, you're feeding the crawns. Clan Yldyllich makes a lot of its money operating a toll road where they guarantee safe passage and charge out the ass for it. Last time I heard of them actually catching bandits on their land, they force-marched 'em to the edge of their territory, where they were in view of the major trade road, doused the poor bastards in asauthec, and lit 'em on fire."

Aster winced. "That's one way to make a statement."

Yeah, I'd found that fire sent an emphatic message. Not that I wanted to dwell on it.

"So," I said slowly, "naturally, any bandits that operate in their territory are both highly skilled . . ."

"And the most vicious sons of bitches ever to take up the trade," he finished, nodding. "Yeah, that crew may not be the worst on the island, but trust me, they're up there."

"Not recruitment prospects, then," I murmured. "Good. That'll be . . . simpler."

Auron eyed me sidelong. "Hm. I was about to ask a stupid question, but . . . Yeah, I guess the honest-to-goddess Dark Lord can wipe out a crew like that, huh? Alone, probably."

"Doing it alone sounds like a needless risk," I said, allowing myself a faint smile, "but yes. I'm not really worried about my chances. If anything, it's needing to hold back that makes things . . . tactically challenging. Solving problems by destroying everything in the vicinity isn't the most productive strategy under the majority of circumstances, but *damn* does it save time."

"I'll bet," Auron agreed in a carefully neutral tone. "Anyway, that's one of the few crews that might not even answer to Highlord Caldimer. There are only a few gangs on the island he doesn't control—the ones that're either too wild to handle, too weak to be worth it, or have an ideological issue like those do-gooders out east. I dunno for certain, but given the risks he'd be taking by sending forces into Clan Yldyllich's territory, I bet it's a blank spot in his map."

"Even better. Nobody will miss them." Taking their territory might not be immediately productive as it sounded like I wasn't ready to throw down with the Yldyllich Clansguard, either, but it would give us a relatively safe corridor to the valuable central territory we'd just seized, which I needed to assert control over before Clan Olumnach or someone else moved in. This group would definitely be my next target.

"Then to the south," Auron continued, "in the area surrounding Gwyllthean, you got a bigger number of smaller gangs with a smaller territory each. That's farming country, divvied up by dinky little Clans that're direct vassals of Clan Aelthwyn. Y'know, the brown-haired ones whose 'fortress' is a house with an unusually high garden wall, and whose Clansguard is five guys who take turns carrying the spear. Clans like that are pretty much helpless, and since Clan Aelthwyn doesn't seem to give a fuck . . . you get open banditry *way* closer to the city itself than there should be. Those gangs're the poor bastards Caldimer's been using to push in on Lady Gray's territory in the Gutters. Way I hear it, that woman's an even bigger monster than that gang over there on Yldyllich land."

"Yeah, I've had the pleasure of her acquaintance," I said dryly.

"I reckon you'll find that more fertile ground, Lord Seiji. Lot of those boys and girls are that first type of bandit I mentioned, folks who're desperate and grabbing at the only job they can hold down because it's that or starve. Especially with this turf war going on—nobody wants to mix it up with that psycho bitch and her crews. There's the—holy shit!"

"Ah," I said, quite pleased at the reaction. "Home sweet home."

My conversation with Auron hadn't started until we'd been on the road a while; I'd been busy supervising the departure and making sure everybody was moving with no problems before moving ahead to hold a conversation. Thus, we had only just drawn close enough to see the towers and battlements of North Watch between the khora branches ahead, rearing up out of the forest itself with the mountain dramatically framed behind it.

"We're way up in . . . No *way*," Auron breathed. "That's *North Watch*! Holy shit, I wouldn't have believed this heap was still standing!"

"Well, mostly," I said modestly. "You'll be able to see better once we're inside, but it's, ah, still kind of a work in progress."

"Uh . . ." His impressed expression transitioned to one of worry. "It's . . . an actual fortress. Like, yeah, I can definitely see the advantage of that, but . . . Lord Seiji, once the Clans find out you're running a massive bandit operation out of a real *fortress*, it's gonna be war. I mean, actual, for real, armies-on-the-march war. I'm honestly surprised you haven't already stirred up the lizardfolk; they get pissy whenever any shenanigans happen too close to Viryan territory. You . . . haven't had trouble with the lizardfolk, have you?"

"Haven't even seen 'em. Don't worry, Auron, I know exactly how much of a provocation this is. I have a plan."

He didn't look terribly reassured, so of course I didn't elaborate that my plan was actually several possible plans depending on how events unfolded from here, and several of them boiled down to 'Immolate everybody until they fuck off out of my business.'

"We should be just about in time for breakfast—a good time to get you lot settled in. We'll get a hot meal in you and then you can rest off the hike for a couple hours, since we pretty well ruined your cozy night's sleep. This afternoon you can join up for training."

"Training?" He turned a surprised look on me. "No offense, Lord Seiji, but we've been doing this for a while. Everybody here knows which end of a crossbow to use."

One of the Alley Cats snorted loudly, and two others laughed.

"Auron," I said kindly, "I have good news and bad news, and both are that you're not a bunch of bumbling fuckoffs rolling around in the forest anymore. We are here to get shit *accomplished*. Welcome to the Dark Crusade."

That incited cheers from those behind me—including, to judge by the male voices joining in, from some of our new "hires."

I, however, frowned. "Biribo, do I really *have* to call it the Dark Crusade? That's just so . . . edgelord."

"Boss, the nice thing about being Dark Lord is you can do whatever the fuck you feel like. But you gotta earn that privilege by demonstrating you have the power to do whatever the fuck you feel like and kick the shit out of whoever tells you not to. It's gonna take some time to build to that point. In the short term, it's probably best to play along with people's expectations."

"Ooh, can we call it the Pink Crusade?" Lionit chirped. "We could get matching uniforms! I look great in pink."

"Okay, note to self," I said aloud. "Lionit is *never* to be in charge of decorating anything."

"Aww."

"How about Seiji's Circus of Terror?" Aster suggested, grinning.

"How about the Bad Bitches?" added Noraen.

"Ugh, that's even worse than the first one," Mierit groaned.

"As of right now," I stated, raising my voice, "the Dark Lord is *not* accepting proposals to rename the Dark Crusade!"

"Boo!"

"That's not fair!"

"You used to be fun, Lord Seiji!"

"*When* did he used to be fun?" Aster demanded.

"This . . ." Auron had to stop, blink, and clear his throat. ". . . is not what I was expecting."

I sighed and patted him heavily on the shoulder. "I feel you, man."

6

In Which the Dark Lord Outsmarts Himself and No One is Surprised

I handed my new minions off to my older minions while accepting Junko's customary exuberant greeting. Minifrit, as usual, was up and about and in control bright and early. She smoothly swept up the new arrivals and ushered them off in the custody of herself and a few girls she had designated as her helpers to get something to eat. Breakfast was being served in the mess hall, which was the usual tumultuous affair because, despite my best efforts, this was a castle full of mostly ex-prostitutes and not any kind of military encampment. At this point, I figured the disorder fostered camaraderie and didn't demand too much of my people, which was probably better for them while they were all still adjusting to such a massive change in life circumstances.

Breakfast sounded good to me, too—that and a nice long nap. However, there was, as usual, no rest for the wicked, and I spotted something scampering through the mess hall which reminded me of a task I needed to perform. Six somethings, in fact. And I didn't so much spot them as almost get run over by them had I been less adroit on my feet.

"Oi!" I grabbed Gilder by the collar, causing a pileup as the five children chasing him failed to stop in time. "There's a whole courtyard out there for you to run around in. What the hell is wrong with you? People are carrying food in here!"

"Sorry, Lord Seiji!" he said, trying unsuccessfully to give me the big puppy dog eyes without first erasing his characteristic irrepressible grin, because Gilder had never been sorry for anything in his life.

"Being a good influence on the new kids already, I see."

"You know it, bossman! We'll have 'em trained up proper in no time!"

"Great," I said sourly, looking past Benit and Radon at the three younger children who were bringing up the rear of the pack. "That's another *fun* conversation with their parents I have to look forward to."

I had been mildly but only briefly surprised to pick up a few strays in the process of recruiting nearly all the prostitutes in the Gutters. There were others adjacent to them who had eagerly bought what I was selling, and a few who'd taken the opportunity to extract their loved ones from the city to my fortress, if only because said loved ones were likely to become the targets of a very pissed-off Lady Gray if they remained. I had not expected brothel bouncers to be family men, but a couple were, and their families were now my responsibility.

In the final tally, I had picked up ninety-three ex-prostitutes, six madams, eight bouncers, three housewives attached to said bouncers, and subsequently, three children in addition to my original three Gutter Rats, plus five johns who'd been nearby and really liked my speech. Well, there was also that one guy I'd spoken to during the long hike back from Gwyllthean, who'd quietly admitted he knew falling in love with a whore was the stupidest thing a man could do, but if she wasn't a whore anymore, he figured if he stuck close he might have a shot. This was definitely not the first time someone had joined a rebellion or criminal syndicate for that exact reason, so I didn't have the heart to tell him what an idiot he was.

Well, okay, that's not true. I refrained from telling him what an idiot he was because that would have a negative effect on morale, and anyway, the guy seemed well aware that he was an idiot, so who was I to judge? I was the Dark Lord, not his dad.

All of which had brought up the additional problem that I now needed to address.

"All right, we need to have a talk," I said, putting on a grim tone. "You three! Go get some breakfast, *politely*, and eat it *with your families*. You've got all day to run around like lunatics; it's too early for this."

I'd pointed at the three newer kids immediately behind my trio and immediately regretted my approach. All three looked terrified; one managed an abortive two-armed twitch that might have been an attempt to fold down hands at me before they all turned and fled toward the kitchen.

"C'mon, Lord Seiji, they're just softy town kids," Gilder said reprovingly. "We've told 'em you're nice, but they ain't had time to *see* that yet. Gettin' told off by the fuckin' Dark Lord's just gonna give 'em nightmares."

"That won't make their parents happy, either," Benit added solemnly.

I agreed and hadn't meant to spook them that badly, but this was no time to show weakness. "I don't want to hear it," I said severely. "With me, now. I want a word with the three of you. And no trying to run off or I'll have Junko drag you back."

Junko obliged by barking emphatically, causing multiple nearby adults to wince. Understandable; she was loud in an echoing space like this, not to mention a big, scary-looking dog. Everybody who hadn't actively scritched or played with her seemed nervous around Junko. I had decided not to discourage this.

"Now you done it," Radon muttered, knuckling Gilder in the ribs. "Good job."

"Biribo," I muttered as I turned and led them away, "I need a private spot for a chat."

"Gotcha, boss," he replied equally quietly, right next to my ear. "South gatehouse tower was clear when we came in. I think it still is."

The trio followed me without trouble, I suspect in part because Junko slipped to the rear to herd them. Thanks to the effects of Tame Beast, she sensed and acted on my needs even better than an actually trained dog. Often, I didn't even have to give her commands. Sometimes I only gave her commands to remind people that I had a big dog who could bite their necks off. It was funny how that could sometimes be a more pressing threat than my known ability to cause spontaneous human combustion.

We did indeed find the tower empty, lit only by a bottled light slime. By this point they had all but replaced asauthec torches throughout the fortress. This was, I noted in some surprise, the very room into which Virya had first dropped me when I arrived on Ephemera. I hadn't actually been in here since then. The memories weren't great.

I waited for Benit to shut the door behind us before I grinned at them.

"Relax, kids, you're not in trouble. I just needed to put on a little show for the onlookers so I could get a word with you away from snoopy ears."

"Oh *ho*," Gilder crowed, perking up immediately. "Just like the good old days! What's happening now, Lord Seiji?"

"Old business first," I said, pulling out a chair from the room's table and seating myself. There were two chairs; I didn't know whether this was the one the dead peddler had been in or the one I'd kicked at Kasser, and frankly, I didn't want to know. "How's exploration going? I hope you haven't involved those three townies; they don't seem as scrappy as you guys."

"Yeah, no worries, we leave 'em out of it," Radon assured me. "They got families who take up some of their time. Gives us a good excuse to ditch 'em."

"We haven't found anything really interesting yet, Lord Seiji," Benit reported more quietly. "We haven't looked everywhere yet, but at this point, I don't expect to find much."

"Hey, you never know!" Gilder said, cheery as always. "It ain't over 'til it's over!"

"I'm not expecting much, either," I agreed, nodding at Benit. "I'd be pretty surprised to find either treasure or booby traps in a dump like North Watch, but still. There's no point in having three sharp-eyed little scouts if I don't use you, now is there?"

All three puffed up visibly.

"Just remember my rules," I added in a more severe tone.

"Always carry a light," Gilder chimed.

"If we see anything weird, poke it with a stick before using our hands," said Radon.

"Exploring the fortress is not an excuse to dig through the personal belongings of people actually living here," Benit finished.

Truthfully, having the three of them poke through the as yet unrefurbished chambers and back corridors of North Watch was pretty pointless in terms of productivity; there was nothing back there but dust, crawns, spiders, and the moldy leavings of the fortress's previous occupation by the Kingsguard and the local cat tribe. All of which was decayed to scraps and mush by now. But I figured playing explorer would give the kids something to do that'd stave off their inevitable boredom, which out here was likely to result in them wandering off into the khora and getting grabbed by cat people.

"Very good," I said approvingly. "Now, I have another job for you."

"You can count on us, Lord Seiji!" Gilder said, beaming.

"Believe me, you've more than proved that. So, as you know, we've now got over a hundred people in this fortress, and that means we've got security risks that weren't a factor before. There's no way for me to know or keep track of everybody here as personally as I did when my gang was just six bandits and the three of you. Added to that, some of our new arrivals are only here because I made it too dangerous for them to stay in Gwyllthean; at least a few are bound to resent that. *Plus*, we've got recruits from several of Lady Gray's former gangs, *and* the sheer number of people, so the circumstances have to have created the opportunity for an operator as sharp as Gray to have slipped a spy or two into the ranks."

"You don't know who you can trust," Benit said seriously.

"Not yet." I nodded at her.

"So you need us to do some good old-fashioned Gutter Rat snooping!" Gilder said with a proper Gilder Grin, the kind that made him look like his face might split in half.

"Sort of, yes, but also *definitely not*." I made my own expression more solemn to compensate. "I want *no active snooping*, and here's why. Among my other pressing needs, I have to manage the morale of this crew. They're pretty fired up after our successes, but things are inevitably gonna get more monotonous around here, and we will eventually lose some of our battles. I have to do everything possible to make sure everyone feels safe, welcomed, and part of the group. That can't happen if they think I'm having my personal spies rummage through all their shit as soon as their backs are turned. Understand?"

All three of them nodded, wearing the incredibly serious expressions that only children and insufferably pompous people could wear.

"What I *do* want you to do is actively keep your eyes and ears open," I continued. "Don't go looking directly into people's business, but don't forget all those skills you learned working for Uncle Gently. Take note of anything you spot that pings your instincts. Don't follow up without direct orders from me, but do come to me if you spot anything that seems like it *should* be snooped into. I'll decide how to proceed from there, on a case-by-case basis."

"You got it, Lord Seiji!" Gilder assured me, puffing up his thin chest.

"I'm serious about this," I warned. "If I start getting complaints that you three are sticking your noses into shit without my permission, I'm gonna have to call off the operation *and* come down on you. Don't put me in that position."

"We won't, Lord Seiji," Benit said, nodding.

"You can always count on us," Radon added.

To be truthful, while my argument about morale was correct and important, the greater part of my concern was that anybody spying on behalf of Lady Gray wouldn't hesitate to silence and dispose of a child. That argument would impress Benit, but the boys were frustratingly oblivious to the concept of their own mortality. Hopefully this would keep them engaged enough to ward off boredom, not put them in danger, and also might even lead to useful intel if we did have a mole or two. While I was motivated in large part by my guilt over the way I'd used and endangered the kids in the past, the fact remained that they were *very* effective little snoops. They'd been trained for it from the cradle.

"Good!" I stood back up, dusting off my trousers, and Junko also rose from the seat she'd taken next to me. "I do love knowing who I *can* trust around here. Thanks, guys."

"Are you gonna stay in the castle for a while longer, Lord Seiji?" Benit asked.

"Sorry," I said, grimacing. "I've left the situation in Gwyllthean unattended for too long as it is. I need to get back there and tie up some loose ends."

"Just . . . be careful," she said, her eyes big and focused. "Lady Gray may've been hurt, but she'll just be madder because of it. That bitch won't stop being dangerous 'til well after she's dead."

"Don't you worry, I'm well aware of what a piece of work Gray is," I assured Benit, patting her head. "And putting her down for good is a big part of why I need to check up on my interests in the city. I've gotta get back there as soon as possible. Which'll probably be tomorrow, considering the night I've already had. Let's go get some breakfast, and then the Dark Lord needs some actual sleep."

"Yeah, I hear naps start to get important, later in life," Gilder said in an excessively solemn tone. "It must be really hard being old, Lord Seiji."

"Well, I have good news, you little shit—keep talking to me like that and you'll never have to find out."

He laughed, which made me feel a bit better about the misunderstanding earlier. At least some people around here knew I wasn't an indiscriminate murderous madman.

I really hoped they were still right about that.

"Some of these are going to be easier to get than others," Cadimer Auldmaer said the next day in his office as he studied the list of our material needs I'd given him. "Grant me an hour to work on this, and I can have it divvied up into what I can supply directly, indirectly, or not at all, with notes on where and how you can go about acquiring the objects from each category."

"That'll be perfect," I agreed, nodding. "And in fact, while you're doing that I'd like you to keep in mind a change in procedure. My organization's needs have grown beyond the ability of your company to directly supply them, and I don't want to put an unnecessary strain on your resources. For the same reason, our ability to acquire liquid capital has substantially increased. I'd like you to pivot the focus of your support from directly supplying us to assisting me in meeting our own needs without leaving an annoying paper trail."

"Splendid, that's the best thing for us both, Lord Seiji," he said with a grin. "And thank you for sparing me the embarrassment of bringing it up."

"How are things looking for you so far?"

"Oh, this has been a satisfyingly profitable relationship," he said cheerfully. "Two months isn't a lot of time for big investments to bear fruit, but those nice, conservative, boring investments we talked about have done very well in the interim, especially with you discreetly trimming some of the competition. The 'losses' you took from my own caravans have barely nibbled at my profit margins. I am about at the point of sniffing around for my next big opportunity, now that the company has a solid base from which to move. On that subject," he added a bit more hesitantly, "and please understand I mean no disrespect, Lord Seiji, I think I'd prefer to pull this off without your assistance, if possible."

"No disrespect is taken," I said, giving him a slight smile. "I get it. All these months spent looking innocent aren't going to amount to much if every windfall you have comes violently at the expense of your competition. Best to save your trump card for emergencies."

"Just so," Auldmaer said with clear relief. "I will, of course, keep you informed, in case such an emergency pops up. Now, in the meantime, we just need to draw up this month's list of necessary, irrelevant, and hands-off targets."

"I do need you to broaden the scope of those," I said. "As I mentioned, we're expanding operations, and I don't want to accidentally cause problems for you. Also, there's another variable to factor in—I've recently learned that we're now in direct competition with Clan Olumnach for the same general objectives."

"Wasn't that true from the outset?" he asked, cocking his head.

"Only in a strictly technical sense," I admitted with a grimace. "That Crown Rose incident aside, up 'til now we've been strictly small potatoes as far as somebody like Olumnach is concerned. Starting now, though, I fully intend to cut into his business in a serious way. A massive way. As in, I'm going to take *all* of his business. I'll be proceeding in such a way that the name 'Lord Seiji' never comes into it; the last thing I want is to accidentally create a trail back to you. By all means, profit from Clan Olumnach's misfortune, just no more than any of the other merchant companies."

"I can do you one better," he mused, a sly little smile flicking across his features. "With a little . . . surgical accounting and some help from you, I can arrange for one of my most annoying competitors to profit significantly from Clan Olumnach's misfortune. And then let nature take its course."

"Now, that is creatively vicious," I congratulated him. "Good show."

"Fortunately, I'm ahead of you on this one, Lord Seiji. Everybody knows what Olumnach is doing, even if nobody dares call him out on it openly. There's a cottage industry among the information brokers down at the Trader's Guild to keep on top of his investments for the specific purpose of *not* stepping on his toes. All of us in the business have a vested interest in not antagonizing the bandit lord of Dount. The Auldmaer Company was previously too small to need to worry about that, but I've recently begun to patronize them. Staying out of Highlord Caldimer's hair should be simple enough, especially if you forewarn me what you're planning to do."

"I'll keep you posted. Olumnach should be a more distant threat, at least for the time being. Right now, our big problem is the difficulty in communicating with you. I'm afraid Lady Gray is *good* and mad at me at present, which makes it . . . interesting . . . to get in and out of the city."

"Yes, I wondered about that." Eyebrows rising, he glanced back and forth between me and Aster, who was leaning against the wall by the door. "Dare I ask how you got here this time?"

"Oh, it was easy," she said, deadpan. "We paid a teamster to smuggle us in on his cart. In crates that were supposed to be full of nails. It was *extremely* comfortable."

"You don't get to complain," I stated, pointing at her. "*My* crate actually still had nails in it."

"Things like that will work in the short term, if you don't mind the indignity," Auldmaer said carefully, "but every time a trick is used, its future utility diminishes. Especially when you're dealing with somebody like Lady Gray, who knows all the tricks to begin with. I appreciated the warning you sent about her; I've improved security here at headquarters and around my other interests. Launching a direct attack on me isn't a viable move for her, but someone like that has all kinds of indirect means of getting her point across. At the very minimum, I would expect her to already have my place under surveillance."

"Dealing with Gray for good is high on my priority list," I assured him, "but as you no doubt understand, that's not something I can just saunter out of here and *do*. The necessary arrangements have to be careful. In the short term, are you reasonably confident she *won't* come after you personally?"

"Oh, it's not even about me," he said with a grin, waving away that concern. "Lady Gray's entire business model depends on the Clans' disinterest in what lowborn do to each other. I'm a moneyed middleborn in the middle ring who's financially connected to bigger trading companies and several of the Clans. If she sent thugs up here to mess with me or my business, it's not my business that would motivate the Clansguards to stomp her back down. They won't stand for a Gutter criminal wandering too close to their own spheres of activity."

"Yes, so I've been told. My concern is that in my own interactions with Gray, I have found her . . . *frustratingly* competent. She's crafty and maneuvers fast. Like you said, there have to be ample ways for her to mess with you and not call down the wrath of the Clans."

"Well, yes, that's the weakness in that particular defense," he agreed, his smile fading. "Nobody in the upper rings is going to bother moving on my behalf *unless* the Gutters' crime queen steps visibly out of her place. To counter her more oblique moves, I would need the kinds of connections I don't have. You, Lord Seiji, are my only asset against measures like that. And while your commitment to ending her permanently is reassuring, in an *eventual* sort of way, in the shorter term . . ."

"It's the cause of your problem, not the solution," I acknowledged. "To that end, I can still help. I've already primed Rhydion to be looking into Gray's business; if I introduce you to him, then Gray putting even a plausibly deniable finger anywhere near you will call down a level of wrath even she isn't prepared to deal with."

"Rhydion?" He straightened up in visible shock. "The *paladin*? How would you—that is, forgive me, Lord Seiji, but I, ah . . . You don't seem like the *type* of person he would associate with. Very much the opposite, to be frank."

"Well, you're not wrong," I said, grinning. "For now, Rhydion wants something from me, so he's being unusually tolerant of my charmingly irascible antics."

"The problem with that plan," said Aster, "is that Rhydion doesn't want anything from a trading company this size. No offense, Master Auldmaer, but he's already got more money than you, *and* follows a way of life that disdains material comforts."

"Yeah, but there are those adventurer friends of his," I said. "His new party of locals—that priestess and the asshole with the mustache."

"Oh, that is a *very* exploitable angle," Auldmaer said. I could practically see the wheels turning behind his eyes. "Adventurers are always in need of goodies. You don't even have to bribe them with artifacts or anything so munificent. Let's see . . . A case of potions with my compliments, and the offer to sell them more at a steep discount. They always want potions. Yes, that would set the hook *deeply*. I'm not actively in the potions trade right now, but I've got a contact I can leverage to get them at cost."

"Try the same with the city guard," I suggested. "They're broadly useless as an actual city guard, but the nice thing about them being a bunch of thugs is that they're probably up for off-the-books thuggery, if they like you and/or you spend some money. I've already set my good friend Captain Norovena on Gray's trail, too, so the pump is primed."

"Paladins and guard captains," he said, staring at me. "You know, Lord Seiji, for a bandit, you keep *very* peculiar company."

"Oh, Norovena's not such a surprising contact," I explained with a pleasant smile. "I bribed him. A lot. He's very interested in my continued survival and financial solvency."

"I do think that'll do it," Auldmaer said slowly. "Prestigious adventurers and crooked guards . . . Those are exactly the kinds of friends who quietly make problems go away. Guards are almost laughably easy to get on your side, too, at least in this country. If you can provide me the actual names of those party members of Rhydion's, in a handful of days, I can have myself set up such that even Lady Gray will hesitate to poke at me with the longest stick she has. If she's already watching my comings and goings, as I strongly suspect, she'll even know that I'm off limits without having to learn the hard way. I must say, Lord Seiji, for all the trouble you cause, you are admirably conscientious about mitigating unfortunate consequences."

"I do what I can," I said modestly, reaching into my coat. "And on that subject in particular, there's something else I wanted to ask you about. I have a short list of people who are connected to people who are connected to the bloody lip I recently gave Lady Gray. Can you possibly locate any of these without drawing attention to them? There are limits to what I can realistically do, but if I *can* protect any of them from blowback, I consider it my responsibility."

The list was pretty short, for having been drawn from everybody currently at North Watch who'd been invited to participate. Apparently, few of them had connections in Gwyllthean, and of those, a lot had had the foresight to bring their connections with them.

"I can give it a look, but please understand there's very little I can do in that regard," Auldmaer cautioned me, accepting the sheet of paper and examining it. "Given the near certainty that Gray has eyes on me already, I have very little chance of pulling off anything without her notice. Me investigating anyone through the channels I have access to would just lead her directly—oh! I know this guy."

Something in his expression and tone made a prickle run down my spine. Apparently not just mine; Aster unfolded her arms and took a step closer to us.

Auldmaer set the list down on his desk and pointed to one name. "Cwynnar Alsiada. He's a porter who works at the Trader's Guildhall. I've seen him now and again, but I doubt I'd have remembered him before this morning. He came by my offices just today."

"Oh, let me guess," I whispered.

"I thought at the time it was pretty odd," Auldmaer said gravely. "He claimed he'd gotten a message from me offering to hire his services for the day. Obviously, I had no idea what he was talking about. Poor fellow was rather miffed, but we put it down to somebody playing a somewhat dull practical joke on him. Of course, in light of this . . ."

Cwynnar Alsiada was the brother of one of Minifrit's bouncers who had joined my army. Supposedly, the only family he had.

"She deliberately brought him to your attention," Aster whispered. "And if she's got people watching these offices, she probably knows we're here . . . Oh *shit*. She outmaneuvered us again, didn't she?"

"Of *course* she fucking did," I spat, already rising from my chair. Beneath the annoyance and self-recrimination, though, I felt something else rising up. Something dark, and avid—the all-consuming rage that had kept me on my feet and fighting all through the battle in Cat Alley. The thing that had all but blotted out my personality and replaced it with pure, homicidal destruction.

She had flanked me yet again; her ambushers were undoubtedly closing in already. And a big part of me *welcomed* it.

All right, Gray, you know I'm here. This time I don't have a whole district full of people to protect. Round two, new rules.

7

In Which the Dark Lord Has a Brilliant Idea

Wait!" Auldmaer rose abruptly from his chair, holding out a hand to forestall me as I started to turn toward the door. "This doesn't add up. There's always time to think, Lord Seiji; give me a moment to lay this out."

The rising surge of incipient violence was practically tingling in my limbs, but I did pause and turn back to face him out of sheer curiosity if nothing else. "I'm listening."

"We are assuming," he said slowly, sinking back into his chair with an intent expression, "that the point of this was to make sure I'd recognize this guy Cwynnar's name, just *in case* you came here asking about people connected to participants in the Cat Alley fiasco, so I could tell you where he is, so you could wander into a trap?"

At that recitation, even some of the rising bloodlust began to cool back down. "Well . . . yes. But when you put it like that . . ."

Auldmaer nodded. "Because that's a *bad plan*. Especially since it happened this morning and you've only just turned up now. It hinges on multiple variables—the timing, my reactions, your reactions—that she can't even predict, much less control."

"So you think Cwynnar coming here was . . . just a coincidence?"

"Not when he'd been sent on that particular fool's errand," he said, leaning back in his chair and frowning. "Coincidences *do* happen, but in my experience, any event that inexplicable *and specific* speaks of intelligent action. And with all due respect to Master Alsiada, I doubt he's all that interesting to anyone but yourself and Lady Gray—certainly no one else who's connected to my company. Which makes the central question—does Lady Gray make bad plans? Is she prone to being reckless and disorganized? I only know the woman by reputation, Lord Seiji, so I'll yield to your expertise on the subject."

"No," I admitted, "definitely not. In fact, I'd say Lady Gray's overall high competence is her most annoying trait. Well, you know, in addition to being generally horrible. You're right—this doesn't add up."

"Which means," he said, nodding, "*this* is not the plan. We're seeing one very small and, perhaps, not very important part of it."

"You're thinking this is . . . what?" Aster tilted her head in confusion. "Misdirection? A feint?"

"Still too random; it would still need to be a well-laid plan for that to work," he said, his frown deepening. Auldmaer began drumming his fingers on his desk, staring intensely at the wall behind us. "Let's step back, consider the overall situation. Lady Gray can't operate *openly* inside the walls without bringing down the wrath of the Clans. And likely the Convocation and the King's Guild, to boot. Her ability to gather information up here is not really hindered—anyone with any combination of time, connections, and coin can do that. It's only assertive action that would get her in trouble."

"Right," I prompted when he paused for thought. Aster was right, this was really annoying when other people did it.

"And from what I've heard," he mused after a moment's consideration, "even her ability to act is somewhat eclipsed right now. She should still have all but total freedom in the Gutters, but even a minor antagonism toward the power structure by making a mess in the middle ring could spell her doom. Her resources are significantly thinner than they were a week ago, and getting thinner by the day as the outlying bandit gangs are growing bolder in their raids."

I pulled out the chair in front of his desk and sat back down. "That's the long and the short of it, yes. It sounds like you've put it together in a way that reveals something I missed, Master Auldmaer."

His eyes came back into focus, meeting mine. "Hm. With all due respect, Lord Seiji, I think you may have fallen prey to Gray's basic strategy already. A strategist must work upon his opponents' minds—for example, by creating the impression that your own expertise means you will always have the upper hand, while making them so angry that they go right for a direct attack at the first sight of you."

I grimaced. "Well, ouch."

"Hell's revels, you have to know all this stuff to be a *merchant?*" Aster demanded.

That bought her a grin from Auldmaer. "Well, I have a personal fondness for books on military history and strategy, but . . . yes, this kind of thinking *does* help in the trade. Business is war. My own battles are usually more cerebral, but many of the underlying philosophies still apply! Ahem, speaking of which, the point is that Lady Gray has primed you to assume she is more dangerous than the reality."

"There's nothing more dangerous than a cornered animal."

"Indeed, but it makes a difference if that animal has had half its claws and teeth removed. Here's my read on the situation. The actual trap or traps will be in the Gutters, where she can safely inflict violence. The key is *getting* you there. Up here in the middle ring, she'll have been exercising what contacts she has to extract information and attempt to catch your attention whenever you showed up. That silly gambit with Cwynnar Alsiada only makes sense as one of a bunch of similarly half-assed measures—a wide net cast in the hope of catching something. That smells to me of desperation."

"Mm," I grunted. "She's still Lady Gray, though. She's good at improvising and very detail-oriented even under pressure. I think . . . if she's set out multiple baits like that, she'll have done so in such a way that noticing *which* I spring for will tell her my angle of attack. That's the only reason I can think of why you were only primed to recognize one of the names on that list."

"Good insight! So if you leave here and head for the Trader's Guildhall, Gray will know to prepare you to think she's taken Alsiada hostage."

"Wait, *think* she's taken him hostage?" Aster demanded. "What's to stop her from actually doing it? I know, I know, middle ring and so on, but c'mon. Nobody in power cares about a guy like that."

"Even less than they care about my modest little trading company," Auldmaer agreed. "What they care about is someone like Lady Gray taking any aggressive action too close to their interests. She *might* risk it, but I think it's more likely she'll misdirect him out of everyone's way again and *claim* to have him, to get you into the Gutters where she can spring the proper trap. However, that is an assumption, not a fact, and whether or not it proves correct, there's a choice to be made. So before we make our own counter-strategy, Lord Seiji, you must decide whether you're willing to leave Cwynnar Alsiada in Lady Gray's hands, if it comes to that."

I drew in a soft breath and let it out slowly. "I suppose you're going to tell me next that he's not worth taking a risk over."

"It's not my call to make; I have no stake in his well-being," he said, shaking his head. "I'm a merchant, after all. I can't help but weigh the costs and benefits. Sometimes, though, you can't make a choice based on pure merit. Only corporations can be utterly rational; a man has to live with himself."

"You have corporations here?" I asked, blinking in surprise.

"Oh goodness, no, not here. The practice is banned in most Sanorite countries. In Dlemathlys I suspect only merchants, diplomats, and goblins even know what the word means." I could see the intrigue on his face; he was dying to ask how *I* knew what a corporation was, but didn't waste any more time on that tangent. "Regardless, that's the situation. Gray won't be coming here to force your hand, but she *will* make her move as soon as you emerge from these offices. That buys us time to make our own plan, so these are the questions we need to answer first. The other central one that I can see is what *her* assessment of *your* threat level is; that will determine what lies waiting for you in the Gutters. A repeat of her strategy up here, with several potential traps for you to stumble into? Or will she try to hit you with all of her resources?"

"All of it," I said without hesitation. "Plus . . . Probably additional assets she'll have sought out in the last week, specifically because I won't know to expect them. She won't be taking any chances."

Auldmaer nodded; again I could see him desperately wanting to ask why I merited so much attention, but again he refrained. "Then I propose that we divide our response. I have an idea to flush her out of the middle ring, but when it comes to striking back at the enemy directly, I must yield to your expertise."

"All right," I replied, slowly. "Give me a moment to think."

"You have it, my lord. Allow me to make preparations while you consider." He shifted over in his chair to pull a cord which dangled beside his desk, causing a bell to chime in the warehouse outside. I stepped to the side of the office next to Aster, leaning against the wall and rapidly considering my options.

Preparation and maneuver, those were her assets. Mine was simple power. Whether or not I had enough power to trump her new preparations . . . even thinking that way made it a quagmire of attrition. Somehow, I needed to flank her. Even a small victory in strategy, a minor tactical edge, could tip the scales in my favor.

How? Well, that was the question. If I knew that, I wouldn't be over here dithering.

The office door opened and a man entered. I didn't remember his name, but I'd seen Auldmaer's secretary around during my visits to the office; he looked like an odd combination of librarian and teamster, with his narrow spectacles, omnipresent clipboard, and the sleeves of his neatly creased shirt always rolled up to display brawny forearms bearing the faded scars of years of what must've been hard work.

"Sir?"

"Merdion, change of plans." Right, that was his name. Auldmaer had spent the seconds between his ringing of the bell and Merdion's appearance rapidly scribbling on some documents, and now pushed these across the desk as the secretary approached. "A big change. I need every outgoing shipment scheduled for the next . . ." He paused to quickly peruse his recently modified papers and jotted something down on one of them. ". . . two days, three as a stretch goal, to depart tonight by dusk at the latest. Simultaneously."

Merdion boggled so hard his glasses almost fell off. "Every . . . for the . . . you can't mean . . ."

"As much as we can arrange on such short notice. This will mean borrowing wagons and porters, of course. Whatever we can get our hands on."

"Of . . . course," said the secretary, recovering a bit. "I'll send Rhan down to the—"

"I'm afraid not," Auldmaer interrupted with an apologetic grimace. "We can't have any direct contact with the Trader's Guild until they ship out, or send any of our people too close to the Guildhall. You'll have to make do with whatever can be loaned or rented to us from other companies nearby."

For a second I thought Merdion was going to either faint or start shouting at his boss. Before he could do either, Auldmaer picked up one sheet from the top of the pile and wagged it at him.

"We need to adjust the routes, too. The shipments have to go out right before the gates close for the night, from *every* gate, and disperse as widely as possible down every available road departing the city."

"Sir . . . even if we can arrange all this in the next few *hours*, sending out shipments *at dusk* is practically begging for bandit attacks!"

"I'm aware. We don't have anything of particular value slated to go out for the next few days anyway. Special orders for this occasion only—instruct the teamsters to proceed as quickly as possible to the nearest safe waystations on their routes, and if attacked, hand over any cargo and flee. Also, they only need to leave the city itself on a wide divergence of paths; they can reroute back onto the main roads from there as soon as possible."

"This is going to cost . . ." Merdion shot me a suspicious look, then pinched the bridge of his nose, displacing his glasses. "Master Auldmaer, how exactly do we profit from this?"

"Business requires foresight, Merdion. Some actions are meant to bring a profit directly; others are to set up a chain of events that will be profitable later."

"But—"

"Hopefully, in the near future, there'll be time for me to explain everything to you," Auldmaer said in a quelling tone, "but for now, this is what I need you to do. Quickly; there's a lot to arrange and very little time. And send Larinet up here. I have a job for her, too."

"Yes, sir," Merdion groaned, finally accepting the stack of papers. He gave me a particularly filthy look on his way back out, no doubt suspecting whose fault all this was, and shut the door harder than was necessary.

"All that sounds . . . expensive," said Aster as soon as we were alone again.

"It's only money," Auldmaer replied with a wink. "You have to spend it to make it, and I expect to recoup my losses. Lady Gray is bad for business, and I'll gain a fortune in goodwill and connections by playing a role in hobbling her. Lord Seiji, do you need a rundown on what I have in mind?"

"I believe I follow you already," I replied. "And now that you've laid it out, you've given me an idea. I know exactly how to turn this around on her."

"Perfect!" the merchant said with a broad grin. He was so amiable and occasionally squeamish about violence, it was easy at times to forget when I first met him he'd been carrying poison around, just in case he needed to murder someone over a civilized drink. "Then while we've got time, let's talk details."

I made my own move in the late afternoon, well before Auldmaer's caravans were ready to roll out. The next stage of my own plan needed to be executed before that happened. In the meantime, it went without saying that anybody watching the Auldmaer Company's headquarters would be able to tell shenanigans were afoot. But that was the neat thing about executing bonkers nonsense—a strategic thinker wouldn't see the pattern in it until it was too late. Undoubtedly, Lady Gray would figure out what we were up to once she realized what was happening, by which time it would be too far into motion for her to stop.

Hopefully. Man, it'd be *really* nice to put one over on her for a change.

I made it two blocks in a straight line toward the Trader's Guildhall before the expected countermove occurred, just long enough for me to start worrying whether this was actually going to work. But before I could despair, a man stepped out of an alley right in front of me, blocking my path.

"Lord Seiji, I presume," he said with a knowing little smirk, folding down his hands at me.

"I have a funny feeling you're about to presume a lot more than that."

He was one of those borderline cases in the caste system, a fellow who might have been upper lowborn or lower middleborn, to judge by his lightish brown complexion and slightly wavy hair, which looked a shade of deep chestnut under the sunlight but probably appeared black when in shadow. At least he was dressed well enough that he probably didn't get too much direct suspicion from the guards.

"Now, now, let's keep this civil, shall we?" he said, still wearing the slight smile of a man who believed himself to hold all the cards. "With you being in such a hurry to go check on your . . . let's say, friend of a friend? It wouldn't do for some rash action on your part to cause him undue . . . discomfort."

"Rash action? Oh, you mean like this?" I whipped out my artifact rapier, hard enough to make it hiss hungrily on the way out of its sheath.

Immediately, foot traffic around us stopped and all those nearest backed away, while everybody safely outside rapier range commenced gawking avidly.

"Whoa! Hey, now, this is a *respectable* part of town," my new acquaintance protested, raising both hands in a peaceable gesture. I had succeeded in wiping the smirk off his face, at least. "Let's not go and create a scene, Lord Seiji. We wouldn't want to have any unpleasantness."

"Interesting proposal," I mused, idly making figure eights with the tip of my sword. Not at his face or heart—aiming directly for his crotch. He backed up another step. "What's in it for me?"

"Well, I should think—"

"Because any unpleasantness is only going to be unpleasant for *you*, my friend." I grinned broadly at his visibly increasing unease. "I expect to find it *hilarious*."

"Listen," he protested, trying to lower his voice so as not to be obviously threatening me in front of all the suddenly attentive onlookers. "You *don't want to do this*. All right? Your *interests* require you to—"

He tried to evade me, but I was wielding a Rapier of Mastery and wearing Surestep Boots, and part of this fellow's "respectable citizen" disguise clearly involved going unarmed; he had no chance. I closed the gap in a single lunge and sank the tip of my sword into his thigh just above the knee. That *could've* been a killing thrust, at least within a few minutes, but I deliberately missed the femoral artery. Thanks to the artifact's enchantment, that was apparently something I could do.

The henchman went down on the street, clutching his leg, howling bloody murder, and squirting blood everywhere. There were a few incidental screams from the onlookers, as well as at least two distinct cheers.

"Are you *crazy*?" demanded my new opponent as soon as he found the wits to form words instead of miscellaneous shrill noises.

"Hah!" I flicked the tip of the sword at him, splattering his face with his own blood. "If you think *this* is crazy, wait 'til you meet my other personality. I say, guards!" I bellowed. "Assault! Mayhem! Assassination! Jaywalking with malice aforethought! Somebody come—ah, there you are."

Unlike my previous encounter with the middle ring guards, I didn't get an entire squad this time, just a pair of Kingsguard soldiers apparently on patrol; they came pounding up the street, the crowd dispersing around them.

"All right, what's all the—Lord Seiji?"

"Oh hey, Sergeant Sanaida!" I greeted him cheerfully. "And it's Tannor, right? They finally moved you guys to middle ring patrol! Congrats, man! I love to see talent rewarded."

Considering their "talent" was taking bribes to let me bring suspicious characters through the gate, this was literally the opposite of that, but I saw no reason to hurt the poor guys' feelings. Not when I had a use for them, anyway.

"Thanks, my lord, it's definitely a less boring gig. As you can plainly see." Sanaida and Tannor silently caught my customary greetings—thrown coins—studying the scene before them with clearly no intention of physically stepping into it. "So what's all this, Lord Seiji? This asshat giving you a problem?"

"*He* stabbed *me*!" the asshat shrieked.

I poked him—gently—with my sword. "Shush, the grown-ups are talking. I don't suppose you gentlemen happen to know this character?"

Tannor spat in the street. "Fuckin' jumped-up Gutter trash, Lord Seiji. Yeah, we know this clown. There's a pool down at barracks going for when he'd finally get knifed. Glad I didn't throw coins in; I wouldn't've expected you, m'lord."

"Or in the leg," Sanaida added. "Future reference, Lord Seiji, if you poke 'em in the gut or heart, you don't have to listen to their bullshit no more."

"Oh, I'm well aware, lads. As it happens, I specifically want to listen to more of this one's bullshit. Or rather, I think the good folks down at headquarters need to. Anyway, in this case, he was quite correct. I did, in fact, stab this unarmed man with no—okay, actually, with *very little* provocation. You should probably arrest me."

The two guards had already pocketed their coins. They now exchanged a loaded glance, then looked in almost comical unison down at the bleeding man, then back at me.

"You . . . *want* to be arrested, Lord Seiji?" the sergeant asked carefully.

"Well, I think that would be best, don't you? Actually, give me just a second, would you?"

"Sure thing, m'lord."

"Are you *serious*?" screeched the previously well-mannered thug. "I'm *bleeding* here!"

"You're makin' a mess on the street, is what you're doing." Tannor kicked him on the shoulder. "Quiet down before I add littering to your charges."

Meanwhile, I was turning in a slow circle with my eyes upraised, until I spotted Aster poking her head over a rooftop across the street, the tiny shape of Biribo hovering above her shoulder. She gave me a thumbs-up and then ducked back down behind the eaves.

"All right, then!" I wiped the blood off my sword with a kerchief, gave it a flourish, and sheathed it. "Thanks for waiting, gents. Now let's all head down to the barracks and explain all this lah-dee-dah to the Captain."

"Yeah, I got a feeling he'll wanna hear this one," Tannor commented. "C'mon, you, up you get. It's not *that* bad, you can still walk. That, or you can get dragged. No skin off my ass either way."

"So, I guess you're under arrest, Lord Seiji," Sergeant Sanaida said apologetically. "This way, if you please. Mind your step, m'lord, street's a bit slippery just there, what with the blood."

Off we went to the Kingsguard headquarters. I have to say, the constant cursing of Lady Gray's henchman was deeply gratifying. You have to appreciate the little things in life.

8

In Which the Dark Lord Avoids at Least One Cliché

An hour later, I found myself reflecting that this, finally, must be what it truly meant to be the Dark Lord.

All this time I'd been mostly working with my own two hands, facing my enemies head-on, and when I had to involve others, leading from the front. Now that I thought of it, that was mostly Hero stuff, right? Boots on the ground, spilling my own blood and sweat to smite the wicked and defend the innocent—and I suspected my motivations weren't any more selfish than a lot of past Heroes, if Sanora tended to choose shut-in otaku for the role. I knew what those people were like.

But now? I had finally begun to lead from the back, filling the more organizational role, which was how the Dark Lord had been described to me. Issuing commands from his dark throne and leaving his minions to do the actual dirty work. Now that I'd tried it, this was extremely stressful; I *itched* to burst out of here and deal with things myself again. Instead, I had to trust that events would unfold more or less as I had foreseen, and that if they didn't, the people I was counting on would be able to adapt on the fly. Trusting other people to do anything right did not come easily to me. Even worse, I had at least one good friend out there facing that danger in my stead, and I couldn't be there to Heal her if things went wrong.

This Dark Lord business was nerve-wracking.

It really didn't help that I was having this epiphany while folded up in a box, being hauled through the streets on what must've been the bumpiest cart Auldmaer could find.

After playing through the entirety of Ravel's "Bolero" in my head twice, there was nothing to do but mull on how my evil plan was unfolding outside my reach. Well, okay, half of it was Auldmaer's evil plan, but I'd helped. At least *he* got to fret from the comfort of his office, and he was used to this anyway. It must be something like this, to send out your caravans and wait weeks to learn whether you'd turned a profit or some disaster had befallen them. Though I imagined I had a bit more on the line than he did.

It was going so *well* so far, which just made the anticipation worse; between how my plans tended to go and the presence of Lady Gray in the background, disaster was like a spider in my bedroom that had vanished the second I'd taken my eyes off it. Little bastard was lurking *somewhere*, I just knew it.

For once, I hadn't even needed to bribe Captain Norovena. I'd just dropped off the goon who had accosted me and dismissed the two guards who'd "arrested" me—because I was in too big a hurry to politely pretend I hadn't usurped his control—and explained my plan. For that, I got the sincerest smile I'd ever seen out of the man. At least, I was pretty confident it was sincere, since it was also the most openly sinister expression he'd ever shown me.

Auldmaer's initial plan was to send out every wagon he could simultaneously so as to smuggle out myself and Aster, plus Cwynnar and whoever else we could rescue from the list, based on the theory that Lady Gray didn't have the manpower to hit every single one, and even sending her forces to hit as many as she could simultaneously would make enough of a spectacle to draw ire she couldn't afford from Clan Aelthwyn. That way, at least some of us could likely slip out.

A good plan, but I wasn't going to settle for escaping when I saw an opportunity to really ruin Lady Gray's evening. Now, Auldmaer's wagons were all going out with a Kingsguard escort. Specifically, Norovena had assigned his most openly corrupt men to them, one to a wagon. Soon enough, probably before they were outside the city, each crooked guard would find himself alone with a cart full of cargo and no witnesses, save an underpaid driver, who had been loudly told in said guards' hearing range to prioritize their own safety and not resist any theft attempts.

What happened next would be pitifully inevitable.

And sure, in actuality, it would be the result of Auldmaer, Norovena, and myself maneuvering these hapless goons into indulging their greed under circumstances wherein the boss lady couldn't possibly reach most of them in time to stop them. To an outside observer, though, it would sure *look* like Lady Gray had just launched a massive, coordinated attack on a middle ring trading company and the Kingsguard itself.

Add to that the man we'd already apprehended and the ones Aster would be rounding up right now—which would look like either a kidnapping or blackmail operation in the middle ring, depending on how Gray had decided to go about getting leverage on me—by dawn, Norovena would have a report to give Archlord Caludon of Clan Aelthwyn of an unprecedented provocation by Lady Gray. Come noon, she'd be the personal target of every Clan on Dount that could muster forces to Gwyllthean.

If, of course, everything went according to plan.

By this point I was taking it as a given that Lady Gray would pull off one of those last-minute bullshit maneuvers she was so good at to at least mitigate the damage, but I was confident she wasn't coming out of this unscathed. At the moment, I was more concerned about Aster. The last I'd seen her she'd just given me the signal that her own operation was a go; with Biribo's help, she'd identified the watcher who was keeping tabs on my own confrontation with Gray's stooge, and she would track him back to whatever field command he was set up in and take that down. Since Biribo hadn't already come back, I had to assume it was an actual secondary unit and not overseen by Lady Gray herself; I'd given Aster strict instructions not to tackle Gray alone. But at best, she was still left to deal with a bunch of armed enemies.

Between her Impregnable Chainmail and Greatsword of Mastery, Aster was basically a human wrecking ball. In addition, she had Biribo's tactical help. I had also given her a healing slime stuffed into a wineskin that Auldmaer had donated in case of emergencies. All told, Aster was one of the deadliest people in this city. Probably only Rhydion, Lady Gray, and I could even hope to take her on.

And yet, the last person to own those two artifacts had died with both equipped, falling into a pit trap dug by some shifty bandit.

I was worried.

It came as a great relief when I got the signal to move, especially since there'd been a real chance of no such signal occurring. My chosen cart had been assigned the single most disreputable guard available, handpicked by Captain Norovena for being corrupt, stupid, and mean, even by the standards of the Gwyllthean Kingsguard, and routed through one of the most disreputable patches of the Gutters Auldmaer could nominate. We had *wanted* this cart to be hit, at the very least by its own guard, and hopefully by worse, and stacked the deck as best we could to make that happen. Still, the guard might have opted not to get sticky fingers for once—and even more likely, we might not have been intercepted.

But sometimes, things worked out.

"Stop the cart!"

I perked up as much as I could, having been stuffed in this box for most of the last hour. *Showtime.*

"Who the fuck are you?" demanded the driver. A thump followed; I didn't *think* it sounded like a person being struck, but it definitely shut him up.

"Hey, the hell do you think you're doing?" demanded our assigned guard. "You blind or just stupid?"

"Don't start with me, Aefryd," snapped the first voice. "Your dumb ass is lucky I got to you before you decided to jack this load yourself. Get rid of this guy."

"Don't worry, I'll deal with this," said Aefryd. "You haul ass back to your boss, tell him to send more men to retrieve what's left of this. I'll get rid of this guy and stand watch 'til then."

"What's left of it, huh," the driver drawled. "If you're gonna stand watch, why's any of it gonna go missing?"

There came a similar thump, and this time I noticed the tremor from underneath me. Ah, they were emphasizing their instructions by hitting the cart with weapons. Classy.

"You heard Master Aulder—"

"Auldmaer."

"*I don't fucking care.* Get outta here!"

Despite my muffled surroundings, I could hear the man's exasperated sigh, followed by the shifting of the cart as he got down from the driver's seat. "At least leave the dhawls alone, will ya?" he said as he stomped back up the street.

Now, there was a fellow I could respect. No fear at all in the face of rampant thuggery. I guess hauling cargo in a place like this made you hard to ruffle.

"Real fuckin' subtle, Aefryd," snorted the new arrival.

"Yeah, yeah, have your fun. It's . . . Lamm, right? Well, you had to butt in, and I don't feel like tussling, so step on up. Let's see what we got."

"Keep your fucking hands off that cargo, dumbass. That's what I'm here to tell you, and I don't have time to play slap-a-hand, so you listen good. Orders from Lady Gray herself. All these Auldmaer Company wagons leaving the city right now are *hands off.*"

There was a momentary pause, and honestly, I could've made my move at that point, but I was almost compelled to wait for the right moment. Not tactically; as soon as the driver was gone, everything was set up the way I needed it to be, but I craved a suitable verbal cue.

Presentation *matters*, damn it.

"Bullshit," Aefryd decided after thinking it over for a second, a process which I suspected took real effort. "You're just lookin' to shoo me off and get first pick. You think I was born yesterday?"

"Listen to me *very carefully*, you stupid sack of goose pellets. I am not going to have first pick or *any* pick of the cargo, and neither are you. I am *just* here to give the message, and now I gotta go stop as many of these fucking things as I can manage before the *rest* of your asshole shellcap friends crack theirs open. I've seen your face here, Aefryd. I know it was you, and I know where this cart was stopped. If so much as a black disc is missing from it, I'm gonna make sure Lady Gray knows, too. Then you'll only get to live long enough to see your family gutted and strung up in your own doorway. Understand?"

"That was the wrong fucking thing to say, corebait," Aefryd retorted, accompanied by the rough whisper of a sword leaving a scabbard. "I don't take well to threats. Especially not from a gray disc alley pounder who just told me himself I'm only gonna have problems if he leaves here alive to squeal on me."

"You've been wearing that shellcap too long, Aefryd," Lamm retorted. Unlike his excitable counterpart, he actually lowered his voice when promising violence. Personally, I found that more theatrically effective. "It's cutting off blood flow to your brain. There's only *one* law in the Gutters, and you're one more stupid move from pissing her off."

That would do.

Given that my box was far from airtight, the pink flash of Heal must have made quite a spectacle in the darkening street. It would make sure both members of my audience had turned to stare at it directly, just in time for me to fling the lid off and burst upright.

"KONO SEIJI DA!"

Windburst!

My first clear sight of my two new acquaintances thus involved them being blown over—Lamm against the front of a building, Aefryd clattering boots over eyeballs up the street in his colorful armor. Akornin was lighter than steel; he tumbled a respectable distance.

"Oh shit," Lamm wheezed, apparently not too winded by the impact. He'd dropped his sword, though, and now fell to hands and knees in the street, groping for it while gasping to himself, "Oh fuck, not him . . ."

"And it is a pleasure to meet you, *too*," I declaimed, sweeping an elegant bow from atop the cart. Behind me, one of the dhawls snorted and stomped a foot, but that was it. They were far more placid in temperament than most Earth creatures put to similar use, which was helpful in situations like this.

"Oh, you are fuckin' *dead*, corebait!" Aefryd snarled, getting to his feet and grabbing his own sword.

"Yeah, go for it, Aefryd," Lamm suggested, shooting me a sharp sidelong look. "I think you can take him."

While I could see where the brains were distributed between this pair, suspicion of Lamm accomplished what basic common sense apparently could not, and at this advice Aefryd paused, reconsidering.

"Boo, did you have to go and spoil my fun?" I pouted at the thug. He looked kind of . . . miscellaneous, among all the street toughs I'd seen, apart from the fact that he had a sense of style. His coat was of the cut that noblemen wore and seemed to have actual gold trim, though it was frayed, threadbare, and patched in multiple places. Some highborn's castoff, no doubt, but it made a serviceable affectation for a guy like this.

"Look," he said, getting slowly to his feet with his sword held out to the side. "I don't want any trouble with you, Lord Healer."

"Yeah, I'll just *bet* you don't. Stand right there, I'll deal with you in a moment."

Slimeshot. Slimeshot.

Lamm twitched violently as the slimes whipped past his head to either side, splattering against the wall behind him. One left a visible dent. I winked at him.

"And I'll deal with you much less *gently* if you do anything . . . unwise. Now, then!" Whipping out my rapier, I flourished it dramatically and pointed it at Aefryd, who was standing in the street in a semicrouched pose as if he couldn't decide whether to attack or run. "You, sir, are a disgrace to your uniform! For *shame*. I hereby place you under citizen's arrest for blatant corruption!"

"*Citizen's arrest?*" Aefryd repeated incredulously. "What the *fuck* are you on about? Have you been hitting the dust?"

"Oh, is that not a thing here? Figures. All right, let me rephrase that." I stepped down off the stack of boxes to the rear lip of the cart and leaned forward to give him my best, coldest smile, holding out an open hand and conjuring a Firelight to make sure my face was properly illuminated for spooky effect. "I have paid your Captain more in the last week than he's paid you in the last year, and *I can kill you with my brain*. So, Aefryd, provided that you have the sense to stay out of my face and do as I say, you've got better than even odds of still being alive and not in prison by this time tomorrow. Should you decide to do otherwise, I can make no promises. Therefore . . ."

I flicked the tip of the rapier down at his boots.

"Sit, boy."

He stared at me, glanced at Lamm, swallowed heavily, and then sat down in the street.

"Good boy. Now, Lamm, I *know* you're not doing something so *unwise* as trying to sneak away," I said, turning back around to find that he'd sidled almost a meter away down the street.

At finding himself once again the focus of my full attention, Lamm froze. He remained frozen while I hopped down from the cart and stepped within rapier range—which exceeded the reach of his scimitar. That was important in case he went and got twitchy on me.

His eyes tracked the tip of the sword as I raised it to point at his throat.

"Where. Is. She."

Lamm's response wasn't what I expected. "That's Tinod's sword."

"Correction, it's *my* sword. I assure you he doesn't need it anymore."

"Yeah, no shit." He actually barked a rough laugh. "Way I hear it, you blew his head clean off."

"Off, yes. 'Clean' isn't the word I'd use."

"Mm. You do know that's an artifact, right? Complete waste, bein' carried around by the wrong kinda Blessed."

"Well I was gonna pawn it, but I just fell in love with the swishy sound it makes." I whipped the rapier's tip back and forth in front of his eyes, making him twitch, and then eased forward, pressing it against his shoulder. "None of which is providing me an answer to the important question I just asked you. Do I *seem* like a patient person, Lamm?"

He drew in a deep breath, his shoulders shifting, and let it out slowly, then raised his chin and stared me in the eye, having clearly steeled himself for what he knew was next.

"Look, it's not like I don't know what you can do. The fact is, though, I've worked for Lady Gray since before my balls dropped. You're all flash, Healer. It's scary flash, yeah, but she gets shit *done*. I'm more scared of her than I'll ever be of you."

I met his stare evenly. The silence stretched out for a beat. Then two.

Then I lowered the sword.

"Thank you, Lamm. Sincerely, from the bottom of my heart, you have my gratitude. There are few things in life I appreciate more than people who feed me a perfect setup line."

His eyes widened. "Wait—"

Immolate.

I look a judicious step back from the burning and screaming which ensued, finally letting the Firelight wink out. It was sort of superfluous anyway, now. Aside from the spectacle poor Lamm was making at the moment, all was quiet up and down the street—as still and silent as on my first visit to the Gutters, when I'd interrupted Lord Arider delivering a bunch of cash to Lady Gray. People around here had a very good sense of when it was important to draw the curtains and pretend they weren't home.

Turning my back on Lamm's suffering, I faced Aefryd—perfectly framing myself to be backlit from his angle by the column of fire with the screaming man in it, because I'm just that good.

"All right, get up," I ordered. "Honestly, man, have some dignity. Who sits in the middle of a street? Show respect for the uniform, for fuck's sake. It's Aefryd, right?"

"Y-yes, m-my . . . Lord?" he ventured as he straightened up, valiantly struggling to maintain eye contact but compulsively peeking behind me at the spectacle every other second.

"Tell me, Aefryd, you wouldn't happen to be a week from retirement, would you?"

"I . . . what?" He blinked stupidly from behind his helmet. "Me? I'm . . . Uh, that is, even if I stick with the soldier thing and don't get drummed out, I'm ten years from even qualifying for a pension."

"I see, I see. And what about your love life? Any plans to propose to your sweetheart in the near future? Got a baby on the way, perhaps?"

"Uh . . . I'm . . . how to put this. Let's just say I'm the kinda guy whose love life got put a stop when all the whores ran off. Hang on." He squinted at me. "He called you Healer. Was that *you*?"

I stepped forward, giving him my most ghoulish grin, half-lit by the fires of Lamm's torture behind me. "Why? Got a complaint to register, Aefryd?"

The soldier swallowed so heavily I could hear it. "No, sir. My Lord. No complaints of any kind, sir."

"Good man!" I clapped him on the shoulder, pretending I didn't see him flinch. Rather than removing my hand, I gave him a jovial, full-body shake. "And good news, Aefryd. Since you are free of obvious doom flags and, let's face it, not doing anything worthwhile with your life, I have decided to deputize you. Stick with me and I'll make sure you get what's coming to you, have no fear of that. We're gonna go on an *adventure*."

Aefryd wasn't stupid enough to miss the threat lurking unsubtly beneath the promise. He gulped again—hard enough that it looked painful—and tried to say something, managing to produce only a hoarse squeak. Having failed at that, he contented himself with a rapid, jerky nod.

Obviously, I saw no reason to explain that "deputize" was an overly charitable term. I wouldn't have trusted this guy to accomplish anything useful even if I'd had the luxury of a week to train him first. Given the remainder of my plans for the evening, though, I could think of several potential uses for a disposable meat shield. If he lasted through the night, I promised myself I would bribe Captain Norovena to let him off the hook for his attempted shakedown.

The fires of Immolation were beginning to recede, finally. I gave Aefryd another pat on the shoulder before releasing him, then turned to watch Lamm gradually flickering out. By that point he was curled up into a sobbing ball.

They all curled up. What is it about pain that turns humans into pill bugs? It wasn't like that ever helped. They burned just as merrily in any configuration of limbs.

I waited until the spell had fully subsided before igniting another Firelight over my palm, noting the way Lamm twitched at the burst of illumination. Then I waited three more seconds before walking back toward him.

Slowly. One deliberate step at a time, putting my feet down just hard enough to make my artifact boots clack ominously against the pavement. From Aefryd's position behind the wagon, it was seven steps until I was standing over him.

There, I stopped and did nothing. It took him almost a full minute to gather enough courage to peek out from between his own arms, whereupon he beheld me looming over him, the orb of Firelight positioned to cast my face in flickering orange semishadow, painfully reminiscent of what he had just gone through.

I met the thug's wide gaze and held it in dispassionate silence for two more seconds, then smiled. A gentle, kind smile.

He flinched.

"So, Lamm," I said in my most pleasant tone. "How scared of me are you now?"

9

In Which the Dark Lord Almost Gets Away With It

Shepherding two unwilling recruits who were only along because they were terrified of me obviously required a great deal of my attention, which spared me the opportunity to get *too* lost in my own thoughts, but even so, I had plenty of time to worry as we made our careful, stealthy way through the back alleys of the Gutters. Much of that energy I spent wondering what the hell was going on with Aster and why Biribo hadn't come to report back yet. Surely he'd let me know right away if some disaster had befallen, right? So no news must be good news.

Obviously that didn't stop me from worrying.

"That's it," said Lamm, pointing at the vista before us.

Our current perch provided a pretty good view. Not trusting either of my companions to be anywhere near Lady Gray, I had directed Lamm to take us to a spot with altitude from which I could see the planned ambush site, but not within shouting range. The structure we'd climbed was not unoccupied, but was quiet at this hour and had a handy set of exterior stairs by which we could get to the roof without having to go through the inhabited rooms. Before us stretched one of those half-ruined areas that seemed to mark a good quarter of the outskirts of Gwyllthean. The city had lost enough population and economic activity over the last ten years that a sizable chunk of its fringes were abandoned.

"Mm, good place for a hideout," I said, examining the cluster of three old warehouses with boarded windows, arranged in a cul-de-sac whose inner courtyard faced to the south, its entrance blocked from our view. "Does she do a lot of business out of there?"

"It's not a hideout, just the spot Lady Gray chose for this particular ambush," said Lamm, his voice tense. It was a *perfect* ambush spot; hide your forces inside the warehouses and you could instantly flank anyone dumb enough to wander into the courtyard. Which, obviously, I was not going to do.

"Is she there?"

"Originally, yes. The plan was for her to lurk behind the Blessed she gathered, let them soften you up, then finish you off." He glanced at me again, still with the same well-contained fear, but also curiosity peeking through. I knew Gray had deliberately not explained to her people who or what I was that required so much effort; obviously he would wonder. "That was before she got word about the Auldmaer Company wagons going out the way they were. She had to leave the ambush to coordinate a response and stop the rest of her gangs from picking them over."

"Any captives?"

Lamm shook his head. "Too complicated. I wasn't part of the teams sent to pressure you into the trap, so I dunno what the deal was with that. They either got somebody or were pretending to. I dunno."

I turned to the third member of our little party, who had just gotten his breath back from the climb. To be fair to Aefryd, he was in full armor, which couldn't have been great for ascending three flights of stairs. Besides, I was just gratified not to be the most out of shape leg of the tripod. It had been a *rough* two months, but all that labor had had its benefits.

"You familiar with this spot, Aefryd?"

"Sure," he said with the faintest hint of a wheeze. "Been there a few times. Popular spot for shady shit."

"Been there busting up the shady shit, or participating?"

"Uhh . . . yeah?"

That was the Gwyllthean city guard for you.

"Okay, then." The artifact rapier's enchantment activated as soon as I touched the handle, enabling me to draw it in the smooth, lightning-fast and *precise* motion of a master swordsman; Lamm tried to shy away, but he only succeeded in removing himself from the range at which he could have struck back at me, remaining well within the long reach of the rapier. I brought the tip to rest against his throat. "I guess this means I don't need you anymore."

Lamm had frozen the instant the blade touched his neck. Now, he inhaled sharply, but did nothing else. He didn't even try to argue, just staring at me with his hands half-raised at his sides as if to reach for weapons, he now didn't dare. I held the sword there, and held his gaze. His expression was . . . oddly detached. Anticipatory, but he seemed more resigned than afraid.

And why not? With the kind of life this guy had led, he knew what happened to people like him as soon as they became more of a risk than a utility. He'd probably seen this coming, and been playing along in the hope of somehow turning the situation around before it got to this point. Now, there was nothing left for him to do. I had the tip of the blade right against the side of his throat. One flick of my wrist and it would tear through the carotid artery, jugular vein, and windpipe. There would be no coming back from that, not when the only person who could Heal it was the one killing him.

I stared into the eyes of the man I was about to murder and found a weary void of feeling where my conscience was supposed to be. He was in my way; that was all. It'd have been nice if I could recruit him like the bandits back at North Watch, but the situation was too unstable and he too untrustworthy. It couldn't be risked. This was just . . . strategy. A pragmatic necessity. Lamm was probably just like Donon or Twigs, someone who'd fallen into a life of crime because the society around him was disintegrating too fast to offer him anything normal. I'd have offered him my hand if I could, I just couldn't risk it this time. I stared at him and felt nothing.

So why was I hesitating? A long span of seconds had ticked by already. If anything, drawing it out like this was needlessly cruel.

After all, where did I even get off questioning the violence at this point? I was no better than any of these people, and worse than a lot. I didn't actually *know* how many human lives I had deliberately ended, because most of them had been during the chaos of battle. I knew I had laughed at and mocked at least several of them. I suspected my kill count rivaled most of Japan's serial killers from the modern era, and probably that of quite a few Warring States-era samurai. I was *well* past having any right to maunder about this. Hell, I had callously tortured this very man minutes ago.

Besides, this guy's hands were probably even bloodier than mine. Of all people, he didn't deserve mercy.

Which, of course, was not the point.

Whenever you can, be kind.

God dammit, Aster. She had better be all right.

I lowered the sword. Lamm inhaled deeply; I realized it was the first breath he'd taken since that sharp one when I'd put the blade to his neck.

"I believe in fairness, Lamm," I said. "I realize you don't see a lot of that in Fflyr Dlemathlys, so I'm instituting it. The fact is, I owe you one. No, scratch that—two. You've helped me out significantly tonight, and before that there was . . . you know. With all the burning and screaming."

"Yeah, I remember that part," he said, still tense. He hadn't tried to move, which was smart, considering his vulnerable neck was still within rapier range, and I had shifted the blade to point at his midsection from a few centimeters away, not lowered it to my side. One swift lunge and he was still a goner.

"You won't forget that anytime soon," I agreed. "If it makes you feel better, I get nightmares, too. Life's like that, at least on this shithole world. So, I owe you two, and here they are. First, your life."

"Appreciate that, Lord Seiji," he said with a jerky nod.

I nodded back, more smoothly. "And second, some free advice. Lady Gray is over. Understand? *Done.* It's impressive that she spotted part of the plan and moved to intervene, but let's face it: she doesn't still have the organizational capacity or sheer manpower to stop all those wagons from being looted in her name. *Maybe* most, but not all. And that wasn't even the whole plan. You may not know what she sent to get my attention in the middle ring, but I do, and I've already tied that up with a neat little bow. The fact that it happened in the middle ring is the linchpin. By this time tomorrow, she will be at the top of Clan Aelthwyn's shit list. This time next *week*, Clan Olumnach will be picking over what's left of her bones. Even if I fail to wipe out her Blessed squad tonight, it's over."

"So I should sign on with you instead; that's what you're saying?"

"I believe I've already pointed out that I have no more use for you," I replied with a lazy smile. "At least for tonight. No offense, but I don't think I'm quite ready to trust you at my back."

"None taken." He actually managed the ghost of a smile himself.

"So here's your advice, in thanks for your help. Go to the guard headquarters, tell them Lord Seiji sent you to talk to Captain Norovena. Tell him you helped me, and then tell him *everything you know* that even *might* help him round up and finish off Lady Gray. Next time I see him, I'll ask if you did, and if he's got you in custody, I'll vouch for you. In fact, I'll pay to get you out of a cell if that's what it takes; though by then he'll be in such a good mood after finally getting to nail Gray that it likely won't come to that. So those are your options, Lamm. Sit this one out, and you've got a chance to buy your way out of the hammer that's about to come down on her whole organization. Or you can go back to her and be just another anonymous goon rounded up and put to the sword when the Kingsguard and combined Clansguards rampage through Gwyllthean starting tomorrow."

Lamm continued to stare at me without moving, though his eyes narrowed slightly in concentration as he weighed his prospects.

"Of course, there's option three," I added. "Fuck off out of Gwyllthean entirely before the shit goes down. That's what *I'd* be doing if I wasn't already neck-deep in this business. It's about to get ugly around here, and between you and me, I'd just as soon miss it."

His shoulders shifted slightly in a minute sigh, and he opened his mouth to answer, but I overrode him again.

"That said, if I see you again tonight anywhere *near* the rest of Lady Gray's operation, or looking like you're heading in that direction, I'll kill you. I promise, no bloody vengeance, nothing like what happened before; at this point I figure we're square and you don't owe me anything. But you've already seen all the hesitation out of me you ever will, Lamm. Cross me once more and you die. Clean and fast."

Lamm nodded once. "I hear you, Lord Seiji. Thanks for . . . the advice. I'll just . . ."

"You're free to go," I said with a magnanimous gesture of my sword when he tilted his head inquisitively toward the stairs. "Just be very careful which direction you go. Wander too near those warehouses or any of Gray's local safehouses and I'll assume the worst. I can very easily finish you from up here."

"Right. Got it." He folded down his hands at me, then turned and bolted down the stairs.

I moved at a more decorous pace to the edge of the roof and watched Lamm emerge from the alley below. He turned onto the street and made a beeline for the walls on the most direct route possible, a street that would take him right to the main avenue from which he could reach the gates. Those were closed at this hour, of course, but every gatehouse had guards posted all night, and with everything going on, I suspected anyone on duty would know to contact Norovena if somebody showed up with a message like that.

Lamm turned to look back and up at me once as he fled. I gave him a jaunty salute with my sword; he ducked his head and resumed course. Moments later I lost sight of him behind a rooftop. Of course, he was more than capable of ducking down an alley and circling about to get up to who knew what mischief as soon as he was out of my line of sight. Given his years of loyalty to, and fear of, Lady Gray weighed against my own threats and offers, well, I could see that going either way. But I just didn't have the luxury of riding herd on him any further, and if the rest of my business proceeded according to plan, it wouldn't matter. Whether anything else would proceed according to plan was, of course, the eternal question.

Logically, I should've just killed him. But it was like Auldmaer had said, "a man had to live with himself."

"All righty, then!" I said brightly, turning to Aefryd with a big smile.

He took a step back, eyes widening, and raised one gloved hand to cover the vulnerable gap where his breastplate didn't cover the throat.

"Relax, Aefryd," I said in my most condescending tone. "I already know you're one of the good guys. See, you've got a uniform and everything."

"Yes, Lord Seiji," he said warily, smelling a rat but unable to pinpoint it. Not the brightest star in the firmament, was Aefryd.

"So! Down there in that trio of warehouses," I pointed at the distant target with my sword, "a trap has been laid for yours truly. It is my intention to spring it when I am not in the middle of it. And that's where you come in."

"Oh no," he whimpered.

Naturally, I allayed his fears with all the sympathy he deserved. "Oh, man up, you big baby. I know you've been on the take from Lady Gray's organization. Aefryd, *don't waste my time*," I interjected as he started to protest. "I know it, you know it, Captain Norovena knows it, *everybody* knows. Don't worry, I'm not here to litigate that. In fact, it's exactly what makes you so useful to me right now, see? They know you, and they know what you're all about. If you head down there and offer to sell them info on my whereabouts and plans, there's no reason they won't believe you. So what I want you to do is go down there and sell me out."

"You want me," he repeated very slowly, clearly laboring to parse this, "to . . . sell you out?"

"No reason you shouldn't make a few halos out of all this, right?" I asked encouragingly, clapping him on the shoulder. "You're going to go in there, tell them I ambushed Lamm and took him out, and lead them back to the spot where we left the Auldmaer Company cart. Tell them I stayed by it to wait for backup. That'll lead them right past here, so I can hit the would-be ambushers from behind. Get it?"

"Ohhh." His expression clearing, he nodded. "Yeah, I see what you mean, Lord Seiji. That's a good plan!"

"Isn't it? Now, time's wasting, so get a move on."

"Uh . . . What if—"

"Aefryd, we've been at this too long already. Don't worry, you'll do *fine*. Just get down there and tell them the story, get your payout, and skedaddle. Come tomorrow, I'll tell Captain Norovena how helpful you were, and as far as you're concerned, all this unpleasantness will be over with. Now *move*!"

Chivied along by my insistence, he scrambled down the stairs almost as fast as Lamm had. As before, I stayed up there to watch as he descended to ground level and turned to head in the opposite direction, toward the distant warehouse cluster. Aefryd paused twice to look back, and I gave him an encouraging wave each time.

As soon as an intervening building blocked my line of sight, I took off at a run, vaulting over the gap to the next roof and heading away from the spot I was in as fast as I could, because I'm not an idiot.

A hypocrite, sure. After all my soul-searching over not killing Lamm, I had just blithely sent Aefryd to what might very well be his death. It made a difference, to my way of thinking, that not only was I not doing it with my own hands, but in fact I was only putting him in a risky position of exactly the kind that his own actions were undoubtedly going to accidentally engineer sooner or later.

The thing about Aefryd was that he was as dumb as a bucket of goldfish. I'd known the man for half an hour, and even I could tell that much. I gave it fifty-fifty odds whether he'd stick to the plan I'd laid out or try to *actually* sell me out with every real truth he knew, and even if he didn't turn on me, it probably wasn't going to go well.

I'd been serious about my offer, though; if Aefryd actually came through and they didn't knife him or something, I fully intended to go to bat with his captain. If nothing else, a guy who was dumb and easily corruptible would be fantastically useful, and once *I* was running the crime on this island, it would serve me well to know which guards were exploitable.

Which was most of them, this being Fflyr Dlemathlys, but screw it. Given the danger I was putting him in, I owed Aefryd a break if he came through.

And so I circled around, bounding over the rooftops at a pace I wouldn't even have considered without my Surestep Boots, with the intent of being as far as possible from the last location Aefryd could place me by the time he met with the ambushers in the warehouses.

Midway during this, the night started to look up even further.

"Boss!"

"Biribo!" I grinned as he zipped out of the darkness to hover over my shoulder in his customary place, but didn't slow. There were still people soon to be after me, and by this point I was fit enough to parkour and talk. "It's about time! How'd everything go? Is Aster okay?"

"Smooth as butter sauce, boss!" my familiar reported, zooming along with me. "We spotted the lookout watching you get that guy arrested, then followed him back to his base. It was a fuckin' treasure trove! Lady Gray put together a whole operation with written notes on people connected to Cat Alley personnel she might be able to use to lean on you. Just, *piles* of evidence. We took so long cos there were *other* connected operations, and Aster wanted to wait and track them before busting up the central one. I thought it was a good call, and it's a good thing cos the two other cells we tracked were actually doing kidnappings. They had three people between 'em. Lady Gray was *serious* about baiting you, and you were right—she laid a network of one lead per possible target, so she could track and anticipate your movements based on what you did."

"*Excellent*. Feels good to have all her careful planning turned against her for once. Are the captives all right?"

"Safe as babes in their cribs, boss. Norovena's got them in custody, watched by men he actually trusts. I have no idea who any of 'em are, by the way. They weren't on Minifrit's list nor mentioned by any of the Alley Cats that I heard. Must've been connected to 'em somehow, or Lady Gray wouldn't have reached for 'em."

"It's not news that she's got a broader intelligence network than we do. What about Aster; is she okay?"

"Perfectly fine! She hit all three safehouses like a falling wall with a big-ass sword. No survivors among Gray's personnel. But that suits the plan just fine—no need to have witnesses who might contradict our story. Right now Norovena's going through the paperwork we collected, organizing it and doing a little massaging so it looks like the blackmail operation we want Clan Aelthwyn to react to. Aster's there, waiting on you to come back."

"Hot *damn*, I love it when things actually work out for once!"

"Yeah, no kidding. Speaking of, what're we running away from?"

"Ah, this isn't a retreat. Just a . . . repositioning." In fact, I stopped, having arrived on another rooftop from which I had a clear view of the warehouse cluster some ten blocks away. For Biribo's benefit, I pointed at it. "That's allegedly where the ambush was laid. I've sent a pawn to poke the trap, and then we'll see what happens."

"You wanna hit 'em from behind when they move out, boss?"

"Well, that was my original intent, because I wasn't willing to assume everything in the middle ring would go according to plan. No offense to you or Aster; it's just . . ."

"No, I get it, boss. Don't forget I've been along for this whole ride, too. That old bitch just keeps running circles around us."

"Exactly. But if all that has actually succeeded, I think it's smarter not to risk my own perky ass against anything Lady Gray cooked up specifically to kill me. If I just disappear and let the avalanche we've set in motion come down on her tomorrow, all her careful work down there is meaningless anyway. Since we're at a safe enough distance, though, I do wanna see if I can get a look at what she's laid out for me. And *if* a golden opportunity happens to present itself, well, I see no harm in taking out a few of her top people from a safe ambush of my own."

"That 'if' is doin' some heavy lifting, boss."

"Yeah, we'll call that a distant contingency. This is probably it for our part tonight, Biribo. Still, no harm in having a look."

"Hell yeah, you're talking to the living embodiment of information. Even if Gray gets the ax, we can only benefit by knowing who and what she considered a trump card for you. At least some of 'em are likely to still be around after tomorrow."

"Exactly. And speak of the devil!"

"Wait, devil?" He swooped about in apparent alarm. "Where?"

"It's just an expression. Settle down, lemme get a look at this."

I pulled Arider's trusty spyglass from its padded case and aimed it at the edge of the warehouse cluster, where people were now emerging. Seven of them, I counted as they stepped warily into the open. All lowborn with the exception of one guy who wore a noble-style coat, though he wasn't *much* paler than the rest, and his hair was brown, not blonde. No sign of Aefryd.

"Biribo, can you get anything on this group from this distance?"

"Focusing on 'em, yeah. Not much detail from this far back, but they're all Blessed with Magic."

So, seven sorcerers to take me down? I was almost insulted; surely Lady Gray remembered how easily I'd torn through her hit squad of Blessed with Might. Then again, according to Lamm's account, she was planning to just use them to soften me up so she could deliver the coup de grace herself.

"Hang on, boss, something happening. That one's casting—wait, I think that's—"

One of the lowborn casters, a woman in a light tan longcoat with a red scarf, was indeed doing something. She held up both hands, and through the spyglass I thought I saw her mouth open as she enunciated a spell. Around her a transparent sphere of blue-green light sprang up, and was quickly marked off by intersecting lines laid out like the latitude and longitude markings on a globe.

"Boss! We gotta move!"

And then one blinking point of light appeared on her globe, obscuring her expression as it was directly between me and her face, despite the long distance separating us. Almost as if it was pointing . . . at my location . . .

The sorceress turned her head to say something to her companions, pointing her finger right at us.

"Oh, *bullshit*," I complained.

10

In Which the Dark Lord Tries Something He Saw in a Movie Once

Is that an attack?" I shifted my feet in preparation, but despite Biribo's exhortation to move, I didn't yet take a step. This seemed like a bad situation in which to run around in confusion.

"No, there's no offensive element," he said impatiently. "The spell's called Locate. It's one of those that varies a lot based on the strength of the Blessing of Magic. It's got some neat perks at a higher strength, but it looks like all she can do is point at her target. Which is plenty to *find* us, unless we book it!"

"Hang on." Below and in the near distance, the seven sorcerers had started moving. In moments they'd pass into the shelter of the surrounding buildings. I focused through the spyglass and brought forth the press of magic in my mind.

Slimeshot.

The theory I was testing was proved correct. The spell itself handled targeting automatically, and I now learned it adjusted for factors like distance, which meant that the slime I launched flew at an upward trajectory, arcing into the night sky before descending straight at the group of magic users below. Specifically at the woman who was casting Locate. I'd been afraid the range might be too great, but evidently not.

"Seriously?" Biribo exclaimed. "You with the slimes!"

"Not ideal ammunition, sure," I agreed as I watched the airborne slime descend, "and also *not my fucking idea, Virya*, but given how far that thing's falling it should hit like a—aw, come on!"

One of the other sorcerers, a young-looking man with no coat and his sleeves rolled up despite the cool evening, had dramatically thrown his hand forward, and a barrier of light flashed into place over the whole group. It looked like a subtly dome-shaped panel of greenish honeycomb, made of linked hexagonal segments, one of which flickered as the slime arced out of the night to splatter against it, hard enough to send droplets spraying in all directions. Honestly, I was impressed he'd even managed to see that coming. Impressed and annoyed.

"Well, that's that," said Biribo, "so let's—"

"Hang on." The group had stopped running to huddle behind the shield, which gave me an idea.

Slimeshot. Slimeshot. Slimeshot. Slimeshot. Slimeshot. Slimeshot. Slimeshot. Slimeshot. Slimeshot. Slimeshot. Slimeshot. Slimeshot.

I began chain-casting, holding the spell in the forefront of my consciousness and pushing at it steadily as my eyes flicked across the group, targeting each in a split second of attention. Slimes machine-gunned out of thin air, hurtling through the night with devastating accuracy and hammering at the shield of green light.

I had the pleasure of seeing the shield caster buckle under the onslaught; I couldn't make out his expression between the distance, the intervening shield, and the residue of slimes rapidly accumulating on it, but he took a knee, clutching at the arm he was holding out as if it were physically keeping the spell up.

He said something to his companions before the shield shattered, causing them all to break ranks and disperse into the cover provided by the nearby walls and roofs. I *almost* managed to hit the man casting the shield, but he knew his limits well enough to be on the move before the barrier collapsed, unfortunately. He got splattered with slime residue, but, unsurprisingly, I failed to land a direct hit on a moving target from that range.

"Well, I hope that was fun for you," said Biribo in an acerbic tone.

"A bit, but it was also instructive. Now I have a general sense of how much punishment that shield can take, *and* a way to make them break formation and scatter. Time well spent!"

"If you say so," he replied doubtfully. "But regardless . . ."

"Yeah, let's get outta here." I was already turning around and set off on another series of bounds across the rooftop and the open alleyway beyond. "Keep your attention on them. Let me know if they draw closer, and I'll disperse 'em again. All we need to do is get to the walls. Even if the gatehouse guards haven't been told to let me through, I can persuade or bribe my way into the exterior fortification. Lady Gray's thugs won't dare assault the walls, not when she's trying to do damage control."

Each gate had two gatehouses—a small exterior one used to impound people or property entering the city illicitly, and a larger interior barracks for the guards themselves. They weren't connected internally, meaning that anyone besieging the city would have to actually bring down the gates; there was no conveniently penetrable side door. Still, there would be guards posted in the exterior gatehouse overnight, able to communicate with those above who controlled the doors in case of an emergency.

And all I had to do was get there. The wide arc I'd taken to reposition myself for a good vantage over Gray's ambush site had drawn me farther out from the walls themselves, and specifically even farther from the southern gate, which was still the closest. That movement had made sense at the time, but now I had cause to regret it.

Almost immediately I had even more.

"Shit, we've got problems, boss."

"*New* problems, or are you just making conversation?"

"That group is gaining on us, boss. Fast! Never mind getting to the walls—they'll be on us within another minute at this rate!"

"What? Bullshit! How?"

"Several of 'em are casting magic. They're still far enough I can't tell details, but there are lots of spells that can influence a whole group. Probably party-wide stamina and speed buffs, boss. This is why fighting a whole group of sorcerers is a headache; once they start enhancing and supporting each other, they can come up with some really creative shit."

Well, this wasn't going at *all* to plan. So, just another Tuesday on Dount.

"Okay," I puffed, thinking rapidly. With all the running and jumping *I'd* been doing recently, I was feeling the effects. Not that I was on the verge of collapse or anything, but I couldn't draw this out too much. "Get me to a position where I've got a vantage over an open area they'll have to pass through."

"Got it! This way!"

Biribo pulled ahead of me, veering to the left, and I followed. Moving this way was liberating, despite the tense circumstances; the Surestep Boots meant I barely had to pay attention to where I put my feet. I practically glided over sloping shingled rooftops, vaulting across gaps between buildings as lightly as a cat. The only real barrier to my speed was my own flagging stamina. As long as I could figure out a way to end this before they caught up or my legs gave out . . .

"Up ahead, the roof with the blue shingles! You can see right down that street, boss; they'll be coming along it in seconds."

"Good work!"

I bounded across the last gap, one of the widest I'd jumped yet, but I was also descending a story. Hitting the shingles in a roll, I let my momentum carry me in an angled slide, turning just as I reached the lip of the roof.

Just in time to see my pack of pursuers round a corner. They were moving *crazy* fast, so much so they looked blurred. Never mind the speed, it was incredible they could move like that around corners without losing their footing. Magic really was cheating.

And I was pretty good at cheating, myself.

This time I didn't play around; they were moving too quickly to be feasible targets, anyway.

Immolate. Immolate. Immolate!

That broke their formation, the three in the lead skidding along the pavement with their own momentum as they crumpled into screaming fireballs. Apparently one of them had been sustaining the speed effect, since they all slowed abruptly.

Then one guy wearing a black coat shouted something I couldn't make out from this range, and the flames around my three victims winked out, leaving them gasping on the ground.

"What the hell?!"

"Oh, *fuck*," Biribo agreed.

"How did—never mind!"

Slimeshot! As luck would have it, the shield caster hadn't been one of those I'd Immolated. He either saw it coming again or knew to expect it, and my incoming missile splattered against the wall of light. Picking him out visually by the dramatic gesture with which he'd cast the spell, I tried again.

Immolate!

The shield winked out and he went down in a column of fire, which was snuffed a half second later. The first three were already limping to their feet. They'd suffered seconds rather than the minute or two the spell usually took, but being incinerated from the inside out was something nobody could just walk off immediately.

Details were vague from this distance, but they didn't even look burned, which pissed me off. If they had a spell to snuff out Immolate, shouldn't it leave them *actually* Immolated in a state from before the healing magic kicked in? But nope, no visible effects, save the trauma of horrific pain. Fucking bullshit; this game was rigged.

It was the guy in the black coat; he still had one hand outstretched. I zeroed in on him.

Immolate.

Nothing. It wasn't quite like trying to cast it on an unacceptable target, like Lady Gray with her stupid spell-blocking artifact; I could feel the magic activate, but its actual physical effects didn't emerge.

"Oh, son of a bitch, that guy's casting Null," Biribo hissed. "Boss! As long as he's got that up, *they* can't use magic, either! Hit him with a slime!"

"Right!" **Slimeshot!**

The distance was enough to give them warning; the Null guy proved a bit too slow on the uptake, but one of his companions tackled him aside as the slime ripped through the space where he'd been, grazing the second man across the back and sending them crashing to the ground in a spin.

Again, the group had scattered, including those who'd been burning seconds before. I guess life in a Gutters gang made a person pretty tough. Even the one I'd winged with a slime hit the ground in a roll, immediately grabbing the Null caster and shoving him into the nearest alley.

But with his concentration broken, Null was down, which meant I could do this:

"**Immolate!**" I shouted aloud, just for the sheer satisfaction.

I didn't get much in the way of that, as the guy burst into flames and just as quickly winked out as the spell was Nulled immediately. I caught a last glimpse of his legs awkwardly kicking as he stumbled into the alley after his companion.

"Okay, what the *fuck* is going on?" I demanded, turning and sprinting away across the rooftop. It took me a few seconds longer than normal to get my speed up. I began to have the sinking feeling that I wasn't actually winning this one.

"We got *big* problems, boss," Biribo said, zooming around me in agitated circles. "Remember I told you Heal almost *had* to have been put there by Virya because it's such a rare and powerful spell? Well, Null is another one like that. It's the ultimate antimagic spell, the absolute apex of what's a pretty obscure school of magic to begin with. Counterspells aren't common and you kinda gotta specialize into 'em, ordinarily. That guy was *way* too young to have acquired it the normal way, and anyway, somebody who can cast Null has no business faffing around a backwater like Gwyllthean."

"*Sanora,*" I hissed without slowing. Motherfucker, of *all* the times for her to add her finger to the scales! As much as I suspected Virya had been subtly helping me, it was stupid of me to forget she wasn't the only one playing this game, and that neither of them played fair.

"Maybe," said Biribo. "I dunno, boss. I mean, yeah, when something that powerful and out of place pops up too close to either Champion, I smell shenanigans, but Sanora cheating has a certain *look* to it and this isn't that. She likes to work institutionally, through her established religious organizations or powerful members of 'em. I thought for sure if Sanora was gonna cheat, she'd send Rhydion after us. Putting a spell like that in the hands of some bandit . . . Well, that seems more likely to bite Yoshi on the ass than you."

I shook my head, even as I leaped across another rooftop. Dammit, I could feel myself slowing . . .

"All she had to do was put it *on* Dount somewhere. I left Lady Gray unsupervised for a whole week, and highly motivated to scrape up something to defeat a powerful sorcerer. Of *course* she found it before Yoshi did. Gray's probably not even on Sanora's radar, but right now she's a hundred times the player Yoshi is on his best day."

Good to know that the goddesses weren't infallible, even when they were subverting their own rules, but that was a matter for later. First I had to get out of this mess more or less intact, a possibility which was looking more remote by the second.

"Oh, fuck—boss, more trouble!"

"*Seriously*?!" Honestly, I wasn't even surprised at this point, just pissed off.

"We got incoming from the other direction, over the rooftops! *Dozens* of 'em in groups, heading at us. No Blessed . . . but they're armed! Crossbows, swords . . ."

I skidded to a stop right at the apex of a tall sloped roof. "Shit. *Shit.* Lady Gray left the ambush to coordinate a counter response . . . Biribo, could she be in contact with those sorcerers?"

"Two-way communication would mean the kind of artifacts even she hasn't got, but there are a number of spells they could be using to send her messages."

Great, and *now* I was in the middle of a pincer. As usual, right the fuck where she wanted me. Why had I *ever* thought counter ambushing her ambush was a good idea?

"I know you didn't ask, boss, but these are just gangsters. If it's them or the sorcerers, well, you've already tossed her street soldiers like a salad."

I turned and almost began to descend the slope of the roof toward the walls, then abruptly stopped, only the preternatural balance of the Surestep

Boots saving me from taking a neck-breaking tumble. ". . . no. *She's* there. She's the only one who could get them all moving so fast. Biribo, I need an exit! Get me out from between them and away from both!"

He didn't bother to argue. "This way, boss! We're gonna have to swing wide and backtrack; she's sent the gangs at us in a wide formation that's arcing forward at the edges. It's an enclosing maneuver, move fast!"

I did so, following his darting form over the roofs and through the darkness, no longer sparing the breath to explain myself. Fortunately, he didn't ask me to, probably well aware of my train of thought.

I was willing to tackle Lady Gray one-on-one, but this would be me against her and a shit-ton of her street soldiers with crossbows. I could *probably* handle them—massed enemies were easy to take down with Windbursts and Slimeshots. All she had to do, though, was herd me into a position with enemies on all sides and stall me long enough for her sorcerers to catch up. As soon as that guy started casting Null, half my advantages disappeared. Then she only needed to land *one* lucky hit, and I wouldn't even be able to Heal it.

In hindsight, I could see how badly I'd blundered by thinking an aggressive action by me would be needed to tip the scales. My plan with Auldmaer and Norovena was still working, and would set forces in motion that would land on her first thing tomorrow. I should've just waited and let the wheels of fate turn. But I hadn't trusted that to work without taking direct action to help, and now here I was with my neck stretched across the chopping block.

Well, live and learn. Hopefully.

Biribo led me on a frustrating course that gradually gave most of the ground I'd just gained toward the walls—frustrating, but necessary. I couldn't sense my pursuers the way he could, but even from his terse description, I had a mental image of what they were doing. The gangs set across the roofs in a bowed formation designed to shift me toward the center and prevent me from doing what I was currently trying to do. Having a familiar to guide my steps was the decisive advantage that would—with any luck—enable me to evade that. As a secondary perk, my artifact boots meant I could move faster across the roofs than any of them, and I didn't even need to pay attention to where my feet were. Which meant that once I could see my pursuers I could attack them more easily than they could attack me.

That became relevant a lot sooner than I would have liked.

"There he is! That's him!"

Courteous of them to give away their position by yelling; I was therefore looking in that direction when two crossbow bolts came whizzing at me.

Neither connected, having been hastily fired in the dark by men trying to run along a sloped rooftop at the same time. Unlike them, I didn't have to slow or concentrate to retaliate.

Slimeshot. Slimeshot!

All I could see of them were dark shapes silhouetted against the distant city walls, but at that range that was enough. I sent two hurtling into space on the other side of that roof, one apparently too winded to scream, and the three other shapes, which had been raising weapons instead ducked back down behind the roof in panic. Not exactly disciplined soldiers.

That marked the point at which they were closing in enough that I could see them, though. There was another group . . . Shit, dead ahead. And one beyond that. They'd succeeded in encircling me.

"Biribo?"

"Casters are catching up, boss! We lost 'em for a minute but they've figured out which direction you're going!"

The rank and file were moving in small squads, rather than a single contiguous net; there was a tempting gap between the two ahead of me. I dissuaded both groups with Slimeshots and made for the opening.

Then changed course.

Gray was here, somewhere, I *knew* it. She would make a beeline for me as soon as she figured out my position. The only question was whether she'd hang back until her trap closed around me, or intervene to push me into it. If it looked like I was about to slip the net, that'd settle the dilemma for her. Which meant that one way or another, I was about to encounter the boss lady herself.

There wasn't a lot I could do to maximize my chances here, so I'd have to do what little I could. For the sake of unpredictability, I didn't go for the obvious hole in her net, where she would probably be moving to intercept me already. Instead, I adjusted my trajectory and charged right at one of the gangs.

Not the one on the end, either. After all, the net ceased for all practical purposes to be a net once I was beyond it; then it was just a bunch more people chasing me, people I had to worry about a lot less than those sorcerers.

Bolts whizzed at me as I rushed the group of shadows on the next roof over; one grazed my leg, snagging my pants but not hitting flesh. Trusting in my Amulet of Final Luck and ability to Heal, I ignored the incoming fire, instead peppering the entire rooftop with a spray of rapid Slimeshots. Two of my opponents I was able to nail directly, while the rest were taking cover behind chimneys and gables. As I approached the gap, I added a couple of Windbursts to rock their position, followed by more Slimeshots.

It was a brute force approach, but that was where I did my best work. I had to hammer the entire area these guys occupied because I simply couldn't spare the attention to snipe them properly; my focus had to be on what was beyond. Gray couldn't let me get past them—this was where she'd strike.

I flashed a broad Light Beam as I vaulted off the edge of my current roof, sailing across the street toward the one still holding a couple of enemies. They reared back, yelling and cursing at their loss of night vision. I was already spouting Sparksprays nonstop before I landed, trying to reveal the invisible opponent I knew had to be there.

"Windburst!" shouted a voice that was not mine, and suddenly my clean jump across the street two stories down turned sideways.

The gust of air ripped me off course and sent me sailing straight down the street. For as much street as there was, anyway; this one forked mere meters ahead, with a narrow structure positioned between the two branches. Narrow as it was, I was hurtling *straight* for it, because apparently my luck is shit when my evil patron goddess isn't tweaking the game in my favor.

Windburst!

Thanks to what little mitigating fortune I had, I was at least flying head on, so I could see it coming and cast. My own spell impacted the shabby akorshil planks of the wall less than a second before I hit, reducing my velocity and also shaking some of the planks loose.

Because, as it turned out, this particular building was one of those half-ruined ones that were common in this part of the Gutters. I smashed through what remained of the second-story wall and immediately discovered that the second story no longer had a floor. Fortunately my trajectory sent me plummeting into the gap beyond at a steep enough angle that I wasn't decapitated by the broken planks poking out from the edge of the hole; less fortunately, that sent me tumbling down to smash into a pile of . . . I don't know what it was a pile of, but it broke with a loud clatter and wasn't what I'd call cushiony.

So that was what being on the other end of a Windburst felt like. Yeah, I did not care for that.

"Boss! Boss, you gotta get up! We have to move!"

I blinked. Everything was hazy . . . Shock, I realized, my senses coming slowly back into focus. Then pain.

Heal! I cast the magic before I could begin making sense of exactly what was broken. There came a few more sharp stabs of pain as several bones were wrenched back into their proper places, and then I was in one piece and relatively alert.

I rolled to my feet and spun in a circle, getting my bearings.

"**Fire Lance!**" somebody shouted, and the wall in front of me shuddered, hot orange sparks flashing through the gaps in its dilapidated akorshil boards.

Ah, so that was the direction from which I'd come. I turned and bolted in the opposite direction, down a hallway. There was a second shout of "**Fire Lance!**" from behind me, followed by a much louder crash, as apparently they managed to burst through the wall entirely.

Oh sure, the random-ass bandit got an awesome fire-throwing spell. What did I get? *Slimes.*

I hated this planet.

Crawns fled as I stomped into what used to be a kitchen, currently full of skittering and the stench of decay. Like many Dountol kitchens, this one had an exterior door, which I burst through. I didn't have time to throw off pursuit by closing it, but that didn't really matter; they'd figure out where I'd gone immediately, and also the whole thing flew off its hinges when my shoulder hit it.

I was on a narrow stretch of sidewalk fronting one of the canals. The sound of rapidly flowing water was almost as overpowering as the stink of it. Most of the canals flowed fairly gently, but the bigger ones had a significant current, carrying away all the refuse people dumped into them in lieu of an actual sewer system. No wonder this area was abandoned; I wouldn't want to live next to this, either.

There was a bridge arcing over the canal just a few meters to my right, offering a tempting path out of this box. Too tempting? I could try to bolt to the sides to throw off pursuit, but I'd be terribly exposed either way.

"Biribo?"

"They're closing in, boss! It's clear on the other side!"

That decided it. Already hearing multiple bodies crashing through the abandoned house behind me, I sprinted for the bridge, turning onto it in seconds.

As soon as I crested the apex of its arch, a figure popped into existence right at its other end, blocking my path. And aiming a crossbow at me.

Even in the dimness, I could see the glint of Lady Gray's teeth as I closed in on her. Grinning, or snarling? Didn't matter. Not even slowing, I raised my hand as the bolt whipped right at my face.

It grazed my temple and nicked my ear. She was undoubtedly too good with that thing to miss such a shot from this close. *Bless* this artifact amulet.

"Windburst!" She tried to dodge aside, but the spell sent her tumbling. **"Null!"**

Fuck. I spun, turning to aim a Slimeshot back the way I'd come.

Nothing happened. Of course.

She'd be back on her feet in seconds. I couldn't afford to hesitate, and even without spells I wasn't helpless. Drawing my rapier, I pivoted and charged back at the caster.

I could see him, that lowborn guy in the nice coat, holding out his hand and grimacing in concentration as he maintained the counterspell on me.

I could also see his reinforcements. They weren't coming through the house, but down the walkway along the canal—two of his sorcerer buddies and what looked like a whole squad of crossbow-wielding thugs.

"Windburst!" shouted the woman in the scarf who could cast Locate, aiming at me. She was still too far away for the spell to hit me with its full impact, but that did mean she was far enough behind the guy casting Null for it to activate. And once cast, it wasn't magic that hit me, but just wind.

Distant as it was, I was sent careening backward, pinwheeling my arms and barely managing not to lose my footing thanks to my artifact boots. My retreat was halted by the painful impact of the bridge's railing against my lower back.

I half-turned to chance a peek at the waters below. Was this an escape route?

Nope, I decided. Aside from smelling like shit and decay, it was a drop of a good four meters into *actual rapids.* This part of the Gutters was so decrepit and Gwyllthean's government so inept that the canal had been allowed to be full of all manner of trash. Broken boats, wagons, and who knew what else half-clogged it, forcing the rushing water into a violent torrent as it had to course through the narrow path left through the obstructions.

Nobody could swim in that. I'd probably bash my brains on the first chunk of debris, and even if not . . . casting Heal while actively drowning just sounded like a creative way to waterboard myself.

"Well, Seiji," Lady Gray drawled, "this sure has been fun."

Fuck. Could I get past her? With the rapier I was as good a combatant as a person could be . . .

She was staring at me with a manic expression that didn't bode well. One hand was on her sheathed invisibility dagger; the other held a murderous-looking scimitar, which I didn't doubt she knew how to use. Looking into her eyes, I could tell she knew. She *knew* how my schemes had undone her. Killing me was likely to be her last act as the fearsome crime lord of Gwyllthean. I was facing a cornered animal.

And, naturally, pushing past her was my *least* terrible option.

I now had three spellcasters and at least twenty crossbowmen aiming at me, a second squad having arrived on the rooftop. Without my magic, there was no way of punching through that. And I already knew my Rapier of Mastery meant at best a stalemate against Lady Gray. In this situation, a stalemate would last just seconds until the rest of them hit me from behind.

The rock and the hard place.

"Everybody freeze!" I bellowed, raising the sword to press its edge against my own throat. "Nobody moves, or the foreigner gets it!"

Absolute stillness descended as everyone gaped at me.

". . . boss?" Biribo asked hesitantly.

Look, I don't know. It wasn't even a conscious decision, certainly not any kind of plan. There's no accounting for what springs to the forefront of a person's brain when it's running on pure adrenaline and zero good options.

"Weapons down! I swear I'll do it!" I shouted. "Drop 'em or I'll gut this bastard right now!"

The silence of pure incredulity continued to reign, and I found myself suddenly appreciating the phrase 'just stupid enough to work.' For one blessed moment, sheer disbelief and confusion held everyone still, and I felt an unwise glimmer of hope that just *maybe* I could parlay this brief distraction into a way out of this mess.

"What in the f—" Lady Gray cut herself off, turning her wide-eyed stare of perplexed fury from me to all her lackeys, who were currently just standing there in uncertainty. "Why is no one *shooting* him?!"

So they all shot me.

11

In Which the Dark Lord is Adopted by a Pack of Feral Noblewomen

The only good thing about being shot by a bunch of crossbows is that it happens too fast for you to dwell on how much it's going to hurt. Which, it turns out, is a lot. Fortunately for *me*, I immediately discovered so many new sources of pain that I didn't even have time to properly register.

I was toppled over the railing by the force of the blows, feeling impact more than penetration; with that many bolts in flight, it felt less like being stabbed and more like being hit by a moving wall. Blood sprayed above me for the all too short second I descended, and I just had time to be grateful for the artifact amulet that had prevented any of these from being lethal shots before I hit the stinking water and instantly plunged under it.

It was acrid, stinging my eyes and my *numerous* puncture wounds, and the force of the current instantly swept me away. I squeezed hard on the handle of my rapier; there was no prospect of swimming, not in this torrent. I was hauled off so roughly by the deluge that the sheer force of passing water kept my arms trailing in front of me, despite my attempts to correct course. Then, almost immediately, I slammed into something hard.

Even as I was swept aside and down the next channel, what little breath I had was driven from my lungs and an unwise reflex made me try to gasp. I had the good fortune that my head was in the process of bobbing above the surface at that moment, so I only choked on a slosh of the foul slurry of the Gutters' refuse rather than inhaling a whole lungful of it.

The current yanked me under again; the world went dark and sound became too muffled to make sense. I could feel myself bleeding out and choking and knew I had no option.

Heal!

Much of the pain abated, and while I knew that Healing myself with so many crossbow quarrels still in me was going to cause big problems very soon, it had been necessary to avoid immediate death. I had little time to dwell on it, as the current of the canal rammed me against something else.

I was forced down and I'm pretty sure scraped through the mud on the bottom of the canal before being ripped away again, tossed bodily out of the spray and actually bounced across the top of the next obstruction. Half-drowned and dazed from repeated impacts, with no idea which way was up, I didn't even realize what had happened until it was far too late; by the time my hand desperately tried to grab at the object, I had already tumbled into the water on the other side and was swept who knew how many meters away.

Heal!

It was an act of desperation because I could do literally nothing but exercise my brain at that moment, and because I remembered the last time had brought a moment of increased clarity to my oxygen-starved brain. I couldn't Heal *instead* of breathing, but it temporarily abated the worst effects of drowning. And then they immediately came back because I had still inhaled too much water, and no amount of consciously knowing how dangerous it was stopped my body from instinctively trying to cough, which of course only brought in more water.

I couldn't even get my bearings, just swept along, bashing repeatedly into obstructions and the sides of the canal, confused and unaware of which direction was up. I cast Heal whenever I could focus on it, but those episodes were becoming fewer and further between. I'd been right; Healing while drowning was basically waterboarding myself, and I was soon too wracked by reflexive convulsions to focus on anything at all.

Something hard impacted me yet again, and somehow I was hurtled completely free of the water, tumbling through blessed air, but attempting to draw a deep breath only made me choke and heave against the fluid already in my lungs. Then I landed again, back in the canal, and went under.

H-heal . . . The magic flickered weakly, barely responding to my will. The darkness receded from the edges of my vision, but only for a second. Too much damage done. Something had changed . . . I was being swept along without smashing into things now. Or had I just grown completely numb to the impacts? This was definitely what drowning felt like. It was excruciating, my body injuring itself by thrashing in its own panicked inability to breathe as blackness closed in on me.

A thought pierced the gloom with surprising clarity—should've cast Windburst. That might've thrown me clear. But I didn't even have enough mind left to summon the magic. And then I didn't have any more thoughts at all.

Something was pushing on my chest. Hard, repeatedly. Something pressed against my face—my mouth. Wait, was that . . . The person whose lips were sealed to mine exhaled forcefully, shoving air into my sodden lungs and making them involuntarily expand. Then another hard blow to the chest shoved them back in—

I wrenched myself to the side and heaved, fouled water surging out of me and spraying the ground. The ground! I was out of the water . . . And in a moment, hopefully I'd have the mental wherewithal to be properly grateful for it. I curled up, coughing up a torrent of disgusting sludge water as somebody helpfully pummeled my back. And then, for the sake of thoroughness, I violently threw up.

It took a few repetitions and several long minutes to empty everything from my lungs and stomach. But when it was over, I could breathe! Not *well*. I was still bruised all over and thwarted by a sharp stabbing pain when I tried to inhale, but at least the air could get *in*.

Heal.

That helped a lot. But not, I discovered, with the breathing . . . Yep. Looking down, I beheld what I had unfortunately expected—two crossbow bolts sticking out of my chest, both broken off close to the skin. Well, at least they'd missed my heart.

Someone's hand was still resting on my shoulder.

"You know CPR," I said aloud in surprise as my brain caught up with the last few minutes, finally lifting my head to see my rescuer.

"Sorry, who?" Her eyebrows drew together. I decided not to pursue it, peculiar as it was that that piece of knowledge existed in this backward culture.

The woman I was staring at from centimeters away was almost unfathomably gorgeous, with one of those perfectly proportioned faces that looks like someone drew it. She had gracefully pointed features, an alabaster complexion, and big eyes that were so black they looked like they had no irises. Her hair was blonde, though currently sodden with brownish canal water. And her ears were long and pointed.

"You're an elf," I said, very intelligently.

The elf grinned. "And you're a pincushion!"

I looked down at myself and winced. "I have to give you that one, yeah." Broken stubs of crossbow quarrels were sticking out of me all over. My clothes were shredded and soaked with a vile mix of blood and fouled water. Fortunately, I wasn't given long to dwell on this state of affairs.

"Lord Seiji!"

"Boss, you doing okay?"

Raising my head to finally take in my surroundings, I discovered that we were on the bank of a river. I had to half-turn and look over my shoulder to see Gwyllthean rising up in the near distance behind me; apparently the canal had washed me entirely out of the city. And I was not alone with the mysterious elf who had apparently rescued me. Biribo hovered less than a meter away, darting back and forth in agitation, while right at hand were two of the last people I'd expected to see—Goose and Twigs.

Both looked extremely worried, for which I couldn't blame them. There were more shapes standing around, I noted, shifting my gaze to take in the scene. A whole cluster of women stood watching, all of them pale and most blonde, though I noticed a couple had light brown hair like Twigs. In addition to the humans—there was only the one elf that I could see—it seemed they each had one of those bird-lizard-dinosaur things I had seen used as mounts. They apparently weren't common; this was the most I'd seen in one place.

Well, why not? If they were willing to pull me out of the river and resuscitate me, these ladies were welcome to be as weird as they liked.

"Okay, first things first," I said aloud. "I am so very grateful to everyone present that I almost don't care what the fuck just happened. Still, for practical purposes I think I should probably ask what the fuck just happened. And is still happening."

"You are welcome," the elf said, grinning cheerfully. "I think *mutual* explanations are called for. To begin with, I am Aelthwyn Nazralind, and absolutely delighted to make your acquaintance, my Lord Mister Dark Lord, sir."

"The pleasure is mine, and did you just say *Aelthwyn?*"

"No, I said Aelthwyn." She tilted her head, like an inquisitive bird. "What was that? Erutoween? I have *never* heard an accent like that."

"Okay, Naz, there's no need to pick on him," Twigs said reproachfully. "Look at the state the poor man is in."

"Quite right," said Nazralind, ducking her head and actually looking abashed. "My humble apologies, Lord Seiji."

"Well, hey, after saving my life, I figure you're entitled to tease a little," I acknowledged. "Speaking of which, **Heal**."

She jumped in surprise as the pink light flared around her, blinking. "Oh! Wow, that *tingles*. Thank you, but I wasn't injured."

"No, but you were clearly just swimming in that river, which I can tell you from experience is just begging for some kind of infection or horrible disease if it's not immediately addressed."

"I take your point." Nazralind wrinkled her nose, then grinned at me again. "I don't know if you've noticed, but we smell *exciting*."

I groaned, starting to get up and discovering that that was going to be more complicated than I'd realized. I had crossbow quarrels in one thigh, both arms, and seemingly every muscle in my torso. I was no longer *injured*, per se, but those things had been Healed in place, which forced all the muscles in question *out* of place. My range of motion had been drastically cut, and doing basically anything hurt.

The news wasn't all bad, though.

"Oh hey." I discovered, looking down at my hand. "I didn't drop my sword! Thank fuck, I *really* like this sword. If I'd dropped an artifact in the river, I would've been pissed. Honestly I have no idea *how* I held on to it."

"Not so surprising," said Nazralind, hopping nimbly to her feet and offering me a hand. "A drowning person will tend to keep a death grip on whatever they can. That's how I knew you weren't as dead as you looked when I went in there after you. You still had one hand free to hang on."

That made me wince again, and not just from what it felt like to stand up, even with help. "I see. I, uh, sincerely apologize if I accidentally groped you."

She tried to make a stern face at me, but that irrepressible grin broke through almost immediately. "You know, if you *had*, that comment would be very suspicious. But no, you'll be glad to hear it was all perfectly chaste flailing and clawing."

"That's a relief." I finally found a standing position that worked; one of my legs didn't want to flex properly with the bolt stuck in the thigh muscle. "Ow. How did you even find me?"

"You have your familiar to thank for that," she said.

"Biribo just *appeared*, right in front of us," Twigs added. "It's lucky we were camped this close to the river, though that's not exactly a coincidence. It's just a couple days 'til the harvest festival that you told me to shoot for, if we could, and our campsite . . . Well, you'll understand when you see it. We were just settling in and making plans to find out what was happening in the city before moving on to North Watch, when . . . Poof! There he was."

"Just, outta thin air, right in the middle of us," Goose added. "I never knew he could do that."

"Neither did I," I agreed, turning a surprised look upon Biribo.

"Congratulations, boss!" he said cheerily, doing an excited loop the loop around me. "You just unlocked a new Wisdom perk!"

"Oh, let me guess. It's activated by being in mortal peril."

"Well, finding yourself in mortal peril in very specific circumstances! If you're about to die, *and* there is an ally close enough to intervene, your familiar gets automatically teleported to them to call for help. Sorry, boss, I'd have warned you, but you know how it is."

"Forewarning me would've made the power not unlock, I remember," I sighed. "Fuck it, I'm too tired to be grumpy about how badly designed these Blessings are."

"Oh, that's *bad*," Twigs whispered. I decided to forgive her, because I was also too tired to be grumpy about that.

"Good work, Biribo," I said. "And good work, Goose and Twigs. I'm *really* glad to see you two again. You have excellent timing."

"Twigs." Nazralind shook her head. "I don't think I'll ever get used to that."

"Well . . . you don't have to call me that," Twigs said, smiling and stepping over to throw an arm around her shoulder, apparently not minding the horrible river sludge all over her. "I think I kinda prefer to keep it, though. It's not much of a name, but I've gotten attached. And it has fewer bad memories than the old one."

"I can see how that would be true," the elf agreed, putting an arm around her in turn. "Crap, now I wonder if I should've changed mine."

"Naz, you wouldn't last an hour being called something undignified," said one of the other women standing by, earning several chuckles from the onlookers.

"Sorry we didn't do more," Goose added, looking actually contrite. "Especially after leaving you alone for all this time. I wanted to go in myself, but, uh . . . I swim like a brick."

"No sense in both of us drowning," I agreed. Man, it was hard to breathe . . . "Ladies, once again, you have my gratitude. But, um . . . I'm going to need to do something about my current condition before I can do much else." I poked at one of the shafts sticking out of my chest and winced.

"How is he even upright and talking with all those sticking out of him?" one of the nearby women asked in a tone of fascinated horror.

"I told you, Lord Seiji can cast Heal," said Twigs. "But, um . . . I think this is going to be problematic."

"You Healed yourself with those inside you, didn't you?" Goose asked.

"Yeah, I'm well aware of the consequences," I grimaced. "But it was that or immediate death, so I stand by my decision."

"Yeah, right call," she agreed, nodding. "But . . . I won't lie, Lord Seiji. Fixing this is gonna be *rough*. Each one has to be cut out, completely. And since you'll need to Heal each wound afterward, that means we can't even get you properly drunk first. It's . . ."

"Well, not quite how I wanted to end my day," I wheezed, starting to sigh and then immediately regretting it. "Could be worse, though. I'm alive, thanks to you girls. So, Twigs! These are your . . . friends?"

"Well, yes and no," she said, looking around. "It's a bit of a story . . ."

"And with all due respect, Lord Seiji, we're gonna want to hear just what the *fuck* has been going on in Gwyllthean and elsewhere," Goose added. "And I definitely don't think trying to cut those things loose out here on the riverbank is a good idea."

"*Being* out here on the riverbank in general is making me Thaila in the glass tomb," added another of the surrounding blondes. "I know it's late, but this is awfully close to the city, and whoever did *this* to the Dark Lord is probably motivated to come make sure it took."

"Right," Nazralind agreed, suddenly with the decisive tone of a person accustomed to giving orders. "Good points, all. We need to take this back to camp. Lord Seiji, are you able to walk?"

I took a step and almost fell; Goose caught my shoulder, causing me to bite back a yell of pain as half the muscles in my arm and chest pulled excruciatingly against the shafts embedded in them.

"Not . . . quickly," I admitted. "Or well."

"I was afraid of that," said the elf, nodding. "Fortunately, we have a solution. Newneh! *Hepep ikkitik.*"

Nazralind clicked her tongue, and one of the horse-sized bird things paced forward. It was a little hard to tell in the moonlight, but I thought this one seemed to have brown plumage with yellow and black accents. The creature stopped next to the elf and nuzzled her shoulder with a beak that, up close, I saw was full of murderous-looking teeth. Rather than being terrified of this like a reasonable person, Nazralind slipped an arm around the thing's neck and actually kissed the side of its face.

"There's my girl! Good girl. Now, Newneh, this is Lord Seiji. Lord Seiji is a *friend*. I need you to give him a ride."

Newneh and I stared at each other. The bird-lizard ruffled her feathers, adding significantly to her apparent size, and emitted an obviously skeptical croak.

"Yeah, I'm with the bird on this one," I said.

Getting me onto Newneh's back was an ordeal that required Nazralind to hold the bird steady, Goose to physically lift me up, Twigs to help position my bad leg on the other side of the saddle, and all six onlooking noblewomen to offer mocking suggestions and encouragement.

I was also informed in *great detail* by Nazralind that these lizard-birds were called gwynneks, that they were very intelligent and loyal companions, that they were perfect mounts much superior to horses in most respects, and so on at length. Looking around at all the surrounding women standing next to their own gwynneks and nodding along with her comments, I was suddenly reminded of my grandparents' farm in California. Specifically their neighbors, a really nice middle-aged lady and her three daughters, who for some damn reason liked to ride their horses around to visit people.

So, I'd just discovered the Ephemera equivalent of horse girls, and in classic Ephemera fashion, it involved horrible monsters instead of anything that made sense. Well, they *had* saved my life, and I was in no position to criticize.

"Nazralind is the only one of them I knew personally before all this," Twigs explained as we made our way along the riverbank, passing into the darkness of a patch of khora forest. I hadn't realized there was any this close to Gwyllthean.

"Not that anyone was interested in being the Librarian of Lastnor to her about it," said Lady Noraene. I'd gotten all of their names and was pretty sure I wasn't going to remember them all, but she was one of the two brunettes. "Lady Elemyn is definitely one of us! It sounds like she held up amazingly well after getting separated from Nazralind."

"Well, I did have Goose," Twigs said modestly. "And later, Lord Seiji. That gang was kind of a nightmare when that cretin Rocco was in charge, but Lord Seiji's made things a great deal better in all respects."

All of them gave me thoughtful looks, except Nazralind, who was walking alongside me leading Newneh by her bridle.

"Whoa!" I exclaimed, making Newneh turn her head to look at me, as a pale glow of light rose around Nazralind. "What's—how are you doing that?"

Everyone stared at me.

"She's an elf," said one of the noblewomen, whose name I had already forgotten, as if this were too obvious to be worth explaining.

"Elves . . . glow in the dark?" I asked.

Everyone continued to stare at me.

"Ahem." Biribo bobbed up in front of me, causing Newneh and two other gwynneks to turn their heads to look at him, but none of them spooked. Apparently, they were less skittish than horses, at least. "The rumors and legends are true, ladies. Dark Lords and Heroes are summoned from another world entirely. Sometimes Lord Seiji needs to have things explained that might seem like universal knowledge to you."

"And there's no need to be rude to him about it," added Twigs.

"That's a fair point," agreed the woman who'd just commented. "My apologies, Lord Seiji. Sometimes I can be a real Westbridge Watchman with new people. I assure you, no personal slight is meant."

"None taken." Oh right, I'd forgotten Fflyr nobles talked like this. It was gonna get tiresome very quickly, I could already tell.

"We elves are chosen of the Goddesses, so the story goes," said Nazralind, raising her chin and smirking in a manner that deftly mimicked the stereotypical hauteur of nobles while also mocking it. I was really starting to like this particular elf. "Sanora's children are blessed with the gift of light, while the dark elves have the gift of shadow."

"So . . . you can make light at will," I said slowly, "and the dark elves can make it dark around them?"

Nazralind shook her head. "No, they go invisible."

"It's a little more nuanced than that," Biribo interjected, "but basically, yeah. Dark elves have an innate gift of stealth. And you should know, boss, that the more gifted ones have one of the few types of stealth a familiar can't see through. You should be glad you haven't done anything to get their attention yet."

"Great," I muttered. "Just what I need, more invisible enemies. Serves me right for thinking that one would be unusual." I started to slide sideways off the unfamiliar mount, and my instinctive shift of balance to correct made me stiffen in pain and start sliding the other way. Goose immediately grabbed and steadied me, and I realized that was why she was walking so close to the gwynnek. "Thanks."

She nodded and let go of my leg.

"And here I thought the dark elves would be your allies," Nazralind said casually. "Children of Virya and all that. Historically, they naturally flock to the Dark Lord."

It occurred to me that I still knew almost nothing about these women. There had to be quite a story explaining why a bunch of noblewomen had turned to banditry, and yet another to explain why they were now willing to throw in with the Dark Lord. Hopefully I'd get those explanations very soon, but I couldn't afford to be too reckless around them in the meantime.

"So I'm told," I said, "but I am also told that they are . . . um, let's say, difficult."

"Yeah, you wanna stay away from dark elves until you're in a position to impress them and command some obedience," Biribo agreed. "You're actually kinda lucky you didn't get started in one of the major Viryan civilizations, boss. More than one Dark Lord has ended up effectively the political pawn of some dark elven empire. Including the last one."

"Great," I sighed, then winced, then had to be steadied again by Goose.

"Really, Yomiko was under the control of Savindar?" Nazralind asked, tilting her head in that same birdlike gesture of hers. I wondered if she'd picked it up from the gwynneks. "I'd never heard that. I suppose it matches well enough with the history I know, though."

"Yeah, there's a lot of details that didn't make their way into the books," said Biribo.

"The books are written by the victors, after all," she agreed. "So, Lord Seiji. Elemyn tells me your big plan was to recruit the prostitutes of the Gutters to your side. And it's all set to unfold on festival night?"

"Ah, right, you two have been gone," I wheezed, managing a smile for Goose and Twigs, both of whom turned to look up at me. "Some shit's gone down, ladies. The short version is I've already done that. We've got over a hundred new recruits training at North Watch, and as of tonight, I have effectively destroyed Lady Gray's organization. But then she had me shot full of quarrels and dumped in the canal, so . . . I guess we're callin' it squaresies."

"Yeah, you cling to that hope," Biribo muttered.

"Because I've been wondering," said Nazralind, again in that casual tone that made my attention sharpen. "Did you choose this . . . unconventional approach because you found personal sympathy for those women? Or are you just using them for your own purposes, like everyone else has?"

Carefully, carefully. I knew a pivotal conversation when I'd stumbled into one; this was no time for any of my characteristic shooting off of the mouth.

"Let me answer that with a question," I said. "You ladies are all highborn; may I assume that means you've had the benefit of a proper education?"

"Well, the Clans aren't generally in a hurry to educate women," said Nazralind with an ironic grin, "but to be Fflyr is to be well-read, and high-born more so than most."

I nodded, and immediately regretted that, but managed to finish my answer. "That's a relief. I'm glad to be talking about this with people to whom I don't have to explain that more than one thing can be simultaneously true."

Nazralind cocked her head at me again, and several of the other ladies gave me considering looks. Goose, though, had to raise one hand to muffle a grin, and after a moment Nazralind nodded, seeming satisfied with that answer.

"Something tells me we have a lot of interesting conversations ahead of us, Lord Seiji," said the elf, "but we've still got some unpleasant business to get out of the way first. And what good timing! Here we are."

It hadn't been a long ride; considering how quickly they'd been able to reach the riverbank and find me, that made sense. The river itself was now out of sight through the surrounding khora, though I could still hear the water. Now, the khora opened out to reveal a wide area surrounded by the shells of old buildings.

This place had clearly been abandoned for many years; none of the structures were fully intact, and many had khora growing through their broken walls. Just as clearly, though, the place saw *some* kind of semiregular use. What had once been a square amid these old houses was still flat and clear, with no encroaching underbrush. Also, there were no less than three firepits that seemed permanent, and they were encircled by stones and chunks of akorthist; one had a flame going with a pile of fresh reeds nearby. Several of the broken-down houses showed signs of subsequent patching, including ragged hides hung over entrances whose doors were long since gone.

"Huh," I said aloud, peering around in the glow of Nazralind's aura. "This . . . doesn't look like any of the architecture I've seen so far on Dount." The akorthist of which these buildings were made was all white, and they had a distinct style to them that was unlike the organic construction Fflyr preferred, or the spartan utilitarianism of North Watch. They were all rigidly straight and laid out at precise right angles, softened with curved buttresses and columns that looked way too elaborate for what appeared to have been a small village once.

"Dark elves," Nazralind explained. "This was one of their settlements, before Fflyr Dlemathlys was founded."

"And this is all just . . . right here?" I asked, again almost sliding off the gwynnek in my incredulity. "This is within easy walking distance of Gwyllthean!"

"And Gwyllthean's the reason the site isn't still used as a village," she said. "A lot of its waste is dumped into that river. As we have discovered. *Phew*. Fortunately, there is still a water source, so you and I can get properly cleaned off, but it's just a tiny little trickle of a spring, not enough to support a whole village, now that the river's not usable as a water supply. But while all the muck isn't good for people or animals, it's *great* for certain kinds of khora, which is why all these are growing here. They yield harvestable reagents that are very valuable, and also provide habitats for a species of shellback that has useful akornin but doesn't do well in captivity. Also, both of those things are very poisonous, which means people stay out of here unless they're on specific business; and by the way, don't wander off or touch anything, Lord Seiji. This stretch of forest is kept here to be hunted and gathered, but only by professionals. Fortunately for us, the seasons for that are in the spring and winter, so right now there won't be anybody in this forest but possibly bandits."

"I think you mean *other* bandits, Naz," said Lady Ismreth with a grin.

"Right, yeah," Nazralind grimaced. "My point is, nobody we'd need to feel bad about shooting."

"All right, Lord Seiji, let's get you down from there and get started," said Goose in a tone that was both apologetic and grim, reaching up to help me out of the saddle. "This is gonna suck mightily, but we need to get those things out of you sooner rather than later."

"Yeah," I agreed with an anticipatory wince. Seemed like my night was going to get much better, but not until after it had gotten a *whole* lot worse.

12

In Which the Dark Lord
Uses Someone's Tragic Backstory
as a Sleep Aid

Of course, it wasn't as simple as jumping right to carving me up like a chunk of roasted beef, which was both good and bad, because while I enjoyed *not* being carved up, stretching out the anticipation wasn't great, either.

Seven of the noblewomen-turned-bandit gang had come to retrieve me from the river, not including Twigs and Goose, but as we settled in to the ruined village, more trickled in from scouting and guard duty. Others left to relieve them, and they didn't all introduce themselves (I was going to need more than one round of introductions to remember all these names anyway), so I didn't get a final head count yet, but I got the impression there were around twice that many overall. Hadn't Maugro given me a number originally? If so, I couldn't recall it.

What was more important for the moment was that they proved quite welcoming. Extremely curious about me, and some morbidly fascinated with my current status as a human repository of broken-off quarrels, but welcoming nonetheless. Clearly Twigs had done a good job of talking me up while she'd been gone.

Apparently, the nearby spring was small enough that getting any quantity of water out of it took time; enough was drawn for me to generally rinse off and Nazralind to have a more thorough wash while I did that. As Goose pointed out, I was about to get covered in blood again, so it made sense to put off properly washing and just get myself clean *enough* that I wouldn't get river sludge in all the incisions we were about to make. It would take a while to gather enough water for that anyway, so it worked out.

Which was my punishment for thinking the anticipation couldn't get worse.

The ladies busied themselves around the camp while Nazralind and I washed off to our differing degrees. It turned out the people were going to sleep in the open, because we could all be warned not to screw around among the poisonous khora, but gwynneks had to be housed inside the old buildings to make sure they had no accidents. And given the amount of space the creatures required, that filled the village's surviving structures to capacity; even the bathing spot had to settle for being behind broken walls in terms of privacy. Food was prepared, though on Goose's orders, I didn't partake as I was shortly going to have a knife applied to my organs.

I was, at least, offered a change of clothes, though obviously putting them on would have to wait until after I was done being sliced into and then washed off properly.

"Fortunately we've all grown accustomed to men's clothing," said Lady Ismreth, whose name had stuck in my mind during the round of introductions because it was by far the least pronounceable of them. "So much more practical for an outdoor lifestyle. If I'm any judge, these should fit you adequately, Lord Seiji. Though, with apologies, they may not be as stylish as what you're accustomed to."

"They're certainly more stylish than what I had on when we met," I said as cheerfully as I could manage, gesturing to the pile of blood-and-filth-soaked rags at the edge of camp that had been my outfit. I was currently sitting near the fire, draped in a couple of old blankets; given my partially washed state, they had obviously given me the ragged ones they'd be willing to throw out. At least I'd gone to Gwyllthean wearing a cheaper than usual outfit, in a futile gambit to avoid Lady Gray's notice, so I hadn't lost my nice red-and-black ensemble that I'd grown fond of. "Thank you kindly, my lady."

"'Tis our pleasure, my lord," she said with a smile. "We'll have no Ladnevin Foresters in our company. The accommodations may not be lavish, but a guest is a guest!"

"Plain speech, Izzy," said a young lady whose name escaped me, a brown-haired girl who looked scarcely older than Yoshi. "Remember, you're talking to Conzart in the bookshop."

"Hey, hey, I recognize that one!" I protested. "Conzart's the one who's always doing something stupid!"

Several of them laughed, and the girl who'd spoken flushed bright pink.

"Lhaenit was helpfully reminding us to be polite and not overuse literary references with someone not native to our culture," said Nazralind, emerging from behind a building in fresh clothes and wet hair. She gave Lhaenit a very flat stare as she stepped into the firelight. "It was a kind thought, which Conzart over there chose to express in the rudest, most ironic way possible."

Lhaenit, now beet-red, made a complicated hand gesture at me—nobles seemed to have a bunch of intricate ones rather than the simple folding down hands I was used to—before fleeing into one of the houses where the gwynneks were stabled.

"Okay." Goose's low, even tone cut through the rising mirth; we all knew what it heralded. She rose from her seat on the other side of the fire, where she'd been carefully running a whetstone over her belt knife, which she'd already thoroughly washed and oiled. Clean and sharpened to a razor edge, it was now as close to a surgical tool as we were going to get out here in the wilderness. Goose, being a surprisingly thoughtful sort for looking like such a big lug, had positioned herself where I didn't have to see the preparations and could barely hear them over the soft hissing hum of the asauthec fire. Now she stepped to my side, knife gleaming in the firelight. "Looks like we're ready. Let's not put this off, Lord Seiji."

"Yeah, the sooner this is done, the better," I agreed, shrugging out of the blanket draped over my shoulders, which left me just in the one covering my pelvis for modesty. I had kept my Amulet of Final Luck on, since it wasn't really in the way, and if Goose slipped it might end up having work to do.

One of the noble bandits let out a wolf whistle, prompting several laughs and one exasperated "*Really*, Sadhith?"

"I'm sure you're just trying to make me feel better, and I appreciate the thought," I said, putting on a grin that I hoped didn't look too forced.

Goose knelt at my side and gestured for me to lie back on the ground. "Okay, I'm gonna start with the two in your chest up here. I can tell you're having trouble breathing, Lord Seiji, which means they're in your lungs. Once we get these done, you'll be able to breathe properly, which'll help you a lot, and I also expect these'll be the worst to get out, so I wanna have 'em out of the way as quick as possible."

"Sounds good, I agree."

"After that I'll get these four here in your gut. Once that's done and you can get something down without fucking up your insides, we'll take a break to get some food and ale into you to give you energy and soften up the rest of this. Not too much ale; you're gonna have to stay lucid enough to Heal after we're done with each cut. After that, cutting the rest outta your arms and leg won't be nearly as bad. *Then* you can get washed up properly and finish off the bottle if you want to, which I probably would if I was you."

"Damn, Goose, and here I was thinking medical aid was my department. You sure you were never a doctor?"

She shook her head, smiling grimly. "Just common sense and an interesting life, Lord Seiji. I've had to cut into a few people I wasn't trying to kill. Just takes a steady hand, which I've got. Okay, I know it's asking a lot, but try to breathe slow and shallow."

"I'll do my best." I watched the firelight gleam on the blade as it descended toward my chest, alarmingly close to my heart, and that was the point where I chickened out of watching. I'm not proud, but dammit, I refuse to be ashamed, either. I looked away, barely suppressing a hiss when she began slicing the skin around the quarrel. Goose worked quickly, but that skin was *attached* to the akorshil bolt, thanks to the effects of Heal, which meant it was a lot of detailed little cuts to avoid having to gouge a giant hole in me. Twigs joined her with a pile of rags and hot water, immediately working to sop up the blood that welled up.

And, as always when I was stressed, I found myself flapping my yap without actually having decided to.

"So, how do you and Nazralind know each other?"

Nobody upbraided me for the foolishness of making chitchat during surgery; I think they understood. It was a poor substitute for anesthesia, but it was what we had.

"We were raised together," Twigs said. Her voice was full of forced cheer, and I appreciated the thought, even if she wasn't very convincing. "I was one of Naz's maedhlou."

"No idea what that is."

"Ah, it's likely you wouldn't!" Nazralind sat at my other side, joining in without hesitation. Not afraid of the sight of blood, this one. "That's a Fflyr highborn custom which is unique to Dlemathlys. You see, Lord Seiji, when a Highlady reaches the age of six, she is assigned two maedhlou from families of lower nobility. They move into her home and for all intents and purposes, all three are raised as sisters. Well," she added with an apologetic grimace for Twigs, "sisters who are never allowed to forget their difference in rank. Maedhlou are not exactly servants, but their role is to support and assist their Highlady. And, ultimately, when she is married, her husband gains the two maedhlou as concubines in addition to a wife."

I was trying not to breathe too heavily, and couldn't really make faces as I was already grimacing. Goose was trying to work quickly, but trying harder to work carefully, which meant I had to feel her digging in little cuts around that shaft as she went down into muscle. A steady hand, yes; a surgeon, no.

"That sounds like something an isekai writer would come up with."

Nazralind blinked. "Forgive me, I don't understand the reference."

"Perhaps it is good for your Ladyship to know what that feels like."

She grinned in, as far as I could tell, genuine good humor, black eyes sparkling in the firelight. "A fair hit, sir. Reference aside, I do catch your hint of derision, and rest assured, I agree. Hard."

"Well, it's not without its benefits," said Twigs, still dabbing blood.

Nazralind stared at her. "Elemyn, of *all* people to defend this practice—"

"Oh, don't mistake me, no one's saying the tradition wasn't set up so delicate men who've never picked up anything deadlier than a dinner fork could carry on like conquering warlords. But it *does* help the country. Maedhlou and the Convocation's prohibition on family fighting each other are all that keeps the peace in this country. The Clans are all full of each other's members, raising each other's children. So they scheme and screw each other over at every opportunity, but it's never come to outright civil war. Not even once. Something set up for vile, selfish reasons can still yield positive benefits. In this case, the only reason Dlemathlys is stable at all."

I really wanted to interject that Dlemathlys was about as stable as a house of cards during an earthquake, but I was feeling the undeniable sensation of a knife cutting *into my lung*, and Nazralind was frowning at Twigs with rising signs of open anger; I decided we all needed a distraction.

"What about—hh—the lower highborn—ow—men? How're there—*nngh*—enough wives . . ."

"From this point I need you to stop talking, Lord Seiji," said Goose, her voice apologetic but firm.

"That's asking an awful lot," my trusty familiar commented from where he was hovering above us. "Look who you're talking to!"

"Come on, Biribo," Twigs objected, frowning up at him.

"All part of the system," Nazralind answered me. She had also picked up a rag and gently swabbed sweat from my forehead. "Lower highborn men *very* occasionally get the opportunity to marry up, if their Clan's schemes can arrange it, but usually they wed women from foreign nobility, or wealthy middleborn families. It brings in fresh blood and money, and gives the lower-status Clans the opportunity to breed themselves up or down, depending on how good they are at arranging marriages. So we highborn aren't as badly inbred as you might expect," she said with a wry grin. "Certainly not as bad as the nobles of *some* countries. We don't have much to boast about here in Dlemathlys, but we've got that! High literacy and less inbreeding than you'd think. They should embroider that on the flag."

I had my doubts about how this system could result in anything *but* inbreeding, but I couldn't focus my mind on the particulars. I could feel my flesh being cut into; I couldn't breathe, my own blood was pouring into my lung, I was *drowning in my own—*

"Got it!" Goose held up the broken quarrel, its head still intact and crimson, with an alarmingly large chunk of flesh attached.

Heal!

Pink light blazed, and I started to gasp for breath before the pain from the other side of my chest stopped me. Still, I could definitely breathe more easily now, at least on one side. Tentatively, I expanded my chest, trying to feel the motion. As far as I could tell, there was no fluid there . . . Did Heal fix that, somehow, or was I just wrong? It wasn't like I had a stethoscope.

The sound of Goose throwing aside the crossbow bolt covered in eau de Seiji was muffled by the sound of one of the nearby women being violently sick.

"Hell's revels, you honking geese!" Nazralind exclaimed in exasperation. "If you don't have the stomach to watch a surgery, *go somewhere else*! Or do you really think what this situation needs is *more* bodily fluids being spilled?"

I was too focused on breathing to comment, but in fairness, it probably didn't make much difference. Nobody looming over me was wearing a mask and I had my suspicions about how thoroughly they'd washed their hands. If not for Heal, this medieval approximation of surgery would probably kill me as sure as getting shot a bunch of times was meant to.

"I'm sorry about that, Lord Seiji," Goose said, grimacing as she wiped off her knife. "I think I fucked up a little, there. I was trying to be careful, but down in the . . . I mean, I couldn't really see what to cut in there with all the blood and it ended up being a mess anyway. Your spell worked great, though!" She carefully wiped blood away from the incision site, shaking her head in amazement. "Not even a scar."

"Yeah, Heal has some arbitrary limitations, but I'm not a hundred percent sure of the rules," I wheezed. "It doesn't restore missing limbs or things like eyes, but . . . It seems to've filled in that hole just fine. On the next one, maybe focus on being faster? I mean, please don't just hack me apart, but . . ."

"I get your meaning, Lord Seiji, don't worry," she assured me. "I think you're right. Taking too much time just caused more harm than good. I'll try to find a balance more toward speed without getting sloppy. Okay, here we go."

"So," I said desperately, clamping down on a spike of animal terror as the flashing blade descended toward my chest. "If you're supposed to have two of these maid people, where's . . . ?"

Goose started cutting, and I bit down on my lip, resolving to simplify this by ceasing my talking earlier this time.

"That's at the core of why we're all here, really," said Nazralind. Again, she stepped in to fill the quiet and distract my attention, though I could tell this subject had gotten harder for her. Twigs's expression had suddenly gone distant, too. "Well, I had my marriage arranged, and . . . You see, it's customary for a prospective groom to spend time alone with his fiancée and her maedhlou, but of course no sexual contact until after the wedding. Well, Highlord Rhanider didn't care for that rule. Obviously he wanted his *bride* to be chaste for the wedding night, but why not sample the rest of the goods early?" Her expression was twisted in a complex blend of dark emotions. "Minyrit refused, of course. I don't think anyone had ever refused that boy anything in his life; he went completely insane. He got his hands around her neck, and he just didn't stop . . ."

Silence fell. I could hear the wet sound of Goose slicing my flesh, feeling the hot, bright pain of it. The distraction of her voice was sorely missed in that gap, but I couldn't fault Nazralind for having to stop there. Christ, this couldn't be much easier on her than it was on me.

"Our sister," Twigs whispered, "the person closest to us in all the world . . . He killed her right in front of us. *Right in front of us.* And . . . and we just stood there. We were *ladies*. We just . . . went blank. Shut down. I couldn't . . . I couldn't . . ."

"It was a scandal," Nazralind said in the cold, tired tone of someone who was far away in her mind. "Because . . . it would be *embarrassing* to Clan Aelthwyn if the details were known. So my uncle fixed the official story, that there was an accident. The wedding was to proceed as planned, and Highlord Rhanider received an extra dowry payment, since he was only getting one concubine out of the deal. *They paid him for it.*"

"That moment of realization is a hell of a thing," Twigs said when Nazralind trailed off. "When you realize . . . this man is going to *kill me*. And all the people who are supposed to love me will just let it happen. He won't even be punished. Highborn ladies are meant to be decorative and passive; we're trained from the cradle to accept things and not . . . not make a fuss . . .

It's funny how different things suddenly become when it is literally life or death. Funny what suddenly isn't unthinkable anymore."

Nazralind grimaced, staring at me but, I think, seeing something else entirely. "Our escape did not go well. We only got as far as we did because Goose helped. She was our bodyguard; young Highladies often get female veterans from the King's Guild to help look after them. A lot would've just turned us in to our Clans, but Goose understood. Even with her help, though, getting away was . . . Well, obviously, they didn't want us to go. There was a lot of money and prestige riding on us, you see."

"We got separated," Twigs whispered. "I thought you *died*. I've hated myself for leaving you . . ."

"It was the right call, and I'm glad you did," Nazralind told her fiercely. "We both lived. You lived because the two of you *ran*, and stood by each other. I . . . found my own help, as I told you. If you hadn't, we never could have met each other again. And I've built up all this, because . . ." She raised her head, eyes glistening with moisture, to look at the other ladies standing silently nearby. "I swore to myself it would never be like that again. The world may be full of nightmares, but I will never again be frozen, or indecisive. I will never again *stand there and watch*."

My fingers scrabbled across the dirt and found her hand. The elf immediately grabbed it and held on, squeezing almost hard enough to hurt, just as I did her. The gesture wasn't really characteristic of me, and I suspected not of her, either, but in that moment it felt right. She was reliving a trauma while I went through a fresh one.

Sometimes, you just need to hold on to someone.

"It's out!" Goose said, drawing in a breath she'd apparently been holding off in concentration. I felt a lightness in the agonizing spot in my chest where pressure was suddenly withdrawn.

Heal!

I inhaled deeply, fully. Sweet, blessed air filled my lungs. It wasn't *completely* normal; the expansion of my chest caused little spikes of pain from the bolts still embedded in my diaphragm muscle below. But I could breathe again. *I could breathe.*

"You're doing great, Lord Seiji," said Goose, resting one big, calloused hand over my forehead. "Need to take a break? This is some real shit, I know."

"Are you kidding?" I croaked, grinning feebly. "I could do this shit all night. Try to keep up."

Nazralind squeezed my hand once more before letting go. "Every woman here has a story like that, Lord Seiji. Hell, I suspect every living person in Fflyr Dlemathlys does. This country is rotten to its broken core; there have to be far more people here ready to fight back than otherwise. They just need someone to show them how, convince them it's possible—someone who has the *power* to back up their promises. I was raised attending temple services just like anyone, hearing the Goddess's dogma, but . . . Screw her, it's not as if she's ever done anything for us. I don't care which goddess you follow. If you can break this horrible system and build something just a *little* bit better, I'm with you. We all are."

"Breaking things is a lot easier than building them," I said, still breathing heavily. "I have absolutely no idea how to put a nation together, Nazralind. We still need to find the right kind of help for that."

"We can . . . tell you a *little* about it," she said with a wince. "Growing up close to power, you pick up a few tidbits from sheer exposure. But . . . yeah, you're right. I was arrogant enough to let myself think I could be the one to save this country, but I was right in the process of learning how wrong I was when Elemyn and Goose found us. Oh, by the way, I forgot—thank you kindly for paying our protection money to that horrible goblin. Considering the trouble that was looking for us, you very likely saved all our lives."

"Maugro's not so bad," I said, awkwardly patting her hand. "But you're welcome. Okay, Goose. Let's get on with tonight's business before we move on to saving and/or destroying the world."

I must've been tougher than I thought; it was a while after that before my Wisdom perk kicked in and I found myself elevated above the pain and trauma of the ongoing cutting, floating on a frozen cloud of logic and observing my suffering from a distance, as if it were someone else's problem. What did it in the end was the smell, the sudden acrid stink of human shit as Goose accidentally opened my intestines while digging out a quarrel.

Nazralind was alarmed when I went stiff and expressionless, but Biribo hastened to explain. I was focusing fully on lying as still, and breathing as shallowly, as possible, because that was the rational thing to do in that situation, and I no longer had anything else in my brain. It certainly made the rest of the procedure a lot more bearable. The Blessing of Wisdom: better anesthesia than a tragic backstory.

The effect lingered; I declined food and ale when Goose finished with my abdomen, simply asking her to move right to getting the rest of them out of me. In that emotionless void, I couldn't even feel properly celebratory once I was fully quarrel-free, Healed and whole again. It was in the same icy fugue state that I mechanically downed some refreshments, went behind a ruined house to properly wash myself with the aid of an Orb of Light and some surprisingly fragrant soap the noblewomen had, and rejoined the group by the fire, just in time for it to wear off.

Which was *loads* of fun, because I was still having an adrenaline crash at that point. The result was that I didn't have much clarity as to the rest of what happened that night, but I sure as hell took Goose up on her offered bottle then, downing it almost fast enough to choke.

Someone gently guided me to a blanket on the ground and I curled up under it. Like a pill bug . . . Like an Immolate victim. Head spinning with alcohol and trying not to sob out loud. It was over; there was no need for this. So I told myself, but my body seemed to want to torture itself further and wasn't cooperating with me. I just wanted to sleep . . .

Most of them had the courtesy to leave me alone at that point, though I could hear soft voices in my vicinity as my wobbling consciousness finally began to flicker out from fatigue and drink.

"Even after your warning, he's . . . not what I expected."

"But in a good way?"

"Yeah, I think so, mostly."

Dead drunk, I couldn't assign a face to either voice, but the deeper one which chimed in had to be Goose. "There's a good kid in there, under all the layers of flamboyance and grumpiness. He's a lot like you ladies. Wasn't a noble or anything in his own world, but it sounds like it was a much easier place. You know what it's like to be wrenched out of comfort and suddenly have to fight for your life."

"Yeah. Yes, we do. I couldn't speak for what the goddesses are up to, but I wonder if Virya hasn't sent us exactly what . . ."

Finally, I disappeared into the darkness of sleep. It was a relief, at first, before the nightmares began.

I had some new ones now.

13

In Which the Dark Lord Learns About Unintended Consequences

Oh shit," I commented upon seeing the line of stalled merchant caravans blocking the major highway into Gwyllthean. It was still early in the morning, but from this distance it already looked to be close to a kilometer long.

"Yeah, and that's only the khora's fronds," said Nazralind, patting me on the shoulder. "What you stirred up last night is going to . . . Well. Just remember, whatever their consequences, some mistakes are *understandable*. I had to learn this one the hard way myself."

I tried to give her a piercing look, and quickly had to turn my head the other way to suppress a smirk.

Nazralind was dressed in a ragged lowborn longcoat, with correspondingly battered-looking trousers, shirt, and boots, all a size too large for her and padded underneath. She had also bound her chest down, but what kept making my lips twitch was the work done above the collarbones. The elf had obscured her alabaster complexion with actual makeup, the results a lot better than Twigs's desultory efforts to smear herself with dirt. Her skin was now a lowborn brown, and it definitely didn't look quite right up close, but the slight discolorations here and there could be taken for dirt on Dountol skin, which was believable with the rest of her shabby disguise.

The best part was the shaggy black wig and fake beard. That plus a big, scraggly, wide-brimmed hat concealed her ears, but the beard was definitely my favorite part. This wouldn't win any Hollywood costume awards, but I supposed it was serviceable so long as nobody examined her too intimately. Nothing could be done about her black eyes—lowborn usually had pale irises in a variety of colors not seen on Earth—but she kept the brim of her hat pulled low and her face angled toward the ground. From a distance at least, Highlady Nazralind had successfully transformed herself into an impoverished man with a much heavier frame and a permanent hunch.

Obviously, all of the ladies in Naz's little revolutionary squad were wanted fugitives. Wanted for various crimes, yes, but far more urgently wanted by their families back behind fortress walls, properly behaved and not embarrassing their Clans. They couldn't show their faces near civilization, so they'd apparently mastered the art of putting on different faces.

For a given value of "mastered," anyway.

From the river, we approached the main road cross-country at first, passing through a few freshly harvested fields until we reached a small trail between them that eventually took us to the main road. It probably would have been simple enough to slip into the Gutters from any direction, since Gwyllthean's actual defenses didn't start until most of the way into its urban area, but Nazralind's ladies had been out scouting since before I even woke up, and based on what they said was happening there today, we judged it best to try the open approach. Under the circumstances, people trying to sneak into the city ran the risk of being shot on sight. I, at least, had a good chance of getting in so long as I brazenly walked in. Even if I was accompanied by such a scruffy-looking character.

The ladies had outfitted me in their fanciest costume, a nobleman's ensemble in beige cream with a light blue coat trimmed in silver, which did not suit me *at all* but at least looked rich enough to command some respect. It was a little tight on me, but it would do. Nazralind was carrying her bow and quiver—most of her followers appeared to have taken up archery, to judge by the arms they carried—and while a nobleman being accompanied by a huntsman might be a bit uncommon, it was less so than my Asian face and at least told a story that would make sense to anyone we met.

We turned onto the highway and made our way toward the city, passing another caravan as it was forced to stop by the queue. There was a great deal of grumbling and cursing, some directed at the two of us as we strode right past the parked wagons. This morning it was just Nazralind and me because after my experiences yesterday I had been easily talked into not trying to do things alone. Once more I was without Biribo, having sent him to find and discreetly update Aster first thing this morning.

I'd have hoped he would have the initiative to do so alone while I slept, but apparently it was fundamentally uncomfortable for familiars to be separated from their masters. Biribo had grudgingly acknowledged that

Gwyllthean, from our current position, was about as far as he *could* safely travel from me, and carrying a quick message shouldn't take too long. He hadn't returned yet, which meant he'd have to wait for an opening, now that we were in public. I had faith in his abilities, though, and at least now Aster wasn't left twisting in the wind.

"Good luck to you," said the sweaty-faced merchant in charge of the foremost caravan as we passed him, directing a scowl at the military blockade closing off the highway right at the city's outskirts. "These oafs are *completely* impervious to reason!"

"Yeah, talk like that'll get you in *much* faster," rejoined the guard who appeared to be in charge before turning to me. "Sorry . . ." He took in my foreign features, scruffy companion, rich clothing, and rapier, and chose to err on the side of caution. ". . . my lord, traffic in and out of the city's closed until further notice. Major security situation."

"Yes, I should say so," I replied pleasantly. "That's what I'm here about. I need to speak with Captain Norovena immediately."

"Captain who?" he asked in open irritation. "Look, I'm sorry, my lord, but I have my orders. Nobody in, nobody out; I was told no exceptions."

"Well, you're already having more luck than I have, m'lord," drawled the merchant. "Got more of a semblance of courtesy out of them, at any rate. What say we stab the blighter? It's about all I've not yet tried."

"If I thought you'd ever stabbed anything meaner than a sausage in your life, your fat head would already be flying upwind," the guard retorted, laying a hand on his sword. "All of you, *back up*."

I sized him up, considering my options. The local Kingsguard were eminently bribable, and also a lot of them knew me as a source of bribes and friend of Captain Norovena, which greatly contributed to my freedom of movement in the city. These were not Kingsguard, though. Not only had I not seen these individuals before, their uniforms were different—they wore armor of green akornin which had the iridescent quality of polished raw shell that hadn't been painted, and also was cut in bigger plates, which still held the shapes of its animal origins rather than the overlapping scales of the Kingsguard uniforms. They also had tabards on over that, green fabric with a convoluted-looking sigil in black over a white outline. My Blessing of Wisdom didn't enable me to read the symbol, so it wasn't a word. Unfortunately, my standard strategy for guards wasn't going to work here; if these guys could be bribed, the well-dressed merchant would already be inside.

"Lord Seiji!" Pounding boots distracted me from my inner debate over how to get past this without causing more trouble than I needed; I looked up to behold a soldier in the more familiar Kingsguard uniform, approaching down the road with one arm waving overhead. To my chagrin, I didn't remember this fellow's name, but he clearly remembered me. "It's all right, that's Lord Seiji; the Captain wants to see him. Let him through."

The guards in green frowned uncertainly, their spokesman half-turning to address the new arrival without taking us completely out of his field of view. "My orders were—"

"Fuck your orders and your grandma, you shroom-picking oaf," the Kingsguard roared, actually drawing his sword and causing all the men in green to back up from this burst of unexpected aggression. "Lord Seiji's toe corns have been more use to this operation than the goblin-fucking lot of you! Get outta the way or it's *your* ass!"

"Whatever. Not my responsibility," the guard muttered, dutifully backing away. "Hang on—"

"He's with me," I interrupted as he started to reach for Nazralind, who had immediately followed me through the gap. The guard looked at me, at the scowling Kingsguard still brandishing a sword, and shut his mouth.

"Thanks for the assistance," I said.

"No worries, m'lord. I'm right glad to see you hale. Some of the Guttergrubbers we've been rounding up were claiming you got gorked. Figured they were full of it, but it's still a relief. Sorry about the holdup back there." Sheathing his sword finally, he directed a last filthy look at the blockade before turning to accompany us up the road at a fast walk. "It's a right mess today, Lord Seiji. The Archlord called in the Clansguards to support us in rounding up Gray's gangs. Sounds good on paper, but on the ground it means we spend half our time trying to keep these countryside shitkickers in order. Not a one of 'em knows which end of a sword to stab with and which to jam up his arse."

My own observation so far was that the mobilized Clansguard differed from the Kingsguard chiefly in that they followed their orders and didn't take bribes, but I saw no need to share that insight with him.

The soldier gave Nazralind a curious look, but apparently my say-so was sufficient authorization in his mind, so he forbore comment. "Captain Norovena left orders he wants to see you as soon as you turned up again, m'lord. He's straight up this road here, been running the mission out of the south gatehouse. Awfully sorry not to provide an escort, Lord Seiji, but each of us is doing six men's work and I gotta get back to mine or it'll be my bum with a boot up it. You'll have no more trouble if you stick to the main road, though. In this quadrant all the Clansguard recruits are manning barricades on the outskirts where they belong, and our own lads should know you. I'd not stray into the Gutters proper until the Captain can set you up with a solid escort, m'lord. We've not tied down all the bastards yet by far."

"Thanks for the tip," I said, flipping him a gold disc. "I'll stay out of trouble. You'd best do the same; don't let me be the reason you get an earful."

"Right you are, m'lord!" He gave me a grin and a salute, then turned to dash off down a side street, presumably to rejoin his squad.

"You're on right good terms with the guards, me lord," Nazralind commented as soon as we were alone.

I had to stop and give her a long look before resuming my stride up the street. Apparently she was too committed to break character as long as the disguise was on. Which was how I learned that Nazralind's impression of a gruff lowborn huntsman sounded exactly like a young woman putting on an imitation of a gruff huntsman. Or at absolute best, a boy too young to have a beard like that. Well, at least the beard wasn't crooked and she seemed intelligent enough not to talk unnecessarily.

"I bribe them," I explained tersely as we walked. "A lot. And I've made friends with the local Kingsguard captain. By bribing him, a lot. Law enforcement in this city is a disgrace and the first thing I'll be replacing when I'm in charge, but in the meantime it makes more sense to spend coin to have them help me than spilling blood and adding to my problems."

"Wouldn't've been my approach," she grunted, but fell silent. It was a little hard to tell under the disguise, but I *thought* her frown looked more contemplative than disapproving, so I decided not to pointedly ask which of us was succeeding in his rebel movement and which had just gotten chased out of hers.

"What in the *hell* are they *doing?*" I demanded, mostly rhetorically, now that I was in a position to get a good look at what was happening in the Gutters today.

The main highway looked downright eerie with no traffic at this time of morning, but the area was far from silent. Though the sounds of shouts, crashing, and screams were relatively distant, they came from all directions. Down every side street we passed I could see the aftermath of destruction. Shattered windows, doors off their hinges, belongings smashed and strewn across the pavement, and most chillingly of all, no sign of the residents; every person who lived and worked around here and hadn't been rounded up was obviously hiding in what remained of their property. The omnipresent food and vendor stalls lining the highway itself were more often broken than not, several of them appearing to have been torched.

They were made of akorshil, which *didn't fucking burn*. The ashes and scorch marks I saw meant someone had gone *well* out of their way to be destructive, toward no purpose that I could see.

Whatever was going on had apparently made its way a good distance from the main road on the outskirts, but the sounds drew closer the farther in we proceeded, and within a few minutes we got our first live glimpse of the ongoing purge of Lady Gray's assets. Or, in this case, what appeared to be a bakery. Men in Kingsguard uniforms—including a couple I recognized as affable fellows who were always good for town gossip—were in the process of hurling fresh bread into the street. As I slowed to watch, one punched the shop owner who'd been pleading with them, sending the man tumbling to the ground and prompting a woman's scream from inside the store.

"Don't." Nazralind caught my arm before I realized I'd started down that street. "You'll only make it worse."

I shrugged her off. "Why the *fuck* are they *beating up bakers*?! They're supposed to be—"

"This is what I meant," she said urgently, her voice low—her normal one, not her awkward Batman impression. "Light a fire under the highborn and it's the low who get burned. The ability to deflect consequences to others is the *essence* of power. I've gotta say, I never kicked off a mess on quite *this* scale, but only because I stayed away from the city. This was more or less the exact consequence of my first efforts to fight back. In one little village after another . . . this."

"I don't . . . I can't even tell what they're trying to *accomplish*. This is just pointless carnage!"

"Let's go. It's done, Lord Seiji. Now we have to be smart and not exacerbate this." She shook her head, gently but firmly nudging me forward up the street. "This is exactly what I expected to see, knowing my uncle. You have to think about highborn and what matters to them; think about how exactly you maneuvered them into cracking down on Lady Gray. They never cared that she was a powerful criminal. You made them think she was fighting against the social order that keeps them on top, remember? So getting rid of the powerful criminal was only part of the goal. With that done, they have to reinforce the social order. Uncle Caludon doesn't care about lowborn preying on each other; he cares about lowborn forgetting their *place*."

I fell silent, because nothing that came out of my mouth right then would have been constructive. I just walked, listening to the sounds of breaking windows, of screams, of guards' truncheons beating down doors and impacting flesh. The sound of a city being beaten for the crime of . . . possibly, theoretically, being inclined to get uppity at some hypothetical point in the future.

Which I had set off in order to strike at my enemy, because I was just so very *clever*.

My god, I might as well have burned down the Gutters entirely to smoke her out. Oh wait, an Ephemeral city wouldn't burn. Maybe I should've looked up the recipe for Greek fire back when I had internet access. Just cut out the middleman next time and commit my own crimes against humanity in person.

Nazralind kept quiet while I walked and stewed in self-recrimination. If she'd been down this road herself, she likely knew what words would help, which was none of them. So we walked, lengthening our strides to get this over with quickly, hearing the chaos growing ever closer the farther in we went.

Fortunately, I didn't have to go all the way to the gatehouse to find a proper distraction. A little more than halfway up we met none other than Captain Norovena himself, striding out of a side alley in the company of three soldiers, an obvious bureaucrat scribbling on a clipboard with a pencil, and a priest in the white, crimson, and gold robes of the Radiant Convocation. Norovena was wearing a heavy scowl and resting one hand menacingly on the pommel of his sword, but his expression cleared upon spotting me.

"Lord Seiji!" He changed course so fast only his soldiers kept up, the two tagalongs getting left behind in their confusion. "Goddess's grace, I'm relieved to see you! Half the gangsters we've rounded up are claiming they saw you die with their own eyes."

"Some of 'em had a go at it, but it didn't take," I said. He held out one hand, and I hope he didn't note my momentary hesitation in clasping it. This was the man overseeing the brutalizing of the city's lowborn populace happening *right now*, at my instigation. I was already in too deep to get squeamish. "They did succeed in chasing me out of the Gutters, though. I couldn't get a clear path back to the walls, so I had to lie low overnight in the fields. Thanks to my friend here it went pretty smoothly, but I decided not to risk going back through the city until I could see your soldiers had it under control."

"A solid plan, my lord." He did a small double take after looking at Nazralind; an experienced city guard seeing her disguise up close could undoubtedly recognize something amiss, whether or not he could discern exactly what. My endorsement continued to prove a sufficient passport, how-ever, and he let it go without peering too closely. "I regret the rough night you must have had. Rest assured we'll get you a proper break once safely back inside the walls. I'm afraid your bodyguard has been beside herself."

I bit back a litany of complaints about what was happening. I wanted to grab him by the collar and shake him until some basic human decency fell out, but what would be the point? If there was any still in there to be jarred loose, his men would club me to the ground well before I found it.

And it wasn't as if I had any right to throw stones.

"How'd it go in my absence?" I asked. "Did you get her?"

Norovena grimaced, shaking his head. He gestured as he turned to stride back up the street toward the gates and I fell into step alongside him, Nazralind sticking to my other shoulder.

"Of course we bloody well didn't. Oh, don't mistake me, I can't call the operation anything but a rousing success! Thanks to our plan, and the intel we received, we've got the vast majority of Gray's people in custody or dead in the street where we found them. Huge swaths of her assets seized and her organizational capacity—for all intents and purposes—gone. But Gray herself . . . no."

"Typical," I muttered. "I've just about lost patience with that fucking cockroach of a woman."

"This is about what we expected, going in," said Norovena. "She's a pow-erful Blessed with powerful artifacts, and vast familiarity with the terrain. The point was always to strip her of her organization. With no network and no assets, she's just another rogue Blessed. The King's Guild will finish her off sooner or later. Our job here is done, and with all due modesty, we've done a damn fine job, Lord Seiji."

They were smashing stores and beating civilians. Over a perceived threat to the racial hierarchy. Thanks to *me*. I had kicked off a fucking *ethnic cleansing* here, and now this guy wanted me to feel as self-satisfied as he clearly was. The guilt was a lump of ice taking up my entire gut, and trying to rise up my throat. I swallowed it back down, clinging to my outward equanimity.

Performance mode. Nazralind was right—I couldn't do any good by complaining about this. Had to play along for now. I could do that; I was Omura fucking Seiji—performing was my entire identity.

It was a lot harder than usual today.

"On the other hand, with nothing left to protect, she may go on the offensive. I could see her throwing everything away for revenge against the people responsible for this. Which, need I remind you, is the two of us and Master Auldmaer."

"Possible, but I doubt it. She's always been self-controlled and profit motivated. The better move in her current position is to flee Dount and try to restart operations elsewhere. Even with that famous dagger of hers, being the top of the Gwyllthean King's Guild's kill list is going to hamper her ability to do anything on Dount. And Lady Gray, as we've discussed, is no fool."

He was wrong, and I had seen the proof. Lady Gray could have fled the city as soon as she realized what we were up to last night, but she'd stayed and hurled everything she had at *me*, showing up in person to make sure the job got done. She was what, fifty? Her life's work was in ruins and starting from scratch would barely be a prospect. No, she'd come for revenge; it was all she had left. The problem was, I wasn't sure how much Norovena knew about the scope of my powers or what had happened last night, which meant it could be a fatal mistake to just blurt it out. How to convince him without revealing I'd tangled with her personally, twice? That was Dark Lord–caliber shit, not something "Lord Seiji" should be able to boast about.

"The *really* unfortunate news is we haven't found her headquarters. Oh, various counting houses and armories and the like, mostly locations we already knew of, but nothing that looks like Gray's personal hideout. That wasn't among the details we got from your informant, Lord Seiji. Fine work sending him along, by the way. That's twice over your maneuvering cinched the operation for us. But she *does* still have a hole to go to ground in, along with whatever resources she'd kept hidden away there. That, in my judgment, will work against her. Those assets are all she has left in the world, and she won't abandon them. Trying to smuggle them out of town will hamper her ability to move. That's how we'll get her."

"My informant? *Oh*, did Lamm actually—"

I realized I was talking to the air. Norovena had suddenly turned and dashed down a side street, this time so abruptly that even his soldier escort were left confused for a moment. But they followed, as did the rest of us.

As soon as we saw what he was going for, I drew my rapier and Nazralind nocked an arrow to her bow, but Norovena got there before we did.

Three Kingsguard had seized two women in front of an akorshil carver's shop, right out in the street in broad daylight; two were holding back a screaming and struggling middle-aged matron, while the third pressed the younger woman against the wall, fumbling with the back of her dress.

The captain was on them so fast they didn't see him coming, yanking the soldier off the girl and then smashing his face against the wall. Then doing the same twice more before hurling him to the ground. Both the other guards released their captive in shock, stepping back, and the freed girl fled into the woman's arms, sobbing. Then the rest of us finally arrived.

"Membership in the Kingsguard carries certain privileges," Norovena stated in a tightly wound tone, looming over the fallen soldier with his sword out. The man wasn't unconscious despite the beating he'd just received, no doubt thanks to his helmet, which was now visibly cracked. He stared up at his captain in wide-eyed apprehension, the tip of Norovena's sword centimeters from his face. "Certain liberties which are understood to be part of the job. Men who have a *future* appreciate that, and recognize when to stop. But there are always a few who just can't help themselves, who *always* have to step across the line. And then I end up down a soldier, because some of those lines are immovable. Haul this idiot back to the barracks and put him in a cell," he ordered the men who'd been escorting him. "I will finish dealing with him when I have time."

"Wait, Captain," the guard stammered, trying to scramble upright in a panic. "I was just—"

One of Norovena's escort kicked him in the head, sending him back down, and then he and his companion grabbed the man by both arms and yanked him upright. Clearly these two were loyal to the captain; they frog-marched the offender away without an instant's hesitation, nor any sign of sympathy on their grim faces.

"You two," Norovena said in a tone of ice, turning to the pair of accomplices, who shied back from his expression. "Amvadi and Lassindh. Black list. You put one *toe* out of line during the next *year*, so much as a failure to muster or *one* citizen complaint, and it's the gallows for the both of you. Now *get back to work*."

"Sir!" Both men saluted, then turned and fled down the street.

The captain turned his back on the two women without another word; they took this as license to flee as well and scurried inside the shop. I had to inhale and exhale slowly twice to repress the variety of things I wanted to say about this incident. Nazralind's expression was fortunately obscured by her beard and hat. A least she put the arrow back in her quiver and said nothing.

"Like as not, those two will desert the moment things cool down around here," Norovena grunted, stalking back toward the main road with the stiff demeanor of an offended cat. "If they're caught, they hang; if not, they become someone else's problem. And unfortunately, that's the best outcome I can hope for. You see my fundamental problem, Lord Seiji, and the reason I've got soldiers out breaking in doors instead of executing an actually useful search grid. The precious handful of men I've got who're both trustworthy and competent are fully occupied keeping the rest under some semblance of control, and that's not even counting the administrative nightmare it's been organizing the Clansguards who have oh so helpfully rallied to Clan Aelthwyn's banner. You came in from the south highway, my lord? Then you'll have seen Clan Algumond's men in action. I expect I needn't explain any further."

I didn't reply, my mind already elsewhere. This . . . didn't hold up. Norovena *had* to know what would happen when he unleashed his men on the Gutters with orders that amounted to "beat any spark of defiance out of whoever you see." Scenes like the one he'd just angrily broken up were beyond doubt happening all over the city *at that very moment*. He was far too intelligent a man not to understand that. Also, he was corrupt to begin with, hardly a shining beacon of professionalism. The first time we'd met, he had been awfully blasé about this exact thing happening to Yoshi's friends in his own jail, until I bribed him to put a stop to it.

So . . . What was that display about? Was he putting on a performance for my benefit? Did my opinion matter that much to him? Or maybe it was for the guy with the clipboard and the priest still trailing along with us, who hadn't said a word since I'd joined him but silently watched everything. There were obviously political undercurrents here I didn't begin to understand. A wrong move from me could very well ignite . . .

Well, not worse than I'd already caused, surely. But that didn't mean I could afford to get careless.

"Clan Algumond's three brown-hairs with a country manor, me lord," Nazralind said unexpectedly in her unconvincing lowborn rasp. "Them what we met on the road's the entire Algumond Clansguard, like as not. Must be a real trial fer the Cap'n here ta keep all them diff'rent troops facin' the same direction, aye aye."

Again, the entire group stopped as everyone turned to stare at her. Only through a supreme act of will did I not clap both hands over my face. I'd assumed she *understood* that the point of a disguise was *not* to draw attention, but suddenly it felt more like I was working with an excitable theater kid who didn't know when to shut up.

Captain Norovena peered closely at Nazralind's half-covered face, then glanced at me. I could literally see him decide that whatever the hell was going on here, he had too much on his plate already to fool with it. Saying not a word, he resumed course, the rest of us falling in alongside.

"I'm acquainted with the general caliber of your men, Captain," I said after gathering my thoughts for a moment. "It's always impressed me you get as much use out of that lot as you do. To be honest, I'm a little surprised they were all that successful against Lady Gray's gangs."

"Oh, don't give them too much credit," he said bitterly. "The King's Guild mustered every available hand at the crack of dawn; *they* formed the first strike teams that hit the major gangs. The Kingsguard are cleaning up the remnants, which is more our speed. In any case, Lord Seiji, you can rest assured the bulk of the work has been done. We'll let you relax soon, I promise—you've earned it—but if I could prevail upon you for just a bit longer, there's something else we'd like your help with. Operations have been this successful in no small part because this Lamm character dished every detail on the current disposition of Gray's forces. By and large, his intel appears to have been accurate. He said you'd vouch for him."

"Ah, that I do. Lamm was extremely helpful to me last night. Not out of the goodness of his little heart, of course; I promised I'd put in a good word if he threw in with us."

"Well, between the help and your word, I'm inclined to be positively disposed toward him. But obviously he is in custody right now, and some of my superiors will be less than understanding about giving a reprieve to a career criminal, no matter how useful he was at the last moment."

"Ah. Hence needing my help."

"You do have a gift for . . . circumventing obstructive bureaucracy, my lord." Norovena shot a flat look at Mr. Clipboard, who tightened his mouth but just scribbled a note and continued to say nothing. "Today's work being as important as it is, I would like to see it done as well as we can manage with the resources available to us. I hope you don't think me presumptuous for counting you among them."

"Not at all, Captain, I'm flattered. Rest assured, I'm with you. I helped start this, after all; I can't very well leave it half-done."

"The Kingsguard, as always, appreciates your civic-mindedness, Lord Seiji."

We proceeded up the road to the gates, while behind us the Gutters screamed as the Kingsguard rampaged through them, punishing the innocent just for being there.

I didn't look back. I had to keep my image up. But I listened. Those sounds were going to ring in my head for a long time.

I could only think it was the least of what I deserved.

14

In Which the Dark Lord is the Lesser Evil

In keeping with the established pattern of everything good on Ephemera being horribly tainted somehow, my first hug from Aster was delivered at high velocity while she was wearing chain mail.

"Oof!" I actually staggered under the impact.

Hugs are nice, but chain mail is *hard*. I couldn't help wincing, even as I tentatively raised my arms to give Aster a light squeeze in return and pat her on the back. Actually . . . chain mail aside, this was okay. Now that I thought about it, I hadn't had a hug from anybody since my last girlfriend, which was . . . a year ago? No, two. Two and a half? Something like that.

"We are *not separating again*!" Aster declared, pulling back just enough to glare at me, grab my shoulders, and give me a violent shake.

I gently pried her fingers loose. "Well, well, look who's suddenly barking orders at whom."

"Oh, *no* you don't. This is not an area where you get to pull rank!" She leveled an accusing finger at my nose from distressingly close. "No matter who you are, there are two people you don't outrank if you want to live: your doctor, and your bodyguard!"

Captain Norovena emitted a little huffing noise that might have been a cough or cleared throat . . . or suppressed chuckle. I shot him a look, catching the man biting down on a smile.

"I never have inquired about your home country, Lord Seiji, but in every military and aristocratic hierarchy in every society I'm familiar with, that is indeed the rule. It's good advice, too. Miss Aster's capable head is surely as valuable an asset as her sword."

"Look, Aster, I'm *fine*. It all worked out! Just ran into some unexpected difficulties, that's all."

"And *my* job is to be between you and the unexpected difficulties! Do you have any idea how worried I've been? The gangsters we rounded up were saying you'd *died*! Never again, Lord Seiji!"

"You know, if you keep yelling at your employer like this in public with *no* regard for rank and decorum, the Captain here is going to assume we're sleeping together."

Aster finally fell silent, apparently out of pure outrage. She was so obviously throttling me inside her mind that I could practically see it reflected in her eyes.

"We are not, for the record," I added to Norovena. "It's just that . . . well, you're right, Captain, she really is *very* good at her job, plus other miscellaneous tasks. I find the quality of Aster's service well worth putting up with her backtalk. Which is unending and *spicy*."

"Yes, I've been quite positively impressed by her capabilities during this whole operation," he said in a diplomatic tone. "Anyway, glad as I am to see you two reunited, this situation is still ongoing, and I asked you to accompany me for a reason, my lord. If you would follow me, please?"

At my nod, he led the way out of the main area of the middle ring guard headquarters in which Aster had intercepted us. The place looked busier than usual, as I might have expected given what was going on; soldiers were scurrying about, and there were, unmistakably, others present, including an obvious noble directing small groups of men, plus several well-dressed middle-aged middleborn whom I took for government bureaucrats. The one who'd been shadowing us all the way through the city stepped aside to speak with the aristocrat, while the Convocation priest peeled off down a side corridor. Those two hadn't said one word within earshot, which I couldn't help but think was ominous.

The civil service types were all business, but several of the passing soldiers were grinning at us as Aster and I fell in line behind Norovena, Nazralind bringing up the rear. What can I say, even when it's not my idea, I put on a good show.

In the corridor outside, I carefully leaned over to nudge Aster with an elbow. She shot me an inquisitive look, and I gave her one right back, raising my eyebrows in a silent question. Comprehension dawned in Aster's eyes, and then she flicked them significantly toward Nazralind behind us, tilting her head infinitesimally.

Naz, noting the tiny gesture, waved cheerfully. I couldn't actually see whether she was grinning behind that big fake beard, but it would've been on brand.

I gave Aster a nod and a thumbs up. She grimaced faintly, expressing her doubt about our new ally, but did nod back and pat the bulging exterior side pocket of her overcoat, the one in which she kept a semipermanent nest of cloth scraps.

Even as I looked down at it, the flap shifted just enough for Biribo's tiny black snout to poke through. He flicked his tongue out at me once and then disappeared back into hiding.

Good. Finally, we had the gang back together. Aster was entitled to a lot more explanations, but they would have to wait until we had a modicum of privacy.

Norovena led us through a set of heavy doors, from behind which a horrific din exploded as soon as he opened one. Wincing, I repressed the urge to cover my ears as I followed him. Before us was a sizable hallway crossing with wide corridors branching out to both sides and directly ahead; along one wall was a smaller door, but the rest were lined with metal bars.

The city's prison. I was a little surprised to find myself suddenly here, having expected to descend into a dungeon to see this, but I immediately realized how foolish that was. Ephemerans were afraid to dig or go underground.

"Apologies for the noise, my lord." Captain Norovena had to raise his voice to a near shout to be audible at all, what with the constant roar of men yelling from in their cells, and guards shouting back and occasionally whacking at the cell bars with clubs. "We're *well* past capacity, and these animals are about the only people having a worse day than my men."

On the contrary, I suspected *everyone* in the Gutters was having a worse day than either, considering they'd done nothing to deserve it. That would've been a pointless thing to say in this company, however, so I took the excuse of the noise to just nod at him without answering.

The Captain marched straight to the sole door and opened it, beckoning us to follow.

Inside was an office. The walls were covered with blueprints of the prison and various charts, save for the wall behind the sole heavy desk, which was a floor-to-ceiling rack of pigeonhole shelves mostly full of scrolls. At the desk sat a heavyset middleborn man in a Kingsguard uniform without armor, looking up at the interruption with his bushy eyebrows drawn together in an intense scowl. I couldn't blame him; all four of us had just trooped into his office uninvited, and Norovena had shut the door behind us.

He pretty much had to if he wanted to carry on a conversation in here. We could still hear the roar of the prison through it, just muffled.

"Warden," said Norovena. "Apologies for the interruption, but I'll need to borrow your office for a few minutes."

"Captain," the Warden replied, scowling even harder. "If you haven't noticed, I'm having a *rather busy day.*"

"We're all having the same day, Warden Divanno," Norovena said in a tone that invited no further commentary. "Nor am I asking you to twiddle your thumbs in the hall. I need to have today's *guest of honor* moved from the secured cells to an interrogation room. Given who else is packed into all your crates this morning, I'd be happier if you tended to that personally and make sure nothing goes awry."

With some effort I kept my mouth shut. The *secured* cells? Then what the hell were the rest of them?

Divanno's eyebrows lowered further, the eyes beneath them narrowing to slits as they darted between the three of us. "You *are* talking about the informant? Lamm?"

"The same."

"Hmf. Well, it's not as if I'm making any headway here," he finally grunted with ill grace, tossing his pen down atop the papers on his desk and rising. "If you're planning to have *that* matter tied off, it'll be at least some of this bullshit squared away. By your leave, Captain."

We cleared a way for him to reach the door, resulting in a momentary squeeze against one wall.

"If I could prevail upon your servants, Lord Seiji," Norovena said, raising his voice above the hubbub as Warden Divanno stepped out. "Perhaps if they watch the door and inform any visitors that the Warden is not in, it will spare us any interruption."

It didn't take two people to do that; he wanted privacy. Which meant this was probably something I'd want to hear.

"Good idea. Aster, and . . ."

"Oh, just call me Gulder, Miss Aster," said Nazralind in that raspy drawl which failed to quite obscure her lovely contralto. "Common huntsman, I am, an' right proud t'be of service to Lord Seiji, yup yup."

Aster stared at her, then turned a classic Aster Look on me.

"Gulder is trustworthy," I said with a smile. "He's a friend of Twigs. I'll explain everything when it calms down a bit."

"Of course, Lord Seiji," she said, sighing.

Norovena wasted no time getting down to business as soon as the door shut behind them. "This Lamm character presents a wrinkle, Lord Seiji. He appears to be the highest-ranking member of Lady Gray's organization who's ever voluntarily turned on her. The information he gave has been largely responsible for the success of the King's Guild's initial raids early this morning; and even with Gray herself out of the picture, his insights into crime in Gwyllthean are an absolute treasure trove. Left to my own devices, I'd like to keep him secured here for . . . well, the foreseeable future, at least until confinement erodes his cooperative spirit, and then I'd rather see him bribed with security and comfort to keep helping us as long as his help stays good. There's some precedent for turning skilled criminals into skilled law enforcement."

"Oh dear, all that was extremely positive," I said, wincing. "That means the 'but' I hear coming is going to be enormous."

"The biggest 'but' of them all," Norovena sighed, running a hand through his light brown hair. "Politics. The downside of involving the Clans in this matter is . . . the Clans are involved. Mostly smaller Clans with holdings close to Gwyllthean, firmly under Clan Aelthwyn's control and not daring to upset the haycart too much. But they're also keenly interested in taking advantage of all this furor, seeking ways to score influence with the Archlord, and it's taking the form of a bunch of small proxy battles, which are *already* making my job needlessly difficult. Lamm has become just such a flashpoint. Some of the highborn who've chosen to insert themselves into my business agree with my take, but others are agitating to have him made an example of, as a deterrent to other criminals."

"Wow. That's . . . *impressively* stupid. Do these lordlings actively want to discourage people from siding with the government against bandits and crime lords?"

Norovena indulged himself in a momentary grimace before smoothing his expression and folding his hands behind his back in parade rest position. "These are small households which control about a square limn each of farmland or at most a khora plantation, Lord Seiji. Their interest in seizing this opportunity to get involved in politics doesn't mean they understand the first thing about the politics in question. However, a Highlord is a Highlord. The favor of the Goddess does not differentiate by skill or prestige." His lips twisted for a second as if he could barely spit out that mouthful of irony without choking on it. "It's not for the likes of me to explain to my betters how my job works. I believe you don't reside in the city itself, my lord?"

"That's correct." As if he didn't know.

He nodded. "If you are willing to arrange it, my lord, I think the best solution to this dilemma is for Master Lamm to join your household for the time being. That way we can retain access to his knowledge and skills, and once he is removed from Kingsguard custody the point becomes moot and the Clans will drop it."

"Won't him suddenly disappearing from under their noses just rile them up?"

"Not if it's done in the proper way." Norovena smiled thinly. "Fortunately, nothing in this entire country is on the up and up. For a man like me who has seen and had to facilitate *countless* schemes of the nobility which affect my duties, it's quite simple to create or *not* create the requisite paper trails and suggestions of influence to convince the Clans that one of them pulled strings to make this happen. Continuing to pursue the matter with the Kingsguard will then be too dangerous for these smaller Clans, lest they antagonize their patron, the Archlord; and besides, they will set to scheming against one another to find out who has Lamm, because that is what Fflyr aristocrats do. You, Lord Seiji, are not considered part of their system; most of them aren't even aware of you. If you can take custody of the man himself, I can arrange the necessary cover."

I hummed softly in thought. "Mmm. The catch is I'm not really equipped to keep someone prisoner in the long term. I see the value in your idea, but it'll depend on Lamm. If he's not inclined to sign on with me specifically, me removing him from the city is just going to give him an opportunity to disappear."

"I considered that," the Captain acknowledged, nodding. "I believe the risk warranted in this case, my lord. You have a proven knack for befriending the high and the low alike, and Lamm in particular has already been persuaded to turn on his former mistress in favor of you."

"I guess he has, at that." Shit, this was going to complicate things. Well, I'd already recruited some of Gray's minions. Norovena was right that Lamm had chosen me over Gray once, but it remained to be seen how he'd react once he learned who and *what* he'd be working for. "I gather that's why you wanted him put in an interrogation room."

"It seemed to me that a chance for you to speak with him in private would give you sufficient opportunity to persuade him, my lord."

"I'm flattered by your confidence, Captain," I said dryly.

A pause fell, and I felt myself about to make a mistake.

I *knew* it was a bad idea. I was logically aware that the smart play here was to politely avoid the topic. I knew even if I could somehow win my case here verbally, there would be no chance of changing any of the real-world outcomes and nothing to be gained by pushing it with Norovena. But god *damn* it, I was only human. There were some things that couldn't be hand-waved away without so much as a word.

"On the subject of things which are stupid," I said, impressed with the evenness of my own tone, "with the greatest possible respect, Captain, what do you hope to accomplish by having your men stomp through the Gutters breaking shit?"

Norovena stared at me with a singularly neutral expression for a long enough span of seconds for me to reflect on what a pointless thing my big mouth had just done, yet again. There was no way this slippery crook of an official was going to reveal, much less *do*, anything useful here.

Then he nodded, once, slowly. "Thank you for phrasing it that way, Lord Seiji. I, for my part, I have no expectations. Not good ones, at least. Your plan was put to Archlord Caludon himself, as the only man on Dount with the power to put it into action. He made his own . . . amendments. What's now happening out there is the foremost of those."

"You mean to imply that you don't agree with it?"

His smile tried to be bland, but was a touch too razor-thin. "I am but a humble servant of the King and Clan Aelthwyn. It would simply never occur to me to question the dictates of my betters."

"Of course," I said. "Captain, men like us can never cut the bullshit entirely; we both know that. But at this point, surely we can . . . lower the volume a smidge? After all, it's not like there's any possible benefit to me in getting you in trouble. What am I going to do, take a gamble that the next Kingsguard Captain would be as amenable to working with me and then start from scratch befriending him?"

That bought me a more sincere-looking smile. "I do so enjoy your . . . elegant pragmatism, Lord Seiji. Very well, to . . . lower the volume . . . what's going on out there is a prime example of how the perspective of a man in my position differs from that of my superiors. To the Clans, this is reinforcing the order of society, an unpleasant but banal task that must be done every once in a while, like pruning the bladegrass. To *me*, it represents an incoming period of every part of my job being harder than it needs to."

He paused, turning away to regard one of the charts of the prison layout. Knowing he was staring past, not at it, I remained silent for a moment while he gathered his thoughts.

"The last such crackdown was four years ago, just after I attained my current position. It was much smaller in scope, and in response to an actual rebel movement. The lowborn blamed the rebels, who never had much popular support to begin with, and the whole thing passed . . . relatively quietly. The time before that was, let's see . . . twelve years ago. That was just after I'd joined the Kingsguard, yes." He paused, his shoulders shifting in a quiet sigh. "Much more on the scale of what's happening today. The outcome of a feud between two Clans, which had nothing to do with the commoners at all. The Convocation stepped in to mediate a truce, and so that no highborn were forced to lose face, the infighting was blamed upon an entirely fictitious conspiracy against the King. It was a lie, and everyone knew it was a lie. And after the Kingsguard finished beating the Gutter-folk into submission, it was two *years* before they stopped trying to dump chamber pots on us out of second-floor windows. It's only been within the *last* two years that my men have been able to get any cooperation from Gutters citizens that's not coerced at sword point." He sighed again, more heavily. "Well, at least I have the experience to know what my people can expect in the immediate future."

It was hard to come up with something to say to that. Or rather, hard to come up with something germane and useful. I'm pretty much never without any comment at all.

"I've gotta say, that doesn't make it sound any less foolish. Even if it's not their pretty clothes getting mussed on street patrol, the highborn are still supported by the income of the country itself. In other words, the people. Imagine how much richer and more powerful they could be if this place were managed with an iota of common sense."

"Makes you wonder, doesn't it?" He gave me a wry smile sidelong. "We must simply be content with the assurance that the Goddess's chosen know what they are doing."

Yeah, we definitely knew what they were doing.

"Aren't you worried about riots? Seems like the consequences of provoking a mob could be worse than chamber pots."

Norovena turned away again, this time staring at the wall of scrolls behind the desk. He was silent for such a long span of seconds I opened my mouth to prompt him when he abruptly spoke.

"You have noticed, I'm sure, that at least a quarter of the Gutters is abandoned. Close to a third, by some estimates. Gwyllthean had a significantly larger population recently enough that all those buildings have not had a chance to completely decay."

"I have," I said slowly.

"That event I spoke of," Norovena continued, his voice unusually soft against the muffled background noise of the prison outside, "the feud between Clans—it was Olumnach and Rhaednyl, specifically. The whole thing happened just after the harvest. Just after Archlord Caludon ascended to the high seat of Clan Aelthwyn and the fief of Gwyllthean. His first act as Archlord, while the feud was escalating, was to have all the harvest brought into the middle ring and stored in warehouses there, to protect it from unrest. That was not popular with anyone, of course, but at the time it was just . . . an inconvenience and an odd decision, the sort of things the Clans do all the time. No one considered it worth raising a fuss over. None of us realized what he was planning." He hesitated, rolling one shoulder as if it had stiffened. "Then came the truce, and the crackdown. And then there were mobs and riots. And then . . . Caludon closed the gates."

Norovena turned back to face me directly, staring right into my eyes.

"He not only secured Gwyllthean's defenses as if its lowborn population was a besieging army, he mobilized the Kingsguard and Clansguards loyal to Clan Aelthwyn to secure the landbridges off Dount. All except the northern bridge out of Dlemathlys entirely. And then, with no way to escape the island and *all the food* locked behind the walls with the upper classes . . . he waited."

For once, it was I who was spellbound listening to someone else's performance. He wasn't even all that great a storyteller, but the sheer horror of what unfolded kept me transfixed while the Captain recalled the details for me.

"It took nine weeks, all told, for him to relent. Time enough for the food to run out, for people who had just expected to benefit from the recent harvest to begin starving. The Clans were forewarned what was happening, and they immediately hoarded everything they could in their fortresses and sealed their gates, instead of even trying to share with the common people. Many of those common people died trying to storm the fortified landbridges or Clan fortresses. Many died because they fled north to Godspire, which either kept them outside the city walls in squalid refugee camps or used them as fodder against gladiators in their Grand Arena. There's no telling how many attempted to survive in the wild khora and were killed by beastfolk or the dark elves, who would have considered that an invasion. Obviously, a lot just starved. The Convocation tried to intercede and were rebuffed. The King attempted to send food as aid to the people; Archlord Caludon turned the caravans back at the landbridges. This was before Lord Vanderhoen's reforms; the King was much weaker then than he is now, far too unsure of his authority to risk forcing the issue.

"Caludon Aelthwyn himself made a daily ritual of standing on the outer walls of the middle ring and throwing bread. Not *enough* bread, of course—just enough to *make people fight for it*. And he demanded that they fight, brawling in the streets like animals. If the amount of bloodshed satisfied him, he would throw more bread. If the people tried to exercise some solidarity and share what little there was, there would be no bread the next day. He played similar mind games with the nobles inside the walls. Those who participated in his little . . . diversions earned favor. They would pelt the commoners from the battlements with mixtures of food, offal, and chunks of masonry, just to earn a smile from their Archlord. Any who refused . . . well. There are consequences for being out of favor with the ruling Clan.

"It took nine weeks for the pressure to mount on all sides to the point that he was forced to relent. That was enough time for his point to be made. Dount has still not recovered, as you can plainly see by walking through the Gutters. Economically, productively . . . This is a rich island in terms of the luxury goods it can produce, but we're not nearly where we were before Caludon's Siege. The Radiant Convocation has *never* forgiven Clan Aelthwyn, and that causes him no end of political trouble. Absolutely nothing good resulted from the whole disaster. And his Lordship still speaks fondly of it as his greatest success."

It was a few seconds after he stopped talking before I could find words.

"Wow. That's . . ."

The most evil thing I've ever heard of, and I've met the actual Goddess of Evil.

". . . creative."

Norovena tilted his head slightly, studying me. "In a number of ways, Lord Seiji, you remind me of Archlord Caludon."

"Captain, all I know about the man is what you've just told me, and I have to say, my feelings are hurt."

"Oh, you are far more personable than he. I suspect his Lordship has never considered anyone's opinion to have enough value that learning to be personally charming was worth his time. But you do have notable points in common. The same flair for drama and disregard for convention, a certain . . . highly flexible imagination. When your plan was presented to the Archlord last night, he was absolutely delighted by it."

And wasn't *that* just the kick in the balls I didn't need right now.

"To answer your question," the Captain said, shaking his head, "no, I am not worried about riots. Even if this were not a population who are *vividly* aware of the consequences of resistance, that kind of pressure takes time to build up. All morning I have been under observation by various bureaucrats and Clan representatives, and *diligently* creating the impression that this morning's business is reaching its natural endpoint. So long as I get clearance to pull my men back before noon, I think things will settle down. But you understand, I cannot *suggest* that, even by implication. It would only make me a target for the malice of . . . well. All I can do is understand what the people watching me value, and guide their perceptions to the conclusion that it's in their best interests to stop. But in the meantime . . . no. They won't riot."

I nodded slowly. "Three percent."

Norovena cocked his head again. "My lord?"

"Sorry. Never mind. It's just a statistic I read once. So, no riots, just . . . chamber pots?"

"Oh, there will be plenty of anger after today," he grimaced. "But they know better than to express it in any organized fashion. It will be smaller—individual outbursts delivered from hiding wherever possible. And always at fellow lowborn in uniform who represent the Clans, never any of the highborn themselves."

"And thus, the Clans remain in power."

"They have it down to a science," he said, nodding.

The office door cracked open, emitting a torrent of noise, which was actually good timing. We were pretty much done here, and I could use a break to process what I'd just heard. Nazralind poked her disguised head inside.

"Beggin' ya pardon, me lord, Cap'n sir, but th' Warden's back, aye aye he is."

The door swung the rest of the way open, and Warden Divanno pushed in past her, giving Nazralind the most vivid "what the hell is this idiot supposed to be" look I'd ever seen. Apparently he didn't dare express that verbally in front of his superior officer and his superior officer's rich friend, though.

"The prisoner's moved to an interrogation room as you requested, Captain," Divanno reported. "Good instincts, sir. I dunno how they got wind, but the scum jamming up the cells seem to know who ratted on 'em. Just moving him through the corridors required a full soldier escort, and it's got those animals riled up something fierce."

I honestly couldn't tell from here; the noise sounded about the same.

"Ugh." Norovena bared his teeth in a grimace. "I don't have any more men to spare you, Warden, but as soon as I can pull a squad back I'm going to station crossbowmen at the prison wing's entrance. Those riffraff aren't destined for anything better than the whipping post if they're lucky, and I've no time to play gently with them. At the first sign of one of those cells bursting open, I want everyone in it dead."

"I'll see those orders relayed, sir," the Warden said, nodding. "Might come to that, but I don't think so. Thank the Goddess we just had that renovation; all the bars are sound as of last year. Not for nothing did the Kingsguard spring for iron fixings."

"All right, we'll give you back your office," said Norovena, ushering me toward the door with a gesture. "Let's go see to our man, Lord Seiji. And, my lord, concerning what I just told you . . ."

"Yes?"

He fixed me with another serious look as we passed back out into the noisy hall, raising his voice just enough to be heard. "Archlord Caludon was very interested in learning about the man who devised last night's strategy. You have his attention, Lord Seiji. I gather he'll be keenly following your progress in the future."

Nazralind stiffened up visibly, raising her head to give me a clear view of the suddenly terrified look in her eyes under that floppy hat. Even Aster tensed, instinctively reaching for the handle of her huge sword.

I didn't need those signs, or Norovena's significant tone, to recognize that that had not been a compliment, but a warning.

15

In Which the Dark Lord
Realizes His Mistake

We had to pass through a cell block to get where we were going, which meant sticking to the center of the path, out of reach of the arms extended through the bars. Those cells were overcrowded to an extent that would've resulted in human rights complaints on Earth. Well . . . parts of Earth. All these men had been crammed in there like livestock, and while I could understand their cage-rattling fury, they helpfully went out of their way to remind me that I had good reason to lack sympathy for these individuals in particular.

Oh, they recognized me, all right. Lord Seiji was a distinctive figure among the population of Dount, and at least some of these assholes had been diligently trying to kill me last night. At least a handful had apparently thought they'd succeeded. I got even more catcalls than Aster, who was the target of no end of invective simply for being a woman in view of this bunch of thugs. I glanced at her a couple of times, but her expression was just wry.

No matter how many times I was reminded, it always came as something of a shock, just how used to depravity and horror the Dountol were. Especially the women. It occurred to me now that the only ones I'd seen actually scared had been guards or gangsters—men accustomed to having at least a measure of power over others. Even the Alley Cats being faced down by Gray's men had just seemed angry and resigned.

"Were you able to arrest any of the Blessed working for Lady Gray?" I asked Norovena as we finally turned a corner onto another hall not lined with open cells. "I ran into several last night."

"It was the King's Guild who did the initial wave of arrests, and they definitely kept custody of any Blessed prisoners. The Guild has facilities and personnel to contain them, which I do not. I have no authority over the Guild; they were courteous enough to notify me that there *are* Blessed prisoners, which frankly was more than I expected."

I nodded, thinking ahead. What I needed to find out was what happened to that guy who could cast Null. If he was going to be rambling around my island, I wanted a firm handle on his whereabouts.

"This is the room," Norovena stated as he brought us to a stop, nodding at the prison guard standing at attention next to the door. The man saluted without otherwise moving. "I apologize, Lord Seiji, but today of all days I'm not at liberty to attend you in person for the rest of this."

"I can imagine. No worries, Captain, I believe I can handle this part alone."

"I think it will go better if you do," he agreed. "Assuming he agrees to cooperate with you, I can't just release him into your custody with no more fanfare than that, you understand."

"Of course, there's a procedure," I nodded. "How would you like me to handle this?"

"Unless there's some further crisis outside the gates, I intend to be here in the Kingsguard headquarters for the immediate future. I'll send a man to escort you to me when you're done. I see no harm in your followers joining you in there, if you feel they will be of use, but if you prefer to leave them on watch in the hall they should be fine. If my opinion is welcome, however, Miss Aster is quite intimidating for someone so pretty." He gave her a smile, which she did not reciprocate. "A show of force never goes amiss with men like that."

"Mmm . . . perhaps. On the other hand, you and I have both used the stick liberally since last night. Let's try the carrot, instead."

Norovena blinked. "The . . . carrot?"

Oh, right. Now that I thought of it, I hadn't seen any of those in Dlemathlys. "It's . . . carrots are a sweet root vegetable. Good for the eyesight. It's a metaphor, Captain, about methods of motivation. Punishment and reward."

"Ah." He nodded, his expression clearing. "Well, in the end, it was you who originally got him to change sides midbattle, my lord. In this case, I think it best to trust your judgment. With that, I must beg your leave."

"Of course, Captain."

He folded down his hands at me, nodded once more to the door guard, then turned and strode back down the hall toward the cell block.

"All right, ladie—ah, lady and lad," I said while the guard turned and unlocked the door. "Join me, if you would."

"Sure y'don't want me t'mind th'door, me lord?" Nazralind suggested.

What I didn't want was her standing around unsupervised; I had a bad feeling leaving her outside; the warden's office had already pushed our luck. My first meeting with Nazralind had involved her saving my ass, which I was starting to realize may have left me with an exaggerated perception of her competence. It was worth remembering that she was only here because she and her gang had tried to do more or less what I was doing, failed spectacularly, and gotten chased halfway across the island. Her antics since we'd entered the city had begun to make me worry about what the rest of those girls were up to outside. Hopefully, Goose would keep them under a semblance of control . . .

"I'm sure this gentleman is perfectly able to do his job without your help, Gilden," I said out loud.

"It's Gulder, me lord."

"That's what I said. C'mon."

Aster was looking increasingly peeved by our new recruit; I was really going to have to explain everything to her as quickly as could be arranged.

It was no surprise that the "interrogation room" of a medieval prison looked nothing like the interview rooms I'd seen on police dramas. Never having been arrested (in Japan), I didn't even know how accurate those depictions were, but this . . . It was just a plain brick room, no table or chairs or anything. There were multiple hooks bolted into the walls at intervals, which I could tell were for chains to be attached because two were currently in use, keeping Lamm affixed to the wall. They had generously left him enough room to stand at ease rather than hanging from his wrists or something, but he clearly couldn't take more than a step away from the far wall. It didn't look like he'd even be able to sit down.

"The hell is this for?" I demanded as the guard outside shut the door behind us. "What do they think you're going to do, run out there to your ex-partners and get shanked?"

"I see you haven't spent much time on the wrong end of the guards' favor, Lord Seiji," Lamm answered wryly. "And here I was just thinking what a good sign it was that I was being treated so gently."

"This is just fucking . . . Shit, we can't let him loose, can we?"

"I suspect the Captain and the Warden wouldn't appreciate that," Aster agreed. "It's kind of moot, since we don't have the keys."

"I appreciate the thought, anyway," said Lamm. "Nice to see you again, my lord. You're not what I expected when they brought me in for another round."

"I hope you haven't been handled too roughly."

He shrugged, causing a rattle of chains. "Helps a lot that I showed up voluntarily, and it seems my information's been useful to the cause. Also, and I'll admit this surprised me a bit, invoking your name seemed to help. With the rank and file, that is. Made that Captain pretty keenly interested in me, too, but not as . . . warmly. I gather his affection isn't as easily bought," he added with a smirk.

"I have a question for you, Lamm," I said.

He grinned, tugging idly at his chains. "A question? Well, now. That'll be a departure from how I've spent the day so far."

I looked back at the door. The guard was standing right outside . . . But the door was decently thick, and it muffled the prison noise even better than the warden's office had. So long as we didn't raise our voices excessively, this should provide at least a bit of privacy.

"What made you decide to take my advice and switch sides?" I asked.

Lamm's grin faded. After a second, he looked away from my eyes, jaw working. "Yeah, well. I . . . You're probably gonna laugh."

"If I find whatever you say next funny, I'll probably be too surprised *to* laugh."

"*Hn*. Yeah, I guess I could see that." Suddenly he looked right back at me, his expression steady. "You showed me mercy, Lord Seiji. And that made me really stop and *think*."

"I can believe you're not accustomed to seeing mercy."

"It wasn't that." He shook his head. "I've seen it, all right. And usually, seen it immediately punished. That's the law of the Gutters; only the weak are soft. Someone who gives shit away for nothing is someone who's about to lose everything they have. Strength is the only thing that matters—that's the rule Lady Gray lives by, and you better believe she enforced it. The thing is, most of the time she didn't even *have* to. It's just life. There are the people who have power and use it against others. Then there are the people who try to be . . . charitable, and whatnot. They're the ones who get stepped on by the strong. Try to help a beaten enemy, and they'll just stab you the first chance they get."

He paused. I waited.

"But you set up that scheme in Cat Alley," Lamm continued finally, now frowning at me with a faintly quizzical expression as if he couldn't figure me out. "And then the strategy you used against Lady Gray last night. Not just the pre-laid plan, but what you adapted on the fly that *beat* her at her own game. You're definitely not stupid. And . . ." He finally broke eye contact, flinching at a memory. "You definitely aren't soft."

I could recall the sound of Lamm screaming, the sight of the flames consuming him. How little it had moved me.

"No," I said quietly, "I'm really not."

Not anymore.

"Yeah . . . It made me think." He raised his gaze to meet mine again. "Here's a man who's powerful. More powerful than Lady Gray, apparently, and also no fool. And you offered *mercy*. Look, I'm not stupid, either. I can see how much my intel has helped your side in this. I know there was strategy in your decision. But I also know that wasn't all it was; you would've taken me to the guards yourself in that case. That's what I would've done. Or Lady Gray. You could have done that, or killed me, and either would've been the smarter thing as I understood it. But you decided to do something . . . kind."

He winced again, as if expecting to be punished just for using that word. I simply regarded him in continued silence.

"It made me think," he repeated. "If there's someone who's powerful enough that he can afford to be merciful, and decides to *do* it . . . Well. Maybe there might be a future with you in charge. That's the one thing Lady Gray can't offer, you know. Everything under her is temporary. Her top people have power and make good money, along with everything that comes with it, but it never lasts. As soon as they're not useful anymore, they're gone. As soon as they start to look like they even *might* be successful enough to challenge her . . . gone. I never really thought it was an option before, but suddenly . . . I wanna have a future."

I glanced at Aster and caught her giving me a subdued but proud smile. Yeah, it always came back to that, didn't it? *Whenever you can, be kind.* Apparently, compassion had strategic uses as well as helping to keep the soul relatively intact. Who knew?

Slowly, I nodded. "I'm gonna level with you, Lamm. I'm none too sure how much of a future there is for any of us."

"Well, shit, I know *that*," he said, grinning again. "Any fucking day there might be a plague or a bad harvest or a shardhail storm. If you've got enemies, eventually one'll get lucky, or just be better than you. Or, hell, you could slip in a pile of dhawl shit and break your neck on the pavement. I knew a guy who went out like that. Nobody can offer forever, and I'd be seriously rethinking this if you tried. But . . . What do you think, Lord Seiji? Do you think things can be just a little bit less shitty until whatever inevitable thing happens?"

I had to laugh. "Well, damn. Usually I have to explain that part, Lamm; you're the first one to beat me to it. Yes, that is the deal. I'm gonna keep picking fights with bigger and bigger assholes until there are either no assholes left or I lose one, and I think we both know which'll happen first. But *until* then, what I offer the people who'll stand with me is a place in an organization where we show some goddamn fucking decency to each other, and get a chance to hit back at those who've wronged us. It's not much, but this is Ephemera. I really don't think anybody on this world is going to get anything better than that."

"Yeah . . . yeah, I think you're right," he agreed.

"So!" I said more briskly. "Here's the situation, Lamm. Captain Norovena appreciates your assistance and is inclined to keep you safe and provided for in exchange for it."

He nodded warily. "But?"

"*But*, this operation has drawn in some of the smaller Clans, who are sticking their stupid fingers into everything and trying to play politics. Some of them seem to want to make a big, messy example out of you."

Lamm looked resigned. "Yeah, that sounds like Clan Aelthwyn all right."

"It's actually not them," I said. "I don't think the Archlord even knows about you."

"What would be the *point* of that?" Aster demanded. "I mean, the Archlord is a sadist and hates lowborn; everybody knows that. But smaller Clans are usually more careful about dealing with commoners. What would they *gain* by turning on somebody who took a risk to take their side?"

"They're nobles, they are," said Nazralind in her obviously fake rasp. "There ain't necessarily *reasons*, or at least not good 'uns. It's just fer his Lordship's attention."

"They want senpai to notice them," I explained.

Lamm's eyebrows drew together. "Who?"

"Never mind. The point is, depending on how this pans out, you might end up safe, or possibly sent to the gallows for no particular reason. Norovena would rather you stay alive and be able to continue offering him intelligence."

"So he wants me to join you," Lamm finished.

"You're impressively quick on the uptake."

He frowned, lowered his eyes, then shook his head before meeting my gaze again. "Norovena already told me about this."

I felt a prickle on the back of my neck. "Oh?"

Lamm's shoulders shifted as he drew in a breath. "He offered me a reward to join up with you, and keep him . . . appraised of anything interesting you did or said."

"That shifty son of a bitch," Aster hissed.

"No . . ." I heaved a sigh. "No, let's not get offended, people. That's pretty much par for the course. Norovena is an ally of convenience, not our friend. And this is a pretty smart thing to do in his position. No need to take it personally. But you told me instead of going along with it," I added, studying Lamm's eyes.

He nodded once. "Same question, same answer. A Kingsguard captain knows all about bribes, but *he* doesn't have a future to offer me, either. On the other hand, he's accidentally given me something I can use to increase my value to *you*, Lord Seiji. Long as you've got me around, you can use me to feed him whatever information you want him to know, and nothing else."

"I see," I mused. Of course, that left the obvious question—could I *trust* him? The answer to that was an unequivocal "fuck no," preceded by derisive laughter. Still . . . This, I figured, was enough to buy Lamm the opportunity to *earn* trust. And in the meantime, I could keep a close eye on him, maintain tight control over what information he passed along. Yeah, this would work.

Still. I'd been planning, when I stepped into this room, to take the opportunity of this moment of privacy to bring Aster up to speed on who Nazralind was, as well as inform Lamm of the Dark Lord angle. But considering Norovena had arranged it specifically such that I couldn't just walk out of here with him, and would have to leave Lamm in his custody a while longer . . . Oh yeah, now I could see why he had set it up that way. He'd be able to get his first report from his double agent on whatever I'd said in this meeting before handing the man off to me.

This was definitely not the moment for any big, dangerous revelations.

"Then it seems we have an arrangement." I smiled, and Lamm immediately looked wary, for which I couldn't blame him. "Welcome to the team."

Norovena was as good as his word, which I suspected he scrupulously would be under any circumstance in which I could check. He'd sent a second guard to stand outside the interrogation room door; as soon as I knocked to be let out, the man escorted us back through the prison and then the barracks to the Captain.

He was not in his office, but in the busy front area of the Kingsguard headquarters from which he could direct traffic. And there was still a great deal of that; with the operation against Lady Gray theoretically still ongoing and the brutal persecution of the Gutters ongoing very much in actuality, harried-looking soldiers, clerks, bureaucrats, and the odd priest or noble were rushing hither and yon through the corridors, many clearly demanding a slice of the Captain's time.

I shot a warning look back at my two companions as we approached him. Aster's expression was politely blank. I wasn't really worried about her; Nazralind was another matter. I had noticed that she shared at least some of my own difficulty in keeping a shut mouth.

Catching my eye, she winked at me over her big fake beard. That . . . wasn't exactly reassuring.

"Good, then get them back here," Norovena was curtly ordering a man in Kingsguard armor. "The rest aren't to let up until we are so ordered by the Clans, but right now I need that squad reinforcing the prison. Make sure they're outfitted with crossbows before they report to the Warden."

"Sir!" The man saluted and dashed off.

Spotting me, Norovena turned and immediately strode over, to the visible disappointment of two more men approaching him, but apparently they didn't think themselves important enough to press, simply hovering about in the near distance and waiting for an opportunity.

"Ah, Lord Seiji. How did it go?"

"He took some persuading," I said, putting on a self-satisfied little smile. "Poor chap seems to've had a rather hard day. I believe I have him on board, however. It's all about making the most . . . palatable offer."

"Yes, that's always the way with men like that," he agreed, matching my smile perfectly, the scheming bastard. "Splendid news, my lord. If you will kindly remain in the vicinity, I'll finalize the arrangements as quickly as possible. Best we get this matter squared away before it becomes more complicated."

"Very good, Captain. Just point me to a place to stand that's out of the way."

"I'll be impressed if you can find one." He grimaced, flicking a look around the busy front hall of the barracks. "Never fear, my lord, it's for common soldiers to get out of your way, not the other way round."

I spotted a well-dressed blonde man in nearby consultation with a priest and some kind of clerk; the highborn glanced up at Norovena's last comment and smirked before returning his attention to his own conversation.

Christ, I was learning to hate nobles. Nazralind and her girls were cool, but I urgently wanted to line up the rest of them end-to-end across the island and then go down the row smacking them each in the face with a shovel.

"Captain!" A man I recognized dashed up, wearing a worried frown. This was the fellow who'd arrested me back when Yoshi's party had picked a fight in the street. Lieutenant something-or-other. I knew he was Blessed with Magic; he'd cast Windburst at Flaethwyn, which had been immensely satisfying to see. "Sorry, sir, but you said to report if . . . Well, there's another one."

"Oh, Goddess send me patience," Norovena growled. "Of all the bloody . . . Which station was it this time?"

"Here, sir, at headquarters."

"What? *Here*? Tell me you're joking."

"Sir, it's me, Lieutenant Vanori," he replied grimly. "The man you're always insisting has no sense of humor."

"Hell's fucking revels, I'll take that over whoever's sick sense of humor *this* is." Norovena rubbed at his forehead, momentarily obscuring his scowl, and I was struck by the change in his demeanor. He was a tightly controlled man usually; even his anger was directed and precise, as when he'd intervened with his men who'd tried to assault that girl earlier. This was the most openly disturbed I'd ever seen him.

I cleared my throat. "I can see you're having an even busier day than expected, Captain. We'll get out of your hair."

"Wait." He turned to me with an intent frown. "I think . . . Lord Seiji, this may be a matter relevant to you specifically. I believe you have an established fondness for the Gutter Rats?"

That cold, hard weight suddenly reappeared in my gut, colder and harder than ever. Suddenly brimming with sick dread in addition to the guilt over what I'd already set in motion in this city. I did not know what was coming, but it was not going to be good.

"I have been specifically generous to a few particular Rats who I've used to gather information," I said, shrugging. "That's just sound policy for informants, isn't it? Can't say I have much of an opinion about the breed in general."

"Makes sense, my lord. Still, considering . . . If you'll indulge me a moment longer, I think this may be something you should see. Vanori, where is it?"

"It was left in front of the service door on the south side, sir. We moved it off the door, obviously, but I left a man keeping an eye on it out there. It's a kicked hive in here today, and I don't know of a good place to put such a thing at the moment."

"Good thinking, Lieutenant. My lord, if you would?"

"Lead on," I said with a deliberately languid gesture, concealing my unease with the skill granted by a lot of recent practice.

He guided us through the halls with notably more urgency than before, which did not make me any less nervous about whatever we were headed toward. It did at least mean there was less time to simmer in the anticipation. In just a few minutes, we reached what I gathered must be a less-used side door, to judge by the relative lack of traffic in this part of the fortress. Norovena yanked it open and strode out, leaving us to follow.

Beyond was an exterior alley behind the guard headquarters. This door opened next to a dead end where the Kingsguard's complex was built right into the city's exterior wall; in the other direction the short alleyway led to a small courtyard, which even from here I could see was encircled by another wall with a gate leading to the street outside. It would be pretty difficult for anyone unauthorized to get into this space at all, much less carrying . . .

I heard Aster draw in a sharp breath with a painful-sounding hiss, followed by a half-strangled noise from Nazralind as she forgot to put on her fake voice while trying to repress what sounded like a mingled retch and sob.

Near at hand, a particularly grim-faced Kingsguard was standing over the body.

It was all too familiar—not individually, but the general aspect. Painfully thin, wearing too-loose pants held up by a knotted cord and a too-tight shirt about to be outgrown, threadbare and dirty, and stained with blood from the deep wound in the chest. This one was . . . bigger than Benit, a year or two older, maybe. Not as big as Gilder.

It was a Gutter Rat. A dead child. *A murdered child.*

"Do you recognize him, Lord Seiji?" Norovena asked quietly.

I shook my head, for once bereft of words. The Captain let out an angry sigh.

"This is the fifth one today."

I managed, barely, not to double over. It sure *felt* like he'd just kicked me in the gut.

"One at each of the wall gatehouses, and now this," Norovena continued, his face set in a darker glower than I'd ever seen on him. "*Someone* with exceptional mobility, an unparalleled gift of stealth, and not even the dimmest little *spark* of humanity has decided to send us a message."

I didn't even realize how close I was to melting down completely until it all went away. The Wisdom perk hit me like a falling piano, crushing down emotion and leaving me adrift above it, my perspective wrapped in ice. From within that stark observatory of the mind, I could see it all so clearly.

I had already determined that Captain Norovena's assessment of Lady Gray was wrong. She wouldn't flee the city; after what we'd done to her, she would seek revenge above all else, even her own survival. Now, I understood the misconception under which I had been operating. She wouldn't try to kill me. Not yet.

Not when she knew how to hurt me.

16

In Which the Dark Lord
Suffers the Little Children

I finally learned about Fflyr funerary customs that day.

They did cremate their dead. Not in crematoriums, though; they used open-air pyres. It turned out the khora-based asauthec could be properly blended and concentrated to burn at ludicrous temperatures. There was, in fact, a specific funerary blend, which was not only intensely hot and not very bright, but scented.

As the priest in the mourning chapel explained to me—the resident ignorant foreigner—burning human flesh results in the smell of roasting meat, which apparently is universally appetizing and thus deeply disturbing to people attending a funeral. Fortunately, I had never had to think about things like this, but it made a horrible kind of sense. Funerary asauthec, I was told, smelled overpoweringly like rain and lightning, and was the reason the Fflyr associated storms with death. So, petrichor and ozone, basically. I wondered how they got refined khora oil to smell like that. Alchemy was pretty spooky stuff.

Mourning chapels were the Radiant Convocation's equivalent of funeral homes. They were all owned and run by the central church and staffed by priests. Apparently there were a lot more of them in Gwyllthean than actual temples meant for worship—because obviously—and were a major source of the Convocation's income. Thus, while the priests in the nice middle ring mourning chapel raised their eyebrows when I wanted them to conduct services for five Gutter Rats, one look at my coin and they were instantly all solemn professionalism.

Salvation awaits those who can pay. As it always was and always will be.

The proper time for the actual ceremony was dusk, according to my quietly delivered crash course in Sanorite religion. The daylight was Sanora's domain while Virya ruled the night, so the dead were sent off in the twilight between them, so as to be fairly judged by both sisters. To do so during full daylight or darkness would be to try to tilt the disposition of the soul toward one or the other, which would have unpredictable effects on the judging and likely invite punishment for the mortal mourners from either goddess, or both.

It was funny. On Earth I'd dismiss all this as superstition. Here, I knew for a *fact* that the goddesses were real, and I was still forced to dismiss it as superstition, because I also knew for a fact that they didn't care.

Obviously, I didn't criticize their religious practices. Ultimately these things are for the people left behind, not for the dead. It was truly comforting, having a ritual surrounding death, even if the ritual was unfamiliar to me and based on bullshit. As the main beneficiary of this solemn routine, I just embraced it without comment.

For the entire day leading up to the cremation, the dead were laid on altars beneath the dome of the mourning chapel, which was surrounded by benches upon which the mourners would keep a vigil until dusk fell. The priests cleaned the bodies and dressed them in simple white robes; goddess coins were used to weigh their eyelids closed, and strips of white cloth draped across that, their ends weighted atop the altar to each side of the head by small carved figurines. Apparently these were mythical creatures unique to the Radiant Convocation's customs, an incorporation of Fflyr folktales into Sanorite practices. Food was prepared and placed by the deceased—their favorite meal in life to give them a comforting send-off to the other realm. Nearly heatless torches burned around the room with another unique blend of scented asauthec, this one with a smooth yet spicy aroma that apparently repelled insects and crawns.

I hadn't known these kids. I didn't even know their names, much less what they liked. I'd bought each a couple of those meat and vegetable skewers in pepper sauce that Gilder, Benit, and Radon had all loved so much, as well as sour strawberry tarts and some of the taffy-like chewy candy also available from the street vendors. Stuff I figured children would enjoy. Funny enough, these were much higher-quality and more expensive treats I'd purchased from middle ring eateries, because the vendor stands in the Gutters were all in ruins, thanks to me.

And then there was nothing but to keep the vigil. The priests retreated politely, leaving us alone with the dead.

It was just the four of us; none of these children's actual friends could even get here in the middle ring, nor could I reach out to them with the pogrom still winding down. And even if I could, my suspicions about who must have enabled this would have prevented me. So they were seen off to the next world by strangers. Me, the interloping asshole responsible for their deaths, and my handful of minions.

Aster and Nazralind were suitably solemn for the occasion. At some point while I was making arrangements, they'd apparently found time for a chat, because Aster had stopped treating Naz like an annoying idiot and more with the uncertainty of someone who'd never been in the company of a Highlady before, and was doing so under circumstances in which none of the familiar social hierarchies applied. Lamm had been smuggled out of the prison by Norovena during the hubbub, and was with us as well. I didn't consider it safe for anyone with me to be out of my sight, and therefore the range of my Heal spell, so long as we were in Gwyllthean. This was undoubtedly not what he'd expected of his first duty in my employ, so he just kept his mouth shut and played along. Smart man.

The entrance to the mourning chapel was cleverly designed to allow ingress without any noise to disturb the mourners. While it was in use, the front doors were propped open, and its entryway was a winding sequence of sharp ninety-degree turns with multiple heavy curtains to muffle sound from outside. Thus, I didn't realize someone else had arrived until I heard his boots on the tile floor as he approached the altars, and even those were quieter than they should have been.

When I raised my head, Lamm was already closely watching the new arrival, but saying nothing, clearly detecting no threat. The other two looked up in surprise at his approach.

He paced slowly across the floor, his armor unnervingly whisper-quiet when it seemed like it should have clanked like a bag of cans. That armor gleamed under the light of the torches and narrow windows as if it had just been polished, which I suspected wasn't true. It was just that magical. Plates of silvery white metal that almost resembled platinum, revealing a black mesh undercoat at the joints which looked to me more like modern Kevlar than any chain mail I'd seen, and its pristine tabard and overcoat of Sanorite colors—white and red, trimmed in gold. The knight in shining armor stepped softly up to the nearest of the altars and knelt.

Rhydion lowered his head and remained in that posture in silence while we all looked on. It took me a confused moment to realize he was probably reciting a prayer, just not out loud. We watched from our respective seats on the benches around the walls until, minutes later, the paladin finally stood. I straightened my back, waiting for him to approach.

Instead, he stepped over to the next altar and knelt by the head of the girl there. She couldn't have been more than nine.

In the silence of the chapel, Rhydion paid respects in full to each victim, taking whatever time it took for every prayer without hurry. This took him on a circuit of the periphery of the chapel, as the priests had arranged the movable altars in as symmetrical a position as they could, with each body's head facing outward.

Only when the business of his faith had been fully attended to did the paladin of Sanora rise again and approach me. Armor still making only the softest of whispers, he seated himself on the bench at my side, less than an arm's length away.

"I mourn with you," he said. His voice was soft, but still prominent amid the stillness of the dead.

I nodded once. It was quiet for another moment before I found myself speaking without really having planned to. "You must've had a busy morning. I heard the King's Guild formed the first line of attack."

"All of us who were present in the city," he said, his helmet shifting in a slight nod of his own. "And I have spent the remainder of the morning in the Gutters. For me to forcibly intervene with the Kingsguard would create . . . repercussions. I avoid causing such shockwaves, as they are always felt by the countless innocent rather than myself. As you have seen today. Still. I find that soldiers are less inclined to brutalize commoners on a street on which I am standing, staring at them with a sword in my hand."

I let out a shuddering breath, distorted by just the faintest echo of the bitter laugh resonating in my brain. "Well. You've just always gotta show me up, huh. Least that's *something*. And here all I've done today is murder five children."

Aster's head turned toward me in a sharp motion, her face tensing in an expression of pain. I didn't meet her gaze.

"That is a difficult claim to credit," Rhydion murmured, "coming from a man who has repeatedly shown a soft spot for orphans. And who clearly grieves their deaths."

My left shoulder jerked in an involuntary semishrug. "Yeah, well. I showed a soft spot for orphans and then antagonized a soulless monster, so it comes down to the same thing, pretty much. This outcome was . . . mathematical. There was no excuse for me not to see this coming, and I did nothing to stop it. Whoever actually held the knife, this is on me."

Rhydion's helmet shifted slightly as if he were looking at me sidelong, and then after a moment returned to facing forward, toward the bodies in the center of the room. "I confess, I was prepared for you to blame me for failing to act on your urging sooner."

"What . . . oh. Y'mean that business where I tried to use you as a human shield without explaining what was actually going on while you repeatedly told me you weren't interested?" I shrugged again. "I guess if I tilt my head and squint *real* hard I could probably come up with a way for this to be your fault, but . . . Meh. My heart's not in it."

"It still amazes me," he said in a bare whisper that was only audible due to the quiet of the room, "how even in the midst of mourning, you can be so utterly consumed by rage."

At that, I turned toward him, frowning. "The hell are you even talking about, man?"

What was *with* this guy?

I mean, well, he was right. The rage was there, the same blinding torrent of white-hot madness that had impelled me through Cat Alley in a whirlwind of magic and blood. It twined around me like an affectionate cat, its purr a muffled roar of incipient violence. I deliberately kept it stoked to a low simmer; I was going to *need* it very soon. The business of this moment required quiet and calm. But this business would end at dusk, and then I was going to unleash carnage such as this blighted little kingdom had never imagined.

But *he* didn't know that. And even if he somehow did, this was hardly the time or place.

Clearly I wasn't the only one who thought so. Aster rose smoothly to her feet, took the three steps over to stand alongside us, and stared down her nose at the paladin with an icy expression.

"This is a *vigil*."

Her tone was quiet, as suited the setting, but it was pure steel, and it brought me a surge of warmth toward her. The last time she and Rhydion had been in the same room, she'd been agog with hero-worship. Now . . .

His helmet dipped once in a nod, and without rising he held out his hands and folded them down. "Very right. That was an utterly thoughtless thing to say. I apologize most humbly."

Aster raised her chin, her expression not lightening, but after a moment she gave him a jerky little nod and retreated back to her own seat.

"All's forgiven," I said with a sigh. "Now of all times I've got no room to complain. I mean, unless *you've* murdered five children recently, who the hell am I to criticize?"

His helmet shifted again, angling toward me. "Lord Seiji, I will speak frankly."

"Oh good. Great. That's fantastic news."

"As I would to any less experienced comrade, and as one who has walked this road backward and forward and knows what you need to hear right now. If your failure has led to this, then you will have to find a way to live with that."

I flinched. I hated myself for betraying that kind of weakness, especially in front of him, but it happened before I could even think to control myself.

"You must take responsibility," Rhydion continued inexorably, "and above all, be certain you *understand* your mistake, so as never to repeat it. And you must not forget that it *was* a mistake. Life is unpredictable, and we are imperfect. Terrible events will happen, and we will all fail at some point. But what defines a person is their decisions. What we choose to *do* with the inscrutable fates we are given."

He lifted one hand and grasped my shoulder.

"You say you as good as murdered them yourself, and in that, you are crucially wrong. *You did not choose this*, Seiji. I know it doesn't feel like that matters now, when you're sitting amid the ruin, but I promise you. The difference is all-important."

I tried to draw a steadying breath, but it still shuddered embarrassingly on the way back out. "Well. Much as I'm annoyed by you preaching at me right now, of all times, I get the feeling that's actually really good advice. So . . . thanks."

The helmet shifted again in another slight nod. "The first time my own ineptitude caused a disaster like this, I was told something which helped me a great deal at the time, and has ever since. Evil is an *aberration*, and anyone who has not dealt with it intimately can be forgiven for failing to expect it. It is one thing to know, intellectually, that it exists. It's one thing to see all the violence people do to one another in their fear and greed and anger. But this . . ." He stared at the five slain children, and shook his head. "No one *normal* could do this, or even think of it. You failed to anticipate it because you are not diabolically insane. That's not a personal failing; quite the opposite. Now, you know better, and will be prepared next time."

"I honestly don't know how you can look around at the world and think that. People are the only real monsters. Most avoid being outright evil purely by being too stupid to pull it off."

"Nihilism can seem like it offers comfort," he said, "but that is a trap. Like drink or drug, a small amount now and then will do you little harm, but once you come to depend on it, it has already destroyed you. In my experience, nearly all the harm people do to one another is rooted in ignorance. People want to live good lives, to work well and care for each other, to be part of something greater than themselves. All too often, the confusion of life can make it seem the only way forward is to step on another's back. That is just part of the mortal condition. This . . ." He looked again at the bodies on their altars, and lowered his tone. ". . . is another thing entirely."

Fucking hell, this guy and his platitudes. Gods spare me the attention of religious people.

"So that's your line, then?" I retorted, hearing a depth of bitterness I didn't intend in my own voice. "People are basically good?"

"People are basically people," Rhydion said quietly. "Let the philosophers debate good and evil. Those of us with our boots in the mud have more urgent things to do. We are all just . . . people. Every one of us, flawed beyond repair, but *defined* by our capacity to be something greater than the brute animals nature would make us. I think there is no greater loss than the sudden end of all that potential." His armor made only the faintest of rasps as his shoulders shifted in a sigh, his gaze still fixed on the dead. "No greater crime than to inflict it."

I studied the paladin for a few seconds, but there was nothing to see but that inscrutable visor. My own gaze returned to the children without my willing it, and I shook my head. "Well. Guess we can agree on that much."

"What will you do next, Lord Seiji?"

"I should think that was obvious," I said softly, staring at them. "First, tend to the dead. Then, the soon-to-be dead. The children deserve the proper respect; it's completely inadequate, but there's nothing more I can do for them now. Then, I'm going to go find those responsible and make such a horrific spectacle of their annihilation that no one on this island, no matter how depraved, ever *considers* doing something like this again."

From the corner of my eye, I saw Lamm's face shift toward me for a moment, then back to resume his watch over the chapel's entrances. He nodded slightly as if to himself. There was a man who understood.

"I've tried that," Rhydion said, just above a whisper. "It doesn't work. I think if you're being honest, you don't really expect it to. The real disappointment will come when it doesn't make you feel better."

"Thanks for the tip."

Again he sighed faintly, then rose. "Regardless, I will not interfere or dissuade you, Lord Seiji."

"Oh?" That actually surprised me.

"There are some lessons that can only be taught by experience. And besides . . ." The paladin looked at the dead children for another moment before turning away. "Even knowing I *should* feel otherwise, I cannot make myself see any suffering visited on the monster who did this as wrong. Useless, at worst. I will keep the children in my prayers, Lord Seiji. Goddess guide your steps."

"Oh, she will," I whispered.

He studied me in quizzical silence for a moment after that cryptic comment, then nodded once, turned, and departed the chapel.

"I'm a little surprised," I murmured after he had been gone for a couple of minutes. "I was expecting him to try to recruit me again. He has every other time we've talked."

"This is hardly the time or place," Aster said quietly. "Of all people, a man of faith would recognize that."

"So that was the great paladin," Nazralind murmured. "He was . . . nice. And pompous. I feel oddly let down, but now that I've said that out loud, I don't know what else I should've expected."

Lamm cleared his throat. "Still a vigil, here."

Naz was still in her disguise; I couldn't see her blush under the makeup and beard, but from the way she ducked her head, I was pretty sure she had. For my part, I didn't feel a need to call her down. Sanorite tradition notwithstanding, we were here to honor five Gutter Rats. I had a feeling they'd enjoy being sent off with some friendly banter a lot more than pomp and ceremony.

A familiar buzz heralded a much more welcome visitor. I looked up to behold Biribo descending from one of the upper windows, making a beeline for his usual place at my shoulder.

"Mission accomplished, boss," he reported. Even he kept his voice to a hush in recognition of the atmosphere; I guess some things are universal. "The ladies are up to speed and sitting tight at the old village, awaiting orders. Goose says they've had no sign of anyone approaching them or being in that patch of khora at all. I told 'em it'd be tonight, and was assured they'll be ready to move."

"Good work. Thanks, Biribo." Good, that was the last end tied up for today. Norovena had immediately moved to secure everyone on both Minifrit's and Lady Gray's lists, so all those who Gray thought even might be tied to me were under watch and being prepared to move out of the city. I was told a lot of them were understandably quite unhappy with this, for which I couldn't blame them, but they would have to suck it up unless they wanted to get knifed by an invisible maniac. It wasn't fair, but that was life on Ephemera. Auldmaer's company now had a permanent King's Guild presence keeping watch; thanks to his invaluable assistance in the plan last night, it was even financed by Clan Aelthwyn. He was reaping a grand harvest of prestige and business connections out of this; for him, it would be a huge win as long as he stayed unmurdered. "I need you to do some discreet scouting for the next phase."

Biribo actually sighed, dropping several centimeters and letting his head hang as if exhausted. "Got it, boss. What's the plan?"

Instead of relaying the plan, I paused, studying him closely. It was a little hard to tell, him being a small lizard and all, but now that I looked, his body language really did seem worn out.

"Hey, Biribo. I still don't know all the rules about this Blessing stuff; is it true familiars suffer if they're not near their . . . person?"

"Well, not . . . I mean, yes and no, boss." He flicked his tongue out to taste the air. "A familiar has a strong compulsion to be near their Blessed. Long as we *are* near, it's not noticeable. The farther we go from them, and the longer we're away, the more it builds up, 'til there comes a point where no familiar has enough willpower to stay away and we have to come straight back. The only way it gets to the point of *suffering* is if we're actively prevented from staying close. That's like . . . having an itch you can't scratch, everywhere at once. Doesn't take much of that to drive somebody crazy with misery."

I nodded slowly, glancing up at the window through which he'd come. It was still early in the afternoon; there was time.

"Okay, never mind scouting just yet, then. Hang out with us, catch your breath. We can do that when you're feeling recovered."

"Thanks, boss," he said in clear gratitude. "I appreciate it."

To my surprise, Biribo actually settled down on my shoulder rather than hovering over it as he usually did. That was . . . different. Not unpleasant, I supposed, and the quiet better suited the vigil than the buzz of his wings. I leaned back against the wall behind me, letting the silence resume. The five of us, now, kept watch over the dead as time slowly ticked past.

It was another hour into our silent watch before the next visitor arrived. This one was quieter even than Rhydion had been in his obviously magical armor. She didn't need stealth artifacts to avoid making noise, though. I undoubtedly wouldn't have seen her coming had Biribo not muttered a warning into my ear and then darted away to hide inside my coat.

But he did, and so I had turned my head to watch the entrance when she crept into view.

It was a Gutter Rat. The girl was . . . ten? Eleven? For as much as people seemed to associate me with children, I sure wasn't any good at guessing their ages. The rest was obvious, though, from her threadbare clothes, wild ratty hair, hollow cheeks, and the smudges of dirt ground into her skin.

Tiptoeing in well-practiced silence, she was staring ahead at the altars . . . at the bodies. I saw the moment of recognition, saw her face crumple, and felt it like a knife in my own gut. Then she saw me watching her and froze, every bit the startled rabbit on the verge of bolting.

"It's all right." I kept my voice low, calm, and moved nothing but my mouth. I feared the merest twitch would send her into flight. "I think you have every right to be here."

The girl hesitated, tense; she glanced around at everyone else in the room. Aster and Lamm had the same instincts and remained fixed where they were, Aster with a gentle smile. Nazralind . . . She waved, and I could tell she was wearing a welcoming smile, even through her fake beard. She also seemed to have forgotten she was disguised as a scruffy outdoorsman, which made that gesture a very different matter than it would have been coming from a pretty elf.

Fortunately, she was clear across the room, so the creepy bearded man with the skin condition didn't spook our visitor into fleeing, though she hesitated, staring warily.

"What's your name?" I asked softly.

She looked back at me, nervously, clearly considering whether she should answer. But in the end, she did so, barely above a whisper. "I'm Aenit."

"Aenit." I nodded once. "I'm Lord Seiji."

"You're Gilder's ma—uh, contact."

"Gilder's mark, yes," I said with a wry smile. I immediately regretted my moment of humor as Aenit shrank back, obviously expecting me to take offense and dispense punishment. Instead I kept still, and after a second she seemed reassured.

"Is . . . is Gilder . . . Is he like . . ."

"Gilder is fine," I said firmly. Quietly, but firmly. "So are Benit and Radon. They're living at my place now, where they're safe from Lady Gray and Uncle Gently. After the way they helped me, I do everything I can to protect them and make sure they're okay. I wish . . ." To my mortification, I had to pause and physically swallow down a painful lump that rose in my throat. "I wish I'd thought to protect the others. It just never occurred to me she'd do something like this. It's so . . . This is my fault." My eyes turned back to the five bodies, unable to look away.

"This is . . . That's just life. That's the Gutters," Aenit said. I could see her struggling to push down the tears, even as she stared at the bodies. The look of hard disinterest didn't suit her at all, but she was working to perfect it. "There's no sense in getting . . ."

"Hey." Slowly, I turned toward her. Not getting off the bench, but angling my body in her direction and leaning forward, bracing my elbows on my lap to look her straight in the eyes. "Don't do that. That's *them* talking, not you. Gray, Gently, every other asshole who lords it over the Gutters. You deserve better than to be turned into a monster like them. When you lose a friend, you should cry for them. *They* deserve that much."

I honestly didn't think the effect would be so sudden, or dramatic, but I guess nobody had ever given her *permission* before. On the contrary, it had probably been openly punished. Aenit managed one choking breath before she broke, crumpling to the floor. Hugging her knees and shaking with violent sobs, to the point I feared she would topple over.

Aster and Nazralind were both moving immediately, but I got there first just because I was closer. All of this was well out of my wheelhouse; I was *deeply* uncomfortable with touchy-feely huggy stuff. But damn it, all of this was my fault, and also my responsibility. Chickening out was not an option. I slid off my bench, took the two long steps to the girl's side, and knelt there, wrapping an arm around her shoulders.

She immediately pivoted and stumbled against me, clutching me and bawling, which was physically awkward in that position and nearly sent us *both* toppling over before I adjusted. Oh well, I'd gone in for a comradely arm about the shoulders, but apparently this was going to be a proper hug now. Also, she was snotting all over the nice coat and shirt Nazralind and the girls had so kindly loaned me.

"Shouganai," I mumbled aloud, just holding the girl while she wept.

That took . . . a while. It was a really strange thing, how something which was so actively uncomfortable didn't leave me wanting to end it in a hurry. I guess crying can be cathartic even if you're not the one doing it. There was also my all-consuming guilt to reckon with; if I couldn't comfort *one* crying child, what the hell was I good for? I was the reason she was crying, after all.

Eventually, though, her sobs did subside. One kid can only hold so much . . . slimy moisture. I was patting her hair while she hiccupped before I judged it appropriate to ask her anything.

"So how'd you get up here, Aenit?"

She said something that was muffled by my chest, but then pulled back enough to be heard, scrubbing at her nose with one forearm. The poor kid looked frightful, streaked with tears and snot. "I hid in a wagon. Listened to guards, found out where you was . . . set up. I'm good at hiding."

"Well, I'm seriously impressed," I said, meaning it. "Even Gilder never got through the gates without my help."

That earned a watery smile. And then Aster was there, bending over and gently dabbing at her face with a handkerchief, which I knew had to be Nazralind's because it was some kind of silk and trimmed with *lace*. Aenit bore this with good grace for a few moments before taking the thing and loudly blowing her nose.

I took that as an opportunity to let go of her and ease back.

"I heard more, in the Gutters this morning," she said, still gulping but clearly on the road to recovering her poise. "From the . . . I was hiding from the Kingsguard, and from Lady Gray's men, and I heard . . . Lord Seiji, it was Uncle Gently. He *gave* them to her. All five of them. Right outta the Nest. They was supposed to be . . ." I could see the thought that caused her to trail off. "Safe," she'd been about to say, but she knew better. Safety was an illusion. Her eyes were already welling up again. "That's our *home*. Uncle Gently's not . . . he's not the best. But he's supposed to take care of us!"

I was already seeing white. I had to close my eyes, force myself to breathe evenly. The mad beast of rage was swelling, clawing its way up, its snarl building up into a roar. I seized control, wrestling with it. Forcing it back down.

Not yet. It's not time yet.

Soon.

"You was . . . I couldn't think of nothing else," Aenit mumbled. "You were good to Gilder. And, and I'm sorry, but I know you're the Healer. It's . . . it's not really a secret anymore. You fought *back*. You *beat* her. I couldn't think of . . . There's not anybody else."

"You did right." I opened my eyes, reached out and squeezed her thin shoulder. "And you did *very well* to make it here with this. You're a goddamn hero, Aenit. What you've pulled off today is more impressive than anything I've ever done. I have Blessings and allies; you did this with nothing but your wits. I know we just met, but I'm proud as hell of you."

Her lip was trembling violently, and more tears poured down her gaunt face, but she was done weeping. Even through the tears, what I saw in her pale red eyes reflected my own. Fire and steel. *Vengeance.* A new Dark Crusader being born right before my eyes, and oh, how that made what was left of my spirit crumble. This was just a child. She should be going to school and playing with friends and having three hot meals a day prepared by someone who loved her, not . . . Not *any* of this vile bullshit.

But that was no longer a choice I got to make. The pain and destruction was in the world already; in this world, it was everywhere. I'd gone and showed people they could strike back; there was no putting that genie back in its bottle. Now, I had to make good on what I'd offered them. All of them.

"And I promise you." I grasped her other shoulder and met her gaze. "*They are going to pay for this.* But that's . . . later. After today. Today, we're going to keep the vigil, and then send them off to rest. Properly, with respect, because they deserve that. Do you want to stay with us 'til the end?"

She nodded, scrubbing at her eyes again with the already soiled kerchief.

"Good." I stood up, holding out one hand to her, and she took it. "For now, Aenit . . . if this is too painful to talk about, that's totally fine; you don't have to. But if you're willing . . ."

I turned to look at the bodies.

"Would you tell me about them? I don't even know their names. I'd like to know . . . who they were. I want to remember."

The little girl smiled up at me through her tears and squeezed my hand, and then led me forward to meet the dead.

17

In Which the Dark Lord Closes In

We moved out right after the ceremony, which put us on the street just as full dark fell. In the gloomy silence of a traumatized city, we made it all the way from the mourning chapel to the south gate before encountering anyone.

There, it seemed, we were expected, and were met by someone I hadn't thought to see again so soon.

"Captain Norovena." I raised a hand in greeting as I came to a stop, eyeing him up and down. "You look like hell, sir. Have you slept at all since the night before last?"

"There are some days when a man's allowed to rest," the hollow-eyed Captain replied, glancing quickly across my little entourage. "Only some. Got big plans, Lord Seiji?"

Maybe it was the fatigue talking, but he seemed unusually terse. The sunken eyes and two-day growth of stubble added to the intensity of the man's expression, but he was definitely more intent and openly tense than I was accustomed to seeing. I'd only come to realize recently just how adept Captain Norovena was at mirroring exactly what I expected from him; undoubtedly, that was a survival skill for a man in his position who had to regularly mollify higher nobility. It made his relatively unguarded displeasure all the more striking.

"I doubt you're here and not collapsing into a bed to experience the simple pleasures of small talk, Captain. What's on your mind?"

Usually Norovena would have blunted my directness with a smile and a compliment, but for once he just answered me straight. "Lord Seiji, what did you do to Rhydion?"

"Rhydion?" My eyebrows shot upward before I thought to control them. "The paladin? He came by the vigil for a few minutes. I didn't think I'd made much of an impression on him. Why, what's he done?"

"He has been exerting his political influence all afternoon," said Norovena, his eyes boring into mine. "Thanks to his string-pulling, the King's Guild *and* the Radiant Convocation have both put out substantial bounties on Lady Gray's head. Mere *hours* after that announcement went out, another bounty on her was posted by Highlord Caldimer of Clan Olumnach. Which resulted in Clan Aelthwyn doing the same in the next hour, to save face."

"Four bounties on one woman? Isn't that redundant?"

"That would be the point, yes. Understand that Lady Gray may be an impressive specimen of a Blessed among the Gutter trash she leads—used to lead, that is—but there are multiple individuals in the King's Guild who could take her on with little trouble, including several who are specialized in the kind of tracking and detection that could penetrate her famous stealth."

I managed not to visibly wince. *I* had been having trouble with Lady Gray; apparently all my Dark Lord powers weren't yet up to tackling hardened adventurers who'd had years to collect all the best spells or artifacts. Sakin was right, I couldn't afford to antagonize the King's Guild.

Yet.

"And that's just our local branch," Norovena continued. "The chance to collect *four* large bounties on a single target will bring the Guild's best from Fflyrdylle and all across the kingdom. Hell, I expect we'll get big players coming from Godspire and Lancor if one of our own doesn't get her in the first two weeks. I realize you feel personally antagonized by Gray, Lord Seiji—she certainly went out of her way to tweak your nose."

I stiffened; that was *one* way to phrase "multiple child murders."

"But she is *done*," Norovena insisted, watching me closely. "At this point it's just a matter of time. Every single move she makes will only create another trail for the hunters to follow. The best thing you can do to finish her off is to step back and let nature take its course."

"If this is such a sure thing, how has she been allowed to run rampant in the Gutters for all these years?"

"You know the answer to that, Lord Seiji," he said wearily.

Of course I did. Because until there was money on the table, *nobody had cared.*

"Right. Well, thank you for the update, Captain—"

"Forgive me for the tangent, my lord, but I was still answering your question. Rhydion has also had his adventurer friends rounding up Gutter Rats all afternoon."

Aenit was holding Aster's hand behind me, but I clearly heard the hiss of her sudden gasp. I myself took an involuntary step toward Norovena.

"He's *what*?!"

"So you *didn't* ask him to do this, Lord Seiji?"

"Of course I fucking didn't! He never does anything I ask anyhow. Have they cleared out the Nest?"

"As of the last report I received, they haven't gone near it. Which, obviously, is because the Rats are as tense and paranoid as everyone else in the Gutters right now—more so than most, probably. Any approach to their home would make them scatter and be that much harder to track down. It seems the adventurers who agreed to help with this have been instructed to be gentle and nonconfrontational about it. They have approached Rats individually and offered to bring them inside the walls to safety, and not insisted when rebuffed. So they've only managed to round up a dozen or so into the Convocation orphanage. Still, that's around half the Nest, by my reckoning. It's more headway than anyone's ever made with the kids before. They must be especially shaken after what happened today."

That was closer to a quarter of their number, according to Aenit's description, but I didn't bother to correct him. "This orphanage. How will they be treated there?"

"Better than under that Gently character's care," Norovena said pointedly. "It's a Convocation institution, so discipline is strict and religious precepts enforced. They run orphanages specifically to train future priests. But this is a middle ring institution and a better opportunity than lowborn orphans could have asked for *until* that paladin involved himself."

Damn that self-righteous recycling bin! Even when he finally decided to get up off his extra-shiny ass and do something *useful*, it managed to throw a wrench into my plans. Well . . . still. This was probably for the best in the long run. I had my suspicions about this Convocation orphanage, but if I was honest with myself, it probably was at least as good a deal for the kids as I'd been planning to give them. More importantly, if Rhydion had his buddies out gathering them up, that would mean some hope for those I didn't manage to gather tonight.

"I guess that's for the best, then," I said grudgingly. "Well, if that's—"

"I don't think you realize the implications of this, Lord Seiji." If anything, Norovena's tone was suddenly grimmer. "Rhydion is famous for his tunnel vision. It's the reason he can go anywhere in the kingdom and not hurl everything into political disarray simply due to his presence; everyone knows he will focus on whatever matter brought him and leave other considerations aside. He's here on Dount to investigate the zombie sightings in the southwest khora forest, which have been going on at least since the Liberation. *Now*, suddenly, the man has taken a hard turn into current events and thrust his sword into the center of them. Can you imagine the ensuing panic among the Clans?"

"Oh, but I'm *sure* such upstanding citizens as our beneficent Highlords would have no reason to be perturbed by a crusading paladin," I said sweetly. "After all, it's not like they would *ever* be up to anything that might offend his sensibilities."

"I'm glad you're amused, Lord Seiji," he shot back. "This is altogether less funny from my position. Standing between the highborn and the low is tense even when things are calm, and things right now are very much not calm! I haven't even begun to address the matter of Highlord Caldimer."

Uh oh. "That's Caldimer Olumnach, you said? Seems like I've heard that name."

"No doubt you have," he said with a particularly piercing look. "He is already making a move to seize the territory freed up by Lady Gray's ouster. Outlying gangs began moving into the Gutters *perilously* soon after my men withdrew, a thing they would not have done without a much more powerful hand cracking their reins. All things being equal, I could not ask for a better replacement for Gray's influence."

Oh, this might be a problem. I'd been operating on the assumption that Norovena was motivated purely by his own self-interest, but if he was actually going to be pro-Olumnach, our days of useful cooperation were coming to an end. Lady Gray's removal as a player left me exactly one possible target for my next campaign.

"And you favor the Highlord for next crime lord?" I asked in as neutral a tone as I could manage.

"I favor *stability*. What Gwyllthean urgently needs right now is a period of *nothing of any interest* happening. The Gutters must have time to rebuild and let any simmering anger over today's events subside; otherwise we risk an *actual* uprising. All things being equal, a Highlord as the de facto crime boss would go a long way toward ensuring that. *He* would be motivated to stifle any threats to the hierarchy and refrain from too audaciously antagonizing the other Clans."

I pounced on the one ray of hope in this analysis. "Are things equal?"

"Not even remotely," Norovena spat. He glanced around; we were alone on the street, the only visible people being his own men guarding the city gate a few paces away, but still he stepped closer to me and lowered his voice.

"Clan Olumnach used to hold the fief of Gwyllthean before it was given to Clan Aelthwyn, and they have been obsessed with this humiliation ever since. Their schemes were one of the causes of the last big crackdown, and Highlord Caldimer in particular has always shown more ambition than restraint. And that was at the *best* of times. Since Lady Gray had his son murdered two months ago, the man has been nearly as berserk as she is now. If he gets a foothold in Gwyllthean, I can't imagine him *not* trying to move aggressively against the Archlord, however hopeless the attempt."

"Let me guess. That would mean a repeat of today's crackdown, but worse."

"I am *concerned*, Lord Seiji." He nodded, holding my gaze with uncharacteristic intensity. "I have a riled lowborn populace in need only of an excuse, a criminal power vacuum, and agitated Highlords who are sharing an island with a man personally powerful enough to smash all their defenses and politically connected enough to *get away with it*. That would be a volatile mix if that were the whole of it. But on top of it are Caldimer and Rhydion, two powerful men whose next moves I cannot *begin* to predict, save that nearly anything either does is likely to set a spark to the whole barrel, and they are all but certain to end up at cross purposes! Do you *see* my problem, Lord Seiji?"

"I believe I do," I said slowly. "I'm not sure how I can help you, though, Captain. I don't know Highlord Caldimer in the slightest, and I have no control over Rhydion. I sincerely apologize if it was something I said that set him off, but really, the man has never listened to me before."

"You can help me by not doing anything that will kick up a massive disturbance, Lord Seiji, and that is what I came here to ask of you." His eyes panned across my entourage of Lamm, Aster, and Nazralind in her shabby disguise—undoubtedly a group of people looking for trouble if ever he'd seen one, plus the added touch of Aenit clinging to Aster's hand just to add to the unpredictability. "I'm almost afraid to ask, but what precisely are you planning to do outside the gates tonight?"

I looked back at the four of them, then back at him, and put on a winsome smile. "Well, Captain, I won't lie to you. I am planning to kick up a massive disturbance."

Norovena's right eyelid began to twitch. "Lord Seiji—"

"*But*," I continued, raising one hand, "it's a disturbance Rhydion will approve of, Caldimer won't care about or likely even notice, and the population of the Gutters will diligently ignore. I'm going to excise one last little remnant of Lady Gray's power structure. And then I intend to remove myself from the city, along with as many of the Gutter Rats as are willing to go with me. Oh, you'll see me again, Captain, and probably fairly soon. But my need to tend to other matters of my own for a few days lines up nicely with your desire for some peace and quiet around here, I think. Does that meet with your approval?"

He exhaled sharply through his nose. "I have deliberately not pried into your business, my lord, but in this case . . . To be clear, you are planning to rid us of Uncle Gently and *nothing else?*"

Deliberately not pried into my business, my ass. He'd only *failed* to do that because Lamm had a good sense of which horse to back.

"That," I agreed quietly, "and nothing else. For now."

"I suppose that's better than I should have hoped," Norovena said with a sigh. "Very well, then, Lord Seiji. I wish you good fortune in your task. And I mean that very sincerely." His eyes hardened for a moment. "The bastard deserves *no mercy.*"

"He'll get none," I promised quietly.

The Captain nodded once more, then turned and barked over his shoulder in a carrying voice. "Crack the gate, Sergeant. Lord Seiji's party is going out."

I returned his nod in farewell, then proceeded on my way with my followers on my heels. They shifted into single file for a moment to get through the narrow opening; I exchanged a nod with the soldier on duty, and then we were descending the long ramp into the Gutters.

This part of the city was quiet, too. Licking its wounds and waiting to see what fresh nightmare tomorrow would bring.

"Aenit," I said softly once we were out of earshot of the gatehouse. She released Aster's hand and trotted forward to walk alongside me. "I know I've already said this, but it bears repeating. You *don't* need to do anything else, okay? You've already single-handedly made a huge difference. There's no need for you to take any more risks tonight. If you want to back out, I will fully support that."

The girl shook her head. "You don't have anybody else who can do it, right?"

"I've got other people meeting up with us in the city. Experienced scouts who can do this kind of work."

"Wilderness scouts, you said, and definitely not Gutter Rats," she retorted scornfully. "I'm sure they're good, Lord Seiji, but never send a hound to do a Rat's job. I can do this. I wanna help. I *need* to."

"I definitely understand that," I nodded, squeezing her hand as she slipped it into mine. "You know, if I were a remotely decent person I wouldn't *let* you involve yourself any further, after everything that's already happened."

"We don't gotta be decent, Lord Seiji. We just gotta get shit done."

"Well put," I sighed. "Brutally, tragically well put."

The plan required some preparation. Fortunately when we linked up with ten of Nazralind's highborn followers and Goose, they'd already brought the materials I had asked for. While the crew organized themselves for the next step, I changed into the provided getup, a serviceable rendition of the low-born longcoat, mask, and cloak of the Healer. It probably wouldn't matter too much that they weren't the same ones; the effect was similar enough to be recognizable, and anyway my old ensemble had been too torn and bloodstained after the battle in Cat Alley to see further service.

I was impressed by how efficient and willing to play along the noble-women were. Nobody even asked why I wanted the hammer, paintbrush, bundles of akorshil planks, quick-drying alchemical glue, and set of huge akornin spikes almost the length of my forearm used in heavy construction. They just brought them, and waited expectantly. That was for the better; if I told them what I was going to do with some of those, some of them would likely refuse to help.

"The girls are used to making do with scant supplies on short notice," Goose explained quietly when I expressed surprise that they'd managed to gather all that up so quickly. "Even with them avoiding the city, and as sub-dued as the Gutters are tonight, they've made friends and connections all over the island. Most places on Dount, they can hook you up with whatever you need. Within reason."

This crew really was proving to be a worthwhile acquisition, even if I was now seeing the signs they all shared Nazralind's happy-go-lucky attitude and general belief that this was all some grand adventure. I was simultaneously impressed with their versatility and resilience, and increasingly aware of just why they'd ultimately been uprooted and forced on the run by the Clans.

Aenit's familiarity with the Gutters was a godsend. She directed us to an empty house barely a block from the Rats' Nest—well within screaming distance, that was important—where I had the ladies prepare themselves for the next phase, and also begin to fortify the structure with the planks and glue.

Lady Gray was out there, and she had to know her antics today would draw me *here*. I gave it fifty-fifty odds whether she'd come at me tonight. There was still a chance Rhydion's adventurer buddies had driven her thoroughly underground already, but as clearly obsessed as she was with hitting me, that was far from a sure thing. So I set them to boarding the windows and kitchen entry, because I needed this house refit to have *one* way in and out. A single door that Aster could hold for at least a few minutes.

Two different stages of the plan would have everyone here, and me alone at the Nest for several long, crucial minutes. That would be Lady Gray's opportunity to strike, either to finish me off, or try to hurt me by going after my people. Aster with her artifact armor operating at the full strength of the Dark Lord's Blessings could, I hoped, fend her off at a single chokepoint long enough for me to get there. Then, she would be the anvil and I the hammer.

"How're we doing?" I asked Nazralind as she approached me in the kitchen, finally cleaned of makeup and sans fake beard. She hadn't changed her clothes, but the slightly scruffy lowborn outfit was pretty well suited to her present path in life. Well, that, and the new addition to it.

"It's quick work; the girls'll be finished in just a few more minutes," she reported with a cheery grin. "We're over halfway there, and it's not hard or time-consuming. You said fast-drying glue, so they got the *good* stuff."

"Thanks. Good work." I paused, eyeing the dramatic midnight-black cloak now draped over her shoulders, plus a loose bit of fabric around her neck that I recognized as a mask that would conceal her lower face when pulled up. I had also seen some of the other women not actively boarding up the windows put these on. "That's a nice touch, the cloak. Very . . ."

"Edgy?" Naz winked. "Yeah . . . Bit of a story, that. We were pretty new to skulking around in the dark, so when someone we helped out offered us a deal on a bunch of black fabric, of course I jumped on that. Had the cloaks and masks all made up, ready to make ourselves invisible as dark elves in the night. And guess what we immediately found out?"

"I'm almost afraid to ask."

"Turns out black is *extremely* visible at night, especially if it's moving. Yeah, apparently actually black objects are rare in nature, so in low light they tend to pop out to anybody whose vision is adjusted to the darkness. For stealth, you want deep gray, earth tones, even really dark jewel tones in a pinch. Black only blends into pitch black—as in, zero light at all, in which case you could be wearing bright orange stripes and be just as invisible."

"Oof." I had to wince. "Well, if it helps, I didn't know that, so I'd have made the same mistake."

"And instead, you get to learn from ours!" She shrugged, swishing the fabric of her cloak with one hand. "So that was a bust. But, it turns out they *look* really dramatic, and we already had 'em all made, so . . . rather than waste them, we changed approaches. Now we use these when we *want* to be seen, and send a message."

"Is the message 'we are fourteen years old and think this is scary'?"

"You're a jerk," she said with a fond smile. "But seriously, that works better than you'd think on Sanorites who live uncomfortably close to the last bastion of Viryan civilization on these isles. Everyone around here who wants to keep any degree of power or influence makes use of Sanorite iconography; even bandits tend to avoid looking too overtly sinister. As soon as it looks like you're *actually* Viryan-aligned, things get a lot more serious, and until the Convocation knights come to stomp you flat, people get legitimately wary."

"And to think, when you started doing this, you didn't even know you'd be working for the Dark Lord one day."

"Life sure is a grand old joke," she said, her expression growing wistful. "Be nice if it wasn't at our expense, for once."

"I'm working on that," I said. "But since the solution involves ascending to heaven, grabbing both goddesses by their divine coiffures, and clocking their heads together . . . don't hold your breath."

"Well, that was an exciting note to walk in on," Goose stated as she returned to the room. "They're just finishing the last rooms upstairs, Lord Seiji. Quick-drying is a relative term; the glue's solid enough to hold boards in place as soon as it's applied, but I'd give it half an hour before it'll stand up to solid impacts."

"It should have about that long anyway." I drew in a breath and exhaled slowly. "All right. Aenit, you ready for your part?"

"Let's do it, Lord Seiji." The girl nodded, her eyes full of that same deeply ingrained fury. God, what must this poor kid have had to endure before Gently's final mistake pushed her over the edge? I related far too well to that soul-deep, all-consuming rage. No one her age should have any idea what that felt like.

"I'll send Biribo with the signal when we're ready," I said, stepping through the house to the front door with Aenit on my heels and the familiar buzzing along at my side. "Naz, you're in charge."

"We'll be waiting, Lord Seiji," she promised.

We stepped out into the street, whereupon I discovered that this party was bigger than I'd planned.

"Aster—"

"Don't even try," she snapped. "I *told* you, Lord Seiji, we're not separating again."

"Aster, this is Aenit's job. I'm only coming along to keep watch in case Lady Gray tries to pounce on her during the one minute she'll be out of my sight."

"Good plan. I'll keep an eye on *you*, for the same reason."

"Every additional person is another risk—"

"Do you wanna stand here arguing about this, or get it *done*?"

"I need you covering this door in case—"

"Goose is fully able to do it for the few seconds it'll take us to get back here."

I scowled at her. She raised her eyebrows, staring challengingly right back.

"Must be nice having somebody who always watches over you," Aenit commented innocently.

I threw my hands up. "Ugh, *fine*. Let's just go."

They were both silent as we strode to the end of the street, not that they needed to speak. I could *feel* the smugness radiating from both. Again, I reflected, this was all my fault. I was the idiot who had the bright idea to surround myself with women. Dark Lord or not, there was no telling them anything.

"Okay, it's a straight shot down this street to the Nest," Aenit reported, stopping at the corner. "Don't peek out, Lord Seiji. If they see you coming they'll all bolt, including Uncle Gently. Should only take me a couple minutes to switch out with whoever's on lookout tonight. Nobody's gonna want to be up on the roof with everything that's been going on, so they'll be willing to trade duties with me. You sure you don't need me to send up a signal?"

"Biribo will be able to tell as soon as you're in position," I assured her. "Is there a convenient way onto the roofs nearby?"

She nodded and pointed back the way we'd come. "First alley there, the last one we passed. Owner of that house lets us keep a ladder propped up for access. Everybody in this neighborhood does favors for the Rats. Keeping on our good side is the only way they don't get robbed blind." Gilder would have grinned while delivering that remark, but Aenit paused, staring up at me intently. "Back at the house, with those nobles, what they were saying . . . Is it true, Lord Seiji? You're the new Dark Lord?"

"It's true," I said simply.

Many people reacted to that revelation with terror; even Lady Gray had been spooked. Gilder, Benit, and Radon had all been excited. Aenit just nodded again.

"Good," she said quietly. "That's good. There's no saving this stupid country anyway. It all needs to burn."

She turned and scampered around the corner, her light footsteps quickly fading.

"Biribo?"

"Don't worry, boss, I'm keeping track of her. Quick little sprout—there we go, she's in the door. No sign of Gray or anybody else."

"All right, thanks. Let's get up top."

The ladder was right where she'd indicated. In moments, the two of us were on the roof, carefully taking position behind it, where we wouldn't be spotted by the lookout atop the Nest, but ready to bound across the gaps as soon as the signal came. Until then, there was little to do but stand and welter in the tension.

"I need a way to beat that dagger," I mused aloud. "That's the problem with her. She's not *that* powerful. Skilled, experienced, smart; I'll give her credit for that stuff, but every time I've gone head-to-head with her, sheer Dark Lord brute force has got me at least a draw. The problem with Gray isn't how dangerous she is; it's just the sheer *fucking* cockroachiness of her. I *need* a way to counter that stealth. She'd have been dead every time we crossed paths already if she couldn't just fucking *disappear*."

"You and everybody else, boss," Biribo commiserated.

"I'm not just making conversation, Biribo. How can I counter the dagger?"

He darted back and forth in momentary confusion. "Boss, if I knew something feasible, don't you think I'd have already—"

"Then forget feasible, go for far-fetched. I know you can't tell me about Wisdom powers or they won't unlock, but what about spells? Artifacts? *Something*. Norovena thinks some of the King's Guild adventurers have ways to beat it. They have to exist. Not right this instant; we're busy, but think on it, okay? I want a list of everything that even *theoretically* can neutralize her advantage, and then we'll work through it and see which I have the best chance of getting my hands on."

"You heard the Captain," Aster said quietly. "With all the heat Rhydion brought down, there's a very real chance someone else will get her before the two of you even have a chance to clash again. That is, if she doesn't try us again tonight."

"Unacceptable," I whispered, staring into the dark alien sky and feeding morsels of rage to the beast inside me. "I will *maybe* settle for Olumnach getting to her first. He's a sufficiently evil fucker to do the job right, and he's good and pissed. Any of the rest? She won't die as painfully, or as slowly, as she needs to."

Aster stared at me in silence.

"Aenit's on the roof," Biribo reported.

"Kid works fast," I said approvingly.

"No joke, boss. That one's a good find. I'm still impressed she got inside the walls. Gutter Rats almost *never* pull that off. All right, the other kid on the roof just went back inside; we're clear!"

"Any other watchers?"

"Neighborhood's quiet, boss. I'd guess it'll be another day or two at least before everybody in the Gutters lets up on minding their own business as hard as they can."

"Good. Let's move."

We rounded the corner of the roof and dashed across them. Our steps were undoubtedly heavier than the patter of Rat feet the residents were accustomed to hearing, but Biribo was right; I doubted anybody around here would be in the mood to be inquisitive after the day they'd had. Aster and I bounded across alleys and ran over shingles with no trouble.

The Rats' Nest was . . . a house. From the outside, it didn't look like much of anything. A big house, sure, with the windows boarded, but other than that, just a shabby structure that fit in with the rest of the neighborhood. As we drew close, Aenit popped up from behind a gable and waved to us.

After pausing to consider the situation, Aster and I got a running start and then leaped across the street to the building next door to the Nest, so as not to alarm our targets by landing heavily on its roof. From there, the alley separating the two was narrow enough that we could simply step across.

"You work fast," I praised Aenit in a whisper.

"I know my business," she replied without false modesty. "Okay, Lord Seiji, there's seven exits apart from the front door, including two on the roof up here. We should leave one of those for last so I can get back inside, but I'll show you the rest in order. Finally gonna get some justice," she growled, her little face creasing in a scowl.

"That's not really how we do things, Aenit," I warned her. "Not most of the time, and *definitely* not tonight. You should never set the Dark Lord after anyone who deserves a scrap of mercy. Forget about justice. As soon as I get my hands on Uncle Gently, I'm going to do something Evil."

Having so declared, I began summoning slimes.

18

In Which the Dark Lord Seizes the Means of Abduction

We worked quickly, Aenit pointing out each of the bolt holes used by the Rats to escape the Nest and me summoning bound slimes to plug them. The mindless creatures were easy to direct in these relatively small numbers, especially after my previous exercises in trying to control hundreds at a time. Stepping as lightly as possible so as not to alert the Nest's occupants to the adult-sized weight on the roof, I moved to each spot and filled it with slimes, giving them the mental order to hold position once each aperture was fully blocked off. Apparently most of the windows were boarded, which left only relatively few escape points. From the roof, I had to lean over and direct the amorphous blobs to slither into crevices at ground level and one halfway up a side wall to plug every hole.

A person could probably push through them, but anyone would be very reluctant to try—slimes up close were gross and slightly caustic to the touch. I didn't feel *great* about trapping the Rats, given the rough day they'd already had, but it was a necessary part of the plan. I required a captive audience to break them from Uncle Gently's control. After that, they'd be free to go.

Biribo returned from the errand on which I'd dispatched him seconds ago. "Still clear on the streets, boss. The girls are on their way."

"Good. Now then . . ." I straightened up from the edge of the roof, looking around. "So, uh, Aenit. This is a little embarrassing . . ."

"Two roofs over that way, Lord Seiji," she said with a smile, pointing. "There's an easy drop to a landing on the second floor, then stairs down to the alley."

"Right. Thanks. You ready?"

She nodded solemnly. "Gotta move fast once you seal me inside, Lord Seiji. The Nest is always packed; even with a bunch of Rats moved to the orphanage or . . ." Aenit paused and swallowed before continuing gamely. "I won't be able to go more than a minute or two without being noticed. If I'm lucky. Not long after that before somebody asks who's on watch."

"Right, clock's ticking." It already was anyway; all it would take was one bored or inquisitive kid looking for some fresh air to notice one of their hidden exits was packed full of slimes. "I'll move fast as I can. If you get in trouble, try to get to the front door; I'll be heading there immediately."

"Got it." She opened the last unslimed exit, a trapdoor set into the roof, and slipped back inside. "Good luck, Lord Seiji."

Aenit shut the thing after herself, and I summoned a pile of bound slimes to ooze into its edges, both holding it down and ready to discourage anyone from poking at it from inside. Then I turned and stepped as quietly as I could to the edge of the roof.

Aster had already gone ahead and vaulted across the alley. I followed suit, and we dashed across the next two roofs with much less circumspection, finding the staircase exactly where Aenit had said we would.

By the time we returned to the front of the Nest, the others had arrived— Goose and Lamm at the head of a column of women in black cloaks with masks over their lower faces. I had to hand it to Naz; this actually was pretty ominous-looking, especially in the falling darkness of the quiet neighborhood. Only ten of the girls were with us now, the rest having stayed to secure their campsite for our arrival, Twigs being among them.

I greeted them with a mute nod, getting several in return. Then I turned to the front door of the Rats' Nest and paused for a moment. With the brief lack of active distraction, I was keenly conscious of the pressure rising within me. All day I'd pushed down that lurking beast, but it was like the rage smelled blood, like it knew it was about to be unleashed. I didn't know whether conceptualizing that omnipresent, simmering fury as something separate from my own mind was making it easier or harder to manage.

Maybe I should take Minifrit up on her offer of whatever passed for therapy here. Man, a real psychiatrist would probably have a field day with me. Fortunately, I'd never have to find out.

My cloaked followers had gathered around, forming an ominous human wall encircling the entrance, which was the closest we were going to get to operational security. I grabbed the latch and yanked the door open, stepping into the Nest.

It immediately burst into a scurrying panic like a kicked . . . well, nest. It was impossible to get a head count of the kids just in the front room as they all bolted, streaming away through doors, down hallways and upstairs toward their various bolt-holes, as was the sensible thing for them to do when their home was suddenly invaded.

Within seconds, the first shrieks resulted as they discovered what was *in* their escape hatches.

To discourage anyone from trying to force the issue, I reached out with my will toward the bound slimes I'd placed there, prompting them to ooze aggressively inward, extending pseudopods and dripping extraneous goo in what I hoped would be a sufficiently intimidating display so the children wouldn't want to try pushing into them. Indeed, I sensed no one bodily disturbing my gloppy minions, though that was the extent of the sensory data I could extract from them.

Not that I was going to leave it at that; people will try almost anything when cornered and desperate. I needed them cornered, so it was necessary to remedy the desperation.

"PEACE." I held up my hands, speaking in a carrying voice that I knew would echo through the halls of the Nest. "I'm the Healer. I haven't come to harm you, Rats. Everyone will be kept safe and allowed to leave once I'm done."

That seemed to help . . . a little. Obviously they were not going to take me at my word, but the level of panicked noise diminished at the reassurance. Still, nobody was trying the slime barriers.

And then the one door through which no one had fled opened, and out stepped a man. Calm, unhurried, and staring at me with no sign of fear.

This was him. This was it.

Showtime.

"Well, well, well," drawled Uncle Gently, eyeing me up and down with ostentatious contempt. "And here he is. The great Healer himself. Come to finish your work, is that it? Haven't you done enough harm to my precious little ones? I guess that'll teach me to hope you were only interested in the Alley Cats."

He was lowborn, middle-aged, honestly pretty unremarkable save that he had a noticeable paunch and jowls; most of the common folk I'd seen in Gwyllthean did not seem to get enough nutrition to put on extra weight. Also, he had a noticeable sense of *style*. Trousers, boots, coat, all of it was in the highborn fashion—except that it was all mismatched pieces that clashed with each other, and all was noticeably frayed and patched. A bright pink scarf was draped around his shoulders, embroidered on the ends with crimson and purple. Absolutely hideous. I knew highborn didn't leave their castoffs lying around where the poor could pick them up; there was too much caste significance attached to the different styles. If he could get these clothes, he could get good ones, which meant this scruffy, eclectic, and *flashy* getup was something he'd cultivated deliberately.

Between that and the assertive, deliberate *presentation* with which he confronted me, I could tell I was dealing with an opponent who understood the significance of stage presence.

While the pair of us sized each other up, my followers streamed into the room, spreading out across its front and making the entire place rather cramped as the Gutter Rats, who hadn't outright fled the front chamber, retreated further.

Uncle Gently ignored the show of force, which was definitely the act of a fellow dramatist. When I declined to argue back as he paused, he pressed his advantage.

"So, what will it be, oh great Healer?" He spread his arms in a gesture I'd found myself using a lot recently, the expansive body language taking command of the room. "Have you come to do your dirty work with your own bloody hands for once? Ah no, that isn't your *style*, is it. Always goading someone else to fight and die for you. First the Cats, and now the Rats. At least you gave the whores the courtesy of a choice! Already today you've killed *five* of my little ones. What will you—"

"You're blaming *him* for that?" snarled Lady Imren—I think her name was Imren. I hadn't memorized them all yet, and anyway, she was masked and cloaked—taking a belligerent step forward.

I held up one hand, bringing her to a halt, and spoke in a sepulchral tone, projected throughout the room and beyond. "Let him talk."

Uncle Gently had betrayed a moment of satisfaction as he got a rise out of one of my followers, but at that he paused in opening his mouth to continue, reconsidering. The suggestion that he was playing into my hands made him think again about his chosen strategy.

"Goose," I said, in the same soft but carrying tone, shifting my head to nod at the door through which he had entered the room. "There."

She nodded once in acknowledgment and strode forward. There were no Rats between us and Goose's destination, but those clustered against the walls pressed back anyway. With one notable exception.

As Goose stepped up to the door, suddenly an older boy who had to have been pushing thirteen scooted in front of her, planting his body in her path and holding his arms wide to bar her way. He glared up at her, which frankly impressed me; Goose was taller than most men, and more muscular.

"You can't go in there!" the Rat snarled. "That's Uncle Gently's room! *Nobody's* allowed in there."

"I wonder why that is," I mused aloud, causing multiple Rats to look at me with narrowed eyes. The building was still secure; we were blocking the front entrance, and my slime barriers were all in place. One had been tested, which I'd put a stop to by directing the slime that was poked to begin crawling up the arm that had poked it.

"Son," Goose said quietly, staring down her nose at the boy attempting to block her, "move. Or be moved."

The bravado leaked from him visibly as he stared up at her and got no support from his fellows. None of the rest of the Rats put themselves forward in his defense—and most damningly, Uncle Gently failed to speak up on his behalf, currently staring at me in consternation. He'd probably intuited the general shape of my plan, and now squandered his one chance to steal a march on me.

After a few silent moments, the boy hunched his shoulders and crept back out of the way, staring at the floor.

Goose grabbed the door latch, which served only to reveal that it was locked. With a grunt, she seized it in both hands, shifted her stance, and lifted one leg to plant her foot against the door frame. Muscles bulged like the steel cables holding up a suspension bridge for all of two seconds before the aged akorshil planks gave up the ghost. Goose didn't even stumble as the entire latch mounting was ripped out of the door, simply stepping backward in a controlled retreat. She tossed the broken latch aside and pulled open the loosened door without another word.

"Biribo," I said.

My familiar zoomed toward the door to Uncle Gently's room, veering aside for a moment as Gently opened his mouth to speak and then gasped and staggered back, covering his face with his arms. Which is what *most* people will do when something the size of a squirrel that buzzes like a wasp dives right at them. It was only a momentary course correction, though, and Biribo immediately resumed his flight path, ducking through the broken door and past the heavy curtains that covered its other side.

On the signal, the rest of my followers flowed into action. Goose retreated, joining Lamm in blocking the door behind me with their bodies, while Aster stood behind *them* on the Nest's stoop, sword in hand, to discourage the curious and hold off Lady Gray should she put in an appearance. The ten black-cloaked noblewomen streamed forward, into the room beyond, where my familiar was already waiting.

I'd not found occasion to use this yet, relying instead on Biribo's ability to sense the presence and position of people, but apparently familiars were also intuitively aware of the shape of structures around them, including any gaps therein. Which made them the perfect instruments for sniffing out hidden compartments.

"Oh, *now* I see," Uncle Gently spat, drawing himself back fully upright and making of himself a spectacle of fearless offended dignity. The man was good, I had to give him that; it was obvious how he'd wrangled all these kids through sheer force of personality. "It's *me* you're here to blame for your crimes. Your big plan is to leave them alone and vulnerable to that mad-woman *you* created. Going to take away the only person who cares for them, who *protects* them, is that it? Come in here and destroy their only safe haven? You surprise me, *Healer*. I dared to hope that you would at least strike quickly and cleanly if you came to bring your chaos and destruction upon my little ones! But no, you'll leave them to suffer, *slowly*."

I continued to stand there in silence, letting him dig his own grave. It was at that moment that the first of the women emerged from his room with an armful. She was followed by three more, all of them laden down with bread.

Wyddh was a kind of flatbread the Fflyr made that reminded me of naan, except that it didn't come in a "plain" variety, and Donon had stared at me like I'd grown a second head when I suggested baking some. The Fflyr loved their tongue-bustingly strong flavors, and they baked their wyddh with *all* of them; it came in spicy, sour, sweet, and savory varieties, and it seemed like every vendor, restaurant, and family had their own handful of unique recipes. Uncle Gently had taken advantage of the stuff's ability to keep for a very long time at room temperature to gather a nice variety. The girls set down piles and *piles* of the flattened loaves in every color and texture. Wyddh with sour syrup, with sugary glaze, with various kinds of meat or fruit baked right in. Enough wyddh alone to have fed this whole orphanage for a week or two.

And that was just the beginning.

"Oh, let me *guess*," Uncle Gently spat, growing more overtly hostile as he saw the writing on the wall. Behind him there came a crash from inside his room; Biribo's senses didn't reveal *how* to open hidden compartments, which was only an impediment to people who cared about not busting up the place.

"You would stuff the poor dears full of rich crap? You know *nothing* about raising children—just what I should expect from a violent whoremonger! Children need discipline, boundaries. They need the care of someone able to wisely portion out their daily bread. Do you know how, Healer? Can you judge the right amount to give them the energy they need, to help them grow, without making them *sick*? Of course you don't. You'll—"

He shied back from a cloaked woman who had just set down a cracked jar trickling out candied nuts from within his room; she had rounded on him with a fist upraised. Nazralind grabbed her shoulder.

"Hey. Not yet, Iloryn. Lord Seiji is handling it."

For the moment, I simply waited, while Uncle Gently desperately talked and the girls systematically brought out his entire stash, creating a huge pile of food in the center of the floor. It was a *ludicrous* amount. What the hell was he hoarding it for? One man couldn't eat all this in a month. And it was definitely hoarded; everything was of a type that would keep well. Expensive and delicious varieties, that is, of foods that kept well. In addition to the flatbread, he had jars of preserved . . . everything, really—meats and countless pickled vegetables. Candied nuts, dried fruit, dried meat of multiple varieties, fruit jams and preserves, potatoes and potato-adjacent Ephemeral roots I didn't recognize.

I knew this wasn't the stockpile of food from which the Rats were fed. Aenit had told me *their* food was kept in a locked pantry in the kitchen controlled by a few of the older kids Uncle Gently favored, while Gilder had talked about the way he would pass out candy and gourmet treats as rewards for his particular pets when they pleased him. Even had I gone in blind, though, I would have known it from the way the surrounding Rats stared at the growing pile of delicacies.

"And who are *you* to judge?" Gently raved at me, now baring his teeth in a desperate snarl. "You know nothing. Nothing! Do you *know* these children? No, you don't! You don't know how to teach them strength, how to cultivate good behavior and the character they'll need to survive in this cruel world! You can't punish effectively and with loving gentleness, all *you* know is how to cast spells and slaughter people! For years and years I have raised these precious children to have the best lives they could hope for; without me, they'd be starving and begging in the canals! I give them what they need and teach them what they need to thrive when they outgrow this place. I have *earned* their trust!"

Several small mouths audibly hissed at that last line. Rats had been trickling back into the room, with their ability to flee cut off; small faces were peeking around door frames and over the second-floor landing, staring down at this ongoing spectacle. Many were blank-faced, a lot gazed at the food pile in hungry fixation. Quite a few were now staring at Uncle Gently with open fury. Not a one looked sympathetic toward him.

I continued to stand in silence while he ranted and my people filled the floor with his hoard. Having brought out all the food, they now carried in small bags and lockboxes, all full of coins; Nazralind paused to forcibly crack open each one, revealing the discs and halos glittering within. They brought piles of fabric, bedding, and clothing of silk *much* finer than the deliberately tattered outfit he wore.

The man owned a shirt made of shimmersatin—the same stuff I had ensured Auldmaer's monopoly on two months ago. I'd thought it was going to the highborn ladies. Where the *hell* did he even plan to wear it?

"Hell's revels!" a female voice shouted from inside his room. Its owner emerged through the heavy curtain a moment later, brandishing a bottle. "He's got a twenty-year silver brandy! My own *family* wouldn't have let me touch one of these, and we own that vineyard!"

"It goes on the pile," Nazralind ordered. With visible reluctance, the discoverer of the bottle obeyed, while her compatriots brought forth and added an amazing selection of wines and spirits.

Uncle Gently had given up by this point, just glaring silent hatred at me. I could have told him his gambit was futile. I know better than anyone the power of a good, emotionally manipulative speech, but you *don't* want to try that right in front of someone who is silently demonstrating how full of shit you are. He had nothing but talk, while I had action, and he'd been fool enough to prove it in front of the audience for whose attention we were vying.

Biribo came back to hover over my shoulder, and the last of the noble-women set down a set of silver candlesticks—as in actual silver, the *metal*, not pale akornin—and the rest took up positions in front of the room they had just emptied of hoarded wealth.

"These kids look hungry, Uncle Gently," I stated into the ensuing silence. My voice was soft but projected, carrying and echoing through the house. "Why do these kids look hungry?"

"This is *your fault*," Gently hissed. "*You* did this. All of it! Lady Gray was always *rational*, logically motivated. It was easy to stay on her good side. Until *you* came along and riled her up, drove her mad. She *forced* me to give up five of my own precious little ones—I *had* to, or she would have slaughtered who knows how many! And all. Because. Of *you*."

I stared at him in silence from the darkness under my hood. The assembled Rats watched the confrontation with grim anticipation. My own people loomed at both ends of the room, a silent threat.

"He's right, you know." I raised my voice slightly and raised my head, directing myself to the onlooking children. "I set all of this in motion. Lady Gray attacked you because of me—because I was kind to three Gutter Rats, and took them far enough away that neither she nor Uncle Gently could harm them again. She thought she could hurt me by hurting you. So she did."

Gently was still baring his teeth at me, but his expression was now uncertain; once again I'd reacted in a manner he hadn't anticipated and couldn't understand the purpose of. No surprise this guy had never risen higher than manipulating children.

"Shit happens," I said. "Life is hard. Lady Gray is . . . just part of the shit that happens, to all of us. Somebody recently told me that what defines a person is what they *choose* to do when the shit goes down. Well, when Lady Gray *happened* to us all, Uncle Gently and I both proved who we are. Both of our reactions got people killed. I fought back with everything I had, and broke her control. *He* served up five of your own on a silver platter to appease her."

The man himself took a belligerent step toward me, opening his mouth.

Windburst.

The spell slammed him against the wall, cutting off whatever he'd been about to say. Almost no reaction ensued from the tiny watchers. Christ, these poor kids had already seen more violence in their short lives than most soldiers back on Earth.

"Shit happens," I repeated, "and life is hard. What *matters* is knowing who you can trust to have your back when it goes down."

I stared down at the winded Uncle Gently, where he was coughing weakly on the floor. Was he trying for sympathy now, or had it really hit him that hard? Well, the guy didn't look to be in particularly good shape.

"I'm gonna tell you kids a secret," I said, lifting my head again to address them. "Something nobody in power wants you to know. Not Lady Gray or Uncle Gently—even the Highlords and the King use this secret. It's about how people stay in control, you see—the secret of power. It's *why* they're always so quick to punish anyone for any sign that they are *soft*."

Pause for effect, shift hood to make it clear I'm looking around at each of them . . .

"Because, oh yes, I am soft. I care about people, and it hurts me when they're hurt. That's why she did this. Why they always do this—because being *soft* means being *connected*. When you care for others, feel what they feel, you have bonds that strengthen you both. Two people acting together are many times more powerful than the same two people alone. The more connections you have, the stronger you are. And so, the people in power want you *isolated* and *alone*. A bunch of individuals is a lot easier to beat down than people with a common purpose. You've seen this yourselves. Think how Uncle Gently keeps control here in the Nest—how he makes you compete, and turns you against each other whenever any of you become *too* close as friends."

I'd heard enough from Gilder and Benit about his methods to be able to describe them, but frankly, I could have intuited that much just from the state of this place.

"It's the same thing Lady Gray does with her gangs," I continued, watching their faces. It looked like most of the Rats were present now; a lot of them were still blank-faced, many obviously suspicious of me, but some were squinting in thought as they considered what I told them. "The same thing the Highlords do with the lowborn—the same thing the Archlord and the King do to the Clans. The same thing the Lancor Empire does with Fflyr Dlemathlys and all its other surrounding nations. It goes *all the way up*, and it doesn't stop until you reach the goddesses themselves. It's the universal strategy—*divide and conquer*. And to beat it, all you have to do is unite."

I held up one hand, forefinger upraised.

"Which is why they'll *immediately* move to crush you if you try. That's why Gently, Gray, and every asshole running the Gutters teaches you not to be *soft* toward each other, and punishes you if you do. That's why it's so hard to break out of this cycle, kids. But there's a trick to it, and I'm going to teach it to you. Wanna hear it?"

Nobody answered—verbally, at least. They were still tense and standoffish, which was only wise in this situation. Almost half of them nodded, though.

On the floor, Gently drew in a breath, but went still when I shifted to look at him. In his position, I would've done or said *anything* to salvage the situation, at least go down fighting, with the full knowledge that letting the Healer talk was only pounding more nails into his coffin. He quailed visibly at the memory of being slammed into the wall, though. In the end, he was a coward.

Must be nice to have the luxury of cowardice. I'd really like to try it sometime.

"Today, Lady Gray and Uncle Gently moved together to cut off a threat to their power. They decided to *punish* me for being soft toward the Gutter

Rats by killing five of you. When someone does that, you have to punish them back, even harder. So *now*, I have to make such a dramatic, *ugly* spectacle of what *happens* to assholes who *murder children* on my watch that nobody in this rotten town even dreams of trying it again."

"Yes," Gently rasped. "You heard it from his own mouth, my precious ones. They are few, but *we* are many! Protect your Uncle Gently and push these bastards out of our home!"

I wasn't actually sure how we'd deal if the mob of thirty-odd preteens zerged us; there were a lot more kids in here than Norovena had estimated. It didn't matter, though. Some of them were still staring obsessively at the pile of food and wealth. Some glared down at their Uncle Gently without a trace of pity. Some were watching me speculatively, several just . . . watching, with neutral expressions, to see what would happen. Even the boy who'd tried to stall Goose earlier was just staring silently at the floor. At some point Aenit had pushed out of the back to stand closer to the cloaked shape of Nazralind than any of the others had dared; she was giving Gently that same look of barely restrained contempt and fury I'd seen in her eyes back at the mourning chapel.

No one raised a finger, or said a word, in his support.

In the silence, Uncle Gently turned slowly to look up at me, and the look on his face told me he saw only doom.

He didn't know the half of it.

19

In Which the Dark Lord Spreads it Around

Jassner," I said aloud into the echoing, expectant silence, "wanted to be a messenger and travel to different cities. He would hang around the trade roads, watching the couriers pass by and ask any who'd talk with a Gutter Rat about their travels. I wonder, Uncle Gently—did you pick him as a sacrifice because he was more likely than most to escape your control?"

To his credit, Gently drew in a breath, straightening his shoulders and hardening his expression to answer me.

"I—"

It was a rhetorical question.

Immolate.

Shell-shocked the Gutter Rats might generally be by the reality of their lives in the Gutters, but nobody can watch *that* unprepared and not react. It had taken me a depressingly high number of repetitions of that spell to stand there in cold silence while it ran its course, feeling nothing.

Many yelled, a few fled the room; several started crying. But in a sight that made me suddenly, crushingly depressed despite how neatly it played into my own agenda, quite a few of the children watched the only caregiver they'd ever known screaming while he burned alive with expressions that were as cold as mine, or even overtly satisfied.

My god. Kids will bond with anyone who looks after them; many people will rally to the defense of even the most openly abusive parents. What had he been *doing* to these poor children, to create such a cavernous vacuum of loyalty? If it wasn't playing out right in front of my eyes, I wouldn't have believed it.

I guess teaching your children to be hard-hearted and rely on no one can backfire pretty badly, when it's your turn to need someone to care about you.

As usual, it took around a minute for the effects to fade. Uncle Gently was left quivering on the floor, his mismatched and bedraggled finery singed and smoking in a few places.

"Ladhnet," I said loudly.

"No," he croaked. "No more—"

"*Ladhnet* was a fan of mine. She was getting closer to the age when you turn Rats out of the Nest, and did *not* want to become an Alley Cat—which you were trying to pressure her into, because you got a kickback from one of the madams. She laughed and *cheered* when the whores beat the shit out of the gangs. I'm seeing a *pattern* in the kids you decided to get rid of."

"No more—!"

Immolate.

From the corner of my eye, I saw Lamm's jaw working soundlessly as he watched this, the flames of ultimate torture making a bright reflection in his eyes. A few of the ladies had averted their cowled faces from the spectacle of Uncle Gently's suffering, but just as many were staring down at him in ruthless satisfaction. They hadn't had it as rough as the Gutter Rats, but all of them were harder than the spoiled highborn ladies they'd once been.

There was just something about seeing the obviously guilty *punished* that helped cleanse a soul stained by the suffering those guilty had caused. Even if it wasn't the same man who'd harmed them, there was catharsis in the symbol alone. In the revelation that the mighty burned and bled just the same as the weak they victimized.

"You always thought Tonnon was a waste of space," I said inexorably when the flames subsided again. "He didn't talk, didn't acknowledge most people. You only kept him around because he was a genius at catching crawns. He loved crawns, knew all the different varieties, where and how they lived, how to catch each kind at any given time of year. When he cried because he couldn't handle the noise or the crowd, you'd have the bigger boys douse him in canal water and lock him in a closet. Where I'm from, we know what the autism spectrum is; a boy like that could have been cared for by people who knew *how* to care for him." I was usually so good at staying in control when I was in performance mode, but the white-hot beast inside me was snarling, clawing its way up; I was struggling to keep it under a semblance of control. It broke through in the roughening of my voice, the way I had to clench my hands into fists, gouging my palms with my own nails for focus. "And there is a deep, *dark* crevice in hell for monsters who abuse those children. *Let me give you a taste.*"

Immolate!

He screamed less this time. I knew the healing effect of Immolate would remedy even the damage done to the throat from overwork, but I also knew my healing powers were ineffective on mental trauma. I guess everybody reaches a point where they can't scream anymore.

Some of the Rats were refusing to watch now, but only some.

"Sildnit wanted to be an adventurer," I said, raising my voice above the noise of Uncle Gently's quiet weeping after the third round of fire receded. "Just like so many children. You never got on her case about that, because you considered it a hopeless dream for any of your Rats—because you don't actually think they have any value or potential. No, you only punished her during the spring and summer, because she kept leaving the city to pick flowers instead of begging or stealing the way you told her. Sildnit really loved flowers. She said they reminded her there was more to life than the Gutters. Can't have *that*, now can we, *Uncle Gently*?"

"P-please—"

"Save your begging for Virya; she has more of a sense of humor than I do. **Immolate!**"

Even the most horrific of things can become routine amazingly fast. I was starting to feel that much of the terror had been leeched from the room through sheer repetition and overexposure. Faces were growing dour and tired, bodies less stiff and tense. Even Gently made less and less noise with each Immolation.

The blinding rage had . . . not settled, but calmed. It was not going anywhere; it was willing to wait. The moment was coming.

"Nadro was a real smooth-talker," I said once there was quiet enough to speak again. "Very good at wheedling coins out of people. Seems like it'd be a valuable skill to you, Gently. He was also really good at talking his way out of punishment when you were annoyed—even better at getting the bigger kids you liked to have bully the others to back down. Maybe that was why you decided you could do without him, yeah? Because in the end, none of them matter all that much to you. All that ever mattered was your *control*."

I fell silent. This time, he didn't beg, just hunched his shoulders and waited for it.

I waited, too. The seconds ticked on, the anticipation built. Until finally, Gently dared to peek up at me, his face twisted with the uncertainty that was the closest thing he had left to hope.

Then I cast **Immolate**.

Because punishment was one thing—punishment was a *start*. But I was in the business of vengeance, and I had come here tonight promising to commit Evil. I'll never again be able to claim I'm a decent person, but I am a man of my word.

"Lord Seiji." Goose's voice was quiet, but audible even through the crackling of flames that wreathed the twitching shape of Uncle Gently spasming on the floor. He was currently in that later stage where a person *couldn't* scream even if they wanted to, because you can't really do that without lungs or a larynx. "I thought the plan was *not* to do this part in front of the children."

I nodded, slowly. "Yeah. Change of plans, though. I learned recently that no less than the paladin Rhydion is sponsoring the Gutter Rats in general to have a place in the Convocation orphanage in the middle ring. He's had King's Guild adventurers down here all day making the offer." I looked around at the assembled Rats; they were listening, most now watching me. A few were sneering at Uncle Gently's suffering, but I doubted they were too focused to hear what I was saying. "And *that* is a good offer. I came here planning to take responsibility for the havoc I've caused, to take any Rats willing to come with me under my protection and get them out of Lady Gray's reach. But you know what, the Convocation can do that, too, and probably offer them a better life. No—*undoubtedly* offer them a better life."

Uncle Gently was flickering out yet again. He didn't seem to even have the strength left to stay curled up; his twitching limbs splayed out across the floor as he struggled for breath. I gave him a long, contemptuous stare before finishing my explanation.

"After seeing this . . . I assume most of the kids will prefer the orphanage. It's a chance for some peace and a future, anyway. Only a certain kind of person needs me, Goose, and I'll take any who do. The ones who need to be able to *strike back* in order to find any peace—I'll have opportunities for them. The chance to even the score, and hurt the people who built this system that's grinding us all down. Or those who'll only feel safe again with the biggest monster of all protecting them. And I do offer that. I make mistakes, I can be hurt, and I've lost people. But only through mistakes. No matter what happens or what is at stake, *I will never abandon my people.* If someone has my back, I have theirs. Period."

I had to draw in a steadying breath and let it out slowly before I could continue, raising my eyes to address the room at large.

"If that's you . . . if you want to be part of our revenge against this whole fucking mess of a world, from the gangsters to the goddesses and everything in between . . . or if you just can't trust in these systems anymore and need to stay with the one lunatic who's dumb enough to have your back no matter what happens or what it costs . . . then you come with me. I have a place far enough from Gwyllthean to be . . . well, *relatively* safe, for now. It's big enough to have room for everyone. Everybody gets their own bed and as much as they need to eat. None of this bullshit about rewards and punishments; I will make sure nobody goes hungry if I have the power to prevent it, and I have a *lot* of power. There'll be work, but no more Rat work—no skulking or stealing or risking your necks. Chores around the place, yeah; everybody has to pitch in. But just helping to clean and mend things, nothing dangerous. Lessons in reading, arithmetic . . . whatever I can find someone to teach you. I want everybody to grow up with as much of an education as they can get. And *when* you're grown enough—not before—for those who still want to, the chance to fight and topple this whole fucking country. And then the next country."

I raised both hands and lowered my hood, revealing my face. Not much reaction ensued, beyond a very minor stir. My features might be foreign, but that was nothing compared to the spectacle they'd already seen. Besides, apparently the fact that Lord Seiji was the Healer was an open secret by now.

"If that's not you, then that's completely fine. You can go and I won't interfere with you at all. Everything I can offer, except the chance to fight back, the Convocation can offer better. I expect their discipline is harsher than mine will be, but maybe that's not such a terrible thing. It's a chance for a life in the middle ring and a career in the priesthood, which is a *big deal* for lowborn orphans. I would honestly recommend you take that deal and find a chance to thank Rhydion if you can arrange it, *unless* you're one of those who feels the need to stay with me."

A large part of me wanted to tell them all to just go to the orphanage. But . . . there was Aenit, expectant and fervent, and hers wasn't the only expression like that. Children had no business in a Dark Crusade. I already had a few, though, and there would be others who needed what only I could offer them. If I sent those away, they'd just get killed trying to fight back against a system that could crush them without even noticing they were there. At least . . . If they came with me, at least I could make sure they had a place in a nice, safe fortress and ensure they stayed *out* of the fighting until they were old enough. Maybe some would even grow out of wanting it. A few of the Alley Cats had already declined to fight, and there was plenty of work for them helping support the place.

It was fucked up no matter how I looked at it, but it was the best I could do for them.

I pointed at the pile still sitting in the middle of the floor, mostly food but accented by coins, expensive fabric, and a few other odds and ends way too pricey for these environs.

"If you're going to choose to leave, then you grab as much of the stash as you're able to carry. This stuff belongs to you kids; it was your hard work that earned it all. Anything you don't take will go with us, to help support whoever decides to join me. I suspect the orphanage may not let you keep much . . . Still. You can try to go it alone out there with whatever you're able to grab, but I wouldn't advise it. Lady Gray's still out there and she's lost her fucking mind. I strongly recommend the orphanage. Go to the south gate and ask the guards there to let you into the city."

"Shellheads won't let us inside the walls even in broad daylight," an older girl scoffed. "No fuckin' *way* they'll open gates for Gutter Rats in the middle of the night!"

"That's why I said the *south* gate," I said, nodding. "The guards on duty there right now were recently privy to something that may change their minds. If you stay together and go to *that* gate and no other, ask them if they'd like to help Captain Norovena get on Rhydion's good side."

Several of the orphans frowned at me, while others exchanged doubtful looks.

"It may not work," I admitted. "It'd be the smart move for them, but if they were ambitious and smart they probably wouldn't be in the Kingsguard. If they give you shit instead of helping, just back away and find a place to hole up for a few hours. Come tomorrow, the adventurers will be out looking for Rats again. Find one of them—"

"Can't," Uncle Gently rasped, laboriously dragging himself up to his hands and knees. "You *can't* take my precious little ones. They *need* me. Only their Uncle can—"

Immolate.

He dissolved into fire and screaming again, forcing me to raise my voice.

"I'm sure you already know that some of your number have already gone with the adventurers to the orphanage. Gilder, Benit, and Radon have already come with me and are safely at my place. If that makes a difference with regard to who you want to see again. If you're going toward the city and the guards won't let you in, I suggest hunkering down on the ramp within sight of the gatehouse. Lady Gray's less likely to try any bullshit right under the eyes of the Kingsguard with the whole island hunting for her head. Now, those who are leaving, let's not have a mob, yeah? Come *one at a time*—that's it, form a line—and pick up whatever you want from the pile. Do *not* take all of any one thing, leave enough for everybody else. Get some coin, some food, and something to wear. And . . . leave the booze, okay? Sorry, but alcohol is not for children. It'll stunt your growth and mess up your brain chemistry."

Uncle Gently had gone through the whole cycle while I talked, down to flickering out again, and now produced the absolute last sound I expected from him—a laugh. Not *much* of a laugh; it was definitely the weak, hoarse chuckle of a man who'd had all the fight beaten out of him, but it was enough to make me turn toward him in surprise.

He didn't try to get up again, but looked up at me with a truly maniacal grin—the rictus of a broken man who knew there was nothing in his future but more pain and then death, and thus was past fear serving him any purpose.

"You have no fucking clue," he rasped, with a giggle that trailed off into coughing. "No idea how to raise children. You must be *consistent*. Consistency! *Especially* with punishment. They need clear rules, clear boundaries, clear expectations. Off to a bad start, Healer. You established a pattern, but broke it. A name, then a reason, and *then* the fire. How are they going to trust you if you can't respect your own rules?"

He did finally push himself somewhat upright, bracing his hands against the floor to raise his torso and sneer up at me.

"That was cheating, that time. Where was the name and the reason, *Healer*? Where's your *consistency*?"

I paced slowly across the room toward him. Barely a meter away, I stopped and lowered myself carefully to one knee, bringing my head down until my face was just slightly above his.

"My name is Seiji," I said quietly. "Fuck you. **Immolate**."

At that range, it singed my eyebrows a bit. Totally worth it.

Straightening, I turned back to the children, who were watching me with dancing fire reflected in their eyes.

"All right," I said through the sound of Uncle Gently howling, backlit by the flames. "Like I told you, single file. Grab a good mix of things, and don't be greedy."

It started slowly, but picked up as the children were satisfied that I was seriously going to let them walk out unharmed with whatever they could carry.

After the first made it out with a pocketful of coins, an armful of wyddh, and a silk bedsheet draped around his shoulders like a cloak, the rest grew much more confident.

Most of them went back into the Nest for a moment; I knew they didn't own much, but it stood to reason a lot of the kids would have their own little treasures that held sentimental value to them, if nothing else. Probably encouraged to comply by my displays of terrible power and looming black-cloaked followers, none of them gave us any trouble with the single-file system, and only a few gentle verbal corrections were necessary to prevent any from trying to grab *all* of the money or a whole jar of candied nuts the size of their own torso. Or in one case, a bottle of wine. Many selected carefully from the pile while watching me and Nazralind for approval of their selections.

In the end, about two thirds of them decided they agreed with my own assessment that I was bad news. I didn't see where they went once they were out of the Nest; I *really* hoped they continued following my advice, stayed together, and made for the south gate. Ultimately, though, I felt I'd done more than enough to them by sliming them into their orphanage and then torturing their caregiver right in front of them. If they didn't want my protection after that, well, that just seemed like good sense. I had no more right to impose on them.

We were left with twelve Gutter Rats, including Aenit. They seemed to be between about seven and eleven and shared Aenit's—and Benit and Radon's, for that matter—intense stare and quiet demeanor.

Man, I really hoped I could do more for them than offer a warm place to sleep and the Dark Lord's protection. Surely *some* of the huge number of women I'd gathered at North Watch must be good with kids, right? A few were actually mothers themselves. I would only be able to consider this venture a success if, eventually, these children stopped staring at me like combat veterans.

Kids should laugh, and cause trouble, and get underfoot like Gilder and the others. If there was any mercy in this rotten world at all, they'd remember how.

Once those who chose to leave had left, I had the rest of the children and noblewomen gather up the rest of Uncle Gently's hoard and retreat to the house we'd boarded up, to wait for me to finish the next part. This time, at last, Aster was convinced to accompany them. She wasn't happy about leaving my side so soon after her angry declaration that she wouldn't again, but matters become different once there were children to protect. They needed her holding that door in case Lady Gray decided to make her presence known.

And *I* wanted them in that house and not this one. Close enough for the screaming to be audible, which was the one glaring flaw in my plan. I'd have much preferred they not be able to hear. But Gray was still out there, and I'd left the ladies with orders to howl like banshees if she turned up; at the first sound, I would drop what I was doing here and run to their aid.

Once they were gone, it was finally time to use the hammer and spikes.

Goose and Lamm stayed behind with me, which was necessary, as I needed their assistance. Uncle Gently wasn't so broken that he didn't struggle once he realized what I intended; anyone would have. But he was one out-of-shape middle-aged con man, and we were two thugs and a sorcerer. In the end, the only real difficulty he gave us was by being heavy.

Goose held him up against the exterior of the Nest by a grip on his neck, next to its front door, stoically ignoring his attempts to kick her. Lamm grabbed and wrestled his arms into place, one at a time as I worked, the gangster easily more than a match for Gently's attempts to pull away. Both my accomplices executed their role in this new war crime with the icy expressions of people embracing a justifiable evil.

And I used the tools.

I let the rage take me over, finally. Unleashed the beast and let its seething fury pound through my veins as I pounded in the spikes. Letting go of performance mode, letting my face twist into an animal snarl of hatred even as it was splattered with blood. I needed that rage, needed it to course through me, because a mentally normal person is not capable of hammering spikes into screaming, struggling human flesh.

"You have no idea what you've done," Gently rasped at me as Goose and Lamm finally released him to hang from the front of his house by his own nailed arms. He found the strength to lift his head and glare at me with an insane hatred that mirrored my own, his legs pressing desperately against the wall behind him to lift his body up so he could breathe enough to talk. "No clue what you've unleashed, *Dark Lord*. She was always so controlled. Always a plan, every action had a purpose. She has *never* been like this, killing my Rats just to make a point. But you *broke her*. Do you even know what the Dark Crusade is? *It is the end of EVERYTHING.* Nations will burn, landbridges will fall, islands will be scoured clean of life, cities will be inhabited by only the dead. You think you're going to *save* these people? Pfaah!"

He spat blood at me. I was honestly impressed he could still make a speech in his condition.

"You don't save *shit*, Seiji. You're nothing but destruction. There's no future for anyone on Ephemera as long as you're alive. Lady Gray looked into the void you represent, and *this* is what you turned her into. This was *one gangster* in *one small town*. You think *this* was bad?" He grinned maniacally, his teeth running red with blood. "Wait 'til you see what a Highlord does when he looks into the same void and breaks like she did. Or a King. Or an Emperor. It'll all burn. *Starting with everyone you've tried to help*. Remember that as you watch them die—your whores, my children, everyone. *This. Is. Your. Fault.*"

"You don't have to listen to this horseshit, Lord Seiji," Lamm stated. "Lemme break his windpipe."

"He can talk," I said quietly. "That's all he has left. And I want to send him to hell with the knowledge that his last act of defiance was a useless waste of breath, one he only got to indulge in because *I allowed it*."

I could have silenced him, of course, but I was arrested by what he said. Unable to tear my attention away from the prospect he foretold . . . Terribly afraid that he was right. But I'd have nailed *myself* to the wall before letting him know that.

The beast reared up and roared, and I willingly embraced the searing rage that blotted out everything but the act of violence right in front of me as I drew back the hammer and, with two methodical strokes, smashed his kneecaps.

Uncle Gently's scream was cut off as he slumped down the wall, unable to support himself any longer. The position was cutting off his air. That was how victims of crucifixion died—suffocation. The Romans would only break the victim's legs as a last cold mercy, so they went in minutes instead of the days it took them to lose the ability to push themselves up and keep breathing. This man didn't deserve even that paltry mercy, but I had gorged my fill of barbaric cruelty and had no more appetite for it. Already I was growing sick with what I'd just done.

It was such a strange feeling, to hate it so much, and yet not regret it.

The last tool was the paintbrush. Uncle Gently was providing plenty of crimson material with which to work. I dipped the brush in the blood pooling beneath him, and carefully scrawled my last warning in Fflyr letters across the front of the building alongside him:

CHILDKILLER

And that . . . was enough. I threw the brush down next to the discarded hammer and remaining nails, already in a puddle of the pouring blood.

"Somebody could still get him down from there," Goose pointed out as I turned to go.

After that? Without the kind of healing only *I* could provide, he'd never again use his hands, or walk.

"Then he can be their problem," I said. "Come on. Let's pick up the kids and go home."

I left behind a single, summoned slime below the dying orphan master, slowly turning crimson as it feasted on blood.

20

In Which the Dark Lord
Has His Work Cut Out for Him

It was not one of the best trips back to North Watch, but it definitely wasn't the longest or most difficult; that honor still went to the previous one, when I'd been escorting most of the population of Cat Alley, along with their various hangers-on. This group was smaller, and while the kids slowed us considerably, the ladies were experienced wilderness survivalists and did a great deal to compensate. We didn't rush, taking frequent breaks and pausing overnight to let the children get enough sleep, and in the end made it in a day and a half.

As it turned out, some of the young noblewomen were quite good with children, keeping them engaged in conversation and playing games as we walked, once we were far enough from civilization for that to be safe. As we gained some distance from Gwyllthean, the kids started lightening up noticeably. Walking in nature can do that for a person, especially if they're not used to it.

By far the worst part was the looming specter of Lady Gray, whom we all expected to jump out of every shadow. She never made an appearance, though. Not in the Gutters, and at no point during our journey back.

Undoubtedly, this had to do with the immense amount of pressure Rhydion had laid down on her while I was seeing to the dead. Still. I hated not knowing where someone like that was, or what she was up to.

"We're almost there," I said. "Should see it within the hour, maybe less."

"Less, I think," Aster added. "We're closer than that."

"I'll take your word for it; every patch of this hell forest looks the same as every other to me."

Aenit, who was walking in the lead with me, just nodded, eyes ahead. She didn't really talk unless she had something specific to say that she judged worth the effort.

I had wondered, initially, why Aenit hadn't been among the kids Gilder considered trustworthy to recruit, and whether I might be making a mistake by relying on her, but since then, I'd figured it out. He probably just hadn't known her that well. She was generally not interested in being known, and hadn't been very sociable even with the other Rats who'd come with us. Aenit had latched onto me as a source of . . . I dunno, safety, I guess? She still didn't say much, but watched and listened and kept close by. Not unlike Benit, but more intense.

That was when I heard it. So did Newneh, the gwynnek raising her head and chirping a warning to her rider.

"Ah!" I grinned, craning my neck to peer up through khora branches. There it was—the distant battlements of North Watch, and the frantic barking of Junko racing toward us. "Kids, ladies, we're home. I'll go ahead, calm the dog and wait by the gates. Biribo, you can guide 'em the rest of the way, right? See you in a minute."

I set off ahead of the group at a brisk trot while a few confused voices made acknowledging remarks behind me. Biribo, at least, I trusted to figure out what was up. Probably some of the others, too, but mostly I didn't want to scare the kids. With Biribo's senses and Aster's artifacts, if Lady Gray chose the brief moment of my absence from the group to jump out at them, they could hold out long enough for me to run back. Hopefully.

And meanwhile, I would find out whether what I feared had come to pass.

I was pretty sure at least some of the others had had the same thought. Aster definitely, probably Goose. We'd been operating for a while now under the assumption that North Watch was a secret which could not be kept, and Lady Gray was highly motivated not just to destroy my organization as I'd done hers, but to *hurt* me. She had been notably absent since depositing her last grotesque message outside the Kingsguard stations. I had thought, when I decided to spend that day in a vigil and that night excising the cancer that was Uncle Gently, that she would hover around Gwyllthean for the chance to strike at me while I was there. But during the day and a half we'd been heading back, I had realized that, if she wanted, she could have stolen a march and reached North Watch before us. That was what none of us had said aloud, because there hadn't been a moment when we could be certain none of the children were listening.

The fact was, I did not know what I would find in the fortress when I got there and had reason to fear the worst. It was a good sign that Junko was alive and apparently normal, but . . .

The dog met me with her usual ecstatic yipping and jumping about, and I gave her a quick hug and a scritch behind the ears because how could I not? But mindful of the group behind me quickly catching up, I kept moving forward, ordering Junko to heel.

Perceptive of my mood as always, she instantly fell into step alongside me, tail furiously wagging in her happiness at being reunited, but otherwise alert as I almost ran the last meters to the gates of North Watch.

Two women I couldn't identify from down below were on watch above the gates; one waved at me. So far, so good. I didn't begin to properly relax until the actual welcoming committee, who were probably alerted to my approach by Junko's barking, met me in the open gates themselves.

My people hadn't been sitting on their hands during my Gwyllthean adventure, I noted with approval; khora had been cleared back from the fortress's outer walls in both directions, and just inside and off the main path, the pair of huge gates looked to be in the latter stages of renovation, waiting to be finished and hung once we acquired the necessary hinges and fittings. Akorshil was sturdy stuff; they looked pretty good for having been buried under a trash pile for years. I took all this in with a glance before focusing on the three who'd come to meet me.

"Is everything all right?" I demanded.

Minifrit raised her eyebrows, taking a long drag on her pipe. Sakin grinned a very Sakin grin, which might have meant anything or nothing. Standing right between them, Kasser looked somewhat harried, and it was he who answered.

"No notable problems, Lord Seiji. Some scuffles and . . . Well, putting this many people together in one fortress when they aren't used to it obviously causes tension, but Minifrit's been handling it very well. Are *you* all right? Where's Aster? Where's *Biribo*?"

"They're coming with the others," I said impatiently. "You haven't been attacked? No casualties? Unexplained . . . incidents?"

Even Sakin stopped grinning by that point. "We're renovating a fort in the middle of the wilderness, Lord Seiji; weird shit happens out here," he said. "What *kind* of incidents are you looking for?"

"Others?" Minifrit asked pointedly.

"In a minute," I said, still terse even as I was beginning to relax. Okay, the worst had not happened, nor apparently even the notably bad, but this was no time to get complacent. "We're moving to a defensive posture, and I want everyone on high alert. I need watchers on the walls at *all* times, each one positioned where they can see and be seen by at least two others. Minifrit, adjust the duty schedule in whatever way is necessary to make this happen. Some kind of impediment *has* to go across this opening until the gate is finished, and I want every exterior window accessible from outside the walls boarded up."

Now all of them had gone still and sharp-eyed, Minifrit staring particularly narrowly at me.

"Lady Gray knows where we are," she guessed.

"I don't know that for a confirmed fact, but it's my assumption North Watch is a secret that cannot be kept much longer." I glanced over my shoulder, hearing the steps of the others catching up. "I'll tell you the long version later, but in brief, I accidentally finished destroying her organization, but she survived and escaped and appears to have gone utterly batshit insane and is . . . miffed at me."

Kasser let out a low whistle, raising his eyebrows. Sakin laughed aloud in apparent glee, very nearly earning himself a slime to the pelvis, and Minifrit just grimaced for a moment as she exhaled smoke through her nose.

"And you are alone and empty-handed," she said pointedly. "Any luck acquiring the supplies which were the primary purpose for your trip, Lord Seiji? Or the *people* you went to secure?"

I winced. "Ah . . . As you might have gathered, things did not go according to plan. Everybody we could identify as a possible target is under the protection of the Kingsguard or the King's Guild or the Convocation, and a lot of them are being taken off the island. Auldmaer has my shopping list, but we're gonna have to make a separate trip soon to pick everything up. I didn't come back empty-handed, though!"

They proved me right with perfect timing, the group beginning to straggle into view around the last bend of the path, Aster in the lead with Biribo buzzing about her head. Junko turned back and barked a greeting at them, tail wagging furiously. Nobody appeared to be distressed; Gray had still not made an appearance.

"Is that . . ." Minifrit stared past me with open incredulity, a rare lapse in her normally controlled expression. "Lord Seiji, did you really just acquire two dozen blended Gutter Rats and . . . somehow . . . noblewomen?"

"Oh yeah, you would not *believe* the shit he drags home," Sakin cackled. "One time it was a stray dog. And then a whole mess of whores!"

Both of them gave him sidelong looks, Kasser apprehensive and Minifrit openly scathing. I started to wonder if there were long-running tensions here I should worry about, though frankly it came as a relief to me to have someone as strong-willed and smart as Minifrit on hand to counterbalance whatever Sakin might get up to.

"Your eyes do not deceive you, Minifrit," I said aloud. "I'll need your help getting everyone settled in."

"Well, you arrived at a good time," said Kasser. "Dinner's being served in the hall right now."

"Gwynneks," Minifrit said sharply. "You brought . . . fifteen gwynneks. *What* are we supposed to do with these?"

"Yeah, we sort of don't have a stable anymore," Sakin commented.

I could already see several of my new nonhorse horse girls stiffening up in offense and intervened to avoid starting everybody off on the wrong foot.

"Gwynneks are extremely useful creatures," I told Minifrit. "I've already seen how fast they can move through difficult terrain like the khora forest. Considering a cornerstone of our strategy is going to be controlling disparate bandit territories from *this* extremely noncentral location, they'll be absolutely priceless."

"Oh yes," she said, smoke dripping from her lips with every syllable like a visible manifestation of the sarcasm in her voice. "Not only that, but they're a fine military addition. Absolutely vicious in combat and far more willing to fight than dhawls or even horses. Clever, too. Altogether a tremendous asset, Lord Seiji. Do you know, then, why every nation doesn't bother to keep a gwynnek cavalry?"

I blinked. ". . . do they not?"

"Because," she said acidly, "they are carnivores *the size of horses*. Not only are they notoriously difficult to train and uncooperative with anyone other than individuals with whom they've bonded, they require *meat*. Lots of it, daily! You've brought us the most expensive and difficult possible mounts at a moment when, last I checked, we were little more than a week from running out of food."

"That's actually not a hardship on largely wild and underhunted territory like most of Dount," Nazralind broke in, smiling reassuringly at her. Minifrit looked unimpressed, Sakin . . . well, like Sakin. Kasser, though, was visibly uneasy to find himself facing an actual elf. "We've been keeping them without trouble in forest camps. This is *perfect* land for it, in fact! They can hunt not only for their own needs, but add to our meat stores for the personnel."

"Mmm." Minifrit finished another long drag and blew a streamer of spicy smoke directly at Nazralind, who, fortunately, was too far away for it to reach her before dissipating. "I don't suppose Lord Seiji thought to inform you, my lady, that North Watch is in the territory of—in fact, quite close to the main village of—a tribe of catfolk with whom we have a tense and ambiguous relationship. Who outnumber us roughly two to one, and who *will* take it as a hostile act if we start hunting in their lands."

". . . ah." Nazralind turned a wide-eyed look on me. "Well, that's . . ."

"Wait, you can't *hunt*?" Lady Loreith peered about from atop her own mount. "Or even gather? How else are you *feeding* everyone in this wilderness?"

Okay, so these details had slipped my mind, but I wasn't caught without an answer.

"The plan was already to take out nearby bandit gangs and absorb their territory," I soothed. "We've already started on that with Auron's gang, remember? Once we wipe out the gang over there on Clan Yldyllich lands, we'll have access to a whole lot of wild khora with no one claiming it. And *those* are the assholes who like to murder and rape people for sport, so it'll be a quick and clean operation. No recruitment or difficult parts like last time, just killing them all. We can have it done tomorrow."

"Just like that, hm," one of the ladies whom I couldn't see muttered.

"So the big plan is to *hunt* on Clan Yldyllich's lands?" Minifrit said, her voice tight. "Lord Seiji . . ."

Nazralind turned over her shoulder. "Hey, Mimi! Care to weigh in on this?"

Another rider guided her gwynnek forward, stepping carefully past the Rats, who eased out of the way. They'd relaxed around the huge birds considerably over the last few days but were still wisely careful not to go anywhere near those massive talons.

"That's actually not a bad idea," the woman who'd come forward said, nodding to Nazralind. "The Yldyllich Clansguard's reputation for brutality will discourage competition, but the truth is the Clan only cares about protecting their toll road. The Clansguard doesn't even patrol deep into the khora; that's the only way a bandit gang could have survived in there. Poaching is only a problem if the Clan in question values its hunting rights, which Yldyllich doesn't. Long as we're careful not to be seen and don't bother anybody on the road, hunting and trapping in there shouldn't be a problem. I also have contacts I can reach out to that might make our movements easier. Safer, at least."

"You are . . . remarkably well-informed, my lady," Minifrit said warily.

The woman Nazralind had called Mimi grinned and released her reins to fold down her hands, which made Minifrit blink in surprise. "Lady Yldyllich Miriami, at your service."

"I know you're aware we've accumulated enemies, Lord Seiji," Nazralind added, "but we also have friends all over this island, both commoners and even a few highborn. I assure you we'll pull our weight."

"I never doubted it," I said, winking. "Satisfied, Miss Minifrit?"

The ex-madam heaved a sigh, tendrils of pipe smoke curling away into the evening air. "It seems you have indeed planned appropriately, my lord. Forgive my skepticism."

"Not at all, that inquiring mind of yours is one of the things that makes you so useful. Now, as for getting everyone settled in . . ."

She looked critically over the group. "Mm. These children look exhausted. Please take them directly to the mess hall for something to eat; I will make sure there are . . ." Minifrit's eyes darted across the group, lips moving soundlessly for a moment as she performed a rapid head count. ". . . twelve beds prepared when they're finished. Ladies, we are going to have to improvise some shelter for your mounts. I gather you would prefer to see to that before your own meals?"

"Correct," Nazralind said with a grin. "They won't need much, though. We're all accustomed to roughing it in the forest."

"Why doesn't the famous North Watch have a stable?" Sadhith demanded.

"Oh, it used to," Sakin said seriously, "but Lord Seiji turned it into a bath house."

All of them perked up visibly and there ensued a general chorus of "Ooh!"

"Kasser, if you would accompany us?" Minifrit suggested. "This is no time for anything too complicated or permanent, but we may need to rig up some semblance of a pen. Even if they don't need a roof, we do *not* need anyone accidentally wandering into a bunch of surprised gwynneks in the middle of the night."

"Uh . . . sure." Kasser actually took a step backward, now staring at the gwynneks with visible unease. Junko was also staring at them, pressed against my leg and no longer wagging her tail. She wasn't trembling or anything, inferring from my own relaxed demeanor that there was no danger here, but I couldn't blame her and Kasser for their reactions. If you weren't familiar with these escapees from a dinosaur movie, they were extremely alarming to see up close.

"They're all very well-trained," Nazralind assured him with a winsome smile. "Don't worry, Newneh is quite sociable, in fact. You want to pet her nose?"

She guided the bird forward slightly, and Kasser retreated to widen the space between them.

"No! I mean . . . No thank you, my lady."

"Naz, please don't give Kasser a hard time," I interjected. "Kasser, the birds are safe, I promise, as long as you don't do anything stupid around them."

"Define stupid," Sakin requested, grinning maniacally.

I ignored him, turning to the Rats. "All right, that's enough of that drama. C'mon, kids. I dunno about you, but I could *really* use a hot meal right about now. Sounds like they have 'em ready, too."

"Hot food?" Aenit said skeptically. She was usually the first to speak, the others following her lead. "Like . . . whole meals? For us? Why?"

"D-did she say *beds*?" stammered a boy half-hiding behind her.

Minifrit's face momentarily tightened, mirroring the sensation that gripped my own chest at this. The Alley Cats and Gutter Rats had had an unfriendly relationship back in the Gutters, but with all that in the past, it was reassuring to see that she felt the same pain at the spectacle of deprivation these poor kids made.

"I told you," I said as gently as I could, "I take care of my people. Food, beds, clothing, and whatever else you need. That's what you're here for, after all. C'mon, you should be able to meet Gilder and the others inside; they never miss a mealtime."

"I bet they don't," Aenit muttered as she and the rest of the Rats trailed along behind me toward the central fortress, whose main doors opened conveniently onto the foyer that led right into the mess hall.

Immediately, I could tell this wasn't going to go as smoothly as I had hoped, to judge by the raised voices I could hear from inside. Shrill voices that sounded like they were on the verge of transitioning from screaming to fists.

Great.

Fortunately, it was a small confrontation, despite its volume, and almost everyone in the room was eating their dinner rather than joining in. Mostly half-turned to gawk, but at least not making it worse. No, it was just Sicellit and Ydleth nose-to-nose in the middle of the aisle and evidently on the verge of violence.

Not what I'd expected. Sicellit was one of Minifrit's unofficial lieutenants and usually pretty even-tempered. Ydleth was a former prostitute from one of the poorer brothels, who I mostly remembered because back when I was doing weekly healing trips I noticed she tended to get beaten up more than most.

"Who the fuck are *you* to tell me—"

"You have *no business here* if you're going to act—"

"Nobody put you in charge of me, cunt!"

"*At least I have—*"

"Ara, ara, *ara.*" I projected hard from the diaphragm as if I were commanding a stadium, my voice cutting through the shrieking match without the indignity of yelling. Everyone stopped what they were doing, turning to stare at me. Including, fortunately, the two combatants.

I kept my features composed, even as I was internally cringing at myself.

Goddammit, I did it again! *Why did this keep happening?* I'd never said "ara ara" in my *life* before I came to Ephemera, I swear.

"*Well?*" I prompted, raising my eyebrows. "Is someone going to *explain* this nonsense I had to walk in on?"

Both women turned to stare at me and pointed at each other, swelling up like angry bullfrogs. Ydleth was faster to speak by a hair.

"*She—*"

"Wait!" I held up one hand, silencing them both. It was gratifying I still had at least that much control over this situation. "Ladies, is this going to be an *involved* explanation?"

"Oh, just wait 'til you hear about *this*, Lord Seiji," Sicellit snarled.

"I was afraid of that," I sighed. And to think ten minutes ago I'd been afraid they were dead. "I will be with you in a moment, girls. Hey, Gilder! You in here?"

"Right here, Lord Seiji!" He popped up from one of the tables nearest the dais—where, I noted, Donon had set up the big meeting table as a serving station with big cauldrons of stew and piles of wyddh.

"Perfect, are the others with you?"

On command, Benit and Radon poked their heads out from behind the crowd, though they didn't speak up, as was fairly typical.

"Great, c'mere. I have a task for you. See, kids, I told you they were fine."

"Holy shit!" Grinning, Gilder came skittering forward in such a hurry that he actually dashed between Sicellit and Ydleth, though Radon and Benit circled around them more warily. "Inon! Tamin! Dony! And is that Aenit? Wait, where's everybody else? What happened?"

"I was planning to help you kids get settled in personally," I said, turning back to Aenit and the others, "but as you can see, I now have to deal with whatever *this* is. So. Gilder, please take Aenit and the others to get some dinner and give them a rundown on how we do things here. Aenit, while you're eating, please catch Gilder and the others up on what went down in the city. I promise I'll be available to talk about it later if you want, but it'll have to wait a bit."

"Huh." Gilder folded his skinny arms, brazenly looking Aenit up and down. "How come *you* got top name in this crowd?"

She curled her lip, meeting his stare. "How come *you* did?"

I tensed in spite of myself for a second, fearing I had just created yet another pointless argument I was going to have to settle before getting back to the first one, and before I could actually eat and get off my feet . . .

But Gilder, bless him, only matched Aenit stare-for-stare for a moment before grinning amiably. "Well, hell, fair enough. C'mon, you guys look fuckin' starved. Let's go get something hot into you. You're gonna love this, the food's *real* good and they let you have as much as you want! Long as you don't piss off the cooks, I mean. You'll never believe who they got running the kitchen—it's Gannit, that old lady from the Jugs! Stay on her good side. Oh, but that's Donon up there at the tables, he's cool. Don't filch anything, that'll just get your hands whacked an' there's no point, he'll give you more'n enough anyway . . ."

His running commentary didn't let up for a moment, only diminishing slightly in volume as he led the rest of the children up to the front toward Donon's serving table. I tuned them out after a moment, deciding this was probably in good hands. Donon had been good with the kids so far. So had Gannit, for that matter, though she was more inclined to whack grabby little hands with her ladle.

I turned back to Sicellit and Ydleth, putting on a cold smile that made them both ease warily backward. That was a good start; I was not in the mood for whatever bullshit this was, and so much the better if they knew it.

"Thanks for your patience, ladies," I said pleasantly. "So! What in the hell is the matter with you two?"

21

In Which the Dark Lord
Lays Down the Law

"I don't mind sleeping in a barracks with other women," Sicellit stated in a particularly tightly wound voice. "I *understand* those are the available accommodations out here and it's not much of a hardship. Hell, it's more comfortable than my own room back at the Cat *because* I specifically do not have to worry about men climbing on top of me in there!"

"Oh *please*," Ydleth sneered, dripping disdain. "Absolutely no one—"

"Well, not *yet*!" Sicellit snarled back.

"Whoa, hold up, I'm confused." I sure as hell was. *Surely* nobody had tried to assault Sicellit—or any of the women here? Everybody in this place knew most of its population were ex–Alley Cats who'd just slaughtered a bunch of thugs over exactly that kind of thing.

"Just . . . This doesn't need to be your problem, Lord Seiji," Sicellit said, visibly trying to restrain her temper. "I just don't want to share a dorm with a man. I don't think that's *unreasonable*. Miss Minifrit can have him moved—"

"Oh, *fuck you*, you self-righteous twat!" Ydleth shrieked. "*I'm* not moving because *you've* decided to be a bitch about something that's *none of your fucking business*!"

"Then why are you in here making it *everyone's* business at the top of your lungs in the middle of dinner?!"

"*You started this!*"

"*Like hell I did!*"

"Shut up." I spoke more sharply than I'd intended; the confusion was not helping my already fatigued mental state. "Sicellit, *what* are you on about? Is there a man in your dorm?"

Wordlessly, she pointed at Ydleth. There was some muttering from around the room, but mostly anticipatory silence that warned me any action I took here could have far-reaching consequences.

I blinked at Ydleth, who looked furious enough to kill. And also, now that I looked closely, on the verge of tears. Past the verge, in fact; she angrily scrubbed at her eyes while I stared, failing to disguise the trembling of her lower lip.

Wait . . . What?

Ydleth was tall, sure—taller than me, in fact—but fine-boned and even somewhat scrawny. She was one of those people who'd probably look awkward in motion if she hadn't so mastered the exaggerated swaying walk and flirtatious mannerisms prostitutes were so good at. I knew her as someone excessively fond of off-color jokes and irrepressibly cheerful despite how constantly she seemed to acquire black eyes and bloody lips. This fury was as out of character on her as it was on the normally unflappable Sicellit. The only thing about her that really stood out among the Cats was that she wore one of those high-necked tight undershirts instead of showing off cleavage like every other . . .

Oh.

It occurred to me that I might have just blithely waded into something far more complicated than I was prepared to deal with.

"How long have you two been at this?" I asked, stalling frantically for time. "Frankly, outbursts like this are out of character for both of you."

"Oh, it's been *all* day, Lord Seiji," said Keffin from a nearby table. I vaguely recalled her being one of their roommates. "Sicellit saw Ydleth changing, Ydleth freaked out, and it's just gone from there."

"They're being a pair of big fat children about it," added Jadrin, folding her arms and looking condescending. "Both of 'em keep pissing away opportunities to de-escalate and clawing for each other's eyes instead."

"Sicellit's not wrong, though," someone muttered from behind me, *just* loud enough I knew she meant to be heard but could pretend otherwise.

"Oh, fuck off," snapped Leiret, a woman who'd worked in the same brothel as Ydleth, jumping to her feet across the aisle. "Ydleth's a sweet girl, and her business is none of anybody else's!"

That, of course, was the cue for everybody who had an opinion about this—which was evidently most of them—to begin offering them all at once. Ydleth looked like she wanted very much to die on the spot. Somewhat to my surprise, so did Sicellit.

I pointed one finger in the air and fired a Sparkspray at the ceiling, causing instant quiet.

"Okay," I said carefully. "Ydleth, not to be indelicate . . ."

"Oh, here it comes," she growled, folding her arms.

That caused a spike of irritation to flare through me, which caused Junko to lay her ears back and growl. Ydleth immediately looked wary, and I continued with a lot less hesitation.

"So I gather that back in Cat Alley you were a provider of *specialty* services to customers of very particular tastes?"

It could be hard to tell with the brown-skinned lowborn, but Ydleth's cheeks definitely darkened in a blush. She put on a defiant posture, however, tossing her hair back and raising her chin.

"Yeah, what of it?"

"So . . . Just saying, if you don't have to do that anymore—"

"*This is who I am!*" she snapped, taking an aggressive step toward me.

Junko barked sharply and she immediately backed off again, which I judged adequate remonstration and refrained from calling her down further.

"So. Just to be clear. You are a woman?"

"*Yes! I am!*"

I shrugged, turning back to Sicellit. "Says she's a woman. Seems like she'd know. We done here?"

No, I didn't actually think that would work, I'm not an idiot. It was worth trying, though. At that moment I'd have tried anything that even *might* get me out of this debacle. Give me murder and carnage, anything but *awkwardness.*

"*He has a cock!*" Sicellit roared, pointing at Ydleth.

"Did she try to stick it in you?"

That spilled out of my mouth before my brain could catch up, causing Sicellit to gape at me and several of the onlookers to snicker.

"Wh— I don't—"

"Cause I didn't think this really needed to be said, considering who we've got gathered here," I continued sternly, "but I will absolutely not stand for that kind of bullshit. Anybody forcing themselves on anyone else in my fortress is asking for me to invent an exciting new way for them to die. So I'll ask you again, Sicellit—did Ydleth try anything like that with you?"

"I—*no*, it's just . . . He doesn't belong in—"

"Then what's the problem here?" I demanded. "If you don't get along with your roommate, fine, talk to Minifrit about changing rooms. I can't see any good reason for either of you to be screaming in the mess hall or dragging each other's personal business in front of the whole place."

"I—you can't—that isn't—" Sicellit seemed on the verge of some kind of episode, which was clearly not being helped by Ydleth's growing expression of smugness. "You can't just *decide* you're a woman! Lord Seiji, you *can't* tolerate this!"

"*Really*, Sicellit? You wanna live under an authority that investigates and enforces the contents of your pants? Can't think of a *single* way that might backfire on you?"

I knew that was the wrong thing to say the instant it was too late. Multiple people cackled with glee, including Ydleth, and Sicellit clenched her fists in impotent fury. I already knew there was more going on here than the question of Ydleth's junk; these two had been at each other at least all day, and even that had probably been building up since before the big reveal this morning. *I* didn't care about their personal business; I just needed to keep the peace and lay down some rules of conduct, and humiliating Sicellit wasn't going to accomplish any of that. It would just alienate her. Which could cause me trouble with Minifrit, who I knew relied on Sicellit a lot.

Ugh, what a fucking mess.

From the corner of my eye, I saw movement from the direction of the door. Kasser had just slipped in, watching all this warily and keeping well back from it. No sign of Minifrit or Naz and the girls; apparently they were still getting the gwynneks squared away and had decided they didn't need his help.

Wait. *Kasser.*

Of my initial bandit crew, he'd been the most hostile to me at first, which I'd put down to having Immolated him that time, but it had to be said I had responded to his abrasiveness with my own and that had definitely not helped. *Until* the episode with the Spirit. I'd shown Kasser some kindness, and then started giving him responsibility, crediting his successes and granting him a high position as he proved himself capable, and now here he was, one of my most valuable supporters.

And that reminded me of my impromptu rant in the forest, about how stupid it was that he and Harold were given such a hard time over something that didn't affect anyone else.

That was it—that was my out. A way to accomplish my goal of using this incident to establish some standards for the overall group, without taking sides in this ridiculous catfight or declaring a position on the oh-so-pressing issue of Ydleth's crotch, because the *fuck* I was touching that.

"Hush," I ordered, and the laughing ceased. Not as instantly, this time, but it trailed off within a couple of seconds.

I took a few steps to the side and leaned against the edge of the clearest table in range, half-sitting there. For four more seconds I let the silence hang, ratcheting up the anticipation, and then spoke in a deliberately more thoughtful tone.

"Sicellit, have you ever given any thought to *why* you do the things you do?"

She scowled at me, clenching her fists again, and I shook my head.

"Sorry, that was poorly phrased. I'm not trying to pick on you."

I paused again, suggesting by my expression that it was for thought, but in actuality for dramatic effect.

"People have an inherent need to *categorize*. We need to know how to define something or we'll be bothered by it, and seeing a thing out of its proper place is like an itch in the brain. Come on, everybody's had that experience from time to time. You see a thing where it doesn't go and it's like somebody poked you in the eye."

A couple of chuckles at that, and a lot of nods. Good, we were making progress.

"So obviously, that trait is really easy for the people in power to turn against you. All they have to do is create the suggestion that somebody doesn't *belong*, that they aren't *right*, and boom! Instant scapegoat. And then, that gives them other levers to pull. Bullying, for example, is a huge problem in every society that's ever existed because it's inherently a *bonding* activity. Ganging up on somebody brings us closer together! It's pretty fucked up, but it's true. Nothing binds people into a group quite like having an enemy to fight—and in the absence of an enemy, having a victim to pick on creates exactly the same effect."

"You think I was *bullying* her?" Sicellit burst out.

"No," I said with open exasperation, "I think *you two* are suffering from a personality clash and a collective lack of maturity. Seriously, I expect better public behavior from Gilder."

"It's not hard, girls," Gilder himself piped up from the other end of the room. "Just mind your own business and don't be an asshole. Super simple; give it a try!"

I felt the beginning of what promised to be a truly spectacular headache blossom directly behind my left eye.

"I am simply making it clear," I said loudly before this could derail any harder, "since you've decided to have this out in front of damn well everyone, why I will not be tolerant of any bullshit directed at Ydleth over this in the future. Because—and this is the important part—all that stuff I just talked about? *We will not be doing that here.*"

I stood up again, slowly turning my head to take in the whole room, noting with approval the intent attention fixated on me from all sides.

"As far as enemies and bonding activities go? We are *more* than covered. There are plenty of people who want us all dead; we will be directing our aggressive energies at *them*, and not at one another. Look around you, folks. We eat together, train together, work together, and together we will systematically cut the ground out from under our enemies and smile as we watch them die with our boots on their necks."

That got me a round of cheers, which I rewarded with a grim smile.

"The people you see in this room are everything you have in this world. And together, out here in the wilderness, we are *free* of the expectations that were only forced upon us all in the first place to keep us under control. I want you all to think about that—about what you were taught is and isn't allowed for people to be and do, and *why*. In the Dark Crusade we have no need to force individuals into some universal mold. Here, you can *be who you are*, and nobody but you gets to decide what that means.

"I don't care what your background is. Lowborn or high, human or goblin or beastfolk or *whatever* else might eventually join us, we're all equally valid. You can love who you love, however they're willing to let you, and nobody but you gets to determine your identity. If Ydleth says she's a woman, that is the beginning and end of the matter. If Donon over there decides he wants to be a really tall, oddly colored goblin with stunted ears and weird teeth, then fine, he can be a goblin. You don't need to agree with or even accept someone else's claims about themselves, but you need to leave them alone and mind your business if you can't. Understand?"

Donon raised his hand. "Uh, just to be clear, I don't think I'm a goblin. I just like them."

Laughter ensued, further throwing off my rhythm. Motherfucker, so help me I was gonna go over there and kick him in the jewels . . .

"It was just an example, Donon," I said patiently. "For now, have I made my expectations plain?"

"Yes, Lord Seiji," Sicellit said stiffly. She definitely didn't look happy, but I thought she seemed . . . I don't know, less wound up. Hopefully this wasn't going to become a recurrent *thing*, at least.

"With all that said," I continued, "personalities are what they are and people who legitimately can't stand each other, for whatever reason, don't necessarily need to share sleeping quarters. If you—or *anyone*—is having a roommate problem, talk to Minifrit about getting a new room."

Ydleth snorted loudly, folding her arms. "Hell, why should she get to scurry off after all the shit she's pulled today?"

I rather think the look I directed at her was sufficient warning that she was one more careless word away from an in-person demonstration of Dark Lord magic, even before Junko growled a pointed agreement with my change of mood. I had been *that close* to defusing this, and the brat had the pig-headed gall to start it up again?

"I'm just saying," Ydleth protested, "that's like rewarding someone for being *dhak!*"

Minifrit, in that improbably swift and stealthy way of hers, had materialized seemingly by magic and rapped Ydleth sharply between the eyes with her pipe.

"Learn to pick your battles, girl," she said in a tone that brooked no further nonsense while Ydleth reeled backward, clutching at her forehead. "And, in general, pick *fewer* of them. Both of you, *sit down* and eat. I will deal with you both in *detail* later, and I cannot advise strongly enough that you draw no further attention to yourselves in the meantime."

The pair hunched their shoulders and slunk away in opposite directions. Fortunately for them, they didn't have to be the target of any further group derision as a splendid distraction had just appeared. Gasps and mutters swelled throughout the mess hall, and people turned to stare at the front doors, where the rest of my new arrivals had just come in.

At their head stood Nazralind, head uncovered to display her pointed ears and implausibly beautiful features—likely the first elf many of the low-born around me had seen in person, and undoubtedly the first who wasn't an enemy. Behind her came her whole coterie of pale, dark-eyed and mostly-blonde friends. Even in their travel-stained masculine clothing, the Fflyr caste system made it clear that we had just been joined by our first defectors from the ruling class.

"Oh, that smells *fantastic*," Nazralind said cheerily, striding straight down the central aisle with no indication of unease. "Thank the Goddess we got here at dinnertime. I would kick my own mother down the stairs for a hot meal right now."

"That won't be necessary," I said dryly. "Go on up to the serving table, ladies. Donon will get you set up with everything you need."

"Much obliged, Lord Seiji," the elf said, folding down her hands at me, and then followed my directions with the rest of her coterie trailing along behind. I was impressed by how utterly unperturbed they all seemed by the whispering and staring that followed them everywhere.

I could certainly do with a meal myself, but in that moment, I felt a pressing need to get out from under the expectant regard of . . . everyone. Ideally before I fell asleep standing up or had a lapse of temper, which would damage morale. I made my way carefully toward the far door that led to the kitchen, watching as Nazralind collected a plate and casually asked several dumbstruck former whores at the nearest table if she could join them. The rest of the ladies did likewise; there was room in the mess hall for them to cluster together at one of the unoccupied tables near the front, but instead they dispersed, politely slipping into open spots among the rest of the crew and visibly turning on the charm.

Now *that* was a smart move in their position, and I didn't doubt for a second that it had been preplanned. That was Nazralind—useless in the strategy and tactics department that she might as well have just been isekai'd here from some high school drama club, but her social skills were absolutely on point. The benefits of a noblewoman's education.

"Hey, Biribo," I said as I ducked into the dark corridor leading toward the kitchen, "how much trouble is it going to be integrating the . . . philosophy I just laid out with an actual Viryan culture, when we start having to deal with one?"

"Boss, that might as well have *been* Viryan philosophy. They're all different in a variety of ways, but that emphasis on self-determination and the worth of the individual? Classic stuff. You should fit right in."

"Good, one less future headache," I muttered. I really wished I had bothered to learn about political philosophies beyond "they're all stupid." Which, to be fair, they *are*, but when I'd had internet access I had never imagined I would one day need to implement one. I had *definitely* not handled the revelation about Ydleth very well, but fuck it. I wasn't trying to build some kind of utopia out here; I just needed these people to *fall in line*. "At least that mess is settled."

"I really admire your optimism," Aster said, making me jump; I hadn't noticed her following me, "if you think that is in any way settled."

"It is *settled*," I declared with a scowl as we stepped into the kitchen. "I have *settled* it. And anyone who *unsettles* it is going to spend some time burning and screaming. I have had enough of this asinine drama."

"If you do that," she said flatly, "I will stab you myself."

I rounded on her, and instead of following up on her threat, she reached out and took me by both shoulders, giving me a fond smile.

"That was a *good start*. I get how frustrating it is, but this is now past the point where shows of force are going to help. What these people needed was guidance and expectations, and you just gave them that. In that uniquely Seiji way, where you're apparently well-meaning and not even wrong but still manage to be the biggest possible prick about it. *Now*, let me and Minifrit and the others take over, okay? Trying to *enforce* good behavior isn't really going to work; it has to be encouraged, guided."

"Yeah, no shit," Gannit commented from where she was dishing something up from a cauldron over the fire. "What's this about you *burninating* people, Dark Lord Crankypants? Bad boys gotta eat in the kitchen with the help."

I realized what she was doing was setting up a serving of bread and stew on the kitchen table, and now pulled out a chair for me with her characteristic saucy grin. At the sudden reminder that *I* was one of the only people in this place who hadn't yet eaten, my stomach growled embarrassingly.

"Well said," Minifrit agreed, stepping into the kitchen. "I mean Aster, of course, not Gannit."

"Oh, up yours," Gannit cackled. "And put out that fucking pipe in my kitchen! What the hell is wrong with you, girl? Don't spray *smoke* where people are cooking."

"*Thank you*," I exclaimed, seating myself and grabbing the spoon while Gannit added another setting for Aster. "I keep telling her about that damn pipe, but does she listen?"

"On the subject of people who don't listen," said Minifrit, sliding into the seat opposite me, "Aster does have the right of it, Lord Seiji. Sicellit is not a cruel or judgmental person; I rather think she would have been supportive of any less quarrelsome girl in Ydleth's situation, but *that* one has a big mouth and a chip on her shoulder. I will effect a reconciliation there, regardless of how much extra work it will be, because that is by far in the best interests of both them and the organization. Threats or violence at this point would only solidify mutual hatred."

"Yeah, well, threats and violence are all I have to work with," I mumbled around a mouthful of bread. My god, it was delicious. Hunger really is the best sauce.

"That isn't true," Minifrit said gently, smiling at me. "Not anymore. You have *us* to step in where your own talents don't apply. Thank you for what you said out there, Lord Seiji, that was surprisingly well-handled. You've done your part, now have a well-earned rest and let me do mine."

I had the vague sense that immediately surrendering control over whatever I had just set in motion might come back to bite me later, but by that point I just didn't have the energy to fuss over it any further. I was famished and now that I was sitting down and eating, the fatigue hit me like a truck. It had been a *brutal* few days.

For once, somebody else could clean up the mess.

22

In Which the Dark Lord
Does Not Bring Home the Bacon

Things were changing around North Watch.

It wasn't practical to entertain business guests in the kitchen, now that the kitchen was actually serving its intended purpose—preparing food for over a hundred people three times a day, plus cleaning up after all that food prep; it was bustling with activity more often than not. The night of my return from Gwyllthean I'd been able to catch it in a lull during dinner while everybody but Gannit was out in the mess hall, and taken advantage of the quiet (once I got some food down) to shout down the goblin tunnel.

Maugro wasn't in, but a little green fellow I hadn't met before jotted down my information request and promised his boss would visit in the morning.

So here we were, in the conference room, which necessitated letting Maugro get a good look at my operation as he was led here from the goblin tunnel, but that couldn't be helped. At least I'd finally managed some proper accommodations. At my request, Kasser had been at work on that goblin-friendly furniture I'd casually promised way back when Maugro and I had first met. He had built a goblin chair, which impressed me and seemed to please Maugro to no end. The seat and back were goblin-sized, and it was elevated enough that when pulled up to the table—well, nothing would make Maugro as tall as the rest of us, but it put him more on our level—the chair's legs splayed outward slightly for stability, and the rungs bracing them were flattened to serve as steps. It even had hinged armrests which could be lifted so a goblin could climb in, and then lowered into place for comfort.

After praising the seat, to Kasser's visible satisfaction, and partaking of some actual breakfast and tea—I did like having real hospitality to offer my business associates—Maugro got down to the first matter on which I'd called him to consult.

"The kid's name is Rhaem Flaerdwyd," he said, setting down his teacup. "All of nineteen years old and freshly Blessed—basically the last person you'd expect to be walking around with a spell like Null. But that's the thing. He's a ward of Clan Yviredh."

"Ahh," Nazralind said, nodding as if this explained everything. I'd called my full council of lieutenants and advisors to this meeting, and added her to it.

Fortunately, Maugro had better sense than to assume her political knowledge of Dount's Clans applied to the rest of us and continued explaining without acknowledging the interruption.

"Yviredh's small potatoes as far as Clans go, one of the vassals of Clan Aelthwyn that holds the parcels of land immediately surrounding Gwyllthean. They have a few little farms and one village surrounding their fortress; that's it. You can stand on the walls of Caer Yviredh and see past their domain in every direction. The one significant asset they *do* have is a Spirit on the grounds of the fortress, nicknamed Head Start. It's hard to please, but if people pass its trial, it not only grants the Blessing of Might or Magic, but *also* a single beginner spell or artifact to go with it."

"Ooh, that's a rarity," Aster commented. "I've never heard of a Spirit that'll give you more than just the Blessing itself."

Now, *this* sounded interesting. "What's the Spirit's trial?" I asked.

"That's kinda up in the air," Maugro admitted, grimacing. "It's a talker. Something . . . philosophical and intellectual, it asks a lot of questions and wants to hear input on all kinds of subjects, but to this day, nobody's really sure what it's looking for. The conversation's different for every person and the results seem kinda random. Only hard rules that seem consistent are that you fail if you lie to it or try to tell it jokes. That's what the Clan tells people who take the trials, anyway. Which they let people do twice a year; they hold a little festival in their village for it. Subjects of Clan Yviredh's authority and invited guests can try it free on festival days, and there's a fee for anyone else who wants to have a go."

I nodded, suppressing a grimace. *That* was definitely a goddess cheat lever. In fact, I suspected that *every* Spirit was a means for them to put a finger on the scales, but this one wasn't even trying to be subtle about it.

"So, the Spirit is Clan Yviredh's main business," Maugro continued. "Aside from the access fees, when one of their lowborn vassals gets Blessed from it, they *generously* sponsor their adventuring career. Gear, potions, King's Guild membership dues, the works—all on loan, with nothing owed up front and at interest. It's pushing the limits of the law, of course; the whole point of the Guild is so the Clans don't have control over adventurers. But Clan Yviredh gets away with it cos they're not *directing* 'their' adventurers to do anything, just financing 'em and then profiting. It's such a central part of their income that they even have their indentured farm laborers take the Spirit's trial, since that's the biggest source of fresh blood that's under their direct control. And whaddaya know, less than a month ago an indenture named Rhaem Flaerdwyd walked in there and walked back out Blessed with Magic—and able to cast *Null*, of all the damned things."

And I even knew *which* goddess was leaning on the scales this time. From the sound of it, Sanora couldn't even have intended this spell to go to Yoshi; she was just dropping something on Dount that would be likely to ruin *my* day. I frowned, leaning back in my chair. "Hm. Has the Spirit ever given somebody that spell before? Or one similarly valuable?"

"Not that I was able to dig up a specific account of, but it's a known phenomenon. You know how it is with Spirits and dungeon rewards. Everything's random, within certain tolerances; sometimes somebody gets lucky. These are the stories that keep wide-eyed young adventurers out doing the stupid shit that gets most of 'em killed."

Minifrit exhaled a streamer of smoke, which nobody else seemed to object to in this enclosed room over breakfast. Oh well, I guess Fflyr culture was more tolerant of disruptive behavior, and anyway, it wasn't *that* unpleasant. Smelled more like incense than tobacco.

"How did this boy go from the control of this Clan to Lady Gray?" she asked.

"Now *that's* where the story gets interesting," Maugro said with a wide grin, clearly enjoying his role as storyteller. "So, a sorcerer who can cast Null belongs on a whole other level than a dinky little Fflyr Clan like Yviredh operates on, see? *Kings* would pay to have somethin' like that in their arsenal. And since this kid *is* legally indentured, the Clan can all but literally sell him. Seems like a hell of an asset to risk in some scheme of Lady Gray's, right? Well, here's the thing—the likes of Clan Yviredh can't just *approach* anybody able to afford to hire or outright buy their Null sorcerer. People like that don't entertain random propositions from nobodies telling unlikely stories like this one. We're talkin' international diplomacy here. Only access they have is to the Fflyr authorities, the King or Clan Aelthwyn, and *they* can just straight-up take the kid without giving the Yviredhs shit for their trouble. Can, and would. Clan Yviredh needs to keep him secret from their superiors in the Fflyr hierarchy, *while* using him to gain either connections or the shit-ton of money that'll *buy* them connections, because he's the only asset they've got that could even do that. And there's limited work in that field. A Null caster is the ultimate anticaster caster, and . . . not much else. So yeah, working with the likes of Lady Gray was obviously a huge risk, but she was not only desperate enough to pay out the ass for Flaerdwyd's services, but probably the only option they had."

I drummed my fingers on the table, thinking rapidly. I could feel a plan forming; I'd started this line of inquiry on the assumption that the Null caster was a loose end I would need to brutally tie up, but this situation was more complicated—and if I was careful, potentially beneficial to me.

"What's the status of this guy now?"

"Safe and sound, back home with the Clan," Maugro reported. "Apparently made it out of Gwyllthean the *minute* Lady Gray allegedly finished you off. Glad to see that account was exaggerated," he added with a wink. "The speed and severity of the crackdown that followed seems to've spooked Clan Yviredh good an' proper; they've had their whole fortress locked down and on alert ever since. Flaerdwyd's in there, secured along with whatever Lady Gray paid them. Oh, and here's another tidbit—a couple weeks ago, in the fuckin' *middle* of bringing in the harvest, Clan Yviredh suddenly freed all their indentured laborers and didn't replace 'em, instead paying for much more expensive freeman labor to finish the work. So we know what he's used up his leverage with Clan Yviredh on."

"Damn, now I kinda like this guy," Nazralind said, grimacing. "Do we really need to kill him, Lord Seiji?"

"First of all," I said with a sigh, "we don't need to discuss our strategic plans in front of the neutral information broker."

Maugro grinned, Sakin cackled, and Nazralind lowered her eyes, blushing.

"Generally speaking, I mean," I added. "In this case, though . . . I think not. Sounds like my argument is not with Flaredud—"

"Flaerdwyd."

"That's what I said. Anyway, it's Clan Yviredh I need to talk to. They've apparently got no problem with me, and it sounds like they don't want trouble. There *will be a discussion* about *my* trouble and what I'm owed for it, but that can be as polite as they're willing to make it. Maugro, I know the Clans are a little out of your purview, but what can you tell me about this family?"

"Hey, Lord Seiji, it's me! Maugro!" He brandished his teacup, not quite sloshing it but prompting Minifrit to lean away. "Clan politics might be over my head, but I can still getcha full profiles on all Clan members and a strategic rundown of their Clansguard and fortress."

Nazralind cleared her throat loudly. "Lord Seiji, *I* can provide you all of that for free. I can also get you *into* that fortress—through diplomacy, subterfuge, or over the walls in the night, whichever approach you prefer."

Maugro gave her a very even look, which she met with a big, simpering grin. Nazralind had definitely not forgiven him for that business of him charging her protection money and then selling her out to me when she couldn't pay.

"Sorry, Maugro," I said with a shrug. "I value your business, but there's no sense in paying for what I can get free."

"Ain't that the truth," he agreed, nodding with no outward display of displeasure. "I never blame a man for showin' solid business sense. Well then, that's *that* matter. Concerning the other subjects you asked me about, I can't get an exact head count or names, but I can assure you that *most,* if not all, of the Gutter Rats remaining in Gwyllthean are now residing in the Convocation orphanage in the middle ring. That seems to've caused a stir among the middle ring itself, but with the paladin Rhydion backing this arrangement, nobody's willing to raise a peep about it. The Clans are generally watching him *real* careful-like since he went off-script in the first place. You know, you scared the hell outta those kids," he added, frowning. "I had to reach outside my usual sources for info on Convocation business, and the priestess I managed to contact made sure to emphasize that quite a few of 'em are still having nightmares about what the Healer did."

"That's fair," I sighed. "Nightmares go away in time." I really hoped they did, anyway. *Mine* hadn't shown any sign of it, but in my case there was some fresh horror every fucking week. Hopefully the Rats would have time to heal. "And the most important matter?"

"The least useful answer," the broker admitted with a wince. "I hope you're realistic enough not to be *too* disappointed, Lord Seiji, but right now everybody in the country wants to know where the fuck Lady Gray went, and nobody knows jack shit. Those five kids she killed were the last anybody heard from her, and then . . . poof. You better believe I've got ears to the ground and while there are other clients interested, I promise you're at the top of the list. When I know something, you'll know something. I do happen to know the last person who had direct in-person dealings with Lady Gray, but unfortunately, *somebody* nailed him to a wall."

"Mm." I sipped my tea. "Shame about that." I probably should have asked him some questions, yeah, but . . .

"Can I ask you a question, Lord Seiji?" Maugro was watching me closely, but with a neutral expression.

I tried for a wry expression. "Oh, should I be charging for this?"

"You want to?"

I enjoy banter as much as the next fellow, but my heart really wasn't in it these days. I just sighed again and shook my head. "Go ahead, Maugro, what's on your mind."

"What'd you do that for?" he asked, still studying me. "It ain't like anybody ever doubted Uncle Gently's career would end badly, but *that* was . . . a bit . . . much."

"I'm pretty sure I made my point clear at the time. Spelled it out, you might say."

"Yeah, everybody got it, no killing kids. Good rule. Thing is, though, nobody was doing that *anyway*. The Gutters are a rough place and the Rats met bad ends fairly regularly, but people were not out deliberately murdering them to make a point. You'll notice that Lady Gray doing that shit was the exact thing that set the paladin on her case, which will undoubtedly be what ends up killing her. You know me, I'm an information guy; anything I don't understand chews at the back of my brain 'til I get answers. You've always been so admirably pragmatic and far-sighted, Lord Seiji; it's one of the things I enjoy most about working with you. *That* business . . . I don't get why that point needed to be made that . . . hard."

For a moment I just met his gaze, silently pondering an answer.

"Some people just need to get nailed to walls, Maugro," I said at last, my voice quiet.

"Hear fuckin' *hear*," Sakin agreed. Aster and Nazralind exchanged a loaded look, while Minifrit frowned and shook her head, exhaling smoke through her nose. Kasser sat rigidly in his chair, apparently believing that the conversation couldn't see him if he didn't move.

"Well, okay," the goblin said with a shrug.

"Find me Lady Gray," I said in the same soft voice, "and I will make it as worth your while as I possibly can within my not inconsiderable means. I mean it, Maugro. This is priority number one. *I want that woman's head.*"

"I will do everything I can," he said very carefully. "You know there's a *lot* of competition for that, Lord Seiji. Still, bein' frank, I suspect you've got a better chance than most—and probably without my help, much as it professionally pains me to admit it. Lady Gray wants *your* head just as badly. You may not have to go to her."

I didn't need the reminder.

"That being said, just because she's priority one doesn't mean there are no other priorities. All right, people, we've got a lot to get done, both generally and before tonight's operation. Maugro, I'll have someone see you back to the tunnel. Always a pleasure."

"I can't help feeling that was anticlimactic," Adelly said about fifteen hours later, standing in the middle of a campsite full of corpses.

It was the middle of the night, and we were in the base camp of the bandit gang Auron had identified as too brutal to bother recruiting. In fact, we'd used the same tactic by which we'd taken out his gang—Kastrin sniped the lookout with her sedative-laced stinger, then lobbed an alchemical sleeping bomb into the middle of the camp and I'd ignited it with a Spark. It worked just as flawlessly.

Except this time, the operation was faster and cleaner. There was no tying people up, no airing grievances, no *showtime*. Once they were out, we swept in with blades and silently finished them off.

"Good," said Sakin, wiping blood off his sword. "Cherish that feeling, Adelly. Anticlimactic is the absolute *ideal* for discreet ops, and things will all too rarely go this well."

"Boy, ain't that the truth," I muttered. "Half of what I try to do blows up in my face. Biribo, any holdouts?"

"Nope. Clean sweep, boss. We got seven bandits, and seven corpses. Well, except . . ."

As it turned out, I'd brought more than twice their number; even had we not killed them asleep, the advantage would have been ours. Hell, I probably could have taken them out alone. Now, though, I turned to my familiar.

"Except? Is there trouble?"

"There's . . . Uh, trouble's a word. No danger, boss, but . . . Hell, you'd have found it anyway when you swept the camp for supplies. Over there, that wall of crates? That's food storage. And behind it is, uh, food prep. You'd better have a look, boss."

"Well, this is good and fucking ominous," I muttered, stalking in that direction and taking my Firelight with me. At least I could be assured the camp was cleared of enemies. Whatever he was being coy about, Biribo took his job seriously and would have warned me had there been an actual danger.

I stepped past the incongruously neat stack of boxes to an area that was clearly used for meat butchering and storage. Obviously this gang had hunted to feed themselves. There were knives and a rusty-looking cleaver lying casually on a big, roughly flat chunk of akorthist, which made an impromptu table; even in the orange light I could tell it was bloodstained, as was the ground. Around that they'd erected several racks and hung cuts of meat to dry, with a few more nearby holding stretched pieces of leather in the process of being tanned. Behind the table was a pile of bones, though it looked like any inedible soft tissue had been disposed of elsewhere. Made sense, you don't want your compost near your food storage. At any rate, this was clearly the source of the smell that wafted over the camp.

For a few seconds, I just peered around, seeing nothing but a primitive butcher's setup. Meat was meat, and I wasn't completely sure I'd recognize all the Ephemeral animals from around here even if I saw them intact. I didn't put it together until I happened to see the distinctive shape of one of the skulls that had rolled away from the bone pile. Not an old skull, one with scraps still attached. Then, amid the dawning horror, I found there were *other* recognizable shapes among the pieces of meat hung up to dry.

I didn't realize Kastrin had come up behind me until she staggered away and was violently sick.

"Holy *fuck*," Auron wheezed, having arrived just after her. I'd brought him along on this operation as an approximation of a local guide. "Hell's bloody revels."

"Well, you did warn me these guys were assholes," I said, pleased that my voice was even despite the roaring in my ears.

"Assholes, yes! Murderers and worse. I didn't know *how* much worse! Goddess's loins, what the *fuck* has to go wrong in somebody's head before they start to do *this*?"

I turned around, as much to put my back to the scene as anything, and found most of the rest of my strike team clustered around gawking; those who hadn't already turned away. Kastrin wasn't the only one losing her dinner.

"This is . . . I don't . . ." Lady Miriami of Clan Yldyllich, who was with us for much the same reason as Auron, looked like she'd just been punched in the gut. "This is *good land*. There's *game*. My family doesn't even hunt it! There's plenty of . . . They didn't *need* to do this!"

Aster gently took her by the arm and led her away.

"It gets to people, sometimes," said Nazralind. Her own face was just bleak; she wouldn't look at the butchery. "The isolation. Being separate from society and its rules. Some of the gangs in the really wild country . . . Well, they start doing . . . things."

"Fucking hell, Naz, how many cannibal gangs am I going to have to clear out?" I exclaimed.

She shook her head rapidly. "Lord Seiji, I'd have told you if I knew of anybody doing *this*. I know you don't have a high opinion of Fflyr Dlemathlys, but *this* is beyond the pale. Something went *horribly* wrong here."

I started to inhale deeply to steady myself, and the smell immediately made me abort that attempt. "I think we may have killed these guys too quickly."

"Boss, your paladin buddy's interested in the zombies on this island, right?" said Biribo. "That's way to the south of here, but still. If there's a necromancer behind it . . . Well, necromancy sometimes results in, uh, peripheral cannibalism. Once you're only thinking of people as meat to be used, and taking parts off 'em for the purpose, well . . ."

"Great, one more asshole I need to kill. If having Rhydion's eyes on me at all times wasn't a fucking nightmare scenario, I might be tempted to take him up on his offer after this. Okay, everybody, let's finish up and get the *hell* out of here. Go through their stuff, grab anything useful. We especially need food, but we're in no position to leave behind anything that might have value."

I hesitated.

"Except . . . Ditch any meat you find."

No one answered verbally, but they all nodded at me and got to work. Anything was better than standing around *thinking* about this.

It was a few minutes later, while I was in the process of transferring a set of akorshil carving tools into a gwynnek's saddlebags (Kasser would be pleased), when Biribo spoke again. He actually landed on my shoulder this time, moving his mouth close enough to my ear to speak in a bare whisper.

"Boss, we got incoming."

I hesitated, then finished tucking the rolled-up leather tool belt into place without showing outward signs of unease. If Biribo chose to be discreet, it was probably best to play along. I even remembered to pat the bird on the haunch, causing her to turn her long neck and give me a skeptical look that was frankly terrifying. The ladies insisted that gwynneks were very friendly, but you had to make an effort to befriend them. Allegedly, it was only scary for the first few weeks until they got to know and like you.

"Details?" I murmured as I turned and went back toward the crate Kastrin was in the process of unpacking.

"Single figure, heading toward us from the northwest. Stealthy—and fast, clearly used to operating in wild khora. Obviously coming *right* at the camp. They just went up a big khora, good vantage to watch us from above or get the drop if they wanted."

I immediately thought of her. How could I not? My hand made a reflexive twitch toward my sword, and the block of mental weight which was Immolate formed unbidden in my mind, ready to be cast, before I made myself stop and think. This didn't *sound* like Lady Gray. She was a city person; I didn't specifically know she wasn't skilled at silent movement in the forest, but nobody had suggested it was among her talents. Besides, if she wanted to stealth up on us, she'd have been using that dagger, which would have prevented Biribo from knowing she was coming.

"He's overhead," my familiar whispered. "Almost directly. Don't look up, boss, but you see how that big khora shell splits? The branch that arches over us; he's leaning over the right side, out of range of the light. About four paces straight up and two to your left."

He? I didn't ask for details; the fact that Biribo didn't offer any more suggested this interloper wasn't about to attack us. Honestly, it made sense anyone in this wilderness would be curious about what was going on, especially in this camp. In another, less perilous world, I might have been able to let a mysterious neighbor satisfy his curiosity and go on his way.

But this was Ephemera, and I was the Dark Lord, and I couldn't have unknown entities prying into my business.

I arched my back, grimacing and knuckling the base of my spine, and then stretched, which brought one of my arms into position to aim at the general spot Biribo had indicated.

Light Beam!

There came a cry, followed by a rustle, and then a heavy thump as somebody landed on the ground, narrowly missing the corpse of a bandit. I winced; that did not look like a comfortable landing. Not to mention that blast of light right into his dark-adjusted eyes had to have been awful.

Well, omelets and eggs.

My people whirled into action all around me, dropping the supplies they were sorting through, bringing up weapons, and swiftly encircling the intruder. Poor guy was surrounded by armed Dark Crusaders before he could see again.

I, however, could only stare. The fellow on the ground in front of me looked a few years younger than myself, shaggy-haired and unkempt. What jumped out at me, though, were the triangular ears poking up through his disheveled mop of hair, and the bushy black tail which protruded behind him.

"Holy shit, it's a beastfolk."

23

In Which the Dark Lord
Gets to Know the Neighbors

What? Lord Seiji, that's not a beastman," said Mimi.

"Wh— He isn't?" I pointed at the fallen man, who was still partially curled up and wincing in pain after the tumble he'd taken. "Look, he's got the ears and the tail and everything."

"Exactly. Ears and tail, nothing else. That's just a halfbreed."

"*Don't* call people halfbreeds," I blurted in annoyance before my brain caught up with my mouth. "That's not just rude, it's nonsensical. Having dual parentage doesn't make you half a person. If anything, the opposite."

"A good point, Lord Seiji, my apologies." Mimi, or Lady Miriami, was as smooth and discreet as all the young aristocrats I'd taken in. It was funny how they all had abundant skills in outdoor survival, social maneuvering, and basically nothing else, but they were definitely easier to talk to than the more rough-mannered lowborn I'd been hanging around with. "I mean, this fellow clearly has human *and* beastfolk parentage. Wolffolk, to judge by the tail."

"Isn't that a fox tail?" said Nazralind.

"Well, if he's not a beastfolk, what the hell do *they* look like?" I demanded.

"They're beast . . . folk," Aster said uncertainly. "Um. Folk who are like beasts. I don't know how else to describe it."

Sakin, grinning as usual, cleared his throat. "For example, Lord Seiji, the local catfolk—picture a cat the size of a man, walking upright like a man, with limbs arranged like a man's. That's a catman. Furry all over, animal heads, fluffy tails, and some weird musculature especially in the limbs. Plus big ol' bappy paws for feet. So yes, this guy's half-human. Maybe more than half, by the look of it. Which also explains why he's faffing around alone in the forest, dressed like a hobo."

"Oh, let me guess," I sighed.

"Yes, I'm afraid half—ah, that is, individuals with dual parentage are usually not accepted by either kind," Nazralind said, grimacing. "Human settlements chase them out. I don't know exactly how the beast tribes deal with them, but I've heard it's more or less the same."

Poor guy. Sakin was right—his clothes were threadbare, ill-fitting rags which had clearly been scavenged and were not going to serve him very well in the coming winter. His mane of black hair looked like it had never been combed in his life, much less cut. He wasn't dirty, though. The clothing was stained, but he had the clear complexion and shiny hair of somebody who bothered to bathe when he could. I guess there were fresh water sources out among the khora, after all.

I was starting to feel bad about all this. The guy had the tense, livid expression of somebody who was terrified and determined not to show it— and also, that had been *quite* a drop and I was pretty sure he'd landed right on his tailbone.

"Well, then. **Heal**." Pink light flashed in the dimness, and he twitched, jerking upright. His furry ears straightened up fully, then laid flat against his skull, and I despised how adorable that was. "Sorry about the rough greeting, friend, but in my defense . . . Here we are in a bandit camp we just cleared out, and there you were lurking in the khora overhead. What was I supposed to think?"

He just stared at me, squinting suspiciously, then glanced at several of the crossbows pointing at him. His whole body was obviously tensed to spring—but by the look of him, he'd much rather run than fight. It was clear that only the fact he was surrounded by armed people prevented him.

"What's your name?" I asked.

The wolf-eared boy narrowed his eyes to slits, staring at me in cold silence. Yellow eyes just like a wolf's, I noticed; though, this being Dount, that didn't prove anything. Aster's eyes were almost the same color; Dountol lowborn in general had light irises in every shade I knew from Earth, as well as tones of red, yellow, and purple.

"You know I can just kill you, right?" I prompted. His tail bushed up, but he didn't otherwise move. A few of my followers gave me dubious looks, but I just kept talking. "Pragmatically speaking, that's what I ought to do. You're an unknown entity spying on my business in the middle of the night. In fact, killing you outright would've been a *lot* easier than knocking you off that perch. So you can tell from the very fact that you're still alive that I do not intend or *want* to harm you." I held up one hand. "*However.* As I'm sure you can see, our business is not the kind that does well with . . . witnesses. So help me out here, buddy. Let's have a pleasant chat, determine where we stand, and decide how to resolve this in a way that lets you go about your business and doesn't require me to do something I'd rather not. Kay?"

One pointed ear twitched sideways, twice.

I inclined my upper body in a very slight bow. "My name is Seiji. And you are . . . ?"

Finally, I got an answer. Grudgingly, but it was progress. "I'm Sato."

"Sato," I said in surprise. "Huh. That's a Japanese name." A surname, but still . . .

"I have no idea what that means," he said tersely.

Sure, it was probably a coincidence. It was just two syllables, after all; that might pop up in almost any language. Still . . . I couldn't help looking closer at his hair. Lowborn hair was black and always curly, with a glossy sheen when clean; elven and therefore highborn hair was yellow, but very stiff and coarse in texture and didn't shine under light the way European blonde did. This guy had straight, black hair that was thick and, despite its disheveled state, glossy. Like mine.

Probably a coincidence. But I was certain Virya had not told me everything about how this game of hers worked, and I had my suspicions about that Vanderhoen character who'd turned up to advise the King of Fflyr Dlemathlys and started implementing reforms that smelled to me suspiciously of modernization.

"He's not bad looking, though," Keffin piped up in the momentary pause, which fell as I considered this. "I never actually met a halfbreed before."

"Lord Seiji *just* said not to use that word," Kastrin muttered at her.

"How about it, cutie pie?" Keffin cooed at Sato, striking a pose—one leg out, hips cocked to the side, leaning forward to give us all a nice view down her neckline. "Wanna share some quality time? Let me pet those ears, and I'll rearrange your whole view of the cosmos."

For my part, I had to clench my eyes shut for a moment against a flash of remembered panic, the lovely expanse of Keffin's cleavage triggering an instinctive clench of horror and grief from something I'd seen while healing in Cat Alley. At least it was a brief and minor flash this time, hopefully gone before anyone noticed my stiffening up.

It'd been a few days; good to know my mind was still unraveling. That was what passed for comforting familiarity for me anymore.

"Keffin," I said aloud, "do you *mind*? We are *working*, here."

"What? I was! I'm just— Oh, right, new job. Sorry, Lord Seiji! Force of habit."

A mixture of groans and cackling ensued from her comrades; Kastrin gave her a particularly scathing look, and Adelly lightly swatted the back of her head. Poor Sato looked absolutely bemused by this exchange, on top of still being quite reasonably afraid for his life.

"So, anyway," I said loudly, "what brings you out here to skulk in the khora over our heads, Sato?"

"I saw lights, heard voices," he answered, still terse. "This gang was bad news. Pays to keep track of what they're doing."

"So you crept onto a khora branch right over the camp? Points for balls but not sense, there. You do know these bastards were eating people, right?"

"I know. I'm not sorry they're gone. But I could tell it wasn't them from a long way off. Figured it'd be smart to see what was happening. Specially when I realized it was *you* guys."

That last bit was delivered with a scowl and a biting tone that seemed more personal with the rest.

"Why," I said mildly, "whatever is wrong with *us* guys?"

"*You're* the idiots who moved into that old fortress," he accused. "You have any idea how much trouble that's going to cause everybody in this forest? Once the Fflyr find out, there'll be a whole army marched out here."

"Hmm."

Yeah, that tracked with what I'd already been told. I considered my options, here. Killing him *was* still the practical thing to do, but I was never going to be okay with casual brutality toward people who'd done nothing to deserve it. For god's sake, I had enough blood on my hands from assholes who forced me to kill them; I did not need to add *silencing witnesses* to the things keeping me up at night. But failing that, I still needed to do *something*. Just letting this rando scurry off into the forest to tell fuck knew who all about my ongoing campaign against the other local bandit gangs was not a good idea.

Then again . . . There was the lesson of Kasser and Ydleth fresh in my mind. The principles I was trying to teach my followers. Now that I thought of it, this dilemma might actually be an opportunity.

"How'd you like to join us?" I suggested.

Only a few of the women surrounding me looked surprised; Auron and Nazralind actually grinned.

Sato met this proposal with an incredulous scowl. "What?"

"Wanna come live in my castle?" I clarified. "There's work to do, it's not a vacation spot, but you don't *have* to do banditry or kill off the competition if you don't wanna. Fighting is the core point, but there are plenty of tasks involved in maintaining a whole-ass castle to support some conscientious objectors. You get a warm place to sleep, regular hot meals, and some proper clothes and weaponry. We're kind of running a deficit at the moment, but once we're pulling down enough income, I plan to introduce some profit-sharing measures when it comes to spoils."

He curled his lip in a belligerent sneer. His upper canines were subtly but definitely elongated.

"Oh sure. And you're just gonna offer me all that out of the goodness of your little bandit heart."

"Hell no," I said frankly. "I intend to use you to demonstrate a political point."

Sato's glare morphed into a confused squint and his ears perked up, which remained *offensively* cute.

"I'm establishing something new," I explained. "In a word, equality. We don't have class or racial or gender divisions in my organization. I insist that people treat each other fairly and without prejudice. Which is easy to *say*, but we are still a relatively homogeneous group, so opportunities to get people used to this are kinda scarce. Sure, we've got a few highborn and one elf, but they're all so single-mindedly good at making friends that it's almost not a fair test."

I got a couple of chuckles at that, and Adelly playfully poked Nazralind with an elbow, getting a similar jab in return.

"So you can see how you'd be a big help to me just by being around," I said, crouching on my heels to bring my eyes closer to Sato's level. "What I'm offering is the chance to live like everybody else, without being chased out or abused just for being who you are. I'm not gonna promise there won't be *incidents*. It takes time to get people accustomed to such things. But I will promise anybody who gives you shit will be swiftly dealt with, and you'll always have people in your corner, starting with me. So yeah, Sato, my motives aren't entirely altruistic, but I'm selfishly offering you the best deal you're gonna get from anybody on this island. Probably the best you could get in Dlemathlys, possibly the world. What do you say?"

His face was a little hard to read due to the sheer intensity of emotions concentrated in it. Sato's left ear kept twitching to one side, but that could've meant anything.

"If it'll sweeten the deal," I added, "apparently Keffin's DTF."

Sato had a lowborn's complexion, so I couldn't see if he was blushing, especially in this low light, but he instinctively glanced at Keffin, and then immediately below the level of her eyes. She made another pose and blew him a kiss, causing him to avert his gaze abruptly.

"To be clear, you don't *have* to shag Keffin, or she you," I clarified. "We're big on consent and personal autonomy in this organization."

"You people are completely crazy," the wolf boy whispered.

"Maybe," I agreed. "Doesn't mean we're wrong. Life's like that."

His ears swiveled back to lay flat against his skull again. "That's just . . . You're not gonna be around long, don't you get that? You're riling up the *real* powers on this island. The dark elves are already onto you."

That made me straighten back up. "What do you mean?"

Sato seemed to think he'd said too much, hunching in on himself and staring up at me with his lips compressed into a thin line.

I regarded him in silence for a moment before deciding to try a different approach. "Well, if you're not interested in joining up . . . it seems you're in possession of information that's relevant to my interests. How about we work out a trade?"

Up went the ears, and I suddenly found I couldn't blame Keffin for wanting to pet them. Maybe it was for the best if wolf boy didn't join the crew. I wasn't sure how long I could deal with this.

Sato did not want to go inside the gates of North Watch, and forcing him to do so would hardly have been hospitable. I was trying to create a particular impression here, so I met him halfway. Even though that resulted in the lot of us standing around on the road outside the gates in the dark while the girls with me and those on watch up on the walls catcalled each other.

We were kept waiting longer than I'd expected, the reason for which becoming obvious when Minifrit emerged from the fortress along with Mimi, my designated messenger. The madam had drafted the noblewoman to serve as beast of burden, but at least Mimi looked more amused than anything as she hauled one of Kasser's khora-transporting sleds, currently piled high with fabric and leather.

"For god's sake, Minifrit," I protested, "I said we needed *one* winter coat!"

"Oh yes?" she drawled, smoke trailing from her lips. "And you wanted what? For Miriami to just grab something at random from the facilities team's storeroom? Most of them were made with a specific person in mind, but luckily they've produced enough variety that we should find something serviceable. Honestly, how do you expect me to select a coat for someone without even knowing his size? I wouldn't expect you to understand customer service, Lord Seiji, so kindly leave it to those of us who do. Now, you are the young man in question, I trust? Sato, was it?"

Sato gibbered something vaguely affirmative, struggling mightily and with limited success to keep his eyes above her collarbone. I got the feeling the poor guy wasn't used to being around women. Fortunately, Minifrit just seemed amused, which made sense given her history.

"Hey, don't talk to me about customer service," I protested as she grabbed a dark gray coat from the pile and held it up against Sato's chest, critically examining the fit. "I worked in a game shop before I came here. In *Japan*."

"You know very well I don't have the context to understand the significance of that. Hold out your left arm, please, Sato. Hm, you have a rather small frame . . . But I think several of these might work. Anyway," she added to me while selecting three other coats from the sled, "there is a difference between running a successful business and getting fired from a succession of them because you spent all your time either snapping at customers or seething at the indignity of being consigned to such labor, which is the only way I can imagine *you* working behind a counter."

"Wow, you're really convinced you've got my number, huh. I'll have you know I held down that one job for over six years, and I would have kept with it until I saved enough to move to America. I'd still be there if not for . . . events outside my control."

"Mmhm."

"Didn't you tell me once that store was owned by a friend of your father's?" Aster said innocently, the damned traitor.

Minifrit paused in holding up another coat against Sato's chest to give me a knowing look.

"Yes, well, that doesn't mean—"

"Also that you got away with being an ass to customers because you were pretty sure it was . . . what did you call it . . . Either a tax dodge or a money laundering operation, right? I remember because I had to have you explain what that meant. Basically the place was deliberately run to lose money."

"What a fascinating country this Japan must be," Minifrit commented smugly. "Here, Sato, I believe we have a winner. Dark red should even be a decent color for camouflage, at least in this kind of khora forest. The blue one would also work for that, but it would be too baggy on you. Try this on, see how it feels."

Sato took the coat from her and shrugged into it, eyes wide. It was a pretty standard lowborn-style work coat, deep maroon in color, with the standard wide cuffs, high collar, and knee-length hem. This one appeared to have a fleece lining that would be very handy once it started snowing.

"It's *new*," the wolf boy whispered, his ears twitching violently, and I had to control my face lest it betray sentimentality unbecoming a Dark Lord. Poor guy had clearly never owned new clothes in his life. I could tell because this was the exact expression and tone the Gutter Rats had all had when we put them in fresh clothing.

"We are blessed with a supply of fabric and leather," Minifrit said. "We have people working to supply winter clothing for everyone; there is enough to share. So that was probably not made by a professional tailor, but I didn't bring out anything that isn't serviceable. It should last for years. The leather will be stiff for a while, but it'll soften as you wear it. And *please* return the next time you find something to trade for," she added, looking him critically up and down. "Before the snow starts, ideally. Just look at the state of you, boy. You need some proper shoes at *least*."

"It's long," Sato observed, twisting and watching the drape of his new coat flare with his movements.

"Yes, that's the common style," Minifrit answered. "The extra drape will help keep your legs warm. Hm . . . I suppose it might be an impediment moving through the khora if you're not used to it. We don't have many garments of highborn cut, but I could see if—"

"I like it!" Sato stepped back, protectively wrapping his arms around himself. "I . . . I like it. It's perfect. Thank you."

"Yes, thank you, Minifrit," I agreed. "Excellent work."

"The only kind I do," she said, inclining her head and looking even more pleased with herself than usual.

"And she was correct," I added, turning to Sato. "Anything else you find out that I might want to know, feel free to come back and I'll compensate you well for your time. In fact, if you want to actually come inside to do business, I'll throw in a hot meal. Not to trade for, just to talk over. That's just basic hospitality."

"He's serious," Nazralind added when Sato looked openly skeptical. "He even feeds that horrible goblin who peddles information."

"Naz," I said, exasperated, "I *just* got finished making a point about how we don't discriminate here. If you have problems with goblins, please keep them to yourself."

"Hey, I have nothing of the kind!" she protested. "I've been shown great integrity and frankly amazing compassion by goblins, and I certainly know what it's like to be despised and cast out by the society of this country. When I call Maugro a horrible goblin, I mean it *very* personally."

"Yes, feel free to stay awhile if you do visit again," Keffin purred, slinking up to Sato while he was distracted, and winding herself around his arm in such a way that it pressed right into her bosom. "I'll make sure to show you *all* our hospitality."

Sato made a very entertaining high-pitched noise and jumped away from her.

"Heel, Keffin," I ordered. Man, I was glad I'd left Junko in my room; her usual greeting probably would have sent the high-strung wolf boy fleeing for the horizon. "Sorry about her, Sato, she's harmless. Now then, if you are satisfied with our end of the deal, shall we move on to yours?"

"Oh! Yeah. Yes, this is . . . It's great." He nodded earnestly. "Thank you. Okay, I'll show you. The nearest one is . . ."

Sato edged away from the group. Sakin subtly shifted his feet, preparing to spring, and Kastrin casually reloaded her stinger with a sleeping dart, but I made a soothing gesture at them. Sato's nervous demeanor did suggest he'd been looking for an opportunity to flee the whole way back here, but after watching him all this time, I suspected he wasn't actively planning to. He was just nervous, generally.

Besides, between Biribo and Kastrin, the boy wasn't going anywhere unless I chose to let him.

"That way." Sato pointed off into the darkness. "Sorry, got a little turned around. I usually stay off the road and away from the fortress, specially at night. But it's this way."

He stepped off the path with no more ado, the rest of us hurrying to keep up. Sato picked his way through the darkened forest floor with the ease of somebody very much accustomed to it, though with me holding up a Firelight it wasn't that much harder for the rest of us.

"You live in this area?" I inquired as we moved. "You have some relation to the cat tribe, then?"

Sato gave me a mistrustful look, ears swiveling backward for a moment, but he then relented.

"None of the tribes want anything to do with a halfbreed. My mother was wolf tribe. Their land is south. They hunt me if I even go into their hunting grounds. Cat tribe is gentler. They'll chase me away from their village, but they don't mind if I roam here. Not very competitive about foraging, either. The last few years, at least," he added in a mutter, his ears flattening again. "It's been pretty good hunting. Haven't found out what their manners are like during a lean year. They've been getting more nervous since *you* showed up, you know," he added accusingly. "Hunting parties yell and throw stuff if I get close to them. Used to be hunters would talk, sometimes trade. Now they're tense, scared."

"Well, they have nothing to fear from me," I said lightly. "So long as they continue to mind their manners, that is. Personally, I would much rather be on friendly terms with the cats, but they're so standoffish."

"You should tell them that," Sato muttered.

"It's hard to strike up a dialog with people who run away at the sight of you. And I'm concerned going too close to their village would just rile them up."

"Yeah," he nodded. "Yep."

So far, so useless. I mentally shifted the cat tribe back to my list of problems to be dealt with when the more urgent ones where settled. The cats were *many* steps below Lady Gray, from whom I still had not heard a peep.

Our guide didn't take us far at all; I could still see the well-lit walls of North Watch through the khora branches when he stopped, pointing wordlessly up at the trunk of a large khora growth. I raised the Firelight, catching a glimpse of what he indicated, but that didn't help a lot in the dimness, so I dismissed it and cast a Light Beam directly at the target.

Affixed directly to the khora somewhat above arm's reach, shaded from rain by one of its hard fan-like growths, was some manner of totem. It took me a few seconds of puzzled staring to recognize that the main piece was the skull plate of one of those shellback animals that were hunted around here. I had not seen one in person, but they were used for meat and akornin. On it was painted in vivid blue pigment an elaborate sigil which, thanks to my Blessing of Wisdom, I found I could read, despite not even knowing what language it was in. Actually it was more reminiscent of a kanji than the alphabetic script the Fflyr used—the symbol could mean "protection" or "warning" depending on context. Long, colorful feathers had been affixed to the skull in a fan-like arrangement hanging downward from it.

"Aw, balls," Sakin muttered.

"What am I looking at?" I demanded.

"That, boss, is a Shylver totem," Biribo explained. "The local dark elves use them to communicate with the beastfolk without having to actually talk to them. They're secretive and standoffish people, but also an elf is an elf, and elves generally won't lower themselves to consort with whoever they think is beneath them. No offense, Naz."

"None taken," she shrugged. "When you're right, you're right."

"I've seen totems like this before," said Sakin. "They mark off areas the dark elves don't want the beast tribes going near."

"There's more of 'em," said Sato, pointing off into the darkness. "If you go through the khora in the daylight and look carefully, you'll see them. They make a ring around your fortress."

I drew in a long breath, letting it hiss through my teeth. "So . . . this means . . ."

"Boy was right, boss," Biribo said seriously. "The dark elves know we're here, and they don't want anybody messing with us. Probably because they're still deciding how they want to proceed. One thing's sure, though—they are watching."

24

In Which the Dark Lord
Comes to Dinner

ere's the thing, though," Biribo continued, weaving back and forth in
the air as if slightly worked up, "these are *gwynnek* feathers."

"These are *our* gwynnek feathers!" Mimi exclaimed in outrage, pointing. "Look, Naz! Melon blonde with red striations and black tips, those are
from Blanci!"

"Wait, are you saying dark elves *plucked* one of your gwynneks?" I
demanded.

"No, no," said Nazralind, frowning up at the totem. She also looked
unhappy, though less agitated than Mimi. "It's molting season. Their winter undercoats are coming in, and they're losing some of the bigger wing
and tail feathers; those come in annually. We've been *really* careful to pick
them up so we don't leave obvious trails everywhere, but . . . I guess we
missed some."

"Some, yeah, but you've done a better job than this," Biribo chimed
in. "I've taken notice, boss; they've grabbed most of the dropped feathers.
Someone could probably make one totem from what they missed, but not
enough from one single bird to match this way, and *definitely* not enough to
make totems to encircle the whole fortress."

"What are you saying?" I asked.

"Whoever made and hung this thing has been *inside* North Watch,"
Biribo said gravely. "They've been in the gwynnek pen itself. This person
picked up dropped feathers from around the birds, without being seen,
heard, or *smelled,* at a time when the birds in question are tense and uneasy
about being in a new home. Naz or any of the girls can explain how freakin'
difficult that would be."

"I'd frankly scoff at the idea if this thing weren't hanging right in front of me," Nazralind agreed. "Sneaking up on nervous roosting gwynneks is a *terrible* idea. We should have found the half-stripped skeleton of anyone who tried it."

"Which fits the evidence," said Biribo. "A Savindar shadow scout could do that; presumably a Shylverrael equivalent is just as good. Lady Gray couldn't have pulled it off, even with that dagger of hers. And they've done all this since *yesterday morning*, when we moved the birds in."

Ever since getting home to North Watch from our last triumphantly disastrous trip to Gwyllthean, I'd lived with a constant prickling on the back of my neck that came from the knowledge that an invisible assassin might spring out at me at any moment. That had suddenly intensified tenfold.

"Excellent," I muttered. "This is precisely what I don't fucking need."

"I *told* you," Sato muttered back.

"Boss, I haven't explained the important part yet," Biribo said, zipping back and forth in agitation. "This thing is *incorrect*. These totems are supposed to be made with harpy and naga feathers!"

"Wait, naga have *feathers*?" Aster exclaimed. It was a relief not to be the dummy asking ignorant questions for once. Finally, someone else's turn over the isekai barrel.

"Instead of hair, yeah. But that's the *point*—it's a declaration of power. The beast tribes make decorative and communicative art like this using shells and feathers and whatnot from animals they hunt, so the dark elves make them from the *sapient races* they control just to flex on 'em. It does the trick; the local tribes do *not* fuck with the dark elves."

"Nobody does," Sato agreed, nodding fervently.

I squinted up at the hanging totem. "Then . . . what's the significance of making this with junk scavenged from the fortress? Doesn't that undermine their point? Or are they making a statement about how they can get in there?"

"It wouldn't have the same import; there are gwynneks all over Dlemathlys," said Sakin. "Even wild ones, on Dount. I dunno if there are any flocks close to here, but beast tribes can undoubtedly get feathers like this from hunting."

I turned to look thoughtfully at Sato, who immediately flattened his ears.

"I didn't know that," he said defensively. "I didn't! I only know a little bit about . . . tribe stuff. The important things. My mom warned me about totems like this, to stay away from anything guarded by them. You don't take risks with dark elves."

"I believe you," I said. "The question is whether the cat tribe will recognize the difference, and what they'll make of it."

"I . . ." He seemed to shrink in on himself. "Maybe? I . . . don't know . . . what the cats know. Probably their shaman would . . ."

"They can tell," said Biribo. "*We* know this was made by a real shadow scout, because we know where those feathers came from, but *they* might think they're fake. It's hard to say what they'll do in that case. Speaking of which, boss, two important points about the dark elves—first, Shylverrael has been developing in total isolation for a century and a half, so nobody knows what they're actually like; and second, the Savin culture they're descended from was prone to elaborate intrigues and scheming. So literally the only thing we can assume about the Shylver is they plot in complicated patterns. I think it'd be a big mistake to make any assumptions about their plans or mindset."

"Let's put that on hold for a second," I said. "All right, Sato, a deal's a deal. We're square. You sure you're not interested in joining us?"

He backed up a step, eyes flicking up to the totem, and shook his head. "I don't . . . Maybe if you, uh . . . make some kind of . . . arrangement with the dark elves, we can talk. I'm not gonna be in there when they storm the fortress. You don't even have your *gates* up."

"Fair enough," I agreed. "My offer still stands, though. Find me anything interesting or useful and I'll trade fairly for it. And I don't mind putting a hot meal in you in the process, if you're willing to visit long enough. So don't be a stranger."

Sato glanced rapidly around, at the armed people surrounding him and the dark forest beyond. "I can go?"

"I won't stop you," I said, nodding. "Just keep in mind what I said."

He carefully slipped away, Adelly and Mimi making room for him, and paused at the edge of the circle to look back at us and self-consciously run his hands over his new coat.

". . . thanks."

Then he was gone, bounding away into the night.

"Bye, cutie!" Keffin hollered after him, waving. Kastrin groaned and rolled her eyes.

"Biribo?" I murmured.

"Boy's making tracks, boss," my familiar reported. "He's a lot more interested in getting far from us than snooping, clearly."

Sakin coughed. "So, no offense, Lord Seiji, but what was the point of all that? We know these have only been here a couple days at the most. Kasser's cutting teams would've found 'em; they're not far from the fortress. *And* now that kid's out there loose, knowing who and where we are."

"Well, it's not as if we could have imprisoned or killed him just for knowing that," Nazralind said belligerently.

He gave her an exceedingly bland smile. "It is, in fact, precisely like that, my lady."

"Button it," I ordered, seeing Naz swelling up and Sakin beginning to grin more widely. "Neither of you are qualified to be my conscience. That was a calculated risk, Sakin, and it was worth paying him off with a coat. Our *entire* strategy hinges on our willingness to offer people a better deal than they'll get under the Clans. I'm not going to abuse anyone just because I have the power to; that would undermine the whole campaign." I turned to face him directly. "Or do you feel I have been insufficiently ruthless toward my enemies?"

"I don't think anyone would make that claim," said Aster.

Sakin folded down his hands at me, grinning hugely now. "Quite right, Lord Seiji; that makes sense. I do feel the need to mention . . . alternatives . . . but if your strategy is proceeding as planned, that's what matters."

"Good. All right, then, analysis. What *can* we conclude about this?"

"Well, it seems the dark elves aren't hostile," Sakin said, still grinning as if this were all a delightful puzzle for us to solve. "Whether or not they know who you are, Lord Seiji, assassinating you and your whole inner circle while we all slept would've been a lot easier and less risky than this business."

"That's reassuring," Aster said sourly.

"Sarcasm aside, yeah it is," said Biribo. "Up to a point, at least. Just cos the dark elves don't want us dead doesn't mean this isn't going to be *serious* trouble, boss. It would be very much in character for Savin and presumably Shylver elves to watch carefully and gain an understanding of you before they make whatever move they're going to—unless they wanted you dead, in which case they'd've just done that. Right away, the main issue I see is that the elf or elves who did this clearly don't have access to the official resources they'd need to make the totems properly. Which suggests . . ."

"A renegade," I finished, turning back to frown up at the totem.

"Again, dark elves are prone to complicated schemes, and we *don't* know what they're thinking, so assumptions are dangerous. With that said . . . Yeah, I think the likeliest explanation is that this is the work of a rogue individual or faction not authorized by Shylverrael itself."

"If they're renegades, that could be why they're out here in the forest when dark elves love to keep to themselves," Adelly suggested. "Shylverrael might still not know we're here, Lord Seiji."

"Assumptions," Biribo warned.

"So," I growled, ire rising to drown out the unease, "not only do I get my long-awaited introduction to an actual Viryan culture *right* when I'm busy and don't have time for their shit, but they've decided to introduce me by plunging me neck-deep into their fucking politics."

"Boss, I dunno how to break this to you," Biribo said hesitantly, "but that is pretty much the only introduction *anybody* gets to Viryan cultures. Especially dark elves."

"I mean, they're still Viryan," Sakin pointed out. "If you introduce yourself by Immolating the ones who annoy you, the rest will fall in line. Unlike Sanorites, they'll probably be positively impressed by it."

"That's a pretty sweeping oversimplification, but there's a kernel of truth in it," Biribo admitted. "Also, boss, this isn't without an immediate upside. The intelligence operatives of a culture where everybody can go invisible are stealth experts by default and *counter*-stealth experts by specialization. If there are Shylver shadow scouts enforcing our hands-off status, Lady Gray isn't getting within bowshot of the walls alive. Trust me, I've seen that woman in action; dagger or no dagger, she's not a match for them."

I had to draw in a deep breath and let it out slowly to steady myself against the surge of emotions that brought. It would be a relief not to have that ax—or dagger—looming over our heads, but the thought of someone else getting the kill made me start twitching. I wanted that woman dead, by my hand. I wanted to hold up her severed head so I could watch the stupid look on her face while the last of her oxygen dripped from her brain.

I also *wanted* that fucking dagger. Oh, the havoc I could cause with that . . . And also that anti-spell-targeting artifact—that would spare me having to worry about half the Blessed who might come after me.

All of it I laboriously pushed aside. Feelings weren't important right now—in fact they pretty much never were, in my experience. What I needed now was to plan.

"All right," I said aloud after an expectant pause in which everyone stared at me. "I'm moving up our timetable. Let's head back inside. Naz, Mimi, you two need to get a good night's sleep; tomorrow I need all of you heading out on that planned hunting trip."

"Tomorrow?" Nazralind asked, raising her eyebrows.

I nodded. "Sorry to put you right to work like that, but we can't afford to wait around."

"It's the opposite of a problem, Lord Seiji." She shook her head. "We came here to do our share, not to hang out and relax."

"Glad to hear it. We need fresh meat—especially if we're gonna keep those gwynneks; they've already eaten most of what we had stored. Scout the territories we've taken over, gather meat, and above all, move *fast*. I'm sending you in particular because Lady Gray cannot catch up with you on those mounts, and I'm betting even the dark elves can't, no matter how sneaky they are. You have one week, then I need everyone back here. We are going to spend that week buckling down on training. Then, before the dark elves or Clan Olumnach or *whoever fucking else* can steal another march on us, we're moving in force."

I immediately decided to be straight with my people; when I addressed everyone at breakfast the next day, I emphasized that the dark elven presence meant we had a measure of protection, but I didn't try to mislead anyone about the seriousness of this. I needed these people to trust me, which meant I could not afford to deceive them.

It was a strange constant of my life on Ephemera that I kept getting railroaded into doing the right thing just by exercising basic sense and not acting like Darth Vader on cocaine, which seemed to be the baseline for the ruling class here.

So it was *tense*, knowing that an unknown number of dark elves of uncertain motivations were apparently prowling through our own fortress with impunity. I instituted security procedures requiring people to be in groups of at least two at all times. The only real resistance came from the Rats when I decreed that children had to stay inside the walls and be accompanied when out of public areas; I mollified them by putting them in charge of hunting elf tracks and instructing anyone tasked with chaperoning them not to obstruct this extremely critical duty.

For my part, I kept Junko with me at all times. If the dark elves could sneak under the collective noses of the gwynneks, the dog probably wouldn't be able to sniff them out, either, but hell, it made me feel better, and she loved the attention.

Ultimately, I was proud of how they handled it. Everybody buckled down to their combat practice and the improvements were noticeable. I had to say, I personally enjoyed having Goose back and resuming my personal training routine, even if I had an artifact sword that practically did my fighting for me now.

At the end of the week, Nazralind and the ladies returned, carrying scouting reports and saddlebags full of meat. I gave them the night after their return to rest up from the trip, designating the bathhouse for their exclusive use, and the next day we moved out for our first major strike.

It was time to bring the fight to the Clans. So to speak.

Caer Yviredh was a laughable excuse for a castle, fortunately for us.

We arrived just after nightfall to find basically a sizable manor house, with some decorative crenelations around its steep tiled roof but little in the way of actual defenses. The manor's grounds were surrounded by a garden wall less than half the height of North Watch's battlements. The only actual defenses were the gatehouse which encompassed the main entrance, on the road leading straight up from Clan Yviredh's nearby village, and watchtowers at two corners of the estate, one of which had a small exterior door that could only be opened from the inside.

Since fucking around with the gatehouse would risk our being spotted from the village, the rear tower was our in.

"You're up, Adelly," I murmured when our thirty-strong strike force was gathered in the nearest available cover, a stand of khora between two farms some thirty paces—*meters*, dammit—from the wall.

She handed the Lightning Staff to Nazralind and, grinning eagerly, pulled the Featherweight Tunic on over her head. "All right. Wish me luck!"

"Don't be lucky," I advised, "be *good*."

"You got it, Lord Seiji!"

"There's one man inside the tower," said Biribo, "currently not near a window or the roof ladder. He's sitting down. Whatever he's doing, this is your opening."

Adelly took the stinger Aster handed her, already loaded with a tranquilizer dart, and flashed us all a wide grin. "Ittekimasu!"

Then she was off, bounding across the slope toward the walls and leaving me blinking.

"Wh-when— Did she just—"

"Means basically 'I'm off,' right?" Aster murmured. "You say it when you leave the fortress. A lot of the girls are making a deliberate effort to pick up your little phrases, Lord Seiji."

"That's . . . not exactly what I . . ." Well, I figured there was no harm in it.

The way Adelly was moving reminded me of an astronaut on the moon, and also reminded me why I hated using that damn tunic. It was the artifact that got the least use among us, since the Featherweight enchantment was incompatible with the Surestep and Mastery enchantments. As the name implied, it reduced the wearer's weight by something like four-fifths without reducing their strength or sturdiness, enabling them to jump incredibly high and fall huge distances without getting hurt.

That meant it played poorly with enchantments that corrected your body's movement as they didn't account for the magically diminished weight. Using the Mastery enchantments on Aster's or my swords, or the Surestep on my boots, would cause our bodies to automatically move in ways which would send us flailing to the ground if our weight were so hugely reduced, probably with a dislocated limb in the process. All three of us had trained with it, but since Aster and I liked our artifacts, actually putting on the Featherweight Tunic during operations fell to Adelly, our only other Blessed with Might.

She vaulted over the wall effortlessly, leaving us to watch the manor in tense silence. Fortunately for my nerves, our girl was quick and precise. The tower door swung open moments later and Adelly leaned out, beckoning to us.

"Advance team on me," I ordered, stepping out of the khora. "The rest of you know your jobs."

At the somewhat jumbled chorus of affirmations, I silently reflected that Adelly might have the right idea. There was something to be said for a short, concise "hai" in response to orders.

I dashed up the slope with the advance crew of fifteen tailing me, made it to the tower in seconds and slipped inside, immediately making for the door to the inner grounds and noting the unconscious guard with a dart still stuck in his cheek.

That made me wince. Well, at least she hadn't hit his eye. I'd have felt obligated to Heal that, and then we'd have to re-dart him. Guy could live with a swollen cheek.

"Nice work, Adelly," I said in passing.

"Thanks, Lord Seiji!" Adelly had already shrugged out of the Featherweight Tunic so she could walk normally again, and now collected the Lightning Staff from Nazralind.

The grounds were pleasantly landscaped. Feathery vines climbed the walls, and there were some statues, but apparently small decorative khora weren't a thing. Made sense; I thought I remembered someone telling me they spread from underground root systems, which was why the plantations could only exist on an island that already had wild khora.

"Biribo?"

"We're still clear, boss. There are seven men in the front gatehouse, all but one asleep—that's gotta be most of the Clansguard. The shrine with the Spirit is over there by the other tower. Eleven people in the manor house; the biggest concentrations are six in what I think is a dining room and three in the kitchen where the rear entrance is. One individual upstairs and one over by the front door."

"Kitchen's where the servants will be," I said aloud for the benefit of my followers spilling out of the tower behind me. "We need to subdue them and get information. Everybody remember to pull your punches, we're not here to spill blood, and we *definitely* don't want to harm working class folks just surviving in this place. Aster, take the rear and watch for any guards. Kastrin, Ismreth, you're on point. Don't let anyone raise an alarm, but don't fire if you don't have to."

"Right!"

"Understood, Lord Seiji."

Kastrin and Lady Ismreth were our best shots with the little stingers, and both were also cool-headed enough that I trusted them to act appropriately and not do unnecessary harm. Kastrin was a tad trigger-happy but not malicious.

We hustled across the grounds to the kitchen door under Biribo's direction. I grabbed the door handle and pulled it open, stepping aside to make room for Kastrin and Ismreth to insert themselves into the kitchen doorway, weapons first.

From within came one half shriek, aborted by the twang of a stinger firing. I rushed in after them, the rest of the crew on my heels.

Three servants were in the kitchen—a middle-aged woman in a splattered apron, looking shocked and furious as she backed against the counter; a visibly terrified young man already cowering in the corner; and an unfortunate maid unconscious on the floor with a sleeping dart protruding from her chest. Ismreth was the one with a dart still loaded, and she had wisely trained it on the woman whom I took to be the cook. I suspected that was the only thing keeping the woman under control; she looked mad enough to charge us, though her eyes were on the miniature crossbow in Ismreth's hands.

"Where is Rhaem Fladdurd?" I demanded.

"Flaerdwyd," Nazralind corrected from behind me.

"I just said that!"

"Oh, no you *don't*," the cook snarled, snatching up a rolling pin and brandishing it at me. "I don't care who you are, you plundering bastard, you leave that boy *alone*! He's been through enough without . . . whatever in the Goddess's name *this* is!"

"Protective of the young," I mused, stepping fully into the kitchen and letting the rest of my followers crowd in behind me, weapons up. "Defiant in the face of overwhelming force. I very much approve. Madam, you have my sincere respect."

I slowly turned to face the corner, where the poor lad huddled there flinched at my mere gaze.

"You, though," I said thoughtfully. "Something tells me I'll respect you . . . less. Kastrin, aim for his nuts."

She had just finished slotting a new dart into her weapon and now turned on command, leveling it at his midsection.

"The dining room!" the unfortunate young servant blurted, hunching forward and protectively covering his crotch with both hands. "He's eating with the family!"

"Oh, *Kesper*," the cook said in clear disgust.

"Don't judge the boy too harshly," I said. "I have that effect on people. So, Clan Yviredh inspires loyalty in their servants and invites indentured lowborn to their table. I'm beginning to like them just a little bit."

"They're not terrible people, as aristocrats go," said Nazralind.

"They had indentured farm laborers until *very* recently," Aster snorted. "This guy Flaerdwyd *still* is."

"Yes, that's among the things I will now discuss with them," I said. "Four of you, secure this room and keep the—"

The cook roared in sheer fury and charged at me with the rolling pin upraised, making it all of two steps before Ismreth shot her and she went down like a sack of potatoes.

"You know, I like her," I said. "A house just doesn't feel like a home without an irascible cook. Anyway. Four of you secure the room. Make sure that kid doesn't do anything particularly stupid, keep these two poor ladies comfortable, and hold the entrances. The rest, with me. Biribo?"

"This way, boss!" My familiar buzzed ahead and I followed, my fellow invaders close behind.

It was extremely considerate of the Yviredhs to keep my secondary target with them. I'd been expecting to have to trawl all over the mansion, tranquilizing servants and guards, to retrieve a recalcitrant Blessed and have to bring him to the rest of them. This was going to save me a lot of time and aggravation.

In a hushed voice, Biribo directed us to the dining room, which was sensibly right near the kitchen. It had no less than three entrances, one serving door from the kitchen corridor and two from the front areas of the house from which the highborn would enter. I diverted our forces, stationing three under Nazralind's command at the servant's entrance with orders to move in as soon as they heard the rest of us do so. We navigated as quietly as possible to the public halls, dividing the remaining group in half with Aster taking one door and me the other.

I wasted no more time; the very second both were in place, I yanked open the door and the four crossbow-wielding women surrounding me streamed through, followed immediately by those posted at the other entrances.

It must have been a terrifying experience, to have your dinner interrupted by an entire gang of masked women in black cloaks. Going for dramatic effect rather than stealth, we had borrowed the cloak gimmick from Naz's group, augmented with long strips of black fabric wrapped around everything but the eyes. This made an impressive showing, if I said so myself, and served the additional purpose of concealing the identities of the highborn among us.

There were shouts, two female screams, and a man's angry demands as the women took positions around the perimeter of the dining room with weapons up. I unhurriedly followed suit only when the stomping of feet ceased. Calm and collected, moving only when I was good and ready, emphasizing my control of the situation.

Because it was *showtime*, and every little touch mattered.

One lowborn man in servant's livery was pressed back in a corner, holding a serving tray in front of his chest as a makeshift shield, while the four living members of Clan Yviredh were seated around the dining table, along with Rhaem Flaerdwyd. Yep, that was him. I had only seen him from a distance, previously, but I recognized his face nonetheless. You don't quickly forget the man responsible for dunking you in a shit river with a brand-new collection of crossbow bolts.

I could see Clan Yviredh's situation just by looking at them. The Highlord was a blonde human, his wife brown-haired; they had a brunette son in his midteens and a dirty-blonde daughter a few years younger than that. Their gambit to leverage Flaerdwyd for riches and status wasn't so much greedy as desperate. Under the absurd laws of Fflyr Dlemathlys, if their Clan didn't have a blonde male able to take over as Highlord and continue the name, the lack of yellow hair would be taken as a sign of insufficient elven blood and thus, the loss of the Goddess's favor. Noble status would then be stripped from them, along with any hereditary fiefdom, which would probably include this estate and the Spirit. That had happened to the Auldmaer family and, I suspected, the Norovenas.

It was hard to be sympathetic to the highborn, the way they acted, but it had to be said that this country's stupid, crooked, and broken situation wasn't even good for *them*.

"It's him!" blurted Flaerdwyd, rising from his chair. "My lord, run! I'll hold him off! **Null!**"

He held out both hands toward me, invoking the spell that stifled all my powers. This close in a well-lit room, I could see that Null caused a visible distortion effect in the air, which had not been apparent during the nocturnal kerfuffle in the Gutters.

Silence hung in the dining room for three beats, the power of that spell shimmering in the space between us, and then there came a muffled snort as one of my armed followers snickered.

The Rapier of Mastery whispered hungrily as I drew it from the sheath, taking two measured steps forward and raising the weapon. I calmly extended the blade right between Flaerdwyd's outstretched hands, bringing the point to rest against his clavicle, and invoked my counterspell.

"Sword."

Highlord Yviredh covered his eyes with a hand and his young daughter closed hers, groaning; at least three more of my bandits began to giggle behind their masks.

"Sit down, boy," I said, not unkindly.

And *now*, finally, I got to have some proper fun. I did so love playing to a captive audience.

25

In Which the Dark Lord Spills the Tea

Flaerdwyd lowered his hands, dropped the spell, and sank back into his chair, looking sickly and terrified. I followed him for a moment with the tip of the rapier before finally removing it, and sheathing the weapon.

Behind me, Nazralind separated herself from the women along the dining room walls and pulled out a chair at the end of the table. We hadn't discussed this, but I immediately saw the symbolic importance—Highlord Yviredh sat at the table's head, flanked by his wife and son, with his daughter and Flaerdwyd at the places below that.

I seated myself, trusting Nazralind's instincts when it came to aristocratic pageantry.

"What have you done with our people?" the Lady of the house demanded. Naz had told me her name was Elidred, which earned her at least a little pity from me. "Our guards? Servants?"

Lady Elidred was looking at me with an expression that suggested she would have already lunged with her steak knife if her children weren't in the room and in crossbow range. Flaerdwyd and the kids looked frightened by all this; the Highlord himself just wore a resigned expression.

"They have been regrettably inconvenienced, nothing more. I beg you not to punish those currently asleep at their posts; you have my assurance they had no choice in the matter."

"I certainly would not have," she said icily. "Asleep? Is that a euphemism?"

I shook my cowled head. "The alchemy costs more than crossbow ammunition, my lady, but I consider it worth the investment to avoid spilling blood, particularly that of people with whom I have no argument."

Lady Elidred actually seemed slightly mollified. Angry enough to murder, sure, but no longer on the cusp of trying.

"Then let me assure you, ah . . . Lord Healer," her husband interjected, "your sole argument is with *me*. I alone set these events into motion. As you have shown concern for the less fortunate and those caught between us, I beg you to dismiss my wife and children from this room and your attention."

Sure, to rouse the guards and do god knew what else. I sympathized with him, but strategically? No.

"I did not come here with the intention of harming anyone, Highlord . . . It is Highlord Adver, I believe?"

He grimaced faintly and enunciated. "Nearly. My name is Adver."

That's what I just said, you fucking—

I kept myself still and let the moment pass. "Unfortunately, what I intend does not always come to pass. For now, I prefer to remain in full control of the situation, so as to *ensure* no one comes to unnecessary harm."

Lady Elidred curled her lip in contempt, while her husband just gave me a long, flat look.

"If you have a family of your own, my lord," he said, "you will understand what a paltry assurance that is."

"I encourage you to judge me by my actions rather than words," I replied with a magnanimous gesture of both hands. "Of course, you haven't yet seen for yourself that your people are unharmed—but you *can* see that I have gone to the trouble of doing all this when it would have been *far* easier to wait four hours, kill you all while you slept, and loot this place to the ground."

All of them stiffened in alarm at the thought, understandably, but the two adults both frowned in comprehension.

"For that matter," I continued after giving it a moment to soak in, "if I were out for revenge, I wouldn't need to exert myself at all. It would suffice to notify Highlord Caldimer *or* Archlord Caludon that Clan Yviredh is harboring a sorcerer who can cast Null and aided Lady Gray in her battles."

"I assure you, as someone for whom it has been a pressing concern of late, it is not so easy to gain an audience with greater powers than oneself."

Highlord Adver managed to be wry and self-deprecating in the face of fourteen loaded crossbows; he didn't trouble himself with pretending he was not afraid, but controlled it masterfully.

"Granted, the likes of them have no business with any scruffy Healer." I reached up with both hands and lowered my cowl, letting the light fall across my features. It *felt* like a bigger moment than it probably was; this was an open secret around the Gutters already. I was pretty sure even Norovena knew. Still, the first time I'd deliberately unmasked myself in front of high-born. "So, naturally, it would not be the Healer who approached them."

"Are we meant to have some idea who you are?" Lady Elidred demanded scornfully.

Well, so much for that.

"If you knew anyone who mattered, you wouldn't be in this situation. What matters is that Caludon is interested in Lord Seiji. That can happen when one takes a lead role in destroying crime syndicates in his domain instead of helping prop them up."

They flinched.

Just as I opened my mouth to move on to my main point, the boy suddenly surged to his feet, thrusting his chair violently back. Immediately several crossbows swiveled to point at him but fortunately my people weren't trigger-happy enough to shoot the kid.

"Enough!" the boy barked, brandishing an accusing finger at me. "I'll not sit here and tolerate these insults! *You*, Lord Seiji, will prove your merit on the field of skill or prove the frailty of your character!"

"Ediver, sit down," his mother hissed.

"You are *embarrassing* us in front of the *bandits*," added his sister in a low growl.

Lord Ediver, who couldn't have been even Yoshi's age, stood his ground, pointing and glaring at me while I blinked, struggling to parse his demand. It took enough seconds that several of my masked followers began snickering again, causing the boy to flush bright scarlet. It had probably never occurred to him that being laughed at by lowborn was something that even *could* happen.

"Ah," I said finally. "So this country has a dueling tradition? How quaint."

"What say you then, brigand?" Ediver said, raising his chin and striving to look commanding despite the vivid pink of his ears.

"Lord Ediver, *he will kill you*," Flaerdwyd stage-whispered urgently.

"No one's killing anyone," I stated, holding up both hands. "Thank you for the offer, my lord, but I'll pass."

"Hah!" He folded his arms, tilting his head back in a misguided attempt to look down his nose at me. "Then be known as a coward!"

"I'll tell you an important secret, young man," I replied in a mild tone. "When you hold someone's life in the palm of your hand, you don't need to care whether he thinks you're a coward."

"Son," Highlord Adver began.

"That's just the kind of . . . of moralizing I would expect from a *coward*!" Ediver sneered.

I don't think "moralizing" was actually the word he wanted there.

"Don't like that one, hm? I have more. For instance, you'll note that your father, to whom you should be looking for your cues in matters of both rank and familial piety, did not offer to duel me. So, either you consider *him* a coward, or you are undermining his chosen strategy. Which is it, Lord Ediver?"

The kid blushed harder, to the point I actually began to be concerned for his blood pressure. Finally, with clear trepidation, he turned to look at his parents for cues. From his father he got only a hard stare.

"Young Lord of Clan Yviredh, you will be *seated and silent*," Lady Elidred said in a quiet voice that held six winters' worth of ice.

Ediver just sank, shame-faced, back into his chair, not even noticing that one of my armed and masked followers discreetly held it for him. His mother did, then did a tiny double-take as she saw the pale skin and dark eyes above the mask. I couldn't tell which of the noblewomen it was; Nazralind was over here by me.

"I appreciate your restraint, Lord Seiji," said Highlord Adver, nodding to me.

"Courage is a valuable quality," I replied. "Once he learns to temper it with some circumspection, the lad will go far. Anyway, I hardly consider it restraint; I don't tolerate harm to children. Now, where were we?"

"I believe we were at your mercy in our own home," Lady Elidred replied in a tone which had gained no warmth.

"Waiting," her husband added, "to discuss what amends we might offer for the inconvenience Clan Yviredh has inadvertently caused you."

"Inconvenience," I enunciated slowly. "That is certainly a way to put it. Ah, I know! Master Fur— Rhaem, why don't you bring everybody up to speed?"

He gave me a sidelong look filled with terror. I returned a benign smile.

"If you would, recount how our last meeting ended. The very moment of our parting, specifically."

Flaerdwyd cringed; his eyes darted around to the various crossbows in the room, several of which were pointed right at him, and he swallowed heavily.

"I . . . I cast my spell to . . . to stifle your magic," he said weakly. "And . . ."

"Go on," I prompted after a prolonged moment in which he seemed to struggle for words.

"And they shot you," he whispered, "with crossbows."

"How many times, Rhaem?"

"I . . . I didn't . . . It's not as if I could have counted, L-Lord S-Seiji . . ."

I smiled gently, which he did not appear to find reassuring. "Guess."

"I-it had to be at least a dozen."

"Almost! It was thirteen. Not to worry, Rhaem. That must have been hard to spot in all that chaos in the middle of the night. They were much easier to count while being pulled out."

All of them cringed at that. Even Lady Elidred averted her eyes in evident shame.

"Please continue," I said, still smiling. "What happened next?"

Flaerdwyd gulped again. "You . . . you fell. Into the river."

"The river containing all the filth and refuse of Gwyllthean," I said, smiling wider. "Bleeding from thirteen impalements. If you've not had the pleasure, by the way, it is quite impossible to swim in that river due to the current and obstructions; you'd drown even if you weren't full of quarrels. I wonder if any of you would care to hazard a description of what that *feels like*."

All of them were now pale and looked sickly at the thought. With one exception.

"How did you survive?" the youngest child of Clan Yviredh asked breathlessly. I hadn't been paying her much attention, but she was now staring avidly at me as if this were a story arranged for her entertainment. Well, I am nothing if not a performer.

"I always survive," I replied, giving her a wink. "Ah, but that *must* sound like a tall tale! Perhaps a demonstration? I know! Someone provide the Highlord with a weapon."

"That really isn't—"

Highlord Adver's interjection was cut off by one of my followers stepping forward and plunking a loaded crossbow down in front of him, next to and halfway on top of his half-eaten meal. He looked down at the illegal weapon on his dining room table as if it were a live snake. Ediver, into whose plate one of its arms protruded, leaned uneasily away, while Lady Elidred curled her lip in disgust.

"Go on, then," I said pleasantly, spreading my arms. "Take a free shot, Highlord. No hard feelings for it, upon my word. Only at *me*, I should clarify; if you harm any of my people, the ensuing discussion will be less civil. But I can take it, as you will soon see."

Silence reigned for a moment.

"All things considered, Lord Seiji," Adver finally said in an admirably controlled tone, "I believe I am inclined to take you at your word."

"And I prefer to have no violence in my *dining room*," Lady Elidred added sharply, "or I suppose I should say no *further* violence. You have discomfited my servants quite enough without forcing them to scrub *blood* out of absolutely everything."

Pretty rich, coming from someone who had never scrubbed anything in her life and didn't plan to. Still, not without a point.

"Quite right, my lady, how ill-mannered of me. My humble apologies." I gestured and the woman who'd yielded her weapon stepped forward to retrieve it. Hard to tell with the masks and cloaks, but by her height I thought it was Ydleth. "We were discussing the details of my previous encounter with Master F— with Rhaem here."

I hesitated for a fraction of a second, then changed tactics. My next line hadn't been part of the original plan, but I considered what I'd seen of these people and their household up 'til now and decided to play a hunch.

"Tell me, Rhaem. Or my lord and lady, if you happen to be aware. Do you know specifically *why* you were brought into conflict with me in the first place?"

"Not out of any spite toward you, Lord Seiji," Adver hastened to answer. "It is undoubtedly of no consolation to you, but it is the truth. Our intervention was motivated purely by an urgent need for profit. Clan Yviredh bore you no personal grudge."

"I am well aware of that," I said mildly, "hence the relatively civil tone I have chosen to take toward you. No, the grudge was Lady Gray's, which you chose to assist her in prosecuting. I am asking if you know the *reason* for it."

"We are hardly versed in the details of criminal gang warfare," Elidred replied, raising her chin.

"Oh?" I gave her a pleasant smile. "That being the case, getting *involved* in it would seem singularly unwise." I waited to see the lowering of her eyebrows and the darkening of her cheeks in acknowledgment of my point before continuing. "Rhaem? You spent the evening in the company of Gray's best and brightest. You must have been told some details."

"She— They said . . . You, um, were moving in on her territory," he mumbled.

"Oh, is *that* what they told you. That I'm just another gangster, hm? You must have found it *rather* confusing when the Kingsguard turned up to back my plan against her."

"That's not what *I* heard," the girl said unexpectedly. Nazralind had told me her name, but I couldn't remember. She seemed to be about twelve or thirteen. "The Healer went around the Gutters helping prostitutes, isn't that right?"

"Avelit, *where* did you hear such things?" her mother demanded.

I was starting to like this kid, so I rescued her.

"Exactly that," I said, nodding graciously to the girl. "I healed the women of Cat Alley. Made them less dependent on her, and ultimately, free of her entirely. I cost Lady Gray tremendously in money and prestige—not by taking over her businesses, but by wiping out a large source of the human suffering from which she drew a profit."

All five of them raised their eyes, looking around at the crossbow-toting figures surrounding them; up close, the cloaks did not conceal that these were women. I watched the nobles and Flaerdwyd put it together, and gave them a beat of silence in which to do so.

"A lot of them were indentured to various brothels in which Gray had a stake," I continued. "Most—nearly all, in fact—fraudulently. If I really wanted to put you off your dinner, I would describe the beating, deprivation, and abuse these women suffered there. It makes my own little dip in the river seem like nothing, crossbows and all. I sincerely hope you were paid *well* to aid Lady Gray in trying to put them back in their place, and punish me for liberating them from it."

I gave them another three beats of silence, watching their faces. Elidréd had closed her eyes, looking pained, and even Avelit seemed to have had the enthusiasm knocked out of her. Ediver looked like he might be sick, Highlord Adver was staring morosely at the center of the table, and poor Flaerdwyd was a portrait of human misery.

"Are you *proud* of yourselves?" I asked quietly.

In unison, all five flinched, hunched their shoulders, and lowered their faces, and I knew my little gambit had paid off. These were nobles who blithely profited from a horribly abusive power structure—well, except Flaerdwyd—but they weren't bad people. At least, they didn't want to think they were. It must have taken a lot of deliberately cultivated ignorance to protect that self-image, and tearing a hole in it had hit them harder than any physical attack I could threaten.

The man of the house rallied first, fittingly enough. Highlord Adver inhaled deeply, squared his shoulders, and deliberately lifted his head to meet my gaze directly.

"I will offer no excuse, Lord Seiji, only repeat my assertion that the full responsibility for these actions is my own. Even Rhaem's part in this has been under my control and not through his own agency. I cannot imagine what recompense I might offer for what you suffered, but I shall hear your demands and do the best I can. My *only* request is that no punishment befall my family, my staff, or any other innocents caught up in this. I am at your mercy."

I held his gaze in another long moment of silence, then drummed my fingers once on the table.

"I think you have the right of it, Highlord. You cannot imagine what recompense would be appropriate. Nor can I. Having lived through that experience, I really could not put a price on it in coinage. So, I suppose I *could* simply take my vengeance . . ."

All of them stiffened, and I let them twist for a second.

". . . but really, what would that accomplish? It would only create a new host of problems and, to be honest, probably wouldn't even make me feel better. No, the truth is, I didn't come here to punish you. On the contrary, I wish to do business."

All of them looked wary now, save Avelit who was back to being interested and excited, though she remained quiet.

"I disdain the idea of making common cause with a criminal," Lady Elidred said, grimacing, "but I suppose we have rather divested ourselves of the right to make that claim, have we not?"

"I salute your self-awareness," I said with a cheerful smile. "And I mean that sincerely. It's not a common virtue of your social class. The simple fact, my lords and ladies, is that our interests align. *Your* situation is that the Yviredh bloodline will be stripped of its Clan status by the next generation unless you can somehow arrange a marriage alliance for the young Lady Avelit, with the palest, blondest Highlord you can find, who is also somehow so desperate that he can be prevailed upon to take *her* name rather than the customary reverse. A tall order, even if you somehow manage to obtain the significant riches you hope Rhaem here can provide you. A tall *enough* order that if you can manage to scrounge up *any* such candidate, Clan Yviredh will be unable to afford such further niceties as selecting a prospect whom you can be assured will not mistreat the lady once he can claim a husband's privileges. Not to mention that this will necessarily mean Lord Ediver must abdicate his claim to primary inheritance in order to let this putative stranger take his role as Highlord."

They were all visibly unhappy at this recitation, the two kids both looking distinctly queasy. I felt pretty awful about how all the life seemed to have drained from Avelit on the spot, but hell, *this* part of the mess was no doing of mine.

"In short," I summarized, planting my elbows on the table and leaning forward to stare at them over my interlaced fingers, "you are in trouble."

I gave them a moment to dwell on it.

"Your situation is worse than you know," I finally said, hammering the point home, "and your dangers far more immediate. My appearance here is only the *first* consequence of your extremely ill-advised foray into organized crime, not the worst. The end result will be Clan Aelthwyn and Clan Olumnach learning you have a Null caster, and that you used him in aid of Lady Gray's dying organization. The Archlord will take Furud—Rhaem, of course. Whether or not he'll care about that business with Lady Gray, I don't know. He seems an unpredictable fellow, from what I'm told. But Highlord Caldimer will care *very much*, as I think you know. His obsession with Lady Gray is deeply personal, and he is not a forgiving man."

"There is— I mean, we have no reason to think any of the other Clans even *could* find out," Highlord Adver said, looking a shade paler than he'd been a moment ago. "Ah—that is, of course, once you and I come to an arrangement. Obviously, I will gladly and *handsomely* reward your discretion, Lord Seiji."

I heaved a sigh. "I'm not going to take your money for a service I can't provide, Highlord. The secret *will* get out. Or how do you think *I* found out who you are?"

His eyes widened in realization, and his wife turned a similarly wide-eyed stare on him. They had seriously not considered this until that very moment, huh? My god, these people were as deep over their heads as I was. Worse, in fact.

"I learned of Rhaem and his patrons from a *goblin information broker*," I continued, making them all flinch again. "The knowledge is out there. You are currently sitting in a *brief* reprieve because their Clans are as reluctant as yours to talk to the scurrilous types who could fill them in, but that won't last forever. Clan Olumnach already deals with—well, look who I'm talking to; you know very well how they make their money. I don't know how long it will take, but my guess is not very. The word will spread, and the hammer will fall."

"You are foreign," said Elidred, gamely trying to rally her haughty courage. "The Clans of Fflyr Dlemathlys *do not* spill one another's blood. This covenant has held since the Liberation. It will not be broken over this."

"Okay, let's say Highlord Caldimer isn't too volatile to respect that," I replied, gesturing magnanimously. "I've heard differing reports on the matter, but we'll assume it for the sake of argument. Say all that's going to happen to you is that you lose your Null caster, along with every silver disc you were paid by Lady Gray and whatever other punitive damages the Archlord chooses to impose."

All of them were cringing already, but I didn't give them even a second to regroup.

"There is a *lot* a man in control of this island's bandit gangs can do to make your lives miserable without spilling one drop of your noble blood. I do hope you've enjoyed being able to send or receive anything from this house without having it seized in transit, because those days are about to end. For that matter, I think you will find it rather impossible to defend your lands from bandit raids when your Clansguard is a handful of men barely sufficient to hold your own house against attack. This close to Gwyllthean, you depend on the Kingsguard and your neighbors for protection, am I right? How do you imagine that will go when you have active enemies and the personal annoyance of Archlord Caludon?"

I allowed them to welter in the reality of their situation for four beats. Poor Ediver looked like he was struggling not to cry.

"As it so happens," I finally said in a milder tone, leaning back in the dining chair and favoring them with a languid smile, "our interests align. My own plans focus heavily on the eventual removal of Caldimer Olumnach as a player of any significant import on this island, and in the short term, his *thorough* inability to spare any resources to come after you, or anyone else. I can also provide a safe place to shelter Rhaem beyond the reach of the Archlord. I won't promise not to put his skills to work, should I find a need, but I can guarantee his safe return once the danger passes or a suitable business partner can be found. I will warn you, however, that all of this is contingent upon his willing participation. My organization will not be party to anyone's enslavement."

"I am here by my own agreement," Flaerdwyd interjected, leaning forward and staring fervently at me. "Highlord Adver and Lady Elidred have been incredibly kind to me—they've given me everything. I am *proud* to do my part to secure Clan Yviredh's future!"

"Good, then that's my biggest concern resolved," I said, smiling placidly. "Lastly, but definitely not least, I can promise that cooperation with me will be profitable for all involved. I couldn't say how much of a nest egg you'll need to make the necessary introductions to some power able to barter for Rhaem's true worth, but I should think that every disc helps."

"All this is . . . astonishingly generous, Lord Seiji," Adver said warily, "especially considering the . . . circumstances under which we have . . . become acquainted."

"Oh, do not mistake me." I dropped the smile and leaned forward again. "I'm not offering charity, and you had best not expect generosity. Your blundering got me shot full of quarrels and dumped in a river. *I am displeased with you people*, and my *annoyance* will be reflected in the terms of the arrangement we make."

"I understand your position, Lord Seiji," the Highlord replied, dipping his head. His wife tightened her lips, but did not intervene.

"That said," I continued, relaxing my posture, "I see far too much benefit to me in an alliance to be worth retaliating. So, I will put it to you, Highlord Adver, since you have so admirably taken responsibility for planting yourself right in my way. Will you accept my aid in facing your problems on less-than-generous terms, or shall I simply leave Clan Yviredh to its self-inflicted fate?"

Adver inhaled slowly, then shifted his head to lock eyes with his wife. Elidred met his gaze intently and they seemed to be communicating in silence for a few seconds, before she inclined her head infinitesimally toward him.

He turned back to meet my expectant stare again and cleared his throat.

"What arrangement did you have in mind, Lord Seiji?"

And just like that, I had a Clan on my side. They were a sad little specimen of a Clan, but they'd do for a start.

26

In Which the Dark Lord
Goes Visiting

Instead of sleeping in a warm, cozy guest room in the luxurious Caer Yviredh, we got to camp amid the damp khora and really enjoy that crisp autumn chill up close. I didn't regret the decision, though, because while I had hammered out a foundational agreement for my alliance with Clan Yviredh, we were a long way from establishing mutual trust. I didn't exactly expect them to try to slit our throats in our sleep—and Biribo would have made that a futile attempt anyway—but I preferred to both conceal our numbers and preserve our element of surprise.

"What's that symbol on those pennants?" I asked Nazralind while we lurked in the khora in the damp chill of the early morning, staring at the distant village with the manor rising up atop the hill behind it. The view was actually quite picturesque, especially with Ephemera's oddly colored sky. "It reminds me of a kanji, but I can't read it."

"Ah, that's their Clan sigil," she explained. "Why did you expect to be able to read it?"

"Blessing of Wisdom," Biribo said pointedly.

"Oh! Right, I always forget about that. Sorry, Lord Seiji, that's a rare Blessing—I don't think I've actually met anyone else who has it. But no, sigils are a Fflyr artistic tradition that goes back to before the Liberation. They *start* as glyphs, but you arrange them on top of each other instead of in a line and then adjust the lines according to the traditional rules of the art 'til you get something that looks less jumbled and more . . . well, decorative. Every Clan has a sigil on their heraldry that's made from the glyphs for words they think represent them, but making sigils out of glyphs is one of the traditional arts, and they get put on everything. Buildings, clothes, book covers . . . Most noblewomen are taught to do it. I'm surprised you haven't seen more of them, Lord Seiji."

"I largely haven't been hanging around with highborn."

"Fair point. Are, ah, kanji a similar art form?"

"No, they're a form of writing, like Fflyr glyphs. Our written language uses two alphabetic scripts for its syllabary, one for native words and one for loanwords because we've imported a *lot* of vocabulary. Then we also have kanji, which is an older writing system where a single symbol represents a whole word."

She blinked. "That sounds . . . incredibly convoluted."

"Hey, Fflyr isn't much better. You may only have one alphabet, but you're still using two different writing systems. Where my mother's from, they use a script with two alphabets and no whole-word symbols. One of the alphabets is barely even used; it just designates proper nouns and the beginnings of sentences."

"Now *that* just sounds like all the worst of both ideas. Writing anything out must take *reams* of paper if you have to spell the whole word phonetically every time."

"I've been wondering why the dual system in written Fflyr, by the way. The two don't even look like they were designed by the same culture."

"They weren't," said Biribo. "Fflyr is written using the high elven alphabetic script that originated in what's now Lancor, and the glyphs are remnants of Savin writing. This whole country's history is made of the push and pull between those two cultures, up until the landbridge collapsed and Savindar was cut off. For centuries before that they were both trying to colonize these islands."

"That's why Caer Yviredh is all straight lines and ninety-degree angles, when Fflyr architecture is all about natural khora shapes," Nazralind added, nodding toward the manor on the distant hill. "It's been remodeled multiple times and those *definitely* aren't the original outer walls, but that's an ancient Lancoral fort. Nearly all the Clan fortresses predate the kingdom itself, on this island at least. Clans like to set themselves up on top of water sources, Spirits, and other points of interest, and there were usually fortifications already around those for the same reason."

"Mm." I rubbed my chin, peering thoughtfully up at the manor. In the middle distance, the village was waking up, people beginning to disperse into the surrounding fields. "Should I have one of these sigils?"

"I thought the whole point of being the Dark Lord is you can do business however you want," said Aster.

"What she said," Nazralind agreed. "But having one will make Fflyr respect you more, if you decide that matters to you. If you *want* a sigil, I can make one for you, Lord Seiji. You'd just have to decide what glyphs to use. So, between two and five describing . . . well, you. Your aims, virtues, personal fixations, whatever you'd choose to emphasize."

"Slimes and whores!" Kastrin suggested.

Aster clamped a hand over her mouth, almost doubling over with suppressed laughter; there was no end of braying and cackling from less discreet comrades behind us.

"That's some top-notch lurking, ladies," I said acidly, turning to sweep a glare across the group. "Did you all simultaneously forget we are trying to be *quiet?*"

"They'd best remember quickly," said Biribo. "Our guests of honor are heading this way."

"*Get it together,*" Aster said sharply, as if she hadn't been laughing almost as hard two seconds ago. "Focus up, girls; it's time to work."

It was a couple more minutes before our visitors rode into sight over the hill, by which time everybody had pulled themselves together. I examined them through the very handy spyglass I had "inherited" from the late and unlamented Lord Arider.

"Who're the riders?" Nazralind asked from behind and above me, having hopped into her saddle.

"Hm," I grunted, lowering and collapsing the little telescope. "Interesting choice . . . Almost the whole family. That's Adver, Elidred and Ediver on horseback—oh, they named him a combination of their names; I just got that. Only left Avelit at home, poor kid. And four soldiers on foot. That's gotta be half their Clansguard."

"Why on foot?" Kastrin asked, adjusting her mask into place. "They can't be going far if they expect them to keep up with horses."

"Well, we assumed they were going to lead us into the khora," said Nazralind. "Horses are no good on that terrain. They'd break a leg within ten paces."

She patted Newneh's neck smugly, earning a soft chirp of approval. Indeed, while gwynneks couldn't match horses for either top speed or endurance on flat ground, they could go places horses simply could not, and go *faster* in those places than even the best scouts. Their long, sinuous bodies could navigate very tight gaps, their clawed feet had excellent purchase almost everywhere, and best of all, their little stubby wings had grasping fingers on the joints; the birds could climb better than humans, and even glide for short descents, even with a rider. No one and nothing would outpace gwynneks through dense, wild khora.

Now that I had a squad of gwynnek riders, I planned to make full use of this capability. In fact, it was central to my strategy for the next phase of the campaign.

"You all know your jobs," I said quietly, watching the Yviredhs approach. "Stealth is paramount; stay *just* close enough to keep track of us, and keep your eyes peeled ahead. You'll undoubtedly spot our target before we do. Move to surround them as soon as you have their location and wait for my signal."

"You can count on us, Lord Seiji," Nazralind promised, echoed by murmurs of assent from the rest of the squad.

I nodded at her and stepped forward with only Aster and Kastrin flanking me, while the riders and the majority of my crusaders on foot began melting away into the khora. We waited in the open while the party approached us. One of the Clansguard I recognized—Adelly had shot him in the face with a tranquilizer dart last night. He was glaring more intensely than the others. Fair enough, guy.

"Lord Seiji." Adver reined in his horse with a little difficulty; all three animals started to appear nervous as they approached, prancing and snorting. Oh right, they probably smelled the gwynneks. "I appreciate your punctuality."

"And I yours, Highlord Adver," I replied politely. Politely, but without offering any heirat gesture, to the visible disapproval of the accompanying Clansguard and his wife. "I'm a little surprised to see most of the family, considering the day's itinerary."

"My son is at an age to begin participating in the business of his Clan," Adver replied, "whatever that business might happen to be. He will need to administer the affairs of Clan Yviredh himself one day."

Behind him, Ediver's expression fell, for which I couldn't blame him; despite his father's statement, the actual plan was for Ediver's inheritance to go to someone else to preserve the Yviredh name.

"And, unconventional as it may seem, I am in the habit of including my wife in those of my affairs from which law and custom do not actively prohibit her involvement," Adver added, giving her a fond look. "There is no one whose opinion I value more."

"I do not fear those to whom we have offered shelter and tolerance," said Lady Elidred, lifting her chin. "Besides, it's not as if we are helpless, Lord Seiji. I *presume* you do not object to the presence of our Clansguard—"

She had to break off, reining in her mare as the horse tried to rear, snorting and laying her ears back. The gwynneks had to be gone by now . . . but I guess they couldn't have gone far, since my people needed to stay close enough to follow us.

"Not at all," I replied, stepping forward and raising a hand, ignoring the two guards who grabbed the hilts of their swords at my approach. The horse rolled its eyes, jerking its head away, and Elidred grimaced as she fought for control.

Tame Beast.

It was one of the less flashy spells, the visible effect only occurring in the eyes of the horse itself, easy to miss if you weren't looking right at them. The mare immediately stilled, facing me directly with her ears alertly forward.

"There you go, girl, it's all right," I murmured, reaching up to stroke her long face. "Nothing to worry about." Huh. A horse's nose was a lot softer than I would've thought. And those teeth were a lot less scary to someone who'd recently been getting accustomed to gwynneks.

"How did—" Lady Elidred leaned to her left to stare at me in consternation past the horse's neck. "Mehnny does *not* like strangers."

"Well, I've heard animals are good judges of character," I said innocently, then winked at her. "I guess we just learned otherwise, eh?"

Elidred's eyebrows drew together. She clearly didn't find me amusing, but I got the feeling I had just scored some points, at least.

Highlord Adver dismounted, handing his reins to one of his soldiers, and a moment later his son followed suit. I backed away, yielding room as he stepped over to help his wife down from her saddle. Lady Elidred was clearly a skilled enough rider that she didn't need his assistance, but I found the chivalry of the gesture more charming than I wanted to admit. This country—this *planet*—was such an unmitigated shitshow most of the time that every little touch of wholesomeness was precious, even from people whom I didn't want to like; I actively resented how fast they were making me like them against my will.

Two of the Clansguard peeled off, leading the three horses away by their reins, and I had to wonder what had been the point of the highborn riding such a short distance to meet me. Well, Nazralind had said that aristocrats were keenly conscious of appearances, often to the detriment of sense.

"Well, then," said Adver, "let us not dawdle amid the cold dew. If you will follow me, Lord Seiji, I'll show you to the camp."

I glanced at Elidred and Ediver. "I gather it must not be far?"

"Not terribly, no," he agreed, starting into the khora. I saw, now, that there was a faint but distinct game trail leading into the shadows beneath the huge shells and fronds; the Highlord stepped directly onto it. "Honesty compels me to acknowledge that nothing within my domain is *terribly* far from anything else. One can comfortably patrol the entire fief several times within a day."

His wife walked alongside him, holding his arm, which was tight, but there was space for two to walk abreast so long as both were careful of their footing. I fell into step right behind them, Aster and Kastrin sticking to my back, and I didn't see how Ediver and the two remaining soldiers arranged themselves.

"I must say, I'm surprised at how much you seem to trust these bandits on your property," I commented.

"Oh?"

"I doubt I would lead most of my family right into the lair of a criminal gang with only two guards to protect us."

"*I* am far from helpless!" Ediver said stridently from the near distance behind me. Indeed, he wore the rapier at his waist with the ease of someone accustomed to its weight, though I had a sneaking suspicion he was a less deadly combatant than he believed.

"I believe I told you, Lord Seiji, that I have no fear of men to whom my family has offered succor," Elidred said pointedly, glancing over her shoulder at me.

"Perhaps that's what puzzles me," I mused aloud. "The . . . nature of your relationship with this group."

The big question I had for them the night before was exactly *how* they had gotten in touch with Lady Gray, since the Yviredhs seemed generally too squeamish to involve themselves with criminals, and it wasn't like she publicized her address. As it turned out, Clan Yviredh paid a small, discreet tribute to Clan Olumnach, as did all of their neighbors, ensuring they were left alone by the little bandit gangs which dotted this part of the island. The Yviredhs, however, went several steps further. Whereas most gangs had to eke out their own survival in the deep khora, Clan Yviredh allowed this small crew to live unmolested on their own claimed land, far enough into the khora to ensure them some privacy but well within striking distance had they chosen to launch an attack. Not only that, but they weren't relegated to subsisting on what they could scrounge or steal. The Clan themselves discreetly sent them food and other supplies.

That explained why the bandits had been willing to introduce them to the Gwyllthean criminal element, and perhaps why they were comfortable coming here with me—though I suspected that also had to do with these sheltered highborn failing to appreciate how dangerous this could be—but left me with the question of *why* they would do all this. Last night I had stayed focused on the business of arranging my introduction to their pet bandits, but if there was ever a time to indulge my curiosity, this was it.

"I would not presume to know the weight of a man's soul," said Lady Elidred, again shooting me a look over her shoulder. "That is for the Goddess to judge. What I *do* know is that this island has been wracked by poverty and strife since . . . the events of some years back."

Adver gave his wife a warning look and she paused. Ah yes, the siege. Did she really think *that* was the cause of all the corruption on Dount? Well, it made sense that highborn would be reluctant to badmouth their Archlord, even if he was a sadistic monster. *Especially* if he was a sadistic monster.

"I'm sure there are truly evil people in the world," Elidred continued more quietly. "Undoubtedly such men are drawn to the criminal lifestyle. But I also know that many who have fallen into banditry did so out of desperation. Many are runaway indentures. I will not endorse their failure to repay justly owed debts, but it is also true that men laboring on the farms are as likely to die of overwork as live to earn back their freedom."

Far likelier, the way I heard it. For that matter, I was shocked to hear such sentiments coming from a highborn.

"But Clan Yviredh kept indentured servants to work its own farms."

Both of them paused, since they couldn't watch where they were going while shooting me angry looks.

"*Our* servants have always been justly provided for," Highlord Adver stated, meeting my gaze with pride and no fear for once. "Clan Yviredh holds sacred its duty to kingdom and Goddess. Those chosen by Her will are to lead with virtue and shepherd their people to prosperity. The men laboring in our fields have always been given enough to eat, warm and safe housing, and sufficient time to rest. We meticulously track the value of their contributions and see them released once their debts are paid."

"And yet," I pointed out, "you suddenly released all your indentures."

Adver and Elidred exchanged another married look, suddenly not so prideful, and turned to resume walking.

"Yes, well," the Highlord answered much less assertively, "since bringing young Master Flaerdwyd into our household and conversing with him, we have . . . learned things about the legal system on Dount. Throughout Dlemathlys entire, as it turns out. He told us many of those pressed into indentured service had been so under fraudulent conditions, for debts not owed. Having learned that . . . Well, a change had to be made."

This time it was I who stopped walking in sheer stupefaction, immediately causing a pileup as Aster and Kastrin ran right into me and the two-and-a-half men bringing up the rear barely avoided knocking us all down. Someone muttered a word which I suspected they generally didn't dare speak in the presence of the family.

The Highlord and Lady had turned again at the commotion, and now Adver gave me a wry little smile. "You seem surprised, Lord Seiji. Yes, I was as well. For that reason, I investigated this carefully, and I regret to assure you that it is quite true. I hope you are not too shocked to learn of it."

"Shocked to *learn*—" I cut myself off, dragging a hand down my face. "Highlord Adver, I'm afraid you have the wrong idea. I am *shocked* to learn that you *didn't know*."

Both of them stiffened, Elidred lowering her eyes.

"That may not be entirely fair, Lord Seiji," said Aster from behind me. "Highborn live . . . insulated lives. I can believe that those few not actively participating in this country's corruption have no idea how deep it runs."

My god, these people were hopeless. What had I gotten myself into? Well, access to highborn circles would continue to be useful, even once my business with the local bandits was wrapped up, but still . . . unbelievable. I controlled my expression with some difficulty.

"Anyway. Forgive the interruption, my lord. After you."

Adver opened his mouth as if to say something, then just nodded once, stiffly, and continued through the forest at a pace considerate of his wife in her—now that I noticed—shoes which were entirely impractical for traipsing through wild khora.

I followed in silence.

It was the most pathetic bandit camp I'd seen yet.

For one thing, unlike every other gang I'd attacked, they hadn't chosen a defensible location, or even one with enough space to make a proper camp. These clowns had just planted a campfire right in the intersection of two game trails and laid out bedrolls and miscellaneous satchels of supplies along the trails themselves. A couple of crude lean-to shelters had been constructed against the various khora, which sprouted from the middle of their camp. You couldn't see the whole thing from any part of it, including the center.

For another, it was close to deserted. Highlord Adver had reported their numbers at nineteen men and women as of his most recent information, but we found only six dragging themselves out of their blankets. And not a one of them keeping watch.

"Highlord!" a man in exactly the kind of shabby coat I expected exclaimed, scrambling upright and kicking one of his slower companions. "And—Lady Elidred! Wh-what brings you? I'm sorry, this place isn't fit for . . ."

"It's all right, Master Viarin," Adver said soothingly. "It is Viarin, correct?"

"Ah—that's . . . I mean, yes, my lord. Madon Viarin, your servant." He folded down his hands, the rest of the gang doing likewise. "I'm . . . very flattered you remember, Highlord."

All of them were now upright and nervously studying their guests, especially me and my companions. Kastrin was a cloaked and masked figure carrying a crossbow, Aster had that huge, clearly magical, sword strapped to her back, and I . . .

"Oh shit," one of the men whispered, his eyes widening. "Oh fuck, oh shit, it's *him*."

"Mind your fucking language in front of the highborn," Madon Viarin hissed, and then his eyes widened as he realized what he'd just said. "Ah— I meant— That is—"

"Let's not stand excessively on ceremony, gentlemen," Adver said with an amused little smile, which immediately faded as he glanced around in concern. "Master Viarin, where is everyone? Surely you can't have lost over two-thirds of your number in the last week?"

"Ah . . . I, um. That is, no, my lord. They're all well, last I heard." He ducked his head, refusing to meet the Highlord's eyes. "It's just . . . Th-the *other* Clan. You know."

"Clan Olumnach is fully invested in taking over Lady Gray's abandoned territory in the Gutters," I explained. "He'll have pulled all his gangs out of their usual stomping grounds and sent them into town. There is a narrow window of opportunity for him while Gray's organization is reduced to broken stragglers, and the civilian population is reeling from the Kingsguard's crackdown. And thus, a narrow window of opportunity for *me* to hit his forces from the rear while they are depleted and distracted. Hence my haste in coming here."

"Oh bugger," one of the bandits whispered. "I only just got used to banditry. Are we doing *politics* now?" One of his less eloquent comrades smacked
him quiet.

"So let's not waste any time," I said, then raised my voice, projecting it
powerfully through the forest. "Ladies!"

They came melting out of every shadow on command, with a skill that
made me nearly shed a tear of pride. Cloaked, crossbow-toting women
stepped forward, encircling all of us so suddenly that the two Yviredh
Clansguard whirled and drew their swords in a panic, as did Lord Ediver. The
bandits clustered together, one of them actually whimpering, as the second
ring arrived behind the first—gwynneks looming over the first rank, ridden
by more cloaked figures, the ladies carrying their own shortbows, which they
still preferred to my crossbows. At this, even Lady Elidred drew in a sharp,
hissing breath.

It was *beautiful*. The sheer, flawlessly executed *presentation* of it. That
was how I knew I'd raised my girls right—they understood the importance
of *showtime*.

"And now," I said pleasantly, lowering my hood in a languid motion that
stretched out and added weight to the moment, "we will discuss who has
paid . . . the price."

27

In Which the Dark Lord Enrolls Some Nobles in the School of Hard Knocks

"Ohh no," the talkative bandit groaned. "He said the thing."

Two of his compatriots smacked him quiet this time.

"All right, ladies," I said. "Everyone crowd around, get a good look. You know the drill—sing out if you have a claim to make."

"What's he talking about?" one of the men whispered as my followers shifted position. A couple glanced behind them, clearly considering trying to bolt since the crossbow-toting women were all moving around to the front where they could see the men's faces. Any such ideas were dissuaded by a matching movement of the second rank—the gwynnek riders guided their mounts to form an even more terrifying killbox behind them.

"Yes, what *are* you talking about?" Lady Elidred demanded.

"A moment, please, my lady," I said politely. "This should not take long. Well, any familiar faces?"

"Him," said a voice from the crowd, pointing.

"Me?" squeaked the most vocal of the bandits, pointing at his own face.

"No, to your left."

"Wh—*me?*"

"His *other* left, dumbass!"

The guy to his actual left looked alarmed, as well he should. "What is this? What did *I* do?"

"Yeah, you're right." I recognized the woman who moved forward, despite the cloaks and masks. Thwynit was one of those who still liked to wear her skimpy prostitute dress under the black cloak, and she was nearly as well-endowed as Minifrit; I had begun actively avoiding looking at her out of fear of triggering a flashback. Now, she hefted her crossbow, drawing a hiss of fear from the man indicated as she prodded his chin, forcing him to raise his face into a more visible position. "I recognize him. This is Freebie Guy."

"Well, I mean . . ." Freebie Guy grinned weakly, trying to put on a disarming facade without taking his eyes from the loaded weapon centimeters from his face. "We're bandits. Aren't we all Freebie Guys, by definition?"

"What are you all *talking* about?" Lord Ediver exclaimed in exasperation.

"Hey, it *is* Freebie Guy!" Keffin exclaimed, incongruously cheerful as was her personal brand. "I totally didn't recognize him. Never seen him in the daylight before."

"He'd come into the establishments in Cat Alley to drink with his buddies," Adelly stated in a much grimmer tone. "Paid for his ale and food and left without hiring a girl. He liked to joke about getting 'freebies.' Then, some nights, he'd lurk around the rear exits by the canals. Down at the ends of the street where the poorer cathouses were, the ones without bouncers, to see if he could catch somebody outside. Over the last two years, he raped Lannin and Miarit and another girl whose name I didn't learn, and those are just the ones I personally know of."

"Also Norrie," said Kastrin, raising her own crossbow to firing position.

Silence descended and reigned for a chilling moment as Freebie Guy became the focus of everyone's direct stares. The movement was subtle but noticeable as every single crossbow shifted from covering the group to aiming at him directly.

"Hey, now, let's . . . let's not blow this out of proportion," he said with a nervous grin, raising both hands. The men to both sides of him had already begun edging away from the line of fire. "Come on, now, be realistic. We *are* talking about whores. That's . . . Basically, it's just shoplifting, right?"

It was really amazing how menacing a formerly awkward silence could suddenly become without anybody saying anything.

"I mean, come on," Freebie Guy stammered, starting to take shuffling little steps backward, apparently having forgotten about the bow-wielding gwynnek riders in that direction. "I'm already reduced to living in the forest like an animal. What more do you want?"

I cleared my throat. "Well, then. Anyone have a personal claim?"

"Just a moment," Highlord Adver interjected. "Personal claim to what?"

He was ignored, which was probably a new experience for him. I looked around at my silent followers for a drawn-out moment during which no one spoke up.

"Very well," I said at last. "If no one present has dibs—"

Five separate crossbow bolts slammed into Freebie Guy, one—probably Kastrin's—cleanly through his eye; he was dead by the time he hit the ground. The rest of his gang dived away, huddling into the scant cover of khora outcroppings. Behind me, I heard an abortive scream from Lady Elidred, quickly silenced as she regained control.

"*Lord Seiji!*" Adver thundered, taking an aggressive step toward me and seeming not even to notice the crossbows which were turned on him in response. "I have granted these men leave to stay on my lands! I don't know how things are done in *your* country, but in this part of the world to assault another Clan's vassals within its own domain is tantamount to an act of war!"

I stared at him steadily for a moment, and then looked pointedly at his two soldiers, who had stepped up protectively alongside Lady Elidred. Then around at my encircling armed followers.

This fucking guy, I swear to god.

"I shall have to throw myself upon your forbearance, Highlord," I said, bowing to him. "Unless you would care to have a discussion about what these men have been doing, and your responsibility for it."

That took the wind out of his sails immediately. I let him flounder for two beats before continuing in a gentler tone.

"It's the inherent dilemma of sponsoring bandits. Believe me, I know. As you and your lady wife have so aptly observed, many of those driven to banditry are victims expelled from normal society because Fflyr Dlemathlys is a preposterous heap of nested injustices clumsily masquerading as a nation. Many, perhaps even most, but not *all*. There are also those who would have ended up as criminals in any country due to their own predilections."

"And so you would have them judged by—by *whom?*" Elidred hissed. "A random coterie of prostitutes?"

I turned to her with a shrug. "Who better?"

The Lady gaped at me, lacking an answer to that.

"After all," I said with a pleasant smile, "what's a whore worth? Absolutely no one cares about them. You can do pretty much anything to a whore, and what's she gonna do about it? Go to a guard? They'd laugh, and if she was lucky that's *all* they'd do. The Cat Alley girls all know better than to be caught alone by the Kingsguard if they don't want to get beaten up and probably raped. A judge? Those guys are the reason most of them were fraudulently indentured and ended up in brothels in the first place. A whore is *nothing* in this society. And that means they get to learn *truth*. If you want to know who someone truly is, my lords and lady, you have to watch what they do when their actions have no consequences. Priests, judges, nobles . . . None of them know the weight of men's souls. The whores know. They know better than anyone should have to."

I met the eyes of each of the nobles in turn; Ediver was frowning as if chewing on these ideas, but his parents just looked gobsmacked.

"I'll tell you something else I've learned since coming to your charming country," I said, turning back to the huddled bandits. "Guys like that can never seem to control themselves for long. You, Master Viarin. Tell me, who *else* did Freebie Guy here go after?"

Viarin peeked at me over a large khora root, wide-eyed and trembling.

"No one's going to shoot you," I said gently. "Come on. There was something, wasn't there? Probably a whole bunch of somethings. Little . . . *incidents*. Right?"

"I . . . he . . ." Viarin swallowed heavily, his eyes flicking from one loaded crossbow to another in rapid succession. "Th-there was . . . once, here in the gang. W-we tried not to let Deckon be alone with . . . I mean, around women. But, uh . . . he got to one of the village girls one time. We, um, were more careful about him since that."

"That would be *this* village?" I prompted. "On this land?" Viarin nodded, and I turned a pleasant smile upon Lady Elidred, who had gone bone-pale. "That would be one of your own people, then, who looks to Clan Yviredh for protection. That happened to her because you lot were fostering and *sponsoring* bandits in the nearby forest, with no plan to control them."

"We . . . it's not as if *we* had any ambition to send them against our enemies," Highlord Adver said weakly.

"We laid out rules," Elidred whispered. "They were not to touch our people. They *promised* us."

One of the women surrounding us let out a loud, derisive snort. The remaining five bandits were just beginning to creep out from behind the khora again. Now they all hunched and avoided looking at Lady Elidred.

"Compassion is a wonderful thing," I said quietly. "I wish more highborn had as much as you two. Unfortunately, compassion not tempered with sense and restraint only gets taken advantage of. That's another thing the lowborn know, because they never have the chance to go through life without learning it the hard way."

"You don't know what it's like out here," Viarin said, his own voice barely above a whisper. "Even with the Clan's kindness . . . You depend on the people around you. None of us could make it on our own. We couldn't chase him out because . . . I mean. You learn . . . to *tolerate* things. You just don't know."

"I do, in fact, know what it's like," I answered. "So do all of these ladies. That's why you aren't being shot right now, and won't be. All of us have had to do things we're ashamed of just to get by for one more day, and we'll all undoubtedly have to do more before the end. But together, we can do a *little* bit better. You work for me now, gentlemen, and that means there are rules, and standards. No more standing side by side with rapists, for one."

"I see," Lord Ediver said unexpectedly, nodding and wearing an expression of dawning revelation. "So there *is* honor amongst thieves."

Oh, hell no. I could see the direction of the kid's thoughts and moved immediately to shut that down.

"Do *not* mistake anything you just saw for justice, Lord Ediver," I stated. "It wasn't. Retribution is the inadequate substitute we have to settle for because there *is* no justice in this damn country. You are a member of the ruling class; you have more influence over things than any of us. If you want to *help*, grow up to implement actual justice where you can, instead of just killing assholes where they pop up."

"I understand, Lord Seiji," he said, nodding again and staring at me with a fervent look that reminded me uncomfortably of . . . In fact, no, it was the *exact* same expression I'd seen on Yoshi's face the first time a goddess told him he could be a Hero. The look of a kid who had not listened to a thing I'd tried to tell him and just found a new way to be chuuni about it.

Fuck it, I tried.

"All right," I said more briskly. "Viarin, I'll need to borrow you for the time being."

Master Viarin squeaked rather like a dog toy.

"With Highlord Adver's permission, of course," I added, turning to the lord himself. "We'll need to return to the manor to plan the next step, and the input of someone who's been on the ground out here will be invaluable. Don't worry, Viarin, you're not in trouble."

"I . . . yes, of course," Adver said slowly, seeming slightly dazed by the events of the last few minutes. "That is quite sensible, Lord Seiji. I have maps and knowledge of the island's politics, but I am rather in the dark about the movements of bandit gangs apart from this one. It's a shame Kandwyd was taken to Gwyllthean. Ah, that was the de facto leader of this gang, Lord Seiji."

I nodded to him before shifting my attention elsewhere. "Mimi! Take your team and incorporate these new guys. I want you to bring them up to speed on my expectations and how we do things. Remember what it's like for first-timers and take it easy on them as much as possible. The carrot rather than the stick, when you can. That said, we haven't the luxury of time to dawdle; if any of them try to attack you or flee, shoot them on the spot."

My five new recruits hunched their shoulders in frightened unison, but Miriami just nodded once from astride her gwynnek. "Hai!"

I managed, barely, not to spoil my presentation by outwardly goggling at her. What was *that*? I didn't remember doing that in front of . . . *When* had she picked that up?

"Job one is to establish a new campsite," I said, mastering myself. "A more *discreet* spot, far enough from here that when the Olumnach Clansguard come around to check in on this lot, they won't immediately stumble across it. Our new friends know the terrain and can help you. Take what's immediately useful and *portable* from this site, and we'll retrieve the rest later. I want you to set up a *light* camp, something that can be pulled up and moved quickly, and once you've done that, scout around to find more locations to which you can retreat."

"You want to . . . hide from Clan Olumnach?" said the chattery bandit whose name I still hadn't learned. "Uh, m'lord, this ain't a *huge* khora patch, and out the other side is Clan Fwyndlich land. Scouts who find this spot abandoned will be able to track us."

"Yes, but tracking takes time," I said patiently. "And because you will be keeping a *proper* watch, you'll see them coming and be able to evade. I don't want you throwing down with any Clansguards if it's at all avoidable; the objective is to deny the Olumnachs a grip on you. Congratulations, you are being liberated."

All five of them instinctively looked down at the remains of Freebie Guy.

"What do we do about Deckon?" Viarin asked nervously.

"Ah right, thanks for reminding me. Girls, retrieve your quarrels, there's no sense in wasting ammo."

Viarin drew in a deep breath, visibly steeling himself. "I meant his body, Lord Seiji."

"You mean the bait left out to confuse the Olumnach scouts?" I held his gaze, keeping my face expressionless. "Mimi will catch you up on the rules, but I'll tell you up front that we do *not* tolerate any abuse of women or harm to children in my organization. Anyone who pulls that shit gets left for the crawns. Am I clear?"

". . . clear, m'lord," he said. The others nodded.

"Mimi, once you settle on a spot, send someone to the manor to bring Viarin back to it."

"Hai!" she repeated crisply. "All right, gentlemen, you heard Lord Seiji. Welcome to the team. I want everyone packed and moving—you have five minutes before I start getting *motivational*."

"We should . . ." Everyone had already started separating into groups, so despite Lady Elidred's lowered voice, I clearly heard her since I was just that moment stepping over to rejoin the Yviredhs. They had clustered closer together, Ediver looking puffed up and clearly imagining himself to be his mother's protector out here in the wilderness. Lady Elidred had to pause and clear her throat before continuing, her dark eyes still fixed on the corpse. "Master Viarin, I must learn who this village girl was. This . . . What happened to her was our responsibility, the result of the Clan's actions. She is owed some recompense."

"I, ah . . ." Viarin cringed and dry-washed his hands. "My lady, I don't . . . know. We avoid going near the villagers, like you told us. I *might* recognize her if I saw her again, but . . ."

"Lady Elidred," Aster spoke up unexpectedly. "A young woman with a good reputation would not want attention drawn to something like that. Most likely she would prefer to put it fully behind her. The criminal has been punished, and the other bandits are *properly* under control now. The best thing Clan Yviredh can do for her now is continue to provide the best governance possible for *all* of your people."

To judge by their expressions, neither of the Yviredhs were accustomed to lowborn talking to them out of turn, let alone offering unsolicited advice on how to administer their fief. After the events of the morning, though, both appeared too rattled by everything they'd just seen to object. Especially Lady Elidred. Despite my generally low opinion of nobility as a concept and Fflyr nobility specifically, I couldn't help feeling bad for Elidred, who I could tell was badly shaken.

Ediver, though . . . I turned my attention to the teenager just in time to *see* the moment when he registered that Aster was quite pretty and well-built. Poor kid was probably gonna have a *thing* about women with big swords now. Oh well, there were worse qualities a boy could go for.

Highlord Adver cleared his throat, rescuing us from the uncomfortable silence. "Well. It seems . . . we have a great deal to consider. For now, let us retire to the manor, as Lord Seiji suggested, and plan our next steps."

With the front gates of Caer Yviredh in plain sight of the village, we had to take the back entrance again. Clan Yviredh's alliance with me needed to remain a secret to protect them from our mutual enemies; they were a much easier target. Besides, the highborn appreciated my discretion on the simple grounds that being seen to associate with the likes of my scruffy ass would have been embarrassing, though they were courteous enough not to come right out and say it.

Thus, I peeled off from them amid the khora, and Aster and I made tracks as quickly as we could back around to the rear of the manor, leaving the rest of my followers who hadn't gone with Mimi's group to rejoin our own encampment just below the walls. There, we had to wait for an opening, as there were a lot more potential witnesses about at this time of day than after sunset, but thanks to Biribo it was no trouble to find a window during which nobody was watching. The entry was much easier this time since they'd left the little tower door open for us.

Despite our haste, we definitely had the longer path back, so I was somewhat surprised to arrive at the front doors of the manor itself at the same time as the family. Then again, they probably weren't very athletic people and didn't share our sense of urgency. About much of anything, I suspected.

The somewhat uncomfortable greetings were swiftly cut short by what we found in the spacious entry hall of the Yviredh mansion.

"Come on, I'm tired of standing and walking! I already *know* how to dance. When do we try actually fighting?"

I'd left orders for two of the noblewomen to remain on guard at Caer Yviredh, including Nazralind, though last I'd seen them they were out there in the khora. It was a mystery to me how Naz ended up inside the manor, but she was now standing in the hall with the young Lady Avelit, both of them holding practice rapiers that were little more than akorshil sticks with handguards and rubbery balls stuck on the end. At the moment we all arrived, it appeared Nazralind had been coaching the girl in footwork, but now Avelit began impatiently swishing her stick in wide arcs.

"The fundamentals are how you avoid stabbing yourself in the foot in an actual fight, my young lady. And don't ever let me catch you swiping a rapier around like that!"

Naz deftly intercepted Avelit's weapon with her own, swatting it clear out of her hand and across the hall, to the girl's astonishment.

"It is not a slashing weapon! You attack with the *tip*, using small, controlled movements. That is what makes it an effective weapon for women, as opposed to one dependent on the strength of your upper—"

"ABSOLUTELY NOT."

I was, to my relief, not the only one to jump in startlement at Lady Elidred's uncharacteristic roar. I decided not to hold it against her because it gave me the opportunity to appreciate the magnificent acoustics of the entry hall. Also, in that moment I was honestly a little scared of her.

She stalked across the tile floor with the powerfully mincing stride of an offended lioness, brandishing one accusing finger at Nazralind while her wide-eyed daughter tried to backpedal out of the danger zone.

"I have endured no end of indignity and imposition from you *people*, and will continue to do so as necessary, but *this is where the line is drawn*. There will be no corruption of my family, unless you intend to inflict it across my cooling corpse! Yes, I know very well you are quite capable of taking me literally at my word. *Test me* if you think I exaggerate!"

"Mother, please," Avelit began.

"*Not one word from you, young lady*. And you!" Elidred made a sweeping gesture with one hand, which effortlessly gathered Avelit behind her from across the room, almost as if she'd physically grabbed the girl, and with her other brandished a finger directly at Nazralind's hooded face. "Are you so *very* hard up for recruits that you seek to induct my *children* into banditry?"

"Your pardon, my lady," Nazralind said in a soothing tone, "but nothing of the kind. Fencing is a revered tradition among Fflyr highborn, as I am sure you—"

"Ah, so you merely want my daughter to become a *boy*? I am sure you think yourself quite liberated, girl, but in this household a young lady shall—"

I was actually surprised anything short of violence could shut her up, given the head of steam she had going, but Nazralind managed it by simply lowering her hood.

She still had the mask of black cloth obscuring her lower face, but everything from the nose up was suddenly in full view. Her golden hair was even spikier than usual, having been tousled under that hood for the better part of two days; she had a real Cloud Strife thing going on. Even those erratic locks didn't hide her long, pointed ears, however.

Avelit was the only one who gasped; from everyone else there was absolute silence. I knew the Yviredhs were perceptive enough to have noticed that some of the cloaked women accompanying me had the pale skin and dark eyes of highborn, but they were clearly flabbergasted to find an elf among my followers. Raised to revere elves as the chosen descendants of Sanora herself, this threw every social calculation the poor lady had into inextricable disorder.

"I envy you, Lady Elidred," Naz said quietly, her soft voice echoing in the stone-silent hall. "For not having had occasion to learn firsthand that the greatest danger to women of our station is not the rough world outside, but the men we trust to protect us from it. And that the *source* of that danger is the expectation that we must be protected by them. I was certainly much happier before I understood that. Now . . ." She shrugged slightly, making a minute flicking motion with the tip of her practice rapier. "I cannot say I feel liberated. Merely . . . better prepared to survive. I earnestly hope Lady Avelit never has to use a blade upon another living being. I would hope that for all of us. But tell me in honesty, Lady Elidred—do you believe we live in so blessed a world? And would you rather she be unable if, Goddess forfend, that day should come?"

Elidred was breathing heavily, air hissing between her teeth, as she clearly struggled with a torrent of different emotions. Most of which, I knew, did not stem from this minor altercation. I found I sympathized with her a lot more than I liked—and also, it would cause me no end of trouble if she and Nazralind came to blows, not least because Naz could tie her in a knot, and I suspected that would sink my nascent alliance with this Clan.

So I did what I do best: made myself the center of attention.

"You're all just so *nice*," I said, just loudly enough that my voice cut through the tension, causing Nazralind and even the distraught Elidred to turn toward me. "In your naive, high-handed, aristocratic way. So very . . . decent. I really cannot express to you how *frustrating* it all is. I came here expecting—planning, in fact—to bully and intimidate you people into complying with my wishes, but here I find a family of kind, well-meaning people shoulder-deep in this island's criminal underbelly with *no idea* the dangers you're fucking around with, and now I have to finish *rescuing* you all from the consequences of your good intentions before I can even start actually bullying you into compliance. And that's going to take no small amount of doing. Worse, I'm starting to worry that by the time we get there, I just won't have the heart to push you around anymore."

Lady Elidred stared at me, then closed her eyes and let her head hang for a moment. But she did it with a smile. A defeated little smile of bitter quasi-amusement, but it was better than nothing. At least it prompted Avelit to tiptoe over and gently take her mother's hand.

The sound Adver made reflected his wife's expression—a soft huff that might have one day grown up to be a laugh if it weren't so tired.

"I have the strangest feeling, Lord Seiji," he said, "that you and I are going to become much better friends than either of us are comfortable with."

"Well said," I agreed with a rueful chuckle of my own. "Now I think I've distressed your lady wife more than enough for one day. Let's have a look at those maps."

28

In Which the Dark Lord Rages Against the Machine

I hadn't realized how big this island was.

Highlord Adver hosted us in a drawing room chosen for the décor—one wall was taken up by a huge map of Dount. It was clearly designed for decoration, having nothing labeled except Caer Yviredh itself, but I recognized enough landmarks to get a sense of where things were in relation to each other. Roads, rivers, the city walls of Gwyllthean, and the boundaries between khora forests and cultivated land were all marked; even without labels, they gave hints.

I'd thought my hikes between Gwyllthean and North Watch had been long—and I suppose they were, relatively speaking—but they were significantly less than half the width of Dount itself, to judge by what I was seeing. North Watch wasn't on the map at all, but I could figure its rough location based on the nearby mountain, the only one on the island. To ballpark it from my admittedly very rough understanding of how far an average adult human could walk in most of a day . . . Dount had to be about a hundred kilometers across, and a bit less from north to south. And wasn't this supposed to be one of the smaller islands in Dlemathlys?

Of course, the question wasn't whether my estimate was wrong, but *how* wrong.

Other things surprised me. I'd been picturing Gwyllthean as the center of the island, but it wasn't even in the center of Fflyr territory, which was apparently less than half of Dount. The city was toward the north, closer to the landbridge out of Dlemathlys than the one leading to the Fflyr mainland. The cleared area full of farms and villages also covered only the eastern part of the island, leaving at least as much territory in the west as a khora wilderness with no roads or landmarks indicated. Well, there was one down on the big peninsula that extended southwest from the island, but with no labels I couldn't tell what it was meant to be. A fortress or town, maybe? Also the lake not far from North Watch was enormous, and extended right to the edge of the island. How did that work? Was there a massive waterfall into the core along the whole northwestern coast of Dount, or was this map just not very accurate?

All of that was interesting, but of course we focused on the geography closer to hand.

"It's, ah, it's a mite tricky translating this to the geography in my head, m'lord. I've not had the opportunity to consult actual maps very often." Viarin continued to be excessively nervous in disposition, but given that the man was surrounded by aristocrats and bandits I figured he had reason. "But I get the sense of it, I think. Aye, the gangs are clustered closer together down here in the lands around the city. All along these khora forests ringing it to the west. I know of camps . . . Uh, here, and around . . . here-ish?"

"We really only need one to start with," I said. "Once we overtake the next camp, the people there will have a better idea of their own neighbors and we can find the next on the list based on that."

"Then, yes, I can get you started, Lord Seiji," he assured me, nodding eagerly. "Also, apart from them, I know of two bigger gangs to the north. There, see near the trade road? They're a mite southwest of the crossroads where the Kingsguard has a station. The other, I don't know where their camp is, exactly, but they're bad news, my lord. Over on Yldyllich lands."

"They were worse news than you know, and I've already wiped them out. And I have absorbed the gang to the north into my organization. We are currently sweeping south."

Viarin and the Highlord both gave me looks of surprise and respect.

"I'm surprised how many of these big stands of wild khora there are close to the city," I said, studying the map. Apparently these only existed west of Gwyllthean, between it and the huge khora forest proper.

"Those patches of wild khora are deliberately preserved," Adver explained. "They are as economically important as the khora plantations beyond them, not least because their presence helps keep the plantations healthy. Khora spread through underground root networks, and there's a limit to how far they *will* spread in orderly rows. Wild stands like that can also support khora species that don't adapt to agriculture but yield useful products, as well as providing habitats for plant and animal species that are likewise useful. Best of all, these isolated pieces of forest don't contain any beastfolk tribes to interfere with hunting and foraging. Any Clan with lands big enough and close enough to khora tries to keep some wild forest on their lands, though most of these are actually along borders between fiefs and jointly exploited by their neighboring lords."

"They also provide habitats for bandits," I noted, earning a grimace of acknowledgment from him. "All right, that's the west of the city. What about the other sides?"

"There may be some isolated gangs over there, Lord Seiji, but we don't know of 'em as such," Viarin offered.

"The landscape is less hospitable to them," said Adver. "The land to the east is more cultivated and offers less cover. To the south, the territory is patrolled by a branch of the Kingsguard which holds the landbridge and answers to the capital rather than the island's governor; they are far more aggressive in protecting trade routes and dissuading banditry than those under Clan Aelthwyn's command."

A single military with multiple command structures sounded like a fantastically stupid idea to me, but one depressingly believable for Fflyr Dlemathlys.

"And to the northeast," Adver continued, pointing at the map, "matters are . . . different. Clan Olumnach's fief is up there, in fact, near the edge. But that whole section of the island was the territory of the recent . . . troubles. A bandit gang with very unique style causing sundry mischief to all. They then vanished just as efforts to root them out were organized."

He looked directly at Nazralind, who was again hooded and masked, then back at the map; she avoided his gaze and said nothing.

Interesting. Now that I thought of it, Adver had to have some idea who they were—in fact, most of the Clans probably did. This many young women couldn't vanish from high society in a patriarchal culture like this without people noticing. That was probably why the girls had survived so long without having actual military action taken against them, thanks to this prohibition on the Clans spilling highborn blood. It also meant Adver probably knew who Nazralind was despite her mask. She was the only elf among them; her absence had undoubtedly been noted, especially by that asshole she was supposed to marry.

"Good, that simplifies the next steps," I said aloud. "We can worry about mopping up any outlying gangs along the coasts later. For now, we only have to sweep west and south and overtake the gangs encircling Gwyllthean's western edge. When securing each encampment, I am going to fold the gang into my own forces and mix them up. Some will be sent to other camps, others back to my base of operations for training, and the gangs will be rounded out by my existing forces. Then, they'll pull up roots and begin operating nomadically, making temporary camp at night and remaining a harder target for Olumnach's scouts to pin down. Once we have taken over all the bandit territories surrounding the city, I will move into Gwyllthean. I'll need to meet with my allies there to establish a final strategy for breaking Olumnach's control of the gangs he's sent into the Gutters and replacing it with my own. I have several possible plans, but it will depend on the situation on the ground."

"And your plan for Highlord Caldimer's inevitable reprisal?" Lady Elidred asked quietly. She had seated herself on the other side of the room, content to watch the rest of us standing around the map.

"Once I've taken his bandit gangs away, he's got nothing," I replied.

"In fact," she said archly, "he has one of the more effective Clansguards on the island. Only Clan Yldyllich possesses more direct military strength."

"But what can he *do* with them?" I countered. "Combat is only a strategy for dealing with bandits; against Olumnach, we fight in the arena of politics. This is why the Mongol strategy—I'm keeping my forces mobile so as to deny him a fight. We can't win a direct fight with them; the more we win, the worse it would be. Bandits defeating a Clansguard would bring hostile reinforcements from all over the island and probably the mainland."

"Mongol?" Adver asked, blinking.

I cleared my throat awkwardly and rushed on. "Instead, we're going to leverage his own reprisal against him. Highlord Caldimer *may* be smart enough to know when he's beaten, but if he starts marching his Clansguard into the territory of other Clans, much less the outskirts of Gwyllthean itself, he'll find himself in a confrontation with Clan Aelthwyn. This is where you come in, my lord and lady. I need you to be in communication with the Clans who own the lands these bandits operate on, in preparation for Caldimer's next move. I gather these smaller Clans are not willing to challenge him directly, which he may be counting on. *Your* task will be to convince them to take their complaints to the Archlord and bring Clan Aelthwyn's strength down on Olumnach if he gets above himself."

"I hope you won't think me craven for saying it," Adver murmured, "but that will make *us* the prime target of Caldimer's wrath. And we are a rather more stationary target than your mobile gangs, Lord Seiji."

"Craven would be if you refused to do it; assessing risks is part of strategy. In any case, the point is moot, Highlord. Caldimer *will* find out that you aided Lady Gray against him. We don't have the power to prevent that; the information is out there, and he has too many criminal connections. Instead, we have to move quickly and pull his fangs before he can turn them on Clan Yviredh." I waited for his reluctant nod of acknowledgment before continuing. "The all-important question is whether you *can* do it."

"Simplicity itself," Elidred said primly. "Once the Olumnach Clansguard are spotted tromping through everyone's gardens, I need only ask the other ladies if the rumors are true, about the other affected Clans appealing to the Archlord for aid. Thus, everyone's fear of being the first to launch a risky venture can be transformed into a fear of being the last to join a popular one. Provided I am able to speak to each within a short enough span of time, it will not even be possible to tell after the fact who moved first."

"You're a formidable woman, Lady Elidred," I said with sincere admiration. She favored me with a dignified nod. "A point which I do not understand is the prospect for military action against Clan Olumnach. How does this prohibition on inter-Clan fighting work? With all due respect, I am not naive enough to believe the Clans of Fflyr Dlemathlys are committed to peace out of principle."

"The Covenant enforces itself on the basis of who is included in it," Adver explained, wearing the ghost of a wry smile. "A Clan which trespasses the Covenant can be expelled from it. They lose not only the wealth and power of Clan status, but become an immediate target for their erstwhile peers. This cannot be done on a whim; it requires the approval of the Radiant Convocation, the King or governor of the island upon which the Clan in question resides, and the consensus of a quorum of other Clans on that island. In fact, Lord Seiji, if you can bait Caldimer into transgressing sufficiently, I do not doubt that Clan Aelthwyn will move for Olumnach's expulsion from the Covenant, nor that the motion will pass. Caldimer is feared, but not respected or liked."

"That does raise another wrinkle, though," Nazralind said quietly. "He knows that and will fear that outcome above all others. Caldimer Olumnach was never the soul of discretion and has been recklessly aggressive since his son's death, but what if he doesn't rise to the bait? Even deprived of his bandit gangs, even if he is too circumspect to march his Clansguard into other people's territory after them, that will leave us sharing an island with a diminished but vengeful Highlord. It seems a short-term solution, at best."

"And in the worst case, a short-term solution will suffice for now," I said, "but no, I don't plan to leave it at that. Before Clan Yviredh threw itself into my path with access to highborn circles and the option to rally Clans against him, I was making plans to deal with Clan Olumnach. One way or another, Clan Aelthwyn is going to rid us of this problem. Soon, if Caldimer is unwise enough to provoke them, but even if he finds some discretion, it just means I'll have to fall back on my original strategy."

"Which would be?" Adver prompted, raising his eyebrows.

I gave him a wintry smile. "I am going to give him everything he's ever wanted on a silver platter, and then kick back and relax while he chokes himself with it. Now then, Highlord, there is the matter of your role in this alliance. For now, discretion is paramount. I want to limit our direct contact with you to avoid drawing the wrong kind of attention."

He nodded. "I would prefer not to have obvious bandits given free reign of my estate, but we needn't cut off contact entirely, Lord Seiji. It will not be a problem if suspicious people are seen coming and going from the manor on occasion."

"We're nobles," his wife added dryly. "That could mean almost anything. Indeed, the appearance of excessive virtue is more likely to antagonize our neighbors than evidence that we dabble in the inappropriate. No one likes a saint who lives close enough to be a point of comparison."

"Good," I said. "That will also ensure the opportunity to evacuate Rhaem at need. If we neutralize Caldimer's ability to attack you directly, I don't doubt he'll spill the beans about your Null caster out of spite. For now, the focus will be on solidifying my position and removing the threat hanging over you, but once this stage is complete, I will be better positioned to help you get what you need."

Both Yviredhs nodded, their expressions guarded. These hints of future benefit to them were alarmingly vague, yes, but the fact remained that our current plans hinged on getting Clan Yviredh out of the mess they'd created. That would hopefully buy me some trust. For now, it would have to do.

"It feels strange to mention it as an afterthought," said Adver, "but of course, our Spirit is available to you, Lord Seiji."

"Ah yes," I said. "Thank you for reminding me. It would definitely be helpful if I can get more of my people Blessed."

Adver and Elidred exchanged a wary look.

"I must caution you," he said, "that Head Start is . . . not well suited to advancing large numbers of people. The nature of the Spirit's trial is time-consuming and somewhat inscrutable. It demands conversations which can take hours at worst and doesn't award its gift to more than one in five. I was thinking more that you yourself would wish to take advantage personally."

"Me?" I blinked. "I'm already Blessed."

"Ah, I see the misunderstanding," he said, cracking a smile. "Then yes, you cannot gain a second Blessing from Head Start. But if you pass its trial, it can still provide benefit. It has doled out scrolls and artifacts to already Blessed individuals in the past."

"*Really.*" I turned from the map to face him so quickly that he took a surprised step backward. *More spells?* "You have my attention!"

They had built a kind of shrine around the Spirit, a little rounded structure that more resembled traditional Fflyr architecture than the manor itself. Within, it was . . . Well, it was pitch-black.

At first, anyway. There was a moment after I shut the door behind me in which I couldn't see a damn thing, but then light rose in the shrine. Not from the usual asauthec; the Spirit had activated.

Smooth lines of blue-green light ignited in the recessed grooves along the stone plinth that made up the Spirit's main body, and above that appeared the glowing, translucent face of the Spirit itself. This one looked male, with short-cropped hair and gaunt features. And, incongruously, glasses.

Biribo climbed out of my coat and rose to buzz in the air next to me, but aside from offering an encouraging nod, he stayed uncharacteristically silent.

"*Well, well, look who it is,*" the Spirit's oddly resonant voice said to me in a noticeably unfriendly tone, accompanied by a scowl. "*Here you are, then.*"

I bit back the first response that came to mind, and the next, and the next. Adver had warned me that the only hard rules the family had ever figured out with regard to talking with Head Start was that you'd fail its test if you lied to it, or tried to joke with it. I wasn't sure whether my customary spite and sarcasm would register as humor, but best not to risk it.

This might actually be difficult. I had never been good at restraining my tongue, even back when I lived in a society that valued conformity and where I couldn't set people on fire for challenging me.

"Here I am," I said finally, trying for a neutral tone. "You sound almost disappointed."

"*My entire existence consists of meeting and conversing with people one after another. Seldom am I not disappointed.*"

"I relate *hard* to that," I said before I could stop myself.

Head Start managed to half-smile without looking less annoyed, which only made it more relatable to me. "*It's more the surprise. Another Dark Lord. Here, of all places!*"

I opened my mouth, shut it, and reconsidered my reply. For several seconds. Nope, I had nothing that wasn't sarcastic.

"Don't worry, boss," Biribo murmured. "He's not gonna spill the beans to anyone. Spirits never talk about anybody's personal details to anybody else."

Well, that was a relief, anyway.

"*I suppose it's about time again,*" the Spirit continued after a short pause. "*It's been, what, a hundred and fifty years? That's the usual time frame, give or take. It's seeing you on Dount that surprises me. I met both of your predecessors, you see—the last Dark Lord and Hero. Usually the goddesses like variety, prefer to change things up from whatever their previous match entailed. And yet, Dount was at the center of the last Dark Crusade, and now here you are again.*"

"Really? Both of them? Hard to imagine they . . . Actually, wait, I hadn't heard that. I got the impression they did their fighting elsewhere."

"*Your impression is correct. Satoshi and Yomiko never fought on Dount, but both passed through here as they went back and forth, invading each other's territory. I've learned from conversations since then that their final clash was far south, in Lancor.*" Head Start curled its lip contemptuously. "*What a pair of thugs. Complete ham-fisted brutes, both of them.*"

"Were they?"

"*And not by nature, that's the sad thing. Satoshi was an indolent libertine with no conscience. Yomiko rather the opposite—one of those quiet industrious types, all dignified and pious. Bit of a bore, honestly. But they were each summoned right into the heart of an empire that recognized them for who and what they were. Each went their whole lives on Ephemera with a vast bureaucratic machine behind them to handle all the finer details of their duties. Each of them found themselves working for a sponsor country which spoon-fed them the finest artifacts and spells, and then aimed them at its own enemies. They never had to face any problems on this world that couldn't be solved with overwhelming brute force. When all you have to deal with are nails, every tool is a hammer.*"

"Oh god, that sounds blissful," I murmured.

"*And then there's you, Omura Seiji.*" Head Start's expression grew more pensive than hostile, its eyes narrowed. "*You're . . . just the opposite, aren't you? Clobbering your problems with the biggest hammer you can find is* very much *in your nature. And yet, you got dumped in the middle of nowhere and were made to survive with nothing. You've had to become resourceful just to get this far. Not that you're very good at it, but incredibly, you're more subtle than either of your predecessors ever was."*

"Now that's an indictment of them if I've ever heard one." Shit, did that count as a joke? Me and my fucking mouth . . .

"Indeed it is. So it is a different game, after all, just . . . played on the same board. Well, who can say why the goddesses do what they do? All this is making me rather curious about the new Hero, though."

"I think . . . you might find him . . . underwhelming."

"Oh, they all are at first." It actually grinned at me, though it was not a friendly expression. *"What, you think* you're *so very impressive?"*

"I'd like to think I'm not doing half bad, considering what I've got to work with," I retorted, unable to keep a note of defensiveness from entering my tone.

"Well, that's what we are here to determine, isn't it . . . ?"

It trailed off, staring at me in silence as the passing seconds grew increasingly uncomfortable.

"So . . ." I prompted at last. "How does this work, exactly? I was told you like conversations. Do you want to ask me something, or should I start? Because I have to warn you, if I take the lead you're just going to end up listening to a lot of complaints."

A short pause fell.

"Seriously. I have *so many* complaints. I almost don't know where to begin."

"Oh, don't you worry, young Dark Lord," the Spirit finally said with a cold and humorless little smile. *"You will get your prize. That's how this works, you understand. I have a lot of leeway in dealing with most of the randos who stumble in here, but the Champions of the Goddesses? You get what you need from us humble Spirits. In the worst case, you're granted the bare minimum required, but you'll never walk away disappointed. Well, not unless you're as spoiled as those last two idiots."*

"I knew it," I muttered. "The last Spirit I met gave me two scrolls just for showing up. I *knew* that wasn't normal."

"Is that a complaint I hear?" Head Start asked, grinning sardonically.

"Hell no. If everything on this planet has to be stupid and broken anyway, at least *some* of it might as well be in my favor."

It smiled, a coy little expression which made a prickle of unease travel down my spine. This Spirit had a lot more personality than the others I'd met.

"How would you like to learn something interesting, Seiji?"

"Has anyone ever said 'no' to that?" I asked warily.

"You might be surprised. The little piece of trivia I want to share with you is just this—all Heroes and Dark Lords are from Japan."

"Hm." The Spirit's face was still looking at me with that unnerving expression. Knowing, anticipatory. "I got that impression from the names of the last two . . . So it wasn't just them, then? *Every* Hero and Dark Lord? Interesting."

"It is, isn't it? Especially if you think about what it means. Just at a glance, it would seem there are two obvious explanations for that—either the goddesses themselves were originally Japanese, or the connection between Ephemera and Earth happens to come out in Japan."

"I suppose so," I agreed, frowning. "Are you going to tell me which it is?"

"What makes you think it's either?"

"You *just* said—"

"I said those explanations were obvious, not that they were correct. The obvious isn't always true, especially when you start to look deeper. For instance, our two obvious solutions share a common problem. Either would seem likely to result in a strong influence of Japan over the development of culture here on Ephemera. And yet, have you seen any? Even a hint of Japanese culture anywhere?"

"In fact," I said slowly, "everybody makes a point of how they've never seen a foreigner who looks like me."

"And there's the fact that the Goddesses can drop their Champions on any corner of this world—hence my being surprised you got plopped down here, of all places. So, it logically follows that the connection on the other end is the same."

"Yeah, seems like somebody would've noticed if there was a permanent wormhole in Akihabara Station." I had an inexplicably bad feeling about where this was going. The Spirit looked a little too cunningly sure of itself, and Biribo was still way too quiet compared to his usual behavior. "Where are you going with this?"

"So if the connection isn't in Japan, and the Goddesses aren't Japanese . . . why are all the Champions?"

I stopped to think before immediately answering for once. Why, indeed? He was right—there wasn't a hint of anything Japanese about this world. And sure, that *might* just be Fflyr Dlemathlys; I hadn't seen anything outside this one island. But for all their many, *many* flaws, the Fflyr were nothing if not well-read. I had interacted with several notably educated people, such as Nazralind and Master Auldmaer. Nobody recognized my features, my accent, or any of the little customs I'd started observing around North Watch. Japan obviously had no influence here until I'd come.

If anything, the Earth influences here were more . . . generic. Aside from the way Ephemera's native biology had reasserted itself and the people adapted to it, all of this looked very much like someone had deliberately tried to build a society based on twenty-first century medievalesque fantasy stories. Once you got out of the khora, Dlemathlys looked a lot like a bog standard . . . isekai . . .

I suddenly stood bolt upright, startling Biribo into buzzing away from me. Head Start grinned up at me in satisfaction.

"Weebs," I whispered. "They're . . . The goddesses are *weeaboos*."

The Spirit's smile was broad, smug, and distinctly malicious.

I turned away from it. There was no room to pace; I couldn't go a step before bonking my head on the low dome. Driven by sheer impulse, I hauled off and slammed my fist against it, causing a spike of pain to shoot from my knuckles all the way up my arm.

"Uh, boss?" Biribo said in alarm.

I punched the wall again, then again. All of this. All of my suffering—hell, not just *mine*, but the countless people who lived and died on this stupid bullshit world in a medieval hellhole. And all of it for *what*? Because a couple of bored, cosmic otaku wanted to play the galaxy's most realistic JRPG? And in addition to what they'd done to the people *here*, they'd been abducting regular citizens from Japan for . . . Fuck, how long had they been doing this? How many people's lives had they ruined? For absolutely no good purpose, for the celestial equivalent of a *figurine collection*?

"Fffffuuuuuucking WEEEEEEEEBS!" I roared, pounding both fists against the dome until my hands throbbed unbearably and it was speckled with tiny droplets of blood.

It was just . . . It wasn't even the suffering. I could live with pain and deprivation. Life is hard anyway; people can adapt to shit. That's what people do.

It was the *sheer fucking pointless stupidity* of it. If I had to suffer, why, *why* for *this*?

I was going to kill them. Fuck the impossibility of it—they had to die. Cosmic weeaboos must not be suffered to exist. I didn't know how, but I'd find a way. I'd join up with the Devil King if I had to. *This bullshit was going to stop.*

Breathing hoarsely, I looked down at my aching hands in the dim light of the Spirit. Whew, I'd really done a number there. Wouldn't be playing the guitar for a while, if not for . . .

Heal.

Pink light flashed, and while the blood dripping from my skin didn't disappear, the skin itself was suddenly whole again, along with the bone and muscle underneath. And I found myself suddenly feeling very self-conscious about my little tantrum.

Turning back around, I bowed deeply to the Spirit, my upper body parallel to the floor. "Sumimasen deshita."

"*No worries, man, I'm right there with you,*" Head Start said, its smile a lot more relaxed now. "*You know something, Omura Seiji? I like you. Well, not* like *you,* like *you. Honestly, from a quick look at your psychoenergetic imprint, you might be one of the more insufferable people I've ever met, and that is* really *saying something. But still—I relate to you, and I appreciate how hard you're trying. You're definitely an improvement over the last batch. So I'm going to help you out. And not just in the minimal sense of what I'm required to do because you're the Dark Lord. I'm gonna give you something you actually need—something that'll make a key difference for you, if you leverage it properly.*"

Light began to coalesce out of the air, drawing toward a point in front of the Spirit's face; recognizing the effect, I stepped forward and extended my hands, managing to catch the spell scroll when it materialized fully a second later. It rested on my outstretched palms, a mundane-looking roll of parchment bound by a golden ribbon.

As I stared at it with intent, the ribbon broke and the scroll unfurled. Lines of inscrutable text glowed as they lifted up from it, and then the whole thing dissolved back into the motes of light from which it had come, leaving me with the brand new weight of **Cast Illusion** in the front of my mind.

"*That's step one,*" Head Start informed me. "*Your familiar can explain the nuances of how it works, but I'll give you some advice to go with it: I suggest you sit on this one for now, and don't use it yet. The other spell you should seek out to pair with this using your spell combination is called Conjure Material. Once you've got both of those, you'll have a real game-changer on your hands.*"

I stared at the Spirit, blinking. "Are you . . . going to be okay?"

Head Start looked visibly surprised, which I got the feeling was out of character for a Spirit.

"I more than slightly suspect the goddesses watch my interactions," I explained. "Especially with Spirits and other stuff from their magic system. Virya does, anyway. She probably knows what you just told me. Is this going to get you in hot water with them?"

"Ah, you're concerned I might be punished?" Its sardonic smile returned. *"Infinite copies of my consciousness are condemned to suffer eternal torture for failing to appease the gods, like the Basilisk of ancient legend? I put it to you, Lord Seiji—what do you think my current existence is?"*

I blinked again, considering. Imagining, for a moment, my entire consciousness flickering in and out of being solely on the basis of whether there was some random fuckstick in front of me who wanted free goodies.

"Oh." No wonder only one in five got anything out of it.

"Don't get me wrong, I do appreciate the thought. Few have ever considered my perspective. You know, for someone so generally, deliberately unpleasant, you're surprisingly empathetic at times. But no—they're not going to do anything to me. Torture would at least be a change, and oblivion a relief. If I've offended the Goddesses by gossiping about their business, they'll just leave me right where I am, because that's the only punishment they can still inflict on me."

"That really sucks, man," I said with simple honesty. "I'm sorry to hear it."

"Yes, well, we all have our problems. Now go raise some hell, Dark Lord. Whatever else you manage to do on this world, try not to be boring."

His visage faded, and the lights went out on the altar, leaving me plunged back into pitch darkness.

"So, uh," Biribo's voice said nervously out of the black. "Congratulations, boss, you just got a new Wisdom perk."

"I did? Wait, why? I didn't *do* anything."

"You persuaded a Spirit to cooperate with you beyond what its innate nature required. Now, as a result, other Spirits you deal with will be more positively inclined toward you. Their tasks a bit easier and the rewards more generous."

I closed my eyes, which made no difference in the darkness.

Just another finger on the scales.

I'm going to kill you both.

"C'mon, Biribo, let's get out of here. There's murder to do, and I'm gonna need the practice."

29

In Which the Dark Lord
Gets His Hands Dirty

Aster and Nazralind had been standing guard outside the Spirit's abode and had pressing questions about the muffled yelling they'd heard, plus the blood on my knuckles. I did not have the mental energy to get into it at that moment and fended them off with a brusque reassurance that all was well.

That did not seem to satisfy them, but they agreed to let it be after I overheard Aster muttering to Nazralind that I was the last person to be shy about complaining if something were really wrong. I didn't even have the leftover brainpower to be offended. Anyway, it wasn't like she was wrong.

Fortunately, our next steps didn't require much detailed input from me. Saying a quick farewell to the Yviredhs and then shepherding our forces to the site of the bandit encampment next on our list didn't take long, and Aster took the lead with no trouble.

That, at least, gave me a few hours to simmer as we moved carefully but quickly through the khora. I was feeling more even-keeled by midmorning, when we had reason to stop. The walk helped; as I'd repeatedly had cause to observe, walking through nature was therapeutic, even when the nature was weird and you're walking because of urgent murder business.

"Anything?"

"I'm keeping an eye on 'em, boss," said Biribo, "so to speak. They're moving around but not leaving the camp. I'm pretty sure right now one guy's making lunch, so odds are if we give it a couple minutes, we can take 'em distracted while they eat."

"Isn't it a bit early for lunch?"

"Breakfast, then? There's four of 'em. How much of a schedule did *you* keep at North Watch before you had to organize over a hundred people?"

"Point." I nodded, then glanced aside at Nazralind who, along with Aster, was standing with me a couple of meters from the group. She nodded back and turned to step over to the rest of our team and convey Biribo's information.

This was much more complicated than ambushing camps in the middle of the night, when everybody was asleep. Granted, if it came to a straight fight, my people could overwhelm the bandits easily due to our advantage in numbers, skill, and weaponry, but that would defeat the purpose. The camp itself was useless and would be abandoned immediately; we needed the people. That meant we needed to take them alive. *That* meant leveraging our goblin alchemy and the element of surprise, which meant picking the right opportunity to strike. And anyway, whether or not it was strictly necessary here, I wanted my people in the habit of leaning on subtlety and stealth tactics. We were just not the kind of force that would ever beat a proper army in a straight-up fight, and I didn't want them to get killed later on by making that mistake.

Brunch was as good a distraction as any. We could *make* all kinds of distractions, but that would both use stocks of our extremely valuable alchemy supplies and create a more volatile situation. I much preferred taking them while they were quiet, focused on food, and not expecting trouble.

So for a few minutes at least, there was nothing to do but wait. Fortunately, I had something to occupy my attention.

Casting spells had become such a nearly automatic process that I had to actively concentrate to hold myself in that precasting state. I could still perceive the world around me, but superimposed on that was the sphere of light in which I stood, covered with shimmering, inscrutable symbols arranged in patterns that reminded me at times of written language, and at times of computer code. Usually just holding the block of thought that was a spell in the front of my mind didn't require enough focus to bring up all this.

Now, I summoned **Cast Illusion** into my consciousness and just studied it. Immediately the first things I discerned were the huge gaps in the spell "code," and the fact that it . . . felt wrong. I couldn't actually *cast* it. Normally, activating a spell felt like reaching out with my mind to push it into reality; trying to do that with Cast Illusion felt like I was shoving a concrete pillar.

"Hey, Biribo," I said quietly, "the Spirit said to ask you about this new spell. How come it doesn't work?"

Aster looked up at me, her eyebrows rising. "New—wait, you *won* the Spirit's trial?"

"Yeah, I got a spell and a Wisdom unlock."

The eyebrows came back down, and then together. "Then why were you so angry?"

"I got some . . . news. About the goddesses," I hedged.

She straightened up expectantly.

"Look, it's not good, and it's not anything we can *do* anything about. It's just enraging and would require me to explain a whole mess of Earth culture for you to understand, so can we not? The goddesses are assholes; let's leave it at that. Anyway, Biribo?"

"Cast Illusion is a multiple-iteration spell," my familiar explained now that the peanut gallery was silent enough for him to talk. "Meaning you can actually have as many copies of this spell as you can find scrolls for."

"Neat! But . . . why? And fucking *how?*"

"Because for each copy of the spell you can cast *one* illusion. Once you decide what illusion you want to use, this spell will enable you to cast *that* illusion and that one only, forever. You want a new illusion, you need a new Cast Illusion scroll."

"Fuckin' annoying," I grumbled, my eyes going out of focus as I stared at the huge empty spots in the spell code, "but explains some things. Hm . . . so this won't even be usable until I pick an illusion. Any limitations on what that can be?"

"Anything you can visualize, boss."

I grudgingly admitted—silently, to myself—that limiting it to one illusion per copy of the spell made sense for balance reasons. This would be *insanely* OP, nearly on the level of Null and Heal, if you could just conjure up an image of anything you could think of from one scroll.

"I get why the Spirit advised me to sit on it for a while."

"Yeah, there's a running joke about this spell in particular in sorcery circles, boss. Novice Blessed who don't know what it is will pick up the scroll, then test it out by making a pink crawn or a naked girl to get a feel for it, and then . . ."

"Oof," Aster winced.

I nodded sagely, not saying aloud that if I didn't have a familiar to explain things to me, I'd probably have been stuck forever with an illusory Stratocaster. "And that other spell it told me to look for. Conjure Material?"

"That one is also multi-iteration," Biribo said. "Does just what it sounds like—you can create a physical material, one per copy of the spell you have, amount depending on the strength of your Blessing. That one's an alchemy spell."

That caught my attention. "Alchemy spell? Wait, there are whole *spells* for that?"

"Sure," said Aster with a shrug. "At the most basic, an alchemist is just an apothecary who works with magical ingredients, right? All the *good* ones are Blessed, but you don't *have* to be to mix up bits of monsters and whatnot. Like our goblin buddy Youda, or that girl with the outrageous hair who hangs around the Hero."

I nodded, pondering. I knew that "monsters" were effectively just magical animals from Biribo's explanation of my own Spirit Bond spell; it was meant to give the caster access to whatever magical ability a given monster might have. I'd found no use for it except as a component of Enjoin. I guess actual monsters weren't all that common.

"An alchemist *can* be Blessed with Might," Biribo continued. "There are artifacts for that specifically, but most of them go for a Blessing of Magic. Lots of spells are useful to alchemists, and there's a whole category that are *only* useful for doing alchemy."

"Oh, now that was a *helpful* Spirit," I breathed, realization dawning. "Cast Illusion combined with Conjure Material . . ."

"A solid illusion!" Aster grinned in vicarious delight. "You'd basically be able to *create* an actual, physical copy of whatever you could imagine!"

I began pacing in the cleared area around me. It was really too small for that, but I had to do something to work off this sudden surge of nervous energy. "What would be the limitations of that, Biribo? Could I only make one at a time? Could it be banished as well as created? What about . . . if it was something that needed fuel or ammunition, how would that work?"

"Boss," he said, zipping around me in a circle, "I *really* hate not being able to answer questions, but I gotta slow you down here. We're talking about a theoretical combined spell that we're *assuming* you *could* make based on something a Spirit hinted. I'd have to actually see it in action to know the details; I've definitely never seen a spell like this in real life before. Sorry, boss."

I nodded distractedly, still thinking. Depending on how the spell worked . . . Just imagine if I could summon an AK-47 at will. *Oh*, the bullshit I wouldn't have to put up with anymore.

But then, with the whole of modern Earth in my head to pick from, maybe a weapon wasn't the most effective thing I could choose? A laptop would be handy for a few things, but with no internet most of its utility wouldn't exist . . . A helicopter? No, I *definitely* didn't know how to operate one of those, and that seemed like the kind of thing you'd get killed for trying without expert supervision. I'd have to give it serious thought. I certainly had time to do so; all of this was theoretical until I actually acquired a Conjure Material scroll.

"Knowing a specific spell I need to look for," I murmured, "is it going to be easier or harder to find a copy of Conjure Material than, just, spells in general?"

"Harder, I should think," said Aster.

"Although there are opportunities to look for specific spells if you know what you're after," Biribo added. "We're a long way from any city big enough to have a market for scrolls, but there are some Spirits that'll take requests when they hand out rewards. Rare, but they exist. Also, boss, keep in mind that the Wisdom perk you just unlocked will weigh Spirit rewards in favor of things that're explicitly useful to you."

I nodded, still pondering. Damn, sounded like Head Start had really lived up to his name. Of course, it wasn't out of the goodness of whatever passed for its heart. I got the distinct impression the Spirit was unhappy about goddesses in general and eager for the opportunity I presented to throw a wrench into their works. Which, of course, only made me even more sympathetic toward it.

"We got movement," Biribo reported suddenly. "Yeah, I was right, boss; everybody's sittin' down eating. They got one guy standing up on watch at the main entry to their camp, but even he's got a bowl of stew."

"Then this is our window, ladies," I said, turning to nod at Nazralind, who had remained within earshot behind me, close enough to relay orders to the rest of the squad without raising her voice. "Let's move."

It had to happen eventually, and I guess eventually was now—the conquest of this camp proved to be the moment when my established strategy went right to shit.

Not initially; in fact the attack itself went down with delightful precision that gave me a surge of pride in how well I'd trained my girls. We had to vary the pattern of our customary nighttime strike somewhat to account for our targets being alert and only somewhat distracted.

The enemy had set up camp in what looked to be a seminatural depression they had further cleared out, between three particularly huge khora which grew in a cluster that made a nice space between them. Of the three gaps, one had been piled with an improvised barricade of raw akorshil apparently chopped off the nearby trunks, with the other two kept open as entries.

After testing the wind, we positioned ourselves where the fumes wouldn't blow right back into our faces, and then Ydleth and I struck first as soon as Kastrin was in her spot. Ydleth wasn't nearly as sharp a shooter as Kastrin—none of us were—but she had decent aim and a strong arm, and succeeded in landing our improvised bomb—a sack of goblin sleeping powder and minor explosives—right in the middle of the camp. That, of course, immediately got the bandits' attention, so I Sparked it the instant it hit the ground, sending up the plume of sleeping powder and knocking the lot of them out. In a reversal of our usual strategy, that left the lookout as the last taken down. He whirled to see what had happened and got not only a face full of airborne sleeping powder but a dart in the side from Kastrin's stinger for good measure.

Clockwork.

After that, it was the usual. We bound them, I Healed them awake, and commenced *showtime*. By this point my speeches about this crooked-ass country and the necessity of purging its nobles had become almost rote, not that I let that diminish the quality of my showmanship. Some of us are *professionals*, after all. It felt good to be back on track.

Right until everything ran off the tracks entirely.

"I don't have any fucking clue what you're talking about!" the bound bandit snarled, every bit the picture of righteous indignation.

I kept up my public face, despite the sudden sinking feeling in my gut. Meeting the man's protests with a raised eyebrow, I slowly turned to the woman who'd made the accusation.

"You're *absolutely* sure, Menytin?"

"I wouldn't forget something like that!" she barked, nearly as angry as the accused.

"Easy, Meny," Adelly murmured, placing a hand on her upper back.

Menytin had to pause and inhale, but nodded. "It was just the one time; I can't say if he made a habit of it. But it was my *first week* in the Cat, I didn't know what the fuck was going on, and I was paying attention to everything, trying to learn the ropes. This clown beat the shit out of Nimidie, so bad she couldn't *work* after that. He got bounced out and banned, but . . ."

"That's a fucking lie!" the bandit shouted, struggling against his bindings. "I never took a fist to a woman in my life!"

"Well, *that* isn't true, anyway," Jadrin drawled, folding her arms. "I know this guy, Lord Seiji. Cwydar's got himself a temper problem—that's exactly how he ended up out here fucking around in the mulch instead of working for one of Gray's cozy little operations where I first met him."

"And who the *fuck* are you, even?" Cwydar sneered at her. "I don't know you, and you don't know me!"

"You're certain, Jadrin?" I repeated, watching his face for any sign of recognition at the name. He looked too pissed off to notice.

Jadrin nodded, still studying him dispassionately. "Yep. All fists and no cunning, this one. F'rinstance, if he was a *little* smarter he'd've pretended that wasn't his name, instead of giving away that obviously I *do* know him."

At that, the accused just looked madder. Not even surprised, just pissed off.

"Well, she's got him there," piped up another of the imprisoned bandits. "His name is definitely Cwydar."

"Radon, you backstabbing piece of shit!" Cwydar roared.

"Oh, fuck you," snorted the only woman in the group. "Think about how you've acted around here, and ask yourself whether any of us are gonna stick our necks out for you, *Cwydar*."

I shook my head slightly, clearing away the uncomfortable recognition that one of these guys had the same name as the youngest of the Gutter Rats I'd taken in. Well, it stood to reason most cultures had common names that lots of people could be given. I'd killed another guy called Donon, previously. For now, I had more urgent matters to be uncomfortable about.

"Go on, Jadrin."

"Right, so," she said in a disinterested tone, "guys like this're a black disc a bushel, specially on the rough streets. I never ran in a crew with him, but we crossed paths a bunch of times back in the day. Dunno if he made a habit of beating up women, but I believe it. Guy *definitely* caused, and then solved, all his own problems by hitting 'em. He punched out my friend Khannit one time. She had it coming, for the record—rude bitch never had any sense of who not to fuck with—but I do know he's not one of those who're shy about hitting a woman. I could *totally* see him beating the hell out of a whore if she said something he didn't like."

"Which I *saw happen*," Menytin insisted.

"Really, you watched?" I asked.

She blinked, then scowled, looking away. "Well, I mean . . . He took Nimidie to a room, she came out bloody, and the bouncer threw his ass practically into the canal."

"See!" Cwydar shouted. "I *told* you she was a fucking liar!"

"You have an alternate explanation for what happened?" I inquired in my mildest tone.

"None of it happened!"

"Lord Seiji," Menytin began, but fell silent as I held up one hand.

"Anyone else know this guy?" I asked.

There was silence from the rest of my followers. I looked directly at Adelly, who shook her head.

"Menytin's got seniority on me, Lord Seiji. If this happened when she was new, I'd've still been in the King's Guild then."

"*See!*" Cwydar insisted.

"Any comments from you lot?" I inquired. "I gather our man here is not *popular* even among his current circle."

"She's got the right of it," said the woman, jerking her head toward Jadrin. "Cwydar's a mean asshole, is all. Dunno if he's got any problems with women, exactly. He never tried to paw me or any of the girls who were here before the Olumnach people took 'em into the Gutters. Least, not that I know of."

"In a small group alone in the forest, you notice who's like that," added Radon. "We did have a couple of those, but they got taken to town. Cwydar's got problems with *everybody*, but I dunno if I'd say he beats on women more'n the usual."

"More than the *usual*," Kastrin spat, raising her crossbow. Adelly pushed it back down, and Radon cringed, trying to duck his head as best he could while tied hand and foot.

Cwydar just seethed in silence now, apparently unsure how to properly support this decidedly lukewarm defense.

Everyone was staring at me expectantly, Menytin insistently so. I made a show of calm consideration—arched eyebrow, head tilted back, lips just slightly pursed. Don't worry, Lord Seiji is totally in control. It was, after all, still *showtime*, and I had more than enough stage experience to feign composure when some unexpected disaster had me inwardly shrieking obscenities.

Fuck fuck fuck fuck fuck!

What the hell was I supposed to do about *this*? I had only just now realized how glassy-smooth the path had been up to this point. With the first gang, there had been some among the convicted and killed who'd protested, but they were overshadowed by . . . What *was* that guy's name, the strangler? And then there'd been Freebie Guy just this morning, who had clearly been so accustomed to getting by on his charming smile that he had failed to realize the danger even as he condemned himself with his own mouth. Through all of them, and uncountable assholes I'd met previously in the Gutters, there ran this undercurrent of contempt for women and particularly prostitutes that seemed to make people blithely dismiss violence against the Alley Cats. It seemed like it just didn't occur to them that beating up prostitutes was objectionable.

Those previous encounters suddenly felt like they'd been soft-balled to me by a benevolent deity. It had always been just a matter of time until I had to deal with a guy whose accused crimes weren't so cut and dry, and who had the basic sense to deny it and argue for himself. Man, in hindsight those other two had been *really* stupid. Sure, lots of people were stupid, but I had royally fucked up by assuming it was always gonna be that simple.

Everyone was still staring at me, practically breathless with anticipation. I slowly tilted my head to one side, drawing out the tension even as I frantically flailed for a solution.

This was fundamentally *not the same* as the abusers I'd made a show of cutting down, to earn loyalty points. It was a dipshit with anger issues who had committed *one* accused crime of temper—accused by only one person, who had only seen the aftermath, and corroborated only by negative character witnesses. This was just straight up not enough evidence to convict him in any court worthy of the name. And even if convicted, the reasonable punishment was a lot lighter than the only thing I was in a position to inflict. He was probably an asshole who belonged in jail, sure, but after a proper trial.

Jails and trials were things I did not have. And as I'd told everyone often enough, I came promising vengeance, not justice.

That, I realized, was the worst part. Because I had known immediately what I was going to do, and known that it was not going to be the right thing. But I was going to do it anyway, because it was what *I* needed to resolve this situation, and all my mental struggling right now was just a futile effort to escape the corner I'd painted myself into without adding yet another unforgivable crime to my conscience.

And I couldn't. I could not do what was right, what was just, because I needed the loyalty of these women above all. I needed the *fear* of these bandits in the short term; actual loyalty in the long would be ideal, but I could make do with fear. A sacrifice had to be made.

God damn it.

I drew my sword.

"No, fuck you," Cwydar rasped, glaring baleful hatred up at me.

"I will not condemn a man based on nothing but *one* accusation," I stated in a ringing tone. "A life is too much to squander for a matter of one person's word against another's. An accusation with only indirect corroboration is still . . . tenuous."

Menytin opened her mouth, swelling up in outrage, and Adelly clamped a hand on her shoulder, silencing her.

"But I've made myself clear," I stated, pointing the sword at Cwydar and staring down the blade at him. "Abusers of women are not suffered under my rule. Hopefully someday we'll have a system to *properly* administer justice— but let's face it, Fflyr Dlemathlys has never had one of those. Here I have a credible accusation, multiple corroborating character witnesses, and *not one voice* raised in support of the accused."

"You can't *do* this, you asshole!" he snarled, struggling again.

"It's a tough call," I said, my demeanor as icy and merciless as I could make it, "but it's *my* call and I've made it. When the victim is unwilling or unable to raise their own hand, or not present to do so, vengeance is *mine* to dispense."

Cwydar tried to surge to his feet, struggling violently against the ropes binding him, and lasted barely a second. The Mastery enchantment did exactly what the name promised—with the rapier in my hand, I was a master fencer. I stepped forward in a laser-precise lunge, the tip of the blade sinking right through his left eye and deep into his skull. It was as easy as strumming a chord on my guitar.

I stepped back and flicked the blade hard, splattering the ground with gore, as Cwydar slumped back down. He twitched a few more times before falling still.

For two beats, I let the silence hang before speaking in utter nonchalance.

"Any other accusations, ladies?"

A few glances were exchanged and heads shaken. I panned a calm stare around the assembled group, then nodded when no one else stepped up.

"Good. Always a relief when *most* of a group is worth saving. Welcome to the Dark Crusade, my new friends."

"Ah fuck," mumbled the woman in the group, then flinched in clear terror when my gaze landed on her directly. I just gave her a smile. I might've ordinarily gone for a more mischievous note, but I was . . . not in the mood.

"Nazralind, get everybody on their feet and organized; I want this place packed up and on the move in half an hour, tops. Adelly, interview our new comrades and find me a location for our next target."

"Hai!" Adelly chimed, already stepping forward alongside Naz to carry out my orders. Even *she* was doing it now.

While the camp shifted into a rush of activity, my followers streaming forward to sort through the bandits' supplies, I stepped backward twice, to the edge, and then turned around to wipe my sword carefully on a low-hanging khora frond.

Putting my back to the camp gave me a moment in which I didn't have to control my expression. Just a moment was all I needed. It couldn't be all showtime all the time.

Aster stepped up beside me and surreptitiously touched me once on the upper arm as I resheathed the cleaned blade.

"It had to be done," she murmured.

I shook my head. "It did *not* have to be done. I had to do it. Those might have the same end result, but they are . . . very different."

She regarded me in silence for a moment, then nodded once and watched the ongoing preparations along with me. Her own advice from what felt like years ago hung heavy in the air.

Whenever you can, be kind.

I tried, but . . . at what point was there just *no* point anymore? There was already no amount of kindness that would compensate for all the blood I'd spilled. And I was only getting started.

While everybody sorted out the bandits and packed up the camp, not one person so much as touched Cwydar's body. Because I'd told them at the *last* camp what my policy was. Those who break my central rules get left for the crawns. And so he was ignored and left there to begin rotting once we were done and gone.

As I had ordered.

30

In Which the Dark Lord
Battens Down the Hatches

My intended blitzkrieg didn't go the way I'd planned, but in a different way than how things usually didn't go the way I planned.

I was regrettably accustomed to my efforts falling flat or blowing up in my face, but having something more or less work out but *take* forever was . . . Well, actually, that was pretty much how my early campaign in Cat Alley had gone down, but this felt more visceral somehow. My intention had been to sweep through the bandit camps ringing Gwyllthean's western border in a rush; based on the distances involved and how long I knew it took to walk from North Watch to the city, I'd figured it would take two days, tops.

Well, in the end, it went smoothly enough, but that left me in control of the final bandit encampment far to the southwest after we set out from Caer Yviredh.

Sneak up on a bandit camp, ambush and neutralize them with our unconventional weaponry and stealth tactics, then *showtime*. Identify and purge the undesirables, then reassign the remainder. I rarely kept more than one or two, along with the small groups I left to take over their territory, brought one or two with me, and sent any remaining back to North Watch. Clan Olumnach had stripped their numbers so much that none of the remaining gangs had more than six members, some as few as three. Then we took and divvied up what was useful from their supplies, provided them with any necessities from our own, and abandoned the campsites, leaving the new Seiji-aligned gangs to begin a patrol of their territory. With the guidance of whichever bandit my core group had absorbed, we would then locate the next camp. Rinse and repeat.

With the gwynnek riders making a constant circuit, we stayed in contact with the previously overtaken gangs, the field command post I'd sent Goose to establish in Auron's old campsite near the waystation, and North Watch itself. It felt like painfully delayed contact to me, with my recent memories of the internet, but everyone with me seemed impressed by how quick our communications were. Rather than a loose and barely controlled collection of criminals as Clan Olumnach had arranged them, I had made these groups part of a single organization, keeping in touch and moving as one.

Turns out, setting up and maintaining something like that is neither easy nor fast.

If only the delays were my worst problem.

I could not renege on the promise of vengeance to my core followers; I had made it too central to what bound them to me, and I was too reliant on their support to risk it. While I preferred to think that none of my girls would lay a false accusation against some random man out of spite, Aster had quietly warned me that in the aftermath of the battle of Cat Alley, we had several burgeoning misandrists in the ranks. I couldn't entirely blame them, especially because all of this was my own fault. I had maliciously unleashed feminism on this country in much the same way the Yviredhs had been sponsoring bandits—barely understanding what it was or how it worked and with no plan at all to control it, and now people were getting hurt.

Not every gang required blood to be spilled. Two of the smaller ones were all-female already; those took one look at my assembled forces and clamored to join up faster than I could explain what they were joining up *for*. Of the rest, a couple had no members identified by any of my followers as problems.

But there was still vengeance to dispense. I learned that Freebie Guy and the Strangler weren't isolated cases; several more idiots sealed their own doom because when accused of the beating, rape, and/or murder of prostitutes, they seemed nonplussed that this was even worth talking about. In a sick way, the bone-deep rottenness of this country was helping to save my own conscience. Even when the abusers didn't blithely out themselves, they had often made enough of a pattern that multiple voices were raised against them, usually even among their own comrades. Not always, though.

Four more times that week I cut down men based on nothing but the tenuous evidence of an accusation.

Because that was what I needed to do to stay in control.

It was getting harder and harder to sleep. I let myself hope that would be easier back in my bed in North Watch, but the hard dirt and khora roots we camped on were not the problem.

A week after setting out from Caer Yviredh, I stood at the end of a trail of corpses, mentally exhausted and fully reliant on pure showmanship to keep up a good face for the troops. We'd had an unbroken string of easy victories and totally secured the ground needed for the next stage. Conquest was complete. It would've been nice if I could have felt good about it.

Aster and Nazralind joined me a short distance from the last camp, as requested; there was a nice little spot the bandits had been using as a lookout point from which we could watch our people sorting and packing everything without being directly within earshot.

"Ladies," I said pensively, "I believe I have fucked up."

"What makes you think so, Lord Seiji?" Aster said, her innocently solicitous tone giving away the game.

Thanks to my own cultural biases, it had taken me a long time to catch on—and in the end I'd needed Biribo to point it out—but once I did, the pattern was inescapable. Fflyr sarcasm looked a lot like Japanese politeness. It turned out that when a lowborn was being vague, refusing to come out and openly voice something critical, they were making fun of me. I guess that made sense in a culture where talking back to your superiors could get you killed.

I gave her a flat look, getting a bland smile in reply.

"Nazralind," I said, breaking eye contact with Aster after a moment, "do you know of any democratic countries near Fflyr Dlemathlys?"

"*Democratic* countries?" Her eyebrows shot upward. "What, you mean like beast tribes?"

"Um . . . Why was that your first thought?"

She shrugged. "Well, because a nation-sized democracy is fairytale nonsense. I believe smaller tribal cultures sometimes organize themselves that way. The beastfolk, for example. I've read that orc tribes are like that, too, but the nearest orcs are way over on the other side of the Lancor Empire."

"What is a democracy?" Aster demanded.

"Government by popular vote," I explained. "People elect their leaders and usually set policy by public agreement."

Now it was her turn to raise her eyebrows. "That sounds like a pretty good idea to me."

"It *sounds* that way, yes," said Nazralind, "but in practice that stops working if you have more than a hundred or so people to govern. Actual leadership is impossible since it takes so long to get anything done, and democracies aren't so much prone to corruption as inherently riddled with it."

"Well, that does sound pretty nasty," Aster murmured. "I'd hate to live in a corrupt country with bad leadership."

Was she being spicier than usual today, or had I just failed to notice how much of her commentary was full of underhanded jabs? To judge by her expression, Naz had caught that last one, too.

"Governing is a skill," she tried to explain. "That's why none of us know anything about it; skills take training and practice, and innate talent helps. You don't want every peasant helping to set national policy for the same reason you wouldn't ask a baker to shoe your horse."

Aster gave her a very bland smile, and I hastily interjected before she could say whatever she was about to.

"I asked because I was hoping there were native Ephemeral examples of societies transitioning into democracies, but I guess not."

"Transitioning?" Naz wrinkled her nose. "Governments transition all the time, usually through coup, conquest, or usurpation. As for democracies . . . No, I've never heard of such a thing. The nearest analogue would be the few small republics scattered about, mostly governed by coalitions of noble houses or merchant syndicates. Even those rarely grow to be anything bigger than a city-state. What brought this on, Lord Seiji?"

"On Earth, most nations are democratic," I said. Both of them looked surprised, and Nazralind also skeptical. "Well . . . at least in theory. And most of the *stable* ones transitioned from authoritarian to democratic rule slowly. Many of the successful states in the modern era still have figurehead monarchies but are actually governed democratically, including Japan. There have also been a lot of violent revolutions overthrowing tyrants to establish democratic governments, and those . . . usually fail, especially if they succeed."

"Well, of course they do," Nazralind said, shrugging again. Aster gave her another even look.

"*Because*," I continued, "as you pointed out, governance is a skill. It reliably leads to disaster if the people trying to govern don't know how to do anything but slaughter their enemies."

Both of them shifted to look down at the camp and our people working there, expressions clearing.

"Ah," Aster said softly.

"Yeah, so, I fucked up," I said, following their gaze. "Every step seemed like the only step I *could* take at the time, but right now I'm looking at the start of a pattern I recognize from *lots* of history, and it ends in fire and blood and nothing remotely constructive. I have to *fix this* before it gets any further out of hand, and I've got absolutely no fucking clue how to do that."

"You could . . . ask the Yviredhs?" Nazralind suggested with hesitance that didn't suggest she believed deeply in her own proposal. "They do govern a fief."

"Are they really an example worth emulating?" Aster asked pointedly. "They're nice enough people, but . . . come on."

"Recognizing the problem is a start, boss," Biribo chimed in. "You need to find somebody to teach you how to rule. There are options; now you know to look for them as opportunities come up. But is that the most important thing to be thinking about right this second?"

"Once again, the flying sass lizard speaks truth," I sighed. "All right, ladies, this is where we part ways. Don't make that face, Aster; you're coming with me! But it'll be *just* the two of us heading into the Gutters. I want to try to keep this quiet until we get the lay of the land. Nazralind, I'm putting you in charge of my forces here."

"Hai!" she acknowledged.

It'd been a week and I still wasn't used to that. After my awkward revelation about the goddesses, hearing it from people who were clearly not Japanese was still making me a little twitchy, but I had decided not to discourage the practice. If nothing else, it was succinct.

"Retrace our steps and rendezvous at Caer Yviredh. I want you to join and take charge of the group there, with whatever sized force you judge won't attract undue attention. Send the rest of our people to join Goose at the central camp up north; I'll return to collect everybody when I've sussed out the situation in Gwyllthean and finalized a plan."

"Hai!" Yeah, it was gonna take me a while longer to *get* used to that.

"Your secondary objective is to keep an eye on *and* maintain relations with Clan Yviredh. I feel like they'll be less inclined to ponder turning on us if we have an armed presence near them, but at the same time I don't want to antagonize them directly. You're the person for that job, Naz; nobody else would be as good at managing highborn. You seemed to be getting along well with the younger Yviredhs, so keep that up."

"Lady Avelit, yes," she said with a doubtful frown. "I'm not sure Lord Ediver would be as amenable to my influence."

"Nazralind," I said patiently, "you are an *unrealistically* beautiful woman, and he's a teenage boy. It will not be hard. Just try not to give the poor kid an aneurysm or piss off his mother too much."

"I'm not sure I agree," Aster said sweetly. "It will *definitely* be hard. Don't ask the boy to stand up in a hurry."

Biribo cackled so hard he lost some buoyancy and Nazralind blushed, for once having no comeback. For the most part she and the other ladies were fitting in well with the group, but I had noticed that most of them were having trouble getting comfortable with the off-color humor that was inevitably popular in an organization of mostly former sex workers.

"Thanks for that, Aster," I said, shooting her my best Aster Look. "All right, let's not waste any more time screwing around; gods only know what Olumnach's been doing to the Gutters for the last two weeks. I want to make a quick address to the team, and then we need to head out. After that, it's in your hands, Nazralind."

"Hai!"

Fucking hell, I was creating monsters left and right.

The Gutters were still quieter than I remembered. People there didn't have the luxury of not going to work just because they were recently traumatized and afraid for their lives, but even a week and change after the pogrom, the place was noticeably subdued. At least that made our passage through it uneventful as Aster led me to the destination I'd asked for.

It was a public house called the Short Stack, which I privately thought was a little too on the nose, but also pretty much in character for goblins. From the outside, it was a lowborn-built structure like any other, which was to say it looked like something from an illustration of medieval Europe, except in a mélange of pastel colors because the Gutters was built of akorthist bricks and blocks and akorshil planks and beams. Inside, though, I got my first real look at goblin culture.

To my surprise, it was pretty cool.

I had to chide myself for succumbing to Fflyr stereotypes in having assumed goblins would live surrounded by squalor and filth. The pub's main room was as clean as any izakaya I'd ever visited, and more so than a lot of the places in Cat Alley. What impressed me most was that it had a sense of style unlike anything I'd seen in Dlemathlys. Or anywhere, really. Every centimeter of the exposed akorshil wall panels were covered in painted murals, clearly done by multiple artists and showing a variety of styles from realistic landscapes to abstract shapes and several pieces of word art that resembled graffiti I'd seen on Earth. In fact, looking around, I observed a tall rack of shelves full of paints and brushes in one corner. The sign hung on it was lettered in extravagant calligraphy, laying out the fees for buying paints, renting brushes, and the rules concerning what patrons were and were not allowed to paint in the room.

It was my first real glimpse of actual goblin culture, and it showed me I had misjudged them. Whatever else they were, the goblins of Dount were so into art that there was money to be made by letting them paint the walls.

"Damn," I said appreciatively, pausing in the door to just take it all in.

The room took me in, as well. It wasn't very full at this hour of the early afternoon, but a dozen goblins scattered around various tables paused whatever they were doing to turn and stare at me and Aster. This was a Fflyr-built structure originally, so the actual building was human-sized, but all the furniture in here was meant for goblins. Even the bar had a kind of dais lining it, with short steps leading up to a ledge with short stools so the clientele could sit at the bar and be able to see over it. All the red eyes in all these green faces were blank and carefully neutral. Not hostile or welcoming, just wary.

Taking just a second to get my bearings and let myself be seen, I strode across the room to the bar. To actually get up to it I had to lean forward awkwardly with one knee on the steps, as standing would've had me bonk my head into the ceiling. Aster hovered behind me in silence, and the bartender, a young goblin woman whose black hair was dyed with red streaks, approached me while putting on a cheerful customer service smile.

"Well, hey there, tall dark and exotic," she said cheerfully. "You sure you know where you are? Not that I'll turn down honest coin, but if you didn't notice, you ain't exactly the target clientele of this establishment."

"Oh, I'm in the right place, don't worry," I replied, grinning back. "Do you have rooms for rent?"

"Yup." The goblin raised her eyebrows but wasn't surprised enough to be thrown off her business game. "All the doors and ceilings are human-sized, but we've only got goblin furniture. So I can rent you a room, but not a bed, or any of what you'd usually expect *in* a room."

"Well, how about some extra blankets and pillows? The floor won't kill me, so long as it's padded."

"That we can do. Extra services mean extra charges, you understand."

"Aw, c'mon." I put on my own best grin, the one I'd used on girls at the clubs I'd performed in back in Tokyo. "Meet me halfway, here. I should really ask for a discount for not being able to use the bed. Doesn't that all cancel out?"

She matched my grin and didn't budge an iota. "Giving you extra linens means we gotta do extra washing, champ. And you knew what kinda place this was when you walked in here."

It wasn't worth pushing. "Well, when you put it that way, fair enough. Just the room then, with the additional bedding."

"How long you stayin'?"

"Just through the night. I might leave earlier, but I won't need it past dawn."

"All righty then," the barmaid said cheerfully. "Though we won't kick ya out at the crack of dawn; long as you're gone or paid for the next night by noonish, we're all good."

"Won't be an issue. What else can I get here?"

"Well, it's an inn. The public room serves booze and food; not much is cooked at the moment, but if you wander down around dinnertime there'll be plenty. I can even bring something up to ya, if you want, and if there's a decent tip in it for me." Her roguish grin faded by several degrees. "Just to be clear, the front girls will come *to* your door, but not past it. I do not come with the room. That ain't up for negotiation."

I thought about Cat Alley, about Donon, and about what kind of human man probably wandered into this place.

"Furthest thing from my mind," I said, making my smile as bland and reassuring as I could manage. "Not that you aren't pretty, but I'm not . . . in need."

The barmaid's red eyes darted past me to give Aster the once-over, then she winked. "I'll bet."

"Also," I said hastily before Aster could register an opinion, "I need to get a message to somebody in the tunnels. His name's Maugro; I assume you know him?"

"A goblin? This may surprise you to learn, buddy, but in fact, we do not all know each other."

This was delivered in such an earnest deadpan that I honestly couldn't tell whether she was being sarcastic or had had to explain this fact to people in seriousness often enough to not care anymore. Knowing what I did about Fflyr Dlemathlys, I'd have believed either.

"I mean, Maugro's business brings him to the surface often enough, I figured you'd be familiar with him just from working *here*. Can I get somebody to send a message?"

She lifted her hands off the bar counter to shrug, her expression a masterpiece of mild-mannered bemusement. "Dunno where you're from, stranger, but around here, taverns don't tend to double as courier offices. If you know your friend's address, you can probably get an actual messenger service to send somebody? Or go yourself."

"Right, but it's down in the tunnels."

"Ah, yeah." She nodded, looking sympathetic. "And I know how you humans feel about going down there. Sorry, man, can't help ya."

"I'm not asking for a favor." I matched her calm, noncommittal smile to the best of my ability. "Two silver halos to carry a message."

The amount made her hesitate, an expression flicking across her face that convinced me I was being deliberately stonewalled and wasn't just barking up the wrong khora. Then the bland smile was back, accompanied by another shrug.

"Must be important for you to be so generous, champ. You could try asking any bystander with tunnel business, but I really can't recommend handing that kinda coin over to a stranger without some assurances. Specially since, like I mentioned, this ain't a messenger service here."

"Well, of course. Payment on delivery."

"Oh sure," she said, deadpan serious again. "You'll promise the moon glazed with sour sauce for a job, and will *totally* pay up once it's all done. And I'll believe that, because my mom squirted me out *this morning*."

"Ew," Aster muttered.

"How about this," I countered, keeping my tone and face affable. "*Maugro* will pay it, on my say-so. And since the message is just that I want him to meet Lord Seiji here, he can collect it from me when he does. I am that confident that he'll vouch for my trustworthiness."

"Did this Maugro tell you this was the place to get in touch with him?" she asked sardonically.

"Well, no."

"Well, there ya go." Again the shrug, this time accompanied by another shark-toothed grin.

I turned to look behind me at the common room, where two-thirds of the goblins present had silently vanished while we'd been talking. One fellow I caught in the act of slipping out the door; he froze like a deer in the headlights, staring wide-eyed at me as if afraid of what I might do. I just turned back to the barmaid with a shrug.

"Well, my mistake. Worth a shot. I guess just the room, then."

"And the blankets," Aster prompted.

"And the blankets, yes."

"Pleasure doin' business, handsome." The barmaid's countenance turned sunny as if on command. "That's seven black discs or equivalent!"

Obviously, the first thing we did was secure the room. Thanks to Biribo's ability to sense the details of physical surroundings and nearby people, all the spyholes were easily found. We plugged them all with slimes. Then we dragged the dresser over to block off the hidden entrance along one wall and moved the bed so that one leg was pinning down the trapdoor concealed by the rug—and since we couldn't use the furniture anyway, piled the chairs and table on the bed for extra weight. As a final bit of emphasis, I opened the room's sole window and dropped a slime out of it, giving no sign I knew it had landed directly on the goblin crouched there trying to listen. He was good—didn't fall off or even yell—and clearly got the message and made himself scarce before I switched to sharp implements.

"How did you know this place would be so full of peepholes?" Aster demanded as soon as Biribo assured us we had a modicum of privacy. "For that matter, why the hell *is* it full of peepholes?"

"Same way I knew I could get in touch with Maugro here. You said this is the place where the King's Guild always starts its raids on the tunnels when they make them, right? Well, the Fflyr up here might believe goblins are too dense or desperate to move away from a location that gets raided all the time, but you and I have seen firsthand that they're *way* too smart for that, unless they're doing it deliberately."

"You think it's . . . a front?"

"I don't know much about goblin culture, but it's at the very least a place under a lot of eyes down there. Anything we let slip in here will make its way into the tunnels faster than we could get back to our usual contact point. Even if that girl didn't want to take my offer, *somebody* out there will seize on the opportunity to make some money. And if they don't, odds are good Maugro will find out anyway, considering what business he's in and how good he apparently is at it."

"Are you sure he can actually do that fast enough to make a difference?" Aster's frown had not abated. "We know his actual headquarters is way out . . . you know where."

"I've been thinking about this for a while, actually," I said, sitting down on the low bed next to the pile of chairs. "Considering how fast he's kept abreast of our own movements, for example. Somehow the goblins are passing information at *least* as quickly as the Fflyr could do it overland. Suffice it to say, yes, I *am* confident he'll get the message and join us in time to give me a solid rundown on the situation in the Gutters—and particularly, the gang movements that nobody else could lay out for us."

"I dunno," she said doubtfully. "I mean, I follow your reasoning, but it seems like a lot to hang on—"

"Heads up," Biribo muttered, turning to stare at the room's door. Aster cut off, following his gaze.

A second later there came a knock.

"One person," Biribo said in a low voice right next to my ear, "no lurkers, no obvious weapons. Doesn't look like an ambush."

I nodded and he slithered unpleasantly down into my coat.

"Oh, come on," Aster protested. "Even if you were right, we've been up here all of half an hour! There's no *way*—that's just the girl from the bar with more blankets or something."

"It is *not* the girl from the bar," said a muffled voice from right outside. "Open up, Lord Seiji. You wanted to talk, so let's talk."

Muffled or not, it was definitely a female voice. Well, Maugro was a busy goblin; maybe he'd sent Mindzi. I gave Aster my smuggest grin as I crossed to the door and pulled it open to greet our visitor.

The sight wiped it from my face.

"Uh . . . oh. Wrong goblin."

31

In Which the Dark Lord
Gets Cut Down to Size

Yeah, that's great," she said, planting her fists on her hips. "That's exactly how a girl likes to be greeted, thanks."

"Hey, I was specifically expecting someone *else*, and I get the impression you were well aware of that . . . uh—"

"Oh, this is *rich*." Now she looked somewhere between incredulous and bitterly amused. "You have no idea who I am, do you?"

"Of course I remember you," I shot back, and it was the truth. Among all the goblins I'd met, this combination of vivid purple-and-white hair, huge tits, and sour attitude was very distinctive. Unfortunately some of the details had slipped, because I rather disliked this woman's company and made an active effort not to think about her. "Sneppit's so-called *hairstylist* and actually . . . I'm guessing executive assistant or business manager or something, I do not understand how you people assign job titles. What are you doing here . . . Ah . . ."

She folded her arms and raised her eyebrows.

Fuck it, I took a shot. ". . . Zuka?"

"*Zui*," corrected the goblin and Aster in one breath.

"Right, that's *practically* what I said."

"Well, thanks for not calling me Boob Goblin, I guess. An amazing number of you tallboys default to that."

"I thought about it," I admitted. "But then I decided that would be unnecessarily provocative."

"Ya think?"

"So then I thought about it again, but then I considered that you're apparently pretty close to Miss Sneppit, and I should consider how dealing with you would affect dealing with her."

Zui stared up at me in silence.

"So then I thought about it *again*, but then I—"

"All right, enough!" she exclaimed. "I *get* it, Lord Seiji says whatever he wants to whoever he wants and doesn't care what anybody thinks. Can I come in already? This whole conversation doesn't need to be yelled in the hall."

I had to consider that for a second. I *was* waiting for somebody else . . . But, hell, there was no point in pissing off Sneppit unnecessarily, and the fact that Zui had bothered to come here meant she probably had something worthwhile to say. Also, I was curious how she'd managed it so damn fast.

"Sure." I stepped back to allow her through the door.

"Wow." Zui looked around at the room, with its displaced furniture and slimes stuck to the walls in several places. "Y'know, just because it's owned by goblins doesn't mean you gotta trash it."

"We're going to put everything back how it was before we leave," I said in annoyance, shutting the door. "What do you *want*, Zui?"

"It's not what *I* want," she said, turning to face me once she reached the middle of the room. "It's what my boss wants. You suddenly showed up on goblin turf and started beating the bushes, Lord Seiji, which gets *attention*. Among others, you got Miss Sneppit's attention. It's not hard to pick up that something's gone wrong—you're usually one to lay careful plans in advance, not rush off and suddenly do shit like this. Miss Sneppit has a vested interest in your continued financial viability, not to mention having you *not* arrested and being interrogated about your contacts by the Fflyr authorities. Not to *further* mention, she also has vested interests in some of the particular bushes you're beating, hence me getting here so fast. So, what's up, and can we help?"

I stared down at her for a stupefied moment, blinking. "Wait. You're here offering . . . help?"

"Look more shocked when you say that," she snipped.

"I don't think that's *unwarranted*. How much would this putative 'help' cost me?"

"Well, that depends entirely on the details. Though despite what you seem to think, in a lot of the possibilities, the answer could be 'nothing.' Miss Sneppit is a businesswoman, Lord Seiji, not a miser. Sometimes you gotta protect your investments, and it never hurts to be owed a favor."

Damn, this was actually an opportunity. One I feared I wasn't prepared to take full advantage of; my current plans were vague, but drawing on Sneppit's resources was a possibility I hadn't even considered. What *could* I ask for? What could she even offer? And would there be hidden costs? Shit, this was exactly the kind of conversation I didn't want to have without being prepared in advance. Fucking goblins. There was always an angle with them . . .

"How *did* you get here so fast?" I asked, stalling for time to think. "Cos I've noticed you goblins seem to get around a lot quicker underground than we can up here, but *that* was really pushing plausibility. I mean, for a message to get down to Sneppit and you to be sent back up in such a short time . . . Oh. Is her headquarters right under this pub?"

"None of that is anything you need to know," she said, pressing her lips into an unhappy line. From a lot of people, I'd take that for a tacit admission, but Zui looked roughly that unhappy normally. "Look, if it helps you, the fact that you're having this conversation with *me* and not Gizmit is a big sign of good faith. From me, not just Miss Sneppit; orders or no orders, I don't come up to this city and talk to tallboys without armed backup unless I'm pretty confident they mean well. If we can't help you, Lord Seiji, then that's that. No harm done or offense taken. But whatever you're up to, if you need a hand . . . it's offered."

Between my deflection and her little soliloquy, I had actually had a thought that seemed worth asking about. Maugro's help would be necessary to create a map of gang activity in the Gutters, but there was privileged information even he didn't have, and I couldn't get. Unless . . .

"Can Youda brew a truth serum?" I asked.

Zui shot me down immediately. "I can tell you've been in Fflyr Dlemathlys long enough to have read way too many novels. There is no such thing as a truth serum. The problem there is philosophical, not scientific. 'Truth' is a much vaguer concept than it seems, like it should be. Even if you wanna limit the effect to, say, *factuality*, that's way too tricky in practice to be bottled. The conscious perception of reality is inherently mutable enough that everybody's understanding of *truth* is already scrambled even before you scramble it further with drugs. Some basic mental training is all it takes to beat any tongue-loosening effect by turning your revelations into garbled nonsense. Hell, you don't even need training; if somebody's a little mentally unstable, or even particularly *religious*, forcing them to tell 'truth' results in a lot of pointless noise. And like I said, administering mind-altering drugs to someone *makes* them mentally unstable by definition."

"Wow, that was a lot of fancy vocabulary all of a sudden."

She curled her lip in contempt, showing off her jagged teeth. "For a goblin?"

"For a hairstylist," I said sweetly, causing the sneer to deepen, "Look, Zui, I get why you've got a chip on your shoulder, considering the way this country treats goblins, but you can really save that for somebody who deserves it. I've never thought goblins were any less smart than anybody else. Most of the ones I've talked to are noticeably cleverer than the average Fflyr I've been running circles around. No offense, Aster."

"Offense?" She folded her arms and raised her eyebrows, almost exactly like Zui had a moment ago. "You sure as hell haven't been running circles around *me*."

Zui, somewhat to my surprise, actually seemed mollified by my speech. "Well, I suppose. Anyway, what you're asking about isn't *completely* off the table. I just wanted you to be aware of the limitations up front. You cannot feed somebody a potion and then just magically get good answers out of 'em, but there *are* ways to break a person's mental defenses, and the right use of alchemy can enhance that considerably. So you're not asking for a potion, but for the time and talents of the professionals necessary to carry out the process. An alchemist and an interrogator, at minimum. Fortunately for you, Miss Sneppit has those."

"Ah right, of course she would employ an interrogator. Or, forgive me, that would be . . . what? A plumber? Fan dancer? Tactical underwater basket weaver?"

"A maid," Zui said with a dry little smile. "That's just one of Gizmit's many talents. To be clear, Lord Seiji, this is not a small favor; we're already past the point of anything Miss Sneppit is likely to offer out of goodwill, but for you, I think she could agree to a deal. I can't *promise* anything without her approval, but that's my estimate. Also, it would depend on who's being interrogated."

I considered carefully under her patient stare before answering. Just revealing this was taking a risk . . . But Sneppit's organization already knew a lot about me that could cause me serious trouble, and she hadn't betrayed me yet.

"An agent of Clan Olumnach. Possibly a member of their Clansguard."

She didn't even blink. "You got a name?"

"I don't have one in custody just yet," I admitted. "This is an angle it didn't occur to me to pursue until you came along offering help."

Zui nodded. "All right, I'll pass the message to Miss Sneppit. I will warn you up front, Lord Seiji, she's gonna want serious assurances for this."

"I'm honestly surprised the idea wasn't an automatic dealbreaker."

"Oh please." She sneered again, though this time I got the feeling it wasn't directed at me per se. "Nobody in the tunnels would shed a tear for anything that happens to the Clans or their stomp-booted lackeys. But *pissing off* the Clans is another matter; they cannot find out we were involved, full stop. So, assurances."

"Stands to reason. Just let me know what she needs and we can talk details."

"I will pass the message," she repeated. "While I'm here, anything else you need?"

Suddenly I had a stray thought.

"Possibly. Say, Zui, explain something about goblin culture to me."

"No."

"Okay," I said ruefully, "we'll just dance around the issue of why you all have obviously fake job titles. All I *really* need to know is whether those are completely made up, or are you *actually* a hairstylist?"

Zui tucked her thumbs into her belt, on which I had noted the presence of bulging pockets containing a variety of tools and materials, including the protruding handles of a pair of scissors.

"I think you've misunderstood something. Mister, I am *the* hairstylist."

The hairstylist didn't walk around with all the tools of her trade, obviously, but she carried the basics on her person, even when on nonhairstyling business, which I assumed was one of those goblin cultural things I was not allowed to ask about. So, no chair or styling products, but she had scissors and combs, and Aster was able to fetch water from the pub downstairs. In the end, the only real problem was the lack of a mirror. The disparity in our heights posed a hurdle, but it worked out with me kneeling on the floor and her standing behind me. She seemed surprised I was able to hold that position long enough.

"Nihonjin desu," I explained with a grin.

"You *have* to be aware I have no idea what you just said."

"Nobody does," said Aster. "You just gotta learn to ignore it. He talks sense when he needs to."

"Up to a point, I gather," Zui muttered, and then her fingers were rifling through my hair, fluffing it up. "Hm. Hmmmm."

"Hm? What *hmmmm*? Exactly how worried should I be about that sound?"

"Just seein' what I've got to work with, here. Interesting texture."

"Is that going to be a problem?"

"Not for me, unless you want something real fancy done. Goblin hair is textured more like an elf or highborn—stiff and coarse. Easy to style, barely needs any product. This is new. Yours is glossy like a lowborn's, but straight. Fluffy."

"Fluffy," Aster repeated, grinning. "I bet you don't get called that very often."

"Not twice, anyway."

"Yeah, yeah, Lord Bigshot doesn't take any crap from anybody, we know," said Zui in a bored tone. "So you're just looking for a trim? I'll repeat what I said—you're the one who consented to do this without a mirror. I'm *good*, but I won't be held responsible if you don't love what you get. I wouldn't even agree to this if you wanted anything more complicated than a trim."

"It's fine, I just want it the way I used to have it in Japan. Aster remembers what I looked like when I first got here, don't you?"

"Yeah, he was kind of . . . deliberately scruffy. It was longish and on the shaggy side, but it was . . . I dunno how to describe it, exactly. It gave off the impression he had it that way on purpose, to *look* slightly scruffy. Now he just looks like he hasn't had it trimmed in months."

"Say no more." Zui began combing out locks and snipping at the ends; black hair fell to the spare blanket she'd wrapped around my neck. "Deliberately scruffy is a solid look; I can respect that. And you're right, it needs upkeep, otherwise you just look like a bum who can't be arsed to take care of himself. The right tinge of *deliberate* scruff expresses contempt for the lords of fashion. Totally different impression."

"See, I knew you'd get it," I said happily. "It's rock 'n roll."

Zui sighed heavily but didn't ask me to clarify that. "Tilt your chin up, please."

She actually was a professional, tugging my head into place with just the right degree of strength, firm but not rough. This adjustment pulled me backward so she could lean over and get at my bangs, and in the next moment I found my head and neck cradled in the most delicious softness. Warm, plush, and—

"*Please*," the woman in front of me rasped in a faint rattle I could barely hear. I couldn't reach her in time; I wasn't fast enough. **Heal**, *Heal!* The spell did nothing, didn't connect. It wouldn't touch a corpse. The blood was spreading from beneath—

I jerked forward, gasping and clawing at the blanket around me. The inn room came back into focus; Aster had stepped toward me in clear alarm, and to either side of my frame of vision I could see a pair of green hands, one holding scissors and the other a comb, instinctively jerked out of the way.

"I don't usually have to explain this part out loud, but I got sharp implements next to your face, here." Zui snipped the scissors twice in mid-air for emphasis. "There needs to be a maximum of *zero* sudden thrashing around, or the *best*-case scenario is you end up lookin' like a particularly smug haystack."

"Sorry," I whispered, then cleared my throat and repeated more firmly, though my voice still held an embarrassing quiver. "Sorry. I, uh . . . Look, this is awkward, but, um. Can you . . . keep those things to yourself, please?"

"Heh." I'd been afraid she would be offended, but the goblin just sounded amused. "Funny, most customers look for excuses to lean back into 'em. Yeah, I've learned to just ignore it, but if it matters to you, no problem. Can do. I just didn't figure *you* of all people for a prude, Lord Seiji."

I was the furthest thing from a prude, and under other circumstances not even Zui's abrasive excuse for a personality would have prevented me from fully appreciating her impressive chest, but . . . But. Even without the flashbacks, I had *seen* some shit recently. The memory of trauma had passed, and even still, there was a lingering discomfort with the idea of touching a woman that way when she hadn't specifically invited it. I was so much happier before I knew how much *touching* and worse they had to endure.

"Yeah, well," I said weakly, "I'm just full of surprises."

I was rescued from my own awkwardness by a knock at the door. It was *still* awfully soon for my message to have gotten the results I wanted, but at that moment I was too preoccupied with regulating my breathing to wonder about it too hard. Aster crossed the room to answer it while Zui resumed combing and snipping.

"Is this . . . a bad time?" Maugro asked pointedly from the doorway as soon as Aster opened it.

"Maugro!" I said cheerfully. "Perfect! Also, damn, you goblins move *fast*. I wasn't expecting you to turn up 'til tonight at the earliest."

"Yeah, well, lucky for you I was in the area. Maugro's gotta make his rounds, after all. Thanks, doll," he said, nodding to Aster as he stepped past her, not seeing her replying grimace. "Though I admit I wasn't expecting anybody to beat me here. I see you're taking full advantage, though."

"Say, speaking of that! Would Miss Sneppit happen to be headquartered right under this inn?"

"Hey, now," Zui growled, snipping her scissors in front of my face again.

"C'mon, Lord Seiji, you know how this works," Maugro said, grinning. "That kind of intel ain't free. Considering you're asking me to piss in Miss Sneppit's flower garden right in front of one of her top people, it ain't even cheap. You sure it's that important to you?"

"It definitely isn't," I acknowledged. "Certainly not what I called you here for. Thanks for going out of your way, Maugro. Do I need to reimburse you?"

"Oh yeah, *that* little ploy," he snorted. "Y'know, if I was a less honorable goblin, I would totally bilk you for the amount. Two silver halos for a message? You sure know how to stir people up. But no, of course not, because I'm not *stupid*. When I suddenly started getting mobbed by idiots trying to collect that bounty, it wasn't hard to find out what was up without having to actually buy the info from any of 'em. That was either a real clever play, Lord Seiji, or the desperate flailing of a man backed into a corner. Should I be worried?"

"I'm a bit out of my element, but desperate is overstating it. By the way, Zui, are you okay with us talking business while you work?"

"You're kidding, right?" she snorted, snipping away. "What the hell do you think Miss Sneppit does while I'm working on her? Everybody who's *got* business does it while they're getting trimmed. Don't mind me."

"Perfect, thanks. I've been away on business for the last week, so I'm a little out of the loop. I need to know everything there is to know about Clan Olumnach's movements into the Gutters."

"'Everything there is to know' is one of those phrases I keep having to train my clients not to say," Maugro sighed. "It *sounds* impressive, but in reality that'll be a lot of junk intel that you don't need and won't want to pay for. Think in terms of what you're trying to *do* and what you need to know in order to accomplish that."

"Okay," I drawled. "I am *trying* to break Olumnach's hold on crime on Dount, while it's still fragile enough to do so."

"That's a tall order," he said skeptically. "I *know* you're aware he's got a monopoly on the gangs outside the city."

"Correction. *I* have a monopoly on the gangs outside the city. Highlord Caldimer went and left them understaffed and undefended while he focused his attention on Gwyllthean."

That caused a moment of silence. Even the scissors stopped for a few seconds.

"Told you," I said smugly. "I have been *busy* this week."

"Well, damn," Maugro said at last. "I'm not the only one who works fast. Okay, then . . . You'll want to know the locations, strength, and fighting style of the gangs as they stand?"

"That's a good start. Also the relevant data about his own people. I'm assuming Clan Olumnach personnel are of a higher caliber than the bandits he's press-ganged into being fodder for this."

"I can get you a *bit* on that, but there'll be blind spots," he hedged. "For obvious reasons, the Highlord's cagey and has made an active effort not to reveal the full capabilities of his Clansguard and household Blessed. I've never seriously tried to ferret out that intel; the effort would've likely caught his attention and pissed him off, which I all *kinds* of don't fucking need."

"Whatever you've got, then. I have other options for gathering that information."

Maugro glanced at Zui. "Y'know what, I believe you."

"I'm also kind of in the dark about what *kinds* of operations are being fought over, here," I admitted. "I know pretty much all of the gangsters I recently killed, and those I'm about to, are street muscle. Gray's and Olumnach's, both. But I assume those can't be all of the crime in the Gutters."

"Yeah, you're not wrong," he agreed. "Muscle like them did a lot of stealing, both burglary and mugging, and Gray leveraged 'em for the likes of extortion and protection. Olumnach's goons won't have the know-how to do that as well, not right off the bat, but they'll catch on pretty quick. None of it's heart surgery. In fact, getting rid of Gently and the Rats will create more opportunities for spying and pilfering work once things start to settle again. But in terms of actual *businesses*, there are several fences and fixers who do discreet work with the more well-heeled types up in the middle ring; they go where the wind blows and will happily bow to whoever wants to claim they're in charge, so long as they get to keep doing business as usual. Some of Gray's moneylending and debt collecting operations may still be intact, if they're using independent muscle in place of the gangsters who got rounded up or knifed. The rest will just be gambling and drug dens. A lot of those got smashed when the Kingsguard went on their little rampage, but you can't really shut that shit down; it just pops up elsewhere the next night. The one thing Olumnach's people probably know about, that Gray's didn't, was smuggling. Most of that trade goes *around* Gwyllthean, not through it."

I started to nod and Zui grabbed my skull, holding me in place.

"Right," I said instead. "Then I need to know who's doing what, where. As complete a map of crime in the Gutters as you can get me, as up-to-date as possible."

Maugro let out a low whistle. "You're talkin' about a sizable research project, Lord Seiji."

"I know. And I need it fast. As fast as you can manage."

"If I pull all my people and put 'em on it . . . I can get you files by tomorrow. Do I gotta clarify that this will not be cheap?"

"This is no time for cheapness," I agreed. "This is the endgame, Maugro. Whatever you need, I'll get you, so long as you can get me what *I* need."

He studied me in silence for a moment.

"This really *is* it, huh? If you pull this off . . . Gray's broken, and Olumnach would be *out*. It'll be you, lord of all crime on Dount."

"That's the plan," I said, smiling coldly. "Which makes this the last opportunity for anybody who wants to be in good with me to *get* that way before they have to beg for my attention."

Zui snorted, but didn't stop clipping.

"Well, all righty then," Maugro said with sudden good cheer, grinning his shark's grin. "Then here's to a dark and glorious future! Let's talk particulars."

32

In Which the Dark Lord Realizes He Should Dial it Back and Then Doesn't

Among the potential targets Maugro found for me, I selected a "pawn shop," which was known to fence stolen goods for its perfect intersection of several conditions—it had survived the purge relatively unscathed; its proprietor had started voluntarily paying protection to one of the imported bandit gangs to secure his place against other looters; and the Olumnach Clansguard overseers had subsequently used it as a contact point to pass orders and receive tribute. It was the likeliest place for me to find what I needed, especially once Maugro got me info on the Olumnach's schedule. So, the next night, that was where I went and kicked in the door.

That was not a euphemism.

"Konbanwa, motherfuckers!" I shouted cheerfully as the door rebounded off the inner wall.

"We're *closed*," exclaimed the man behind the counter, not unreasonably. "And don't break my door! The fuck is wrong with you?"

Before I could address him, another man stepped directly in front of me, blocking my view—a particularly beefy fellow with a heavy cudgel in his hand. "Private party, buddy," he rumbled. "You need to move along."

I swept my eyes around the room, getting a quick count. One shopkeeper and five bandits. I heard Aster step up behind me and noticed the distinctive eye movements of every man in the room as they took in her huge, obviously magical sword, and the collar of her obviously magical chain mail, then eased back nervously. The customary reaction of low-rent thugs coming face-to-face with Blessed.

"Gentlemen!" I declaimed, spreading my arms wide, "I have come to educate you on the theory and practice of *crime*."

"Oh, for fuck's sake," grunted a man to my right, stepping up and already raising his sword.

Windburst!

He smashed against the wall, everyone else retreated, and the shopkeeper yelled from behind his counter. "Oh, *come on*! Can you not *wreck* the place, at least? That's merchandise you're blowing around, not your mum's wyddh molds!"

Looked like a bunch of junk to me, and anyway I didn't have time for his problems.

"All right, lads, being serious," I said in a suddenly more solemn tone. "We're all men of the world; we know better than to take it personally when someone tries to murder us. Correct? That said, I do need to establish what happens if you *interrupt* me while I am making a speech."

Immolate.

The spell hit my would-be silencer just as he was trying to scramble upright from being blown into the wall. As usual, there was no end of yelling, both from the immediate victim of the spell and the onlookers. The fence, in particular, seemed mightily upset about the sudden bonfire in the front corner of his shop. I couldn't entirely blame him, and it wasn't even my stuff getting singed. That spell was especially intimidating when used indoors, particularly under a ceiling as low as this one. There were going to be scorch marks all over the place. As always, I was glad khora-based construction wasn't flammable.

I waited it out. Yeah, yeah, sound of ultimate suffering, and so on. Nothing I hadn't seen before.

As soon as the unfortunate bandit was smoking and whimpering in pill-bug pose, I loudly cleared my throat.

"Any questions?"

Everyone was pressed back against the walls, staring at me in terror. Except the shopkeeper, who seemed to possess a modicum of self-mastery. He slowly raised one hand.

"Uh, yeah. Can we, um, help you with something, m'lord?"

Nothing like a bit of fire and screaming to improve everybody's attitude.

"You can listen," I said kindly. "So. Crime! As you may be, but probably are not, aware, gentlemen, the ultimate defining characteristic of a state as a viable political body is its *monopoly* on violence. A state is only a state if it has the only say in who does harm to whom. There are all kinds of different ways to organize a government and a society, countless philosophies and religions, but in the end? You have police as the only ones allowed to use violence against the country's own citizens, and the army who has the exclusive right to do it to everyone else. Monopoly on violence. *That* is what a state, at the end of the day, *is*. And that's why Fflyr Dlemathlys has to be considered a failed state, because . . . Well, I mean, look around. You all know what this place is like."

"Why's he telling us this?" one of the bandits stage-whispered to another, who made a slashing gesture for silence at him.

"And thus, crime," I lectured, swaggering further into the shop and leaving Aster to cover the door. "In the absence of any kind of functional governance, we human beings sadly revert to more primitive means of organization. In a way, you can gauge how civilized a region is by the role strength plays in social standing. Under any kind of decent social order, the capacity to kick ass means virtually nothing in day-to-day life. But *here*, where there are—in effect—no laws, save for extensions of the already established power of the authorities to ravage and murder? Once outside their purview, there is only the hierarchy of the pack. *He* knows what I'm talking about."

I gestured grandly to the man I'd just Immolated, who flinched and tried to hide behind a rack of shelves.

"In short, gentlemen," I proclaimed, "I can hurt you with nothing but a thought, a *lot* worse than you could hurt me with every ounce of effort you can muster. That means I'm in charge."

There was absolute silence in the pawn shop.

"Could . . ." one of the bandits finally rasped hoarsely, "could you not have just *said that*?"

I gave him a pleasant smile and a self-effacing shrug. "That's not really how I do things."

Behind me, Aster snorted loudly.

"Well, all right, then," said the shopkeeper, raising his hands. "You're in charge. Glad we've established that. So, my original question stands—how exactly can we help you, sir?"

"You gents are expecting a visit from a representative of Clan Olumnach," I said, smiling. "When?"

Everybody went silent again, looking nervously at each other.

I sighed. "I see I need to establish a bit more of the nuance of this situation. Now, let's see, you lads will have been moved into the Gutters just within the last week. Previously you were part of a bandit gang out in the khora, yes?"

"Aye, that's right."

"*Adler*," hissed one of the other men.

"What?" Adler shrugged emphatically. "He obviously *knows*, and it's not like that's a secret anyway."

"Which group?" I asked, maintaining the same pleasant demeanor. When they all just looked at each other again, I prompted further. "Maybe Kosach's gang? Or were you the . . . *privateers* Clan Fladwych paid to poach on their neighbors' lands? No? Perhaps the lads who had that sweet little gig due west of the city, extorting protection from those two outlying villages near the frontier?"

"Hell's revels, he's well-informed," Adler muttered, then raised his voice, addressing me. "We had a little camp in the border forest between the Clan Luoch and Clan Oliwyn fiefs . . . uh, my lord. Didn't really hit the farms or any travelers; we only stayed there because Clan Olumnach paid us to do some . . . y'know, minor damage and thefts and such in the villages around there. Make the place feel unsafe, cast doubt on Clan Aelthwyn's ability to keep the peace. It was all way more politics than I ever liked, but we weren't bandits to begin with because we had any better options."

"*Ah*! You lot were with Tig, Nannit, and Adiret's group!"

The fellow I'd Immolated hid again; the others suddenly glared, and Adler actually took an aggressive step toward me.

"How'd you know about that?" he demanded. "What did you do to the girls?"

"Oh, they're fine," I assured him. "Better off than *you* are. First thing we did was get a decent meal into them, and then some proper clothing. Camping outdoors in autumn calls for better than the rags they were wearing. I see you boys have yet to catch up."

"Who's . . . we, exactly?" Adler asked. Evidently he was the official spokesman of the group, if not its leader.

"Ah, that's right! Here I forgot to introduce myself. How very rude; my humble apologies." I bowed, shallowly but deliberately, because it wigged out every Fflyr I did it to, and my purposes were best served by emphasizing that I was not going to play by the rules they knew. "I am Lord Seiji, and you work for me now."

"Oh boy," the fence muttered from safely behind his counter. "This just got a lot more interesting than I wanna see in my shop . . ."

The rest of the lads looked at Adler, who drew in a deep breath, visibly steeling himself.

"Uh, look, Lord . . . Seiji. Please don't burnify me for pointing it out, but we're working for Clan Olumnach. Highlord Caldimer is not a man you wanna fuck with. He wasn't even before his kid got knifed and he went berserk, and now I'm uncomfortable enough with him knowin' I exist. I don't mean no disrespect, but just cos you're Blessed doesn't mean you're ready to take him on."

"That is correct." I pointed at him and nodded approvingly. "*This* is why I'm ready to take him on—I'm the guy who dismantled Lady Gray's organization and drove her out of the Gutters. I have the Kingsguard itself in my pocket, as well as the women of Cat Alley and what's left of the Gutter Rats. Highlord Caldimer moved you lot into the Gutters to seize Lady Gray's old turf because *I let him*. While he was doing that, I swept through the countryside and seized control of what was left of your gangs out there, and began stirring the Aelthwyn-aligned Clans up to create a pretext for Archlord Caludon to move against him directly."

I gave them a moment to let that sink in before continuing, putting on a smug smile.

"You're accustomed to thinking of Clan Olumnach as in control of the bandit gangs in rural Dount, right? Well, as of now, *I* am in control of those gangs. Olumnach has lost his grip on the countryside, while I've tightened mine. He's in the process of losing his ability to leverage his Clansguard. You boys and the others like you are the last viable assets he had left—and you're now in the Gutters, where *I* want you. Where I can move the Kingsguard and the remains of Lady Gray's information network as I please. I can walk into a room with the lot of you and let myself be surrounded at will, and not just because I can kill you all with my brain. So long as you're in my city, it is *I* who have *you* surrounded."

Pause again, fade expression to a flat stare . . .

"This is my island."

Pause. God, I loved the drama of it.

"So, gentlemen, I will ask you again, as a generous and merciful lord to his vassals. When, exactly, do you expect the contact from your *previous* master to arrive?"

I gave them a couple of seconds to mull it over. They didn't need more than that; the rest of them looked to Adler's lead, and he spoke after just a heartbeat of silence.

"Should be any time now, my lord. Deal's always that they come to us on their own time, and expect us to wait around at their convenience. It's been a bit trickier here in town than it was out in the forest where we just didn't have much to do. Here, they want us to be pushing on Gray's old contacts to take 'em over, and also bring in income from doing jobs in the city. Which we ain't even familiar enough with to be any good at, yet. And on top of that, we're to wait around in meeting spots with every lad available for inspection. You know highborn, m'lord. The Olumnach people are pretty big on . . . y'know, keeping us in our *place*."

I clicked my tongue disapprovingly, shaking my head. "Now that's just poor management, is what that is. Not to mention disrespectful of you gentlemen and your time. You'll find we do things differently in my organization."

"Differently how, my lord?" one of the other bandits asked, seeming to find some of his nerve.

"There's more listening to speeches, right?" ventured another.

They all tensed, looking at him.

"They're *good* speeches, though," Aster said. I glanced back to note that she was leaning against the wall by the door, arms folded. "Lord Seiji's better than a bard. He gets talking and it's as entertaining as it is informative. More so, often enough."

My loyal subordinate, everyone.

"That," I agreed, inclining my head magnanimously. "More importantly, I look after my people. You're the boys out in the thick of it doing the work; there's absolutely no excuse for you to be hungry and carrying shabby equipment. We'll fix all that at the earliest opportunity, but things are going to be a bit less settled until I finish straightening out the Gutters. Now then! That leaves you, sir."

The shopkeeper to whom I turned put on a big customer service smile and folded down his hands at me. "It's an honor to have you in my humble shop, Lord Seiji. I flatter myself that I'm something of a fixture of this neighborhood. I was in business here before Lady Gray rose to power, and wasn't much surprised to have outlasted her. Here I was prepared to deal with Clan Olumnach's agents as the next established power in the Gutters, but I suppose I needn't get comfortable with the idea, eh? Well, no matter. Good old Laerdh is just as happy to provide you with the same excellent service, my lord."

"All this to say that you're not interested in declaring for me, either?" I summarized in a dry tone.

He shrugged, smiling blandly. "I'm just a businessman, my lord. Just let me know what you're owed for protection, should you be in control of that operation, and we'll get along swimmingly. It's not for the likes of me to take sides in political squabbles. Laerdh will always be here to provide you with the finest curios and treasures that make their way through the Gutters, and to help you turn any such you happen to acquire into good, spendable coin."

"Hm." I looked around the shop, which was too dim to make out many details, but at a glance it looked like . . . well, junk. Everything from clothes to furniture, toys and jewelry, and all sundries in between, none of it of apparently stellar quality. There was no apparent theme; it was just a general-purpose pawn shop.

"Of course, I don't keep the *good* items out here for the riffraff to paw through," Laerdh hastened to assure me. "If your lordship is interested in any . . . specialty items, I can show you some of my discreet selection. Or, if it's a particular treasure you're on the lookout for that's not among my stock, I'm always pleased to put out my tendrils and see what can be found. I don't even mess about with finder's fees! It's enough to see a satisfied customer walk out my door with their heart's desire in hand."

"You got any spell scrolls back there?" I asked hopefully.

His smile faded, and he blinked twice. ". . . spell scrolls?"

"Yes," I explained patiently. "They are scrolls which—and stay with me, this is the complicated part—have spells on them." Aster sighed softly.

"Ah." Laerdh nodded once. "My lord, I hate to be the bearer of bad news, but you're in Gwyllthean. It's a city on Dount—an outlying island in the worst kingdom in the archipelago."

I stared at him; he stared back, and after a moment coughed discreetly and continued.

"Sure, I keep the spell scrolls out back in my invisible tower. That's where I've got the Goddess's underwear, the platinum crowns of the four Queens of Lancor, and the gate key to Shylverrael."

An interesting set of noises issued from the bandits in the shop; at least two hastily muffled snickers and as many apprehensive hisses of indrawn breath.

I studied Laerdh curiously. He was a short fellow, balding and paunchy, with a sharp nose and the generally oily look of a small-time salesman. I'd have expected him to be unctuous and sniveling, especially after that little speech of his; the backbone and sarcasm came as a surprise.

"You." I pointed at him. "I like you."

"My lord is too kind." Laerdh grinned and folded down his hands again.

"That was a bold move, considering the *other* likely response to sassing me would have involved burning and screaming."

"In business, one must take risks. You don't strike me as a man of such fragile ego as to demand bowing and scraping from everyone." He glanced past me at Aster.

"True enough. All right, lads, before he gets here, tell me what I should expect from the Olumnach representative. Any Blessings? Martial skills? Other relevant details?"

"It's not always the same guy," said Adler, "but among those who've been sent . . . Well, if they were Blessed, they never showed it. No obvious artifacts and didn't do magic in front of us. Dunno how much that means, m'lord. We sure as hell never got shirty enough to need such demonstrations. As for martial skills . . . Well, none of them was ever in armor."

"Fighters, though," added another bandit. "You can always tell, by the way they move. Way they ain't scared of bein' around rough lads like us. Every man they sent carried a sword—rapiers, nobleman's weapons." He nodded at my own. "They was all middleborn, too. Well-bred enough, as things go, but probably not of the Olumnach bloodline."

"So, nothing worth worrying about."

"Not weaklings, either," Adler hastened to add. "I suspect these boys are Clansguard commanders out of uniform. And the Olumnach Clansguard ain't pushovers. If you're gonna gork this guy, best do it from behind while he's distracted."

"No, no." I held up a warning hand. "None of that, I need him alive. He's going to tell me every detail about his Clan's operations that I don't already know."

Laerdh coughed discreetly. "Ah, my lord, it's worth mentioning that the kind of men the Highlord uses to herd bandits are bound to him by more than coin and intimidation. They're not spineless, nor destitute. It'll take you more than a pretty speech and some spells to turn them."

"Don't you worry," I said with a wink, "I'm very persuasive when I need to be."

"Yeah, I fuckin' believe that all right," mumbled the guy I'd Immolated.

"Well, can't say he didn't persuade *us* quick enough," Adler agreed.

"You know, you boys are all right," I said cheerfully. "I really hope I don't have to kill any of you later."

They exchanged another round of glances.

"Is, uh . . ." Adler began hesitantly. "Is there any way we might . . . better our chances of not having to be killed?"

"Well, that all depends on how you are with women and children."

He blinked at me in pure bafflement, then turned to one of his comrades for clarification, getting only a shrug.

"Oh, I getcha," another bandit said, his expression clearing. "I see watcha mean, m'lord. Aye, you'll have gotten to know both types, if you've been out gathering up bandits. We get 'em both, lads like us who fell into a spot of hard luck, and them other bastards who were just gonna be bastards no matter what."

"Oh yeah," Adler added, catching on. "I guess that's as good a test as any of a man's worth. Yeah, we've *seen* some shit out there. Some of those fuckstains'd rape their own sisters if they got bored enough. No, I doubt you'll find any complaint with me or the boys, here. Tig an' the others'll vouch for us, I bet."

"Yeah, we ain't middleborn gentlemen with fancy manners," chimed in another, "but the girls never complained that I heard. Ain't hard to be a decent enough sort, even if you're out robbing for a living."

"Good to hear," I said noncommittally. Time would tell.

The shop door opened, suddenly. Biribo hadn't warned me—he was down my coat rather than in Aster's pocket for the specific reason of being able to give warning if he felt it necessary. That he hadn't bothered told me we weren't in danger. I turned around at an unhurried pace to find myself face-to-face with the representative of Clan Olumnach.

He was pretty much as the bandits had just described. Fairly pale of complexion with coarse brown hair, and wealthier than most middleborn, to judge by the extravagant silver trim and decorative chains on his charcoal gray coat. The obligatory rapier hung at his waist; currently he had his left hand resting on the pommel in the quasi-threatening position of a man reminding us he had a sword but not quite on the verge of drawing it.

"What exactly is this?" he demanded, curling up his lip at me. "You idiots were told to be *discreet*. You, foreigner! This is a private meeting. Go elsewhere."

"Wow," I said, impressed in spite of myself. "That was a *lot* of needing to be taken down a peg packed into just a couple of short sentences. I hate him already. Thanks, my guy, that makes the next part easier."

The sneer deepened and he changed the position of his hands, moving the right across his waist to grasp the handle and prepare to draw his blade—a thing I had *not* done because this cramped and cluttered shop was the worst possible place to try and use a long weapon like a rapier.

"If you are considering—"

And that was as far as he got before Aster shot him in the back with a sleep dart.

"*Damn*, but that felt good," she declared, looking down her nose at the rich soldier as he slumped to the floor.

"The hell just happened?" demanded one of the bandits.

"Thank you, Aster," I said. "All right, lads! Welcome to the team. Gather up our luggage, there, and we'll be off. Through back alleys, if you please; the fewer eyes there are on this, the better."

"Uh, sure," said Adler as one of his fellows stepped forward and bent to hoist the fallen Olumnach soldier over his shoulder. "Where, uh . . . Where exactly are we going, m'lord?"

"Don't worry, I'll lead the way," I assured him. Something told me it was best not to mention the goblins in front of Laerdh, as concerned as they were with their privacy. And speaking of which, there was the matter of mitigating the risk of letting him live, because I wasn't quite fallen to the depth of killing people just for knowing too much.

Yet.

I turned, reaching into my coin pouch, and tossed the fence a gold halo. "For your trouble, sir. We both know you won't stay bribed as soon as my back is turned, so we'll call that compensation for any damages caused. And when I say that neither I, these boys, or the Olumnach rep ever showed up here tonight, it is *purely* in the spirit of friendly advice. That's the story that'll keep you maximally out of trouble no matter who ends up reigning over Dount's underworld."

"A very cogent analysis, my lord," he said smoothly, having already made the coin disappear. With a grin, Laerdh folded down his hands again. "Forgive me, it seems I've already forgotten your name and what you look like. It's been a surprising pleasure and I look forward to either working with you in the future or forgetting that you ever existed."

"Good man. All right, gentlemen! Off we go. The night is young, and I have so much more to teach you about crime."

33

In Which the Dark Lord
Has Questions

"So how much of Sneppit's leadership have I got up here?" I quietly asked Gizmit as I accompanied her in checking the perimeter and exits from the old storehouse Maugro had found. She insisted on doing this personally, despite me putting people on watch. Behind us in the near distance, Youda was fussing with his chemistry set next to the still-sleeping Olumnach agent, who was tied to a chair, with Zui hovering nearby.

"Miss Sneppit *is* the leadership," she said. "Zui and Youda are valuable assets, though."

"Right, I just found it odd she would send her top people up here without even a bodyguard."

Gizmit gave me an amused sidelong look, which she had to tilt her head sideways to do. "Clearly Miss Sneppit values her association with you, Lord Seiji. Besides, she generally considers additional security personnel to be extraneous when I'm along."

"I see." Wow, that was a much more graceful way of saying "I can easily kill you" than I usually did it. I had so much to learn. "Well, glad to have you. No disrespect to my new . . . employees . . ."

"You don't need to say it, Lord Seiji. I've met them." The boys from the pawn shop had been positioned at entrances and windows to keep an eye out, but they appeared to be mostly just loafing on the verge of falling asleep, except for the guy I had Immolated, who ever since then had seemed to be having a nightmare while standing up. He flinched whenever our eyes met. "Anyway, you have Zui to thank for Miss Sneppit's investment in this. The boss listens to her and she advocated for helping you. Zui appears to think highly of you."

That brought me to an actual, physical stop, causing Gizmit to get a few more paces beyond me before she turned to see what the holdup was.

"Bullshit." I glanced aside to where Zui and Youda were still at work and lowered my voice further; goblins had proportionally bigger ears than humans. "I'm not falling for that, Gizmit. I've spoken with enough of my ex-girlfriends to recognize when a woman would casually prefer I was dead but doesn't care enough to make it happen."

"Yes, I can believe you've had that experience," she said, deadpan. "Lord Seiji, you've only met Zui when she was on edge and defensive from being on the surface, surrounded by tallfolk, sometimes with Youda's safety also her responsibility. She's the one who usually ends up dealing with the aftermath when one of Sneppit's goblins runs afoul of humans. I think she has the lowest opinion of humans of any goblin I've met who doesn't have a specific, personal trauma related to them. *You* treat goblins like people and don't stare down her shirt. Sadly, that's all it takes to be the best human she's ever met."

"How would anyone stare *down* her shirt? She wears those high-collared—" I stopped, too late. Gizmit was already giving me that sidelong look again, this time with a sly little smile. "Wow, look at that. I walked right into it."

"Don't feel bad, Lord Seiji, I lay good traps. As you may recall."

"Hm."

"Goblin, human, presumably elf, and beastfolk—it always seems men think we can't *tell* when they're ogling. It's so very transparent so much of the time. It'd be one thing if you just weren't into women, but someone as used to it as Zui could *also* tell when you noticed 'hey, those are nice' and then didn't act like a creep about it. Such a low standard to set, but such is the world."

"Humans, men . . . You don't think much of *anybody*, do you?"

"I have a high opinion of some of the people I work with," she said noncommittally, "and I am always willing to be impressed. Looks like they're about ready."

I glanced over at the center of the room; the prisoner's head was still slumped forward. Youda was laying out tools on a tray, and Zui had a sheaf of paper on a clipboard she was now holding. It just looked like more of the same inscrutable preparations to me. "How can you tell—"

"All right, we're set up here," Youda called. "You ready?"

Gizmit gave me another little smile. "I'm a professional, that's how."

I opted not to engage any further with that line of thought. Instead, as we drew close to the alchemy setup, something caught my attention. "Hey, are those syringes?"

"Sure are!" Youda grinned, pleased as always at having his work recognized. "I'm impressed, Lord Seiji! I didn't think any surface folk on this island would recognize 'em."

"I'm from a place considerably less ass-backward than Dlemathlys." Youda was good people; I didn't have the heart to tell him how primitive his equipment was, not after seeing how proud he was of it. The syringes in question were just little inflatable rubber bladders attached to . . . "Are those porcupine quills?"

"No idea what a porcupine is. These are thadnecht quills! You gotta boil the venom out of 'em, obviously, but properly sterilized they work like a charm."

"Huh. Is it a problem with them being curved? I've only ever seen straight needles used."

"Ah well, I can see how that'd make for more precise handling, but unfortunately there are no shellbacks on Dount with the right kind of anatomy."

"Ah. Where I'm from, we just manufacture the needles."

"Really? I gotta say, I dunno how you could carve a hollow akornin needle fine enough."

"Me neither; I've only seen them made of steel."

He blinked twice. "*How?*"

Gizmit, Zui, and Aster all cleared their throats in unison.

"Quite right, ladies," Youda said briskly. "Business before shop talk! Okay, so you've dosed this guy with the tranquilizer serum I gave you, right? Shouldn't be a problem; he'll be coming out of that within a few minutes, and I don't expect any reaction with the drugs I mean to use. The tail end of it should ease the transition, and this'll go smoother if we don't wake him up before administering the dose. For that reason, though, I gotta choose an agent that acts differently on the brain or we risk an overdose. I got plenty of options, though, so no problem. I'm gonna use two derivatives of starleaf extract, a base calming tonic that you pretty much *can't* OD on, short of drowning in it, and a smaller dose of an alchemically accelerated version that's formulated to give pleasant dreams. So this shouldn't impair his memory, but the dream state can specifically interfere with organized recall. I know that's not perfect for interrogation, but no solution would be and this'll at least bypass conscious resistance, which oughta be the biggest issue, right?"

"Whatever you think best," I said, already lost.

"Ah." Youda glanced up at me even as he was positioning one of his rough quasi syringes against the subject's arm. "No offense, Lord Seiji, but

I wasn't talkin' to you. Interrogation is its own science, and the person doin' the questioning needs to know exactly how the subject is drugged so she can properly tailor her approach."

"Oh. Right." I looked at Gizmit, who gave me another one of those coy little smiles. "I gave Zui a rundown on what I need to know from him. I presume you have it written down?"

The smile widened and she tapped her temple with one forefinger.

"Well, okay, then." The man twitched as Youda withdrew the first needle from his arm, beginning to mumble slightly as the goblin alchemist hastened to apply the second drug before he woke up completely. "I'll just . . . be over here."

Everyone was already ignoring me. Youda was holding the man's wrist while staring at his mouth, monitoring both his pulse and breathing; Zui had her pencil poised to note down everything, eyes alert on the proceedings. Gizmit stepped up to the man's other side and spoke, and her voice was low, soothing, and warm, completely unlike I'd ever heard her before.

"Hey there. You're all right, there's nothing to worry about. Can you tell me your name?"

It really was something else, working with *professionals* for once.

I could tell Gizmit knew what she was doing, even if I didn't. She spent a lot of time asking banal questions whose answers I did not care about and that Zui didn't even bother writing down, personal stuff about the guy—his life, family, career ambitions, and so on. Maybe she was coaxing him into a pattern of answering harmless questions, or testing his state of mind? He seemed almost fully asleep with his eyes half-open, speaking slowly and on a delay, but he *did* form mostly coherent sentences and didn't seem resistant to the questioning. At least twenty minutes of this went by without going anywhere useful, but the one time I opened my mouth Zui immediately shot me such a blistering look that I instantly closed it. I dunno how she even saw me; she'd been focused on the interrogation as if anything interesting was happening.

Well, the goblins seemed to know what they were doing, so I opted to let them work.

It wasn't long after that before Gizmit's efforts started to bear fruit, and it happened so smoothly even *I* was lulled in. She had transitioned deftly from aimless chitchat about the guy's work life and gossip about people he knew to details on the Blessed individuals working for Highlord Olumnach. It was so gracefully done, I only belatedly realized we had finally gotten to the meat of the interrogation when Zui's pencil started quietly scratching as she noted down data.

The whole thing took over two hours, but it was easier to sit through once I recognized that Gizmit was indeed in control of the proceedings and competently directing things the way she wanted. She kept her demeanor soothing, actually brushing the man's hair back or holding his hand in the moments when Youda readministered one or the other of his drugs as the dosages began to wear off. Whenever there was any sign of resistance, she would smoothly segue back into harmless chatter, bringing up topics she'd already discussed, specifically those she'd learned would lull him back into a positive and receptive frame of mind, and only gradually meander back into the territory we actually wanted once he was calm again.

All of this had an unfortunate side effect I wasn't expecting. It was one thing to drug and interrogate some insignificant middleborn asshole whose only interaction with me so far had consisted of him being pompous and violent. You could do pretty much whatever to a guy like that and not feel particularly bad. Fuck him, he had it coming.

It became less and less clear-cut the more I got to know the life story of Calim Flaedthwyct, fencing instructor turned enforcer for Highlord Olumnach, and how conflicted he was about everything. Loyal to his Highlord, yes, out of gratitude for how the man had taken him in and elevated his status. Even so, he had a personal attachment to the family, having been an honest friend to the young Lord Arider and beset by grief and rage at his untimely death.

That actually helped me regain some distance, remembering what a vile prick Arider had been and considering what kind of man would call him a friend.

Calim was the middleborn son of a woman of lower nobility, practically sold to a higher-caste commoner with money because her Clan was financially desperate. He'd grown up disliked by the high and low alike until Olumnach had given him a place. He had married well, to a noblewoman who ensured his social place and with whom he shared a kind of congenial dislike. It was his lowborn mistress he really adored, along with the infant son she'd borne him, about whose future he was constantly worried because he knew what it was like to grow up without a solid place in the Fflyr caste system, and *I didn't want to know any of this.*

It was so easy to kill random assholes waving swords at me. When they started having their own lives and perspectives and struggles, things got . . . sticky.

I wasn't the only one, to judge by Youda's and Aster's frequent grimaces. Gizmit and Zui remained completely on point, however, just asking questions and writing down the answers, respectively. In and around the awkward backstory I did get what I needed—more of it than I'd hoped even. Numbers and basic deployments of the Olumnach Clansguard. Names of officers, of Blessed, along with a description of their spells and artifacts, and most importantly, an account of the strategies and organization of the Olumnach agents overseeing his bandit forces in Gwyllthean. Getting that kind of intricate detail out of the drug-addled officer was what took the longest, but we got it.

Gizmit finally stepped back, nodding at Youda, who nodded back and then gave Flaedthwyct—I mean, the Olumnach officer whose name I didn't need to know or want to remember—another shot of something that made him slump forward in silence.

"I believe that's as much pertinent detail as one session can reasonably extract," she said. "Lord Seiji?"

"It's more than I expected," I agreed. "Fantastic work, people. Please give Miss Sneppit my thanks for the loan of . . . well, you."

"If that's all we need here, then all that remains is to finish this guy off," Gizmit said calmly. "Do you wish to do *the necessary*, Lord Seiji, or shall I?"

It brought me up short, I had to admit. After she'd just spent a couple of hours learning the man's entire life story and talking to him in the gentlest tone I'd ever heard from her, it was utterly chilling how she could be so blasé about executing him.

"Hey, Youda," I said, turning to him. "Do you have some . . . potential cocktail of drugs that can erase someone's memory?"

"Well, I mean . . ." He scratched his head, squinting up at me. "Actually altering a person's mind or memories is some pretty powerful magic. You can't just do it with drugs, that's not how *brains* work. Like, sure, there's a number of things I could do to induce mental damage that *tends* to erase memory as a side effect. It does other stuff, too. Dunno if it'd be kinder."

"It's off the table, anyway," Gizmit said in a much flatter tone. "Those methods are unreliable at best. Miss Sneppit agreed to the loan of her personnel and equipment, and sale of alchemical reagents, strictly on the grounds that you would take *all necessary measures* to ensure her security. The Fflyr *cannot* find out about our involvement here. Frankly, you're exhausting any leeway in the arrangement by allowing these five goons to live, and that's only because I have your assurance that they are shortly to be removed from the city."

"Hey," protested one of my new goons.

"I know it's a risk," I said, trying a different angle, "but I am not being sentimental, Gizmit. My long-term plans involving Clan Olumnach do *not* include a direct confrontation. That means I need to minimize provocations, which are already going to be considerable enough. It affects my operations if one of his top people turns up missing or dead and the Highlord figures out who was behind it."

"You're not the only one behind it, or whose well-being would be threatened by Olumnach's ire," she retorted. "We had a deal, Lord Seiji."

"Executing the prisoner was not one of the agreed-upon terms."

"*Security* was," she said with a hint of open exasperation. "Apparently, I was at fault for assuming you would recognize that lesser measures are *not acceptable*."

"Do not give me orders, Gizmit," I said quietly.

Zui and Aster both tensed; Youda hunched his shoulders, avoiding everybody's gaze.

"You know it's not as if I can compel you, Lord Seiji," Gizmit said after a short pause. "The question is whether you consider this guy worth damaging your relationship with Miss Sneppit."

Damn it, I needed these goblins. This was a bridge I couldn't afford to burn. They had real *expertise*, something my organization lacked. Plus, after the last conversational tripwire Gizmit had laid for me, I was pretty sure Sneppit knew about the Dark Lord thing. Knew, and had kept it to herself.

I turned my gaze on the slumbering Calim Flaedthwyct. *Fuck*, why did I have to know his name? I couldn't help thinking about his illegitimate child. What would happen to him without a well-bred, well-connected father in the picture?

Then again, did Calim have a penchant for maiming Gutter Rats, the way his bestie, Arider, had cheerfully boasted about doing?

All of this would be so much simpler if those questions had solid answers, one way or the other.

"No," I said at last. "No, you're right. Obviously Sneppit is more important to me than this asshole. Youda, do you have something in that kit of yours that's lethal in a high enough dose?"

"Uh, Lord Seiji," he said with a weak grin, "it's a basic rule of chemistry that *anything* is lethal in a high enough dose."

"Something painless, specifically."

"Oh hell, that's easy. I can pump him full of a concentrated solution of general anesthetic we use for surgery. Too much of that in one dose will cause the brain to just shut down in a last surge of euphoria. It's not just painless, it's *anti*painful!"

"Sounds perfect," I nodded. "Proceed, please."

"You got it, Lord Seiji."

"That anesthetic is, as he said, used for surgery," Gizmit said with clear annoyance. "It's also derived from components that aren't native to Dount. It isn't *easy* to get the reagents."

"I'll pay for them," I sighed, "as we agreed."

"Selling *that* stuff in particular wasn't part of the original agreement."

"Nor was it precluded by said agreement." I turned to face her directly. "Meet me halfway, Gizmit. And maybe appreciate that I'm doing the same for you. Most of the people I deal with don't get that much courtesy."

"He's not kidding," Aster added when Gizmit hesitated. "Our last big business meeting was with the heads of a Clan. The option he gave them was to do as they were told and like it. And they *took* that deal."

"Well," Gizmit said at last, "I'm not sure how thrilled Miss Sneppit will be, but she will probably prefer to err on the side of diplomacy."

"You know full well she would," Zui stated. "Reagents are replaceable, even if not easily. We'd have a much harder time finding another . . . y'know, him."

"Anyway, it's moot now," Youda declared, withdrawing another syringe from Flaedthwyct's arm. "He's gone."

Gizmit sighed but made no further comment.

"I'll write out my notes in longhand for you, Lord Seiji," said Zui, holding up the clipboard. "Just give me an hour, and—"

"No need." I took the papers from her, which she allowed with a brief grimace of dissatisfaction. "This is fine. Thanks, Zui, I can transcribe any relevant sections into Fflyr if any of the rest of my people need details."

"There's no way you can read that," Zui protested incredulously. "That's my *personal* shorthand, based on Khadzid!"

I gave her my sweetest smile, which only served to visibly piss her off. Wow, Zui really was starting to remind me of some of my exes.

Turning, I made eye contact with Gizmit again, who was now watching me with the kind of blank expression that always conceals intense thoughts. Yeah, she knew. If she hadn't before, definitely now. All of this was a calculated risk.

"Thanks for your hard work," I said. "You can tell Miss Sneppit that her assumption is correct . . . and that her strategy is working. I will definitely remember those who helped me when I needed it."

"I'll be sure to pass that along." Gizmit nodded once, slowly, then smirked. "Your hair looks nice, by the way."

"Of course it does," I said with a benign smile. "Miss Sneppit only employs the very best."

Zui snorted.

34

In Which the Dark Lord
Speaks Softly

The long and short of it was that I had nothing immediately to worry about. Olumnach had several dangerous-sounding Blessed but was unlikely to leverage them at me; he liked to keep them nearby for his own family's protection, and since it was known among the Clans who employed what Blessed, sending them to do anything disruptive in or near Gwyllthean would get him in hot water with the Archlord. I could only hope I could bait him into that mistake, but otherwise, I wouldn't have to face off against his forces unless I attacked him on his own turf. That was not happening for a host of reasons.

Gwyllthean was different from the countryside, and my tactics would have to change accordingly, but the fundamental strategy was the same— deny Olumnach a fight and make him trip over his own feet. Constant retreat could be a winning move in the right circumstances, like how the Russians had crushed Napoleon using . . . Russia.

We made good time once out of the city, and reached Caer Yviredh by late afternoon, just before what would usually be dinnertime for the Fflyr. Having spent most of my time either wandering the island in circuitous routes or making the daylong trek between Gwyllthean and North Watch, it felt downright strange to get between two points on Dount so quickly.

I was pleased to find my people in the khora surrounding Yviredh lands and keeping a proper patrol with lookouts; they spotted Aster and me arriving before we found them, which was exactly what I hoped would happen if they encountered anyone *else*. Nazralind wasn't with them, apparently having gone to visit the family in the manor, so that was where we went directly after I left my five newbies with the girls. Much as I wanted to supervise their first interactions with the rest of the gang, I needed to speak with the Yviredhs.

Aster and I entered through the front gate, this time. The Clansguard on duty opened it for us and escorted us to the house, looking not particularly happy but not offering so much as an utter of complaint. The man seemed leery of us rather than resentful, which I could live with.

"Lord Seiji," Lady Elidred said, entering the second-floor drawing room, to which I'd been escorted in a stately glide. She didn't even so much as glance at Aster, which I guess was the usual custom when it came to nobles and other nobles' servants. It didn't quite sit right with me, but I figured I'd better pick my battles.

"My lady." I bowed, shallowly, which made her mouth tighten but she otherwise let it pass. "Thank you kindly for receiving us. I hope I have not caught you at an inconvenient time?"

"Is there ever a convenient time?" She raised one eyebrow. "I'm afraid you have missed my husband, but you will not be kept waiting long, my lord; he is only down in the village. If you find either of us at the manor, the other will be along shortly. Visits to the homes of other Clans may take us away from our home for a day or two at a time, but our own holdings are simply not broad enough to make the Highlord's rounds all that time-consuming."

"Ah, then my apologies for imposing on you. I should like to speak with Highlord Adver, but we'll not trouble you overlong after that. By the way, I was told my . . . associate was visiting you?"

"Yes, hence this particular parlor," she said with a faint smile, gliding toward the window. "It enjoys a decent view, if you would care to look."

I followed her to the window, which overlooked the manor's gardens. I could see the domed housing of the Spirit off in one corner of the grounds; but closer at hand, Nazralind—mask and all—was on a stretch of open lawn, apparently coaching the young Lady Avelit in the use of a practice foil while Lord Ediver hovered around both of them.

"Ara, ara—" I caught myself in time to bite it off this time. Well, almost. "I hope she hasn't been . . . an imposition."

"On the contrary." Elidred watched her children exercising with my elf, her expression fond but distant. "I have made my apologies to Highlady Nazralind, but I offer them to you as well for my previous . . . outburst. I'm afraid the large number of changes and new sources of stress in my life have made me more volatile than befits a lady as of late."

"Ah, so Naz decided to introduce herself?"

"She has not," she said with another faint smile. "I'm sure you have noticed, Lord Seiji, that Dount is hardly a bustling metropolis. When a daughter of the island's ruling Clan goes missing, it is *noticed*, despite the best efforts of her family. When, shortly after a number of other young noblewomen ran away from their homes, a gang of poorly disguised young noblewomen took to . . . strangely idealistic banditry, well. No one failed to connect the clues. It was scarcely more difficult to make the connection when she arrived here, in the company of a new bandit leader."

"I see," I said ruefully. "In any case, my lady, I feel you owe me no apology. All of this has to have been hard on you. I don't know if it helps you at all to know, but I enjoy *being* a bandit leader exactly as much as you enjoy having to deal with one."

Elidred looked at me sidelong. "It does, a bit. Perhaps you understand the . . . discomfiture, then. But life is surprising and not always comfortable; it is our lot to make do. In this case, I can certainly see how my family's actions have caused many of its own problems. You are not the help I would have sought, but it would be churlish to reject even you. Even had we the option."

Below us, the trio on the lawn passed out of our view, apparently calling their practice to an end and coming back inside.

"Lord Seiji," Lady Elidred said suddenly, "I am in absolutely no sense disloyal to my husband. He determines the course of our family's labors, and I support him, as is the role of a wife under the Goddess's order. I am, however, more of a realist than Adver."

"Is that so?" I was suddenly apprehensive about where this was leading. Surely this woman wasn't about to hit on me? Last I'd reckoned, she could barely stand me, but then, that was what I'd thought about Zui.

"I am cognizant that in the best-case scenario, even our gambit with Rhaem is a long shot. The odds of saving Clan Yviredh's noble status are . . . slim, even with your help. And if that effort fails, it will not be without its upside. I have raised my daughter to honor her duty to family, as any decent Sanorite woman ought. That does not mean I *relish* the prospect of selling her off as a bargaining chip to some overbred reprobate."

I blinked. That wasn't what I'd expected to hear. For once, I didn't have a ready reply.

"Unlike my husband," Elidred continued, gazing absently out the window, "I do not consider the loss of nobility to be the end of the world. Certainly not for my children, who will have to live beyond it. As a mother, I wish above all for them to be happy, to lead fulfilling lives, even if it cannot be as the Goddess's elect. And there are so many ways for the unfolding of events to endanger their prospects, beyond even what social diminishment must."

She hesitated, and I waited.

"Highlady Nazralind has mentioned," Elidred finally said in an off-handed tone, "that you have a particular soft spot for children."

Well, I wouldn't exactly say *that*, but . . . okay, maybe.

"Whatever happens," I promised her quietly, "I will do my very best to make sure they're safe. I don't want to promise beyond my means, my lady. Life is terribly uncertain, and *my* life in particular is more violent than anybody should want. And . . . I have failed to protect people in the past. But whatever I *can* do, I will."

She nodded slowly, still not meeting my gaze. "What is hardest about being a parent is learning that one *cannot* protect them from everything. No, more than that—one *must* not. No one can grow without struggling, without suffering. A child must be allowed to face their own challenges if they are to become the adult they have the potential to be."

I thought about Gilder, Benit, and Radon. About Aenit. About Jassner, Ladhnet, Tonnon, Sildnit, and Nadro, five names I sometimes recited to myself at night, because there was nothing else I could do for them but remember.

"I'll settle for not having to keep any more vigils for them," I whispered.

Elidred finally turned to look at me. Then she stepped back, and to my astonishment, bowed. A little awkwardly, as she had probably never done it in her life, but still.

"No one can ask more of anyone than their best, Lord Seiji. I accept your promise, with a mother's gratitude. And I shall hope you never need be held to it."

"So shall we all," I agreed.

The door opened, blessedly saving me from this conversation. Highlord Adver was the first into the room, followed by Nazralind, who had apparently ditched the kids on the way. Probably the Highlord had sent them somewhere other than where the bandits were; I probably would have, in his position.

"Ah, Lord Seiji," he said, and to my surprise he seemed satisfied to see me. Not *happy*, precisely, but more as if my presence was a sign of things unfolding as they should.

"When did you find time to get your *hair cut*?" Nazralind demanded.

"It's amazing the things that just fall into your lap," I said with complete sincerity. "I'm glad to report my visit to Gwyllthean was productive for more than just cosmetic reasons. How have you fared here on the home front?"

"The plan is unfolding," Adver said with a pleased grin. My god, the man actually seemed to be having *fun*. "We've not yet had the opportunity to begin rallying support among the neighboring Clans, though we are keeping alert to the gossip. My Elidred is truly adept at navigating these tricky social currents. There has, as of yet, been nothing over which our neighbors have reason to complain, but Clan Olumnach has taken note of your actions, and I've no doubt the necessary provocations will be forthcoming, to judge by their . . . *assertive* displeasure."

"Is everyone all right?" I asked, frowning.

Adver waved a hand airily. "Right as rain, my lord. I feigned ignorance of what had happened to our local bandit gang, and freely offered Clan Olumnach's representatives leave to search for them anywhere in my domain. I'm glad to say that your people are both perceptive and swift; undoubtedly the Olumnach scouts found traces of their passing, but did not come upon them in person."

That's my girls.

"No problems on that front, Lord Seiji," said Nazralind. "At the first sign of them, we vacated the area, just as you ordered. They're good, but not great; it's not all that hard to be *better*."

"Our open and hospitable posture toward Clan Olumnach's representatives will help deflect suspicion from Clan Yviredh when the pressure begins to mount among the other Clans," said Elidred with a thin, satisfied smile. "And that will begin as soon as they start treating our peers the way they did us. *They* have no strategic need to tolerate it, and highborn are in many ways more sensitive to insult than injury."

"I have to say, I am both impressed and relieved," Highlord Adver admitted. "When you laid out your plan . . . Well, I could see the logic of it, but it's another thing entirely to watch it start to unfold exactly as designed!"

"Don't become complacent," I warned. "Nothing ever goes *exactly* as planned, and Caldimer is neither stupid nor weak. It always becomes necessary to improvise before all's said and done."

"Yes indeed," he agreed more seriously. "Speaking of that, I hope you have a strategy in place to take Gwyllthean. I fear that evasive maneuvers of this kind will be rather more difficult in the city."

"Indeed, a different battlefield calls for a different strategy," I said, nodding. "Which is not to say I mean to confront the Olumnachs—far from it. On the contrary, I think there's been more than enough bloodshed recently. Lord Seiji has done his part. What comes next is a job for the Healer."

35

In Which the Dark Lord Carries a Big Shtick

The plan didn't call for a mass use of my forces, but after the last time I'd tried a major operation in the Gutters and gotten dumped in the river full of quarrels for my trouble, I was playing it safe. This time I was planning to draw as much attention to myself as I could and couldn't know what might happen, so I put my people in position to intervene if something went wrong.

Their presence should not be required, if all went according to plan, but how often did that happen?

Now, it was time for my revenge on that fucking river.

We emerged from the khora forest at its closest point to the city, at one of the outgrowths between the fiefs of two small Clans where it nearly reached the ruins around the outskirts of the Gutters. From there we picked our way through the rubble-strewn outermost road, seeing almost no one until we rejoined the main trade road leading into Gwyllthean. It would have been vastly more efficient to just go through the Gutters to our destination, but the point of today's mission was not just to do what I planned to do, but to be *seen* doing it. For that, I needed to make a spectacle of myself.

It was nice to do things that actually played to my talents once in a while.

I proceeded with Aster traveling along in my wake, in our full Healer and bodyguard getup with some slight tweaks. The ragged coats on both of us with hooded cloak over mine were the usual. Under both, though, I had adjusted our masks and gloves to be solid black and of finer fabric than the Healer's usual rags.

It was useful to have Nazralind around to explain things like fashion, which my mostly lowborn associates either couldn't afford to care about or had simply never bothered. Black didn't have the same cultural associations here that I remembered from either of my cultures back on Earth. Since nights on Ephemera didn't get truly dark thanks to sunlight filtering through the core of the broken planet, and the Goddess of Evil's colors were purple and green, black was seen as a neutral tone, used as a backdrop to the brighter colors and elaborate decorations the Fflyr liked. In this country anyway, it was often worn by highborn to accentuate their flashier accessories and had no role in heraldry.

Since it was now time to start actively courting attention and cranking up the mystery, I had decided to start making use of it. The association of the color with highborn costumes, plus the finer quality of the fabric, made the point that the Healer was shabbily dressed and hung around with lowborn by choice, not necessity. I had to give credit to Zui for planting that idea in my mind with her comments about my hairstyle. Not that I'd ever do so out loud. Especially where she might hear.

We stepped out onto the trade road, which wasn't yet crowded at this hour of the morning but already had traffic. Perfect for my purposes. I stepped right to the center of it and proceeded on my way into town at a sedate, deliberate pace. People streaming in toward the city gates and a few heading the opposite way streamed around me, and it was funny how I could tell the long-distance travelers from those familiar with Gwyllthean by whether they carefully avoided stepping into the Healer's path or gave me annoyed looks in passing.

More of the latter than the former by far. There was a reason I had done this just after dawn, when the road wouldn't yet be busy enough that the sheer press of people would have run me over for trying it.

"The fuck is the matter with you, idiot?" one particularly annoyed voice shouted from behind me. "Get out of the road!"

I didn't even have a chance to respond before one of the food vendors set up alongside the road shouted back.

"Oy! If the Healer wants to walk, you let 'im walk, roadie!"

"Suggest you mind your business around that one, friend," added another in a less aggressive tone.

It *was* nice to see the vendors back, even apart from their emotional support. The trade roads had already been thoroughly cleaned of all traces of the Kingsguard's rampage, destroyed stands swept away and new ones erected. The men and women working at them had been back to work as soon as they could at all manage, not having the luxury of taking time off. Especially after they'd had to pay to have new stands built.

I came to an outright stop, turning fully around to gaze past Aster up at a merchant wagon immediately behind us, a smaller one pulled by a single dhawl. The dickhead had plenty of room to go around if he'd wanted. I guess road rage predates the internal combustion engine, after all.

"Please!" I raised both hands to either side of me, quieting further rumbling from the onlookers. "Forgive them. They know not what they do."

"He's a local street preacher, boss," muttered the single guard walking alongside the wagon, just loud enough for me to make out. "Blessed with Magic, s'pposed to have some real nasty spells. People don't fuck with him."

The merchant grimaced as if being forced to swallow an entire turd, sucked in a long breath through his teeth, and finally gave me a grudging nod and a gesture with the hand holding the reins.

"Well, go on, then, priest. Let's all be on our way."

I stared at him from within the shadows of my hood, just long enough that his face started to change colors and physically quiver, and Aster minutely shifted to give me a questioning look, and then I turned and proceeded on my stately, languorous way.

The merchant had the good taste to wait a few seconds before guiding his dhawl to one side to pass us, stubbornly refusing to look at either me or the street vendors laughing at him.

On we went at the same pace, which meant it took us a solid half hour to make it all the way to the base of the ramp, which ascended to the city gate. By that point, the road was becoming crowded enough to make my ploy increasingly difficult, though no one had interfered with us on the way. Not physically, anyhow, and the others who complained were also either shouted down or warned off by Gutters locals, depending on whether they liked the Healer or didn't want to see him explode somebody as the rumors said I could. Once there, we could finally turn down the wide side street closest to the towering walls, within the actual shadow of its overhang.

This was on a different side of the city from my first approach, where I'd met Lord Arider Olumnach and subsequently gotten him killed. This one seemed like a normal street to me, fairly prosperous and active. Enough so that I caused a stir by walking slowly down the very middle of it.

I did not look around or behind me, as that wouldn't suit the persona I was projecting, but I thought I sensed from the sound of footsteps and whispers amid the general city noise that people had started to follow me. Good; job one accomplished.

Going around the city walls took even longer than getting to them; it was at least another half hour before we reached our destination, probably more. Even that served my purposes, though. People were definitely following and speculating about my intentions, though so far nobody had approached me directly.

By the time we got there, an actual crowd had gathered, with people following me and others coming to investigate as rumor had spread. I continued to outwardly ignore them as I repositioned myself along the edge of the canal, right where water spilled from the grate about three meters up.

Well, not *right* there, but on the edge a bit downstream. Even that close to its source, the water was foul enough that I didn't care to stand in the spray.

It wasn't the source, which was the problem. The actual water source was beneath Caer Aelthwyn, the towering palace at the very apex of the city. It was this combination of an abundant spring and the defensible hill that had led to the city being built here. Clan Aelthwyn siphoned what they needed directly and let the water pour through the middle ring in a network of actual pipes rather than open canals, distributing it more evenly through the wealthier part of the city. The highborn there had easy access to clean water, and dumped their refuse into more pipes.

It was a blend of this and whatever clean water they didn't use that was funneled into three large pipes which drained into the Gutters to be spread throughout the canals and ultimately discharged into the two rivers, which meandered away from Gwyllthean. Lowborn could gather water easily, or "water" at least, but it had to be thoroughly sifted and boiled before it could be used, and the wealthier among them still added alchemical purifying agents first. The water was befouled by the time it entered the district, whose people didn't even warrant proper sewers and borderline sludge by the time it poured out.

I knew that more intimately than most.

Stopping and repositioning myself there gave me a chance to sneak a glance around. Oh yes, this was a very satisfactory crowd; people completely clogged the street behind me, with more on the other side of the canal. Everyone gave the generous but dangerous sorcerer a wide berth, watching with interest to see what this sudden change in my behavior was about. I spotted four of my own people, three in alleys and one perched on a rooftop. I was pleased to see they all had the sense not to openly display weapons, though at least some of them had stingers hidden away and all should be carrying clubs or short swords under their cloaks.

It seemed I'd also picked up a Kingsguard patrol, which were likewise standing at some distance observing me without intervening.

Satisfied that I had everyone's attention, I began to work my literal magic.

Summon Bound Slime.

The pale blue blob, conjured into being with the effects of my Tame Beast already active on it, appeared at the edge of the canal, causing a stir from across the way and whispers from people behind me, who couldn't clearly see what I had done. Immediately, receiving a mental nudge from me, it slid forward and tumbled over the edge, splashing into the turbulent water and disappearing beneath it.

And so I continued.

Summon Bound Slime.

Summon Bound Slime.

Summon Bound Slime.

Summon Bound Slime.

Summon Bound Slime.

Mutters began to grow around me, mostly of confusion. Aster's head remained in motion, constantly scanning for threats, but she neither moved nor found reason to reach for her sword, so I carried on with my work, ignoring the noise.

I had dumped almost forty slimes in the canal before one of the Kingsguard screwed up his courage.

"Here now, uh . . . Healer. Sir." The young man, scruffy behind his uniform helmet, approached hesitantly, and I didn't need to have been close enough to hear the whispered conversation between his fellows to see that he'd had this duty delegated due to lack of seniority. I recognized him, though not by name; he'd been around on patrol and gate duty, but it always ended up being the more senior guards who took bribes from me in my other persona. "What, uh . . . Watcha doin' there?"

An ugly undercurrent threaded through the sea of murmurs around us. Even had I not been generally well-thought-of in the Gutters, the Kingsguard right now were decidedly not.

I paused in my summoning, turning slowly to face him. The poor boy took a half step backward before he caught himself, swallowing visibly.

"What I always do," I intoned sententiously, projecting my voice at a low register over both the noise of rushing water and mumbling onlookers.

Then I paused for three beats, just to ratchet up the tension, before dropping the final note.

"Healing."

The guard looked at me, then at the roiling surface of the water, then back at me, and swallowed again.

"You . . . Uh, you're . . . putting slimes in the canal."

Very slowly, I nodded my cowl once.

"Look, I don't . . . Uh, how exactly is *this* healing?"

"There are many ways," I stated gravely.

I could see frustration beginning to flicker through the unease on the poor guy's face.

He drew in a deep breath to steady himself, and then by his expression, immediately regretted it. Yeah, I was breathing shallowly this close to the water, too. "Right, well, I don't think . . . That is, are you sure you should be doing this? You're, well . . . littering."

A chorus of jeers rose from the surrounding watchers, and I had to grin behind my mask. It would take a lot worse than slimes to make this canal any filthier. This close to the drainpipe there wasn't any visible flotsam, but everybody knew what the canals were like through the rest of the Gutters.

"I mean," the guard said, clearly flustered, "you're making a mess!"

The displeased catcalls rose, now accompanied by actual laughter. Behind the unfortunate guard, his two companions turned to face the crowd, hefting weapons; that bought them a bit more personal space, but the noise didn't diminish.

"You object to my healing?" I asked, keeping my tone mild while still projecting hard enough to be audible to the whole audience.

"*How* is this healing?" he exclaimed.

"All will become clear," I intoned.

I'd finally made the rookie mad enough to scowl outright.

"Look, mister—"

"Do you require healing, soldier?" I raised one hand, palm out toward him. "Have you paid the price?"

The scowl instantly vanished and he backpedaled physically, raising both hands. "Hey, hey, there's no call for that talk! Just . . . It's my job, all right? I—*we* have to investigate disturbances." He shot an accusing look over his shoulders at his unhelpful patrol partners. "Look, if you're . . . I mean, I suppose that's . . . Listen, man, if those slimes cause any real trouble, it's going to bring the Clans down on us all. You don't want that, all right? Nobody wants that."

"Surely the Clans will not object to me healing the Gutters," I said, turning back to my work.

"Healing, right." The guard had one last try in him. "*Why* are you putting slimes in the canal?"

A better question was why there weren't already slimes in the canal. I couldn't have been the first person to think of this, surely. Superstition, or did the city authorities just not realize that giant biomatter-eating amoebas were basically free water treatment? I was never sure how much the Fflyr knew about anything; this place was solidly medieval, but they had some anachronistic technologies and were way more into literature than most cultures at their general stage of development.

"I go where I am needed most," I said, already summoning another slime. "Where the price has been paid."

"Whatever," the guard grunted, retreating to his comrades and leaving me to my business.

As had become the theme of my recent endeavors, it took longer than I'd expected. I was used to a society of smartphones and bullet trains, and even after a few months of constant hiking, my internal sense of time hadn't fully adjusted for the pace of life at this level of technology.

Most of it was travel time. Now that I had the city's attention, it wasn't strictly necessary to proceed at the same stately pace—at least, not in terms of making a show. *Maintaining* a show was another matter. I needed the Healer to be consistent, unflappable, impossible to be moved from his course by any outside influence. Thus, having set that pace, I had to keep to it. Walking most of the way around the city walls that way ate up most of the day; between that and the time it took to stand in one place and summon slimes one by one until they filled the head of the canal to the point of visibly raising the water level, it was nearing dusk by the time I was ready to head to my final destination of the day.

I was tired and *really* hungry, but I was first and foremost a showman. More than myself, I was concerned about Aster, who had imperturbably shadowed me all day. Well, this would be wrapped up soon, and we could rest and refuel. Also, to be honest, Aster was tougher than I was.

The slimes wouldn't stay conspicuous that long. I had imprinted them with instructions to stay in the water and eat as much as possible of anything that didn't fight back. They should be harmless, especially once they spread throughout the canals of the Gutters. Even the hefty amount I'd summoned wouldn't provide much coverage, but that was the thing about slimes—they were basically made of magic and didn't need to eat to survive. Eating was how they reproduced. Once a slime nourished itself to a big enough mass, it would divide into two slimes, and their numbers would grow exponentially until they'd scoured the Gutters of every speck of filth and started making their way down the rivers.

Hopefully my own purposes here would be accomplished before I had to find out what this would do to the ecosystem. Probably not much; there was a strange lack of aquatic life on Ephemera, or at least on Dount. Some of the shelled creatures that could be harvested for meat and akornin were amphibious, but everyone I'd asked insisted there were no purely water-dwelling animals and were confused by the concept of fish.

Also, slimes were slow and basically defenseless. Hard to actually destroy without magic, but the Dountol *had* magic. If they decided to get rid of a bunch of slimes, that would be at worst tedious, not difficult.

At any rate, that was a problem for another day, and someone else's problem to boot. My own day's journey ended at the largest temple of the Radiant Convocation here in the Gutters.

It wasn't as large or as nice as the temple up in the middle ring, of course, but that meant nothing to me; I had chosen this one for maximum public impact, and in that I had succeeded. The priests had clearly been forewarned of my coming, and no fewer than eight stood in the main sanctuary when I arrived.

Convocation temples were built around a central dome where the actual religious ceremonies took place, with a large column-lined front extension housing a short entry corridor. Being a structure for the lowborn, there were no decorative carvings on the akorthist blocks of this temple, but its interior decorations were nice enough. Mostly depictions of Sanora and various saints and heroes, plus smaller pictures of fhullyr, little mythical critters from Fflyr folklore. According to Aster, the inclusion of these myths in temple practice was one of the core differences between the Convocation and the Radiant Temple, the state religion of Lancor from which it had diverged.

Behind the dome would be housing and workspaces for the priests in residence, as well as a library, another function unique to Convocation temples. I had no need to worry about that, though, as I wasn't planning to go in there. My business was here in the main sanctuary, with the priests.

To my surprise, I recognized one of them. She was clearly the most highly ranked of the priests present—socially, if not in terms of rank within the Convocation, which I didn't know how to tell anyway. But while the other seven were all lowborn, this woman had paler skin, light brown hair, and spectacles with frames of actual metal to match her pricier-looking garments.

I'd met her twice in the King's Guild, once on my first visit, where I indulged her taste for church music and once as a member of Rhydion's party. It was . . . Dannit? Danno? Something like that. Truth be told, I wasn't all that interested in her, though her presence made me look warily around for an armored shape of which I fortunately saw no sign. I wasn't exactly sanguine about encountering Rhydion right now. He *shouldn't* know who was under the Healer's cloak, but that guy had already given me trouble by being smarter than he looked. I didn't want to have to find out exactly how dangerous that artifact armor made him.

It was she who stepped forward, tilting her head back to regard me over the rims of her spectacles and down the length of her nose, which brought to mind that after just two short meetings I quite disliked this woman.

"Welcome . . . Healer." Her tone was laden with skepticism, as was her expression. "You *are*, I trust, a brother priest of the Goddess?"

"In the end, sister," I declaimed, "do we not all serve at the Goddess's pleasure?"

She didn't care for that answer, which I found amusing to no end, doubly so because of the wordplay. Eventually people were going to figure out they needed to clarify which Goddess.

"Sister Dhinell," murmured another priest, stepping up to her shoulder and looking pointedly past me at the entrance. "Let us be mindful of the serenity of this house of worship."

"Yes, of course," Dhinell—right, that was her name—replied in annoyance, restraining herself with visible effort. That was the right call; I'd been followed into the temple by quite a crowd of curious onlookers who had dogged my steps through the city. Enough of a crowd, at least, that none of these functionaries wanted to be seen at odds with a popular local healer. Exactly as I had intended. "What brings you, brother?"

"As always," I intoned, stepping right past her, "I come to heal."

Dhinell said nothing in response, and I deeply regretted not being able to see her face at that moment, but you couldn't have everything. Ignoring her and the other priests, I crossed the open space at the center of the dome to stand behind the altar positioned there.

It had been showtime all day, but now came the *real* spectacle.

Aster had already peeled off to one side, as I had directed her before we'd even come into town. You can't have showtime if the extras don't know their blocking, after all. She remained close enough to whip out her sword and intervene in the unlikely event that it should become necessary without distracting from the center of attention—me.

Stepping up behind the altar, I loomed over it and raised my hands, positioned as if to focus my power on the surface of the altar itself. Which was indeed the plan, as I waited only two beats to ramp up expectation before I began to cast.

Breath of Vitality.

I conjured the spell in a wide spray, sending a gentle, warm breeze through the temple. It didn't travel far, just enough to lightly touch the audience spectating from the entry, but it was enough to ruffle the clothing of the priests nearer at hand. More importantly, it was obviously magical—and impressive magic, to judge from the murmurs that rose from the onlookers and even the clerics. Visible flickers and sparks of pink and green light danced on the enchanted wind, and with it came healing. At that level of diffusion it wouldn't do *much*, but the Breath was pleasant and invigorating to experience, enough at least to make it obvious that this was a healing spell.

I couldn't cast it and the next one on the agenda simultaneously, which I knew because I had tried in preparation for this moment. But, having practiced it, I was able to make the transition look seamless enough that it could be taken for another stage of the same powerful working by somebody who didn't know how spells worked.

Healing Beacon.

The next spell took over the instant I ceased focusing on Breath of Vitality and filled the room with its warm pink glow before the last flickers of its predecessor had faded a few meters from me. The combination of Heal and Orb of Light made an orb that projected healing power at a much higher intensity than the widely sprayed Breath had. Focusing on it this way, I had some fine control over it and it began as a relatively gentle burn.

Then, gradually, ramped it up. Unevenly, letting it flicker weakly now and again to really sell the impression that I was laboriously pouring magic into my grand design, as opposed to holding a level of concentration that was honestly less difficult than just keeping my hands in the air. To judge by the increasing mutters throughout the temple, my showmanship was on point as always.

The Beacon grew in intensity until its light filled the sanctuary, its power reaching to the farthest onlookers and washing healing magic over everyone close enough even to see it. That was a nice ancillary benefit; I could indirectly do some *actual* healing here, since undoubtedly at least a few of the lowborn watching had medical issues and could benefit from this.

But it wasn't the point. I systematically drove it higher and higher, focusing more and more power into the spell, before—and this, again, I had practiced to make sure I could do it right once I had an audience—abruptly dropping it the instant I cast the final spell on the program.

Summon Healing Slime.

It snapped into existence exactly where the Beacon had been, just above the altar, and fell to land atop it with a soft splat. By the time everyone's vision had cleared after having stared at the intense blaze of healing light, they beheld what must have looked like that same spell concentrated into solid form—a single slime, bright pink and softly glowing.

Tame Beast, I added, just to make sure they wouldn't have too much trouble with it.

"What in Her blessed name," Sister Dhinell muttered, squinting at the magical slime through her spectacles.

"I leave this in your care, servants of the Goddess," I stated, my voice ringing through the *excellent* acoustics of the temple. Man, I needed to create more excuses to perform in here—this was fantastically designed for carrying sound. "Keep it safe. Tend it well. Let its power touch all who come in need of healing."

"That's . . ." One of the priests goggled dumbly at the altar, blinking. "That's a slime."

I wasn't about to engage with that. They'd figure it out, one way or another. I simply stepped around the altar and forward, making my way toward the door of the temple.

The crowd parted before me, astonished-looking lowborn—and, I noted with interest, more middleborn than I usually saw here in the Gutters—letting me pass untouched. I left behind a gift that would change everything in the hands of the Radiant Convocation.

If I knew human nature, which I did, what happened next would be as simple and inevitable as arithmetic.

The only question was who would snatch the slime first. It best served my immediate purposes if Olumnach's gangsters were the ones to do the deed, but as soon as everyone understood exactly what they had there, *someone* would. If not the gangs, then Gwyllthean's own highborn, or possibly the Convocation itself. Whoever did it, the lesson would be felt throughout the Gutters—and if I wasn't mistaken, it would be around that time that the canals began to be cleaner than anyone had ever seen them.

I gave, and I took away. The other powers on Dount? They only took.

I would deal with them all in due course. By the time I got around to each of them, the *people* would be mine.

Maybe then I could stop having to do so much killing.

36

In Which the Dark Lord Catches Up on the Gossip

The only tricky part was getting out of the city; we ditched most of my adoring crowd by heading straight into the poison khora grove. Really useful now that I knew it was there. A few stubborn individuals tried to track us further, but with Biribo's help and that of a couple of fast-flowing streams, we gave them the slip. Then we linked up with one of my bandit gangs in the area, who had been told to watch for us via gwynnek messenger. I was almost as glad of the proof that my system was working as for the opportunity to eat for the first time that day and grab a few hours' sleep.

We set out early the next morning for North Watch, just in time to reach it a bit before dusk.

"You're worried," Aster observed quietly that afternoon as we drew close to the fortress.

"Well, yes, obviously."

She shook her head, smiling faintly. "And you're worried about your people, who are now all spread out where you can't reach them, or even see what's happening."

"Exactly," I grumbled. "God knows what they'll get up to."

"And," she said gently, "you won't be there to tank the hits for them, or apply your healing if they need it."

". . . I left every group with at least two healing slimes."

She just looked at me, wearing that damnable, knowing little smile.

"Look, Aster, I'm making a hell of an omelet here; I'm well past fretting about the eggs I've gotta break."

"You know, a couple months ago—hell, weeks ago—that probably would have worked." She patted me gently on the upper arm. "But I've been with you too long now, Seiji. It's all right, you know. It's not a weakness to worry about them. If anything, that's one of the surest indications you're a man worth following."

"Shut up, Aster," I growled. She had the goddamn temerity to laugh and pat me again.

"Oh, there's the alarm," Nazralind said cheerfully from behind, where she loomed over us astride Newneh. "Right on time!"

It was indeed; the upper tower of North Watch had just come into view between the khora fronds, and the distant barking had begun, rapidly drawing closer.

Not bothering to suppress the grin on my face, I pulled ahead of the column, going to one knee with my arms stretched wide as Junko came tearing around the bend. As usual, it took a minute or two to be able to give her a proper hug, she was jumping and wiggling about in such excitement. God, I'd missed this. If you want to experience unconditional love, get a dog. Nobody sapient is capable of being so pure.

Fortunately the delay didn't seem to bother anybody; my followers, as usual, grinned as they watched this little ritual. Good. I wouldn't trust anybody at my back who didn't love dogs. One Sakin per army is more than enough. Once Junko settled down enough for us to resume moving, they kept coming forward in turns to pet her as she trotted along at my side. I allowed this infringement upon my personal privileges, because . . . obviously. I'm not a monster.

. . . well . . .

"That really is convenient," Minifrit drawled, taking a theatrical drag on her omnipresent pipe. Having been away from her for several days, I found myself noting anew how much of a *performance* her every move was, and how well she pulled that off even when it was so very transparent. Maybe that was why I so instinctively respected her. "Very useful, to always know when you're coming. Welcome home, Lord Seiji. It's good that you're back."

Something about that phrasing tickled the worry center of my brain even before Sakin, grinning as usual, chimed in.

"We've had a pretty *interesting* time the last few days."

"Oh no." I stepped fully through the gates, looking around. Nothing was visibly amiss, except that the women and several men drilling weapon forms in the courtyard had stopped to stare at me. "Is everyone all right?"

Minifrit blew smoke. "Mostly. Janyn was stabbed, but we applied a healing slime to her in time. They seem not *quite* as powerful as your Heal spell;

the wound was fully closed, but in the aftermath, the muscles were weakened and sore. It would not be amiss for you to Heal her properly, my lord, if you would."

"Still a better outcome," Sakin added. "That was a killing strike, if we didn't have magic slimes on hand."

"Stabbed," I grated, "by *whom*?"

"We don't *strictly* know," Minifrit said dourly, "but . . ."

"But come on." Sakin shrugged; his grin, if anything, increased by a fraction. "How many people are invisible and have a knife?"

She was here.

It hit me like a kick in the chest. The familiar burn blossoming from just behind my lungs, like a bad case of acid reflux, followed by a surge of nervous energy coursing through every limb. Rising up my spine, pounding behind my temples, twisting my features. That old familiar friend. The *rage*. The searing, mind-destroying promise that *someone was going to fucking die*.

That bitch. She came to my *home*, dared to stick her knife in one of *my people*? She'd had it. I was going to hack off her hands and feet and spend the entire night repeatedly Immolating her until there was nothing left of her mind. I was going to . . . Junko laid her ears back and growled at no one, picking up my mood instantly.

Nazralind took one look at me and loudly cleared her throat. "All right, ladies and gents! Lord Seiji's busy; you can pet the dog later. Everybody inside! We all deserve some hot chow and a real bed."

Everybody took the hint, with none of the good-natured sass and back-talk I'd come to expect from my followers. The column streamed into the fortress; Minifrit, Sakin, Aster, and I were a rock around which they parted in sudden haste to be far away.

"Explain," I said tightly, pleased at how well my voice remained under control.

"The situation has become complicated," said Minifrit, for once not pausing to theatrically inhale or blow smoke before speaking. "The attack on our walls that injured Janyn was only one recent event in a chain; I will begin at the beginning and ask you to bear with me."

"Do."

"First, the catfolk have begun testing our borders."

"The fucking *cats* attacked us?" I exclaimed.

Sakin cleared his throat. "No, Lord Seiji. It's a whole story; let her talk, please."

I bit back my instinctive response. None of this was their fault and taking it out on them would be the worst kind of counterproductive. "Right, sorry. Go on."

Minifrit nodded, seeming to take no offense. "To date, the cats have not actively interfered with us, and in a sense it is not *we* who are being tested. Kasser's cutting teams began to find large collections of pawprints, so obvious that they had to have been left deliberately. They were always *inside* the perimeter of dark elf totems, usually no more than a few strides inside, and near one. It appears the cats are deliberately challenging the elf's authority. At the moment, we don't know how that tangle has been progressing because as things have begun heating up out there, we've stopped sending out cutting teams. That was at Kasser's request," she added pointedly, "but *I* approved it on my authority. If you disagree, no need to take it up with him."

I shook my head curtly. "No, that's the right call. Lives are more important than resources. Has anyone *seen* the cats, or communicated with them?"

She shook her head. "We have the walls lit up, which helps, but . . . As it is, anyone mucking around in the forest at night can see our sentries far more clearly than the reverse, and the cats are undoubtedly experts at stalking."

"Right, makes sense. What happened then?"

"Next came the attack in which Janyn was injured." Minifrit turned and nodded at Sakin, with no indication of reluctance or resentment; if I didn't know how those two got along, I'd never have guessed how much she hated giving him credit. "Sakin's defense plan worked perfectly. Every sentry is always within sight of two others, and the alarm was raised the second Janyn went down. Others reacted swiftly, which is how we got the slime to her fast enough that she survived. It wasn't our people who actually repelled the attack, however. The invisible foe was shot, twice, from the forest."

I blinked, then frowned incredulously. "The cats *helped* us?"

"No, Lord Seiji," she said, allowing a hint of impatience to enter her tone, which given Minifrit's impeccable self-control, was as good as telling me to shut the fuck up already. "We've still had no direct contact with the catfolk, hostile or otherwise. The archer out there was able to *hit* an invisible target, who was in the middle of a fight, *twice*. One was a glancing shot, which enabled us to recover the arrow; the other actually impaled her."

"She's *dead*?" I burst out, having instantly forgotten my decision of three seconds ago to be quiet until the story was finished.

"Could be," Sakin said with a cavalier shrug, "but we've seen no body, and when it comes to that bitch Gray, I'm gonna insist on rifling through her cold pockets my damn self before I believe she's actually bitten it off. Considering our friend out there is clearly trying to get on our good side, I suspect they'd present the corpse as a gift—if there was a corpse."

Aster grimaced. "Well, we know she carries healing potions . . ."

"So we were not *that* fortunate, or so it is probably best to assume," agreed Minifrit, smoke dripping from her lips as she spoke.

"Oh, shit," Biribo muttered, causing everyone to look at him. "This arrow. Was it silvery white, and *really* overdesigned? More like an art piece than functional ammunition?"

"Exactly," said Minifrit. "Beautiful thing. The aesthetic reminds me of higher-quality artifact gear, and the highborn fashion which imitates it."

"Biribo?" I demanded.

He did an excited little loop the loop in the air, flicking his tongue out at me. "Boss! I know that artifact! It's a longbow—never misses a shot, conjures its own ammo when the string is pulled back. *That* ammo, specifically— really pretty arrows that would be way too expensive to actually use as arrows if somebody had to make them with their own two hands. It's a state treasure of Shylverrael."

"I want to see this arrow," I stated.

Minifrit and Sakin winced in unison.

"Oh, what the fuck *now?*" I demanded.

"As I said, we were able to recover it," Minifrit repeated, frowning in irritation. "I had it stored as securely as we were able for you to examine. It was subsequently *unrecovered*, from our vault. Nothing else was taken, but . . . it appears our dark elven friend is particular about what traces they leave behind."

"It's worth pointing out that our *vault* is just the only closet with a solid door and a functioning lock," Sakin cackled. "Nothing that'd more than slow down a Shylver shadow scout."

"That's right, we still need to get the actual vault repaired," I muttered. There was one in the fortress, but someone had torn the door right off and actually knocked down part of the attached wall at some point. I'd directed Kasser to leave that far down the priority list, as we'd not had a problem with thieving among the ranks, and there just *wasn't* much of great value in the fortress. "So to sum up, we're in the middle of a three-way power struggle between the cat tribe, the dark elves, and Lady Gray which is all around and all *about* us but in which we are somehow not even involved?"

"That's . . . more or less . . . not inaccurate," Minifrit acknowledged.

"Well, I know a solution for that," I growled. "Good on you for hunkering down, but now I'm back and so is Aster. It's high time we went to have an actual talk with the cats."

"Everything we previously discussed still applies, boss," Biribo warned. "You sacrifice the position of strength by being the one to—"

"The beautiful thing about that, Biribo, is that I can swiftly *re-establish* a position of strength by Immolating everyone who so much as looks at me wrong in front of all their friends." I felt my lip curling into a snarl as I talked. The rage pulsing in me wasn't even about the cats, but they'd do for an outlet. "I should have done this weeks ago. Waiting on them to make a move was a mistake. If they want to test our strength, I will *show* it to them. And then we will have a calm, polite discussion."

I received a round of skeptical looks.

"A calm, polite discussion," I repeated with more emphasis. "Because the alternative to reaching an accord is to wipe them the fuck out, and while I've never done a genocide, it sure does sound like a whole bunch of messy effort toward no productive end. I've got more important shit to do, and Lady Gray is at the top of that list. The instant we don't have to worry about being shot in the back by angry kitties, I want that fucking forest *torn apart* until she is found and at my mercy!"

"That is a *terrible* idea," Aster said immediately. "We've already been over this, Lord Seiji. *We* have the advantage so long as she's forced to come at our defenses, which are set up specifically to counter her. As soon as we start trying to hunt her in the forest, that situation is reversed. She'll pick off our people one by one."

"You want to just fucking *sit here* and *let* her keep knifing people on the walls until she breaks through?" I exclaimed.

"Healing potions or no, two days ago she was shot twice and fell *off* that wall," Sakin pointed out. "Assuming she *is* still alive, she's not gonna be up to trying that again for a while. More importantly, she's being stalked by an equally persistent dark elf trying to earn our favor, who is *much* more suited for that than we are. Strategically, the most effective use of our strength is to cow the cat tribe into submission so our Shylver ally can work."

"You really want to trust the lives of *everyone we have on watch* to some unknown dark elf against the ultimate assassin—just what in the fuck is so goddamn funny?!"

Biribo had just had the exceedingly poor taste to interrupt me by bursting out laughing so hard he forgot to fly for a second and lost a meter of altitude.

"Ultimate assassin?" he wheezed. "Boss, may I remind you of your first meeting with Lady Gray? When she *failed* to kill you, and then her next move was to *drop her invisibility* and try to intimidate you with a speech. And then *kept doing that.* Assassin, my scaly tail—she's more like you—all charisma and grandstanding. That woman has gotta be the *worst* assassin I've ever heard of. The fact that she has the ultimate assassin's *weapon* is just an insulting waste, is what it is."

"And that's another thing," I agreed. "I *want* that fucking dagger—*and* whatever it is she's using to block spell targeting. If we let the dark elves get her, I'll lose those artifacts. They may want to impress me, but I can't see them just handing over something that valuable."

"I see your point, but I think you're looking at it backward, Lord Seiji," said Aster, shaking her head. "It would be great to get those artifacts, yes, but you don't *have* them now. It's not like you can lose them. Having them change hands from a known enemy to an ally is *still* a win for us."

I hadn't noticed it happening, but my hands had clenched into claws at my sides and were actively trembling. The rage pounded in the back of my throat so hard it was impeding my breathing.

"I *want that woman's head*," I hissed. The sound of my own voice was alien, like the warning rattle of some angry reptile.

"That *cannot* be a priority right now." Minifrit managed to be utterly implacable and nonconfrontational at the same time, a skill that had undoubtedly been perfected over years as a brothel madam. "Do not take me for some priest or moralist; I know very *well* the value and the delicious sweetness of revenge. If your enemies *can* be made to suffer, they *should* be. *But,* never at the expense of more productive goals."

"Grand final confrontations are great for stories," added Sakin, "but life doesn't work like that. The mark of true power is that you don't even have to do anything and your enemies die ignominiously in a ditch somewhere from the sheer inherent blowback of trying to fuck with you. This is you *winning,* Lord Seiji. Don't fuck it up."

"Thanks to you, in the space of a few months, Lady Gray has gone from privilege and power as the uncontested crime boss of the Gutters to scrabbling around in the wild khora, being hunted like an animal." Minifrit's eyes bored into mine, all but visibly willing me to come around to her point of view. "Lord Seiji, you could chain her to a wall and spend an entire night casting your fire spell on her, and it would not be a greater vengeance than what you have already done to her."

I drew in a deep breath to argue, feeling it shudder in my chest.

"You're scaring Junko," Aster said quietly.

That, finally, made me freeze. I looked down; Junko was pressed against my leg, still growling softly, but staring wide-eyed around in uncertainty. She could feel my fury and shared it, but was in her safe home surrounded by friends, seeing no threat. I'd been ignoring her for the last few minutes, and only now realized how the confusion must be wearing on her.

The rage didn't flicker out like a candle—I don't think it really works like that. It began to gutter, though. There were more important things for me to care about.

Slowly, I sank to a crouch, forcing myself to breathe deeply and evenly, and put an arm around the dog, gently ruffling her ears with my other hand.

"Fine," I said after a moment in which none of my lieutenants spoke, just letting me process. "Fine. Then . . . we should figure out how to be more proactive about these dark elves. Even if they manage to solve some problems for us, from everything I've been told about Viryans, that'll only cede advantages to them when they finally decide to show themselves and actually negotiate."

"I'm absolutely sure that's literally why they're doing it this way," Biribo agreed. "Viryans try never to negotiate except from a position of power. If they come to you without having something *major* to offer, along with proof of their worth, it'll mean they're completely desperate. Which, apparently, they are not."

"Dark elf, singular," Minifrit said with a smug smile, blowing a streamer of smoke.

"Now, how can you possibly know that?" I demanded.

"I didn't get a chance to finish my account of what's been happening in your absence, Lord Seiji. If you'll come with me, let's round up Gilder and go to the kitchen. There has been another development, which I think will put you in a better mood."

37

In Which the Dark Lord Leaves an Offering

The mess hall was filling up as everyone settled in for the evening meal that was soon to be served, and Sakin took advantage of the hubbub to slip away. It made me . . . wonder. Shirking duties was not among his . . . let's call them "interesting character quirks," so I could assume his presence wouldn't be needed for Minifrit's thing. On the other hand, he wasn't one to miss out on something that could be important, and he and Minifrit never missed an opportunity to compete with each other.

Minifrit herself gracefully deflected greetings and inquiries, save those of Gilder, who was ecstatic to see I was back. She chivvied the both of us along with wordless ease, also gathering up a quieter Aenit from the children's table as we made our way to the kitchen.

"Oh sure, yeah, let's just march a buncha people in here," Gannit complained loudly as we filed through. "Not like I'm in the middle of gatherin' up dinner for a hundred mouths or anything. And why is there a damn *dog* in my kitchen?"

"Junko's cleaner than Donon," I replied, ignoring his stammered protest. "Never mind the dog, *I* can't get over the fact that Minifrit put out that pipe before coming in here. How the hell did you housebreak *her*? I've had no luck."

Gannit brayed an abrasive laugh, her assistants grinned, and Minifrit gave me an extremely calm sidelong glance that said I'd be paying for that later. Junko panted and thumped her tail on the floor, just happy to be hanging out with everybody.

It was Gilder of all people who got us back on track, clearing his throat loudly and skipping over to the door to the pantry. "So, Lord Seiji, Miss Minifrit wants to show you what we found, right?"

"Indeed," Minifrit drawled. She opened the pantry and glided inside. "Gilder, Aenit, come. Lord Seiji, it will be easiest for you to see what we mean from in here, but more people than that will make it uncomfortably cramped."

Aster sighed, but silently took up her position next to the door, leaning against the wall with her arms folded.

The pantry was kind of a source of pride for me, because it was well-stocked. Dire warnings about the state of our food supply aside, at a glance it appeared we were doing okay. There were shelves, barrels, and bins, well-organized and while not *loaded* with food, amply supplied. Hocks of dried meat and bundles of herbs hung from the ceiling.

"No," I said sternly as Junko went right for the jerky, pointing at the floor by my feet. "Sit down."

She whined and gave me the eyes.

"Don't even try it! It's not like I don't *know* all these suckers sneak you treats. You're gonna get fat."

Gilder and Aenit immediately looked way too innocent and Minifrit rolled her eyes.

"Junko gets plenty of exercise, thanks to . . . well, everyone," she reported. "And in fact there has been much less begging since Harold started making toys for her from leftover hardened leather. I don't know how he got them to smell like meat, but you'll likely be finding one in your bed, Lord Seiji. Everyone else has."

"Right, well," I prompted, as Junko sat by my feet and smiled at us all without a hint of remorse, "we are in here because . . . ?"

"This is where we discerned the nature of our dark elven ally," said Minifrit. "Or at least, some of it. Obviously there remains more mystery than fact, but the balance is tilted a bit further toward our favor, thanks to the ingenuity of the Gutter Rats. The idea was Gilder's, so perhaps he had best explain."

Gilder swelled up with pride, ignoring Aenit's eyeroll. Minifrit had clearly grown adept at handling him, not that it was hard. A little praise went a long way with this one.

"Okay, so it's like this," the boy said with all of his usual animation, skipping over to a fully loaded bin of tubers. The thing had a lid, but it was upright against the wall behind it, the potatoes piled too high for it to close. "Say you wanna keep track of who's filching, right? There was a bunch of reasons to wanna know that in the Gutters—we Rats all had our own stashes of stuff an' was always hunting for each other's, plus sometimes stall owners would give us leftovers if we could figure out who was gettin' into their stock an' put a stop to it. I got a whole black disc for it once! And then there's always the food stores inside the Nest—that's where we got the most use outta our secret technique. Little grubby fingers always gettin' into the pantry. So what you gotta do is, you gotta learn to paint a picture in your head!"

"A picture? You, ah, wanna expand on that?" I asked, frowning.

"Say, these potatoes." Gilder turned and gestured widely at the bin of spuds. "So what I do is, I have a good, *hard* look at the potatoes, right? And I *remember* what it looks like. The important details! See, most people's brains, they turn a bunch of potatoes into mush, right? You see a bin of potatoes and it's just a bin of potatoes, you don't see what each individual potato looks like. That's just how our eyes work, see? So you remember *exactly* what it looks like, and when you check it again, you can see what's different, so you know what was taken!"

"Photographic memory?" I exclaimed. "Holy shit, kids. That's impressive as *hell*." Junko barked in agreement, her tail thumping against the bin of onions behind her.

Gilder puffed up so much he looked like he was about to float off the ground, so of course Aenit had to let some of the air out of him.

"It would be, if we could just do that any time for anything," she said, her soft and even delivery standing in contrast to the boy's. "It takes a lot of focus to remember a single scene, and even then it really only works reliably if we cheat ahead of time."

"Exactly," Gilder agreed, nodding eagerly and looking not at all perturbed by her undercutting of their trick. "It's all about advance prep! See, you gotta know how a filcher *thinks*. And if there's one thing Gutter Rats know, it's that."

"Truer words were never spoken," Minifrit commented. I noted with amusement that she still had her pipe in its usual perch in her hand, though so far she hadn't forgotten herself and tried to pull from it. Her eyes silently dared me to make a comment, which I didn't, only because I was far too busy listening to Gilder's account.

"If you're picking something to filch," the lad continued self-importantly, "there's a bunch of factors you gotta consider. Take these potatoes, right? You wanna pick one that's *good* to filch—but not *too* good, cos really good ones're more likely to be missed, see? And you wanna pick one that's in a *position* where it's not as likely to be missed if it goes missing from the pile. Say, off to the side and toward the back—never the big nice one sittin' on top like a jewel. But because it's in a lower position on the pile, you gotta make sure it's not one that's buried, cos what you *don't* wanna do is disturb the pile. You could be in trouble if it falls and makes a noise while you're grabbin' it, and also the more of a disturbance you make, the more likely the shopkeeper— uh, that is, *whoever* owns the potatoes—will be noticed. Right?"

He covered for his momentary lapse by reaching over to grab a potato and held it up.

"So here's what I do, see? I pick a *perfect* potato—big and nice-looking, but not *too* much, not so much somebody'd have it marked out for their dinner and get annoyed if it goes missing. Then I *put* this potato real careful-like, in exactly the right kinda position in the pile. See?" He leaned over, screwing up his face in concentration, and very carefully placed the chosen tuber in a place just as he'd described, near one edge of the pile and toward the back. "Then I do that, oh, about seven or eight times. Depends on the pile and how many perfect filching spots there's room to set up. So that way I don't gotta memorize the whole damn pile of potatoes! Cos, yeah, too many potatoes turns to mush in anybody's mind. You just remember your perfect filching ones, then you come back and see if any of 'em got filched! That'll trap most any thief, especially if they're going after something like *potatoes*. It takes a Gutter Rat to bother with this kind of detail over something this cheap!"

I blinked, considering the ramification, and looked again over the pantry with fresh eyes. "I think that's even *more* impressive, Gilder."

He grinned again, but somewhat to my surprise didn't try to hog the credit. "Hey, I'm just in charge of potatoes. The girls did a *lot* more work; Benit and Aenit both have super sharp eyes! Aenit especially—she was always best at this, back at the Nest. She sees *everything*."

Aenit gave him a surprised smile at the acknowledgment, though it immediately switched back to a frown. "If you're so impressed, how come you didn't ask me to join when Lord Seiji had you recruit trustworthy Rats? Benit, sure, but you picked *Radon* over me?"

"What've you got against Radon?" he demanded, frowning right back.

"He's a tiny!"

"What do you want me to say, Aenit?" Gilder gave her an exaggerated shrug. "Lord Seiji wanted people who were *trustworthy*, not just smart."

"I'm not trustworthy?!"

"Sure you are, and I know that *now*. But this was then! You're always such a mystery all the damn time, Aenit, nobody ever knows what you're thinking.

Yeah, I thought about you cos I know you're sharp, but come down to it, I couldn't even guess whether you'd throw in or just run right to Uncle Gently."

Aenit ground her teeth audibly, and I decided to cut this off before it progressed any further off course.

"It worked out for the best," I interjected, making my voice as soothing as I could without sacrificing firmness. "Your help made the crucial difference in busting up Uncle Gently's operation, Aenit. If Gilder had recruited you earlier, you wouldn't have been there to guide me. Right now, I'm proud as hell of you kids—you continue to do excellent work. So what did your investigations turn up?"

"The Rats have been monitoring the pantry all week," Minifrit said, interjecting smoothly before either of them could answer. Both kids looked a trifle put out that she took over the story, but considering how readily they devolved into squabbles and tangents, I figured this was for the best. "Thanks to their careful inventory of what was taken, I believe we can be certain that we have *one* person helping themselves very lightly from our supplies. The surrounding circumstances being what they are, I am confident it is our dark elf. A more inept thief would grab at random, and a larger group would scoop up whole handfuls. The Rats' method is perfect to see, specifically, the traces left by a single careful, skillful thief."

"I almost hate to ask," I said, "but how can we be sure it's not just one of our own people stealing? We've got too many in this fortress now to keep tabs on everybody."

"The pantry *is* secured and watched most of the time," said Minifrit, looking significantly down at Junko, "but such terms are . . . relative. Anyone capable of getting into the valuables closet could bypass the defenses here quite easily. Besides—"

"Besides," added a strident voice from behind us, "nobody who eats from *Gannit's* kitchen goes hungry!"

The cook herself stood in the doorway, arms folded, dripping stirring spoon still in one hand. Behind her, I noted the kitchen was considerably quieter already; it seemed Donon and Madyn had wheeled out the serving carts while we were talking in here.

"If it was any of our people stealing," Gannit continued with a scowl, "they'd be grabbing high-value items. The flavorful stuff that's *nicer'n* what everybody gets three meals a day of, what little there is of it. Nobody around here'd be stealing single potatoes, jerky, and unflavored wyddh. Those are survival rations."

"Some people do steal out of a compulsion or for the thrill rather than for acquisition's sake," Minifrit added, "but those would start with other people's personal possessions rather than food items from the pantry. No, Lord Seiji, this paints a very specific picture. We have a dark elf walking through our fortress with impunity, invisible and silent. They are trying to endear themselves to us—but also, they are *hungry.*"

Well, how about that. So you're an intelligence operative with an innate gift of stealth? Well fuck you, *I've* got half-starved orphans! That means I win, apparently. Somehow.

Life is weird.

This painted a whole different picture indeed. I'd been nervous about the prospect of Shylverrael, or even just one political faction therein, keeping its eyes on my operation out here. But one dark elf, alone, starving, desperately trying to prove themselves? Suddenly I couldn't help feeling a twinge of sympathy. Sure, I'd landed in a fortress when I was ripped out of my life and dropped in this wilderness, but I'd had to fight for it. *Everything* had been one damn struggle after another.

Poor elf, they were trying so hard . . .

I cleared my throat. "Excellent work, everyone, I am seriously impressed. Biribo, analysis?"

"Minifrit's right, boss, we got a more thorough picture now," he said, as Junko panted happily at the positive change in mood. "It's a bit contradictory, but that might actually help us narrow down the possibilities. So we're dealing with an individual who possesses one of the most powerful artifacts on this entire island, one of the great treasures of Shylverrael itself. That, plus the fact that they know exactly how to make the warning totems that tell local beast tribes to clear off, says this is somebody with wealth, connections, and a solid education in political affairs. She's Blessed with Might, to be able to use that artifact—with a respectably strong Blessing, at that—and is a skilled shadow scout. Sure, dark elves have an innate gift of stealth, but they don't all have the same inherent strength in it, and the ability to walk around a fully occupied fortress without getting caught says *training.*"

"Wait, *she?*" I interrupted.

Biribo bobbed in the air. "Okay, yeah, true, we don't know this person's gender. But as assumptions go, boss, it's relatively safe. Dark elves are more or less as sexist as the light kind, just in the other direction. If you ever meet a dark elf man who's in charge of anything, you best watch your step; that guy had to outperform the dozen most qualified women to get that job."

"Well, shit, now I kinda like them," Aster commented from just outside, earning a cackle and a punch on the shoulder from Gannit.

"On the *other* hand," Biribo continued, "our girl is alone and clearly cut off from her city's resources, as revealed by the fact that she's unable to make the totems *properly*, lacking naga or harpy feathers, and the fact she's reduced to stealing food."

"Sounds like a noble, all right," Gilder commented, grinning. "Anybody *else* can live just by catching crawns, at least until winter comes. But you gotta know *how* to do that. They're sneaky little bastards if you ain't learned their tricks. Any Gutter Rat or farm boy can catch crawns, but highborn kids don't learn shit like that."

"This does sort of counter-indicate Biribo's theory," Minifrit added. "If this individual is exiled and on the run from Shylverrael, there's no reason to assume they are of the dominant gender there. If anything, I propose that it implies the opposite."

"Could be, I guess," my familiar agreed, though not happily.

"So," I murmured, staring absently at the potatoes, "we're dealing with a deposed aristocrat or a thieving rebel, possibly both, and in either case, someone exiled from Shylverrael. Who either is or isn't a woman, which makes that a *completely useless* data point until we know more."

"All right, fine!" Biribo exclaimed in annoyance. "What's *important* is that we can be certain they're in a weak position just from how they're going about this. A Viryan with any amount of political education would *not* approach us openly until they were in some kind of position of strength. Coming to us for help like a beggar . . . Well, that's just unthinkable if you see the world the way Viryans do. Even possessing an artifact like that bow would just be asking to have it taken away if you showed up at the Dark Lord's feet with nothing else. She—*they*—are trying to prove their value to us by keeping the cats off our back and ridding us of Lady Gray, an obvious enemy. That's why I think Sakin was right—as soon as they actually *kill* Gray, they'll come present her corpse. In fact, that's probably exactly what they're waiting for before revealing themselves."

"That being the case, we ought not disregard how their well-meaning attempt has utterly backfired," Minifrit said archly. "We had no problems from, or even contact at all with, the cat tribe *until* our 'friend' started putting up those totems. Clearly, the cats immediately recognized that they were fake, because of the faulty materials used. I doubt they would challenge the decree of Shylverrael, but from their perspective, someone *not* backed by Shylverrael's power is trying to invoke it. Small wonder they've become aggressive. *Worse*, they most likely assume it is *we* who tried that trick."

"Unless the elf has been putting those fancy arrows in cats," I mused. "That'd settle them down, all right. As far as that goes, we're blind to the situation, since we don't know what's been happening out there."

"Settle 'em down?" Gannit snorted. "Some dipshit elf started shooting *my* pals, I'd get good and pissed off. Maybe enough to take it out on whoever the dipshit's friends are."

I sighed. "Thanks, Gannit."

"You got it, Mister Dark Lord," she heckled, turning to saunter off back to her oven. "You gonna eat with the crew tonight, or should I make you a plate in the kitchen?"

"I'll go out to the mess hall as soon as we're done in here," I said distractedly. Making my presence felt to the troops was a big part of my reason for returning to headquarters, after all.

"Right, well, either way, the dog doesn't eat in here. This is a kitchen, not a damn kennel."

"Before you reach a conclusion on how to proceed, my lord," said Minifrit with a serious expression, "I must raise a point for your consideration. I am not advocating *for* this specific approach, you understand, but merely ensuring that you have considered it."

"Devil's advocate, I understand," I nodded. "Go on, Minifrit, your input is always valued."

She rewarded me with a ghost of a smile as she continued. "I believe you should at least entertain the option of rejecting this individual's friendship. One of the few things we know for certain is that they are one person, isolated and without power or connections. Indications are that their allegiance will not gain you a foot in the door with Shylverrael, and may in fact earn the enmity of the dark elven state. And there *is* the very strong possibility that their ineptitude is the direct cause of our current troubles with the cat tribe."

"Uh, scuze me?" Gilder held up one hand for attention. "This person's invisible, right? With a deadly-ass artifact weapon? And might be in this room *right now*, listening to us? Cos, just sayin', suppose we 'reject their friendship' and they start rejecting people's throats while they're asleep, huh?"

Junko growled softly, and I reached down to give her ears a soothing scratch. I still wasn't quite sure how much spoken language she understood, but she was amazingly sensitive to minute changes in mood, and not just mine.

"You both have good points," I said, "but ultimately neither is what it comes down to. Look around. We have an organization built of orphans, prostitutes, and bandits here. Even in our more elite connections, the Auldmaer Company and Clan Yviredh are poorer and weaker than the entire rest of their social circles, and I gained their friendship *specifically* by approaching them in their hour of greatest need. Hell, even the Kingsguard Captain I've been working with has welcomed me at least partly because he gets no respect and not enough aid from the system he's supposedly serving. Every step here on Dount, I've succeeded by siding with the people who needed my help, not those who had the most to offer me. Now, since we don't know much about this elf, their situation or motivations, all I know for sure is what's worked for me so far, and I see no reason to deviate from it. If anything, the fact that they're an outcast in need of allies makes me more inclined to welcome them. Clear?"

All of them nodded; even Minifrit, who had raised the objection, did so with an approving smile at my answer.

"I always did want to meet a dark elf," Aenit commented solemnly.

"That being decided," said Minifrit, "all that remains is the question of how you wish to proceed."

I considered for a moment, glancing again at the potatoes, the jerky, the wyddh. Survival rations indeed. If this person couldn't catch crawns, they probably couldn't cook; were they trying to eat *raw* potatoes? Yikes.

"Hey, Gannit," I called, leaning over to look out the pantry door.

"Hey, Lord Spookypants," she called back, stepping into my field of view and wiping her hands on a rag.

"Do we have any of those ration packs you make for the gwynnek riders at hand?"

"Sure, I got three different batches, for three different size trips. How long you planning to need rations for?"

"How big is the biggest size?"

"Food for a week of careful eating, plus small travel supplies. Y'know, for mending clothes, starting fires, shit like that."

"Perfect. Could you bring me one of those, please? Oh, and some paper and a pencil. And a kitchen stool!"

"Oh, sure, I'll just bring the whole damn kitchen in there for him," she grumbled, just loud enough to be clearly audible, which had to have been deliberate. "Let's have the old lady with arthritis haul furniture around after a whole day of cookin', that makes sense. Perfect division of labor."

I knew very well Gannit's arthritis was a thing of the past and she generally moved like somebody half her age. But she loved to complain, and I wasn't about to spoil her fun, especially since she produced everything I requested in less than a minute. Of *course* there was paper and a pencil just hanging around in the kitchen; it was a Fflyr kitchen, after all. I wondered how many sauce-stained books they had in there.

"Oh, and an empty wineskin!" I added as she retreated. From outside the pantry there came a loud, theatrical sigh, but Gannit returned in moments with just what I'd requested.

I had already set up the stool in front of the potato bin, set the pack of food and supplies prominently atop it, and now carefully wrote a label on a scrap of paper in Fflyr script, which I then affixed to one of the pack's buckles:

Dark Elf Rations

Hopefully they could read Fflyr. Presumably so, if they were hanging around us.

I then conjured a healing slime; thanks to Tame Beast, it was the work of seconds to get it to crawl into the empty wineskin and remain there. The instruction should hold it, but nonetheless, I tightened the cap and added all the necessary details to the warning label, which I attached to it before setting it on the stool alongside the pack:

For medical use only. Do not ingest.
Keep container closed when not in use.
Gently squeeze and apply a small amount to injured area.
Do not allow it to escape the container or you'll never get it back in.

"There," I said with satisfaction, standing back. "Well? Looks good?"

Junko barked her approval.

"Extremely serviceable, Lord Seiji," Minifrit said in that excessively solemn tone, which was as good as laughing. "A most compassionate gesture."

"It is that," Biribo agreed, "and also, from a Viryan's perspective, a real power move. Putting them back in our debt even as we accept their help, not to mention revealing we know about the thefts."

"Well, I'm not trying to piss them off . . ."

"I doubt our mystery buddy will take offense, boss. A good Viryan will be more likely to be impressed by it. 'Sides, if they succeed in collecting Lady

Gray's head for you, that'll still give 'em enough face that they'll finally be comfortable declaring themselves openly. Most likely they'll take the supplies and leave money on the stool."

"Why would this person have money? I thought we figured they were a starving runaway."

"Probably an aristocratic starving runaway," Minifrit corrected, "or at the very least, someone with a combination of education and deadly skills, which says they were accustomed to power. Such people *always* carry money. It must have been quite a bitter realization that they cannot eat or burn coins to survive in the forest."

"Well, fair's fair," I said. "Let's clear out, everybody. Whether or not our friend takes the deal, they're not the only one who needs to eat. C'mon, we're late for dinner."

38

In Which the Dark Lord Gets Some Help

It ended up being for the best that I had that brief update in the pantry. Part of the reason for coming back to base right now was to make my reassuring presence known to the troops, especially the newbies. If I'd joined everyone in the dining hall while in a mood after learning about Lady Gray's ongoing bullshit, I probably would've just scared people. At least now I was more relaxed.

Undoubtedly, the newer hands still thought it odd that I sat down with my stew and wyddh at the children's table, but the sooner they got used to my peculiar ways, the better. This ain't your daddy's Dark Crusade.

So there I was at one corner seat, with Junko chomping from her bowl on the floor beside me, Benit settled in on my other side, and Gilder and Aenit all but physically scuffling over who was going to sit across from me, when they were upstaged by none other than Nazralind.

"You snooze, you lose, kids," she said, completely unrepentant as she slid onto the bench with her tray and grinned at Gilder's protest. Aenit, looking grudgingly impressed, seized the opportunity to plonk down next to the elf, leaving him to shuffle down the row another space in defeat. Naz herself, meanwhile, grabbed the pair of chopsticks she'd brought, one held upright in each fist, and beamed expectantly at me. "All right! Show me how to use these."

"Where the hell did you *get* those?" I demanded.

"Same place you did. Kasser's got lots of scrap akorshil lying around from all the stuff he has to make; polishing up a pair of little sticks hardly takes any time at all, apparently. It's funny, I was always told akorshil wasn't suitable for tableware because of how it splinters, but apparently it all depends on the type and how you treat it."

"Rookie mistake," Benit murmured. "Never ask Kasser about akorshil. You'll be trapped for *hours*."

"It wasn't *hours*," Nazralind said, then winced. "Technically. Not quite, I don't think."

"*Easy* mistake, though," Gilder added. "That guy won't talk at all *unless* it's about shilworking. I never knew he *could* talk until I broke that lamp stand."

I placed a bite of chewy crawn meat in my mouth with my own chopsticks and gave him the eye. "That was you?"

Gilder was suddenly very busy with his stew. Joke was on him; this was the first I'd heard about any lamp stand.

"Anyway," Naz prompted, gently thumping her chopstick-holding fists on the table.

"First of all, don't ever do *that*," I winced. "Why the sudden interest, anyway?"

"You probably haven't had a reason to ask him, but Kasser's had so many requests for these he actually just keeps them lying around now. It was actually annoying," she added, frowning. "Would've been one thing if I got to listen about akorshil polishing while he was actually demonstrating it, but he just *handed* them to me and went off on this rant . . ."

"What?" I looked around the mess hall. "Who's been . . ."

Benit, Gilder, and Aenit all pulled chopsticks out of their sleeves.

"We've tried," Gilder admitted. "I figured it can't be any harder'n picking pockets. But damn, Lord Seiji, it's hard to even get a proper look at what you're doing with your fingers . . ."

"I stabbed myself right up the nose," Benit mumbled.

I couldn't imagine how anyone could possibly fuck up chopsticks that badly, but it was Benit, so of course I didn't say that out loud. With Gilder I'd have gone for the throat, but she responded better to encouragement.

"It's not just the kids; people want to imitate you," Nazralind said, shrugging. "That's what it's like to be in charge. I'm sure Miss Minifrit has mentioned this, but it's probably a good thing to let folks pick up little customs that help differentiate them from Fflyr society. Soooo . . . ?"

They all stared at me, bright-eyed and waiting. I could see others at nearby tables watching with varying degrees of surreptitiousness.

Well. What could it hurt?

With a sigh, I held up my right hand. "Okay, start by bracing one stick this way, across the base of your thumb and your third finger . . ."

Turned out using chopsticks was easier than explaining how; the motions were so second nature I had a little trouble consciously thinking about it. But I got them all holding them the right way, at least. More or less.

"Bloody hell," Nazralind growled, losing a whole bite of meat from her stew as one stick skittered out of her grip. She hadn't yet managed to lift one all the way to her mouth.

"Excuse me, young lady, you need to watch your mouth at the dinner table," Gilder said severely. "There are children here, for fuck's sake."

"Fuck off, Gilder. You know more swears than I do."

"In at least four languages," he agreed, grinning. "Perk of growing up in a trade city near the border! Aw, bugger." At least he didn't lose his chopsticks along with the chunk of potato that sadly tumbled onto the table.

"I think we picked the worst possible meal to test this," Nazralind grumbled. "Shoulda tried on something solid . . ."

I shrugged, placidly eating another bite. "It's a thick stew; shouldn't be that bad. Back home we usually have a light soup with breakfast."

"And you eat that with *sticks*?" Aenit demanded. "*How*?"

"You pick out the solid parts with chopsticks and sip the broth from the bowl." I was having way too much fun now to tell them that we used soup spoons in Japan.

"In Dlemathlys, that would be absolutely execrable table manners," Nazralind commented.

"Wow," I said, "it's almost as if different cultures have different customs. That's a brilliant flash of insight, Naz. I wonder if anyone's ever put that together before? You should write a book."

"You're such an arse," she said fondly. "All right, here we go. I swear I am gonna get *one* piece of meat into my face tonight . . ."

"Hah!" Gilder leered insanely. "That's what she hmmfffgm!"

Aenit shoved a chunk of wyddh into his mouth, and I'm pretty sure Benit kicked him under the table.

"We have fun, don't we?" I said cheerfully. "Junko, sit back down. You *just* finished yours, I sat here and watched you. Little scam artist."

She whined piteously. And then so did Nazralind, though for different reasons.

I made it a habit to play my guitar a bit before bed; it was a little ritual I had missed while out on maneuvers in the forest and the city, but now that I was back in the fortress . . . Well, it was strange how much like home North Watch had begun to feel. Sitting on the end of my bed, strumming softly with Junko already half-asleep next to me, everything felt more comfortable than camping out with the bandits. I was going to have trouble sleeping regardless of anything I did, but this made it a little better.

Or would have, except that Biribo suddenly buzzed upward from where he'd been hanging out on the "nest" I'd built for him—a pile of cloth scraps and pillow stuffing on a shelf.

"Oh, this should be good," he muttered. "Hey, boss, no worries. I can take the dog for a walk."

Junko raised her head and I blinked. "Excuse me?"

There came a knock at the door.

I looked over at Biribo, who just hovered aimlessly. He didn't seem alarmed, and neither was Junko, so . . .

With a sigh, I stood up, setting my guitar on the chair that was serving as its stand. What time was it? Well after dark, at least. Everybody not on night watch was either in bed or heading there . . . This had better be important.

I opened the door to behold Minifrit standing in the darkened hallway outside. I could just make out her face and not her expression thanks to the shadows; my body blocked the light coming from the bottled light slime I had in one corner of the room. Her eyes glinted subtly in the dimness as they flicked over my face.

"Well?" I said irritably.

And suddenly she had flowed across the space between us. I caught her by reflex and froze in surprise as warm lips pressed against my own. A soft sound of appreciation rose from deep in her throat, her chest pressed against me—by *God*, she was soft. I'd never held a woman quite so—

Panic jolted through me like a physical force. No hallucinations this time, at least, just the overwhelming fear, the certainty that someone was dying while I wasn't there. I had to move, had to find them. I was letting everyone down, and people would die because I wasn't . . .

I jerked my head up, gasping for air, and half-stumbled backward a step before catching myself. Minifrit moved right along with me, but I managed to put a few centimeters between us. And then a few more, because she was *really* abundant in the front; I had to push her away a surprising distance before I didn't have her bosom brushing my chest.

"Woman, you taste like a chimney," I said hoarsely. "How many times have I told you about that smoking?"

Minifrit tilted her head, and raised an eyebrow. "Ow."

I only belatedly realized I had a death grip on her upper arms, my fingers sinking into her biceps hard enough to bruise. With another gasp I released her, half-stumbling backward again.

Once more she followed, this time stopping just inside the doorway as I continued to retreat—but deftly kicked the door closed with her heel, shutting us in my bedroom.

"And *that's* how easy it was," Minifrit said sharply, pointing one finger at my face and cutting off the angry tirade I was already swelling up to deliver. "Lord Seiji, *people are noticing.* Take it from a professional, women have been using sex to distract and disarm men since time immemorial. There's an art to it—a science, even. And even so, it is often unreliable in effect if the man in question is prepared, or not interested. *You*, though, are a tragically easy target. All it takes is one good display and you are *shut down* for several entire seconds. Do you really imagine you have no enemies who will take advantage of this? If you hadn't already recruited most of Cat Alley, someone would have flashed some cleavage and then put a knife through your eye already. Once the highborn realize you're coming for them, they *will* deploy those well-trained middle ring courtesans. And with the right trick, they will *end you*. When, Lord Seiji, not if."

I drew in a breath, hating the way it shuddered.

"Yeah . . . well . . . It's not like you can *fix it*, so . . ."

"Tell me you haven't already forgotten," she said, exasperated. "I *said* I could help with this. I also warned you how important it was at the time. In fact, I seem to recall demonstrating my point with a less . . . aggressive example. Just how brazenly do I need to emphasize this, Lord Seiji? Do you think I'll stop short of flashing you in the dining hall and then licking your face while you have a seizure? I promise you, boy, your imagination is not sufficient to conjure anything that would shock or embarrass *me*. This is not a pissing contest you will win."

"Wow," Biribo muttered. "That was . . . vivid. Look, boss, you really should listen to her, okay? You got a legit problem here, and you *also* got an actual professional who can help with it. Not letting her work is just sheer, straight-up bonkers."

"Well, what can you *possibly* do?" I burst out. "It's not like there are any psychiatrists here!"

"Yes, yes, I know, we're all mud-splattered primitives next to the wonders of glorious Japan," Minifrit said, disdainfully flicking her fingers off to the side. "I can't say I *appreciate* that attitude, but if even a fraction of your anecdotes are true, I'm not willing to argue with it. I have no idea what your old life was like or what expectations you might have. What I know is this world, *my* life, and what *I* am capable of. Lord Seiji, I would not have offered you my help if I did not fully believe I *could* help! Have I impressed you as a woman willing to waste her time?"

I backed up from her, not tearing my gaze away from her relentless eyes until my knees bumped into the foot of the bed. Then, an unbidden sigh dragging itself from me, I sat down, finally turning my head to stare at the guitar.

"I don't . . . I mean . . . How? Exactly *what* are you suggesting? *Specifically.* Tell me that."

Minifrit glided forward, not coming back within arm's reach of me but regaining some proximity. Not enough to spook me, I noted with muted annoyance. I was being *handled.* Not exactly flattering, but if nothing else it was a hint that maybe she did know what she was talking about.

"I have dealt with things much like this, countless times. I will tell you up front that there are no certainties. It is *possible* that my best efforts will accomplish nothing—even *distantly* possible I might make it worse, though I consider that risk too small to be worth caring about. The brain is unfathomably complicated, Lord Seiji, and fixing it is never a certainty. Even so, the symptoms you are showing are part of a consistent pattern that I have seen and helped girls work through many times. There are methods that very often *can* help. It just takes time, and patience, and a willingness to do the work."

"Girls?" I said sardonically.

She smirked. "The great secret is that the minds of men and women are not so fundamentally different as most of us would like to think. I have mostly worked with girls because . . . I have mostly worked with girls. Come, you know what my profession was. The most common cause of their trauma was having been brutalized by men. Well, I couldn't justify providing room and board to a girl who would panic or have flashbacks when a man touched her, so I had to learn how to deal with it. The root problem of trauma is your brain mistakenly learning that something quite banal is incredibly dangerous, and throwing up extreme but false signals to warn you away whenever a reminder of the trauma occurs. With my girls, I used my bouncers. They're all good lads—I do not employ less than the best. Stable and *safe*, without a mean bone in their bodies. Bit by bit, I'd have them get the girls used to being around a man again."

"That's—you're talking about . . . hang on, there's an actual term for this." I thought there was, anyway. I'd read it somewhere, probably online. ". . . exposure therapy?"

Minifrit shrugged, causing me to avert my eyes. Her robe was . . . noticeably looser than usual.

"As good a term as any. It does seem to describe the process well enough."

I barked a short, harsh laugh. "So . . . what? You're planning to bang me straight? One good screw and I'm cured?"

She did not reciprocate the bitter humor. Minifrit moved slowly forward, and sank down on the foot of the bed—next to me, but not too close, eyes serious.

"It will not be that simple, or that fast, or that *easy*. To be frank, Lord Seiji, the way you tend to seize up at any reminder makes me suspect it will take a good bit of time and several sessions at least before you're even *able* to fuck me. And that, when we get there, will be a landmark achievement—probably the most significant one in your progress toward rehabilitation. But even so, it's not likely to be enough. These things can linger for years. You should expect that there will be ongoing pangs for a long time, regardless of my best efforts. What we should aim for is to *soothe* the effects of trauma, not banish them. It's about retraining your brain not to associate sex with terror and pain. Success will be . . . relative. A process that may never entirely end. On the other hand, a complete cure isn't impossible. We simply won't know until we have put in the work."

This was just surreal. I couldn't believe I was even having this conversation. The weirdest part was that her logic actually made a lot of sense.

"You know, if you just wanted to be the Dark Lord's mistress, you could just ask," I said, managing a strained approximation of a light tone. "It's not like you aren't qualified."

She raised a supercilious eyebrow. "Surely you don't imagine that I would hesitate to do so, if that's all I wanted. Lord Seiji . . . I'm accustomed to men refusing help out of simple stubbornness and machismo. Odd as it seems to say, that really doesn't feel like your problem. You have always been admirably willing to listen to advice and accept help—it's one of the reasons I find myself so willing to tolerate your . . . charming personality quirks." Her voice dropped slightly in pitch and volume, becoming gentle without dipping into condescension. It was really impressive vocal control. "What *is* this about? Is there something else you're afraid of?"

I couldn't look at her. I stared at the guitar, at the shuttered window . . .

At my own hands, which I didn't remember clasping so hard, but there they were.

"It's . . . I can't . . ." I shrugged, the motion awkward and jerky. "Look, I know what a hothouse orchid you must think I am already, right? Look at Seiji, he's always mad about indoor plumbing and how hard the chores are. Seiji comes from a glittering palace in the future and can't handle medieval life. I was never . . ." I had to swallow hard against the growing tension in my throat. "All I had to do was *see* it. All those women I healed . . . They just got back up and went back to work. Where the fuck do *I* get off being traumatized? Fucking *bullshit*. I just dealt with it one night a week, did my incredible magic and fucked off back into the forest. They all—*you* all had to go right back to it. It's . . . stupid. I can only imagine how contemptuous you must be."

There was quiet for enough seconds that I eventually, out of sheer dreadful anticipation, had to raise my eyes and find her gaze again. Minifrit wasn't looking at me with any of the contempt I expected. Also not with mercy or compassion, which was for the better; I don't think I could've stomached that. She just studied my face, her expression calm and interested.

"I do see your point," she mused after considering for another long moment. "The way you describe your country sounds downright utopian compared to anything in my frame of reference."

"I assure you, Japan is not a utopia."

"Well, obviously, it's full of people."

"Hah! And people are—"

"Yes, yes, I don't think one of your misanthropic tangents is going to be useful right now. Anything full of people is going to be *imperfect*. But you definitely describe a manner of life which is easier, in almost every respect, than the one I know. And I *can* relate that to something in my experience, if imprecisely. We used to get curious young highborn in Cat Alley, from time to time. And of those visits, there would occasionally be one who saw something . . . some fraction of what *you* kept coming there specifically to see." Her smile was mischievous, bitter, and faintly malicious. "The poor dears. They were so *terrorized*."

"See, that's exactly what I worried about," I exclaimed. "You looking at me like *that!*"

"I would never look at you like that," she replied, and in truth her smile did change. It was subtle, but there; just warm, maybe a little teasing, but without that cruel edge. I was constantly impressed by how Minifrit could manipulate the fine details of her face the same way I handled a guitar's strings. "Lord Seiji, you were yanked out of your whole life, dumped into a world where everything is harder and dirtier and more dangerous than anything you knew. You came to *our* little corner of hell and immersed yourself in the worst it had to offer, the darkest parts we worked so hard to conceal from our clients. And you *kept coming back*."

"Yeah, well, I can't say—"

"You had ulterior motives, I know. That doesn't change the basic fact that you *faced* what you saw and never once fled from it. Seiji." She leaned closer, still smiling, and shook her head. "I never once blamed you for being shocked or horrified by what you've seen. The idea is *absurd* to me. What stands out to me is that you—sour, snide, spiteful little shit that you are—have shown more spine and more *heart* than any aristocrat in this blighted country."

"Not that that's saying a lot . . ."

Minifrit chuckled ruefully. "And so quick to deflect. Well, look at it this way—whether or not you're *justified* in being traumatized is beside the point. If you fell down the stairs and broke your collarbone because you were trying to balance on a ball at their top, the injury wouldn't be any less in need of healing because you got it by being stupid. You require *treatment*. But I will, as the person proposing to administer this treatment, insist on one point for you to remember."

She scooted a bit closer to me, her smile widening as her voice dropped another register, taking on a huskier undertone.

"I am offering to help you mend an injury, because this organization of which I am a part depends on your leadership. But I am *also* offering to go to bed with you. Because . . . I would like to."

My breath caught, and not because I was so very moved. I had to squeeze my eyes shut and fight back a tremor of remembered panic that didn't belong in this situation.

Minifrit, consummate professional that she was, gave me a moment to recover my poise before continuing in a more casual and therefore less dangerous tone. "And also because I believe I can *trust* you not to do something wildly asinine like fall in love with me."

"Ah . . . heh." I shook my head. "Well. I'm definitely flattered, and interested. But, ah, no offense, Minifrit—"

"Here's some excellent advice which you will ignore—if you find yourself about to say something that needs to be prefaced with *that*, close your mouth. Seriously, this may just be the prejudices of my own life experience talking, but I'm firmly of the opinion that a powerful man suffers stresses and pressures which he can only properly relieve in a woman's body. Or another man's, I suppose, if that's what he prefers," she added with another mischievous little smirk. "The point is, it needn't be anything more intimate than that—and between you and me, to be honest, I'll be more comfortable with the assurance up front that it will not be."

Now it was I who raised an eyebrow and smirked. "No offense meant?"

"I wouldn't have said it if you were the type to take it personally," she retorted, grinning back. "Truly, Dark Lord, you're a little rich for my blood. It will be interesting to serve as your outlet for a while, as you establish yourself—quite the notch on my own already well-traveled belt. But we both have different destinies, you especially. A figure like you . . . Well, somewhere out there is a legendary romance—some Viryan witch or dark elven princess, or who knows what, just blithely trotting around without even suspecting the Dark Lord's signature is on the ribbon of her fate. And *when* that destined beauty finally deigns to turn up, I intend to hand you over to her in much better condition than I found you."

She paused, leaned back a bit, and cast her eyes rapidly up and down my form with a critical expression.

"Which is, simultaneously, not saying much and yet will be *quite* an undertaking. You, young man, are a wreck."

"Okay, I take a *little* offense at that one."

Minifrit grinned pure mischief at me, then her eyes cut past me and she cleared her throat.

"Ahem! Biribo, are you able to handle door latches, or do you require help?"

"Yeah, yeah, I got it," he groused. "Dunno why you big shaved apes are so convinced anybody *wants* to watch that anyway. C'mon, Junko, let's go for a walk. Trust me, girl, you don't wanna be in here."

He actually could handle the door latch, somewhat to my surprise; the only hurdle was that Junko required a firm order from me to follow the familiar out into the hall. I suspected neither of them would go far. Biribo seemed to be uncomfortable being separated from me by too much distance or time, and Junko . . . well, she was a dog.

"So, uh." I hated myself for the uncertainty that suddenly fell. For god's sake, it wasn't like I was some virgin. "How, erm . . . Ugh, you must think I'm being—"

"Shush." Minifrit placed one finger on my lips, smiling. "This is specifically unlike any of your previous experiences, in both purpose and execution.

And trust me, Seiji, I've seen boys far more self-conscious than you, with much more reason, and not judged them for it, either. We will go slowly. I'll try things . . . gently, a bit at a time . . ."

She eased closer, until she was almost pressing against me. I could feel her warm breath on my cheek as she murmured.

". . . and you'll try things. Whatever you feel comfortable with. Don't worry about me; I'm impossible to shock, and I don't mind being handled roughly. Still, go *slow*. A bit at a time, as we see how far we can push before you're triggered. Then we will stop, and make sure you're calm again before we try once more. All right?"

I nodded silently, not trusting my voice for a whole variety of reasons.

"There is no hurry," she whispered. Her forehead came to rest gently on my temple; her body eased forward until my arm was nestled between her breasts. Her *bare*— When had she opened her robe? "No further or faster than you can bear. There is no timetable and no rush. We'll stop for tonight before too much longer; you need some proper rest, and this needn't be solved in one day. But one . . . bit . . . at a time . . ."

I turned my head, caught her lips in my own as she tilted her face to accommodate. The taste of smoke, I decided, wasn't *that* terrible. Especially with that spicy-sweet smell about her.

She gently kissed my lips, slowly, repeating soft motions in no hurry. Gradually, I felt some of the expectant tension ease from my shoulders as an episode failed to occur. With a soft murmur of satisfaction, she pressed a little forward, offering her tongue, accepting mine.

So far so good.

I slipped an arm around her waist to hold her; hers wrapped around my neck. A bit further, and I was still okay. I leaned into her, moved my other hand. She made a soft noise of approval into my mouth as I lightly squeezed her breast, lifting its weight—

It was as if all the suspended trauma that should've triggered for the last few minutes hit at once, in one of the worst flashbacks yet. I was drowning, surrounded by blood and the sickly stink of rot. Couldn't breathe, people were dying, women screamed on all sides—

It only gradually receded, and Minifrit was holding me, her grip firm and comforting without a hint of the erotic questing from just moments ago, her quiet voice devoid of that huskiness. Just soothing, like she was talking to a high-strung animal.

"It's okay, you're all right. You're safe, it's fine. That was a good start. It's okay. Just breathe, Seiji. A breath at a time. In . . . out . . . That's the way. There's no hurry."

I realized I was gripping her hard enough to bruise again and winced.

"Uh . . . sorry. **Heal**."

Minifrit smiled through the flash of pink light. "You can probably save that for the end of the night. You're very unlikely to do any real harm in panicked flailing—and I told you, I've no objections to picking up a few little scrapes and bruises. Don't worry about me. Are you okay? Ready to try again?"

"I, uh . . ."

"Don't force it. I'm here to help you, not just playing around."

I nodded. "Just . . . lemme settle my breathing."

"Of course. Take whatever time you need."

"That was a really frustrating place to break," I said, trying for a little levity. "Like, *terrible* timing. Do you *know* how long I've been waiting to get my hands on those things?"

She grinned. "You and everyone else. Don't worry, we'll get there, and I assure you they're worth it."

"If you do say so yourself."

"It's a professional guarantee."

I needed a bit more time to feel calm enough to try again. She didn't push. For the first time, though I was almost afraid to, I began to feel like this might eventually be okay.

39

In Which the Dark Lord Destroys

I did not have sex with Minifrit that night, because as usual she was annoyingly right about everything. The work was . . . exhausting. This might be the weirdest therapy I'd ever heard of and probably wouldn't fly in any doctor's office on Earth, but the fact remained that it was therapy, and it was a lot more challenging than it was enjoyable. Having flashbacks and panic attacks repeatedly triggered will take it *out* of you; we just didn't get that far before I was too wiped out to keep going. I think it was less than an hour, in the end, before she declared that I needed to rest and take time to process everything, and slipped off back to her room. At that point I didn't have it in me to argue.

I was too keyed up to actually sleep, of course, and oddly not because I'd just had an hour of intermittent foreplay that went nowhere; it wasn't that kind of keyed up. The traumatic episodes were just . . . a lot.

At that point, it was late enough that when I went down to take a hot bath, I had the place to myself. And afterward, I slept more easily and more deeply than I had in the longest time.

The nice thing about the morning after was that Minifrit was a consummate professional. There was no awkwardness, or any indication at all that anything of import had happened between us. No, she just turned up at breakfast her usual self—politely pushing at me as hard as she could without actually challenging my authority.

"Let me get this straight," I said, setting down my bowl of porridge. "After *all that* yesterday, you want me to just sit on my thumbs in this fortress all day?"

"Clearly not," she said with subdued exasperation. "There is plenty to be done around North Watch that doesn't involve traipsing through the forest and confronting the cat tribe."

"They *need* to be dealt with!"

"Very much so. Specifically, they need to be dealt with in the most effective way possible—by a Dark Lord who is *well-rested* and at the top of his game. You can take a day to catch your breath."

"I dunno about *that* reasoning, but I do agree with her ultimate conclusion, Lord Seiji," Sakin chimed in.

"This is mutiny," I complained. "I am being ganged up on."

"Kinda the opposite, if you think about it," noted Aster, who was digging into her own breakfast next to me. "They probably have the same opinions as yesterday, but nobody was willing to push you when you were *that* angry. Best we could manage at the time was talking you down from getting yourself killed in the forest."

"You, too, Aster?"

She shrugged, smiled, and chomped another spoonful.

"I confess I find myself curious," Minifrit said, barely short of open disdain as she gave Sakin a look out the corner of her eye. "By what reasoning did *you* arrive at the same conclusion?"

"Why, how could I turn down such a gracious invitation?" he said sweetly. Even when they agreed, these two just had to butt heads about *something*. "But yes, Lord Seiji, you've been gone from the fortress for a while, and we've got a lot of the new faces you've gathered up here. Regardless of how your extended maneuvers out there may have tired *you* out, I think it's an important moment to make your presence felt around North Watch."

"Crack some heads and assert dominance?"

I did not miss the wary glances shot my way from several nearby tables.

"Wouldn't really match up with your leadership style, now would it?" Sakin said airily. "On the contrary, I think it'd best serve to have you around so the new blood can see how positively the old blood reacts to you. You're pretty popular among the troops for a bandit boss, Lord Seiji. That's an asset; you should leverage it."

"Hnh," I grunted, looking over at Aster. "Well, go on, I suppose you agree with them, too?"

"I cannot in good conscience weigh in on this, due to my lack of personal objectivity," she intoned. "We've been stomping around in the wilderness and/or the Gutters for weeks, and I *really* wanna take a day to sit quietly in the castle."

"No reason you can't do that while I go talk to the cats," I pointed out.

She just gave me a vintage Aster Look.

"I'm honestly kind of impressed how you can do that with your mouth full."

"Lord Seiji." Minifrit gave me one of her own masterful looks, no-nonsense and yet gently supportive. I really needed to have her teach me how to do stuff like that with my face. "The situation is stable. Take the day, rest yourself and reassure our people with your presence. *Then* settle the cat tribe when you are at your best."

I sighed, grudgingly, and poked at my porridge with my spoon. Creamed grains with peppers, spices, and little bits of some kind of pickled meat. It was pleasantly filling and not bland; I was actually somewhat annoyed at how much I'd started to like some of the food here. Once you adapted to the sinus-blasting amount of peppers the Fflyr put in everything, it really wasn't bad.

"Fine. *One* day."

So I took the day off.

At least, that was what it felt like to me, coming as it did when I had an immediate need to address the situation with the cat tribe and my plans closer to Gwyllthean were unfolding in my absence. All of this, though, was according to strategy, and as my advisors had pointed out, it wasn't as if there was nothing to do around North Watch.

In the early days, yeah, it had gotten downright boring out here at times. Back then it was just me, Aster, and Rocco's old gang, and we'd kept busy by cleaning and fixing things with the knowledge that the fortress would likely finish collapsing before our meager efforts could finish restoring it. Aster and I would be gone for a couple of days once a week on our Gwyllthean trips, and . . . that was it.

Somehow, since then, this had become a whole *organization*. There was a command structure, divisions of labor, and North Watch was always full of voices and activity. With new recruits brought in and some of my earlier ones dispersed through the khora and bandit camps near the city, the fortress's population still hovered around a hundred, though my total followers numbered close to half again that many. Surprisingly enough, considering we were ultimately a big gang of bandits building up toward an insurrection, the atmosphere around North Watch was cheerful and energetic.

My own role had grown and changed, and ironically, I was less free than before. With a larger and less intimate core of followers—more people than I could manage to have personal relationships with—it became necessary to cultivate my image in place of that. For one thing, this meant I could no longer join in the training sessions that were a big part of everyone's daily activities. Oh, I was still *getting* training, but in private sessions behind closed doors. I still had the martial skills of a musician and part-time store clerk who'd been practicing for a couple months. Right now, most of the people we had giving lessons could kick my ass easily, and that was the problem—you couldn't have the Dark Lord plowed face-first into the dirt a dozen times during a sparring session in front of all his minions. With just a handful of us who had nobody to talk to but each other, that was funny—a bonding experience, even. When we were a nascent army, it was a hazard to morale.

Which was not to say I was a conventional leader; I'd never have been able to pull that off. I bet most Dark Lords, bandit bosses, or military rulers in general didn't provide musical entertainment during lunch and dinner, but fuck it. I'd compromise to the extent of not looking weak for their benefit, but these people needed to get used to me as I was, and they'd pry my guitar from my cold, dead fingers. Happily enough, this seemed to improve my popularity. If anybody thought playing for the troops was unbecoming of a leader, they didn't dare say so.

Most of what I ended up doing on my day off was . . . touring. I stood watch over several training sessions, was shown around areas of the castle that had recently been cleaned out or were in the process of being refurbished, inspected all the defenses. Kasser and Minifrit had been doing very well; the walls were all navigable now, with walkways and barricades of akorshil planks in place of the broken spots. They were also heavily watched—every sentry in immediate view of at least two others at all times, as Sakin had recommended, all carrying alarm horns and with barrels containing healing slimes positioned at regular intervals, as well as bottled light slimes. The refurbished gates still weren't ready to be hung—Harold was working on the hinges and fasteners, but they were *large*, and we didn't have any other skilled ninwrights to help him—so the open gateway had improvised defenses in the meantime. Spiked barricades covered the open space, light enough to be moved but sturdy enough to mess up an enemy charge, and four guards in the best armor we could scrape together stood right behind them in the gateway itself, supported by crossbow-wielding sentries above.

I guess Sakin was right about my popularity, given how a gaggle of whoever wasn't currently on duty kept following me everywhere, except when I was receiving reports in private, like my detailed sessions with Minifrit and Kasser on their progress. Junko stuck by my side every minute; Aster, by contrast, barely put in an appearance all day, evidently serious about wanting a break. I guess this was the first time in a while I'd been in a position where she didn't feel I needed a bodyguard. Others came and went as they had time, though, of course I had my usual hangers-on.

There were a few who seemed to feel a loyalty toward me that verged on hero worship, which I found uncomfortable in the extreme, though how that manifested depended on the individual. Kastrin, for example, was quiet, focused, and generally good company; you could forget she was there, until she suddenly came out with one of those sly jokes of hers. She was my oldest fan, and had always hung around me since I'd first healed her back in Cat Alley. Ydleth's company was . . . less comfortable. After I stood up for her during her embarrassing public to-do with Sicellit she seemed to have decided I was the best thing since wyddh and also hovered around, eager to please. Unfortunately, Ydleth was loud, pushy, seemed to respect no one, and was prone to starting arguments. Fortunately, Minifrit usually turned up to peel her away for some task before she wore down my patience. The handy thing about Ydleth was that she was consistently on some punishment duty or other.

Nothing was perfect, but all told . . . it wasn't a bad day. In the end, I had to acknowledge that Aster and Minifrit—and Sakin, I supposed—had been right. I felt better for having taken time to oversee my people, and they seemed happy to have had me around.

In the quiet wind-down after dinner, I decided on a pure whim to take another quick stroll along the walls, just to stretch my legs a bit before retiring for the night. We hadn't discussed it, so I didn't know whether Minifrit planned on another "session" that evening, though if she showed up I'd already decided, somewhat regretfully, that I would have to ask for a rain check. If the whole point of taking a day of rest was to be fully charged and ready to deal with the cat tribe at my very best tomorrow, spending part of the night twisting my psyche into knots would be counterproductive. Even if it did mean getting my hands all over a particularly magnificent set of curves. Traumatic flashbacks just suck all the fun out of everything.

For what might have been the first time that day, I was alone, nobody having latched onto me as people wandered away from the mess hall after dinner. Even Junko had finally left my side, apparently reassured that I wasn't going to disappear again. She was likely off pestering every sucker in my employ who loved dogs more than they feared the Dark Lord; I was pretty sure Junko had identified every soul in this place who would give her snacks in defiance of my orders.

The sentries greeted me but, to my satisfaction, didn't divert attention from their duty. They'd had a recent reminder that they were the first line of defense against an invisible assassin, after all.

My steps slowed as I crossed a particular section of wall, turning to gaze out over the darkened khora forest with its multicolored fronds waving gently against the stars. This was the same spot where I'd stumbled to a halt in my first minutes on Ephemera as I fled from Kasser and Harold, the place where I'd seen the alien forest out there and it had sunk in just how far from home I was. Instead of a shadowed ruin of a fortress, though, this was now a well-lit stretch of wall, swept clean of rubble, with crossbow-holding soldiers sworn to me at either end of this stretch between the tower and the main building. Strange . . . That had only been a few months ago, but already the memory seemed nostalgic. Given time, filled with experiences, perhaps even the khora could become . . .

No, khora forests were still weird as hell. I missed trees. I guess I was a little more comfortable with it, though.

"They're watching us, boss," Biribo said quietly.

A shiver made its way down my spine, and I rested a hand on the battlements, resisting the urge to duck down behind them.

"They?"

"Cats. They've put sentries out there in the khora. In perches high up."

"Are they going to attack?"

"Hmm . . . Well I can't read minds, but this looks to me like a defensive posture. We got nine individuals, widely separated, up in rough hunting blinds. That seems more like sentries—not even as many as we have on the walls. And only arranged along the side between North Watch and their village, not encircling us. Also there's a bigger group of 'em, way out at the very edge of my senses, but just holding there. If I was planning an attack, this isn't how I'd start. Looks like they're just keeping an eye on us. Standing ready in case we make a move."

"Not unreasonable for them to do," I murmured, staring out in the deep shadows amid the khora fronds, where apparently there were cat people staring back at me. I couldn't see them, but on the well-lit walls, I knew I would be easily visible. "Well. I'll settle them tomorrow."

"This ain't gonna be like anybody you've dealt with before, boss. They're just trying to live in the shadow of greater powers. Most likely they're already afraid of you, and feel cornered. The tribe's less malicious than a lot of the fuckers we've had to deal with, but cornered people do stupid things."

"Yeah, I know. We have a lot more to offer each other as allies, and that's what I'll emphasize. I probably won't get out of there without having to make some kind of show of force, but . . . In the end it comes down to mutual self-interest. Ruling them by force is way too much trouble, and I'm not willing to wipe them out. We'll *have* to settle on . . . something."

He made no reply, just buzzing softly over my shoulder as usual. After another few seconds of contemplation, I resumed my slow course along the wall.

"Lord Seiji," Kastrin said with a warm smile as I drew close. She was in position just outside the tower door, a sensible assignment for our best shot. "Just taking the night air?"

"One last stretch of the legs," I agreed. "It's back to work tomorrow."

"There's always something," she said softly, gazing out into the dark.

"I know you are anyway, but . . . keep your eyes sharp. Biribo says the cats are lurking out there."

"I heard," she said, nodding, "and suspected anyway. We've never *seen* them, but there are those tracks that show up in the morning . . . And we've all noticed it, those of us on night duty. Feels like we're being watched. Sicellit says it's just tension, but . . ."

"Sicellit's probably right, generally speaking, though in this case we actually are being watched."

"Yeah, well, don't tell her that," Kastrin muttered. "There's no living with her as it is."

I chuckled, pulling open the tower door. It blocked my view of the forest as I paused just before stepping over the threshold. "Interested in being part of my guard tomorrow when I go see them? I can't promise it'll be a safe assignment, but I could use a crack shot on hand in case things go south."

She turned from her steady perusal of the forest, grinning, and opened her mouth to reply.

"*DUCK!*" Biribo yelled suddenly.

Neither of us even had time to comply. The arrow whipped out of the darkness, and his shout only gave me enough warning to be watching directly when it slammed through Kastrin's head. She toppled silently off the wall.

To my eternal shame, I was frozen completely by shock for a full second. It lasted until a second arrow hit the door next to me, its head penetrating through the akorshil plank centimeters from my eye.

Warning horns blared from multiple points along the wall; I heard someone scream, and at the other end of the stretch of wall before me Jadrin dropped smoothly to one knee, taking aim between crenelations with her crossbow. She didn't fire, though, unable to spot a target. More shafts whistled as they came out of the night, shooting over the battlements now that there were no easy targets and apparently just peppering the grounds at random.

I filled my lungs to capacity in one breath and roared with the absolute maximum projection my trained voice could manage, "GET THE KIDS INSIDE!"

"Boss, the main group's coming closer!" Biribo shrilled. "The snipers are keeping us pinned down so they can attack! Looks like a force of about forty—it's a full raid!"

I dropped to the floor, lurching to the inner edge of the wall so I could peer over it at the crumpled form at its base.

"Heal!"

I immediately cursed my haste—healing her with that shaft *through* her skull would only . . . But it didn't matter. The spell failed to activate as it had no valid targets. You can't heal a corpse.

This was what happened because I took a day off.

Turning, I rushed inside the tower and down the stairs to the base, intercepting the two armed women in there who were trying to run up the same stairs to reinforce the wall.

"No!" I shouted at them. "Get down and cover the gates!"

We burst out into a courtyard in pandemonium. Unarmed people were fleeing inside the fortress or towers, while others bearing weapons rushed forward to join the fray. I saw someone else drop with a strangled scream as an unlucky arrow landed in them. They were still alive, though, so I diverted my attention for the moment.

As I'd expected, the gate was the weakest point. Three of the watchers there had taken cover behind the walls, but one was lying behind the barricades with an arrow sticking out of her chest. As I turned to take in the situation, the woman nearest me lunged forward, trying to grab her friend and pull her back to safety. She immediately cried out as she was pinned down by another shaft.

Then Aster was there, charging fearlessly into the open. Greatsword still strapped to her back, she bent and grabbed both fallen sentries, hauling them back into shelter. Two more arrows struck her, sticking in her coat and failing to make any impression on the artifact chain mail beneath it.

"Lord Seiji," said one of the tower sentries I'd dragged out with me, "what do we do?"

The rage had washed over me before I'd noticed it coming, but this time it brought crystal clarity and heightened alertness, along with an eerie kind of calm floating over the roaring sea of bloodlust. Not the same as the Wisdom perk that shielded me from pain, just . . . an overdose of adrenaline. And to my own surprise, within its grip, I found myself forming a plan.

"Everyone to me!" I shouted. "Those on this side of the gates—don't cross the gap if you're over there, get inside the tower and up to the battlements! The rest of you, form up behind me. I want a rank—no, three ranks of archers *right* behind this point. See where the arrows have fallen? That's their range, form up within the shelter of the wall and they can't hit you. You! You and—okay, everybody with a *sword* come forward. Crossbowmen behind them, shoot through the gaps. When they come through the gates, *this* is the kill zone. You will *tear them apart*. Aster, take the lead here."

She was already moving into position next to me, sword in hand. To either side of us, bandits with a variety of swords were spacing themselves out to either side of her, leaving room between them for our archers to shoot through. A hasty line of women and a few men had formed behind them, dropping to kneel with a second line still getting into position at their backs, ready to fire over their shoulders. Others were straggling into place in the third rank I'd called for, loading bolts and preparing to take over when the second rank dropped. Fortunately this was one of the maneuvers Sakin had trained them in. Behind *them*, more stragglers were rushing forward with healing slimes to treat the wounded.

"This formation won't hold long," Aster said curtly.

I knew that, but I'd just had an idea. A wonderful, terrible, Dark Lord of an idea.

"Maybe not against a charge," I replied. "But when they come rushing in here in a panic, it'll do. No hesitation, no mercy. When you're out of ammo, *then* consider taking prisoners."

She nodded. "What are you going to do?"

"What I do best. Hold this line, Aster."

I turned and dashed back into the fortress. Through the front gates, to the side and up the angled staircase. Again, I found myself repeating the run I'd made when I first landed in this fortress—this time with the same urgency as before. Except that instead of fleeing for my life, I was charging toward bloody retribution. Ignoring the shouts of those I passed, I made it all the way up to the door to the observation platform where I had first used spell combination, discovered Immolate, and inflicted it on two men who would somehow, eventually, forgive me.

This time, there was a ladder against the wall, thanks to Kasser's ongoing repairs, leading up to a trapdoor that opened onto the actual tower roof. My limbs burning with adrenaline and fury, I practically flew up the rungs, punching the trapdoor so hard its latch tore loose, and in the next second, I was standing on the flat top of North Watch's highest tower, looking out over the fortress all around me, the dark forest spread out at my feet, the shape of the mountain rising up in the distance behind.

Still, my enemies were invisible, snipers hidden among the fronds while those moving forward to attack properly hadn't yet emerged from beneath their shelter. But I was well out of their range up here, if they could even see me.

I fixed my gaze on one towering khora just beyond the front gates and closest to the walls, one of those with huge spiked plates like a moose's antlers which sprouted waving fronds. It occurred to me that I probably should have tested this down there before I'd climbed up here to this vantage; if it didn't work I had just wasted all that energy and abandoned my forces for nothing. But it should work. They were living things, after all.

I pointed and roared into the night.

"Immolate!"

Oh, it worked all right.

Orange fire rent the darkness as every bit of soft tissue in the huge khora combusted. The gently waving fronds disintegrated immediately, giving way to gouts of seething fire. Every aperture in its shell was lit up like a furnace—no, it *became* a furnace, a towering structure of armor plates from within which flames spewed in every direction.

My face was twisted in a grin of cruel triumph.

You want blood? *You got it.*

Immolate! Immolate! Immolate! Immolate! Immolate! Immolate! Immolate! Immolate! Immolate! Immolate! Immolate! Immolate! Immolate! Immolate!

I turned in a complete circle, casting my spell of ultimate horror at every khora in a line around North Watch's walls. In seconds, we were encircled by a ring of fire, and the forest outside became a *very* inhospitable place to be. Then, having come back to my starting point, I began igniting more of them in a line away from the gates, creating a swath of pure hell leading straight over the path the raiders would have to take to our gates.

Attack my home? *My people?* Then you can *all fucking BURN*. And tomorrow, the rest of them would be next!

Savage vindication gave way to confusion when, suddenly, a khora at which I hadn't even aimed yet burst into flame.

What? These things were explicitly not flammable; this only worked because of goddess-granted magic. The underbrush might ignite, but other than that, the flames *couldn't* spread. It wasn't like a forest of wood and leaves . . .

But it did. As I watched, confused, more of them went up. It began extending out from us on all sides of the ring; one after another, khora burst alight, fronds dissolving into hungry tongues of flame. And the more it spread, the *faster* it spread, until my ring of fire was inexplicably racing in all directions past the edge of my vision.

And only then did my stomach plummet as I realized what I'd just done.

I remembered Aster casually explaining, on that first walk into Gwyllthean, that khora plantations could only be cultivated on islands where they grew wild; that they spread through underground root networks. Kasser, excitedly telling me that North Watch stood in what he called a "tangle," an area where multiple different khora species intermixed. He'd been so happy at being able to harvest materials from so many kinds.

They weren't trees; they weren't *like* trees, except maybe aspens. Or mycelium. Each free-standing shell was only the surface part, one node of a vast organism spreading across the island beneath its surface. Of *multiple* such beings.

I had just sent the effects of my Immolate blazing through every one of them, and it wouldn't stop until it covered the entirety of Dount.

My fierce triumph was gone in an instant, and with it the rage, leaving me in mental freefall as I grappled with the enormity of what I had just viciously set in motion.

Dear god, the *plantations*. There was an unstoppable tidal wave of fire racing toward Gwyllthean—right through the half-gathered harvest. Countless little villages and Clan estates stood right on the edges of khora groves, with no idea they were all about to burn. The beastfolk tribes—not just the cats attacking me, but *every* tribe's village. *My people* were out there, encamped amid the khora and totally unaware of what was about to roar across them. Somewhere out there, Sato was alone in the darkness as it dissolved into fire all around him. Somewhere else, the lone, desperate dark elf who'd tried to help us was the same.

Fuck, I'd just remembered that those root systems ran *through the goblin tunnels*; the ability to extract reagents from them directly was most of why goblin alchemy was more advanced than the Fflyr's, despite their relative lack of resources. And to the west, where the khora marched into a swamp that became the lake in which stood Shylverrael . . . All that water was about to flash into steam as the khora themselves began to blaze. Right through the lizardfolk and naga colonies, which answered to the Viryan city. The dark elves were going to have . . . *opinions* about this.

That was as far as I got in my mental tally of the unfolding catastrophe before I suddenly learned something new—khora had voices.

They came in at the edges of hearing, beginning to appear from beyond both the upper and lower registers of human perception. The noise reminded me simultaneously of whale song and the subsonic vibrations of an earthquake, at once piercing and booming. I didn't even know if they normally sang and I just couldn't hear it, or if they only cried out when they were suffering. If their voices only grew intense enough to be heard when they were in the extremity of pain.

I stood on my tower, surrounded by an endless ocean of fire of my own creation, listening to the island itself wail in agony beneath me, cut through by the constant roar of fire. I could barely hear my own unbidden whisper, in English.

"I am become death, the destroyer of worlds."

Then, finally, *blessedly*, the Wisdom perked kicked in and I was floating coldly above it, able to think clearly again.

The immediate situation was . . . probably resolved. If the attackers hadn't been wiped out entirely by this, the rest would probably try to escape through the invitingly open gates of the fortress, the only place *not* actively on fire, only to be cut down by the massed crossbows ready and waiting for them. My plan was working and my people were safe. That was one crisis handled.

There were a whole lot more now unfolding crises I was going to have to start dealing with immediately. First off, I noted that this burn effect was already lasting far longer than Immolate usually did. Was its duration relative to the target's mass? Interesting. The first thing to—

"Boss."

Biribo, I observed, was glowing. *This* I had never seen before. A silver aura blazed around him like concentrated moonlight.

"Wisdom perk unlocked, Dark Lord."

Fucking Wisdom perks. The rules of this system *aggressively* refused to make sense. Still, I would take what I could get.

"Good. What did we get this time?"

"Nothing permanent. This one is more of a one-time gift—a perk available only to the Champions of the Goddesses. When a Hero or Dark Lord first unleashes their power on the world in a way that *cannot* be ignored, they get one . . . freebie. An unfiltered answer drawn from magic itself, unrestricted by the limits of what a familiar can sense by themselves."

Yeah . . . the world would definitely notice *this*. My carefree days of establishing myself in anonymity were about to come crashing to an end. But if I got a free answer out of it, *any* answer, to *any* question . . . Shit, the trouble was picking one. There was so damn much I didn't know; prospects flashed across my consciousness almost too rapidly to tally.

"And how long do I have to decide on a question?"

"You don't pick, boss," he said apologetically. "It's assigned to you. That's the effect of the Blessing."

Effect of the Blessing, my ass. I was about to see whatever tidbit Virya thought would produce the most entertaining show.

"For this one, Dark Lord—your enemy. *She* is here. It was Lady Gray who incited the cat tribe to attack, and she's *with* them, out there beyond the walls. Not killed by the fire, but very much vulnerable to it. And tonight, thanks to this perk, there is no artifact or spell or *anything* that can hide her from *me*."

There were so many things that were so much more objectively important than that bullshit, but in that moment? I could only agree with Virya's choice. Beneath the cold pall of the Wisdom's emotional protection, beneath the horror and the rage that surged outside this unnatural bubble of calm, there was a thread of satisfaction. I grabbed it like a lifeline.

Finally.

Damage control later; right now?

No more fucking cockroach.

"Bring me to her."

40

In Which the Dark Lord Puts His Foot Down

With my uncannily glowing familiar leading the way, I slid down the ladder to the landing below and threw myself down the stairs, which was not just a turn of phrase; I descended in a long series of jumps that, as often as not, resulted in ungainly crashes at the next landing down, followed by a pink flash of Heal so I could do it again.

A distant part of my brain was aware that Lady Gray was no longer a high priority and hadn't been for a while, and that I had seized on this in desperation to feel like I was in control of *something*, but . . . what of it? The truth was there was very little I could immediately do about the disaster unfolding out there. But this? *This* I could finally put an end to. In my blank Wisdom fugue I even recognized it as the strategically correct action right now. She was a problem left unsolved for far too long, and the solution had just been handed to me. It was well past time.

The stairs terminated in the foyer area that stood between the mess hall and the doors to the courtyard; as soon as I hit the ground there I heard voices from behind me, where noncombatants had fled indoors to huddle. Right where any invaders would first burst in, if they made it past the outer defenses. Someone shouted a question at me, indistinct under all the noise.

"Get back to your rooms, shut the doors, and barricade them!" I shouted, already yanking the main door open.

Taking a second to shove it closed behind me gave me a brief opportunity to appreciate my terrible success. The space inside the fortress's open gates was strewn with bodies, and apparently none belonged to my people; I got a brief impression of fur-coated forms with odd limbs and tails and animal heads, solidified as two more tried to dash inside and were immediately shot down, as the only escape route from the fire brought them in front of a line of crossbows behind a line of swords, all in the hands of very angry bandits.

That was as much spectating as I could manage before Biribo, darting ahead to the gates, yelled at me. "This way, boss!"

"What did you *do*?!" Aster shouted as I dashed past. I didn't have time to explain, charging out into the inferno.

Even as I emerged from the shelter of the walls, another cat person came running at me. He threw aside the spear he was holding, waving both hands at me and yelling something completely muffled by the noise of fire and khora, howling now that we were directly in it. Those hands had digits tipped in very long claws.

Immolate, Windburst! I turned him into a comet shooting back into the rest of the fire.

Under the glow of orange flames, I had momentarily lost sight of Biribo; in looking around for him I beheld other cat tribesmen hunkered down against the base of the walls from the outside, getting as far from the flames as they could without risking the gates. Even as I watched, one of them dropped as someone on the ramparts leaned over with a crossbow and shot straight down.

Then Biribo came dashing back to me, bobbing in front of my face for a second before zooming off down the road. Fixing my eyes on his tiny figure, I followed at a careless run. Black and limned by a silver glow, he was only somewhat distinct against the surrounding flames; I knew if I took my gaze off him I'd lose him again.

He led me straight down the road, the familiar path turned into a surreal nightmare of open space beneath an overarching vault of burning, wailing khora. Even the ground was more dangerous; the big red vine-like growths were untouched, but the khora roots that had buckled through the ancient paving were now venting orange flickers and gouts of steam through cracks in their shells. Even as I pounded through the obstacle course, a huge column of that same tubular structure toppled with a tremendous crash behind me, already charred almost to oblivion by the burning of the khora around which it had been wrapped. And still, I understood why the familiar led me this way; this all but had to be where Lady Gray had taken refuge. There might be other sheltered spots out there in the forest, but to get to them she'd have to pass through the roaring chaos. Even here the heat was overwhelming and the air felt thin.

The flame showed no sign of subsiding. It had already been much longer than the effects of Immolate usually lasted; I had no way of knowing how long this would go on. Once it was over, my target's potential cover would become a lot more hospitable again, and chasing her down would become that much harder. That could not happen. This pest and her bullshit were coming to an end *tonight*.

Biribo's shrill cry was barely audible amid all the noise; if it contained actual words, I couldn't distinguish them. But his glow dived forward and began swooping in circles around one person-sized area of space, and that was all I needed.

Windburst!

It sent Biribo hurtling away, unfortunately; that was what I got for casting spells on pure, adrenaline-fueled instinct. But it also hit the intended target, and I got the distinct pleasure of seeing a fallen length of burning vine the size of a tree trunk shatter as Gray was smashed through it. She flickered into view on the surface of the road, losing her grip on her artifact dagger.

I tried an Immolate, but she was still wearing that artifact that made her untargetable by spells. Slimeshot didn't work for the same reason, and the Sparkspray I fired as I closed in was thwarted by just how far I'd blown her; the sparks dissipated before they got there. Meanwhile, she scrambled to her feet, turning and running, and to my great annoyance, immediately found and picked up her dagger, vanishing from sight again.

But it had been enough time for Biribo to return to the fray; he swooped in and began another set of tight circles, now also darting up and down as he dodged swipes of the dagger. This time I concentrated on closing the distance, having learned the lesson of using Windburst under these circumstances.

Before I could reach them, the glowing familiar vanished off the path, following our target as she fled desperately into the burning khora. It was another second before I got there and was able to see the opening into what had been some kind of game trail; much tighter quarters, hotter and licked by angrier surrounding flames, but big enough for a person to pass through, especially now that the underbrush had been incinerated.

I could still see Biribo circling rapidly and had an idea.

Slimeshot!

Well, look at that, I found a loophole. I might not be able to target Lady Gray with spells, but if she was invisible and yet I knew exactly where she was, I could sure as hell target that little slice of "empty" space with a spell.

The direct impact sent her flying forward, once again bursting through a barrier of burning debris where another of those huge vines had landed in a now-dried and crumbling bush. I could just barely see a patch of relative dimness beyond; I'd just shot her into an open clearing of some kind, but the collapsing rubbish immediately tumbled inward to block the path again.

Windburst! I turned the barrier into a spray of burning charcoal shards, charging through the gap before it could close in again. Not a moment too soon, either; I could hear something cracking at an ominous volume, audible even through all the surrounding noise.

But this was the end of the line. This was a patch of clear area in the shelter between three huge khora growths—one of those dome-like structures that looked like brain coral the size of a house, and two enormous trunks of the antler-shaped khora. There were only two ways into the lopsided depression between them, the still-collapsing trail now behind me and another that was completely obstructed by a fallen length of red vine thicker than a car and actively on fire.

Biribo was still marking my target in a tight orbit, but even as I closed in he was sent spinning away with a shrill cry as she finally landed a hit. I fired a Sparkspray into the space he'd been marking, realizing my error a second later—surrounded as we were by fire on all sides, I couldn't even tell whether I'd landed a hit as any lingering sparks on an invisible body were completely indistinguishable from the rest of the flames.

But there was only one exit from this trap, and I was standing in front of it. Bracing my feet, I began firing Sparksprays steadily in every direction; if she wanted out, she was going to have to face me.

From behind me there came another loud crackle, as well as the beginning of a long rumbling crash as more burning lengths of vine that had been suspended in the branches above began to fall.

I knew what it would mean, but I didn't have a choice; I kept flinging Sparksprays, but at random as I risked diverting my attention to look up and make sure I wasn't about to be crushed. Sure enough, I had to take two judicious steps forward to be safe, and she recognized my one moment of inattention and capitalized on it.

Or tried to.

I only knew the direction from which Lady Gray tried to close in on me because, snarling furiously, Junko shot right past my leg, barely making it through the gap before the rubble crashed down, and clamped her jaws down on an invisible leg. The huge dog savagely shook her head, worrying her quarry and likely yanking Gray right off her feet.

A second later Junko let out a shrill yelp and a crimson wound appeared in her side.

I saw white.

"*SLIMESHOT*! Heal!"

The impact hurled the invisible woman away, and the second spell instantly remedied the damage done to Junko. Biribo returned to the fray again, diving down to mark my quarry, but this time I barely needed him. That dagger apparently didn't fool the dog's nose; Junko went right for her again, once more getting her jaws around a limb and jerking viciously back and forth.

This time, the woman popped back into view with a strangled scream, revealing that Junko had bitten down on her right arm, causing the dagger to drop from her fingers.

Behind me came another huge crash, and I dodged forward, half-spinning to look. This time it was due to a massive horizontal sweep of an artifact greatsword, pulverizing the burning wreckage that had fallen across the game trail behind us. It took two more swipes to clear the way properly, but then Aster stepped into the clearing, taking in the entire scene at a glance and then turning to me for direction.

"Perfect timing," I said. Loudly, but I was still more audible than I'd expected; was it getting quieter? "Block the opening. Junko, release her. Fetch *that*."

The dog dropped Lady Gray's mangled arm, instead grabbing the dagger's handle in her jaws and trotting over to me. She dropped the priceless artifact into the dirt at my feet.

"Good girl." I stroked her head once before closing in on my fallen enemy.

It was definitely quieter now. As I watched, I could see the flames beginning to visibly diminish. Not at the same rate all around; the huge dome was still venting gouts of fire through the cracks in its shell, but the branched khora had dimmed noticeably, now only steaming and emitting a faint intermittent glow through the apertures where their burned-away fronds belonged.

And there she lay. Crumpled, soot-covered, her clothes ragged and her body visibly wounded, even aside from the fresh lacerations where the arm she was now cradling against her chest had just been mauled. I could see stained bandages through rents in her sleeves and one wrapping around her upper torso, visible through the open neck of her coat, a reminder of her recent humbling at the hands of my standoffish dark elf ally.

This was just . . . pitiful. There was going to be no grand, dramatic final duel with this . . . creature. Just an old woman, exhausted, hungry, and wounded, now cornered and at the mercy of two powerful Blessed and a huge dog. The fearsome crime lord who had reigned uncontested over the Gutters was long since starved and withered away. I could almost find it in me to feel sorry for *this* bedraggled remnant, had I been able to forget for one second that she had *murdered five orphans just to piss me off.*

The flames subsided further. The branching khora had gone inert and, in fact, were visibly regenerating their fronds overhead. Across from them, the dome was steaming with no more glow. Quiet was descending, the khora no longer screaming in pain and the sound of falling vines occurring intermittently in the near distance. The air wasn't much cooler, but there was little enough active flame now that the noise was faint and not nearby.

Gray coughed, then managed a bloodstained grin up at me. "Well, well. So you finally—"

No, she did not get to make a final speech.

Summon Healing Slime, Tame Beast.

I conjured the slime in my own hands, and silenced her last words by hurling it directly into her face.

Now it was time for the real retribution.

I had given a *lot* of thought to exactly how this particular piece of shit was going to die. In the end, I'd decided the worst thing I could think of was both something I myself had experienced, and something she herself had inflicted on me. I could envision nothing more excruciating than drowning, repeatedly, and being unable to lose consciousness due to constant healing magic. Regrettably, I didn't have a shit-filled river handy to dunk her in—but I could correct the inefficiency of my own desperate, repeated casts of Heal by exchanging them for a single, steady source of that same spell.

Under my mental direction, the healing slime went right to work. Slipping straight into her mouth, oozing aggressively through her fingers as she tried to claw it away. She bit down to stifle the flow, but the remaining slime just began sliding into her nose.

Gray had the presence of mind to pinch her nostrils shut with her one good hand. I let her; it was too late. Enough had gotten in.

I wasn't sure what would happen to a healing slime in the acid of a person's stomach, and I didn't plan to find out tonight. It slid instead into her lungs. She managed to hold the grip on her nose for a few more seconds before the convulsions overtook her and she began to drown in slime. In her flailing, she opened up her nose and mouth, and the remainder of the slime slithered in, rejoining its main body and filling her lungs to capacity, blocking off any access to air.

And then, blazing with powerful healing magic, *refused to let her die.*

"You *really* thought you were something, huh," I said, sneering down at her in utter contempt as she thrashed, her entire body heaving, clawing at her face and throat with both hands, even the one too injured to form a grip. "Big bad boss of the Gutters, feared by all. Figured you were the only *real* person in a big board of game pieces, isn't that right? Fuck all these little people; they're just here to be moved around however you needed."

I watched her face with cold satisfaction at the sheer suffering. I hadn't even noticed the point at which my Wisdom perk had relaxed its hold on me, but I was definitely not in a space of emotionless analysis now. Whatever part of me remained that *should* have been horrified at the cruelty I was inflicting was just too tired and starved to rear its head anymore. Gray heaved and thrashed, instinctive convulsions taking over as her oxygen-starved brain kept trying to give up, while the unbroken flow of healing magic wouldn't let her consciousness flicker out.

"Well, we *learned*, didn't we?" I hissed, stepping forward so I could loom over her. She kicked my legs—apparently by accident in her mindless flailing. Already she was too weak for it to make an impact. "You know what, I'll give you credit. You *far* outlived your allotted role in life. Be proud of clinging to existence for a few more miserable weeks after your fate was finished. You were put on this world for one purpose—to be just the first stone in the path for me to *step on* in my own rise. And you dared, you *presumed* to think you had a chance against me? That you had any significance at all?"

Her eyes were rolling up, but she still couldn't pass out. The wet, hoarse noises emerging from her throat didn't diminish, even as her struggles did. I knew too well the weakness of Heal and any spell derived from it—you couldn't heal natural processes that way. Fatigue would win in the end. Her beleaguered limbs faltered, struggles fading as the muscles wore themselves out and even the magic refused to offer them any relief.

"Who the *fuck* do you think you are? You think you can just come here, kick these people around for your own convenience? Who *cares* about your sad backstory or what pressures you're under? You don't *get* to decide anybody's fate. You have *no fucking right* to dispense death and punishment just because you happen to be the asshole with the big enough stick on a given day. You were *always* going to get what was coming to you. Just like *every other asshole.*"

I seized the slime with my will and pulled; it immediately relinquished its hold, sliding up and out of her body in one long, wet *gloop.*

Gray tried to draw in air, managing the first half second of an aborted gasp before my foot descended on her throat. Something in her neck audibly crunched.

Twitching faintly, eyes wide and wild, she still summoned the will to reach up with her good arm, trying to claw at my leg. All that was left of her strength amounted to an impotent pat on my boot.

I leaned forward, resting an elbow on my knee and bringing my face as low as I could, so I could sneer down into the fading light in her eyes.

"You. Are. Not. Special."

Lady Gray died a broken ruin of a woman, on her back in the dirt, with my boot on her neck. I held it there until all motion had ceased, until her vacant eyes were staring up at the regenerated khora fronds above me, and then for half a minute longer. I was past taking chances with this one.

The corpse barely shifted when I finally removed my boot.

After the carnage of just moments ago, the quiet was terrifying and oppressive. I raised my head to look upward at the sky, visible between swaying khora fronds once again. There was usually a veritable cacophony of clicks, hoots, and other alien animal noises, but all were silent now. Whatever had survived the blaze was hunkered down in hiding. Some underbrush and hanging vines still smoldered, but the most prominent sound now was the omnipresent whisper of wind through fronds as they swayed above us.

I might have been imagining it, but I thought those fronds looked longer and more robust than I was used to seeing. It would make sense; Immolate was, after all, a healing spell. A cruel one.

I lowered my head and drew in a breath, letting it out slowly. The air tasted of ash and smoke. Aster was looking at me, and for a moment I expected her to be appalled by what she'd just seen, but she simply nodded at me once.

Yeah, she'd seen the aftermath of Gray's cruelty too. Sometimes, with some people, there was no such thing as too far.

Aster took two steps forward, bent, and closed her hand around the hilt of the dagger. Instantly she vanished from sight. I watched in a kind of dissociated curiosity as footprints appeared in the dirt moving toward me, stopping just nearby. Then Gray's body shifted as it was awkwardly tugged, and the dagger's sheath was pulled free of her belt. It, too, vanished the second it was picked up. A moment later, Aster reappeared, the sheathed blade in her hands right where she'd just joined the two pieces together.

"Yeah," she mused, holding the artifact out to me, "you were right. *This* is gonna be handy."

"Damn right," I agreed, taking it from her. I just tucked the dagger into my own belt, carefully clipping the sheath on with its provided hook. "The other one will be even better."

"We may as well see what else she's got," Biribo suggested.

"Ugh." Aster curled her lip. "Somehow the idea of rifling through this old bitch's pockets is . . . not appealing."

"Has to be done, though," I agreed with a sigh. "Let's get it over with."

Junko sneezed.

The mystery artifact was a ring, concealed beneath her heavy gloves. I slipped it onto my finger, where it immediately adjusted to fit me perfectly. Just like that, I was spellproof and able to vanish at will. And all I'd had to do to earn it was burn down the entire fucking island.

Gray didn't have much else, a testament to how she'd been roughing it in the forest for the last several weeks. Some unused bandages and jerky, a surprisingly well-filled coin purse. She also had two half-filled vials of healing potion, apparently separated out that way because she was down to rationing them. I debated, but took them, too. Sure, *I* could heal anything immediately, and make healing slimes for my followers to use when I couldn't be near them, but surely a use could be found. There was no sense in leaving expensive alchemy to rot in the forest.

We turned to go, me dragging Gray's corpse by a grip on her ankle. That was far from the most efficient way to haul a body through the underbrush, but fuck it. I had plenty of energy left and was bound and determined to handle her body as disrespectfully as possible. We only got just outside the clearing and back onto the game trail before the next surprise appeared.

A cat person lay face down on the path, shortbow and arrows scattered nearby, with a single arrow sticking out of his back. The most remarkable arrow I'd ever seen. Dropping Gray, I bent to grasp and yank it out.

The whole thing was silvery white and gleamed under the moonlight as if highly polished. Rather than being separate pieces of shaft, head, and fletching like a normal arrow, it was all one clearly wrought piece of the same peculiar material—metallic to the touch, light as aluminum but gleaming like polished platinum—with gracefully sculpted, rigid fins like a missile rather than feathers. About halfway along its length, the shaft separated into two parts, which reconnected in the front in a single thickened point, with intricate traceries between them, apparently just for decoration. The entire thing was twisted in a spiral, making it resemble a helix that ended in a drill bit on one end, except excessively beautiful. I knew the twisting was to make it spin rapidly in the air when fired, which would stabilize its flight for accuracy's sake. That was the only practical thing about it; the rest of the design was ridiculous. No one would *make* an arrow like this if they intended to actually shoot it at anything.

"Well, well," I said softly, lowering the bloody arrow to hang at my side. I turned in a complete circle but, of course, there was no sign of anyone else nearby. I raised my voice anyway. "I appreciate the help. If you'd care to come out and introduce yourself, I would be glad to reward you appropriately."

The forest remained silent.

"We're probably still not gonna see 'em for a while, boss," Biribo said, buzzing up next to my ear. He had long since ceased glowing, the Wisdom perk having apparently exhausted itself once I finished off my enemy. "Remember they were trying to set themselves up to approach you from a strong position by dealing with the catfolk and Lady Gray for us. Well, their plan with the catfolk actually *caused* us problems, and now you've finished Gray off yourself. *And* just made what might be the greatest single demonstration of personal power anybody's seen on this world since Hara's Sin. They'll make a proper introduction when they feel confident enough to negotiate from a solid position. Or when they get too desperate to wait."

I drew in a deep breath, closing my eyes. *Fucking* Viryan bullshit, I did not have time for this. Why did I have to babysit this elf's precious little feelings on top of everything else? If they ever finally deigned to speak with me like a real person, the first thing I was gonna tell them was that their goddess was an ass and all of her advice was bad.

I dropped the impractically beautiful arrow back on top of the catfolk hunter it had killed.

"Well," I said aloud, "the offer stands. Let's get home, everybody. We have a *lot* of work to do."

41

In Which the Dark Lord Gives Peace a Chance

I was right—dragging a body by the ankle over rough terrain was just about the most needlessly difficult thing a person could do.

We'd only just emerged onto the main road before a gwynnek came dashing up from the fortress, fast enough that it had nearly reached us before I identified Newneh with Nazralind sitting astride her.

"Oh, Goddess be thanked," the elf gasped as they came to a halt. "I mean, ah, no offense . . ."

"I'm not really devout," I said. "Situation?"

"Handled." She nudged her mount around to face back toward the fortress, falling into step alongside us. "They surrendered. It seems most of the cats survived. We have them disarmed and under guard."

"Good," I grunted. "Good work. Gotta deal with that, and then . . . go help wherever we can. It's going to be bad out there."

Nazralind nodded, then looked pointedly down at my burden. "Do you need help with that, Lord Seiji?"

"I have it."

"That looks rather . . . I mean, I can walk and put her over Newneh's saddle. It's no trouble."

Newneh lowered her head and made a croak I could only interpret as disagreement.

"You know how when someone important or beloved dies, there's a big funeral? Lots of crowds, all sad and solemn. Possibly a procession, then a long vigil. All care and respect paid to the departed, that whole thing?"

She looked at me askance. "Yes . . . ?"

"This is the exact opposite of that."

Nazralind glanced down again just as Lady Gray's corpse bumped as I dragged it through the burned-out husk of a fallen red vine, limbs trailing awkwardly through the soot.

"All right, then," Nazralind said, shrugging. "Makes sense."

We were met halfway back by an honor guard of men and women with crossbows and another of Nazralind's ladies mounted on a gwynnek. Truthfully, I paid them little attention, focused as I was on the gate. A full contingent of my people stood there, aiming weapons in every direction into the forest, with Minifrit at their center. For once she hadn't brought her pipe.

"The injured are receiving treatment," she reported as we drew close, before I had the chance to ask. "Arrow wounds seem to respond well to healing slimes, provided they are not immediately fatal. That is ongoing; I will notify you if anyone requires further healing, Lord Seiji. We have sequestered the dead, of both factions."

"Thank you." I nodded, and dropped Gray's leg. My arm was really starting to hurt by that point. "Secure this someplace crawn-proof, please. I'll need it later."

Minifrit gave the body a disdainful look, then stepped closer to me and lowered her voice for discretion's sake. "I realize you enjoy being enigmatic, my lord, but in this case it would help to know your intentions. Preserving an entire body under these conditions will be . . . challenging. Do you simply mean to collect the several bounties on her?"

I nodded again. "That, and I'll need her for my plan to reach a settlement with Highlord Caldimer."

"And will that plan require the *entire* corpse, or simply positive identification?"

I considered that for a moment. "The latter should suffice, I think."

"In that case, we only need the head," she nodded. "That can easily be preserved in a glass jar of akhor brine. That's the usual way."

The fucking *usual* way. Of *course* the Fflyr had worked out best practices for displaying people's severed heads.

I wearily quashed my instinctive reaction. It was long past the point when I had any right to condemn anyone else's violent ways.

"That sounds perfect, then. Throw the rest into the forest for the scavengers."

"I will see it done, Lord Seiji."

We stepped through the gates, leaving Gray's body on the ground to be watched over by my guards. It seemed most of the population of North

Watch had come out by now, though, I was glad not to see any of the Rats or other children. A sizable knot of cat people were huddled together, disarmed and covered by enough crossbows to kill all of them twice. A row of catfolk bodies, neatly laid out on the ground, separated them by the line of guards.

Across the courtyard from them was another row of still figures. I felt my chest tighten at the length of it.

"We have treated the injured," Minifrit said in a clipped tone, "as is the standard practice with prisoners of war. Even so, I might have been disinclined to squander valuable medical supplies on *these*, but it costs us nothing to apply healing slimes. Simply leaving them to bleed seemed pointlessly cruel."

I nodded again, silent, and she remained behind me as I stepped over to the row of bodies.

They had been laid out in what I now recognized as Fflyr funerary custom, with strips of fabric over the eyes, weighted down on both sides of the head. Apparently there were none of the little ceremonial statues handy, so coins had been used instead.

Kastrin was at one end of the row. Someone had laid her crossbow beside her, and placed her stinger in her right hand.

Images flashed across my mind, nearly as vivid as one of those trauma flashbacks and only slightly less intrusive. The first time I'd seen her, beaten half to death and as suspicious of the Healer as she was grateful. The night her face had twisted in rage and vindication as she snatched the ax from my hand and felled her abuser. Her cheerful smirk when she suggested "slimes and whores" as the slogan of the Dark Crusade. A hundred repetitions of that satisfied little wrinkle of her nose every time she pulled off a difficult shot on the first try. My perfect little bloodthirsty cinnamon roll. She couldn't have been more than seventeen.

And next to her—

Sakin.

I stared at the ragged wound in his throat, uncomprehending. No, this . . . What? This wasn't how this was supposed to go. I could barely make *sense* of it. He was this nigh-mythic enigma full of impossible skills and knowledge. I was going to gradually unravel it, piece by piece, slowly working out just who he really was, why he knew what he did, what the hell he was *doing* out here in the forest with us. Whether he would turn on me or remain loyal to the last. All of that couldn't just *end*. Not like *this*, to some random, stupid arrow out of the dark in a chaotic night raid by a bunch of savages. It was . . .

Ridiculous. It was just *silly*.

Sakin would have thought it was hilarious. In fact, in his last moments, he probably had.

I continued, pacing slowly down the row while everyone watched me in dead silence. Looking at each face. Thirteen of my people dead, in total. Cat Alley girls, bandits, one of the brothel bouncers from Gannit's old place. I didn't even know all of their names. To my bottomless relief, there were no children and none of the handful of housewives and noncombat family members we'd picked up. To my everlasting self-loathing, I was also relieved that none of the other fallen were strategically important.

I'd lost my best sniper and one of my most important advisors. All the rest were . . .

Replaceable.

God, I hated myself.

"What's the final tally?" I asked aloud, turning back to face Minifrit.

"Eleven of the catfolk are dead," she replied, tilting her forehead momentarily toward the separate row of their fallen.

"Twelve," I corrected. "One tried to ambush us as the fire was dying down. The dark elf got him."

Someone from the knot of two dozen or so surviving catfolk made a soft noise. It might have been a whimper or a sob. Understandable, considering they'd just learned one of their own who they must have been hoping had got away was dead. Unfortunately, it was also the worst thing any of them could have done at that moment.

The rage bubbled up as if from the ground at my feet, coursing through my veins, and I opened myself to it, letting it banish the guilt and exhaustion. I *thrummed* with seething fury, and yet remained outwardly cold. It was an almost Zen state, in a perverse way. Countless times on stage I had kept playing to perfection, absorbing the furor of a crowd that was *truly* rocking out and riding that euphoria, channeling it into precision and fine control. Now I rode the sheer bloodlust to the same effect. Calm and composed, not in spite of the fact that I wanted to foam at the mouth and gouge out someone's eyes with my own two thumbs, but because of it.

Because it was *showtime*.

"So," I mused, pacing toward them in slow, deliberate steps. "Thirteen to twelve. Seems . . . unfair."

All around us, everyone seemed to be holding their breath.

It was my first time seeing cat people up close, and Sakin's description was basically spot on. They were more or less human-shaped, except for the feline heads and the digitigrade lower legs ending in big paws. Also, they had tails, claws on their fingertips, and were covered in a layer of sleek fur. All of them seemed to have black fur, many with subtle brown and gray markings; a few had bits of white thrown in as well. I didn't know if all catfolk were colored that way, or just this tribe.

Obviously I had seen furry art back on Earth, but seeing the real thing in person really emphasized just how like nekomimi these were very much not. The cartoon illustrations do a lot to humanize the faces, especially the eyes. Seeing furry people with animal heads in person gave a straight-up uncanny valley effect. I wouldn't have believed any possible interbreeding took place, if I hadn't met Sato. And if I didn't know what people were like.

I stopped a few steps from the crowd of prisoners, who were huddled together and watching me in obvious fear. Their facial expressions were a bit hard to read, but the way their ears lay down flat above wide eyes gave away the game. Junko padded up alongside me and growled softly.

I held out my hand to the side. Without me needing to say anything, Ydleth stepped forward and placed the butt of a crossbow in it.

"Who's in charge here?" I asked in a deliberately pleasant tone.

There was a muted shuffling among them.

"You are," a female in the front row said after a moment of silence.

I smiled, a gentle expression that went nowhere near my eyes and made her duck her head apprehensively.

"Good answer," I said, still polite and calm. "I meant, however, who leads your group?"

Another short silence fell, until finally a male next to the woman who'd spoken raised his head. His ears came upright and forward, and I had the distinct impression he'd had to force them to do so.

"I can speak for the tribe," he said, raising his head further and only remembering to project bravado at the last second.

"Good." I rested the crossbow in both hands; it was already loaded and fully cocked, ready to fire. "Now. Who would you say is the most useless among your people? The most . . . expendable?"

His eyes widened, the pupils narrowed to frightened slits. "I don't . . . What do you mean?"

"You know exactly what I mean," I said, deadly quiet.

"I . . . you can't . . ."

Slowly, I raised my eyebrows, and spoke in a whisper. "*What* did you just say to me?"

The cat man's breath caught in his throat. His wrists were bound behind him, as all of theirs were, but he jerked his head to the side at the female who'd spoken previously. "Jessak is the least—"

"Touhah, you faithless *slime*," she hissed, baring fangs at him.

Both fell silent as I leveled the crossbow.

"It was a trick question," I said coolly. "And that was the wrong answer. A leader does not throw away his people to save his own miserable hide."

Touhah's eyes widened further. "Wait, no, I can—"

A fully primed crossbow makes an unbelievable mess at that range. The bolt didn't just penetrate his head; it caved his entire face in, splattering Jessak and everyone behind him with blood. A short tussle ensued as several of them cried out in horror and then squirmed as his body toppled backward into the next rank. They fell still almost immediately, mindful of the dozen other such weapons still aimed into the group, though at least two now were weeping quietly.

"There," I said cheerfully. "Squaresies."

I took one step back and held out the unloaded crossbow to the side; it was immediately taken from my hand.

"So! Jessak, was it?" I put my pleasant smile back on, thrilling inwardly at the visible terror it caused. The rage inside me wanted to kill *more*, to *kill them all*. I let it flow through me, riding the wave but not yielding to its control. Instead, I just shrugged, gesturing around at the courtyard. "The hell, man? I thought we were neighbors."

She cowered, staring up at me in apprehension.

I abruptly dropped the smile. "Are you under the impression that we're on a date? Just making small talk? I require answers, Jessak. You will provide them. I promise you'll like the outcome better if you provide them *swiftly*."

"I—we—" Jessak had to pause and swallow heavily. "I . . . am not a shaman or raid leader."

"Aww," I cooed. "Just following orders, is that it?"

Finally, she straightened up a bit, a hint of anger peeking through the fear. "Authority is not given to me to speak for my tribe. But I will not disavow any action I've taken. Everything I've done has been for my people."

I stared down at Touhah's still-dripping corpse, then over at the row of other dead cats, and finally back at her.

"Good job."

Her face contorted in such visible anger, I could interpret it easily despite its weird shape. That was more like it; angry people, I've found, tend to be more responsive than scared ones. It was sickening that that was a thing I had to know, but here we were.

"Why did you attack us?" I demanded, my voice suddenly curt.

"*You* broke the agreement," she retorted. "Your group lived here in peace, on *our* lands, in exchange for tribute. Then the tribute stopped coming!"

"Notice what else you don't see?" I replied, gesturing around. "Rocco. The guy your agreement was with. He's gone, and that left us with no connection to you. I was told about it, but nobody but him seemed to know the terms, or how to get tribute to you, or how to speak with you at all. I figured when it didn't show up, somebody would come to ask and we could settle it. All you had to do was *ask*. But nobody ever came. And now, you do this?" I clicked my tongue, shaking my head ruefully. "Not very neighborly, Jessak."

Her ears had lowered again, but she rallied, straightening her spine. She had more of that than Touhah, at least.

"Well, *then* you started rapidly growing numbers, bringing in weapons and supplies . . . We'd have been crazy to approach you while you were gearing up to attack us!"

"Attack *you*? What do you have that you imagine I would want? We do just fine without you."

"And . . . and then there were those fake totems! Who did you think that would fool?"

"I have absolutely no idea how to make a Shylver totem. There's a dark elf skulking about who put those up. They seem to think they were helping us, but they haven't bothered to introduce themselves, and frankly I'm losing patience with their antics. You see what it's led to."

She fell silent, mouth hanging slightly open and her eyes darting as she quested for something to say.

"Tell me about Lady Gray," I said. "How is she involved in this?"

"The woman? That . . . Fflyr Blessed?" Jessak folded her ears back again. "She spoke with the chief and the elders and shamans. I'm not important enough to have been part of that, but I know what they told us after. She said that you were Blessed with Wisdom, told us how to arrange our hunters to strike before your familiar could give enough warning. That's all they explained to us. I don't know how she persuaded them that attacking was the right thing. The tribe has been arguing about that for months. Just . . . After she talked to our leaders, this was their order."

"I'm afraid she lied to you," I said. Holding up one hand, I conjured a Firelight over it, casting an orange glow which flickered in the eyes of the cats. "Don't feel excessively put upon; Gray was an authentically vile excuse for a person. She lied to everybody, and much worse. She sent you here to die. I am Blessed with Wisdom, yes. *And* with Might, and with Magic."

"No," Jessak whispered, eyes going wide. "That . . . you . . . *no.*"

"I can appreciate your position," I said more quietly, letting the spell flicker out. "Really, I can. It is not . . . wholly unreasonable. Perhaps I should have made more of an effort to reach out sooner. In the end . . . all of this has been a tragic misunderstanding. *Unfortunately,* now you've gone and attacked my home. Killed my people. You see why I can't just let that lie."

Slowly, Jessak's feline face crumpled from an expression of shock and terror and was now scowling up at me.

"Are we not . . . *squaresies,* after all? Fine." She shifted against her bonds, straightening her spine fully to stare me in the eye. "I will take whatever punishment you demand, human. Everything you were going to do to *all* of my tribe. Do it all to me. I accept blame. If you planned to kill them, I ask that you choose a punishment *worse* than death and let me bear as many as you require."

Several of her comrades hissed at her, objecting in hushed voices, though I did note with dark amusement that nobody else volunteered themselves.

"Oh? Did you not just tell me, repeatedly, that you weren't part of the planning of this and have no authority?"

She bared her fangs at me momentarily before getting herself back under control. "I am offering myself to take all blame! If you truly see how all of this has been a sequence of errors, I beg you to let me do this!"

Okay, I liked Jessak.

Again I looked down at . . . what was his name? Oh well. Then, just as pointedly, over at the other fallen catfolk.

"I believe we've settled what needs to be settled," I said after a terribly loaded pause. "Your weapons and anything else confiscated from you are forfeit. Blood has answered blood, and I deem the scales balanced. You will be released, and may take your dead to give them whatever rites are fitting. Tell your leaders what has happened here, and let this show them that the Dark Lord is *merciful.*"

I paused for one beat, then leaned forward until I was looming directly over Jessak.

"Up to a point."

She opened her mouth to speak, but I gently tapped my forefinger against the tip of her nose.

"Be sure to inform them, Jessak, that this is the last time. You have *one* allotment of forbearance from me, and your tribe has now used all of it. If I have any further trouble from your people—so much as a rudely worded greeting should we happen to meet in the forest—you will know nothing but the full wrath of the Dark Crusade. I will descend on your measly village like a living plague and *scour* it from the face of creation. Everything you value will be smashed and burned as refuse, and every last drop of your people's blood spilled to water the khora. You will die festooned with the entrails of your loved ones like holiday decorations, you will watch your elderly *roasted on spits, and I WILL CARPET MY FORTRESS IN YOUR **MANGY PELTS**.*"

My voice steadily rose as I spoke until, at the end, I was screaming so violently into her face that my throat burned and spittle decorated her features along with her tribemate's blood. Jessak's eyes had gone wide as saucers with pupils contracted to slits, her ears plastered flat against her skull in an expression of abject terror. Clearly she took my words literally. Good; in that moment, that was how I'd meant them.

I hadn't even consciously registered it happening, but my hand had shifted from a finger on her nose to a full-on death grip over the entire upper half of her muzzle, with my thumb over the nose and the rest actually inside her mouth, which she'd never closed after I interrupted whatever she'd been about to say. In fact, I was clutching it so hard that her fangs had penetrated my palm. I was bleeding right into her mouth. Strange, I didn't even feel the pain.

There was a truly disgusting sucking noise as I pulled my hand off her teeth and drew it back.

Heal.

Pink light snapped along my arm like lightning, flaring brightly against the small but deep wounds as they closed. Odd; I'd never known it to do that before. Normally the flash covered the whole body, healing indiscriminately.

"Or."

My voice, again, was calm. Perfectly cordial, my expression relaxed. Slowly, I straightened back up, put on an amiable smile, and spread my arms in a shrug.

"We can go back to being neighbors. Staying out of each other's business—and perhaps, when times are hard, lending a hand, as neighbors do. That sure sounds like the better option to *me*. What do you think?"

Jessak's mouth was still hanging open, dripping blood, she started to close it, grimaced in disgust, and then nodded mutely. I realized she probably *really* wanted to spit but didn't dare to do that in front of me right now.

Smart kitty.

"I'm so glad we could settle this like reasonable people." I turned my back and stepped away, folding my hands behind me. "Release them. *Gently*, provided they behave. If anyone struggles, kill them all."

I was obeyed.

Cutting that many people free was a process that took some time, especially since they were mostly too frightened to move. I stood exactly where I was, moving no more than a statue and seemingly ignoring the sounds behind me as, over the next several minutes, the catfolk were released and allowed to gather up their fallen comrades. Only when I heard them begin to shuffle out the gates did I suddenly turn.

"Oh! And Jessak."

She wasn't the only one who flinched; the whole group came to an immediate stop, even those carrying bodies. Jessak hunched her shoulders for a second and started to turn, but that was all the time it took for me to suddenly glide across the distance between us, long strides of my Surestep Boots almost silent. The catwoman only managed half a turn before I was suddenly leaning an elbow on her shoulder, which made her flinch again.

I'd used this exact maneuver on Kasser once before; it was a memory I was ashamed of, now. Back then, that had just been me bullying a subordinate who had entirely reasonably complaints. My theatrical talents were much better used cowing defeated enemies into compliance.

"I realize all this was kicked off by a little uncertainty over territorial rights," I said casually, brushing my fingernails against her fur. "Just so we don't have a repeat of this incident, let me just settle that matter right now."

I leaned more heavily on her, bringing my mouth closer to her ear, and lowered the pitch of my voice without altering its volume.

"*You* are living on *my* land. Is that clear?"

Jessak nodded once. "I understand, Dark Lord."

"In fact," I mused, "you'll find me a more amiable landlord than *you* ever were. You officially have my permission to hunt and gather to whatever extent you require, wherever I have control. And my territory has expanded considerably beyond your old borders. Feel free to follow my scouts and see for yourselves where they go, so long as you don't interfere with them. My people have first rights to hunt, but consider yourselves welcome wherever I hold sway. Contingent upon your good behavior."

Pause for a beat, and finish ever so casually . . .

"If I get one report of you messing with my operations or speaking with my enemies, every last one of you will die screaming. Clear?"

"I understand, Dark Lord," she repeated in a tight voice.

"Smashing." I pulled back and clapped her once on the shoulder, hard. "Off you go. Have a safe and pleasant trip home, now!"

Of course, I hadn't actually seen the cat village. Depending on how much of it was built in or around living khora, it was an open question whether her home was still standing. Or inhabited. To judge by their expressions, it had occurred to them, too.

I stood in the center of the open gate, forcing them to move around me, and just watched in silence until the last of them had vanished into the forest. Only then did I turn around.

"We should've wiped them all out anyway, Lord Seiji," Jadrin said unexpectedly. Her voice was thick; looking at her, I discovered to my shock that she seemed on the verge of crying. I'd never realized Jadrin had any feelings beyond scorn, humor, and scornful humor. She must have been close to one of our dead.

There were several mutters of agreement from the onlookers. I slowly gazed around at them, gauging the mood. Absolutely nobody looked happy, of course. Most of my people were quiet and solemn, but I saw now that Jadrin was far from the only soul wanting revenge.

I sighed softly, then raised my voice.

"That's how they get us, y'know."

Anger shifted toward confusion on several faces, and I let it for a few seconds before continuing.

"Not the cats, they're up to their necks in this as much as we are. I mean the Clans. The Convocation . . . Fuck, just the people in charge in general, you don't need me to run down the list. *This* is why they get to be in charge no matter how obvious it is that they're not morally qualified or even basically competent enough to rule. Because everybody who might be motivated to resist them is always pitted against everybody *else* instead of the people actually responsible for all the problems."

I half-turned so I could stare out into the darkened forest in the direction the cats had gone.

"We have to be able to distinguish between our enemies. To differentiate those who *choose* to be our enemies because they despise what we stand for and will lose their power if we succeed . . . and those who are our enemies because the first group have managed to maneuver us into conflict. The scheme is brilliant in its evil elegance. Once blood has been shed and vendettas declared, the bastards don't even have to *do* anything. We'll all just keep fighting each other while they sit back and laugh."

Turning back, I faced everyone again, adopting a resolute expression.

"No one is more cast out and persecuted than the beast tribes. You heard them; the cats did this because they were frightened and uncertain, because their survival is always at risk and they felt they couldn't afford to take chances. And because they were manipulated into it, in the end, *by our enemy*. Same old story. Well, now they know better than to challenge us. If the cats come back here and are willing to bend the knee and obey, I will welcome them into the fold, same as I have every other outcast.

"We must be willing to forgive our enemies—not because we're saints, because quite frankly, fuck that. But because we must be *strategists*. Because that is what it will take for us to win, and if we can't do it, we're all screwed."

Some of the faces around me seemed mollified—or at least more thoughtful than angry now. Not all, but I could tell everyone was listening and thinking. The anger was still there, but I saw no immediate sign of anyone about to start letting that anger make their decisions for them.

After giving them a couple more seconds to absorb my words, I moved on briskly before thinking could turn into challenges or questions. Stepping back into the courtyard, I moderated my tone to a more businesslike cadence to signal a change in mood.

"Minifrit, I'm going to have to leave this in your hands. I want more than anything to tend to our fallen right now, but it's going to be chaos out there after the fire. A *lot* of people will need a healer, starting with those of our own who were out there caught in it."

"None of them would begrudge you that, Lord Seiji," she said, nodding deeply. "I will see our people sent to rest with all respect and honor."

"Thank you," I said softly, putting weight into the words, before resuming my brisker delivery. "Anybody with injuries the slimes didn't heal, step up now and I'll take care of it. I need people kitted out to move, and supplies prepared to be distributed. Other objectives are going to have to be put on hold; right now we have to go help whoever we can. Here's the plan . . ."

42

In Which the Dark Lord Catches a Break

We could afford neither to waste time nor charge in blind; that was the dilemma.

Step one was to send out the gwynnek riders, loaded down with as many healing slimes as we had containers for, to both distribute among my people encamped in the forest and carry out a damage assessment. I designated one of the mobile camps closer to Gwyllthean as a meeting point, toward which I would head directly with a small support team, just enough people to carry relief supplies to replace what had probably been burned up. For this I picked the spot most equidistant between North Watch and all the other patrol areas into which my expanded territory was divided, so that by the time we got there on foot, the much faster riders would have been able to regroup there with word on where my healing magic was most urgently needed. Based on their reports, I could draw up a plan for how to proceed next.

I set out within minutes of dealing with the catfolk, leaving Minifrit in charge and North Watch on a heightened level of security, because while our immediate threats had just been dealt with, this was clearly no time to get lax. Given the distance to the rendezvous point I selected, that gave me hours—the whole rest of the night, basically—to do exactly the one thing I most needed and least wanted to do.

Think.

I found no answers. Really, all I managed to do was keep going in circles inside my head.

The dead haunted me, of course. Vivid memories of Kastrin tended to flash across my vision whenever I closed my eyes, either lying there or in that horrific instant when the arrow took her.

I definitely spent time dwelling on the people I'd failed and gotten killed tonight, but oddly enough the thing that kept rising up to occupy my mind was Sakin. It's a weird feeling, when someone you're connected to but don't really like dies; it was hard to sort out what I felt, and what I *should* feel. Being honest with myself, though, I was most hung up on the arbitrary nature of it. Maybe I'd blown Sakin up a little too much in my mind. After all, we're all just shambling piles of meat, and death is random and comes blindly out of the sky for lots of people. Still . . . It was *Sakin*. That wasn't how he was meant to go out. It wasn't . . . part of the story.

Except this wasn't a story, and I think the dreadful uncertainty that was now clawing at me was mostly that if something like that could happen to Sakin, why not to anyone? It wouldn't be that exact thing for me or Aster, since we were both wearing artifacts that prevented instant-kill shots—up to a point. But no artifact was perfect, life was terrifyingly unpredictable, and we were up against some of the greatest powers in this world, or soon would be.

Which was the other thing weighing down on me. The immediate future was even grimmer than the immediate past.

There was obviously a *significance* to what I'd done that went beyond the immediate, physical effects of burning down the entire forest. It was the first grand, world-altering action of the Dark Lord; that was meaningful in the goddesses' system in a way that had unlocked a special Wisdom perk, which meant it would definitely be noticed from far beyond Dount. While we walked, I quietly asked Biribo about this.

"That's not *common*, boss," he hedged. "And keep in mind that oracular powers of any kind are always vague. Not much fun for the goddesses if anybody else can see too far along the game board. But . . . yeah, there are things that register events like that. *Rare* things, but there are a handful of Spirits and Wisdom perks that probably noticed you. What you don't have to worry about is any of 'em finding your location physically based on it, that's exactly the kinda detail that's consistently blocked to such perceptions."

Which did me no fucking good at all, if those "rare things" pinged at the exact moment the entire island of Dount went up in flames.

Not to mention that them *being* rare was a mixed blessing at best. Those were exactly the kinds of assets that would be under the control of the most powerful factions in this world. The specific people who would have vast resources and would immediately throw them at the Dark Lord as soon as he popped up.

There was also the issue of Immolate being a one-of-a-kind spell, which a lot of people on Dount had seen used by the Healer. This was further complicated by the fact that enough people now knew, or at least strongly suspected, the Healer and Lord Seiji were the same person that *that* secret was on its way out; I'd already stopped relying on it. Seeing my signature spell used on khora might not immediately be familiar, even to someone who'd seen it done to people, and in any case, all of this would be obfuscated by the fact that all such information took the form of rumor, and rumors distorted as much as they retained. Still, at least some people would put it together, and few of those would be motivated to keep it to themselves. All the work I'd done, building public support for the Healer by cleaning the canals and giving out healing slimes, had likely just gone up in smoke.

And when the powers that be started sending their agents to Dount, there was a big, easily followed trail pointing right to me.

I was fucked.

Biribo, Aster, and . . . Sakin . . . had all been in agreement that I wasn't yet capable of throwing down with the best of the King's Guild, even here on Dount; that Rhydion was way out of my league and any team of the Guild's best was likely more than I could handle. My forces amounted to about a hundred and fifty bandits armed with crossbows and goblin alchemy; my fortress didn't even have a gate that closed. We weren't capable of tangling with even the combined Clansguards of Dount. If they brought over a full Kingsguard army from the mainland, they'd steamroll us, never *mind* what the forces of Lancor could do.

So . . . fucked.

In the whole night's travel, I failed to come up with *anything* to counter the kinds of powers I would very shortly have to contend with. There was just nothing within my own power that could fix this. I was unready; I'd counted on having *time* to build a power base and gather more artifacts and spells. My best reckoning had been that I'd need at least a few *years* to gather enough strength to start conquering openly. The best I could hope for was to be found by Viryan powers who would be looking for me as well after this night's work, and the only one close by was Shylverrael—which was both too small to do more than defend itself and likely pissed at me right now, considering I had just torched their own outer defenses and consorted with one of their exiles.

So very, very fucked.

I preferred to think about the dead.

Dawn was breaking as we linked up with the team whose turf we'd headed toward; they were understandably skittish after the night they'd had, but gave the correct countersignal to our birdcalls after a couple of repetitions. To my great relief, everyone was alive and relatively healthy. They'd been camped inside a large, dead khora shell, and thus had seen the entire forest burn around them but not felt the flames directly.

I hadn't slept since about this time yesterday, nor had most of those with me. We huddled up in the shell ourselves while the gang kept watch, managing to get a little rest during the hour it took for the gwynnek riders to converge on this site. Nazralind was one of the first back, and she gave the order not to disturb me until her whole crew had checked in and she had a full report for me, which bought me two more hours of sleep. That was not the call I would have made and I'm pretty sure she knew it, but I couldn't find it in me to castigate her, especially since she'd brought me good news.

"Turns out burns respond really well to healing slimes. You know how they kind of sting even as they're healing you?"

"Right, because they're still slimes," I said. "Magic aside, they're trying to digest anything organic they're sitting on."

"Yeah, exactly. Apparently that really smooths out skin and tissue while the magic works. It takes a lot longer than your Heal spell, but the people who've used the slimes on burns don't even have scars. Great stuff. We do still have some people in multiple different groups who'll need better healing, though. The slimes don't do as well with broken bones or deep tissue damage, stuff like that. They're keeping people stable for now, but the ones in a bad way are the ones who fell out of khora that caught fire or had run-ins with shellbacks or other wild animals that ran into them in a panic. I've got everybody's reports; gimme five minutes and I'll have a collated list for you, Lord Seiji."

"Thanks, Naz." I took in a deep breath, steeling myself. "And . . . how many did we lose?"

Nazralind shook her head, smiling. "Nobody."

"No—um, by 'lose,' I meant—"

"I understood what you meant, Lord Seiji. We've got injuries that still need your special touch, but no fatalities. It's stable out there, now that everybody's got extra slimes and knows things are under control, and that you're on the way to finish up. Injuries aside, I think the uncertainty was what was really getting to people. No, the biggest losses were supplies. *Every* group lost quite a bit. I've got reports on that, too, for each gang."

I was barely managing to listen to her, suddenly lightheaded. No fatalities? *None?*

"We . . . didn't lose anyone else?" I asked. There was a faint tremor in my voice that I didn't like, but in that moment I couldn't manage to be upset about it. I was stuck in a weird combination of numbness and elation.

Nazralind smiled again. "That's right, Lord Seiji. I was worried, too, but in hindsight it makes sense. Khora shells don't burn, the fire was just vented through the apertures where the fronds come out, and nobody was up in the fronds because . . . well, why would they be? Since it hit at night, most people were camped, which meant they placed themselves in open areas. The only ones who were actually up in khora themselves were keeping watch, so there were some bad falls. But the fire didn't crack most of the shells, so everybody had time to get away from the khora, even the ones who were asleep. Quite a few people were singed, just because there aren't a lot of khora-free places to *go* in the forest, but nobody got cooked. Really, that could only have happened if someone was caught in a *really* unlucky position."

Her face had gone blurry for some reason. I rubbed distractedly at my eyes, fully preoccupied with what she'd just said.

I hadn't killed any of my own people. Not directly, at least. It was . . .

"Th-thanks, Naz, I . . ." Why was my voice so rough? I rubbed at my eyes again to clear them. "Okay, w-we need to . . . I'll . . ."

The lump rising in my throat choked me off, and *now* my legs were tottering.

Come on, what the hell was *this*? I desperately fought to get myself back under control. Where was the sinister Dark Lord, all ruthless and in command, who'd sent the catfolk packing just a few hours ago? It was because I'd just awakened—that had to be it. Nothing good happened when I took a break. Getting a proper *showtime* going required some advance notice. I needed to work on my improv.

"I'm fine, sorry," I muttered thickly, scrubbing at my face with a sleeve. "It's just . . . adrenaline, y'know. And fatigue." Aster had stepped over and placed a steadying hand against my back, undoubtedly noticing my suddenly tottering legs. How humiliating.

"Lord Seiji." Nazralind had taken a step closer, still wearing that small but warm smile. "Feel free to slap me if I overstep, but the thing I've noticed about men, and especially powerful men, is this idea that showing emotion reveals weakness. Not to drag up a sore point, but after last night, the one thing *no one* will ever call you is *weak*."

Off to my left, a man cleared his throat. Auron was with the group I'd brought from North Watch; he'd turned out to be a very good acquisition for the team, level-headed and always willing to pitch in. And to speak his mind, apparently.

"Beggin' your pardon, Lord Seiji, but she's quite right. Everybody signed up knowing there was gonna be some major destruction, working for the Dark Lord. But, eh . . . In all the stories, there's always, y'know, the guy who brings the Dark Lord bad news and gets thrown off a tower for it. It, ah . . . It means a lot to know you care so much about us. Seriously, that makes all the difference."

Ugh, when did this turn into such a fucking hugbox? I took a final swipe at my left eye with the heel of my palm, and cleared my throat.

"Right, well. Thanks. Okay, let's not waste any more time. Naz, how tired are your riders?"

She tilted her head briefly to one side in that little suggestion of a shrug she often did, and looked over at the nearby gwynnek riders. "It's not ideal, Lord Seiji. We've been going fast and hard all night, on no sleep."

"That's about what I figured. I'm sorry, ladies, but I'm going to have to ask you to push it. Not too far, though. I want you all to take a break here, rest up until . . . noon. Sorry that's not much time, but it's a mess out there, and we're all going to have to push hard over the next few days. Once you've caught a nap, I need you to scout and find out the situation in the villages. Start with those closest to the khora; they'll be hardest hit. Bring your reports to the northern camp up near the waystation, and I'll rendezvous with you there once I've helped all of our people. You'll be moving much faster than I can so you should have more time to rest up once you're there. Naz, I leave it to you to organize a search pattern."

"Hai!" I was too tired even to have feelings about that. Or maybe I was just used to it already.

"Lady Ismreth," I continued, turning to her.

"It's pronounced *Ismreth*, Lord Seiji."

I inhaled an entire lungful of air through my nose. Very slowly.

"But maybe that's not important right now," she added in a casual tone. "You know, some people call me Izzy."

"I have a different job for you. I need you to carry the collected reports of every group's lost supplies back to North Watch and turn it over to Minifrit; tell her I want her to organize replacements and send them out with foot teams. It'll take a few days to reach everyone, but we'll be distributing what we brought as we go so nobody should starve. Then stay at the fortress and rest up; I want you posted there in case Minifrit needs to get a message to me."

"Hai!" she said crisply, bending down from her saddle to accept the sheaf of papers Nazralind handed up.

"I appreciate all your hard work, everyone," I said to the group at large. "I'm sorry to keep asking more of you when all this is my fault, not yours. But the fact is, people out there need help—not just our people, but everyone on this island. And we all know their leaders aren't going to do anything for them. It comes down to us."

To my honest surprise, nobody looked resentful; everyone just nodded, faces resolute. I nodded back.

"Let's get to work."

So that was how my week went. That was about how long it usually took to do the complete circuit of the khora. Plus, stopping at each encampment to administer healing, reassurance, and emergency supplies wasn't *much* faster than taking over the gangs in the first place had been. A little bit faster, since we were pushing hard on the march between them, so in the end I got to everybody within five days. A couple of spots only needed some additional food to keep going, and in the end, there were only a few individuals with lingering wounds that needed my powerful magic to sort out. Even those were kept stable and in not too much pain by the healing slimes until I could get there. Ultimately I *had* to call a halt for an uninterrupted night's sleep, or we were going to start collapsing.

I kept waiting for it, but nobody threw any recrimination at me. In fact, all my people were glad to see me, and grateful for the help. I put on a good face for them, since group morale was my responsibility, but the guilt was starting to hollow out my insides.

There was good news, though. As we linked up with every group and got the news, I learned that my initial impression standing atop North Watch and looking out over the sea of fire had been exaggerated. It had sure looked like the whole world was burning from *there*, but as it happened, that tangle hadn't been connected to every khora on the island. Gathering reports from each of my gangs, I gradually put together a mental map of how far the flames had spread, and as it made sense in hindsight, the farther they radiated out from deep in the western forest, the more gaps there were. One group had seen khora blazing in the near distance to either side while none around them had gone up.

They showed me the effects of the damage, dampening my relief some-what. The khora I *had* burned were vibrantly healthy now, in a way they hadn't been before, thanks to Immolate's healing effect. However, those unfortunate enough to be standing close to them had been seared by the fire and were missing fronds, with blackened shells.

It was in the aftereffects that the worst results showed. Every camp had been briefly overrun by animals trying to get away from the fire; those had caused the worst of the injuries among my people. It seemed we had only been spared such a stampede at North Watch because bigger fauna had already cleared out of the area due to the presence of so many humans and catfolk. Crawns were just beginning to trickle back into their habitats; bushes, vines, and other flora that lived in and around the khora had been devastated. I knew from forest fires back home that they, too, would come back healthier than before, but that would be the result of months, not minutes. With winter coming on soon, it was likely to be spring before Dount got to experience the new undergrowth benefiting from ash-nourished soil and cleared space in which to prosper.

By the time we reached the end of our circuit, the last gangs had already received their full resupply from North Watch, thanks to Minifrit's efficiency. Furthermore, at that point the riders had completed their rounds, had a chance to rest up, and it had been long enough that Nazralind sent someone to track me down and check in. That saved some time, as it spared me having to backtrack all the way up north to the rendezvous. Instead, she was able to brief me on the situation in the surrounding villages, and meet up with me at the first one I decided to visit.

There, the news was even more surprising.

"Miracles?"

"Oh aye, it's not just on Dount," the village headman assured me with an amiable grin, nodding. "From the sounds of it, ours was a wee bit *rougher* than most places got it, but I reckon that's as close to special as this island'll ever get. Have you really not heard, Lord Healer?"

"I've been in the forest since the . . . Inferno," I explained, using the term that had apparently sprung up and stuck for my disastrous mistake. It made me cringe, not least because it was pretty accurate. "There are people living out there; they were in the most urgent need of help."

"Whoof, I'll bet," he agreed, wincing. "Wait, does . . . this mean you really haven't heard?"

"About . . . miracles?" I shook my cowled head, grateful my Healer costume concealed my expression. "No, what's this about?"

I was standing in conversation with Aster, Nazralind, and four of the senior members of the village. All four immediately swelled up as they inhaled, grinning with the anticipation of veteran gossips about to break a juicy piece of news to a fresh audience.

"Turns out the Inferno was only *one* such," the headman said, getting to speak first only out of rank; the other elders were still practically vibrating with anticipation. "It's only been a week, mind, so a good half of what we've heard is just rumor, and that much only because everybody who matters is passing word on this as far and wide as they can. But aye, signs from the Goddesses occurred all over the world that night!"

"*Both* Goddesses," added Mother Agit, who appeared to occupy some kind of wise woman status in the village, which I didn't know enough about Fflyr culture to understand. "Very explicit signs from Sanora and the Dark Sister, both."

"Only two I've heard of with any certainty—aside from the Inferno, I mean—and that cos they were both from the lands closest to Dlemathlys." Headman Rouor was quick to regain the floor when she paused for breath. "Up in Godspire there were lights in the sky, and a choir of voices from the heavens proclaiming that a new Hero has come to Ephemera! And then down in Eliphrell, whole fields of crops had great signs burned into them, patterns making the holy symbols of both Sanora and Virya."

"Where is Ellif . . . Uh, that place?"

"Oh, that's Eliphrell Province in the Empire," chimed in a third man, who hadn't actually been introduced to me. "Northernmost part of Lancor. The landbridge from Dlemathlys links to it."

"There's a lot more than that!" added old Cwydder, the oldest man in the village, thumping his walking stick against the ground for emphasis. "My grandson is a Convocation priest, you know, and he's sent me three letters in the last week! The Convocation's got means of getting information that us common folk don't. Wydnar's not ranked high enough to learn important secrets—not yet—but even he can tell that *all* the talk among the Convocation right now is of signs and portents the world over. And not just them; they're in contact with the Radiant Temple. The Empire's stirred up about this, too!"

"*I've* heard stories from beyond Godspire, even," Agit said smugly. "In Vairoth, a huge monument appeared, a black obelisk glowing with Virya's symbols. And in the capital of Savindar, a great army of spirits rushed through the streets, shouting that they were off to join the Dark Crusade!"

"You old squawk, how would you know anything from Viryan lands?" Cwydder scoffed.

Mother Agit aimed a kick at his walking stick. "I'm younger'n you by a decade, you heap of bones and leather! And I have my ways!"

"Right, but there are also more credible rumors from Lancor and beyond," said Rouor, the headman clearly trying to steer this back on track. "To be sure, rumors exaggerate. We likely won't know the reality for quite some time. But the fact that there *are* rumors points to a truth, see? It's coming from all parts of the archipelago."

"Signs and portents," Cwydder said gravely, nodding, and again thumping his stick on the ground. "We here on Dount got only one of many. There's no denying it—the Champions have been called. A Hero walks among us."

"Well, not among *us*," added the other fellow, grinning. "I'd not expect to see a Hero on Dount, of all places. It's surprising enough Dount warranted a miracle, you ask me."

"The fire was off in the west, see?" Mother Agit retorted. "Like as not, it was a message from the Dark Sister, meant to get the attention of the dark elves, not honest folk like us. You mark my words; we'll have trouble with those dark elves by next year's end."

I decided to deflect this conversation away from the idea that there might be a Dark Lord on Dount. "Thank you for the information. Do you know how the other villages and farms have fared, in the aftermath of the Inferno?"

"Aye, we've had word," said the headman, grimacing. "It's much the same as here, Lord Healer. Few enough build close to the khora; that's not easy turf for honest farmers and tradesmen. Not many got hurt by the actual fire. It really upset the animals, though, and the whole island's in upheaval. It was dangerous less because of the burning and more due to the effects that burning had on the land. We're not like to see the end of it for . . . well, years to come, being realistic."

"If you've a mind to go help further, head north or south," Mother Agit agreed. "It's closest to the great western forest that folk are having trouble. Whatever caused the Inferno didn't affect every khora; it must've started in one of those big tangles in the deep forest. Some of the plantations went up, and some of the outlying stands of khora, but less and less the farther you go from the forest. Whole eastern half of the island barely saw a spark, and I doubt the shellbacks will've gone that far. Whole thing's little but a curiosity to folk over there," she added with a sour little twist of her mouth.

I let them chatter on while I collected myself. I was almost dizzy with relief. Both because it seemed I had caused much less devastation than I'd initially thought, and because this business of "signs and portents" meant the entire world's attention was in fact not going to be laser focused on Dount.

I was . . . maybe . . . *not* fucked? Less immediately fucked, at any rate. That'd do for a start.

Though it raised additional questions that became more and more ominous the more I thought about them.

"Then I still have a long way to go," I said, inclining my hooded head to them. "Thank you for the information."

"Ah . . . aye, yes, if you're out to heal folk, we oughtn't keep you," Rouor agreed. "But at least let us send you off with something for your trouble!"

Disengaging from the villagers took some doing, as did refusing the gifts of food and supplies they tried to press on me. I couldn't admit it to them, but there was no possible way I could accept anything from their stocks, not when I had been the cause of a disaster that was likely to make those supplies run thin during the coming winter. It was a few more minutes before we were back among the khora, moving north toward the next village Nazralind had identified as a spot in need of aid. Once we were a safe enough distance, the rest of my gang came melting out of the shadows to rejoin the three of us.

"Biribo," I said as Aster fell back a few steps to catch the team up on what we'd learned.

My familiar buzzed out of his comfy nest in Aster's coat pocket, coming to hover alongside me as usual. "Boss, I think I know what you're gonna say."

"Yeah, I'll bet you do. Why didn't you tell me that causing a sign of the Dark Lord's presence would trigger . . . ugh, *signs and portents* all over the world? Do you *know* how worried I've been about this?"

"Because it *doesn't*!" He began zooming around me in circles in his agitation. "Boss, that's not a thing! Or at least . . . it never has been before. No previous Dark Crusade has been heralded by . . . anything like this!"

Oh, that wasn't good.

"Any idea why the goddesses would suddenly change how they do things?" I asked, hopefully.

"Boss, I really don't think it was them. The most obvious effect of this is to deflect attention away from Dount, which only benefits you—and by extension, Virya. Neither of them could pull off something like *this* without the other's cooperation, or at the very least, awareness, and Sanora wouldn't sign on for you evading the consequences of screwing yourself over. This is . . . something else."

Fuck. I was still relieved, of course, but now I had something new to be worried about. There was another player involved, one who had eyes closely enough on me to know exactly when to trigger a massive worldwide distraction. And one who was *capable* of feats on such an enormous scale. I could think of only one faction that could be, and with friends like those, I didn't need enemies.

"Biribo . . . can devils disguise themselves as people? In a way that would fool even *your* senses, in the long term?"

He settled down into his normal holding pattern next to my shoulder. "Uh, well, boss . . . The awkward fact is there's almost no way to predict what devils can do. They use Void magic, which works entirely outside the system. I will say it'd take a really powerful devil to pull that off over the long term. Boss, you're not thinking the Devil King is responsible for this, are you? Cos that'd be pretty out of character for him, too. He likes to play the long, slow, careful game."

"I can't think of anyone else it could be, though. And I had a wild conspiracy theory just pop into my head. It was Sakin who told me about the Void and the Devil King . . ."

"Oh, *did* he, now," Biribo huffed. "I was wondering about that."

"Hang on," Nazralind interjected. "You're not . . . Are you suggesting Sakin was secretly a devil? That he didn't die, he just *left*, and arranged a cover story for us?"

I shrugged. "It sounds pretty stupid when you say it out loud that way."

"I am really glad you understand that, Lord Seiji," Aster said from behind me.

I drew in a deep, steadying breath and let it out in a long sigh. "Well, whatever the fuck is going on, we have clearly not heard the last of this. It's a reprieve, though. We're not as immediately under threat, which means we should hopefully have time to make preparations before this fresh insanity comes home to roost. C'mon, folks, let's pick up the pace. We've got a lot more people to help before we get down to covering our *own* asses."

43

In Which the Dark Lord
Loses Patience

"So, here's the situation, based on what I've learned."

Ten days later we were back around the conference table at North Watch. With the same number of people as my original council, even, the empty seat having been filled. Not just the same physical chair; Nazralind occupied more or less the same niche as Sakin had. She was more naive in a lot of ways, but she had political knowledge of the kingdom and experience at guerrilla warfare.

"The short version is it's bad, but not as bad as I feared it was going to be," I continued. "To begin with, the food situation. It turns out the harvest was well more than half brought in on the night of the Inferno; and furthermore, most of the agriculture on Dount is done on the eastern half of the island, where the actual burning was minimal to nonexistent. So, some of the harvest was lost, but a small amount overall. It looks like it'll be a lean year, but there won't be a famine."

"There may or may not be relief supplies from the capital, depending on how organized and motivated the King happens to be on a particular day," said Minifrit, "but I rather expect Dount will receive gifts of food from Lancor. Especially with all the talk of signs and portents in the air, the Empire will seek to aggressively position itself as the leader of the Sanorite world."

"Food prices are still gonna rise this winter, and relief shipments probably won't help," Kasser added, scowling. "The problem's not how much food there is, but how it's distributed. The Clans will start hoarding. That's what they do whenever there's a shortage of anything. People will be hungry while piles of grain sit around rotting."

I closed my eyes. My elbows were resting on the table, hands folded in front of me, and for a moment I leaned my forehead against them.

"What can I do?" I wondered—aloud, but talking mostly to myself. "I can put a knife to the throat of any Clan on this island if I really wanna work at it . . . but not without starting a war we won't win."

"Best not to try that approach anyway," Nazralind murmured. "Take it from someone who has. If you squeeze the highborn, it's the lowborn who'll feel the most pain."

"You should talk to Rhydion," Aster suggested.

I raised my head to look at her with a questioning frown.

"You're right about the basic problem, Lord Seiji," she explained. "The shortage will be manageable, except for the greed and paranoia of the Clans. Someone has to get them under control, and neither Clan Aelthwyn nor the King have the power to do it. Well, Archlord Caludon probably *could*, but this isn't something he'd care about. What's needed is a blade to their throats to make them fall in line. This time, you're not the best person for the job."

"She's right," Nazralind said, her eyes widening with dawning realization. "The Clans are scared of Rhydion in a way they never will be of you, Lord Seiji. I'm sorry to say it, but it's true. He's at least as physically dangerous as you are, and . . . Well, it's like the night you ousted Lady Gray from the Gutters. They drew together to confront a perceived attack on the power structure itself, and that's exactly what they'd do if an outsider like you started bludgeoning them into line. But Rhydion is *part* of the system—a powerful part. He could walk into any Clan's fortress and behead the Highlord, and the reaction from the throne and the Convocation would be to start viciously 'investigating' the survivors, because he must've had a good reason."

"Rhydion," Minifrit mused, leaning back in her chair and raising an eyebrow. "This is the so-called paladin who rather notoriously refuses to *see* injustices under his nose, yes?"

"It's true, he's on Dount to deal with zombies or some shit and got tunnel vision about it," I said. "Hm. He *did* finally stir himself to protect the Gutter Rats, after me and Gray and made a big, ugly spectacle of it close enough to him that he risked getting splattered by the blood spray."

"Course, it's hard to say whether that was him changing his ways," Aster muttered, "or a one-off exception that'll make him even less inclined to in the future."

I heaved a sigh. "I think you're right. Rhydion is the solution to this problem . . . And I have something he wants. I bet I can get him to play ball."

"Hang on, Lord Seiji," Kasser protested, "doesn't the thing he wants involve you going adventuring with his party? As their healer? Am I the only one who thinks that sounds like eleven kinds of disasters just waiting for an excuse?"

"No, Kasser, we *all* possess basic sense. Thanks for your concern," I snapped. "It's not as if I *like* this idea. But . . . I have to do something. If this is the only thing I can do, it's what I'll have to do. Never mind it being the right thing to *help people*; all of this is *my fault.*"

He lowered his eyes, frowning pensively. Nazralind gave me a warm smile across the table.

"Speaking of that, though," I continued, "this is *also* exactly the kind of thing a Hero would stick his sword into, and . . . With all respect to Yoshi and his crew, they will definitely fuck it up and cause exactly the kind of blowback Naz was talking about."

"Are they even still on Dount?" Aster asked pointedly. "We haven't heard a peep out of them in months."

"*They* are on Dount to cause trouble for the goblins, which means the goblins are paying *very* close attention to them, and I paid Maugro to inform me if they do anything interesting or give up and leave. He hasn't informed me, so I presume they've been spinning their wheels, basically just like Rhydion has been with his zombie problem. Oh! That reminds me, was there any word from the goblins while we were away from the fortress?"

"Not on their own initiative," Minifrit replied. "I did check in on them while you were away, Lord Seiji. Apparently, Maugro was unavailable when I called down the tunnel, but that junior agent of his appeared, Maizo. He seemed quite . . . harried. I gather events in the tunnels are tense at the moment, but when I asked after the goblins' welfare he rather curtly told me that goblin business was none of ours, and to refrain from summoning them unless we wished to conduct commerce."

"Could be worse, I guess," I grimaced. "Okay, then, the next matter of concern is our strategic position. Nobody I met as the Healer in the last week seemed to connect the Inferno with my, ah, signature spell. It seems like all the miracles in other countries provided suspiciously good camouflage for that, too. But *somebody* will definitely put it together. And we still don't know who or what caused all those . . . ugh, *signs and portents.* Biribo claims that only the Goddesses or the Devil King even *could* have done it, and that all three of them weren't likely to."

"And I stand by that," Biribo chimed in.

"Well, I mean, whoever it was had to have been friendly to us, right?" Kasser offered. "Cos let's face it, none of that *helped* anybody except us."

"Just off the top of my head," said Nazralind, "that was as much a life-saver for the Fflyr government as us. If it became known there was a Dark Lord on Dount, Dlemathlys would be an annexed province of Lancor by the end of the month."

"The Fflyr government, as you just pointed out, isn't even capable of securing its own borders," said Minifrit. "They *definitely* don't have the capability to cause miraculous events in multiple countries simultaneously. You would be hard-pressed to convince me the King even learned of the Inferno in time to order a response, were he even capable of executing one."

"It was just an example," Nazralind said impatiently. "My *point* is, politics are complicated, and they get more so the bigger the scale on which you consider them. *Countless* potential factions benefit from muddying the waters. Anyone who knows where the Dark Crusade is beginning has an advantage over those who don't yet; many would stir up much bigger trouble than this to preserve that advantage for just a little longer. What it comes down to is that *someone* out there did this, and almost certainly for their own benefit. Any help to us is purely incidental. We shouldn't forget that *someone* is going to be coming at us."

"And that's what it comes down to," I agreed. "The material and economic effects on Dount, the strategic implications for us . . . We're looking at mitigation, not salvation. People won't starve over the winter, but it's going to be tight for everyone—starting immediately, and for a good while to come. We don't have the attention of the entire world rushing toward us, but Dount is now *one* of the sites every power on the archipelago is going to be investigating, which means the clock is ticking. We're going to be found sooner than later. There is now an indeterminate grace period until the Dark Crusade has to get kicked off in earnest, which means we need to be ready for it."

"Okay," Kasser said, wincing. "But . . . like . . . how? I hate to be the party pooper, Lord Seiji, but I don't see us being in a position to even conquer Gwyllthean in the next . . . what? Year? Let alone deal with Lancor and whoever else."

"First of all, I'm not Yomiko," I said. "I'm not in her situation, and I have a very different set of aptitudes and resources. Thinking in terms of conquest was always going to be a losing proposition for me; I've succeeded by working surreptitiously. Whatever strategy we pursue next should leverage that rather than brute force. As for *how* to go about getting ready for the big fight . . . I have several potential plans I'm working on, but I don't want to commit to one prematurely. A lot depends on the outcome of my next battle."

"Ah yes," Minifrit said, blowing a streamer of smoke at the ceiling. "Your planned confrontation with Caldimer Olumnach."

"Exactly. We know where his agents are positioned and distributed in the Gutters. The next step is to arrange a meeting. And depending on how that works out, I'll decide what to do next."

"Well, closer to home," Minifrit continued, "Biribo's prediction was accurate."

"Hell, of course it was!" my familiar blustered. "What're we talking about?"

She blew smoke at him, smiling in muted amusement. "The dark elf. Lord Seiji's supplies disappeared from the pantry, replaced by a pile of coins. Viryan coinage. In fact, they rather significantly overpaid."

"Sounds right," said Biribo. "They'd wanna show largesse, since they're in an inferior position."

"That," Aster countered with a grin, "or, like we decided earlier, they're a displaced aristocrat who probably doesn't know the value of basic supplies."

"I'd believe that," Nazralind muttered. "No need to make fun of them for it. That could happen to anyone."

I rested my forehead in one hand. "You know, I wasn't just bullshitting at the cats. I am just about out of patience with this creep and their nonsense. It's nice that they're trying to help and all, but their fucking up has already gotten people killed. Is there any way to *make* them just show up and *talk* to us like a normal person?"

"Boss, a Viryan noble would probably rather die than end up as anyone's servant, even a Dark Lord's. They'll want to be on good footing to present themselves as a valued ally. Keep in mind, this person has been starving in the forest for . . . months, probably, and prefers *that* to the risk of becoming a pawn. With Viryans—especially Viryans who're accustomed to power—trying to force them into subordinate positions tends to trigger the kind of fight other people put up when their *lives* are in danger. If you wanna force the issue, the best approach is to engineer a situation where they have the opportunity to prove their value."

I massaged my temples. "What a fucking headache. All right, fine, I'll . . . try to come up with something. More immediately . . . Aster, Naz, I know we just got back, but now that we've checked in and settled this place . . ."

"We need to head out again," Aster finished, nodding. "I understand, Lord Seiji, there's no time for screwing around. Better deal with Olumnach as soon as possible."

"That's the plan."

It wasn't hard to find Olumnach's people once we reached the Gutters; thanks to the goblins, I had a solid handle on their deployment and schedule. It had been a couple of weeks and the Inferno had happened in the interim, but there was only so much they could change up and still stay in business. On the first day back in Gwyllthean, I cornered a well-dressed man in the process of delivering orders or collecting a report or something from a gang. After tossing the lot of them around a street with strategic Windbursts, I instructed him to carry a message to his boss.

What ensued was a protracted exercise in frustration.

For three days I made a point of visiting the Gutters every night, intercepting and interrogating—*politely* . . . well, relatively politely—the Olumnach agents who were running the new gangs in town. After the second day, they started trying to avoid me, which, thanks to Biribo, was futile. All of them had the same answer—Highlord Caldimer had heard my request and would respond at his leisure.

I didn't kill any of them, or even scuff them up more than was necessary to get them to sit still for a chat. It was tempting, but I was, after all, trying to open a dialogue here.

"What is this guy's problem?" I complained aloud on the third dawn, as we were settling in for our daily rest at Nazralind's old camp in the poison khora grove, which had been untouched by the Inferno. "I'm the guy who killed the enemy he wanted dead, *and* the competitor who wiped out Gray's organization and took a massive bite out of his. That's two reasons he *needs* to talk to me. Is he just an idiot?"

"'Idiot' is a strong word, Lord Seiji," Nazralind answered, fighting a smile, "but, well . . . it's not uncommon for the decisions of highborn to be weighted more heavily toward pride than reason."

"That's a way to put it, all right," Aster said dryly.

"Consider it good practice for when you start dealing with Viryans on the regular, boss," Biribo suggested. "Him and our dark elf buddy back at the fortress. He's asserting dominance by making you wait. Yeah, he undoubtedly *does* want to have an actual meeting, but he feels the need to put you in your place first, so he can go *into* said meeting on favorable footing."

"Yes, that," said Nazralind, nodding emphatically. "Exactly."

"Oh *really*," I growled. "Asserting dominance, is it?"

"Oh, here we go," Aster groaned.

"Here we *go*!" Nazralind cheered.

Starting the next day, I began seeking out and spending time with the gangsters, the ones imported from the countryside territories I had taken over. To begin with, they were afraid of me. Obviously; they were gangsters, so in order to approach them unrobbed, I always had to open with a demonstration of why fucking with me was a fantastically bad idea. But after pushing them around with some flashy spells, I gave out healing, and then I listened to their problems.

Immediately I ran into a roadblock of suspicion, as these boys had heard enough by now to suspect I had murdered a bunch of their friends. It was an issue I could resolve easily enough by sending Naz on a messenger run back to North Watch, to collect reports from Minifrit on how the new folks we were recruiting were doing. It took her a couple more days to do that, since a lot of them were still spread through the forest camps, but once she was back, I quickly made myself the favorite person of the new Gutters gangs, simply by being able to update them on the well-being of their friends. That, and the free healing; these guys managed to get themselves roughed up a lot more than they were used to. Apparently, the population of the Gutters was getting uppity and had less patience with criminals than they did in Gray's day.

For the first entire week, I made a game of tormenting the agents of Clan Olumnach—the rules were that I could only use Windburst and Heal and move at a walk, and the objective was to see how long I could bat them around like a sadistic housecat with a mouse before they managed to escape my clutches. My record, reached on night four, was an hour and a half. I left them shaken and bruised, but never seriously harmed; I made sure of that. I quickly earned the hatred of the Clan, but made myself the beloved dangerous mascot of the gangs.

Class resentment is a hell of a drug.

I gave it fifty-fifty odds whether Highlord Olumnach would care about or even notice the state of morale among his lowborn pawns, but he'd definitely see the shift in the more well-bred lackeys he used to control them.

There was a positive result of Olumnach keeping me waiting, at least. I had time to check on the various other irons I had in the fire in and around Gwyllthean.

Captain Norovena had some details about the island's recovery efforts, which I mentally filed away to direct some later relief of my own where it would do the most good. He was also in a position to have a more complete picture of the damage, which continued to reassure me. Most of the Fflyr didn't actually live in or even too close to the khora, so the Inferno had, for many, just been a terrifying spectacle that posed no immediate threat to people, animals, or structures. A lot of grass fires had been started, and those had resulted in more harm than the actual khora burning. Displaced animals had been the biggest problem for a while, and by now they seemed to be returning to the forest.

Norovena casually mentioned that the Healer had been seen giving aid all up and down the island. The air in his office all but thundered with the pointed questions he did not ask.

Master Auldmaer confirmed Minifrit and Kasser's speculation about economic developments following the Inferno. The wheels had already begun turning; Clans and merchant houses alike were moving to corner every market they could, extending predatory loans to the khora cultivators who had been affected, and beginning to stockpile food from the fresh harvest. He perked up immediately when I said plans were in the works to put a stop to all this behavior. As I'd thought, a man in his position with advance knowledge of something about to happen could surely find a way to profit from it. I promised to give him as much advance notice as I could of whatever was about to unfold.

All the downtime, frustrating as it was, gave me the opportunity to check up on what I'd set in motion in the Gutters, as well. The canals were already noticeably cleaner, all over. It seemed the slimes had spread far enough that the outermost canals ran clear and almost clean enough to drink out of. I say "almost" because nobody I met was stupid enough to test that; if you get your water from a canal, you boil the shit out of it, full stop. Even so, the difference was night and day. The spread of disease was already noticeably down, and for the first time probably ever, *the Gutters didn't stink.*

I was here in my persona as Lord Seiji and the relatively few who had connected the two didn't hang around with the lowborn down here, so I had freedom to move without being constantly mobbed. The Healer, it seemed, had leaped right past "local folk hero" and nearly to the role of saint. Between cleaning the canals, healing the villagers after the Inferno, and donating the healing slime, the Healer's stock had never been higher.

Actually, that was the one thing that had not gone as I'd intended:

the healing slime was still in the possession of the Convocation. It turned out King's Guild adventurers had been brought in to do around-the-clock guard duty on it. The *good* adventurers, the ones nobody wanted to fuck with, and even I would hesitate to tackle more than one at a time. What was more important, the priests were *using* the slime, healing anyone who came to them.

"Plus there are three healing slimes now," Aster reported after a rumor-gathering session, once we were safely private on a rooftop. "They immediately figured out they reproduce just like normal slimes. So it's exponential; as long as they've got trash to feed them, their numbers will keep growing faster until the whole population explodes."

"Well, blow me down, they're actually being *smart* about this," Nazralind marveled, shaking her head. "I thought for sure the Convocation would want to hoard a resource like that, same as anyone else, but . . . Yeah, *eventually* something like that would escape into the environment and become widely available; this way, they get to take credit for doing it on purpose. Hell's revels, they could even get a political leg up on the Radiant Temple by unleashing free healing slimes on Ephemera. And of course, once they're not scarce, nobody's going to bother trying to steal them, so they'll only need the guards at first."

"Huh," I grunted. "Y'know . . . considering my strategy was just foiled, I'm strangely unable to be upset by this. Free healing for the poor? Yeah, that seems like a good day's work."

"Relax, the Healer still gets credit for kicking it all off," Aster said, smiling and gently elbowing me. "There were way too many witnesses for the Convocation to bury it."

"That's true. Also, though, damn. I had better be *really* careful to douse any fire slimes I summon. There'll be hell to pay if *those* get loose."

All this was well and good, but Caldimer Olumnach was still wasting my precious time. I could practically feel the eyes on the back of my head as seconds counted down. All manner of agents from every major power on Ephemera were closing in; undoubtedly some were already poking around Dount, as was every other site that had seen a miracle. Thanks to the plethora of signs and portents, nobody seemed to have connected the spell Immolate with the Inferno, but I knew the trail existed. Sooner or later, somebody good enough to follow it would stumble across its end. And still, the overbred fool *wasted my time.*

So I did what I do best—I escalated.

44

In Which the Dark Lord Wears the Pants in the Relationship

Now then," I said, exercising my full stage presence to make my tone even more condescending than the question inherently was, "what did we learn?"

The nobleman struggled back up to one knee, breathing heavily and glaring pure hatred at me while his clothes smoldered. I had to give the guy credit—most people were crying and begging after one Immolate, but this chap had some actual spine.

"None of this is going to get you what you want any faster, foreigner."

"Well, you'd better hope that's not true," I said reasonably, "as that would mean all of this has happened to you for no reason at all. If I were in your shoes, I feel like that'd make it all worse. Or such is my best guess, anyway. I'm not really sure how you see the world. It's hard to project myself into the perspective of such a loser. But to answer my *question*, the lesson you should take back to your pals is that nobody can cast spells or swing artifacts while *on fire*."

I gave him my biggest, most insufferable shit-eating grin.

"Coming at me with Blessed is not going to help, because *I am better than you*. You, and everyone you know."

The effort of self-control was visible on the guy's face; he made the most fascinating series of grimaces for about four seconds before speaking, but when he did, his voice was impressively even. Impressive for an amateur, that is. Not just anybody can perform to my standards.

"Right. Are we *finished*, then?"

He rose stiffly to his feet and I let him, smiling, before I answered.

"Not quite. As your master's dithering continues to waste my valuable time, I am instituting a new policy with regard to his low-level lackeys. Congratulations! You are being robbed."

The highborn curled his lip in well-bred contempt. "Of course. It's always about money with you sticky-fingered dregs."

"Oh, I don't need your money," I replied with an airy gesture. "Nor, before you ask, any heirlooms or valuables you might happen to be carrying. Nothing so . . . prosaic, no."

I grinned hugely, widening my eyes to look deliberately insane, and paused for a beat to nail the comedic timing.

"Gimme your pants."

Behind me, Nazralind made a choking noise only mostly muffled by her mask.

The aristocrat's face lengthened into an incredulous expression.

"You cannot be serious."

"You may keep your boots, of course," I said magnanimously, "because I am a civilized person. I realize that's a *challenging* concept to what passes for the nobility in this ruin of a country, but now you have me here to set an example. Come now, chop chop, we all have places to be. Drop 'em."

Eyes widened, he took a step back as if contemplating an unwise attempt to flee. "You—you're *not* serious!"

Five minutes later I had his trousers draped over my arm, and we watched the nobleman stalking away through the twilit streets, bare-assed and dangling in the breeze.

"That was incredibly juvenile," Aster stated. "I'm not saying I disapprove; it's just something I felt needed to be pointed out."

I nodded. "Yup."

"Please tell me you have more of a plan for this than just humiliating that guy?"

"Humiliation *is* the plan," I said. "I am increasing the pressure, and for guys like him? This is the way to do it. Nothing enrages people like being humiliated. The lower classes are accustomed to it; they learn to duck their heads and repress. Nobles never learn that skill. Highlord Olumnach doesn't care about what's happening to the bandits working for him, but he depends on a layer of these highborn middle managers to run his criminal empire. He will start to notice if *they* demand action be taken."

"Is ruining that guy's night really going to be enough pressure to shift him?"

"Oh, Aster." I shook my head. "Aster, Aster, Aster."

"Stop that."

"Surely you didn't think we were only going to do this *once*?"

She clapped a hand over her eyes and ruined the gesture by smiling. "Oh no."

"Welcome to the Dark Crusade," Nazralind said cheerily.

Olumnach kept me waiting for another week, during which I pantsed his rich, well-bred lackeys nine more times. By that point I was pretty familiar with all of them; there weren't *so* many men of good breeding who were desperate enough or sufficiently under Clan Olumnach's control to serve as bandit shepherds. They sure as hell got to know me. I suspected it wasn't on the Highlord's orders that they started trying to ambush and assassinate me with their gangsters, but between Biribo and my own combat capabilities, that never went anywhere except to give me another opportunity to humiliate them in front of their own lowborn servants. Whom I then sent on their way with a proverbial pat on the head, trying not to laugh at the mortifying retreat of their half-naked overlords.

During this period, my gambit with Clan Yviredh really started bearing fruit; the Olumnach Clansguard were making increasingly ham-fisted efforts to chase down and engage my mobile bandit gangs, with no result save for irritating the other Clans whose territory they were stomping through. When I visited, Lady Elidred smugly informed me that multiple complaints and petitions had been sent to Clan Aelthwyn about Olumnach's behavior. A united bloc of smaller Clans would have raised the suspicion of an organized campaign, but her ploy had succeeded—by seeding the rumor that this was already happening, she prompted them all to jump independently on the bandwagon, resulting in a seemingly unconnected string of complaints. I knew Archlord Caludon didn't give half a shit what was happening to anyone in his province, but a pretext to pounce on Highlord Caldimer's neck was one of the few things that would definitely prompt him to move.

The pressure was mounting on Olumnach. I was becoming an ongoing hassle he could not afford. I kept the stakes of fighting with me low even as I constantly pestered him, creating a single opportunity to remedy his problems by coming to terms with me. If he took the bait, finally, I could proceed with my next plan.

Finally, one of the Blessed highborn surrendered at the first sight of me—visibly bitter and angry about it, but following his orders. He gave me a time and place at which the Highlord was willing to meet.

I let him keep his pants.

"You are quite late, *Lord Seiji,*" Caldimer spat upon our first face-to-face meeting. "I would think someone so adamantly determined to prevail upon my valuable time could deign to appear at the appointed hour."

When I conjured a Firelight over my palm to see his face clearly in the darkened storehouse, he did not react except to narrow his eyes slightly, though all three of his guards put hands to the hilts of their rapiers. The Highlord of Clan Olumnach was sharp-featured and the shade of very pale blonde that would tend to obscure whether he was starting to go gray. He was a passably handsome fellow, middle-aged, with the beginnings of lines around his mouth, but not so prominently at the corners of his eyes. A face more accustomed to scowling than smiling. I could definitely see the resemblance to Arider.

As agreed, we each had three guards; mine were all masked, but this did not conceal the fact that they were women, which may have prompted the sneers from Olumnach's trio of attendants. Or maybe they were just unhappy to see me; I'd confiscated trousers from all three of them over the past week, one of them twice. I'd brought Aster, Nazralind, and Adelly, my most dangerous hand-to-hand combatants. Not that I was planning on having a fight, but I was done taking risks. Adelly's hands were full with the package, so she currently had the Lightning Staff slung over her back; Kasser had rigged her up a shoulder strap with akornin clips that held it securely while enabling easy retrieval.

"I humbly apologize for my rudeness, Highlord Caldimer," I said smoothly, bowing, which was paradoxically both out of politeness and disdain for Fflyr customs. "Truly, I regret keeping you waiting, but I was unavoidably delayed. I am sure you of all people understand how responsibilities can suddenly spring up with unplanned demands upon one's time. Indeed, were you a less busy person, perhaps I wouldn't have needed to subject myself and your men to frankly undignified antics to merit a moment of your attention."

All three of the armed men glared at me, but Caldimer just made an impatient gesture with one hand, his gaze fixed on the object in Adelly's arms. "You've brought her, as agreed? Show me."

I nodded at Adelly, who stepped forward and set down the heavy jar and whisked off the cloth covering it. She was in great shape, but I wasn't going to make her carry that thing any longer than necessary, even if it meant Highlord Caldimer had to bend over to properly examine the guest of honor.

It was one of our *good* jars, made of the clearest glass, which had previously contained a light slime helping illuminate North Watch's mess hall. The khora-based brine within was remarkable stuff, likewise crystal clear, and had done its job perfectly. Lady Gray's head floated in the liquid, hair drifting with the motion, preserved without a speck of decay and with features perfectly visible.

Eyes fixed on it, Caldimer stepped forward, and then knelt. I obligingly approached as well, lowering my hand with the light over it to afford him a clearer view. His guards objected to this, surging forward and half-drawing blades, which caused Aster to pull out her greatsword and Nazralind to nock an arrow. There they all stopped, though, eyeing each other while Caldimer and I ignored them all.

He stared fixedly at Gray's floating face for several protracted seconds before he curled his lip in a sneer and stood. As he straightened his coat and stepped back, his men eased back as well, resheathing their weapons. At a gesture from me, my guards did likewise.

"Not a countenance I am like to forget, for all that I met her only rarely. Somehow, I always knew our last meeting would be much like this. Since you have denied me the chance of vengeance with my own hands, Lord Seiji, tell me this—was it a clean death?"

I shook my head. "My grievance with this hag was different than yours, but no less personal. She suffered terribly, and for as long as I could drag it out. I think even you would have been satisfied."

His face clenched in a terrible rictus, rage and cruel glee mingling, before he brought his features back under control. "Indeed. For that, and on behalf of my son's memory, I give you my thanks in truest earnest."

I nodded, silent.

"And now, you'll be wanting the bounty I placed upon this very head." Caldimer straightened his coat again, unnecessarily, and raised his voice. "I *regret* that this transaction may not proceed as you'd hoped, *Lord* Seiji."

He looked smug. His enforcers looked smug. I let them.

"Yes, matters are somewhat complicated by . . . well, by the entire rest of our relationship, aren't they?" I gave him a very bland, polite smile. "In point of fact, Highlord, I don't intend to claim the bounty. Not yours, I mean;

there are three others I'll aim to collect, but allow me to open our negotiations by offering you relief from the sum you promised. Not to imply that such a monetary trifle should be of consequence to a man of your prodigious means, you understand. It is simply a gesture of good faith."

I'd talked long enough that they all looked notably less smug. Caldimer kept his eyes fixed on me, but his tagalongs were glancing furtively around the storehouse, specifically at its two doors and the windows near the ceiling. They were hilariously bad at this. To be fair, this guy and his closest cronies probably preferred to do all their skullduggery from a safe distance; I bet they weren't very practiced at being so up close and personal with the enemy.

"Yes, well. That is a courteous gesture, my lord, but we must consider how it weighs against the multiple insults and injuries you have inflicted upon my Clan." He cleared his throat, then raised his voice again until he was very nearly shouting. "I *regret* that the prospects for an amicable relationship between us are quite diminished."

I regarded him with a calm smile for another two seconds. Then cleared my own throat and called out into the night.

"Ahem! I believe that was the secret signal word."

The doors at both ends, behind his group and mine, opened in unison, and armed figures stepped in. Cloaked, masked women carrying crossbows, which they raised as they spread out along the walls, took aim at Caldimer and his escort. All four had now grabbed swords, but were staring around with expressions of grim realization. Rapiers weren't going to help them when they were covered by that many crossbows.

I kept my smile subdued, despite the temptation to give him my meanest grin, the one his buddies had all seen multiple times by now. I had something different in mind for the Highlord.

"And now you understand what urgent business made me late to our meeting."

It hadn't been a *bad* plan; I'd give him that. He'd positioned his forces in a loose ring around the chosen warehouse, far enough out that I could easily get through the perimeter without knowing they were there. He'd even had the sense to use Olumnach Clansguard rather than local gangsters, who were already more favorably disposed toward me than him. Presumably, they were to watch until I entered the storehouse, then close in so they could hear the signal when he gave it and finish me off.

That obviously didn't work on someone with a familiar who wasn't stupid enough to walk into the trap, and whose followers carried stingers with sleeping darts. Locating and neutralizing every one of his ambushers had been trivially easy, thanks to Biribo. Every quiet shot caused a pang of grief for Kastrin, but that was by far the hardest part. It took me barely half an hour to circle around, locating every hidden household guard and having my girls send them off to dreamland.

All this served as a reminder that I was tying up a loose end here, not facing off against a legitimate enemy. Soon enough I'd have to fend off foes who knew what they were dealing with, and it wouldn't be this easy.

"So," Caldimer grated, baring his teeth at me.

"Your men are unharmed, Highlord," I said, keeping my tone even and mild. "They'll be awake in a few hours, quite embarrassed and otherwise none the worse for wear. Needless to say, arranging that was significantly more difficult than just killing them all. Consider it another gesture of good faith, since as you pointed out, I have more amends to make before approaching your good graces. And I have more, still."

I reached into my coat and pulled out the signet ring I had taken from Lord Arider's corpse, contemptuously nudging Lady Gray's jar with my toe and making her head slosh about. "She was carrying this. I've asked around and have been informed that it is the Clan Olumnach sigil."

Caldimer's eyes fixed on the ring, glinting in the glow of the Firelight, and his face twisted again in pain and fury. "That is—you will *give that to me*!"

He lunged forward, gripping the hilt of his rapier; instantly, all the women surrounding us surged forward themselves, raising their crossbows and taking aim directly at him. The Highlord's guards, to their credit, tried to arrange themselves around him, but their bodies couldn't possibly block every shot.

"Please!" I raised my voice, and one hand. "Ladies, enough. A little consideration for a grieving father, please. It goes without saying, my lord; a Clan sigil belongs with its Clan. I brought this to return it, not to taunt you."

I stepped forward, holding out my open palm with the ring upon it. Slowly, as the Highlord breathed heavily in his struggle for self-control, my forces eased back, lowering their weapons—not fully, but no longer directly aiming to kill. Caldimer gathered himself and reached out, taking the ring. He managed enough self-control not to snatch it in haste, simply gathering the signet from my palm before stepping back.

He stared at it for a second, then closed his fingers, squeezing so tightly his fist trembled. Only then did he tuck the ring gently away inside his coat, raising his head to meet my gaze. The man couldn't bring himself to thank me, for which I couldn't entirely blame him.

"That makes . . ." I made a show of counting on my fingers. "Three kindnesses I have done you in the last handful of minutes, Highlord Caldimer. Four, if we consider the fact that I hold your life in my grasp and have refrained from squeezing. Please understand that I am only so gauche as to point it out aloud because you seem like the sort of fellow who mistakes mercy for weakness."

Caldimer was still staring at my face. His shoulders lifted and fell in a deep, slow breath; I was getting the impression that he was better at regaining control than maintaining it. I got to see the process yet again as he slowly straightened up, smoothing out his expression, and finally favored me with a cold, cunning little smile.

"I see. You *want* something. Something you cannot simply take by force. Ahh, *I* understand. You seek *legitimacy*! A place within the hierarchy—the one thing a foreign lord cannot seize with swords, magic, or coin."

"A reasonable guess, my lord. Not correct, but not entirely wrong. In fact, I think you and I understand one another better than you realize."

"You begin to interest me, my lord. Very well, since it seems I am your guest in any case, do elaborate."

I gave Gray's final resting place another disdainful nudge with my boot, setting her aslosh once more. "This grasping, venal creature never understood the value of money the way you and I do, Highlord. Even as she devoted her entire existence to scrounging and hoarding it, never showing more than a kind of base animal cunning in its pursuit, she failed to grasp what it was— nothing more than a means to an end. Such a low specimen has no means of *comprehending* a higher purpose than satisfying base, animal desires. But you and I, Caldimer Olumnach, understand what it means to have a legacy. To be *part* of something—a greater cause than survival or greed. The value of a name—a *heritage*, a reason for being and for acting that impels us to become something greater than what such a common thug, no matter how jumped-up, could even envision."

What a bunch of bullshit. Luckily I'd forewarned my people that I was going to go full ham on this guy and pander heavily to his sensibilities, or I'd probably be costing myself loyalty with this speech. Caldimer, of course, began to look thoughtful, as if I were really making sense to him.

"Perhaps I have misjudged you, Lord Seiji. I confess I entertained doubts that your title was legitimate, but you speak as one who indeed understands the meaning of noble blood in a way that the common folk do not."

Yep, called it.

"I would hardly blame you, Highlord. Circumstances have compelled me to conduct myself in a manner rather unbecoming a gentleman of good breeding. Perhaps that, too, you understand. After all, why else would men like us become involved in crime, if not toward a greater purpose? It is my understanding that Clan Olumnach *rightfully* holds the fief of Dount—or did, once, before it was usurped by the Aelthwyns."

He curled his lip in distaste. "Terms such as 'rightful' are loaded, Lord Seiji. It would not be prudent of me to say such things where they might be overheard. After all, there is no more effective way to steal power than by working *through* rather than against the system."

"Oh, to be sure, I assumed it was something of the kind. Forgive me; I might be projecting my own history a bit onto yours. The theft of *my* legacy was less legal and more brutal. Still, I have only to look around this island to see that Clan Aelthwyn are inept and unqualified guardians of the land."

"I gather a similar fate befell . . . Clan Seiji?"

"Clan Omura," I corrected gently, smiling. "But yes."

He nodded, still watching me with a knowing glint in his eye, the expression of a man who greatly overestimated his control of the situation he was in. "And now you desire my help. But not, it seems, to reinstate your Clan on Dount?"

I shook my head. "Like you, I mean to begin by avenging myself against those who have wronged me, and reclaim what is *mine*. Obviously, I require certain resources to do this. And I will have to *take* those resources on a long journey in order to achieve it. My ancestral lands are . . . well, farther from here than you'd suspect."

"I see. Regardless of the feasibility of that, there remains the matter of what has passed between our Clans already, Lord Seiji. *You* have cost me more than the current generation of Aelthwyn scum, in material resources and respect, if not formal prestige. Step by step you have stolen what is mine, and now you threaten me while begging for my help."

"I think you'll find me too prideful to beg—as, I note, are you, even with crossbows aimed at your heart."

Caldimer half-smiled with the right side of his mouth, and inclined his head momentarily in acknowledgment.

"Indeed. Begging does not become men of good breeding."

"Precisely. And I could argue over who has stolen what from whom, my lord. After all, it was *my* efforts that ousted that beast Gray from

Gwyllthean, and you lost not a moment in swooping in to seize all that I had liberated."

"You snatched a final victory over her after I had spent *years* softening her grip!"

"That's one way to look at it, surely. Another is that you *had* years to break her, and failed to, while I achieved it in weeks. Please!" I held up one hand to forestall his angry rebuttal. "We both know we could argue this all night, Highlord, and it would be nothing but wasted breath. The point is that it would *be* an argument; there are cases to be made for both sides. It is not so clear-cut as one of us having unilaterally wronged the other. Rather than dwell on fruitless questions, let us instead consider the matter of where we stand now. And how we might, together, achieve *both* our goals."

"Oh?" He raised one eyebrow. "You wish to *help* me, now?"

"I've already said I am too proud to beg; I am also too intelligent to imagine I could get the level of cooperation I need from you by threatening your life, my lord. So let me lay it out. You need for Clan Aelthwyn to be brought low, while you simultaneously regain the prestige and resources to regain the fief of Dount. As I understand the system established under your King and Convocation, dislodging a ruling Clan from governorship would require them to have failed in governance so utterly that not only do their superior *and* subordinate Clans agree on the necessity of removal, but also that they haven't the means of forcibly resisting their ouster. Do I have the general shape of it?"

He grimaced, but nodded once. "There are . . . nuances, but in broad strokes, yes. The strict prohibition of Fflyr highborn fighting one another always favors the incumbents, unless they begin the hostilities."

I nodded in return. "Then it seems to me that it would spell the doom of Clan Aelthwyn if the Archlord were to, say, instigate an unjustified attack upon Clan Olumnach, and in the process cripple his ability to govern so that all order on the island collapses. Then, if Clan Olumnach were to decisively vanquish Clan Aelthwyn's forces *and* go on to restore order on Dount, the King and Convocation would have, effectively, no choice but to acknowledge you as the rightful Archlord of Dount."

Caldimer nodded slowly, making a pensive expression as if this hadn't been his entire plan all along. "Indeed, that could work. And such a crisis could be both instigated and easily resolved by whomsoever controlled *all* the bandit and criminal activity upon the island, is that it? Then it does raise the question of why I need *you*, Lord Seiji."

I gave him my politest smile, again. "Why, because *I* control those bandits, Highlord. And those I haven't already taken from you, I easily can. Within the week."

His expression hardened.

"What I think you have *not* considered," I smoothly continued, "is what would happen in the aftermath of such a successful coup. Presumably you thought to continue business as usual, with yourself in control of both the formal government of the island and all its criminal activity. And perhaps that could work—but there is a *better* way to go about it, Highlord. What if you could establish yourself as Archlord of a province with *no* organized crime?"

"Hah!" He expelled a short bark of derisive laughter. "Your people must be even fonder of fairytales than we Fflyr if you think the elimination of crime is remotely possible."

"Oh, to be sure—once removed from Dount, it would begin to crop up again. That vacuum will always be filled by *someone*, and it would fall to you to deal with it in whatever manner you choose. But think of it, Highlord. For that very reason, to *expel* all banditry and crime from a province under your control would be an *unmatched* achievement. No one would expect it to be perfect, or to last forever. Simply by doing it at all, you would gain prestige and favor well beyond that afforded to the governor of one island. The kind of political clout a man of ambition and wit could parlay into far greater power than the fief of one outlying province. After all, why content yourself with restoring the honor of Clan Olumnach, when you could *advance* it beyond the greatest achievements of your forebears?"

He regarded me through narrowed eyes, face now a mask of contemplation. "You sing a pretty song, Lord Seiji. In this scheme you have laid out, you take on the lion's share of the work and the risk, while I reap all the benefits. That raises the opposite question of my previous one—why do *you* need *me*?"

"It comes down to what happens after. I require a replacement for my Clan's forces, and I have found them in the bandits, gangsters, and miscellaneous dregs of Dount. Undoubtedly, they are an unimpressive set of specimens to *you*, but you will have already noticed that bandits you previously controlled with ease have suddenly been running circles around your Clansguard. I am capable of shaping them into a fighting force to be feared—one more dangerous than Clan Aelthwyn will understand, I promise you. And once my ancestral holdings are retaken, I can reward them as one does one's best vassals—with lands, prestige, and a comfortable life once the fighting is done. However, *all* of these efforts will mean nothing if I cannot *get them home*." I hesitated, then put on a grimace. "It's a long journey to my country, and to begin it, we must go north."

Caldimer's eyebrows lifted. "I did wonder what country you hail from; your features and accent are like none I recognize. Are you truly from Viryan lands?"

"Let us say . . . I am from *beyond* Viryan lands, and know how to get through them. Viryans are predictable folk and easily impressed, if one understands how they think. No, my problem is far more immediate."

"Ah." Expression clearing, he nodded. "The eternal gateway to the north. Godspire does not suffer armed forces to pass through their domain."

"*Precisely*. To the rulers of Godspire, I am nothing but a minor warlord leading a horde of bandits—precisely the kind of person they will *not* allow through their gates. To get past them, I require . . . legitimacy, as you said. The kind of prestige and formal acknowledgment I could be lent only by a legal and recognized ruler, able to negotiate on my behalf with the notoriously, stubbornly neutral city-state to grant me safe passage. And for that, Highlord, I need *you*. I can't work with that imbecile Caludon—in addition to being incompetent, he's apparently some kind of insane sadist. Regardless of how much it would benefit him to have the bandits removed from his domain, he derives more pleasure from knowing they are here, keeping life . . . *interesting* for his subjects."

Caldimer sneered in contempt, nodding. Obviously, any trash talk directed at Caludon would earn sympathy from him, and it had the benefit of being true: by all accounts, the Archlord was a fucked-up piece of work even by Fflyr standards.

"And it's not as if I can establish *myself* as the ruler of Dount. Even if that wouldn't defeat the purpose of going home, all the bandits on this island combined aren't enough to face down its unified Clans, which is what I *would* face if I tried to take Gwyllthean by force, never mind what the King would send from the mainland. No, Highlord, the reality is that in order to realize our ambitions, you and I need each other. I have taken control of your bandits, yes—but I need them more than you do, and if you'll work with me on one last, grand plan, you will end up better off for them being gone. With your political acumen to maneuver Caludon where we want him and then cut a deal with Godspire, and my strategy and training to turn these bandits into a respectable force to win our victories, we can achieve together what neither of us has managed to accomplish alone."

I grinned, putting just enough anger and malice into the expression to mirror the faces he had been making all night, and held out my hand toward him.

"Join me, Highlord. Let us put aside our quarrel, crush our shared enemies, and part as friends."

Caldimer looked down at my hand, then back up at my face, not making a move to take it.

"It should go without saying, but as the entirety of this plan rests upon *my* ability to direct our actions, I will expect my orders to be obeyed."

"Just as I expect control of the remaining gangs to be turned over to me with no more fuss," I said, smiling and not lowering my hand. "My plan is explicitly not to darken your lands one moment longer than I can be of service to you. It is no affront to my pride to submit to your leadership until then."

He considered me a moment longer—just to keep me hanging, I knew. I bore it without complaint, because I respect showmanship.

Then, finally, the Highlord smiled a cold little smile, stepped forward, and clasped my hand. "We have an accord, Lord Seiji. Let us discuss terms."

"Clear, boss," Biribo reported some time later, as we stood in the darkened storehouse. "They've retrieved the last of their boys and moved out of the area. We got privacy."

I inhaled deeply, and blew the breath out, letting it puff my cheeks and not caring how undignified it was. In fact, deciding I was done standing up for the time being, I slouched over to the jar and sat carefully down on Lady Gray's head. The wide lid on the jar was just big enough; it wasn't comfortable and I'd have to move soon, but for the moment it just felt right. Welcome to my ass, you rotten old bitch.

I was just . . . tired. There had been a lot of details to hash out—particulars of the transfer of authority for the last gangs, percentages and quotas of plunder to be handed over to Clan Olumnach, procedures for him to send us orders, and me to contact him at need. A bunch of minutiae like that, all of it very necessary but extremely tiresome.

"I hope I don't need to point out that that guy's gonna betray us first chance he gets, Lord Seiji," said Aster.

I snorted. "Oh, he's not going to betray me. He *thinks* he is, but he's not. Caldimer thinks my plan is to leave Dount. He thinks *I* think a feudal lord in this rathole of a country has the authority to negotiate with Godspire. He thinks he has me in a bottle, unable to leave or pursue my own goals until *he* opens the gate for me, which he will never actually have the power to do. I've already got control of most of the bandits and can get the rest without him, and he knows it; the only way he *can* turn on me is to rat me out to the Archlord or the King. And doing that before I get him control of Gwyllthean will lose him everything and gain him nothing. The gangs would all be destroyed and there'd be too much attention on him afterward to rebuild them. No, he'll wait 'til I get him what he wants and *then* betray me. That's the only moment it would make sense for him to do so. Once he has Dount, mobilizing the Clans to crush me and the united bandits will just secure his position. He will never get the chance to do that, because I'm going to betray him first. Needless to say, ladies, we are not putting that fool on the throne in Gwyllthean. Once he finishes picking a fight with Clan Aelthwyn, we're gonna pull back and let him lose it, and good riddance."

"This is all a really roundabout way to kill somebody, Lord Seiji," Nazralind pointed out. "I'm just saying. We've got contacts among the servants of a lot of Clans, including his. The girls and I can get into Caer Olumnach in one night's work and put an arrow in his eye. Zip zap, problem solved."

"Naz, you know better than anyone what would happen next."

She grimaced and lowered her eyes. "Yeah, I know. If bandits kill a Highlord, there'll be a complete purge of the island."

"Exactly." With a grunt, I stood back up; Lady Gray's briny tomb was already beginning to hurt. Even dead, she was a pain in the ass. "Caldimer is our meat shield. Everyone knows him as the bandits' not-so-secret leader, so leaving him in place and giving orders keeps attention off us while we make preparations to deal with all the *other* attention that's going to come our way soon enough. Then, once he goes down fighting Clan Aelthwyn in Fflyr politics as usual, there'll be no reason for a bandit purge. It buys us some breathing room to maneuver. That means, for now, I need Caldimer happy, and to think he's in charge. Unfortunately," I added with a grimace, "*that* means we're gonna have to bow and scrape a bit. I'm really sorry to ask it of you, ladies, after we've made so much progress in getting out from under the Clans' collective thumb, but for the time being I need everybody to play the good lapdog. Caldimer needs to believe he's got us firmly under control until the very moment it's time for him to die. Can I count on you all to play along?"

Adelly cleared her throat. "Lord Seiji . . . Did you really just ask a room full of whores if we know how to manage a stupid man's ego?"

The braying of laughter from every corner of the room was damn well therapeutic, a sudden lightening of the mood that I hadn't realized I'd needed. I found myself grinning right along with them.

"Well, fair enough. All right, girls, let's ditch this depressing hole and go sleep in the forest like the civilized scum we are."

Dount wasn't mine, not yet. My initial goal of taking over the criminal underworld was in the bag, but I still didn't have a direct path from there to overt control of the island, and now it looked like I wouldn't even have time to finagle one before I had to deal with powers on such a scale that control of one island was barely a factor.

I needed to get someone to teach me more about the history, geography, and politics of Ephemera. Nazralind probably could; she had the right education. I'd leveraged Godspire into my plans already, but all I really knew about that city-state was that it was a notorious geopolitical nuisance.

Currently, four days after my negotiations with Caldimer, Naz was busy with ink brush in hand and surrounded by discarded papers, carefully drawing on the most recent sheet in front of her. We were back home in North Watch, loitering in the quiet mess hall long after dinner. Kasser and Harold had crafted shades to put over the bottled light slimes, so it was dimmer in here but not completely dark. I rather liked the effect; it was cozy. A few groups of people were still hanging out and chatting at some of the tables before bed. Closer at hand, Minifrit puffed away at her pipe while Aster lounged against the table next to me and Biribo hovered lazily above Naz's art project, watching it take shape.

"Better deal with the beast tribes first," I mused, repressing a yawn. "After the Inferno they're gonna need the help, and also they're in a weak enough position to be easily taken over. That, and I owe them something."

"I've no idea how many beastfolk there even are on Dount," Minifrit said, blowing smoke. "There are four native *kinds* of them, though. Even discounting the lizardfolk, who answer to the dark elves . . . That is a lot of additional mouths to feed, Lord Seiji."

"They're skilled hunters and foragers, Minifrit. Giving them aid will be an initial investment, but it'll start paying off quickly. Not just in food; with their wilderness skills and knowledge of the land, bringing them into the fold will give us effective control over the wild khora, which is going to *matter* once major powers start coming here and poking at us. We need places to retreat to. Even fully restored, North Watch won't be able to hold against a major military push."

"Just so," she said, smiling. "Forgive me, my lord, I was merely making sure this was a *strategy* you were executing, and not a sentimental gesture. A guilty conscience can cause nearly as much grief as the lack of one."

"Oh, come on. Me, sentimental?"

"Don't worry," Aster said, gently nudging me with an elbow. "We won't tell anyone."

"You're all a bunch of backstabbing ingrates. Anyway, the other thing is that it's a natural progression. Bringing in the tribes will be easier than bringing in the goblins, and I still don't even know where to *start* with the dark elves. I can't even get a handle on the one we've got, much less the whole city of 'em."

"Okay!" Nazralind said brightly, straightening up. "I think I have it! Come have a look, Lord Seiji!"

I stood and stepped over, leaning past her shoulder to examine the sigil she had painted in accordance with the traditional Fflyr folk art of sigil crafting. Supposedly, you needed one of these to be taken seriously as an institution in this country, so it was past time I had one. Traditionally, they were created by noblewomen, and I'd only recently acquired those, so I reckoned I could be pardoned for being a little late to the party.

"I like it," I said, examining the abstract pattern of lines. "Can't tell what the hell it *means*, but it's . . . hm . . . aesthetic, that's the word. It's got a satisfying sort of look to it."

"I'm glad you approve," she said, grinning up at me. "So I started with the two glyphs you wanted, and once I got them arranged in a way that looked pleasing I picked two embellishments. There were any number of those that might be applicable, but more than this made it look all . . . busy, and cluttered."

"Is that a crown line?" Minifrit inquired, leaning forward from the other side of the table. I quickly averted my eyes from the risk of looking down her dress; the fact that I had explicit permission to stick my hands in there only increased the potential for a debilitating flashback.

"It is!" Nazralind pointed at the top part of the sigil, looking up at me again. "It's the horizontal line along the top there, Lord Seiji. Traditionally, the crown line indicates royalty; displaying a sigil like this while *not* associated with the King signals your intent to challenge and replace him. So, of course, it's almost never used, but I thought it was . . . apt."

"Good instincts," I said approvingly. "Is the other embellishment that cross thingy in the middle there? That doesn't look like part of either glyph."

"Exactly, yes! The ascending star—with the long line coming from the bottom—is a symbol of the Goddess, used to signify devotion and allegiance to her. Well, there's not one in the traditional Fflyr arts for the, ah, *other* goddess, so I improvised."

"Ah, and that's why it's upside down, with the long tail on top."

"Precisely! Now, this is just plain ink, but in terms of heraldic colors I think red markings on a black field is appropriate."

"Black is neutral, right? That's what you told me." I patted her shoulder. "Nice work, Naz. I like it; this is the design we'll go with. Make a few copies, please. We'll give one to Kasser and have him start applying it to stuff. I guess I should have a flag, at the very least."

"It's just . . ." She hesitated, sighed, and twisted on the bench to be able to look up at me without having to crane her neck back. "With more complex sigils made from multiple glyphs, it can quickly become impossible to tell what the original words were. With one like this, made from just two . . . Well, anybody with a grasp of Fflyr heraldry—in fact, potentially anyone who can *read* Fflyr—will be able to tell your personal sigil says 'slimes and whores.' Are you . . . *certain* that's the face you want for the Dark Crusade?"

Minifrit and Aster were both grinning.

"I am absolutely certain," I assured her. "I want my enemies to not take me seriously. I want them to laugh and not realize what they're dealing with until it's far too late—and in the bitter end, I want them to perish knowing I never respected them. This is the one, Nazralind. *This* is what I'm about."

I gave my absurd new personal logo another long, appreciative stare, then heaved a sigh and stepped back.

"All right, ladies, let's all get to bed. Tomorrow comes early, and our enemies are closing in. We have a lot more people to disappoint before all's said and done."

About the Author

D. D. Webb is a highly suspicious character widely believed to be up to no good. Any information on his misdeeds should be reported to the requisite authorities.

Podium

DISCOVER
STORIES UNBOUND

PodiumAudio.com

www.ingramcontent.com/pod-product-compliance
Lightning Source LLC
Chambersburg PA
CBHW030918120726
47906CB00002B/385